Ellis Peters has gained universal acclaim for her crime novels, and in particular for her medieval whodunnits, featuring monastic sleuth Brother Cadfael, now into their nineteenth volume. Here she introduces the reader to two more of her charming sleuths: Detective Inspector George Felse and Detective Inspector Musgrave. Originally published in three volumes, each novel is further proof of Ellis Peters' extraordinary storytelling talent:

City of Gold and Shadows

City of Gold and Shadows, like everything else Ellis Peters produces, is crisply written and sharply observed' *Birmingham Daily News*

Flight of a Witch

'Felse, in a class with the best-portrayed British policemen in fiction today, is a fully-dimensioned character . . . This is a deeply satisfying murder novel' *Publishers Weekly*

Funeral of Figaro

'An unusual and well-plotted tale' *Herald Express*

The Detective Omnibus

Ellis Peters

Comprising
City of Gold and Shadows
Flight of a Witch
Funeral of Figaro

HEADLINE

First published in this omnibus edition in 1992
by HEADLINE BOOK PUBLISHING PLC

This omnibus edition was originally published in three volumes in
hardback: *City of Gold and Shadows* in 1973 by Macmillan London
Ltd; *Flight of a Witch* and *Funeral of Figaro* in 1964 and 1962 by
William Collins Sons & Co Ltd; and in paperback in 1989, 1990 and
1989 by HEADLINE BOOK PUBLISHING PLC

10 9 8 7 6 5 4 3 2 1

ISBN 0 7472 4020 5

Typeset by Keyboard Services, Luton

Printed and bound in Great Britain by
HarperCollins Manufacturing, Glasgow

HEADLINE BOOK PUBLISHING PLC
Headline House, 79 Great Titchfield Street, London W1P 7FN

Contents

City of Gold
and Shadows

Chapter One

Mr Stanforth came from behind his desk to meet his visitor in person, and settle her with ceremony into the client's chair, though she was not a client, had no need whatever of a solicitor, and had come here in response to his telephoned request chiefly out of pure curiosity, of which she had a woman's proper share. Mr Stanforth was not entirely what she had expected, but neither, she deduced from the covert glances he was using upon her like measuring instruments, was she quite matching up to his preconceived picture of her. He was small and nimble and immaculate in fine grey mohair, with a clever, froggish, mildly mischievous face, like a very well-turned-out troll from under some Scandinavian mountain. But towards her he was being punctilious in a way which seemed slightly out of character, as though he did not quite know how to approach her, even though it was he who had brought her here.

Her part was easy. She had only to sit back with perfect composure – something at which she was adept – and wait for him to find his way through the necessary preliminaries to the real business of this meeting. After all, he had initiated it. He must have some need of her; she had none of him. This could not even be a matter of learning something to her advantage. Her mind – and she was well aware that it was an elastic and enterprising mind – was quite open. Perhaps that was what baffled him about her. She should have been more concerned, more anxious to know what he had to confide, since he had invited her here for that very purpose.

'Mademoiselle Rossignol, it's very kind of you to spare me a little of your time . . .'

'Miss will do,' said Charlotte helpfully. 'I'm almost completely English, you know, apart from the name, although I've lived most of my life in France. My father walked out on my mother when I was seven, so the English influence came out on top from then on.' Her mother, flighty as a butterfly, had heaved a sigh of relief at getting

3

rid of a whole entrenched family along with Maître Henri Rossignol, who still, perhaps, coloured Charlotte's image of the law, and made Mr Stanforth incongruous, with his pricked ears and his mild, perilous, goatish hazel eyes.

'That certainly makes things easier,' he said heartily, and leaned across the monumental desk to offer her a cigarette and a light. He was just warming up; she knew the signs, knowing quite accurately the effect her looks had on most males of most ages. What she had was not beauty, and she had learned that early, and come to terms with it, being of a practical mind. But there was something more adventurous than beauty in her, a tendency to surge forward into situations somewhat risky in their ambiguity, a taste for accepting any challenge that offered, and a manner and a gait to match the proclivity. Angels might well have feared to tread where Charlotte habitually planted her size four sandals with zest and aplomb.

'You must be wondering,' said Mr Stanforth, approaching by inches, 'why I asked you to come here like this. It was pure luck, my seeing that notice of your concert. There couldn't be many Charlotte Rossignols who happen also to play the oboe. So I made enquiries at the hall. It was an opportunity for me. I hope you didn't mind my asking you to come here. I would gladly have come to you, but I thought we could talk more freely here than in an hotel. Briefly, I need to ask you, my dear Miss Rossignol, if you have had any word within the last year from your great-uncle, Doctor Alan Morris.'

There was a moment of absolute silence and surprise. Her eyes had opened wide in wonder, and the light entered their long-lashed blackness and turned it to a dusky, flecked gold. Her small, delicate monkey-features quivered into childish candour, reassuring him that for all her formidable composure she was, indeed, no more than twenty-three. She had fine, white skin, not opaque and dull, but translucent and bright, with the vivid come-and-go of vibrant blood close beneath it; and she had beautiful hair, fine as an infant's and black as jet, curving but not curling about a very shapely head, and cropped cunningly to underline the subtlety of the shaping. Oh, yes, there was a great deal of France there, whether she knew it or not. And her lips, opening to reply to his question, were long and mobile, eloquent even before she spoke, though she might sometimes go on to contradict what they had intimated.

'Mr Stanforth,' she said now, 'I've never once in my life had any communication from my Great-Uncle Alan. I've never set eyes on him. I know quite a lot about his work and his reputation, and am quite proud of him, but I don't expect ever to exchange one word with him. My mother was his niece, and the only daughter of his only sister, but she was as foot-loose as he, and when she married into France she never kept in touch with her English connections at all. I grew up detached. I'm sorry if it seems almost unnatural. It wasn't out of any want of feeling. No, I've had no word ever from Doctor Morris. I should have been very astonished and concerned if I had. I should have taken it for granted there was something the matter.'

Mr Stanforth massaged his sharp jaw with one finger, and looked thoughtful.

'*Is* there?' asked Charlotte, making connections with her usual rash speed. 'Something the matter?'

'That's exactly the trouble, we don't really know. Naturally I hope not, and the probability is that we're exercising ourselves over nothing. But the fact remains, we can't be sure. I'm not surprised,' he agreed, 'that you've received no word from him, but it was just a chance.'

'I'm sorry to be a disappointment. Was that the only reason you asked me to come?' She was reasonably certain by then that it was merely a necessary preliminary to the real business he had with her.

'Hardly, or I could have asked it over the telephone, and avoided imposing upon you. No, circumstances make it very desirable that we should have this talk, and continue in close touch afterwards, if you're agreeable. I had better,' said Mr Stanforth, philosophically accepting the fact of her total ignorance, 'tell you exactly what the position is. I have acted for your great-uncle for more than twenty years now, and have often been left in charge of his affairs during his long absences abroad, on digs all over Europe and North Africa and the Middle East, everywhere that the Roman and Graeco-Roman power extended. You're familiar with his subject, you know he is an authority, internationally known and universally respected. So naturally he travels a great deal, and is in demand as a consultant wherever Roman sites are being excavated. A year ago last October he planned a year's tour in Turkey. It was approaching the end of the season, of course, but he intended to make a first flying visit to Aphrodisias, where some old friends of his were at work, and then to spend the winter on research in libraries and museums, and have the whole of the following summer for field work. He let his house in Chelsea furnished for the year, with the usual proviso that his own staff should remain to run it – he has a housekeeper who has been with him for years, and one daily maid. All quite in order, of course, he has done the same thing at least twice before. And of course no one expected to hear much from him during his sabbatical year, unless, as you say, something was wrong. But the trouble is that no one has heard anything from him even now that the year is over.'

'Nearly six months over,' Charlotte pointed out. 'Quite an edgy matter for his tenants.'

'Precisely! Finding accommodation in London is difficult in any circumstances, and this couple happen to be Australians who don't intend to stay permanently, but are anxious to see their daughter through her physiotherapy training here, and take her back with them afterwards. It would suit them very well to have the tenancy of the house for at least another year. But without any instructions from Doctor Morris it's difficult to know what to do.'

'And what,' she asked practically, 'have you done about them so far?'

'In the absence of any word from my client, I took the responsibility of renewing the tenancy for six months. They could hardly be expected to agree to less, and they're excellent tenants.'

'And now the six months is nearly up. And still no word! Yes, I see why I represented a last hope,' she said. 'Is this very unlike him?'

'Very. He is a man who has deliberately avoided certain responsibilities in his life, and certain involvements, but those business obligations which do unavoidably devolve upon him he has always observed punctiliously. There are money matters, investments, tax affairs to be considered. It is, one might say, a conscious part of his policy of personal detachment to have all his affairs in scrupulous order, and so obviate pursuit and inconvenience of any kind. To be slipshod is to be hounded, which is the last thing he wants. No, I must say that things have now gone so far as to justify me in feeling considerable uneasiness about his continued absence.'

She gazed back at him in thoughtful silence for a moment, and shook her head doubtfully. 'I don't know . . . he's a free agent, and he has confidence in you. At a pinch, he might very well feel safe enough in going ahead with what he's doing, and leaving all the rest to you. Supposing he got excited about some new discoveries, for instance . . .'

'During the winter months work would be at a standstill. In many places it couldn't open up again before June, late May at the earliest.'

'You ought, perhaps, to start official enquiries,' she suggested hesitantly.

'I already have, more than a month ago. I rather wish I'd taken the step earlier. The trail came to a dead end. One that might be perfectly normal, though it leaves us in complete uncertainty.'

'How much *do* we know? I mean really *know*? Do we even know that he ever reached Turkey? Exactly what did they find?'

'Oh, yes, he got to Istanbul, all right. He caught his flight from Heathrow on the 6th of October, the flight-list has been checked through. He claimed his reservation at the Hotel Gul Bejaze, and stayed there for three weeks. We even know just what he was doing, intensively, during that time. He took a piece of work with him to finish. He was commissioned to write one of a series of monographs on the settlements of Roman Britain, and he took the almost completed text with him when he left England. I knew of that from him before he left, for he was going to spend his last few days before the flight actually on the site, refreshing his memory on certain details. Well, he posted the finished text to his publishers from Istanbul about three weeks after he arrived there. The book has been out several months, of course, now. A few days, after he mailed it, he telephoned his friend and colleague at Aphrodisias, in Anatolia, and called off his visit. He said he was afraid the delay over the book had lost him the opportunity of reaching the city in time to take part in any meaningful work, and promised to join the next summer's dig in June.'

'But he didn't.'

'He didn't. The day after that telephone call he paid his hotel bill and left by taxi for the main station. Attempts to trace one taxi in Istanbul, after a year and more, naturally fell flat. No one has heard from him since, no one knows where he is.'

It began to sound more serious than she had realised. 'Who undertook these enquiries?'

'The police, through their Turkish colleagues. Missing Persons has all the information available. But I'm afraid the trail was cold before I called them in, and we didn't take it the length of broadcasting or advertising. One doesn't want to set a public hue and cry in train after a perfectly rational and responsible person who knows very well what he's about.'

'He may still be that,' she said. 'There may be reasons for his silence, perfectly good reasons if we only knew them. And he may turn up at any moment with a simple explanation, and wonder what we've been worrying about.'

'So I think, too. Though let's admit that personal security has recently become distressingly tenuous all over the world, and the most innocent and uninvolved of people can still find himself made a pawn in all manner of dangerous games. And Turkey has its share of the modern virus. But urban guerillas don't kidnap distinguished foreigners only to keep their exploit secret, hijackers can hardly help becoming news on the instant, and here there has been profound silence. I tell myself that silence is more likely to be a personal choice than an imposed one.'

'There is such a thing as amnesia, I suppose,' Charlotte said dubiously. 'Illness or accident could have isolated him somewhere. I mean, if he did go off into the wilds of Anatolia, or somewhere remote like that – something might happen to him in some village, where he isn't known.'

'Villagers would be all the more anxious to get the responsibility for him off their hands. And there are quite a number of people in Turkey who do know him, people in his own field.'

They looked at each other for the first time with a long, speculative look, weighing up the possibilities honestly and in much the same terms. 'You think, then,' she said, 'that this disappearance is more likely to be voluntary on his part. But in that case, all we have to do is wait, and when he chooses, he'll reappear. And I take it the police still have his case more or less open, and will be looking out for news of him, in case there's something more in it. There isn't much more we can do, short of going off to Istanbul in person to try and find his tracks. And if, for some reason, he has really chosen to drop out for a while, he wouldn't be grateful for too much fuss, would he?'

'You state the position admirably. That's exactly how we are situated – you and I both.'

'I?' she said, drawing back slightly into her crystalline, black-and-white reserve, and becoming in a breath notably more French. 'I realise that I come into the picture as a relative, and I do feel natural interest and concern for my great-uncle. But I can't feel that I have any more positive standing than that in the matter.'

'You have a very *positive* standing, my dear young lady,' said Mr Stanforth patiently, and perhaps a little patronisingly, too, for this was where money entered into the reckoning, and very young concert artists and music teachers with a living to make must surely react to the alluring image. 'Let us suppose, just for one moment, that we are being over-optimistic, and that Doctor Morris will *not* reappear, as, of course, we hope and believe he will. If this situation goes on unchanged, then it may become necessary eventually, for legal reasons, to take steps to presume his death. That need not jeopardise his position if he should subsequently emerge from his limbo. But it would, meanwhile, regularise his affairs and ensure proper continuity, proper attention to investments, and so on. In short, Miss Rossignol, I've reached the point where I must have your approval and consent for whatever steps I take in protection of his financial affairs. Since your mother's death *you* are his only remaining relative, apart from some distant cousins in Canada, several times removed. And Doctor Morris – a remarkable quirk in his otherwise orderly character, I may say – has always stubbornly refused to make a will. There are people,' said the Norse troll, burning into sudden antagonistic fervour across his cavern-desk, 'who hypnotise themselves into believing that they are going to live for ever.' His client's optimism and appetites, with equal suddenness, burned clear in opposition, and Charlotte had a vision of two principles in headlong collision, and chose to ally herself with her own kinsman, by intuition and once for all. 'If we do not see him again – for we must take that possibility into account – you are his next of kin and his sole heiress. That is why I need to consult with you over anything I do, from now on, in his name.'

Charlotte had never in her life felt obliged to examine her relationships with anyone. Her mother, once rid of the armour-plated respectability of Maître Henri and his phalanx of parents, brothers and sisters, all devoted to the law, had married a happy-go-lucky literary exile from Leeds, as nearly as possible his opposite, and the half-English, half-French child had been absorbed into their slapdash household with the greatest enthusiasm and affection, and never given time to doubt or worry, surrounded as she was by joyous evidence of her own importance and value. There had never been too much money, but never less than enough. She had no vision of money as an independent power, or a formidable opponent. It was there to be used, insofar as you had it; and when you were short, you worked a little harder, and made good the deficiency. And foreseeing that necessity, you made sure that you knew something which could earn you money at need. It was as simple as that. She did not even

know what it meant to adapt oneself to another person's requirements for the sake of self-interest. All she had, to enable her to
visualise Mr Stanforth's view of her position, was a vivid imagination and a very acute intelligence. They helped her to understand
him, and even, regretfully, to sympathise with him.

'If you're asking me,' she said carefully, 'to come into consultation
and share responsibility for whatever decisions we have to make
about Great-Uncle Alan's affairs, of course I will, though I don't
claim to know anything about business and I probably shan't be
much help to you. I can't even claim to know what he would want
done, because I know almost nothing about him. But I don't at all
mind saying what I think *I* should want done in the circumstances. I
don't think, for instance, that I should want my death assumed and
my property disposed of too soon, so we won't go into that part of
the affair just now, if you don't mind. He'll probably live to be a
hundred, and make a will leaving whatever he's got to his old college,
and I shan't mind at all. But I quite see that you need someone to
come in on a practical issue like what to do about his tenants. I think
you should extend the tenancy for another full year, if that's what
they would like. It would ensure the house being taken care of, and
the staff maintained, since you say they're good tenants. And even if
Uncle Alan turns up within a month or two, he can hardly complain.
It's his own fault. And the inconvenience will be only slight, he can
always take up residence at his college again until their time's up.'

She made it sound very simple, as young people do; and she hadn't
yet considered the implications for herself, Mr Stanforth reflected
cynically, or she would not so blithely dismiss the matter of the
inheritance. It was not a fortune, but it was a respectable competence, thanks to royalties, which would continue for years yet,
whether the doctor reappeared or remained in limbo. 'I'm gratified,'
said Mr Stanforth, with only the mildest irony, 'that your judgement
agrees with mine. That is indeed what I had intended suggesting to
you, and it disposes of the immediate problem.'

'If you want me to keep in touch, and be available for consultation,
of course I will.'

'Thank you, that will ease my position considerably. And as you
say, all we can do is wait, and continue to expect Doctor Morris to
turn up in his own good time. May I ask what your own plans are?
Do you intend to stay some time in England?'

'I'm making my home here,' she said. 'I'm taking a teaching job in a new comprehensive school, but that won't begin until the September term. That's why I'm trying to fill up the gap with a few concerts, but of course I'm not good enough for the big dates, it will be mostly provincial engagements. I'll let you have word of all my movements.'

'That would be most kind and helpful.'

The interview seemed to have reached its natural conclusion. She picked up her handbag, and he rose from behind his desk to take a relieved and ceremonious farewell. But before they had reached the doorway she hesitated and halted.

'You know what I would like? Could you let me have a list of all the books Uncle Alan's written? If I'm going to be a stand-in for him, even temporarily, like this, I really need to know more about him, and that seems as good a way as any. They must surely convey something about him.'

Strange, he thought resignedly, she's not at all interested in how much her kinsman's worth, only, rather suddenly and rather late, in what he's like. And at this stage, isn't that rather an academic consideration? But he said politely: 'Yes, of course. If you'll allow me, I'll have a few of his titles sent round to your hotel. This last one, the text he sent from Istanbul – the publishers took care of the proof-reading, of course – that one I believe I've got here. Take it with you, if you'd care to. Though it's hardly the most riveting of his works. He found Aurae Phiala, it seems, rather an over-rated site in revisiting it.'

There was a large bookcase in the corner of his office, stocked mainly with leather-bound volumes; but the end of the lowest shelf was brightened by the clear colours of a number of paperbacks. He plucked one of them from its place and brought it to her. 'The Roman Britain Library', the jacket told her, and in larger print: 'AURAE PHIALA', and Alan Morris's name, with a comet's-tail of letters after it.

The cover was a fine, delicately-composed, atmospheric photograph of a shallow bowl of meadows beside the silver sweep of a river, the whole foreground patterned with a mesh of low walls in amber stone and rosy, fired brick and tile, with two broken pillars to carry the accented rhythms up into a sky feathered with light cloud. Charlotte gazed at it, fascinated. A landscape obviously planned, disciplined, tamed long, long since, and long since abandoned to the river, the seasons and the sky; and not a human soul in sight. A less cunning photographer might have felt the urge to place a single figure, perhaps close to the columns, to give life and scale. This one had understood that Aurae Phiala was dead, and immense, needing no meretricious human yardstick to give it proportion.

'But it's beautiful!' she said, and voice and accent had become wholly French for one moment. 'This is where he spent those last few days?' she said. 'Before he caught that flight into Turkey?'

'Yes. He knew the site from many previous visits, though I think he had never organised a dig there himself. The curator is an old friend of his, a fellow-student, I believe. But less distinguished.'

'So Uncle Alan would be with friends, when he stayed there? And he went straight from this place, to catch his plane?'

'So I understand. It is an attractive picture,' said Mr Stanforth, with patronising tolerance. 'Wonderful what a first rate photographer can do with even unpromising material. But you'll see what Doctor Morris has to say about the place.'

'Where is it?' she asked, still viewing the sunlit, fluted hollow with pleasure and wonder.

'Somewhere on the Welsh border, I believe. The text and maps will show you exactly where. The name means something like "the bowl of the gentle wind". Apparently an ideal climatic site. But you'll discover all about the place if you read it.'

Clearly he hardly believed that she would stay the course. She wondered if he himself had survived it. She closed the little book between her palms, and put it away in her handbag. 'Thank you,' she said. 'I look forward to setting foot in my uncle's field.'

She was not sure herself how much in earnest she was, at that stage; and if she had had any other agreeable reading matter to fill up her evening, she might never have started on *Aurae Phiala* at all. But she had no concert, and no engagement socially, since she knew hardly anyone in London, the small hotel in Earls Court was not productive of amusing company, and the television was surrounded by a handful of determined fans watching a very boring boxing match. Charlotte returned almost gladly to the recollection of her morning interview, and in retrospect it seemed to her far more strange and mysterious than while it was happening. She had never been brought face to face with her great-uncle, and never devoted any conscious thought to him. He became real and close only now that he had vanished.

Such a curious thing for an established and respected elderly gentleman to do, now that she came to consider it seriously. How old would he be now? Her grandmother, his elder sister, would have been seventy if she had been still living, and there were several years between them. Probably sixty-three or sixty-four, and according to the photographs she had seen in newspapers and geographical magazines, and his occasional appearances on television, he looked considerably younger than his age, and very fit indeed. Say a well-preserved sixty-four, highly sophisticated, speaking at least three languages, enough to get him out of trouble in most countries, and with a select if scattered network of friends and colleagues all across the Middle East, to lend him a hand if required. And on his last known move obviously still in full control of his actions. A taxi had dropped him and his luggage at the main railway station, he had walked in through the entrance with a porter in attendance; and that was that.

On the face of it, a man about whom the whole world knew, whose life was an open book – no, a succession of books. But what did she really know about him? She roamed back thoughtfully into child-hood memories, hunting for the little clues her mother and grandmother had let fall about him, and the sum of them all was remarkably meagre. A handsome, confident man, who had managed to retain his friends without ever letting them get on to too intimate ground. No wife ever, and (as far as anyone knew!) no children anywhere, but all the same, his kinswomen had spoken of him tolerantly, even appreciatively, as an accomplished lady-killer, evading marriage adroitly but finding his fun wherever he went. An eye for the girls at sixty no less than at twenty; and silver-grey temples, blue eyes and a Turkish tan were even more dangerously attractive than youth. He played fair, though, her mother had said of him generously. Not with the husbands, perhaps, but with the ladies. They had to be more than willing, and as ready as he to part without hard feelings afterwards. Doubtful if he ever dented a heart; more than likely he gave quite a number of hearts a new lift after they'd imagined the ball was over for them.

It seemed she did, after all, know a few significant things about him. He lived as he chose, one foot in home comforts, the other shod for roaming. She understood now what Mr Stanforth had meant by describing him as a man who had deliberately evaded certain responsibilities and involvements, and even kept his affairs in scrupulous order mainly to avoid being badgered, or giving anyone a hold on him. And she thought suddenly, with a totally unexpected flash of dismay and sympathy: My God, you overdid it, didn't you? You were so successful at it that in the end you could vanish without leaving a soul behind sufficiently concerned about you to kick up a fuss – only a solicitor worried about the legal hang-ups, and especially the money!

Sympathy, of course, might be misapplied here. For all she knew, so far from being lonely and deprived at this moment, he might well be taking his mild pleasures in his usual fashion, with some lady chanced upon by pure luck in the wilds of Anatolia. In which case he would surface again when it suited him. All the same, the image of his isolation remained with her, and made her feel uneasy and even guilty towards him.

So it was partly out of an illogical sense of obligation that she began to read his book on Aurae Phiala. Eighty or so acres of Midshire by the river Comer, close by the border of Wales. A recreation city, apparently, for the officers of the garrison at Silcaster, and the legions tramping the long course of Watling Street. The account he gave of it was detailed, detached and distinctly unenthusiastic. A place of historical interest in its small way, especially for its sudden death at the end of the fourth century, after the legions that were its life and its protection had been withdrawn. But otherwise a site very unlikely to repay much further examination, and hardly worth spending money on, while so many more promising sites waited their turn to snatch a crumb of the meagre and grudging funds available. In plan after plan and page after page, Doctor Morris amended the estimates even he had given in articles previously published, and disputed various claims made for Aurae Phiala by other authorities. Their aerial photographs he subjected to destructive scrutiny, the light crop lines they detected under the unbroken fields he dated several centuries later than the sacking of Aurae Phiala, the dark crop marks emerging so strongly in contrast he refused to consider as early Roman military lines, but set well back into pre-Roman settlement. (A light, sandy sub-soil, Charlotte learned, provided a first-class ground for crop-marks, since crops growing over ancient foundations tend to ripen and show yellow while the rest of the field is still green. And the crop-marks that show dark instead of pale are likely to lie along the lines where timber walls stood, prior to the stone.)

In short, Doctor Morris was bored with Aurae Phiala, and succeeded in making it slightly boring for his readers. Charlotte found herself intrigued by his handling of some of his colleagues who took views different from his own. His deference, while he refuted their conclusions, was careful and considerate. Even, perhaps, a little cagey? She felt almost sorry for Professor M. L. Vaughan, who was obviously in the same rank as her self-confident great-uncle, and differed from him on almost every point.

She would have been completely convinced, but for that limpid, lovely photograph on the book's cover, so serene, and pure, and gracious in its emptiness of man, a tragic landscape recognised and captured.

It was one of those cosmic accidents which are no accident, that the next day, when she called in at a bookshop to look for some more Morris titles, she should find on the same shelf the total output of Professor M. L. Vaughan; and among the rest his: *Aurae Phiala: A Pleasure City of the Second Century AD*. She took it down and opened it at random, and the prose caught her by its incandescent fervour. He was Welsh, of course, by his name; this frontier site might be expected to excite him. But he wrote like a sceptic captured and moved against his will.

She bought another of her uncle's books, but she bought, also, Professor Vaughan's; and his was the one she began to read, in the train to a modest concert engagement in Sussex.

Experts do differ, of course, even experts of equal eminence. And yet they were writing about the same place, and both of them knew it intimately, and had known it for years. Every indication Alan Morris rejected, Professor Vaughan accepted and expounded. He gave the city not eighty or so acres of ground, but more like two hundred and twenty, he burned to have the funds to take up lovingly every acre of those two hundred and twenty, and tenderly brush away the dust of centuries from every artifact he expected to recover; and his expectations were high. It was all very odd, very attractive, very mystifying.

Charlotte got back into London rather late that night, and rather tired, but hooked beyond redemption upon Aurae Phiala. It was the last preoccupation of her kinsman before his exit from England, and it was a strangely appealing bone of contention between him and several of his peers. Charlotte lay stretched upon her bed, waiting to relax enough for her bath, reviewing her evening's performance with merciless austerity – the oboe is a tyrannical instrument, and demands lofty standards – and confronting her odd, challenging, unknown English great-uncle, unexpectedly lost before she had ever become aware of him. He was beginning to threaten her personal security, her conviction of her own integrity. He was a ghost – a figure of speech, of course, she was in no doubt of his irrepressible re-emergence – whom she had to placate and exorcise.

She knew, then, that she was going to Aurae Phiala, to look at that charged, controversial, emotional ground-site for herself. It was a gesture without any wider significance, she knew that; she was exorcising and placating no one but herself. But at least she would be treading in his footsteps, and somewhere along the way a clearer picture of him might emerge. The move to Midshire even made economic sense; she had several modest school recitals in Birmingam and the Black Country during the next month, and it would be cheaper to move up there and find a furnished room somewhere, rather than spend the intervening time here in town.

She left by train for Comerbourne the next morning.

Chapter Two

She paid her ten pence at the glass cage of the entrance booth, to a young man who could not possibly be the custodian, Great-Uncle Alan's contemporary, but was clearly something rather more scholarly than a mere gate-keeper. He had a long, agreeable, supercilious face, dark eyes which dwelt upon his latest customer appreciatively but not offensively, and a general style that hovered oddly between the fastidious and the casual. His long hair stopped neatly at the level where it curved most attractively, but his shave was indifferent. Either that, or he had only yesterday decided to bow to fashion and grow a beard. His slacks and sweater were well-styled and good, but he managed to wear them as if they were about to fall off him. His aim had been either hopelessly inaccurate, or else capricious of intent. He had a pile of books, two or three open, and a large loose-leaf notebook at his table in a corner of the booth. It was early in the season yet, and he probably had long periods of inactivity to fill up between visitors; but he was not going to be left at leisure for long this time, for in the gravelled car park outside the enclosure a large bus was just disgorging a load of loud and active schoolboys, shepherded by a frantic youth hardly older than the eldest of his charges. The schools were evidently back after Easter.

Charlotte took her ticket, and went on into the enclosure of Aurae Phiala. Once round the low barrier of the gate-house and the prefabricated museum building, with her back turned on the plateau along which the road cruised towards distant Silcaster, the shallow, silver-green bowl of the book-jacket opened before her, wide and tranquil. There, even on this windy and showery day of late April, there was a stillness and a warmth, and in the flower-beds that had been laid out among the stretches of lush emerald turf the daffodils and narcissi were at least two weeks ahead of their fellows in the outer world. It was a naturally sheltered basin, a trick of the undulating meadows along the Comer. Narrow, gravelled paths led forward into the maze of low, broken stone walls, the pale ground-plan of a dead settlement. Delicately placed on a slight ridge, left-centre and midway between gatehouse and river, the surviving columns of the forum balanced, lifting the eyes to the exactly right focal point in a sky of scintillating, tearful blue feathered with airy clouds. Two groups of higher walls clustered below in the hollow of the bowl. And everywhere the orderly, skeletal bones of foundations, brittle and austere, patterned the brilliant grass.

The distant border of the enclosure was the river itself, sweeping in serpentine curves round the perimeter. From where she stood it shimmered in silver under a glancing sun, though upstream at the inn, where she had seen it close to, it rolled darkly brown and turgid, and laden with the debris of bushes, for the spring thaw had come late and violently, bringing down an immense weight of snow-water from the mountains of Wales. They were constructing a series of weirs upstream, so they had told her at 'The Salmon's Return', which would eventually control this annual predator, but for this year, at least, it surged down irresistibly as ever, biting acres out of its banks as it cornered, like a ferocious animal frustrated. Its wildness and this elegiac calm met, circled each other, and survived. The demon passed, not once for all, but constantly, and the dead turned over in their sleep, and went on dreaming.

From here, where she stood orientating herself to the unknown photographer's vision of Aurae Phiala, and sharing his revelation, even that violent force, at once protection and threat, seemed charmed into tameness, passing on tiptoe by this idyllic place.

'Idyllic! You're perfectly right,' said a voice just behind her shoulder; a male voice, pitched almost apologetically low, to make its uninvited approach respectable and respectful. And she was quite sure she had not said a word aloud! How did he know what she was thinking? It was a liberty. But wasn't it also a compliment? 'That's why they chose it,' the voice said, diverting her possible resentment before she could even be aware of it herself. 'It was a pleasure city, quite unreal like all its kind. And then it turned real – always the beginning of tragedy. People walked a tightrope here, in search of a secure living, just like today. And history walked out on them, and left them to die. It happens to most paradisal places. That's the irony.'

Many times during this pocket lecture she could have turned and looked at her instructor, and put him clean out of countenance merely by looking; but she had not done it because she was so sure that he was the young man from the entrance booth, a licensed enthusiast, and entitled to his brief moments of emotional escape. His bus-load of senior schoolboys were all over Aurae Phiala by this time, gushing downhill towards the river like streams in spate, and no doubt he was free for a minute or two to breathe again and care about his own theories and idylls. Besides, she liked his voice. It was low-pitched and reverentially modulated, a nice, crisp, modest baritone. And knowledgeable! She had a respect for people who knew their subject, and she was here to discover Aurae Phiala; he could be very useful to her.

'Are you doing research here?' she asked, and turned to face him.

Leaning over the glass counter of his booth, the young man in charge was deep in conversation with an elderly gentleman draped with cameras, and she was gazing into the face of quite a different person. The small shock of surprise disturbed her judgement for a moment, and the awareness of feeling and looking disconcerted inclined her to resent him, and to look for and find impudence in an approach which would have seemed perfectly excusable in a resident scholar. For that matter, she might not have been far out in thinking him impudent; his manner was innocence itself, his deference if anything delicately overdone, as though he were ready to come down off his high horse the moment she came down off hers, and didn't anticipate that the descent need be long delayed. He had the wit to keep talking.

'It began as a sort of rest-station and leave resort, as seasonal and artificial as a seaside fun-fair. And then it grew, and traders and service providers thought it worthwhile to settle here and go into business. They brought their families, some of them intermarried with time-expired soldiers who chose to settle here, too, and it grew into a real, life-and-death town, where everyone had a stake sunk so deep that when the legions started to leave, the locals still couldn't get out. Everything they had was here. No, I don't belong here, I'm only visiting,' he ended disarmingly, coming roundabout to the answer to her question. 'It's my subject, that's all. But I could see what you were thinking. It *is* a beautiful place.'

He was taller than she by only a few inches, and slenderly built, an athletic lightweight in a heather tweed sportscoat and grey cords. He had a thick crop of wiry hair the colour of good toffee, and heavy eyelashes many shades darker, as lavish as on a Jersey cow, fringing golden-brown eyes of such steady and limpid sincerity that she felt certain he could not possibly be just what he seemed. The face that confronted her with so much earnest goodwill and innocence, and with, she felt mistrustfully, such incalculable thoughts behind it, was square and brown, with a good deal of chin and nose to it, and an odd mouth with one corner higher than the other. He could have been anything from twenty-five to thirty, but not, she judged, beyond thirty. He did not look like a wolf, but he did look like a young man with an eye for a girl, and techniques that would bear watching.

'How kind of you,' she said, balancing nicely on the edge of irony, in case a few minutes more of this should see him running out of line to shoot, and make it desirable to jettison him '—how kind of you to tell me all about it!'

'Not at all!' he said, and had the grace to flush a little; she even had a fleeting suspicion that he enjoyed the ability to flush at will. 'How kind of you not to resent being told! I get carried away. Amateurs do. And this one I really like. Look at that hillscape over in Wales!' Fold on fold, rising gently from the water-meadows, the foothills receded in softening and paling shades of blue into the west. 'No wonder the men who'd served out their time put their savings into market stalls and little businesses, tanneries, dye-works, gardens. Nobody knew the risks better than they did. It was a brave gamble, and in the end they lost it. But it was a stake worth throwing for.'

'I should have thought,' said Charlotte, trapped into genuine interest and speculation, 'that they'd have built just a little further from the river. Weren't they for ever in danger of floods? Look at the height of the water now.'

'Ah, now, that's interesting. You see, the Comer has changed its course since the third century. Exactly when, we don't know, it may have been as late as the thirteenth century before it cut its way through. Come on down, and I'll show you.' And he actually took her arm, quite simply and confidently, and rushed her on the wings of his enthusiasm down through the green complexities of the bowl, between the crisp, serrated walls, across the fragments of tiled pavement, past the forum pillars, down to where the emerald turf sloped off under a token wire barrier to the riverside path and the waters of the Comer.

Here, at close quarters, the fitful, elusive silver congealed into the turgid brown flood she had seen upriver, a silent surge of water looking almost solid in its power, sweeping along leaves and branches and roots and swathes of weed in its eddies, gnawing away loose red layers of the soil along this near bank, and eating at the muddy rim of the path. The speed of its silent, thrusting passage dazzled her eyes as she stared into it. The snows in Wales had lain long, and the spring rains had been heavy and protracted; the Comer drank, and grew quietly mad.

'That's it!' she said, fascinated. 'That's what I meant. Would you choose to live close by that?'

'But look across the river there. You see how the level rises? Gently, but it rises, look right round where I'm pointing, and you'll see there's a whole oval island of higher ground. In Roman times the river flowed on the far side of that. Aurae Phiala was close enough for fishing, close to two good fords, in all but the flood months, and safe from actual flooding. In a broad valley like this you inevitably get these S-bends, and this was the biggest one. By the Middle Ages the river had gradually cut back through the neck of land at this side of the rise, until it cut right through to where it runs now. You can still trace the old course by the lush growth of bushes and trees. Look, a regular horse-shoe of them.'

She looked, and was impressed almost against her will, for everything was as he said. Alders and willows and rich grass and wild rose briars described a great, smooth horse-shoe shape that was still hollowed gently into the green earth, with such authority that it had been acknowledged in perpetuity as a natural boundary, and a single large field hemmed within it.

'Probably if they ever raise the funds to do a proper dig here, they'll find the town had a guard outpost on that hillock. Not that the tribesmen would attempt anything more than a quick raid by night, not until the legions were withdrawn. And if they ever did set out to open up this place,' he said consideringly, 'there are a dozen more important places to begin, of course.'

'Why haven't they ever? Labour isn't a problem, is it? I thought there were armies of students only too anxious to join digs in the long vacation.'

'It isn't the labour, it's the money. Excavation is a costly business, and Silcaster hasn't got enough money or enough interest.'

'Oh?' she said, surprised. 'I thought it was Ministry property.'

'No, it's privately owned. It belongs to Lord Silcaster. He keeps it up pretty decently, considering, but it's all done on a shoe-string, it has practically to pay for itself. The curator has a house downstream there, among the trees – you can see the red roof. And the only other staff seems to be that young fellow in the kiosk, and I rather think he's working for peanuts while he mugs up a thesis.'

'And a gardener-handyman,' said Charlotte, her eyes following the vigorous heave and surge of the mole-brown water as it tore down past them and ripped at the curve of the bank, lipping half across the trodden right of way. It had been higher still, probably some three or four days earlier, for it had bitten a great red hole in the shelving bank, like a long wound in the smooth turf, and left the traces of its attack in half-dried puddles of silky clay and a litter of sodden leaves and bushes. Round this broken area a big, blond young man in stained corduroys and a donkey jacket was busy erecting a system of iron posts striped in red and white, and stringing a rope from them to cordon off the slip.

'Hey, there's brickwork breaking through there!' Charlotte's companion said with quickening interest, and set off to have a closer look. The cordoned area was much bigger than they had realised, for several square yards of the level ground on top had subsided into ominous, shallow holes, here and there breaking the turf, and the slope down to the river path, once dropping gradually a matter of fifteen feet or so, now sagged in red rolls of soil and grass. The gardener had completed his magic circle, and was hanging three warning boards from the stanchions, with the legend boldly and hurriedly slashed in red paint: DANGER! KEEP CLEAR!

By a natural enough process, this injunction immediately attracted the most unruly fringe of the school party, straying from the group of their fellows in the forum. They came like flies to honey, not the heedless junior element, either, but a knot of budding sophisticates in their teens, led by a tall, slim sixteen-year-old on whose walk, manner and style all the rest appeared to be modelling themselves.

The young teacher, observing this deliberate defection, broke off his lecture to raise his voice, none too hopefully, after his strays. 'Boys, come back here at once! Come here and pay attention! Boden, do you hear?'

The boy who must be Boden heard very well. His strolling gait became exaggeratedly languid and assured. One or two of his following hesitated, wavered and turned back. Most of the others hovered diplomatically to make it look as if they were about to turn back, while still edging gingerly forward. Boden advanced at an insolent saunter to the stretched rope. The gardener, suddenly aware of him, reared erect to his full impressive six-feet-two and stood still, narrowly observing this unchancy opponent. The boy gazed back sweetly, forbearing from touching anything, and daring anyone to challenge his intentions. He was a good-looking boy, and knew it. He was pushing manhood, and much too well aware of that, though he believed himself to be much nearer maturity than he actually was. Twice he advanced a hand with deliberate teasing towards the hook that sustained the rope on the posts, and twice diverted the gesture into something innocuous. The gardener narrowed long, grey-blue eyes and made never a move. The boy stretched out a foot under the rope, and prodded with the toe of a well-polished shoe at the edge of one of the ominous cracks in the grass. The gardener, with deliberation, put down the spade he held, and took one long step to circle the obstruction between them.

The boy gave an amused flick of his head, swung round unhurriedly – yet not too slowly, either – and sauntered away with a laugh, his admirers tittering after him. Distant across the grass, the young teacher, with opportunist alacrity, chose that moment to call: 'That's better, Boden! Come on, now, quickly, you're holding up the whole party.'

'The secret of success with performing fleas,' said Charlotte's self-constituted guide startlingly, diverted even from his Roman passion, 'is to synchronise your orders with their hops. Our unfortunate young friend seems to know the principle, whether he can make it work or not.'

The gardener stood a moment to make sure that his antagonist was really retiring, then turned back to complete his work. His eye met Charlotte's, and his face flashed into a sudden brief, almost reluctant smile. 'Flipping kids!' he said in a broad, deep country voice, with a hint of the singing eloquence of Wales.

'They give you much trouble normally?' asked the young man.

'What you'd expect. Not that much,' he allowed tolerently. 'But that one's a case.'

'You know him?' the young man asked sympathetically.

'Never seen him before. I know his sort, though, on sight.'

'Oh, I don't know . . . he's just flexing his muscles.' He looked over his shoulder, to where the youthful shepherd was fretfully hustling his flock from the forum into the skeleton entrance of the baths. 'He's got a teacher bossing him around who's about four years older than he is, if that, and a lot less self-confident, but holding all the aces. Not that he plays them all that well,' he admitted, thoughtfully watching the harried youngster trying to be as tall as his tallest and most formidable charge. 'And of course,' he said aside to Charlotte, with a devastating smile, 'having a girl like you around doesn't make their problem any easier for either of them.'

'I could go away,' Charlotte offered, between offence and gratification.

'Don't do that!' he said hastily. 'Each of them would blame the other. And you haven't seen half what's here to be seen yet.' He turned back to the gardener. 'When did this slip happen?'

'This morning. Water's been right up over the path two days or more, I reckon it's loosened part o' the foundations under here.' He stood at the edge of the slope, looking down the line of his cordon and into the turgid water. 'Who'd get the blame, I ask you, if some young big-head like him got larking about in that lot, and the whole thing caved in and buried him alive? I don't reckon they'd allow as a rope and three notices was enough. It'd be me for it, me and Mr Paviour and his lordship – ah, and in that order! But they expect us to keep the place open for 'em. We got stated hours, nobody lets us off because the Comer floods.'

His deep, warm western voice had risen into plangent eloquence, indignant and rapt. And Charlotte was suddenly aware of him as a person, and by no means an unintelligent person, either; but above all a vital presence, to be ignored only at the general peril. He was built rather heavily even for his height, a monumental creature admirably suited to these classic and heroic surroundings; and his face was a mask of antique beauty, but crudely cut out of a local stone. She could see him as a prototype for the border entrepreneur trapped here in the decline and fall of this precarious city, the market-stallholder, the baths attendant, the potter, the vegetable grower, any one of the native opportunists who had rallied to serve and exploit this hothouse community of time-expired settlers and pay-happy leave-men. He had a forehead and nose any Greek might have acknowledged with pride, and long, grey-blue eyes like slivers of self-illuminating stone, somewhere between lapis-lazuli and granite. His fairness inclined ever so slightly towards the Celtic red of parts of Wales, an alien colouring in both countries. He had a full, passionate, childlike mouth, generously shaped but brutally finished; and his clean-shaven cheeks and jaw were powerful and fleshless, pure, massive bone under the fine, fair skin. It was easy to see that his roots went down fathoms deep in this soil, and transplanting would have destroyed everything in him that was of quality. There was nowhere else he belonged.

Charlotte said, on an impulse she only partially understood: 'Don't worry about him. In an hour they'll be gone.' And just as impulsively she turned to check on the movements of that incalculable swarm of half-grown children who were causing him this natural anxiety. The boys and their uneasy pastor were moving tidily enough into the first green enclosure which must be the frigidarium of the baths, emerging in little, bulbous groups from between the broken walls of the entrance. She saw the stragglers gather, none too enthusiastically, but not unwillingly, either, and waited for the last-comers. Something was missing there. It took her a few minutes to realise what it was. The teacher, self-consciously gathering his chicks about him, was now the tallest person in sight. Where had the odious senior, Boden, gone, somewhere among those broken, enfolding walls? And how had he shed his train? The numbers there looked more or less complete. He was a natural stray, of course. He needed the minimum of cover to drop out of sight, whenever it suited him. But at least he was well away from here. No doubt something else had diverted his attention, and afforded him another cue to spread confusion everywhere around him.

'There's always closing-time,' said the gardener-handyman philosophically. He lifted one narrowed glance of blue-grey eyes, slanting from Charlotte to her escort and sharing a fleeting smile between them as recognised allies. He was gone, withdrawing rather like a mountain on the move, downriver where the water most encroached. He walked like a mountain should walk, too, striding without upheaval, drawing his roots with him.

'Come down to the path,' said the enthusiast, abruptly returning to his passion as soon as the distractions withdrew, 'and I'll show you something. Round this way it's not so steep. Here, let me go first.' He took possession of her hand with almost too much confidence, drawing her with him down the slippery slope of wet grass towards the waterside. Her smooth-soled court shoes glissaded in the glazed turf, and he stood solidly, large feet planted, and let her slide bodily against him. He looked willowy enough, but he felt like a rock. They blinked at each other for a moment at close quarters, wide-eyed and brow to brow.

'I ought to have introduced myself,' said the young man, as though prompted by this accidental intimacy, and gave her a dazzled smile. 'My name's Hambro – Augustus, of all the dirty tricks. My friends call me Gus.'

'I suspect,' she said, shifting a little to recover firmer standing, 'that should be Professor Hambro? And FSA after it? At least!' But she did not respond with her own name. She was not yet ready to commit herself so far. And after all, this could be only a very passing encounter.

'Just an amateur,' he said modestly, evading questioning as adroitly as she. 'Hold tight . . . the gravel breaks through here, there's a better grip. Now, look what the river did to one bit of the baths.'

They stood on the landward edge of the riverside path, very close to the lipping water. Before them the bevelled slope, fifteen feet high, cut off from them the whole upper expanse of Aurae Phiala, with all its flower-beds and stone walls; and all its visitors had vanished with it. They were alone with the silently hurtling river and the great, gross wound it had made in this bank, curls of dark-red soil peeled back and rolling downhill, and a tangle of uprooted broom bushes. At a level slightly higher than their heads, and several yards within the cordon, this raw soil fell away from a dark hole like the mouth of a deep, narrow cave, large enough, perhaps, to admit a small child. The top of it was arched, and looked like brickwork, the pale amber brick of Aurae Phiala. Bushes sagged loosely beneath it; and the masonry at the crown of the arch showed paler than on either curve, as though it had been exposed to the air longer, perhaps concealed by the sheltering broom.

'You know,' said Gus, as proudly as if he had discovered it himself, 'what that is? It's the extreme corner of what must be one hell of a huge hypocaust.'

'Really?' she said cautiously, still not quite convinced that he was not shooting a shameless line in exploitation of her supposed ignorance. 'What's a hypocaust?'

'It's the system of brick flues that runs under the entire floor of the caldarium – the hot room of the baths – to circulate the hot air from the furnace. That's how they heated the place. Narrow passages like that one, built in a network right from here to about where the school party was standing a few minutes ago. They'd just come in, as it were, from the street, through the palaestra, the games courts and exercise

26

ground, and into the cold room. The chaps who wanted the cold plunge would undress and leave their things in lockers there, and there were two small cold basins to swim in – two here, anyhow – one on either side. The sybarites who wanted the hot water bath or the hot air bath would pass through into the slightly heated room one stage farther in, and undress there, then go on in to whichever they fancied. The hypocaust ran under both. If you were fond of hot water, you wallowed in a sunken basin. If you favoured sweating it out, you sat around on tiered benches and chatted with your friends until you started dissolving into steam, and then got yourself scraped down by a slave with a sort of sickle thing called a strigil, and massaged, and oiled and perfumed, or if you were a real fanatic you probably went straight from the hot room to take a cold plunge, like sauna addicts rolling in the snow. And then you were considered in a fit state to go and eat your dinner.'

'By then,' she said demurely, 'I should think you'd want it.'

He eyed her with a suspicious but quite unabashed smile. 'You know all this, don't you? You've been reading this place up.'

'I could hardly read up this bit, could I? It only came to light today.' She strained her eyes into the broken circle of darkness, and a breath of ancient tension and fear seemed to issue chillingly from the hole the river had torn in history. 'But they're quite big, those flues, if that's their width. A man could creep through them.'

'They had to be cleaned periodically. These aren't unusual. But the size of the whole complex is, if I'm right about this.'

She let him help her back up the slope, round the other side of the danger area, and demonstrate by the skeletal walls where the various rooms of the baths lay, and their impressive extent.

She had no idea why she suddenly looked back, as they set off across the level turf that stretched above that mysterious underworld of brick-built labyrinths. The newness of the scar, the crudity of the glimpse it afforded into long-past prosperities and distresses, the very fact that no one, since this city was abandoned overnight, had threaded the maze below – a matter of fifteen centuries or more – drew her imagination almost against her will, and she turned her head in involuntary salute and promise, knowing she would come back again and again. Thus she saw, with surprise and disquiet, the young, dark head cautiously hoisted out of cover to peer after them. How could he be there? And why should he want to? The incalculable Boden had somehow worked his way round once again into forbidden territory, had been lurking somewhere in the bushes, waiting for them to leave. The twentieth century, inquisitive, irreverent, quite without feeling for the past, homed in upon this ambiguous danger-zone with its life in its hand.

She clutched at her companion's arm, halting him in mid-spate and bringing his head round in respectful enquiry.

'That boy! He's there again – but inside the rope now! Why do they *have* to go where it says: Danger?'

Gus Hambro wheeled about with unexpectedly authoritative aplomb, just in time to see the well-groomed young head duck out of sight. He dropped Charlotte's hand, took three large strides back towards the crest, and launched a bellow of disapproval at least ten times as effective as the hapless teacher's appeals:

'Get out of that! Yes, *you*! Want me to come and fetch you? *And stay out!*'

He noted the rapid, undignified scramble by which the culprit extricated himself from the ropes on the river path, followed by ominous little trickles of loose earth; and the exaggerated dignity with which he compensated as soon as he was clear, his slender back turned upon the voice that blasted him out of danger, his crest self-consciously reared in affected disregard of sounds which could not possibly be directed at him.

'Those notices,' announced Gus clearly to the general air, but not so loudly as to reach unauthorised ears, 'mean exactly what they say. Anybody we have to dig out of there we're going to skin alive afterwards. So watch it!'

It was at that point that Charlotte began seriously to like her guide, and to respect his judgement. 'That's it,' he said, tolerantly watching the Boden boy's swaggering retreat towards the curator's house. 'He'll lay off now. His own shower weren't around to hear that, he'll be glad to get back to where he rates as a hero.'

She was not quite so sure, for some reason, but she didn't say so. The tall, straight young back that sauntered away downriver, to come about in a wide circuit via the fence of the curator's garden, and the box hedge that continued its line, maintained too secure an assurance, and too secret a satisfaction of its own, in spite of the dexterity with which it had removed itself from censure. This Boden observed other people's taboos just so far as was necessary, but he went his own way, sure that no values were valid but his own. Still, he removed himself, if only as a gesture. That was something.

'You did that very nicely,' she said, surprising herself.

'I try my best,' he said, unsurprised. 'After all, I've been sixteen myself. I know it's some time ago, but I do remember, vaguely. And I'm not sure it isn't all your fault.'

She felt sure by then that it was not; she was completely irrelevant. But she did not say so. She was beginning to think that this Gus Hambro was a good deal more ingenuous than he supposed; but if so, it was an engaging disability in him.

'I was going to show you the laconicum,' he said, and he turned and snuffed like a hound across the green, open bowl, and set out on a selected trail, nose to scent, heading obliquely for the complex of standing walls where several rooms of the ancient baths converged. The amber brickwork and rosy layers of tile soared here into the complicated pattern of masonry against the pale azure sky.

'You see? That same floor we've been crossing reaches right to here, one great caldarium, with that hypocaust deployed underneath it all the way. And just here is the vent from the heating system, the column that brought the hot air directly up here into the room when required.'

It was merely a framework of broken, blonde walls, barely knee-high, like the shaft of a huge well, a shell withdrawn into a corner of the great room. Over the round vent a rough wooden cover, obviously modern, was laid. Gus put a hand to its edge and lifted, and the cover rose on its rim, and showed them a glimpse of a deep shaft dropping into darkness, partially silted up below with rubble.

'Yes – it would take some money and labour to dig that lot out! Wonder what happened to the original cover? It would be bronze, probably. Maybe it's in the museum, though I think some of the better finds went to the town museum in Silcaster.'

'This is what you call the laconicum?' she asked, drawing back rather dubiously from the dank breath that distilled out of the earth.

'That's it. Though you might, in some places, get the word laconia used for small hot-air rooms, too. They could send the temperature up quickly when required, by raising the cover – even admit the flames from the furnace if they wanted to. Come and have a look round the museum. If you've time? But perhaps you've got a long drive ahead,' he said, not so much hesitantly as enquiringly.

'I'm staying at "The Salmon's Return", just upstream,' she said. 'Ten minutes' walk, if that. Yes, let's see the museum, too.'

It was a square, prefabricated building, none too appropriate to the site, but banished to the least obtrusive position, behind the entrance kiosk. It was full of glass cases, blocks of stone bearing vestigial carving, some fragments of very beautiful lettering upon the remains of a stone tablet, chattering schoolboys prodding inquisitively everywhere, and the young teacher, perspiring freely now, delivering a lecture upon Samian ware. Boden was not among his listeners, nor anywhere in the three small, crowded rooms. By this time Charlotte would have felt a shock of surprise at ever finding that young man where he was supposed to be.

They made the round of the place. A great deal of red glaze pottery, some glass vessels, even one or two fragments of silver; tarnished mirrors, ivory pins, little bronze brooches, a ring or two. Gus, tepid about the collection in general, grew excited about one or two personal ornaments.

'See this little dragon brooch – there isn't a straight line in it, it's composed of a dozen quite unnecessarily complex curves. Can you think of anything less Roman? Yet it is Roman – interbred with Celtic. Like the mixed marriages that were general here. This kind of ornament, in a great many variations, you can locate all down this border. In the north, too, but they differ enough to be recognisable.'

She found the same curvilinear decoration in several other pieces, and delighted him by picking them out without hesitation from the precise and formal Roman artifacts round them.

'Anything that looks like a symbol for a labyrinth, odds on it's either Celtic or Norse.'

It was nearly closing time, and the school party, thankfully marshalled by its young leader, was pouring vociferously out into the chill of the early evening, and heading with released shouts for its waiting coach. The last and smallest darted back, self-importantly, to inscribe his name with care in the visitors' book, which lay open on a table by the door, before allowing himself to be shepherded after his companions. On impulse, Charlotte stopped to look at what he had added in the 'Remarks' column, and laughed. 'Veni, vidi, vici', announced the ball-pen scrawl.

'You should sign, too,' said Gus, at her shoulder.

She knew why, but by then it was almost over in any case, for when was she likely to see him again? So she signed 'Charlotte Rossignol', well aware that he was reading the letters as fast as she formed them.

'Now may I drive you back to the pub?' he said casually, as they emerged into the open air, and found the studious young man of the kiosk waiting to see his last customers out, one finger still keeping his place in a book. 'I'm staying there, too. And as it happens, I didn't walk. I've got my car here.'

The car park was empty but for the elderly gentleman's massive Ford, which was just crunching over the gravel towards the road, an old but impressive bronze Aston Martin which Charlotte supposed must belong to Gus – it sent him up a couple of notches in her regard – and the school bus, still stationary, boiling over with bored boys, and emitting a plaintive chorus of: 'Why are we waiting?' The driver stood leaning negligently against a front wing, rolling himself a cigarette. Clearly he had long since trained himself to tune out all awareness of boys unless they menaced his engine or coachwork.

And why *were* they waiting? The noise they were making indicated that no teacher was present, and there could be only one explanation for his absence now.

'He's lost his stray again,' said Gus, halting with the car keys levelled in his hand.

'Here he comes now.' And so he did, puffing up out of the silvered, twilit bowl of Aurae Phiala, ominous at dusk under a low ceiling of dun cloud severed from the earth by a rim of lurid gold. A glass bowl of fragile relics closed with a pewter lid; and outside, the fires of ruin, like a momentary recollection of the night, how many centuries ago, when the Welsh tribesmen massed, raided, killed and burned, writing 'Finis' to the history of this haunted city.

'Poor boy!' said Charlotte, suddenly outraged by the weariness and exasperation of this ineffectual little man, worn out by a job he had probably chosen as the most profitable within his scope, and now found to be extending him far beyond the end of his tether. 'Whoever persuaded him he ought to be a teacher?'

'He's not that far gone,' Gus assured her with unexpected shrewdness. 'He knows when to write off his losses.'

The young man came surging up to them, as the only other responsible people left around. 'I beg your pardon, but you haven't seen one of my senior pupils around anywhere, by any chance? A dark boy, nearly seventeen, answers – *when* he answers! – to the name of Gerry Boden. He's a professional absentee. Where we are, he is most likely not to be. Sometimes with escort – chorus, rather! This time, apparently, without, which must be by his own contriving. I'm missing just one boy – the magnate himself.'

Between them they supplied all they could remember of the encounter by the roped-off enclosure above the river.

'He never did come back to us,' said the young man positively. 'I always know whether he's there or not. Like a pain, if you know what I mean.' They knew what he meant. He shrugged, not merely helplessly, rather with malevolent acceptance. 'Well, I've looked everywhere. He does it on purpose, of course. This isn't the first time. He's nearly seventeen, he has plenty of money in his pockets, and he knows this district like the palm of his hand. We're no more than ten miles from home. He can get a bus or a taxi, and he knows very well where to get either. I don't know why I worry about him.'

'Having a conscience does complicate things,' said Gus with sympathy.

'It simplifies this one,' said the teacher grimly. 'I've got a conscience about all this lot, all of 'em younger than our Gerry. This time he can look out for himself, I'm going to get the rest home on time.'

He clambered aboard the coach, the juniors raised a brief, cheeky cheer, half mocking and half friendly, the driver hoisted himself imperturbably into his cab, and the coach started up and surged ponderously through the gates and away along the Silcaster road.

Charlotte turned, before getting into the car, and looked back once in a long, sweeping survey of the twilit bowl of turf and stone. Nothing moved there except the few blackheaded gulls wheeling and crying above the river. A shadowy, elegiac beauty clothed Aurae Phiala, but there was nothing alive within it.

'When did it happen?' she asked. 'The attack from the west, the one that finally drove the survivors away?'

'Quite late, around the end of the fourth century. Most of the legions were gone long before that. Frantic appeals for help kept going out to Rome – Rome was still the patron, the protector, the fortress, even when she was falling to pieces herself. About twenty years after the sack of Aurae Phiala, Honorius finally issued an edict that recognised what had been true for nearly a century. He told the Britons they could look for nothing more, no money, no troops, no aid. From then on they had to shift for themselves.'

'And the Saxons moved in,' said Charlotte.

He smiled, holding the passenger door open for her. By this time he would not have been surprised if she had taken up the lecture and returned him a brief history of the next four centuries. 'Well, the

Welsh, over this side. Death from the past, not the future. A couple of anachronisms fighting it out here while real life moved in on them from the east almost unnoticed. But their kin survived and inter-married. Nothing quite disappears in history.'

But she thought, looking back at that pewter sky and narrow saffron afterglow as the Aston Martin purred into life and shot away at speed: Yes, individuals do! Perversely, wilfully or haplessly, they do vanish. One elderly, raffish archaeologist in Turkey, one uneasy, spoiled ado!escent here. But of course they'll both emerge some-where. Probably the boy's halfway home by now, ahead of his party, probably he thumbed a lift the other way along this road as soon as he got intolerably bored. That would amuse him, the thought of the fuss and the delay and the inconvenience to everyone, while he rode home to wherever home is, in the cab of a friendly lorry.

And Doctor Alan Morris? He could be accounted for just as easily, and much more rationally. Total absorption in his passion could submerge him far below the surface of mere time. Somewhere in Anatolia, as yet unheralded, a major news story was surely brewing, to burst on the world presently in a rash of photographs, films, television interviews – some new discovery, one more Roman footprint in the east, stumbled on happily, and of such delirious interest that its discoverer forgot about the passing of the year, his minor responsibilities, and his fretful solicitor.

Over Aurae Phiala the April dusk closed very softly and calmly, like a hand crushing a silvery moth. But her back was turned on the dead city then, and she did not see.

Chapter Three

'The Salmon's Return' lay a quarter of a mile up-river, and dated back to the early seventeenth century, a long, low, white-painted house on a terrace cunningly clear of the flood level of the Comer, and with ideal fishing water for some hundreds of yards on either side of it. It was small, and aware of the virtues of remaining small, lurking ambiguously between hotel and pub, and retaining its hold on the local bar custom while it lured in the fanatical fishermen from half the county for weekend indulgences and occasional contests. Its ceilings were low, and its corners many and intimate. And it belonged to a family, and reflected their stubborn conservative tastes, with a minimum of staff providing a maximum of service. The only relatively new thing about it was its romantic and truthful name, which someone in the family had thought up early in the nineteenth century as an improvement on 'The Leybourne Arms'; for the Leybourne family had been extinct since the fourteenth century, while salmon regularly did return several miles up-river from this house, and were regularly taken for a mile on either side. Downstream, the nearest weir was a tourist sight in the season, flashing with silvery leaps as the salmon climbed to their spawning-grounds.

From the narrow approach lane a gravel drive swung round to the side door of the inn, and then continued, dwindling, to the rear, where there was a brick garage and a half-grassy car park. Gus halted the Aston Martin at the doorway instead of driving straight on to the garage, and was out of the driving-seat like a greyhound out of a trap, to dart round to the passenger side and hand Charlotte out. His meticulous performance slightly surprised her; there had been moments when they seemed to have achieved a more casual contact, and he couldn't be still trying to impress. However, she allowed him to squire her to the desk, without comment and with a straight face, told him the number of her key, though keys were almost an affectation at 'The Salmon's Return', more for ornament than use, and let him take it down for her and escort her to the foot of the oak staircase, which wound in slightly drunken lurches about a narrow well, the polished treads hollowed by centuries of use.

He stood back then, and let her go, and she mounted the first flight, and the second, planting her fashionable square heels firmly on the beautiful old wood, which was austerely and very properly without covering, and recorded her movements accurately for anyone listening below. She didn't look back, and she didn't linger, but her ears were pricked at every step. She felt, rather than heard, how he turned smartly and loped back across the panelled hall towards the door, no doubt to drive the car round into the garage. No doubt! Except that he was in no hurry about starting it up. Its aristocratic note was not loud, but proudly characteristic. Though she had no car of her own just now, Charlotte had been driving, and driving well, for more than four years.

The second landing was carpeted, the wood of the flooring being slightly worn and hollowed. Her steps could no longer be heard below, once she reached the corridor. She did not even go as far as her room – the sound of the door being unlocked, opening and closing again should surely not carry down to the hall. She kicked off her shoes on the carpet, and slid back silently to listen down the well of the staircase; and picking up from this level only minor and ambiguous sounds, she went quickly down again one floor, to where she could lean cautiously over the glossy black banister, and train both eyes and ears upon any activity in the hall below. Visually, her range was limited. The acoustics were excellent.

She had no idea, until then, why she was acting as she was, or what she suspected, or why, indeed, she should suspect anything but a straight pick-up, and one so simply and attractively engineered as to be quite unalarming; a normal minor wolf on the prowl, with a long weekend to while away, and an eye cocked for congenial company, preferably intimate, but in any case gratifying. And yet she held her breath as she leaned out from the cover of the first-floor corridor, and hung cautiously over the oak rail.

Mrs Lane was there just below her; she could see the top of the round, erect, crisply waved head of iron-grey hair, and the bountiful bulges, fore and aft, of the pocket-clipper figure below. Mrs Lane was the miniature goddess who controlled her large, tolerant, good-humoured menfolk, and made this whole organisation work. And at this moment she had a finger threading the maze of the register, and one hand already vaguely gesturing towards the key-board.

'Well, yes,' said the comfortable border voice, pondering, 'I can give you a single room, but only for two nights, I'm afraid. Weekends we're usually booked up in advance, you see, even in the close season. There's a club meeting here for a social weekend – I think they like to keep their places warm here for when coarse fishing starts again. Number 12, if two nights is any good to you?'

'Better than nothing.' said Gus Hambro's voice heartily, but with circumspect quietness. 'I'll take it, and gratefully. This is a dream of a position you've got here, with the path down-river. You ought to keep rooms for archaeologists as well as fishermen.'

'They're not so predictable,' said Mrs Lane practically, 'and they do so tend to camp, you know. The fishermen are good men for their comforts, and then they do patronise the bar. After all, you need an audience when you talk about fish, and salmon especially. You don't fish yourself now, Mr Hambro?'

'I never really had time,' said the winning baritone voice. 'You might convert me, at that! Number 12, you said? And I can move my car round into the garage? Fine, I'll find my way. I'll sign in when I've put her away for the night.'

Charlotte withdrew into cover, and hoped no one on the upper deck had fallen over her discarded shoes. Gus was plunging away out of the door, contented with his dispositions, and Mrs Lane, apparently satisfied of his *bona fides* – and Mrs Lane had an inbuilt crystal globe, and took some satisfying – had subsided into her private enclosure and was lost to sight. Charlotte climbed the stairs to her own room, and let herself in silently, with considerable doubts about her own situation.

She sat on the edge of her bed and thought it out. It need not, after all, be so abstruse, or so deeply suspect. He was young, alert, very much aware of the opposite sex, and with a personal taste which apparently inclined strongly towards her type. When she had revealed that she was staying here, he had simply decided to hook up and join on. But no, that wouldn't do! She chilled, remembering. She had told him where she was booked, and at that stage he hadn't reacted at all. Not until she had signed her name in the book, at his request, and his long-sighted eyes had read it over her shoulder. Only after that had he said: 'Let me drive you back, I'm staying there, too'. As he had certainly not been, it seemed; not until now.

But what could her name mean to him? It wasn't Morris, it wasn't identifiable, even to a keen archaeologist – not unless he happened to be all too well informed about the experts who had interested themselves in Aurae Phiala, and even in their heirs and heiresses, down to herself.

But why? What could he be after, where could he fit in, if this was true? No, she was imagining things. He had simply hesitated to take the plunge and stake on a worthwhile weekend with her, and it was pure chance that he had made up his mind just after he had learned her name. Logic argued the case for this theory, but instinct rejected it. Unless she was much mistaken in that young man, pure chance played very little part in his proceedings. His manipulation of impudence and deference was too assured for that. Whatever he was about, there was method in his madness.

Well, she thought, it won't be difficult to judge how right I am, if I pay out a few yards of line for him. If he isn't just amusing himself, then I can expect total siege. And I shan't be making the mistake of attributing it to any charms of mine, either. And even if I'm wrong – well, I might find it quite amusing, too.

She had not intended changing for the evening, country inns being the right setting for good tweed suits; but now she took her time about dressing, and chose a very austere frock in a dark russet-orange shade that touched off the marmalade lights in her eyes. Why not use what armoury one has? If he was setting out to find out more about her, she could certainly do with knowing a little more about him, and her chances were at least as good as his.

He was sitting in the bar with a drink and the evening paper when she came down, and though he appeared not to notice her quiet descent until she was at the foot of the stairs, she had seen him shift his weight some seconds before he looked up, ready to spring to his feet and intercept her. The look of admiration and pleasure, she hoped, was at any rate partly genuine.

'May I get you a drink? What would you like?' No doubt about it, he meant to corner her for the evening. If he had been simply playing the girl game, she reasoned, he would be getting steadily more intimate, and here he is reverting to deference. Because I'm Uncle Alan's niece? But she could not believe in him as that kind of reverent fan, whatever his enthusiasm for his subject.

'Since we're both alone here,' said Gus, coming back from the bar with her sherry, 'will you be kind enough to have dinner with me? It would be a pity to eat good food in silence, don't you think?'

'Thank you,' she said gravely, 'I'd like that very much.' Not that she intended accepting any favours from him, but she knew he was booked in for two nights, which gave her time to return his hospitality if she could not manipulate tonight into a Dutch treat.

'When you get bored with my conversation,' he said, 'I promise to shut up. There's even a telly tucked away somewhere.'

Boredom, thought Charlotte, as she made her way before him across the small panelled dining-room, is one thing I don't anticipate.

By the time they reached the coffee stage it had become clear that he was doing his best to pump her, though she hoped he had not yet realised how little result he was getting, or how assiduously she was trying, in her turn, to find out more about him. The process would have been entirely pleasant, if the puzzling implication had not lingered in her mind throughout, like a dark shadow without a substance. And his method had its own grace.

She saw fit to admit to her musical background. Why not, since some of her Midland concerts would be advertised in the local press, and inevitably come to his notice? 'I call that one of the supreme bits of luck in life,' he said warmly, 'to be able to make your living out of what you love doing.'

'So do I. One you enjoy, too, surely? Don't tell me you don't love your archaeology. But how does one make a living at it? Apart from teaching? Are you attached to one of the universities?' Her tone was one of friendly and candid interest, but she wasn't getting many bites, either. We should both make better fish than fishermen, she thought.

'There aren't enough places to go round,' he said ruefully, 'and I'm not that good. Some of us have to make do with jobs on the fringe.'

'Such as what? What *do* you do, exactly?' No need for her to be as subtle as he was being. She had, as far as he knew, no reason to be curious, and therefore no reason to dissemble her curiosity. It was an unfair advantage, though; it made it harder for him to evade answering.

'Such as acting as consultant and adviser on antiques generally – or in my case on one period. Valuer – research man – I even restore pieces sometimes.'

'Freelance? It sounds a little risky. Supposing there weren't enough clients?'

He smiled, rather engagingly, she admitted. 'I'm retained by quite a big outfit. And there's never any lack of clients.'

It was at that point that the stranger entered the dining-room, and stood for a moment looking round him as if in search of an acquaintance. Charlotte had seen him turn in the doorway to speak to Mrs Lane, whose placid smile indicated that she knew and welcomed him. He looked like a local man, at home and unobtrusive in this comfortable country room as he would have been in the border landscape outside. He was tall and thin, a leggy lightweight in a dark-grey suit, with a pleasant, long, cleanshaven face, and short hair greying at the temples and receding slightly from a weathered brown forehead. He was of an age to be able to wear his hair comfortably short and his chin shaven without eccentricity, probably around fifty. Middle age has its compensations.

There were only a few people left in the dining-room by that time, two elderly men earnestly swapping fishing stories over their brandy, a young couple holding hands fondly under the table, and a solitary ancient in a leather-elbowed tweed jacket, reading the evening paper. The newcomer scanned them all, and his glance settled upon Charlotte and her companion. He came threading his way between the tables, and halted beside them.

'I beg your pardon! Miss Rossignol? And Mr Hambro? I'm sorry to intrude on you at this hour, but if you can give me a few minutes of your time you may be able to help me, and I'll be very much obliged.'

Charlotte had assented to her name with a startled bow, but without words. Gus Hambro looked up with rounded brows and a good-natured smile, and said vaguely: 'Anything we can do, of course! But are you sure it's us you want? We're just visitors around here.'

The stranger smiled, still rather gravely but with a warmth that Charlotte found reassuring. 'If you weren't, you probably wouldn't come within my – strictly unofficial – brief. We locals don't frequent Aurae Phiala much, we've lived with it all our lives, it doesn't excite us. I gather from the visitors' book that you were both there this afternoon, that's the only reason for this visit. May I sit down?'

'Oh, please!' said Charlotte. 'Do excuse us, you took us so by surprise.'

'Thank you!' he said, and drew up a third chair. His voice was low, equable and leisurely; so much so that only afterwards did it dawn upon Charlotte how very few minutes the whole interview had occupied. 'My name is Felse. Detective Chief Inspector, Midshire CID – I mention it only by way of presenting credentials. Strictly speaking I'm not occupied on a case at the moment, and this is quite unofficial. If you were at Aurae Phiala this afternoon you probably saw something of a party of schoolboys going round the site with a teacher in charge. A coachload of them from Comerbourne.'

'We could hardly miss them,' said Gus. 'They were loading up to leave just when we came out.'

'Including a senior, a boy about seventeen, who was probably subjecting his teacher to a certain amount of needling?'

'Name of Boden,' said Gus. 'We had a modest brush with him ourselves. Incidentally, they'd lost him – the coach set off without him in the end.'

'Exactly the point,' said Chief Inspector Felse. 'He still hasn't come home.' He caught the surprised and doubtful glance they exchanged, and went on practically: 'I know! He's perfectly competent, well supplied with money always, and it's no more than a quarter past nine. Probably you'd already gathered that it isn't the first time he's played similar tricks, and that he's a law to himself, and comes and goes as he pleases. The simple fact remains, he's never yet been known to miss a meal. Suppose you tell me exactly where and how you last saw him.'

They did so, in detail, each supplementing the other's account and refreshing the other's memory.

'Odd as it seems, that's the latest mention of him I've got so far. He drew off and went back towards his party?'

'Not directly,' said Charlotte. 'I suppose we just took it that he would, and weren't surprised that he made a pretence of being unconcerned and going his own way about it. What he actually did was to stroll away downriver, right along the perimeter. I watched him as far as the corner of the curator's garden, and saw him turn in alongside the hedge. I didn't pay any attention afterwards. I just took it for granted he was on his way back to the group.'

'I've talked to his particular friends. None of them saw him again. He never rejoined his party.'

'Have his parents reported him missing?' asked Gus.

'No, not yet. His father happens to be a close neighbour of mine in the village of Comerford, that's all. Young Collins – he teaches Latin for his sins – reported to the Bodens when the coach got back to Comerbourne, not to complain of the kid, but so that they shouldn't be worried about his non-arrival. They know their son, and are more or less resigned to his caprices, but they know his consistencies,too. He likes his comforts and he likes his food. When he failed to show up by half past eight they did begin to wonder. I happen to be three doors away, and dropping it in my lap is a discreet step short of making an official report. Easier to back out of, and sometimes produces the same result. This isn't a case. And if it ever becomes one – God forbid! – it won't be my case. But the odds are Gerry's merely run into something more interesting than usual, worth being late for supper.'

'A girl?' suggested Gus dubiously.

'It happens. Though up to now he's been too much in love with himself,' said the chief inspector frankly, 'to show much interest in girls. He's not a bad kid, really. Just the only one, too spoiled, and too clever.' He rose, and restored his chair to its place at the neighbouring table. 'Thanks, anyhow, for pin-pointing the actual place and time. No one seems to have caught a glimpse of him since.'

'You don't think,' said Charlotte, suddenly uneasy, 'that he could possibly have missed his footing and slipped into the river? It's running so high, and so fast, even a good swimmer might not be able to get out if he once got caught in the current.'

'No, I don't. He *is* a good swimmer – quite good enough, and quite mature enough in that way, to respect flood water. And he wasn't attended by his admirers at that stage, so he had no inducement to show off by taking risks. No, I feel confident he absented himself deliberately, for some reason of his own.'

'Then he'll reappear,' she said, 'in his own good time.'

'In all probability he will. As soon as he begins to think pleasurably of his bed.' He smiled at her. 'Thank you, Miss Rossignol, and goodnight. Goodnight, Mr Hambro.'

He turned and left the room, threading his way between the deserted tables to vanish in the warm, wood-scented half-darkness of the hall. In a few moments they heard a car start up and drive away. Downriver, Charlotte thought. Perhaps he wasn't as completely convinced as he made out that a lost boy, however bright and confident, could not have ended in the Comer. And perhaps he wasn't going to wait until morning before launching a search.

Gus Hambro was sitting quite still, his brows drawn together in a tight and abstracted frown, and the focus of his eyes fixed far beyond the panelling of the dining-room.

'Of course he'll be all right,' said Charlotte, all the more firmly because she was not totally convinced.

Gus said: 'Of course!' in a slightly startled voice, and visibly withdrew his vision and his thoughts from some distant preoccupation in which she had no part. He looked vaguely at her, and quickly and intently at his watch; but at least he had returned to the consciousness that she was present. He even managed a perfunctory smile. 'He'll turn up when it suits him. Don't worry about him. What do you say, shall we see what's on television?'

Her thumbs pricked then. She let him accompany her into the small lounge where the set was kept in segregation from the vocal and gregarious fishermen, and settle her in a comfortable chair, cheek by jowl with a single elderly lady, who seemed pleased to have company, and disposed to conversation. That suited him very well. Charlotte was counting the seconds until he should extricate himself, and he did it in less time than she had expected, and without even the pretence of sitting down with her.

'You won't mind if I leave you to watch this without me? There's a letter I really ought to get written tonight – I hadn't realised it was quite so late, and I can get it off by first post if I do it now.'

'Of course!' she said. 'In any case, I shall be going to bed very soon, I am rather tired.'

'I'll say goodnight, then, if you'll excuse me.'

'Goodnight, Mr Hambro.'

It sounded absurdly false to her, as though they were playing a rather bald comedy for the benefit of the elderly lady, who was dividing her benign attention between them and a quivering travel film. He withdrew quickly and quietly, closing the door carefully after him. Charlotte strained her ears to hear whether he would slip out by the side door and make straight for the garage at the rear of the house for his car, but instead she heard the crisp, light rapping of his heels on the oak staircase. Room 12 was on the first floor. Arguably he must be bound there now, but almost certainly he had no intention of staying there.

'Oh, dear!' said Charlotte, groping in the depths of her handbag, 'I seem to have left my lighter in the dining-room. So sorry to keep disturbing you like this, I must go and get it.'

She closed the door after her no less gently and purposefully than he had done, and snatching off her shoes, ran silently up the two flights of stairs to her own room. It was a risk, for she might well have run headlong into him on the first floor landing, but she had luck, and was round the next turn of the stairs when she checked and froze against the wall, hearing his rapid steps on the oak treads below her. Very light, very hurried steps, but the bare, glossy wood turned them into a muffled drum-roll. Down to the hall again, and across it to the front door. She had made no mistake; he had an errand somewhere that would not wait.

She ran to her own room, plunged frantically into her walking shoes, and dragged on a black coat. She had a small torch in her case, and spared the extra minute to find it and thrust it into her pocket. Even this brief delay meant that he would be out of sight and out of earshot, but did that matter at this stage? She knew, or she was persuaded that she knew, where he was bound. And he had gone out by the front door, presumably to present an appearance of normality if he should be seen by any of the family – a late evening stroll before bed being a simple enough amusement – while she could save the whole circuit of the house by using the back door close to the kitchen. At this moment she did not care at all whether she was observed, or what the observer might think of her. The curiosity which was quick in her had now a personal urgency about it. He had picked her up of intent, had followed her into this inn for some purpose of his own. And now for some purpose of his own he shook her off, and with almost insulting lack of finesse. Charlotte was not a commodity to be picked up and put down at will, and so he would find.

She saw no sequence in what was happening, and no coherence, but she knew it was there to be seen, if only she could achieve the right angle of vision.

Her walking shoes had formidable soles of thick, springy rubber composition, remarkably silent even on the staircase, and gifted with a firm grip even in wet river mud. The right footwear for venturing the riverside path, short of gumboots. She let herself out softly by the family door, and made for the silver glimmer of water in haste. The trees that sheltered the inn fell back from her gradually, and the vast, chill darkness of the sky mellowed by degrees into a soft, lambent un-darkness, moonless but starry, in which shapes existed, though without precision. By early habit she was a countrywoman, she could orientate herself by barely visible bulks and air currents and scents in the night, and she was not afraid to trust her feet in the irregularities of an unknown path. The torch she hardly used at all; only once or twice, shading it within her palm, she let it lash upon the paler gravel of the path, to align her passage alongside the faintly glowing water, and then snapped it out again quickly, to avoid reliance upon its light as much as to conceal her presence here.

She walked steadily, using all her senses to set her course accurately. And it was several minutes before her quick ears picked up, from somewhere well ahead of her, the snap of a broken branch under a trampling foot. A sharp, dry crack. Dead wood, brought down in the flood water and cast ashore perhaps two days ago. She eased her pace then, knowing he was there in front of her. She had no wish to overtake him, only to maintain her distance, and keep track of his movements if she could. He was on his way downriver, by the waterside path that enjoyed right of way through the enclosure at Aurae Phiala. Ten minutes' walk at most, by this route.

After that, she did not know. All she had to do was follow, and find out.

She knew, by the looming bulk of the bank on her right hand, when she reached the perimeter of the enclosure. To make sure, she risked using her torch, shielded by her body, and saw the single strand of wire, a mere symbol, that separated the path from the city site. Then, distant beyond the broad bowl full of skeleton walls, she saw the headlights of a car pass on the road to Silcaster, sweeping eerily across the filigree of stonework and grass, and vanishing again at the turn of the highway. Twice this random searchlight lit and abandoned the past, all in marvellous silence, for the trick of the ground siphoned off all sound. After every such lightning, darkness closed in more weightily. Then she went cautiously, losing ground but keeping her bearings. The river was dangerous here, still gnawing at the rim of the path. In the night its silence and its matt, pewter gleam were alike deceptive, suggesting languor and sleep, while she knew from her memories of day that it was rushing down its bed with a tigerish fury and force, so concentrated that it generated no ripples and no sibilance. One slip, and it would sweep you away without a murmur or a cry.

She had lost track of the movement ahead of her. It was vital here to pay proper attention to every step, or the river would claim forfeit. A mysterious line of pallor, the nearest thing here to a ripple, outlined the rim of the Comer as it lipped the gravel. She judged that she was somewhere very near to where the bank on her right had subsided, shattering the outer corner of the hypocaust. But so much of her attention was now centred on her own immediate steps that she had no leisure to orientate herself in a wider field. Curiously the darkness seemed to have become more dark. When she lifted her eyes, she was blind. Only when she looked down, fixing upon her own feet, had she at least the illusion of vision. A degree of light emanated from the silently hurtling water, which she felt as a force urging her forward, as though she were in its grip and swept along with it.

She was concentrating with exaggerated passion upon her own blind, sensitive footsteps when her instep caught in some solid, clinging mass, and threw her forward in a clumsy, crippling stumble, from which she recovered strongly, and kept her balance.

The block, whatever it was, lay still before her, lipped by the faintly phosphorescent rim of shallow water. All she saw was a rippling edge of pallor, but she felt the barrier as a solid ridge barricading the path. She fumbled for the torch, and thumbed over the button with a chilly hand, and the cone of light spilled over a man's body, face-down in the shallow water, glistening under the abrupt brightness in violent projections of black and white.

She turned and lunged into the crumbling bank with the torch until it lodged and held still, focused upon the motionless bulk below. Then she plunged forward with both hands, took fast hold of the thick tweed jacket, and dragged the inert body out of the river. He was a dead, limp weight, but the smooth mud greasing the path made her task easier. Clear of the encroaching water of the Comer, she collapsed across her salvaged man, and crouching on her knees beside him, turned up to the tight circle of light the wet, white face of Gus Hambro.

Chapter Four

She stooped with her ear against his lips, and could detect no sound of breathing, spread her fingers against his chest under the sodden jacket, and felt no faint rise and fall. Yet he could not have been long in the water. She had not been far behind him, and yet had heard no sound to prepare her for this. She felt nothing now but the urgency of her own role, and acted without thought or need for thought. She wound her arms about his knees and dragged him laboriously across the gravel into the safe, thick grass; his right cheek suffered, but he was hardly going to hold that against her if he survived. In the soft turf she turned his face to lie upon that grazed right cheek, and spread his arms above his head. Somewhere in the depths of her mind the fact was recorded, and later recalled, that from the shoulders down his back was dry, and even in front, from the knees down he was merely damp and muddy from the slime of the river bank. His head and his chest were soaked, and streaming water into the grass.

But at the time she had no awareness of any such details, though her senses missed none of them. She was entirely concentrated on the curved grip of her hands on his loins, and the rhythmic swing of her body as she leaned and relaxed, forcing the water out of him and dragging the air into him, and waited, holding her own breath, for the first rasping response out of his misused lungs. At first it was like leaning into a thick, inert sponge, and that seemed to go on for an age. Actually it was only a matter of perhaps fifty seconds before the first convulsive rattle of protest shook his ribs, and then she felt the first thread of breath drawn out long and fine under her coaxing fingers as she sat back from him. She dared not halt upon so tenuous a promise. She went on industriously compressing and releasing, but now she felt the breath of life responding to her touch, following the pressure of her hands in and out, lifting the body under her, until she was only orchestrating the performance, and signalling its progression by the measured touch of her palms and undulation of her body.

She ventured at last to sit back on her heels, let her hands lie in her lap, and listen. And palpably, audibly, he breathed. She heard him catch at air, and cough up the last slime of the river. Then he heaved in a breath that must have gone right down to his toes, and his whole body arched and stiffened, and then relaxed on as prolonged an exhalation. She waited, for a time renewing the light, guiding pressure on his back, afraid to leave all the labour to him. By then he was breathing so strongly and normally that she was able to extend her consciousness to details, every one of which was stunningly unexpected and astonishing, even the flickering yellow eye of the torch still beaming upon the recumbent body. She looked up, and became aware of the vault of faintly luminous sky over them, and the silence. An absolute silence.

She understood then that if she had had leisure to listen at the right moment, she might have heard the faint, suggestive sounds of a third presence. For men do not come out by night with the intention of lying down to drown in eight inches of water at the edge of a riverside path. Not cocky young men with roving eyes and a nice taste in girls. Now, of course, there was nothing to be heard at all, nothing to be seen but the sudden, wheeling pallor of one more set of headlights taking the curve in the Silcaster road, far beyond Aurae Phiala.

She leaned down to check closely upon the steady rise and fall of his chest, and the slight, rhythmic warmth of the air expelled from his lungs. The pulse in his wrist was vehement and strong. Cold, if he lay here too long, might be a greater enemy to him now than anything else. And if one thing was certain, it was that she could not get him from here alone. Probably he needed a doctor, but certainly he needed warmth and shelter and a bed. Twice she turned from him, and again turned back to make a double and treble check. The third time she clambered stiffly to her feet and looked about her, dazed by the darkness outside the circle of torchlight, and switched off the beam to acclimatise once again to the starry night. It was like enlarging herself tenfold into a chill but resplendent vastness, like taking seisin of the night. She gave herself a full minute to find her bearings in this mute kingdom, and her senses made the adjustment gratefully. Gus Hambro – ridiculous name, she thought, with wonder, exasperation and affection, for he enjoyed it now by her grace – continued to breathe strongly and regularly in his oblivion. And she knew that she not only could, but must leave him.

Her memories of Aurae Phiala were sharp, but now she could not be sure how accurate. The entrance with its kiosk and museum was away at the far side, and not inhabited by night. But before her, downstream, was the hedge of the garden hemming the curator's villa. Gerry Boden, the lost boy, had made off in that direction when he was hunted out of the dangerous area. Somewhere along that hedge he had last been seen, and by her. By this time he was certainly in his own home, fed, unchastened, and ready for fresh mischief tomorrow. At this moment she did not believe in tragedies; she had just averted one.

She took the torch, using it freely now because speed was of the first importance, and stealth of none at all, and went on down the slippery path towards the thick box hedge, behind which the invisible red roof hung, representing help and companionship. There was a narrow gate opening on the pathway, as she had expected there would be. Within it, the curator's garden climbed in three steep terraces, concrete steps lifting the level at each stage. The house loomed undefined, a large bulk between her and the milky sky. She found herself facing a glass-pannelled door, with the luminous dot of a bell set in its frame. She pressed the spark, and seemed to feel a warmth in it. There were people on the other side of that door. She was not accustomed to wanting people, but she wanted them now.

She seemed to wait a long time before she heard footsteps within, and then a light sprang up beyond the frosted glass. There was an interval of clashing bolts and keys turning – she had to remind herself that it must be nearly eleven by this time, and that this was an isolated spot – before the door opened. But at least it opened fully and vehemently, offering every hope of a welcome within. Somehow she had expected six inches. of semi-darkness, and half a face enquiring suspiciously what here business might be at this hour.

This was not the front door, but a garden way to the river. She saw a white conservatory full of plants, soft light filling it, a few flowers making knots of dazzling colour; and at the door, casting a spidery shadow, a long, meagre but erect man, all angles, like a lesser Don Quixote put together out of scrap iron. A well-shaped grey head leaned to peer at her out of concerned hollow eyes, whose colour she could not determine. By this light they had no colour, only an engraved darkness in his ivory face. He had a small, pointed, elusive beard like the Don, and wispy grey moustaches drooping to join it.

'I'm so sorry,' said a high tenor voice, soft and mild in surprise, and apologising even for the surprise, 'but we don't normally use this door, and especially at night. I hope I didn't keep you waiting.'

With distant astonishment at her own efficiency, she heard her voice saying very clearly and reasonably: 'I do beg your pardon, but I came to you as the nearest house. I've just pulled a man out of the river, two hundred yards or so upstream. I've been giving him artificial respiration, and I think he's going to be all right, but we ought to get him into shelter as quickly as we can. Can you help me? Could we bring him here?'

After one stunned instant, for which she could hardly blame him, he reacted with admirable promptitude. The door opened wider than ever. 'Come inside!' he said. 'I'll call my colleague, and we'll get the poor chap indoors at once.'

'I could help you carry him in,' she said. 'We ought not to lose any time.'

'Don't worry, Lawrence is only a couple of minutes away. He has a scooter, he'll be here in no time. You sit down by the fire, you're wet and cold. I'll be back directly.' And he thrust her briskly into a small, book-lined room, and himself went on along a passage to the hall and the telephone, leaving the door open between them. She heard him dial, and speak briefly and drily, almost as though similar rescue operations landed on his doorstep every night. It might not be the first occurrence, she realised. People who live beside flood rivers are liable to be recruited from time to time. Certainly he wasted no time in calling up his reserves. After the click of the hand-set as the connection was cut, she heard him dial and speak once more.

When he came back into the doorway of the room where she waited, he had a duffle coat over his arm, and was carrying a folding garden-bed with a rigid aluminium frame and a patterned canvas cover printed with brilliant sunflowers. Incongruously festive for a stretcher, but she saw that it would serve the purpose very well.

'If you wouldn't mind coming along to light us on the way back? I've got a coach-lantern here in the garden room. I called the police, as well,' he explained. 'You may not know, but we had an officer here looking for a missing boy, earlier this evening. I hope you may have found him for them.'

'No,' said Charlotte quickly, 'this isn't the boy. I do know about that, but this is someone else, a man I know slightly. He's staying at "The Salmon's Return", like me.'

'Oh . . . I see! A pity . . . I called the number the chief inspector gave me, I felt sure . . . Well, never mind, here's Lawrence! Let's get this one in, at any rate.'

The busy sputter of a Vespa came rocking round the bulk of the house, and the young man of the custodian's box put his head in at the open door, gave Charlotte a brief, blank glance, and asked briskly: 'Where is he?'

'By the path, just upstream. Here, take this! I'll lead. And mind how you go,' he said, heading rapidly out through the garden, the lantern held out beside him to light the steps for Charlotte. 'That path's in a very dangerous state until it dries out properly. What was he doing taking a night walk there? A stupid thing to do!'

His voice was detached and impersonal, but she heard very clearly the implication: And what were you doing taking a night walk there? 'Lucky for him you came along,' he said, almost as if he had recognised the implication, too, and was making a token apology for it.

'Listen!' said the young man named Lawrence suddenly, and checked to strain his ears for the small, recurrent sound that had reached him. 'Someone else out late, too. This place is getting like Brighton beach.'

They had reached the gate in the box hedge, and froze in the grass for an instant to listen. Slow, irregular footsteps, audible only by reason of the slight sucking of soft mud at the heels of someone's shoes as he approached along the path.

'I called the chief inspector,' said the curator, advancing again to meet the sound. 'I thought it likely this might be the young fellow he was looking for. But he couldn't be here yet.'

'He wouldn't be coming along here, anyhow. He'll be driving. Mrs Paviour surely wouldn't walk this way in the dark, would she?'

'Lesley's home, twenty minutes ago, and gone to bed. I hope she's sleeping through this disturbance.'

They walked towards the unsteady steps, and a figure took shape out of the darkness, weaving as it came and blinking dazedly as the lantern was lifted to illuminate its face. Wet and muddy, but moving doggedly under his own steam, Gus Hambro lurched into the circle of his would-be rescuers, braced his rubbery legs well apart, and stood dazzled, holding his head together with both hands.

'It's him!' said Charlotte, humanly indifferent to grammar at this crisis. 'He's walking . . . he's all right!'

The young man named Lawrence put her aside kindly but firmly, and took over in her place, drawing Gus's left arm about his shoulders. 'Man!' he said admiringly. 'Are you the tough one! Here, girl, cop hold of this thing, we don't need a stretcher for types like this.'

The curator moved to the other side, encircled Gus competently but aloofly, and handed over the lantern. It was Charlotte who led the way back slowly and carefully through the garden. Mounting steps was what Gus found most bewildering at this stage; his feet made manful efforts, but tended to trail, and he was half-carried the last few yards to the door. And yet he had come to himself unaided, clambered to his feet without even the support of a fence to lean on, and made his way some two hundred yards towards the single light of the curator's open door. A tough one, as Lawrence had observed. Or else his handicap had been rather less than she had reckoned. She was tired by this time, and unsure of her judgement: of stresses, of odds, even of personalities.

'I'm sorry,' said Gus, quite distinctly but as if from a great distance. 'I seem to be causing a lot of trouble.'

'Not to worry, chum!' said the Lawrence youth benignly, puffing a little on the steps but indestructibly cool and amiable. 'See that nice, bright hole in the wall? Aim for that, and you're home and dry!'

The nice, bright hole in the wall stood wide, as they had left it, gleaming with the reflections of white paint within. They bore steadily down upon it. And suddenly the oblong of light was inhabited. A shadowy silhouette materialised, rather than stepped, into the frame, and stood leaning forward slightly, peering understandably into the dimness outside, and curious about the massed group of figures converging upon the doorway. There was an outside light which no one, so far, had thought to switch on. The girl in the conservatory reached out a hand and flicked the switch, lighting them the last few yards, and floodlighting herself at the same time. Appearing magically out of shadow, suddenly she shone there before them, the focus of light and warmth and refuge. She had not the least idea what was going on, and she was smiling into the night in enquiry and wonder, her brows arched halfway to laughter, her lips parted in a whimsical welcome to whatever might be pending.

There was one brief moment while she stood illuminated thus theatrically, and still not at all comprehending that the group which confronted her had had a close brush with tragedy. She had a heart-shaped face, of striking, creamy smoothness, and broader than its length from brow to chin, like the bright, intelligent countenance of a young cat, innocent, assured and inquisitive. Her eyes were so wide-set and widely-opened that they consumed half her face in a dazzling pool of greenish-blue radiance. Her nose was neat, small and short, and her mouth full-lipped and firmly formed above a tapered but resolute chin. She had a cloud of short hair curving in clinging waves about her head, the colour of barley silk, and under the feathery fringe her forehead bulged childishly, with room in it for a notable brain, the one thing about her that was not suavely curved and ivory-smooth.

The details sounded like a collection of attractive oddities. The sum total was a quite arresting beauty. And the most jolting fact about her emerged only by implication. In a nylon jersey house-gown of peacock pattern and iridescent colouring, which clung like a silk glove, she could not possibly be anyone but Mrs Paviour, that same Lesley who walked when the fit took her, last thing at night, and had been home twenty minutes when Charlotte rang the door-bell. Ergo, the wife of this elderly Don Quixote, Great-Uncle Alan's colleague and contemporary, who must be well into his sixties at the very least, and slightly arid and passé even at that. How old was the girl in the doorway? Not a day over twenty-five, Charlotte reckoned – hardly two years senior to herself. Perhaps even less. What an extraordinary mis-match! And not just because of the tale of years involved. The old man was a cracked leather bottle trying to contain quicksilver. She *could not* feel anything for him! It made no sense. And yet she had not the look of a woman cramped or dissatisfied. She glowed with ease and wellbeing.

At sight of her Gus, stiffening into startled consciousness between his supporters, set foot of his own volition on the last step, and his soiled eyebrows soared into his muddy hair, in reflection of the apparition before him. Very faintly but quite clearly he said: 'Good God!' and seemed to have no breath left for anything more explicit.

The moment of charmed stillness collapsed – or more properly exploded – into motion and exclamation. The girl in the Chinese house-coat narrowed her eyes upon the central figure in the tableau before her, and the supple lines of her face sharpened into crystal, and lost their smiling gaiety.

'My God!' she said, in the softest of dismayed voices. 'What's been happening, Steve?' And she went on briskly, springing into instant and efficient comprehension: 'Well, come on, bring him in to the fire, quickly! I'll get brandy.'

She turned in a swirl of nylon jersey, and flung wide the door to the study, where the subsiding glow of the fire still burned. Her movements, as she receded rapidly along the passage beyond, were silent and violent, a force of nature in action. Only gradually did it emerge that she was rather a miniature whirlwind, perhaps an inch shorter even than Charlotte, but so slender that she escaped looking like a pocket edition. When she came back, with a tray in her hands, they had installed their patient by the fire in a deep chair, and peeled the soggy, wet jacket from him. They were five people in one small room, and hardly a word was said between them until Gus Hambro had a large brandy under his belt, and was visibly returning into circulation. His still dazed eyes followed his astonishing hostess around, measuring, weighing and wondering, in forgetfulness of his own predicament. He said nothing at all, as yet, but very eloquently. Charlotte hung back in a corner of the room, and let them encircle him with their attentions. So far he had not even registered her presence, and she was in no particular hurry to enlighten him.

'He should have a doctor,' said Paviour anxiously, standing over him with the empty brandy glass.

'I don't want a doctor,' protested the patient, weakly but decidedly. 'What could he do for me that you're not doing? All I've got is a headache.' He looked round him doubtfully, winced abruptly back to his original position, and clapped a surprised hand behind his right ear. 'What happened?' he asked blankly.

'You fell in the river,' said Paviour patiently. 'I shouldn't worry about remembering, if I were you. The main thing is, you're here, and you're going to be all right.'

'Fell in the river?' repeated Gus like an indignant echo, and stared at the smear of blood staining his muddy fingers. 'I never did! I was keeping well on the landward side of the path, on the grass. And that's where I was lying when I came round just now. All I've got is a welt on the head here. Somebody jumped me from behind and knocked me out.' He looked from face to face, questioning and wondering. 'If I was in the river,' he said reasonably, 'what am I doing here now?'

'This lady,' said Paviour, stepping aside to allow him to follow the mild gesture that indicated Charlotte, 'pulled you out. Not only that, she administered artificial respiration and brought you round, and then came here to get help. Why did you suppose we were setting off with a stretcher and torches, at this time of night?'

'I didn't know . . . I never realised . . .' He sat forward, staring in outraged recognition at Charlotte. 'You mean *you* . . . it was *you* who . . .' He shut his mouth and swallowed hard, and in the space of about two seconds she saw a whole kaleidoscope of emotions flash in succession through his mind. If she's here, if she found me, it's because she followed me! If she followed me, it's because she doesn't trust me, and if she doesn't trust me it's because she knows something, or has found out something. So far she was sure of her ground. And what followed was neither surprise nor mystery to her. For suddenly Gus Hambro performed a minor miracle, by producing a fiery blush that made itself visible in waves of dubious gratitude and indubitable mortification even through the layers of river mud that still decorated his face. Tales of gallant rescues ought not to go into reverse, and cast the lady as hero and the man as helpless victim. Especially when, whatever other circumstances may hold good, the man has been exerting himself to make an impression on the lady in question. Fate, thought Charlotte, gazing innocently back into his admiring, devoted, humiliated and furious face, has certainly given me the upper hand of you, my boy!

'The kiss of life, I hope?' said the young man Lawrence, putting a deliberate finger through the slight tension which was palpably building up within the room.

'Schafer,' said Charlotte shortly. 'The only method I know.'

Gus did not sound at all like a man recently revived from drowning as he said with sharp disquiet: 'Right, that disposes of how I got out, and I'm duly grateful, believe me. But now will somebody please explain to me *how the hell I ever got in*?'

They were all staring at him in speculative silence when the sound of a car's engine circled the house, coming to rest in the arc of gravel before the door. After it died, the silence was absolute for a few moments. Then incongruous suburban chimes jangled from the front porch.

'That must be the police inspector,' said Paviour. 'Will you let him in, dear?'

His wife turned without a word, and went to open the door; and presently ushered in Detective Chief Inspector George Felse, mild, grey-haired and ordinary, a tired middle-aged man who would have been inconspicuous and among his peers almost anywhere he cared to materialise.

'I got a message,' he said, 'that you wanted me here.'

He looked round them all as though none of them afforded him any surprise, though two of them did not belong here, and to his certain knowledge had been elsewhere only a short time ago. So short a time, Charlotte realised with a shock, that he could not possibly have returned home in the meantime, since he was a close neighbour of the Bodens, who lived ten miles from Aurae Phiala. The relayed message must have found him somewhere not far from this house. Somewhere by the river, she thought, downstream. Whatever went into the flooded Comer here would fetch up at one of several spots, no doubt well known to the police, where curves and currents tended to land what they had carried down. The chief inspector had just come, case or no case, from setting a close watch on those spots, in expectation – in foreboding, rather – that the flood would bring some unusual freight aground very shortly.

Only then did she fully realise that if she had been five minutes later the watchers keeping a lookout for a stray boy might, tomorrow, have been hauling ashore the sodden body of Gus Hambro.

Washed, warmed, with a shaven patch and an adhesive dressing behind his right ear and a second large brandy nursed gratefully in his hands, Gus told his story; though not, perhaps, quite ingenuously.

'All I did was come out for a walk before going to bed, and I was about by that place where the bank's caved in, when somebody jumped me from behind. I never heard a thing until maybe the last two steps he took, I never had time to turn. Something hit me on the back of the head, here, and I went out like a light. I remember dropping. I never felt the ground hit me. But I do know where I was when I fell – in the belt of grass under the bank, and facing straight ahead the way I was walking. And when I came round I was in the same place. I took it for granted I'd just been lying there since I went out, and whoever had jumped me had made off and left me there. When I could make it, I got up and made for the nearest shelter. There was a lighted doorway here, I steered for that. And just outside the garden I ran into this rescue party coming out to find me. Now they tell me,' he said flatly, 'that I was in the river, drowning, and Charlotte here pulled me out and brought me round.' He had used her Christian name without even realising it, so intent was he on pinning down the details of his own remembrance.

'When I found him,' said Charlotte, 'he was lying right across the path.'

'*Across* the path?'

'*Across* the path,' she said firmly, 'with his feet just touching the grass on the landward side, and his head and shoulders in the river. His face was completely under water.'

She felt them all stiffen in instinctive resistance, not wanting their routine existence to be invaded by anything as bizarre as this.

'There may be a simple explanation for this discrepancy,' ventured Paviour hopefully. 'If there was a fresh fall of earth there – the bank is quite high, and we've seen that there's brickwork exposed there . . . Perhaps it wasn't a deliberate attack at all, just a further slip that struck him and swept him across the path. After all, we didn't go along to have a look at the place.'

'*I* was there,' said Gus drily. 'There wasn't any fall.'

'I was there, too,' said Charlotte. 'There's something else. When you get a blow on the head and fall forward, whether it's flying stones or a blackjack, you may fall heavily, but even so I don't think you'd embed yourself as deeply in the mud as Mr Hambro was embedded.'

Chief Inspector Felse sat steadily watching her, and said nothing. It was Paviour who stirred again in uneasy protest. 'My dear girl, are you sure you're not recalling rather more than happened? After stresses like that, the imagination may very easily begin to add details.'

'I'm recognising things I did see, and never had time to recognise then. But the other thing is a good deal more conclusive . . .'

George Felse asked quietly: 'How were his arms?'

'Yes, that's it!' she said. 'How did you know? When you fall forward, fully conscious or not, you put out your hands to break your fall. His arms were down at his sides. Nobody falls like that. Even if you were out on your feet, and fell as a dead weight, your arms wouldn't drop tidily by your sides. And that's how his were.'

She was watching the chief inspector's face as she said it, and she knew that he believed her, and accepted her as a good witness. Both the Paviours were stiffening in appalled disbelief, even young Lawrence had drawn a hissing breath of doubt. Probably Gus himself found it hard to swallow, and would have preferred not to accept it, the implications being too unpleasant to contemplate. But George Felse had come halfway to meet her.

'But, good God,' objected Stephen Paviour faintly, 'do you realise what you're suggesting?'

'Not suggesting. Stating. I'm saying that someone, having knocked Mr Hambro cold, dragged him across the path to the water, and shoved him firmly into the soft mud with his face under water, to die.'

In the stunned silence George Felse got up, without speaking, and crossed the room to where Gus's jacket hung on the back of a chair, turned towards the replenished fire, and steamed gently as it dried. He slid his hands into the sleeves, and lifted it to turn the back to the light, and for a few minutes stood studying it closely.

'The back,' said Charlotte, watching, 'was dry as high as the shoulder-blades. Except that I probably made some damp patches, handling him after I got him out.'

'Quite a difference from actually lying in the river.' He spread the jacket between his hands, holding it out for them to see. 'Look in the middle of the back, here, from just above the waist upwards. What do you see?' He turned to look at Gus, with a faintly challenging smile.

'A moist patch – sizeable. Two patches, rather, but practically joined in one.' The warm, heathery colours of the tweed darkened there into a duller, peaty shade, two irregular, fading patches, with a vague dry line between. A thin rim of encrusted mud, drying off now, helped to outline the marks, but even so they were elusive enough until pointed out.

'Well? What do you make of it? You tell me!'

'It's a footmark,' said Gus, and licked lips suddenly dry and stiff with retrospective fear. 'I know what to make of it, all right! It means some bastard not only laid me out cold, and stuck me face-down in the Comer, but even rammed me well down into the mud with a foot in the small of my back to make dead sure of me, before he lit out and left me there to drown.'

They were too numbed by then, and too tired, to do much exclaiming, however their orderly minds rebelled at believing in mayhem and murder at Aurae Phiala. They stared in fascination at the imperfect outline which did indeed look more and more like the print of a shoe the longer they gazed. Lawrence said hesitantly, with almost exaggerated care to sound reasonable and calm: 'But why? Why should anyone want to . . . to kill him?' It took quite a lot of resolution to utter it at all. 'Just a visitor here like anyone else. There couldn't be any personal reason.'

'I think,' said Lesley sensibly, 'I'll make some coffee. We could all do with some.' And she walked out of the room with something of the same wary insistence on normality. It was then still some twenty minutes short of midnight, though they seemed to have devoured the greater part of the night already in this improbable interview.

'Someone,' said Gus, 'didn't want me around, that's certain. But wasn't he still taking rather a chance, if it was all that important to him that I shouldn't survive? I might have revived enough to struggle out, once he was gone.'

'So you might,' George agreed. 'With a river handy, and you past resistance, why not do the obvious thing, and shove you far enough in to make sure the current took you? Even a swimmer with all his wits about him might well be in trouble down those reaches at this time of year. Out cold, you wouldn't have a dog's chance.'

'You comfort me,' said Gus grimly, 'you really do. Go on, tell me, why didn't he?'

'Pretty obviously that's what he intended. He simply didn't have time.'

'Because he heard me coming,' said Charlotte.

'I think so. He needed no more than one extra minute, or two, but he didn't have it. He heard you, and he preferred to run for it. He dropped Mr Hambro where he was, in the edge of the water, and planted a foot between his shoulders to drive him in deeper before he made off.'

'But without reason!' protested Paviour. 'Surely no one but a madman . . .'

'The procedure would appear to be far from mad – quite coldly methodical. And since, as Mr Lawrence says, there could hardly be anything personal in the attack, we're left with the probability that *anyone* who had happened along at that moment would have been dealt with in the same way. You were suspected, in fact, of having blundered head-on into something no one was supposed to see.'

'I didn't see a thing,' Gus said bitterly. 'Not a thing! He needn't have bothered scragging me, if that was his trouble.'

'He could hardly ask you, and take your word for it, could he? Obviously he thought you'd witnessed something you shouldn't have. At best he was afraid you *might* have, and that was enough. But Miss Rossignol was some way behind, and advancing without stealth.' He cast one brief glance at Charlotte, caught her large, clear, self-possessed eye, and one conspiratorial spark of laughter passed between them. He knew she had been exercising what stealth she was capable of, and he knew why, but that was purely between the two of them. 'There was no need to think she'd noticed anything, and whoever he was, he wasn't mad enough to go looking for extra murders. He took a chance – admittedly an almost negligible one – on you, and slipped away to avoid her.'

Lesley brought in a laden tray, set it down on a side-table, and distributed cups in silence.

'In view of the apparent urgency of getting rid of you,' said George Felse, stirring his coffee, 'it might be an idea if you tried to recall what, if anything, you *did* see.'

Gus held his head, and pondered. 'Well, of course there's always some reflected light, once your eyes get used to being out at night. But I didn't meet anyone, I didn't hear anyone. Oh, yes, after I got to the perimeter of Aurae Phiala, where you can see clean across the bowl to the road the other side, I did see cars pass there a couple of times. You get a sort of lighthouse flash from the headlights, as they swing round the curve there and out of sight. The lights cross the bowl gradually, and out again, and then the dip in the road cuts them off. Yes, and the second time that happened it swept across the standing walls there, and in the near end of the caldarium there was somebody standing by the wall. No, not moving, quite still. It was only a glimpse. The light swerves off in an instant, and it's darker than ever. But he was there, all right.'

'*He?*' said George.

'Oh, yes, it was a he. The whole cut of him,' he said, imprecisely but comprehensively. 'No doubt about it.'

'But nothing more detailed? Clothing? Build?'

'Oh, for God's sake!' said Gus irritably. 'One flash of light, and gone. Just a mass, like a Henry Moore figure. He didn't have any clothing, just a shape. All I know is, it was a he, and he was there.'

'And how long was this before you were attacked?'

'I'd say about three full minutes, maybe even four, before I was hit. I didn't think anything of it. He had as much right to be out walking as I had.'

'Not in Aurae Phiala,' said Stephen Paviour, in tones of quiet outrage. 'Not at that hour. Our gates are closed at six – seven in summer. He had no right inside the enclave, whoever he was.'

'No, true enough. But the path along the river is a right of way, and there's only a token wire in between. Anyone could walk up into the enclosure. You'd have a job to stop them.'

'You know,' said Lesley, busy at the coffee-tray, 'I must have been out there about the same time. Oh, no, I wasn't down by the river, I was over on the side next to the road. I often have a little walk along the new plantation there. That's what cuts off the headlights, you see. The site is very exposed on that side, in Roman times there was a woodland there, so it was sheltered. Now we're trying to replace it, to reproduce the same conditions. I was home well before ten, though. I never noticed the exact time, but I was in the bath when I heard the stir down here.'

'You didn't see anything of this man in the caldarium?' George asked.

'No, I didn't. Though I must have been around just at that time, I think. I do remember seeing two – maybe three – cars pass on the Silcaster road, but I didn't notice anything shown up in their headlights.' She hesitated for a moment, poised vulnerably with the coffee-pot in one hand, and the jug of hot milk in the other. 'You know . . . please don't think I'm being funny! – maybe Mr Hambro saw the Aurae Phiala ghost. And don't think I'm crazy, either,' she appealed warmly. 'Look, it's only half a joke. You go and ask in the village. People *have* seen things! You don't have to take my word for it, they'll talk about it quite freely, they're not ashamed or afraid of it.'

'My dear, this is frivolous,' her husband said with frowning disapproval. 'Mere local superstition. We're concerned with realities, unfortunately.'

'*Are* there such stories?' George asked mildly.

'Can you imagine such a place as Aurae Phiala existing without giving rise to its own legends? I have heard loose talk of people seeing things here by night, but I've never paid the least attention, so I can't tell you what they claim.'

'I'm not being frivolous,' Lesley declared firmly, 'and these *are* realities. I don't mean helmeted sentries literally do patrol the walls by night, I don't mean even that anything's actually been seen, but the things that go on in people's minds *are* realities, and *do* influence events. It hardly matters whether there's a ghost there to be seen or not – what matters is whether someone is convinced he saw it. Besides, what's a ghost, anyhow? I'm not a convinced believer, I just don't find it difficult to credit that in these very ancient sites of occupation, where such emotional things are known to have happened, people should develop special sensitivities, racial memories, hypernormal sympathies, whatever you like to call them. I don't see anything supernatural about it, just rather outside most people's range of knowledge. The test of that is, that the local people treat the experiences they claim to have had as perfectly acceptable – almost take them for granted. They don't go challenging them, they respect them, take what's offered but don't go probing any farther. A thoroughly healthy attitude, I call it. Look at Orrie,' she appealed to her husband. 'He's seen the sentry twice. He doesn't run away, or hang out crosses or wreaths of parsley, or ring up the local press, he merely men-tions it to his friends in passing, and gets on with his work. And you couldn't find anyone more down-to-earth than Orrie.'

'Orrie?' George enquired.

'Our gardener. He's local stock from way back. They had the same site, even bits of the same cottage, in the sixteenth century.' She laughed suddenly, the evening's first genuinely gay sound. 'You wouldn't credit what the Orrie's short for! Orlando! Orlando Benyon! The name's been in the family for generations, too.'

'And Orrie's seen the Roman sentry?'

'Listen!' she said, abruptly grave again. 'I've seen him myself, or else hearing about it has put me in a special state of mind, and all the other factors have come up right, atmospheric conditions, combinations of light and dark, what you like, and made me create what I believed I was seeing. Twice! A figure in a bronze helmet, both times a good way off, and both times close to the standing walls. I didn't find anything very strange in it, either. In its last years Aurae Phiala surely did mount a watch every night. Just such a sentry must have been the first to die, the night the Welsh came.'

Paviour's uneasiness and distaste had grown so palpable by this time that his rigid bones looked tensed to breaking point. He said with nervous acidity: 'We're not dealing with atmospheric hallucinations here, but with an attempt at murder. When violence breaks in, something a good deal more material than imagination is indicated.'

She agreed, with an unabashed smile. '*And* when ordinary mundane light like a car's headlights starts making the immaterial perceptible. Now that would be supernatural! I paint a bit for fun,' she said, with a grimace of deprecation for the unsatisfactory results. 'I do know about masses and light, even if I can never get them right. No, this person you saw was a pretty solid kind of reality.'

'And he wasn't wearing a helmet,' said Gus.

'Tonight's haunting was for a pretty compelling reason,' said George. 'But what you've told us is very interesting, Mrs Paviour. We'll see what the village has to add.' He put down his coffee-cup in the tray with a sigh. 'You've been very kind to put up with us all for so long, I'm most grateful. But now I think there's nothing more we can do here, and it's time we left you to get some rest. If you feel fit to go back to the inn, Mr Hambro, I'll be glad to drive you and Miss Rossignol round there.'

Lesley had begun to gather up the remaining cups, but at the mention of Charlotte's name she put down the tray abruptly, and turned with a startled smile. 'Rossignol? You're not *Charlotte Rossignol*? Steve, did you hear that? There can't be two – not two and both connected with Roman antiquities! You must be the niece Doctor Morris mentioned. He told us once his sister's girl had married a Frenchman.'

Charlotte admitted to her identity with some surprise. 'I didn't think he took so much interest in me. We've always been a rather loosely-knit family, and I've never seen him.'

'It's true he didn't often talk about his family, but I couldn't forget your lovely name, I liked it so much. You know Steve is an old fellow-student of his, and a close friend? Isn't it wonderful, darling, Miss Rossignol turning up like this?'

His face was grey and drawn, Charlotte thought, perhaps with pure fatigue, for after all, he was an old man. He favoured her with a slightly haggard smile, but his voice was dry and laboured as he said: 'I'm delighted to meet my old friend's niece. I'm only sorry it had to be in such circumstances of stress. I hope you'll give us the opportunity of getting to know you better, on some happier occasion.' His lips were stiff, the words of goodwill could hardly get past them.

'I'm not quite such a coincidence as I seem,' she said, 'I've just been reading my uncle's book on Aurae Phiala, that's why I came to have a look at the place for myself. He didn't really do it justice, did he? I find it beautiful.'

'Stephen doesn't agree with him, either,' said Lesley, smiling, 'but of course Aurae Phiala is our life. Are you going to stay a little while, now you're here? You should!'

'I have a few concerts in the Midlands, and I thought I'd make my base somewhere close by until they're over. Yes, I think I shall stay on for a few days here.'

'But not at the "Salmon"! Oh, no, you can't! Anyone belonging to Alan Morris has a home here, of course. You must come to us. Look at all the rooms we have, the house is much too big for two. Do come! Stay tonight, too, I can find you everything you need overnight, and we'll fetch your things from the pub tomorrow.'

Confronted by sudden and eager invitations from strangers, Charlotte's normal reaction was one of recoil, not out of insecurity, but to maintain her independence and integrity. She was never afterwards quite sure why she side-stepped only partially and temporarily on this occasion. There existed a whole tangle of possible reasons. She was in search of a closer knowledge of her great-uncle, and here were informed friends of his, one of them of long standing, who could surely tell her a great part of what she wanted to know. She was attracted by this place, and here was her opportunity of remaining. She was held by the disturbing events of the night, and here was her chance to wait out a better understanding of them on the spot. And also there was something in Lesley's appeal that engaged her sympathy in a way she hesitated to analyse. Here was this young creature, beautiful and restless, married to a man almost old enough to be her grandfather, and apparently setting out to make the very best of it, too, with no signs of regret or self-pity; but the prospect of having a girl of her own age in the house, even for a few days, might well matter to her a great deal more than the extension and acceptance of a mere conventional politeness. And Charlotte heard herself saying quickly:

'That's awfully kind of you, and I should love to come for a couple of days, if I may. But I'd like to go back with Mr Hambro to the "Salmon" now, if you don't mind. If I may come tomorrow?'

She had not looked at Paviour until then. Lesley had issued her fiat with such confidence that she had taken his compliance for granted. His long, lean, lugubrious face was dry and rigid as carved teak, and his eyes, sunken between veined lids and deep in cavernous hollows of bone, looked like roundels of cloudy glass with no light behind them. With all the grace and spontaneity of a wooden puppet, but in the most civil and soft of voices, he said: 'We shall both be delighted if you will. We have the highest regard for Doctor Morris, and of course his niece is most welcome. And Lesley will enjoy your company so much,' he added, and the sudden faint note of hope and warmth sounded almost as though he was issuing comfort to himself, looking on the single bright side. No doubt, she thought, a visitor might be a very unwelcome distraction in his entrenched life.

But it was done now, there was no way of backing out. And she need not, after all, stay long. After two days it would be easy enough to extricate herself.

During the short drive back to the inn they were all three monosyllabic, suddenly isolated in private cells of weariness and preoccupation. The occasional remark passing seemed to come from an infinite distance, and be answered after a prolonged interval.

'I hope Mrs Lane won't have locked you out. We should have given her a call.'

'I've got a key,' said Gus, and lapsed into silence again. He made no comment on Lesley's invitation and Charlotte's acceptance of it, none on the curious complexities which had confounded their own relationship since they left 'The Salmon's Return' two hours and more ago. No one said a word about Doctor Alan Morris, and the charged significance of Charlotte's name. There were things all three of them knew, and things all three of them were wondering, but no one cared to question or acknowledge at this hour. Silence, if not golden, was at least more comfortable than speech.

Only as the car was crunching softly to a halt in the gravel of the yard did Charlotte ask suddenly, but in a tone so subdued as to suggest that she had been contemplating the question for some time, and refrained from asking it only for fear of the answer:

'You haven't found him yet?'

The engine fell silent, and there was a brief and pregnant pause. Then: 'No,' said George Felse, equally carefully and constrainedly, 'we haven't found him.'

In the first chilly greyness of dawn, before the sun rose, Sergeant Comstock, of the uniformed branch, who came of a long line of native fishermen, not to say poachers, and knew his river as he knew the palm of his own hand, thankfully abandoned what he had always known was a useless patrol of the left bank downstream, and on his own responsibility borrowed one of his many nephews, and embarked with him in the coracle which was his natural means of personal transport on the Comer. They put out in this feather-light saucer of a boat from his nephew's yard only just below the limits of Aurae Phiala, transport downstream in the spate being rapid and easy – for experts, at least – and the return journey much simpler by portage. This consideration had dictated his choice of nephew. Dick was the one he would really have preferred, but Dick lived well downstream. Jack was not only in the right spot, and the family coracle-builder, but a bachelor into the bargain, so that there was no protesting wife to contend with.

The sergeant had already mapped out in his own mind, with an eye to the wind, the speed of the flow and the amount of debris being brought down, the procession of spits, shoals, curves and pools where a heavy piece of flotsam would be likely to cast up, beginning immediately below the village of Moulden, which lay just below the Aurae Phiala enclosure. Cottages dotted the waterside through the village; and anything which had gone into the water some hours ago must, in any case, either have been brought ashore there already or long since have passed through, before the general alarm went out.

From there they went darting across the boiling surface like a dragon-fly, skimming with the currents where the banks were swept too open and smooth to hold flotsam, swinging aside round the sergeant's paddle in the marked spots; round the shovel-shaped end of Eel Island, which had scooped up a full load of branches, twigs, uprooted grass, and even more curious trophies, but not what they were seeking; a little way down the sluggish backwater beyond, until motion ceased in stagnant shallows, and still there was nothing; out into the flood again, hopping back on to the current as on to a moving belt that whisked them away; revolving out of the race again where the trees leaned down into the water at the curve by the Lacey farm, acting like a great, living grille to filter out debris; clean across the width of the river at the next coil, to where the long, sandy shallow ran out and encircled a miniature beach. Every junk-heap of the Comer on this stretch they touched at and ransacked. It was a game they could win only by losing; every possibility checked and found empty was a point gained, and with every one discarded their spirits rose towards optimism.

The sun was up, and they were a mile or more down-river, in wider and less turgid reaches, where some of the best fishing pools deepened under the right bank.

'Looks like we've had our trouble for nothing,' Jack said, with appropriate satisfaction. 'Anything that's run that gauntlet without getting hooked has got to be brother to an eel.'

It was one more case of famous last words. In the first dark pool under the hollowed bank the steady, rolling eddies went placidly round and round, smooth as cream, their tension dimpling the centre into a slow, minor whirlpool. And in the middle of the slanting span, circling upon a radius of about three yards, and light enough to maintain its place a foot or so below the surface, something pale and oval went monotonously round and round. First oval and single, then weaving as it spun, like a water-lily on a stem, then suddenly seen as articulate in separate petals, a limp magnolia flower.

'Why don't you keep your mouth shut?' said Sergeant Comstock, with deep and bitter resignation, and reached for the boat-hook they'd brought with them. His third nephew Ted had made it to family specifications in his forge in the village of Moulden. 'Cop hold of this paddle, and move us in slow. And hold us clear of him, or he'll go down.'

There was a second drifting flower now, deep below, and greenish brown with the tint of the water between. And presently, as Jack held the paddle like a brake and let them in by inches, a third, without petals, a pale disc trailing tendrils of weed. A spreading darkness wove lazily beneath it, keeping it afloat.

The boat-hook reached overside gently, felt its way under the leaves of dark material, was lifted delicately into their folds, and held fast. The three submerged flowers lost their rhythm, jerked into stillness, and hung quivering. A palpable bulk aligned itself beneath them, a fish on a line, but a fish without fight.

'I've got him,' said Sergeant Comstock gruffly. 'Better take us down a piece, where the bank levels out. We can get him ashore there.'

The fish floated uncomplainingly with them, down to the gentle slope of grass fifty yards downstream. There they brought the coracle ashore lightly, and drew in, with reluctance and the reverence of finality, what they had been hunting with such assiduity, and so persistently hoped they would not find. To have settled something is always an achievement and, of sorts, a satisfaction. This they would rather not have settled, and yet there was a kind of relief in it.

The body came ashore into the grass with monstrous and majestic indifference, for the first time caring nothing at all what impression it made. A long, young body in correct school uniform, black blazer, white shirt, black tie, dark grey slacks. Very like its living counterpart still, because it had not been in the river very long. The Comer had not managed to loosen the knot of the tie, though its ends floated wide, or to hoist off one of the regulation black shoes. He even had a ball-point pen still firmly clipped to the top of his breast pocket.

'That's him,' said Sergeant Comstock, looking down at the slow rivulets of storm-water trickling down out of clothing and hair to wind their way thankfully through the grass back to the river. 'Hang on here, Jackie, while I cut up to the farm and phone.'

Chapter Six

George Felse telephoned his wife from the Sallows farm somewhat after eight o'clock in the morning. By that time he had not only set in motion all the police retinue that attends on sudden and unexplained death, but also attended their ministrations throughout, seen the body examined, photographed, cased in its plastic shell and removed by ambulance to the forensic laboratory, delegated certain necessary duties, placated the police doctor and the pathologist, come to terms with the inevitable grief and rage which do not reach the headlines, and made dispositions within his own mind for the retribution which is so often aborted.

'We found him,' he said. She, after all, had been left holding up the universe over the parents, and in all probability, whatever strict injunctions he issued now, she would, by the time he rejoined her, have relieved him of the most dreadful of all the duties his office laid on him, and somehow, with sense, sedatives and sturdy, unpretending sympathy, have gone part-way towards reconciling the bereaved to their bereavement. 'Dead, of course,' he said. 'Some hours, according to preliminary guesses. Yes, in the river. Drowned? Well, provisionally, yes. Personally, I wonder. Don't tell them that. They're almost prepared for the other. I'll tell them later – when we know.'

'It's all right,' said Bunty Felse. It wasn't, but he would know what she meant. 'I was half expecting it. So are they, I know. When will you be home?'

He had been up half the previous night upon a quite different case, and all this night upon this, which had only just become a case, and his, after all.

'As soon as I can, but it may be three hours or so. I shall take time out to call at Aurae Phiala. They won't have heard officially. I want to be the one to bring the news. I've got to see their faces.'

'Not the Rossignol girl,' said Bunty. It was a little less than half

68

enquiry, and a little more than half assertion. He had called her shortly after midnight, she already knew something of the personalities involved.

'I want to see her face, too. But no – you're right, not the Rossignol girl. On present form,' he said, his voice warming wearily into a semblance of the voice she knew best, 'she only pulls people out.'

His timing was good, though it was determined mainly by the exigencies of the situation. When he drove down the gravelled road along the edge of the site to the curator's house, at half past nine, he found the bronze Aston Martin parked in front of the doorway, and Gus Hambro just handing out Charlotte's suitcases. Both the Paviours had come out to greet their guest, Stephen Paviour long and sad and constrained as ever, Lesley eager and young and welcoming. Her movements as she ran down the steps had an overflowing grace of energy. Behind her Bill Lawrence appeared in the doorway. So much the better. One was apt to overlook Bill Lawrence, who nevertheless was there on the spot like all the rest, and able to move even more privately, since he lived alone in the lodge cottage, further along the Silcaster road. Probably he rode over here for his meals on most occasions. The Vespa was a handy transport for the mere quarter of a mile involved. He wore his usual air of meticulously contrived casualness, and the shadow of beard round his by no means negligible jaw was a shade more perceptible than on the previous day. Apparently he was setting out to grow whiskers of the latest fashion, for his lips were carefully shaved. Probably he knew and cared, in spite of his cultivated disdain for appearances, that he had a very well-cut and intelligent mouth, too good to be hidden. His lazy, supercilious eyes, too, managed their affectation of aloofness without actually missing a trick. It might be a great mistake to overlook Mr Lawrence.

He had been the first to hear the sound of the car approaching, and the quickest to identify it, for he was the only one who looked completely unsurprised as it rolled gently alongside the Aston Martin, while all the rest had checked momentarily and turned to gaze. Recognition halted their breath for an instant. He was there with intent. With news or with questions.

Lesley came towards him, veering from the advance she had been making upon Charlotte. 'Chief Inspector Felse! We didn't expect to see you so early. Is there any news?' The intense blue of her eyes shaded away into a translucent green in a bright light, burning into emerald in her moments of laughter or animation, clouding over into a ferny darkness when she was grave. She gazed into his face, and they darkened. Unexpectedly but very simply she said, with concern: 'You haven't had any sleep!'

'I'll catch up on that soon.' He turned from her to look at Paviour. To him the light was not kind. The contrast with his radiant, vital young wife was blatant almost to embarrassment.

'You wanted to see us? – some one or more of us,' he said. 'If we can help you at all . . .'

'Thank you, but this time I needn't keep you more than a minute. I thought that as I'd involved you all, to some extent, in the enquiries that were launched yesterday, I ought to inform you of the results of our search for the boy, Gerry Boden . . .'

He was listening very carefully, for any exclamation, any in-drawn breath, even, that would single out one person among these five; but they remained anonymous in their concern and foreboding. The issue, after all, was fairly plain. No one is that much of an optimist.

'One of our sergeants took him out of the river about six o'clock this morning, a mile and a half downstream from here. Dead.'

They stood frozen, all transfixed by the same small, chill frisson of shock, but no one exclaimed. He looked round all their sobered, pitying faces, and registered what was there to be registered, but it was not much; nothing more than was due to any boy of sixteen, suddenly wiped out for no good reason. No use looking for the one who felt no surprise, for after the gradual attrition of hour after hour without word they could none of them feel very much.

'How awful!' said Lesley in a resigned whisper. 'Terrible for his parents. I'm so sorry.'

'The poor fool kid!' said Gus. 'I wish to God now I'd lugged him back to his chain gang by the ear. Can't say we didn't half expect it, I suppose, by this time. It began to look . . . But there's always the odd chance.'

'Which in this case didn't come up. I thought you should be told. Sorry to have ruined your day.'

Paviour moistened his pale lips. 'Do you think it was here, on our premises, that he fell into the river? I feel to blame. But the path is a right of way, we couldn't stop it if we tried.'

'It's too early yet,' said George with deliberation, 'to say where and how he entered the water. The forensic laboratory has a good deal of work to do on his clothes, and the contents of his pockets. And of course there'll be a post-mortem.'

'A post-mortem?' The meagre, gallant Don Quixote beard quivered and jutted as though every individual hair had suddenly stiffened to the clenched tension of Paviour's jaw. He relaxed the convulsive pressure of his teeth cautiously, and drew breath deeply before he resumed with arduous reasonableness: 'Is that really necessary, in a case like this. I know you have to be thorough, but the distress to the parents . . . And surely the cause of death isn't in doubt? A clear case of drowning . . .?'

'It would seem so,' George agreed gently. 'But double-checking does no harm, and as you say, we try to be thorough. I doubt if it's an issue that will affect the parents' distress one way or the other.' He was turning back towards his car when he looked back with a casual afterthought. 'By the way, you won't be surprised or disturbed if you find some of our people patrolling the riverside path or inspecting that slip, will you? A routine precaution, that's all.'

He did not look back again, except in the rear-view mirror as he drove away. They were grouped just as he had left them, all looking warily after him. And if he had got little enough out of that interview, at least he had lobbed one small, accurate pebble into the middle of the pool of their tranquillity, and its ripples were already beginning to spread outwards.

A young giant working on the flower-beds along the drive straightened his long, lithe back to watch the car go by, without curiosity though with fixed, methodical attention, his senses turned outwards for relaxation while he took a breather. The reddish-fair head, Celtic-Roman, with chiselled features and long, indifferent lapis eyes, belonged to a statue rather than a man. George knew the type locally, a pocket of fossils preserved among these border valleys, though this superlative specimen was not personally known to him. Orrie Benyon, of course. Orlando, who admitted his ghostly ancestors ungrudgingly into his territory by night. Those cropped military curls, that monumental neck and straight nose, would have looked well in a bronze helmet; no doubt he recognised his own kind, and was at home with them. And indeed his stock might well go back to just such stubborn settlers, survivors after the death of this city, the offspring of time-expired legionaries and the daughters of

71

enterprising local middlemen. Deprived of their urban background, they had rooted into the valley earth and turned to stock and crops for a living. And survived. Tenacious and long-memoried, they had not allowed themselves to be uprooted or changed a second time.

George stopped the car at the edge of the drive, and walked back. He stood watching beside the flower-beds; and after a long minute of uninterrupted work, Orrie straightened his long, athlete's back again, and turned towards his audience the massive, stony beauty of his face, flushed with exertion. At this range the flaws that reduced him to humanity, and a fairly limited humanity at that, were plain to be seen: the stubble of coarse reddish beard he hadn't bothered to shave, the roughness of his weathered skin over the immaculate but brutal bones, the inlaid indifference of the blue eyes.

'Good morning!' said George. 'Nice show of bulbs you've got coming along.'

'Not bad, I reckon,' the gardener admitted. 'Be some tulips out by now if it'd bin a bit warmer. You come round in three weeks or so, they'll be a show worth seeing.'

George offered his cigarette case and a light. Both were accepted tacitly but promptly. 'You take care of all this place single-handed? That's a lot of work for one.'

'I manage,' said Orrie, and looked with quickening curiosity through the smoke of his cigarette into George's face. 'You're police, aren't you? I saw you once when you picked up that chap who was firing ricks, up the valley.'

'That's right. My name's Felse. You'll have heard we fished a young fellow out of the Comer this morning?' Everyone with an ear to the ground in Moulden had heard the news before ever the police surgeon reached the spot. 'He was here with a visiting school party yesterday. You had to chase him off from where you were cordoning off the slip. That was the last you saw of him?'

'Last I saw, *yes*,' said Orrie, with a long, narrowed glance. 'I finish here half past four, Wednesdays, I do a bit at the vicarage that night. I was gone before closing time – the vicar'll tell you where I was. I told your chap, the one who came after me up home, 'bout nine that'd be. Seems there was some others saw him after I did, monkeying about by that cave-in again. But I tell you what,' he said confidentially, 'I reckon I know one place he's been since then. If he hasn't, someone else has. In my back shed. Not the tool-shed where I keep the mower and all that – the one down behind the orchard. I got

72

a little work-bench in there, and me stores of sprays and weed-killers and potting compost. And I can tell when somebody's bin moving me stuff around.'

There were interesting implications here, if Orrie wasn't imagining the prying fingers; as why should he? He wasn't the imaginative kind, and a man does know how he puts down his own tools. The orchard lay well back from the riverside, and the wealth of old and well-grown trees between isolated it from the house. Gerry Boden had last been seen alive strolling negligently along the garden hedge, and somewhere along the course of that hedge he had vanished. Now if there should be a hole, or a thin place, inviting him through into the plenteous cover of the orchard, and the solitary shed in its far corner . . .

'You don't lock that shed?'

'It's got no lock. I keep thinking I'll put a padlock on, but I never get round to it. Him,' he said, with a jerk of his head towards Paviour's house, 'he's always scared of having things pinched, but the stuff in there's mine, no skin off his nose. Folks are pretty honest round here, I'm not worried. I do me own repairs – make me own spares when I need 'em.'

'And there's nothing missing this time?'

'Not a thing, far's I can see. Just somebody was in there, poking around, shifting things, passing the time nosing into everything, and thinking he'd put it all back the way it was before. Which you can't do. Not to kid the one who uses the place regularly.'

'You didn't say anything about this to Detective-Sergeant Price.'

'I didn't know, did I? I hadn't been back here. I only went into the place twenty minutes ago.'

'Fair enough,' said George. 'How about coming down there with me now? No need to disturb the household, if we can come round to it from the other side.'

There was a navigable track that circled the perimeter, and brought the car round to the other side of the curator's house and garden by inconspicuous ways. The shed was of wood, a compact, dark, creosoted building tucked into the corner of the shrubbery. Inside it smelled of timber and peat and wood-shavings. Various small packets and bottles and tins lay neatly but grimily along shelves on one side, folded sacks were piled in a corner, and full sacks stacked along the base of the wall. Under the single window was Orrie's work-bench, a vice clamped to the edge of it, and a rack of tools arranged under the window-sill. He was comprehensively equipped – power drill, sets of spanners, sets of screwdrivers, planes, even a small modern lathe. In the fine litter of sawdust and shavings under the bench the morning light found a few abrupt blue glitters of metal.

George advanced only just within the doorway, and looked round him. There was dust and litter enough on the concreted floor to have preserved the latest traces of feet, though it was clearly swept reasonably often. And if Orrie had not already tramped all over it this morning, since his discovery, nosing out the signs of trespass, there just might be something to be found.

'Did you move about much in here when you came in and realised you'd had an intruder?'

'Didn't have time. I never went no further than you are now, all I come for was my little secateurs, and they were on the shelf here inside the door. I reckoned I'd come back midday and have a look over everything, but I don't think there'll be anything missing. Yes, I did go a bit towards the window and had a quick glance round. That's all.'

'Then what made you so sure somebody'd been in? You were talking about something more than just a feeling.'

'That!' said Orrie succinctly, and pointed a large brown forefinger at the top right corner of the window, where his periodic cleaning had not bothered to extend its sweep.

He wasn't clairvoyant, after all; he hadn't even needed the tidy workman's hypersensitive unease over his tools. In the small triangle of dust the tip of a finger had written plainly GB, and jabbed a plump round fullstop after the letters. The human instinct to perpetuate one's own name at every opportunity, whenever more urgent occupation is wanting, had made use even of this mere three square inches of dusty glass. The act cast a sharp sidelight of acute intelligence upon Orrie's remark about passing the time.

'There's the way things are lying, too,' conceded Orrie, 'but that was what took my eye right off.'

What had taken George's eye was that splendidly defined fullstop. With the morning light slanting in here, and showing up every mote of dust and grain of wood-powder, the individual nodules of that fingertip showed even to the naked eye. Almost certainly the right forefinger, unless Gerry Boden happened to be a southpaw. And he had impressed that print with careful precision – he or whoever it was. It wouldn't take Sergeant Noble very long to find out.

'Do any of the others ever come here?' George asked. 'Legitimately?'

'Could happen,' allowed Orrie indifferently, and shrugged. 'Not often. Not lately. What for?'

'Good! Then stay away from here today. Can you do that? If there's anything you want, take it now.'

'There's nothing I want,' said Orrie. 'It's all yours.'

George made two or three telephone calls from the nearest box, handed over the minute inspection of Orlando Benyon's shed to the appropriate people, made contact with the police pathologist and his own chief at CID headquarters, left strict instructions about what news and reports should be channelled to his home number immediately, and what could wait, and drove with the exaggerated care and deliberation of sleeplessness back towards the village of Comerford, uncomfortably in transition to a suburban area, where he, and the unhappy parents of the boy Boden, lived within three doors of each other. One more hurdle, the highest, and then he could sleep. Whether the Bodens would be able to sleep was another matter. With sedatives, maybe. But not everyone responds to sedatives. Some people feel them as a kind of outrage and violation, and Boden was a strong-minded and passionate man. George was not looking forward to that interview. On the other hand, he would not for any money have delegated it to anyone else.

'I hope you didn't mind,' said Lesley Paviour blithely, swinging the wheel of the old Morris nonchalantly as they negotiated the sharp turn by the downstream bend of the Comer, not very far from where Gerry Boden's body had been towed ashore. 'I had to get away from there for a few hours. Normally I can ride it. I mean, for God's sake, I took it on, didn't I? I don't welch on my bargains, I really don't! But under pressure, I tell you, it gets tight. But *tight*!' She sat back in the driving seat, a neat, competent figure in a deep green spring suit as modest and suave as her own creamy countenance. 'I'm a placid person,' she said deprecatingly, 'I have to be. But I've got my limits. I know when to duck out for a breather. Trouble is, I don't always get such a marvellous excuse. So I know you won't mind being made use of. Am I making you nervous? Driving, I mean?'

'Not in the least. You drive well.' And so she did, with verve and judgement, and certainly with decision. She smiled with quick pleasure at being praised.

'If I had your friend's Aston Martin, now, instead of this old thing!'

Charlotte declined to rise to this fly. They had seen nothing of Gus since he had withdrawn, she suspected with reluctance, after delivering her and her luggage at Paviour's house. He had strung out the conversation, after the chief inspector's departure, or made an attempt to, but without much backing from anyone else, and failing to get any invitation to remain, had finally taken himself off.

'He seems to be a gentleman of leisure, that young man,' Lesley continued thoughtfully. 'Whatever can he do for a living, if he's free to ramble about in the middle of the working week in April? Have you known him long?'

'I don't know him at all, really,' said Charlotte. 'We only met walking round Aurae Phiala yesterday, and then found we were both staying at the same pub. I gathered he's some sort of adviser on Roman antiques – I'm a little vague about details. Maybe to museums? Or collectors.' Those things she knew about Gus Hambro which did not fit into this picture, such as his manipulations over the room at the inn, she did not care to mention to anyone until she herself understood them better. 'He seems to know his subject,' she said. 'At least, *I* couldn't fault him, but of course I'm only a beginner.'

'In spite of having Alan Morris in the family,' Lesley said, and smiled as she drew into the left traffic lane at the lights on the outskirts of Comerbourne. 'Have you really never met him? Oh, you must! You don't know what you've been missing.'

'Nobody's finding it very easy to meet him at the moment,' said Charlotte. 'He seems to have gone off into the wilds of Turkey on some dig or other, and got so interested that he forgot to come back. Nobody's heard from him for more than a year. As a matter of fact, his solicitor is getting a bit worried about his silence.' She did not care to make the point any more strongly, or to admit any anxiety on her own part, not even to this impulsively talkative companion whose goodwill and sympathy were already taken for granted. 'Tell me about him,' she said. 'What is he really like?'

Lesley turned smartly left as the lights changed, and wound her way by back-streets to the parking-ground on the edge of the shopping centre, a multi-storey monstrosity of raw concrete, at which she gazed with resigned distaste as she crept slowly up to the barrier and drove in to the second tier. 'Brutal, isn't it? In a nice

Tudor-cum-Georgian town like this, I ask you! Doctor Morris? Well, I suppose I do know him fairly well, he's stayed with us a couple of times. But of course Stephen knows him much better, he was at college with him, and they've always kept in touch, in a fairly loose sort of way. Don't think I'm being bitchy if I say that Stephen probably resents him as much as he admires him. They began more or less level, you see, and then the one went on forging right to the top, and the other came labouring along always further and further in the rear. They never were less than friends, though, so admiration must have kept on winning out.'

The car slid neatly into its slot, and she cut the engine and opened her door. 'Grab the shopping bag, would you mind? – it's slid over your side. Let's go and have coffee first, and then I've got to call at the bank to get some cash, and dump that package, before we start shopping.'

Charlotte lifted out a large bag of pale, soft leather, so limp as to seem empty, and lifted her eyebrows in surprise at the weight of the small, brown-paper-wrapped box that dragged down one corner of it. And Lesley laughed.

'Yes, that's why I want to get rid of it first. It's something of Orrie's, actually. Country people are odd! He claims he doesn't trust banks, he refuses to open an account, yet he doesn't see anything illogical in asking me or Stephen to put things in our safe-deposit box to keep for him. He's not so dumb, you know. Quite sharp enough to know all about dodging income tax on the odd jobs he does in his spare time. Cash payments and no account books! And every now and again he probably gets a shade nervous at keeping cash under the floor-boards or wherever he puts it, and starts spreading the load.'

Now that she was away from Aurae Phiala, Lesley had flamed into an almost delirious fluency and radiance, she who was bright enough to dazzle even in her chosen prison. She talked incessantly and joyously over coffee in the feminine precincts of the main dress shop: about Aurae Phiala itself, about Orrie, and the village community of Moulden, about Bill Lawrence and his aspirations. She rejoiced in being free from the place, but she talked of it with comprehension and critical affection. Perhaps she needed this interlude only as the lover needs a rest from loving.

'Poor Bill, he has ambitions towards scholarship. I mean the real thing. I could be wrong, but I don't think he has the real thing in him. He's doing a big thesis on the border sites, that's why he's working at our place for a year or so. It doesn't pay much, so you can imagine he's in earnest about his aspirations. He's a nice boy,' she said tolerantly, and a shade absurdly in view of the fact that she was perhaps two years his senior, 'but somehow I don't see him making it to the top. He prowls about the place, you know, on his own, and dreams of springing a dazzling surprise on the archaeological world some day. I don't know! I see him ending up pretty much like Stephen, half-fulfilled and half-frustrated – a third-rater,' she said, candidly and regretfully, 'and knowing it.'

She talked of the limitations of her husband and her acquaintances in a perfectly detached way, quite without personal venom and certainly without any delusions. Charlotte could imagine her discussing her own imperfections, if the subject should arise, with the same critical precision.

The bank was directly across the street from the shop. Lesley rummaged in the depths of her calf handbag for a matching key-case as they crossed at the lights, and flicked out the smallest of the keys on the bunch it contained. 'You won't mind waiting a minute for me? They make a thing of this strong-box business, but ours mostly has rather dull securities and family papers in it. And Stephen's will, I suspect. Not that he ever mentions it, or that I've ever asked him, but he's the type to consider it a sacred duty to have everything in order for every emergency.'

'It could be a virtue,' said Charlotte rather drily, reminded of the unimaginably sudden aspect death sometimes assumes.

'It *is* a virtue. One I envy but am never likely to possess. I'm an improviser, he's a method man.'

She disposed of her errand, and armed herself with cash, and they went to shop, the usual duty shopping for the household, the more esoteric lines which were not stocked and delivered locally; and a few items for her own pleasure. Then they loaded the purchases into the car, and went with free hands to view the delectable older parts of Comerbourne. Lesley set herself to be the most enlightening and intelligent of guides. Her knowledge was wide, and her taste was decisive and good.

'I was born here,' she said, sensing the question Charlotte had not asked. 'Not here in the town, but only about four miles away, in a village. I used to be a typist in Lord Silcaster's estate office. Not a very good one. That's how I got to know Stephen. We used to do any typing that was needed for the Aurae Phiala publications, and for the few little books and articles Stephen occasionally produced. I was the one who mucked up his texts worse than any of the others, that's what made him notice me in the first place.'

'It sounds highly improbable,' Charlotte said frankly. They were leaning side by side on the stone parapet of the oldest bridge over the Comer, and the same river that scoured so savagely at its banks upstream flowed beneath them here full, strong and smooth, partially tamed by two weirs in between. A few black-headed gulls wheeled headily above the water.

'No, honestly I wasn't much good. I wasn't interested enough. And as I had this urge to correct manuscripts as I went along, and couldn't read his handwriting, and didn't know the first thing about Roman Britain, you can imagine he felt obliged to educate me. Looks like being a life-work, doesn't it?'

There was no being certain how serious she was, or how flippant. Her lips were curved slightly in a mild, private smile. But she did not elaborate anything or withdraw anything, then. She took Charlotte companionably by the arm, and they turned back together towards the car park, and the Morris, and home. Not until they were drawing near to Moulden did she suddenly reopen, more gently and more directly, the subject of herself.

'You're wondering about Stephen and me,' she said; a statement, not a question, and with nothing defiant or defensive about it. 'Impossible not to wonder, isn't it?' And that was a question, and required an answer.

'Quite impossible,' said Charlotte, 'since you ask me.' It was difficult to feel any tension or embarrassment while Lesley felt none. 'I do it regularly, about all the interesting people I meet.'

'Good! So do I. But I know we're a rather special case. For one thing, you have to realise that even three years ago Stephen was rather a different person – to look at, I mean, and to be with, and all that. Growing and ageing don't work in a smooth, regular sort of way. A stunted little boy suddenly starts to shoot up like a weed, a plain adolescent turns into a beauty overnight, and well-preserved middle-aged men who reach sixty still looking forty-five suddenly make up the deficit and more than overtake their age, all in a few months. For no good reason that I can see. And for another thing, he began to take an interest in me just when I was on the rebound from a very unhappy love affair – the kind of let-down that alters not just your life but even your nature. He was kind, and attentive, and soothing. And I'd gone off passion. I married for safety, and comfort, and consideration. Not to be alone, and not to be vulnerable any more. Maybe a little for reputation, too,' she said, with a serene air of examining her own motives in the light of a new discovery, and finding them credible, reasonably creditable, and slightly amusing. 'My own family was pretty undistinguished, and Stephen had at any rate a respectable reputation in his own field – though I probably over-valued it at the time. So I married him. I think it was just as big a gamble for him, perhaps bigger.'

They had reached the rising curve in the road, where the plantation of young trees came into view, fringing Aurae Phiala with delicate pales of green.

'Insecure young girls,' said Lesley seriously, 'are often happiest with much older men. They feel safe.' And suddenly she laughed, a gay peal, refreshed by a whole day of escape from her selected cage. 'Doesn't always work out that way, though. Yes, you really must make the acquaintance of your great-uncle. Now there's a handsome old dog! He knows it, too! He must have put in some agile footwork at times, to get this far through his life still single, and yet have all the fun he's had.'

'I've been hearing about his reputation as a lady-killer,' Charlotte admitted. 'Everyone tells the same tale about him, so it must be true.'

'I speak,' said Lesley feelingly, 'as one of the many at whom he made charming and – relatively! – harmless passes.'

'I thought you might!'

'But unfortunately – I suppose it isn't surprising in the circumstances – Stephen is almost pathologically jealous of me, so it wasn't much fun. It was pretty innocuous play, but I had to discourage it. Absurd, but even so it could have been dangerous.'

'I suppose,' said Charlotte casually, 'you haven't heard from him since he left for Turkey? He went straight from here to the airport, I was told.'

'That's right, he did. No, I haven't had any word. He knew it wouldn't be a good idea, you know. Neither has Stephen, I'm sure. But in the ordinary way we shouldn't expect to, of course, he isn't a writing man. Only books! And they've been friends long enough to take each other for granted, turn up when they feel like it, and shut up when they're busy. They always get on well, except that they never can agree about Aurae Phiala. After all,' she said simply, 'it's all Stephen has, and he's never going to excavate it, not really, nobody's ever going to put up the money. But he lives on the hope, and that's enough.'

The Morris rolled briskly through the carriage gates, and down the gravelled drive towards the house.

'And you've never had any regrets?' Charlotte asked.

'Me?' said Lesley, opening her wide eyes even wider in amused surprise. 'I never regret anything.'

Chapter Seven

George slept until six o'clock, and was then awakened by the telephone. Sergeant Noble had a comprehensive report to make, the day's summary of his own activities and those of several others.

'Got a preliminary estimate for you from Goodwin, but he's not through yet, he'll be on the line again later this evening.' The pathologist attached to Comerbourne General Hospital enjoyed Home Office recognition in this region, and he was an old friend, and amenable. 'It confirms what Braby suggested, but we'll have to wait until he's finished the post-mortem. Yes, the father showed up to identify. Very composed, considering. Shall I read it out?'

He did so. Doctor Braby, hard-worked GP and police surgeon to the district, had done more than confirm the fact of death on this occasion, he had called immediate attention to certain peculiarities about the body, and boldly essayed a guess at the length of time it had actually been in the water. A very suggestive guess, too, but there was no acting on it until Dr Reece Goodwin had made a more detailed examination and confirmed or corrected Braby's estimate. Noble's matter-of-fact voice made short work of the interim report.

'And this shed of Benyon's. We've about mapped it, took us most of the day. He was there, all right. We got a set of his prints from the body. The letters on the glass are drawn, of course, but you were right about the dot. Right forefinger tip – a beauty. But besides that, we've collected half a dozen more, various but his, from all round the place. And as good as a complete set off the vice – the metal had the thinnest possible film of oil. He was there, and there for some time, poking into everything. No damage, no mischief, just having a look. Like you and Benyon put it – passing the time.'

'So, alone,' said George.

'That's how it looks. Nearly all the other prints we lifted are Benyon's, naturally. One or two of someone else, probably Paviour himself, but of course we haven't got him on file, and these are where you'd expect 'em, on the door, where you might well finger it if you just looked in to have a word with the incumbent, so to speak.'

'So young Boden spent some time alone in there, alive and active. What about getting in there, considering where he was last noticed?'

'Easy! The box hedge is solid as a wall as far as the corner, but just round there it ends, and that short side is privet, and there's a place in it where an old wicket's been taken out, and the gap hasn't grown in completely yet. Not much doubt he slipped in there and went to earth in the shed, for some purpose of his own. Otherwise *someone* would have seen him again.'

'And waited. For what, I wonder? I can't think he had any date to meet somebody there. He came with the party, and halfway through the visit he was still showing off for his fans and being mildly provocative towards all authority. He wasn't doing any showing off when he slipped quietly away into Orrie's shed. Something happened, something came into his mind, while he was there at Aurae Phiala, that prompted him to disappear and let the party leave without him.'

'He may not have expected them to do that,' objected Noble reasonably. 'They never had before. Maybe he just wanted to make 'em hunt and fret a bit.'

'Look, Orrie's shed isn't any special joy, and this was a boy who liked his comfort, and company, and adulation. He might sit it out ten minutes just to annoy, but not the time it took him to fidget all round the place as he seems to have done. He'd have to have a much more compelling reason than that. It looks to me more as if he wanted them to push off and abandon him. For his own reasons. And that means a reason right there on the spot, otherwise, once out of sight, he'd simply have made off for wherever it was he wanted to be. But he didn't. Where he wanted to be was right there, but unobserved. He camped out and waited. For what?'

'Closing time,' said Noble. 'For everyone to go away.'

'You're not far off target, either, but it's no answer. Look, there wasn't any sign in there of a scuffle of any kind? Even tidied up afterwards?'

'Not a thing. The dust lay peacefully, except where he'd actually trodden or pawed. Nobody'd been fighting in there, take it from me.'

'Then nothing to suggest that – granted he walked in of his own will – he didn't walk out the same way?'

'I was coming to that,' said Sergeant Noble with satisfaction. 'He walked out, all right. I don't know if you noticed, but just outside the door, where the ground's trodden, the grass thins, and there's a slight hollow that obviously holds water every time it rains, and only dries out gradually in between – nice smooth black mud like double-cream. It's in first-class shape just now. I've got two and a half beautiful prints in that layer of mud, heading *out* of the shed. I haven't got the shoes he was wearing, but I have got his spare school pair. They're his prints, all right. If there was any doubt, there's one very nice curl of metal swarf shed from the shoe, bang in the middle of one of those prints. I've got the whole piece of turf under plastic. It looks like the same sort of swarf that's lying under Orrie's bench. I reckon when we get the actual shoes we may find some more. That stuff works into composition soles like nails knocked into wood. He walked in, and he walked out – alive, in case you were wondering . . .'

'For a while,' George conceded, 'I was. It was just a possibility. Knowing what we know.'

'Yes, granted. But there it is. He went out of there alive and alone, after a fairly lengthy stay. And where do we go from here?'

'Home to bed,' said George, 'in your case, and leave me the file. In my case – back to Aurae Phiala.'

It was after nine o'clock, however, by the time he got there, since his route was complicated, and involved calls at the mortuary of the General Hospital, at police headquarters, and a telephone call to the forensic laboratory. He collected the full list of the contents of the dead boy's pockets, and one unexpected item in the collection sent him out of his way to pay a visit to 'The Salmon's Return' before he finally reached Paviour's house.

'Why, Mr Felse!' said Lesley, opening the door to him, and blessedly forgetting to think of him first by his rank and office. 'Do come in! Do you want Stephen, or all of us?'

He said that he didn't mind who was present, that he had something to communicate which might slightly affect the convenience of everyone in residence here, and therefore could be stated in everyone's presence. And he hoped it wouldn't inhibit the activities of anybody here. Anybody, of course, with an easy conscience.

'I don't promise anything,' said Lesley serenely, 'about anybody's conscience except mine. But I don't anticipate any real onslaught from you, somehow. Come along in!'

They were all there, opportunely including E greeted the visitor with immaculate politenes acid disapproval which might well have stemm than nervousness. 'I thought,' he said, in with we had answered all the relevant questions have had access wherever they wished. Is the can do?'

'No questioning is entailed tonight,' said George. 'I called to tell you that we find it necessary to remain on your grounds for a day or two. It might – it's for you to decide – be preferable to close Aurae Phiala to the public for some days. No doubt you'll consult Lord Silcaster about that. We're prepared to cordon off our section if you see fit to continue admitting the public. I'm sorry to put you to any inconvenience, but it can't be helped. What we intend is to take up the area of ground you now have roped off, or a part of it – the broken corner of the hypocaust.'

Paviour shot up out of his chair, for once jerked erect to his full gangling height, which was impressive. He looked more than ever like Don Quixote confronting the most formidable of spectral windmills; and his tenor voice blazed from a reed to a trumpet in his indignation.

'You can't do such a thing! You've no right! Can you imagine the harm you might do? Uninformed digging is disastrous. Lord Silcaster will never tolerate it.'

'Lord Silcaster has already given his permission. On the grounds set before him.'

'I can't believe it! Grounds? What grounds? I quite understand that where there's some reasonable connection, some prospect of information to be gained . . . But surely here, tragic though the circumstances may be, there's no question of a crime? This poor boy fell into the river—'

'I'm afraid your information is not quite complete,' George said equably. 'Gerry Boden did not simply fall into the river and drown. He was knocked on the head, just as Mr Hambro was last night, and *put* into the river.'

Paviour stood rigid, frozen into silence like the rest.

'Put into the river,' said George, studying the circle of shocked faces, 'somewhere on these premises. He showed particular interest in that subsidence, it's reasonable to assume that his object was to return to it at a time when there would be no one around to interfere can also tell you, roughly, at any rate, the time when he the water. It was somewhere around ten o'clock. And you t need reminding what happened here at very much the same ue last night.'

No, they needed no reminding. Charlotte had been the first to make the connection; her eyes lit with a spark of alert intelligence which was meant as a communication, and as briefly acknowledged by a warning flicker of George's glance in her direction. She said nothing. Paviour was the last to understand. His habitual greyness faded into a bleached and waxen pallor.

'We were concerned last night,' said George, 'with the question of what Mr Hambro could possibly have blundered into, to make it essential that he should not survive to talk about it. Now we needn't wonder about that any longer.'

When he left the house, he went down to the riverside, and spent some time considering the extent of the job they were about to tackle, the resources they were going to need, and the best way of setting about it. He came back to his car, parked inconspicuously on the grass by the privet hedge, shortly before half past ten. From the darkness where the thicker growth of box began, a shadowy figure slipped out to join him, and he saw the oval of a girl's face as a paler gleam above her dark coat.

'Miss Rossignol! What are you doing here?'

'I had to speak to you,' she said in a hurried whisper. 'It's all right, they won't miss me. I think they were glad to have a little time to themselves. I said I'd like to walk a little way with Bill Lawrence when he left. I had a sudden thought, when you mentioned the timing. One I don't much like, and can't quite believe in, but it's there.'

'What is it? What's on your mind?'

'I was pretty close behind Gus Hambro last night. I know you realised I was following him. And it was a quiet night, no noise from wind or leaves. Look, I'm no expert at that sort of thing. I was as quiet as I could be, but all the same, I can't help wondering if at some stage he realised I was on his heels. There *is* something curious about him, you know. The way he shook me off, as soon as you left us, and hurried off down the river like that. And even his *being* there at the inn. He pretended to me that he was already booked in there, but he wasn't – I heard him ask for the room afterwards. When he knew who I was.'

'You think that's significant?' George asked, and drew her a step deeper into the darkness of the hedge.

'I think it ought not to be,' she said earnestly. 'But yes, I think it is. So it adds up to something ambivalent about him, so much so that I *have* to wonder. Was he genuinely attacked, because he blundered into murder? That's what the timing suggests, but that's not the only thing it could suggest. The other is that he heard me following, and staged the attack on himself, with the help of some accomplice unknown – for it couldn't have been done alone, could it? – to put himself in the clear, and immobilise me long enough for the other person to get away, and the body to be well downstream. Maybe someone bold enough to improvise like that would even take the risk of getting himself really knocked out and dropped in the water, knowing I couldn't fail to find him in a few minutes.'

'And knowing you,' George added. She sensed that he was smiling, and was a little disconcerted. 'Enough to estimate your capabilities, at any rate. In the circumstances you outline, I agree I'd rather take a chance on you than on most people.'

'Thank you,' she said, 'but I think you're laughing at me.'

'I assure you I'm not. But I'd still be a bit wary of taking a risk like that. Even on you.'

'It would be a pretty desperate choice, though, wouldn't it? It isn't a thought I like, myself,' she admitted. 'But I *know* he isn't what he seems to be. He isn't here by accident, and your news about an unofficial hunt being launched for the boy sent him off in a hurry to this place.'

'As it well might,' said George, interpreting, 'if the boy was already dead, and concealed somewhere here, and Hambro had guilty knowledge of it. The news that the police were interested made it imperative to get the body away at once – and the river was the obvious ally. Is that what you think happened?'

'I hadn't thought as far as that,' she said, quivering. 'It simply seemed a possibility that he was somehow involved.'

'That isn't what I asked you.'

Now it was she who was invisibly smiling, oddly encouraged and reassured. 'No,' she said, 'it isn't what I think. I *don't* think it. But I could be wrong, too, that's why I had to hand it over to you.' And abruptly reverting to painful gravity: '*Was* the boy already dead?'

'It isn't certain yet. We shall get the pathologist's report tomorrow. But yes, I think he was.'

'Not drowned, then?'

'In confidence, though again we haven't yet got the word officially – no, not drowned. I'm trusting you with some part of the background. I'm afraid you saw the beginning of it. This boy had found something very intriguing and exciting here at Aurae Phiala yesterday afternoon. I rather think he must just have picked it up when Mr Hambro chased him away from the cave-in. He didn't dare attempt to go back again until the coast was clear, so he hid himself until everyone was gone. Not until dark, since his intention was to search that patch of ground thoroughly. But he may have waited until it began to be dusk. And someone – someone from close by, someone on or near this site – caught him in the act, and took drastic action. Whoever it was didn't go through his pockets. His find was still there when they stripped him at the mortuary.'

In a whisper she asked: 'What was it?'

'A single gold coin. An aureus of Commodus – that's round about the end of the second century AD.'

'But you couldn't!' she said just audibly. 'You couldn't kill somebody for one gold coin. It isn't possible!'

'People have been killed for less, even taking it at its face value, though its actual value is very much greater. But no, he wasn't killed for that, or it wouldn't have been still on him. No, whoever caught him hunting for more knew that there was more there to be found – knew it because he himself had come out as soon as he dared, to remove whatever was there to a place of greater safety. Don't forget the landslip had taken place only that morning, Orrie Benyon was just cordoning off the dangerous area and putting up warning notices. If someone had valuables hidden in the hypocaust, he must have been waiting on thorns for the chance to get his hoard away, and baulked all day by staff and visitors wandering around. He came at dusk, as soon as he dared, when everyone was gone. So did the boy. Maybe he'd already unearthed what was left, and it was too late just to warn him off and hope for the best. X preferred a final solution.'

'Is this a theory?' she asked in horrified fascination. 'Or do you know it?'

'It's a theory. One that fits. In the last days of Aurae Phiala the coinage was shaky in the extreme, a lot of barbarous, debased pieces were being struck everywhere. But this – I'm well briefed on the subject, this isn't my own knowledge – is a fine, full-weight aureus from two hundred years previously, enormously enhanced in value. And the Romans were hoarders. Now supposing some family here had a store of such good gold pieces at the end, when the Welsh attack was threatening, they might very well bury it for safety, in the hope of recovering it later. They seem to have shut their eyes and hoped to the very end.'

'But can one coin prove anything?' she said hesitantly.

'A very special coin. It hadn't lain loose in the soil for centuries, or even for weeks. It's virtually mint-new. That means it's been kept carefully and put away securely, and certainly not alone. In a pottery jar, well sealed. During the slip falling bricks inside the flue may have broken the jar, and rolling earth carried one coin down the slope, for Gerry to find. Not a dull bit of corroded bronze, but fire-new gold. No wonder he went back to look for more.'

'But if someone knew all about it before, this treasure, why hadn't he removed it earlier?'

'It was safe enough where it was, until the river took a bite out of the hypocaust. It's possible the hoard was actually found somewhere else on the site – say the cellar of one of the houses – and put in the flue for safe-keeping, to be drained away gradually. A whole thicket of broom bushes came down in that slip, as you saw. I think there was a way into the flue all along, under cover of those bushes. Possibly the slip, while it exposed it, also partially filled it in. I think, too, that the find was not merely of coins, but also of small pieces of jewellery and other articles. The indications are that this site may have been exploited for at least a year. You can't dispose of such pieces wholesale. You take one or two, having studied the collectors of the world, and the highly professional fences of the antique market, and place them where they'll bring you in the best and safest return. You lie low for a while, and you disperse a handful of coins, singly, perhaps not to the best advantage, but still it's all clear profit. And when you hit a passionate collector who takes care to ask no questions, then you venture the big deal. But it means dedicated study, exact judgement, and above all, time.'

He could sense, even in the darkness, the enormous wonder of her eyes, fixed unwaveringly upon his face though they saw him only as a bulk solid and still between her and the sky. 'But how do you know all this?' she said. 'About a whole year's robberies from here?'

'I don't yet – not to say know. But for about a year certain pieces of late Roman coinage and art have been cropping up in unexpected places in the international market. Obviously genuine pieces, but of very dubious provenance. Only a few, of course. Collectors are queer fish, you know, liable to banditry without any qualms. But four instances have come to light within the year, through dealers or buyers who did have qualms. And four coming to light argues forty or more in the dark, most likely for good.'

'And there's something to connect these cases with Aurae Phiala?'

'Not until now, not specifically. But period and style are right. You've seen the ones in the museum here, the curvilinear trumpets and dragons, those un-Roman Roman antiquities? Let's say, there was plenty to connect our cases with four or five border sites, of which Aurae Phiala is one. And one such gold coin here, and a cold-blooded killing, are fairly eloquent argument.'

She was shivering slightly but perceptibly, not from cold and not from fear, but with the vibration of some personal and secret tension about which he had, as yet, no right to ask. She might, if he waited, confide in him, but not now; there was no time, if she was to retain her immaculate position in this household. He put a hand upon her shoulder, which was firm and slender, and turned her towards the gate.

'Keep your lips closed and your eyes open, and think about it. And if you want me, I won't be far away.'

'But you won't be here,' she said, not complaining, merely making the position clear to herself, and well aware that her utterance had its ambiguities. 'Not all the time.'

'You won't be entirely unprotected here,' he assured her, 'even when I'm not around. Better get back now, before they come out to look for you.' She sensed that he was smiling again. It wasn't an amused smile, but it was one that sent her away at a brisk and confident walk towards the house, and with a gratifying sense of being respected and appreciated.

The Roman city of Aurae Phiala remained closed to the public next day, and for several days following, an apologetic notice on the gate making known the fact to a largely indifferent general public. The enclosure was never exactly crowded, even in the height of the summer. On the riverside, where the pathway could not be closed, a uniformed policeman paced imperturbably, and occasionally moved people along if they tended to congregate and linger too long. The natives, markedly, did not. They passed, apparently oblivious, intent only on their own business; but hardly a soul in the village failed to pass at some time during that day, and not one missed a detail of what was there to be seen.

Operations had begun early. Breakfast was not yet over at the curator's house when Orrie came to announce that the police were in occupation, and beginning to stake out the ground. Paviour left his coffee without a word, and went rushing away to protect his beloved site, and the two girls followed in slightly apprehensive curiosity. Three uniformed men were there with spades and sieves, and three or four more in plain clothes, with George Felse at the head of operations. More surprising, and to Paviour more confounding and conciliating at the same time, was the presence of Gus Hambro, busy with a large clip-board, charting on squared paper the patch of ground to be taken up, and sketching a hurried but accurately proportioned elevation of the exposed vault of the flue. He had a coloured pencil behind either ear, and a couple more in his breast pocket.

'I knew you wouldn't mind,' said Bill Lawrence, hurrying to account for the phenomenon, a sheaf of plastic sacks and fine brushes under his arm. 'He came along to copy some lettering in the museum, not expecting the place to be closed, of course. When he heard why, naturally he was interested. It was my idea, asking him if he'd like to lend a hand on doing what recording *can* be done on a job like this. He knows his stuff, you know. He jumped at the chance. We shan't be able to do a thorough coverage, I know, but it's a relatively small area, and we may as well keep it under what control we can manage between us. There might be some useful finds.'

'Naturally,' said Gus diplomatically, 'I regard myself as under your orders, sir. If there's any possibility of anything to be gained from this operation – and in the absence of the kind of labour you'd prefer to have on a job like this – I thought an extra pair of hands might be welcome.'

A faint look of baffled pleasure crossed Paviour's harried face and vanished again instantly. However carefully and reverently the job was going to be handled, obviously he expected nothing but disaster. He hovered about the site restlessly, like one barefoot on thorns, all the while they were removing the debris of sagging, uprooted broom bushes, which Orrie phlegmatically loaded into a handcart and wheeled away along the riverside path to be unloaded and burned as far as possible from the sacred precincts. The care with which they

91

examined and photographed those bushes before allowing them to be removed brought Paviour quivering to the spot. With straining eyes he watched small fragments, meaningless to the lay eye, delicately extricated from the tangle of earth about the roots and the soft turf beneath them, cased in plastic, and labelled.

'Not your relics, I'm afraid,' said George, meeting the baffled and frantic gaze. 'Ours.'

He dared not ask, and was not told more. But he could not tear himself away. The operation proceeded methodically once the bushes had been cleared, though the spots where the mysterious fragments had been found were carefully tagged and covered with plastic. The broken fringes of grass were lifted off and stacked well out of the way, the spades began to clear the ground downwards from the arc of russet brickwork, warily because of sinister little trickles of loose earth that drifted down the slope at every movement. Layer by layer the narrow strata of brick and rubble were laid bare. Bill Lawrence, his eyes gleaming with the hunting passion, pounced on the fragments of encrusted ceramic and bone that were left behind in the police sieves, and Gus industriously entered their location in his graph, and sketched in each layer of masonry as it emerged.

Detective-Constable Barnes, large, rustic, intelligent and benign, put down his spade and went to work lovingly with a soft brush on the exposed uprights of the flue, whisking away loose, moist soil that abandoned its hold with revealing readiness. 'Look at that, now! That stuff's only been dropped here a few days. Watch that brickwork dry off in the sun, it'll be as pale as the arch, here, in ten minutes. I reckon there was eighteen inches or so of this passage open till the bank gave way.'

They had just passed that level now, and the darkness that yawned within the flue was black and inviting. Barnes reached a long arm over the ridge of fallen soil that remained in the mouth of the hole, and groped experimentally around within.

'Drops a foot, inside there. The bushes covered it. Nobody walks on a slope like this for choice, only sheep, and they don't let sheep graze this lot. Reasonable folks walk on the level – either up top, or down below.'

'What's it feel like, as far as you can reach?' George asked. 'Still silted over, or any traces of flooring? Tiles? Stone-work?'

'No, rubble. But still dropping. I'd say you'd get clear flooring a yard or two inside there.'

Lesley, watching in fascination from the sidelines, said with conviction: 'You've done this before! I know the signs.'

'Only once, miss.' Detective-Constable Barnes turned his bene-volent gaze upon her with pleasure. He liked a pretty girl. 'I went on a dig with a bunch from Birmingham University. They had me brushing out post-holes on some rubbish dump they said was a castle. Not my idea of a castle. We never turned up nothing like this. My dad was a mason – I reckon he'd have been right interested in these bricks. There's a colour for you! Spot-on what you mean when you say "brick".'

'What's it like above? Never mind further in, how about the first couple of feet?'

'Feels sound as rock. Arched – shallow, like.' His stretched knuckles tapped as far as they could reach. 'Barrel-vaulted, but low. Could be brick, could be stone. But I'd say brick. I can feel the courses.' He withdrew a hand like a shovel, and spread fingers black with the fine dust of centuries and a mere veiling of cobweb. 'Not much for seventeen hundred years, is it?'

The opening loomed before them, sliced into the bank, brushed relatively clean, a narrow, erect oblong of darkness with a rounded roof and pale, red and amber jambs rooted in deep green turf. And within was empty darkness, fenced off by no more than a ridge of soil. George looked round his team, and they were all massive countrymen, well in advance of the minimum police requirements. The slightest person present, leaving out the girls, was Gus Hambro, busy pricking in on his diagram the latest minor find.

'Care to take a look inside for us? You're the ratling.'

'Loan me a torch, and I'll have a go,' said Gus. 'What am I looking for?'

'Whatever you see. Structure, condition – and anything that looks out of place.'

'Right! Hang on to this,' he said to Bill Lawrence, and thrust the clip-board and its records at him. He shed his array of colour pencils, dropping them haphazard into the grass, hesitated whether to shed his tweed jacket, too, and then, considering its worn condition, buttoned it closely for protection instead. The dank darkness had a chill and jagged look.

'Don't go beyond where we can reach you,' George warned him. 'Six feet inside is enough. Just look it over, and memorise whatever there is to be memorised.'

'I'll do my endeavour. Right, give us that floodlight of yours.'

He dropped to his knees in the turf, now trampled into glistening, half-dried mud, and plunged head and shoulders under the ochre-tinted lintel. Torso, slim flanks and thighs, thrusting legs, vanished by silent heaves into the hollow under the slope. He was now nothing more than the neatly tapered ends of corduroy slacks, and a pair of well-worn Canadian hide moccasins. And these hung still, though alertly braced, for more than a minute, while the torch he carried ranged round the interior of the passage, and leaked little sparks of muted light into the outer day. He heaved himself six inches forward, and George laid an arresting hand on the remaining available ankle, and held fast.

'All right, you inside there! Leave it at that!'

Indistinct sounds emerged from within the earth, deprived of sense by the complicated acoustics of the soil. There was an interlude of silence, absorbed and intent. Then, without previous movement or sound, only with a sudden gush of closed and graveyard air, the rotten surface above buckled and dimpled, lolling in sagging bubbles of turf, and sending its under-levels of soil cascading down on top of the ancient arc of bricks that upheld it. Those without heard the ceiling yield, with a muffled, sickening grinding of brick against brick and stone upon stone, and the dull, filtering trickle of soil busily winding its way between.

A hollow yell was forced out with the jettisoned air. And George Felse dived forward at the jerking ankles under the archway, felt his way forward towards the knees, and hauled strongly backwards as the roof sagged slowly and ponderously inwards on top of Gus Hambro.

They dug him out with their bare hands, scrabbling like frantic terriers to clear the soil away from his head and shoulders; and within minutes they had him laid out like a stranded fish on one of their plastic sheets in the grass. All the internal filth of generations, cobwebs and dust and soot, had been discharged on top of him as the joints of the roof parted, but an outstretched arm had sheltered his head and face, and he was not only breathing, but spluttering out the dirt that had silted into mouth and nostrils. They had to brush away the layers before they could examine him for worse damage, George on one side of him, Barnes on the other, feeling urgently at a skull that seemed to have escaped all but the loose, light weight of the fall. They drew off his damp, soiled jacket, and felt at shoulders and arms, and could find no breakages. Everyone hovered unhappily. Little rivulets of loose soil trickled capriciously down the slope of raw earth. Somewhere on the sidelines Paviour could be heard protesting that they could not possibly proceed with this excavation in these conditions, that the risks were too great, that someone would be killed.

'No damage,' said Barnes, breathing gusty relief. 'Just knocked silly. He'll be round and as right as rain in five minutes. All that got him was the loose muck, not the bricks.'

'I'll fetch some brandy,' Lesley offered eagerly. 'And take this jacket to sponge and dry, he can't possibly put it on again like this.'

They were two deep round him in any case, nearly a dozen people hanging on the least movement of a finger or an eyelid. She's right, Charlotte thought, watching dubiously but compulsively like all the rest, one grain of sense is worth quite a lot of random sympathy.

'I'll bring one of Stephen's coats,' said Lesley, and set off at a light, long-stepping run for the house.

Charlotte offered tissues to wipe away the trailing threads of glutinous, dirty cobweb from the victim's eyes, for his eyelids were beginning to contract and twitch preparatory to opening. He lay for some minutes before he made the final effort, and then unfurled his improbably luxuriant lashes upon a bright, golden-brown stare of general accusation.

'What in hell do you all think you're doing?' he said, none too distinctly and very ungratefully, and spat out fragments of soil with a startled grimace of distaste. 'What happened?'

It was a fair enough question, considering how abruptly he had been obliterated from the proceedings. His exit had been brief, but absolute, while they, it seemed, were still in possession of their faculties and the facts. He sat up in the circle of George's arm, seemed to become suddenly aware of his shirt-sleeves and the late April chill, and demanded, looking violently round him: 'Where's my jacket?'

'Mrs Paviour's taken it away to clean and dry it out for you. You were taking a look inside there, and half the roof came down on you,' said George patiently. All the victim's limbs seemed to be in full working order, even his memory was only one jump behind.

'Oh, blimey!' he said weakly. 'Was that it?' And he leaned forward to peer at the spot where two policemen were stolidly clearing away newly-fallen rubble from the mouth of the flue, and a third, well above them on the level ground, was cautiously surveying the crater. 'You'll have to dig for that torch of yours,' he said more strongly, not without a mildly vindictive satisfaction. 'I let go of it when things started dropping on me. That chap up there had better watch his step, there was a gleam of daylight a good two yards forward from where I got to. He didn't put one of those beetle-crushers through there while I was inside, did he?'

'He did not,' said George tolerantly. 'The thing just gave. Mea culpa. I shouldn't have let you do it.'

'The thing just gave. Did it?' He was coming round with remarkable aplomb now, it was with the old, knowledgeable eye that he stared at the ruin of the neat archway which had been their entrance to the flue only ten minutes ago. But all he said was: 'You know what? Either I'm accident-prone, all of a sudden, or else somebody, somewhere, is sticking pins in a wax image of me.'

Some minutes later, when all anxiety on his behalf had ebbed away into renewed interest in the job on hand, when he was sitting hunched with Price's sportscoat draped round his shoulders, and one of George's cigarettes between his lips, and not a soul but George within earshot, he said, softly and with intent: 'Watch it from now on! I'm getting clearer every minute. Somebody'd been hacking at the brickwork inside there. That wasn't any accident.'

'You sure?' asked George in the same tone.

'I'm sure. I lost your torch – and switched on, at that, you won't get much mileage back in that battery! – but I know what I'd already seen. Fresh-broken surfaces, high in the wall. The upstream side was what I noticed. A gash in the brickwork, pale and clean. Even if you have to dig out from on top, now, with care you'll find it. Somebody aimed to bring that flue down.'

'Nobody,' said George, gazing ahead of him at the spot where Price was re-deploying his forces on the level of the caldarium floor, 'can have got into that place ahead of you. Earlier, yes, that I believe. Not since the slip.'

'They wouldn't have to. I told you, at least one gleam of daylight ahead there. More than one hole on top. A crowbar down one of those would be all he needed.' The momentary silence irritated him. He said with asperity, and considering his recent escape with some justification: 'It worked, didn't it?'

'It worked, all right. I'm considering motives. What was the object? To have a second go at you? They couldn't have known you'd even be available, much less put your head in the trap.'

'No, that's out,' admitted Gus generously. 'To seal off the flue, more likely.'

'To hide what's there?'

'Not a chance! There'll be nothing there. To hide the traces of what *was* there.'

Lesley came back from the house with a tweed coat over her arm and a flask in her hand. 'We can also,' she said, looking down at Gus with a slightly quizzical smile, 'offer a bath, if and when you feel equal to it. You can hardly go back to "The Salmon's Return" looking like that.'

He looked down, slightly startled, at the state of his shirt and his hands, and admitted the difficulty.

'And you can't see your face,' said Lesley helpfully, her friendly, candid eyes dwelling upon the spectacle with detached amusement, but not with any apparent repulsion.

'That's immensely kind of you. I'd like to take you up on it, if Mr Paviour will allow me,' he said, suddenly aware of a little chill in the blood that warned him not to leave out the curator from this or any other exchange on these premises.

'Of course,' Paviour said, with prompt but distant courtesy, 'by all means avail yourself. I can offer you a change of shirt, if the size is right.'

'And as I've got lunch on the way in about three quarters of an hour, hadn't you better take it easy and join us? You'll just have time to make yourself presentable. Bill will be staying, too,' she said, firmly arranging everything to her own satisfaction.

This somewhat drastic rupture in her ordinary routine must in its way, Charlotte thought, be a godsend to Lesley, however deplorable the reason for it. She was also reacting in an understandably female way to having a ready-made casualty of pleasant appearance and attractive manners dropped at her feet. For the second time, too! But on the first occasion, even when deposited half-drowned and battered in the Paviour household, he had belonged by rights to Charlotte, who had pulled him out of the river and demanded shelter for him. This time he was, so to speak, legitimate prey, and Lesley intended to enjoy him.

'If you feel like walking up with me now, I must go back and keep an eye on lunch. Charlotte, will you come and help me?'

The three of them walked back together, Gus steady enough on his legs, and only slightly exercised in mind at leaving the excavation, which had now been transferred of necessity to the higher level. There could be no more attempts to enter the flues from the slope, they were going to have to take up all that island of rotten ground and expose them from above. A more thorough job, and a safer, but infinitely slower. They were staking out the limits of the subsidence now, and Bill Lawrence was clipping a new sheet of graph paper to his board. One of the plainclothes men was busy with a camera. And Paviour, torn between the instinct to follow his wife and the desire to pursue George Felse and renew his protests, hovered in indecision. Charlotte looked back once, and saw him standing motionless, gazing after them, lean and desiccated as a stick insect, but with a face all too human in its tormented anxiety; not all, perhaps, about his beloved and ravaged city.

Lesley could, she thought, do a little more to placate and reassure a husband she knew to be almost pathologically jealous. It was easy to believe that she had no regrets about her bargain, and no intention of backing out of it, but in the circumstances this was a reassurance that needed to be repeated endlessly. And yet everything she did had an open and innocent grace about it. If she devoted herself to her new guest all through lunch, she did so out of a pleasurable sense of duty, and not at all flirtatiously. It was impossible to associate the word with her; there was nothing sidelong or circuitous about the way Lesley approached anyone, man or woman.

As for Gus, bathed and polished and reclothed in his own beautifully pressed sportscoat, he trod delicately, dividing his attention as adroitly as he could between the two of them, repaying Lesley's direct friendliness with wary deference, and turning as often as possible to Paviour with leading remarks on Aurae Phiala, to draw him into eloquence on the subject dearest to his heart.

'I imagine,' said Paviour, regarding him almost with favour over the coffee, 'that you'll be interested in seeing this distasteful invasion limited as much as possible. The damage could be incalculable. I suppose,' he said, almost visibly writhing at coming so near to begging, 'you haven't any influence? The authorities, I believe, do sometimes listen to the opinions of scholars . . .' His thin, fastidious voice faded out bitterly on the admission that he had none.

'I'm afraid,' said Gus ruefully, 'that nobody who won't listen to you, sir, is going to pay the slightest attention to me. But I don't believe, from what I've heard this morning, that the police want to take the dig a yard past where it need go. After all, they do have some evidence, apparently, to connect this boy Boden with the place.' He added deprecatingly: 'I think Chief Inspector Felse means to brief us, as fully as he can, this evening.'

'Will you be staying on to see the job through?' asked Bill Lawrence.

'I'd have liked to, but it doesn't look as if I shall be able to. I got my room at the pub for only two nights. From Friday night on you have to be a fisherman to get in at "The Salmon's Return", even in the close season. I've got to get out today.'

'Oh, no!' said Lesley, aggrieved. 'What a shame, when you're being so helpful. Stephen, don't you think *we* . . .?'

She had rushed in where angels might have hesitated to set foot, and almost instantly she recognised it, and halted in contained but palpable dismay. And Bill Lawrence put in smoothly, as if the tension had never communicated itself to him, but so promptly that Charlotte, for one, knew it had: 'Why don't you move in with me?

I've got the whole lodge as bachelor quarters, there's plenty of room for one more, if you don't mind sharing a room? Two beds,' he said cheerfully, 'and acres of storage space. We can run over and pick up your things, if you say the word?'

'Consider it said,' Gus said heartily, 'and thanks! I should have hated to have to go away and miss this chance. I thought I should probably have to go as far as Comerbourne to get a room without notice, and it hardly seemed worth it commuting from that distance. Especially,' he said, with an engaging smile in Paviour's direction, 'as I more or less invited myself to the dig in the first place.'

Lesley had recovered resiliently from her momentary disarray. She sat serenely silent, apparently well content at having Gus's problem and her own solved so economically. It even entered Charlotte's mind, watching, that there were moments when Lesley deliberately made use of Bill Lawrence to pull chestnuts out of the fire for her.

Afterwards, in the car on the way to 'The Salmon's Return', Bill said, after too patent deliberation and in too world-weary a voice: 'Look, it's easy enough living in this set-up, but you have to know the rules. Be my guest, use my experience and save your own, boy. Rule number one: Never even *seem* to get too close to that lady.' His tone was lightly cynical, and a little rueful; there was no knowing for certain how deeply he felt about what he was saying.

'I wondered,' said Gus, 'why you got off the mark so fast and so smoothly. Apart from having a generous disposition, of course.'

'Don't mistake me, there's nothing wrong with Lesley. She's straight, and she means what she offers. It's her old man. He's mad jealous of her. Oh, he'd have backed up her invitation, all right, if he'd had to. Very correct, very hospitable. But then he'd have made life hell for you, her, and above all himself, by being suspicious of every glance you gave her. It's better to keep a nice safe distance, and be a bit of the landscape, like me.'

'And you've experienced that yourself?' Gus asked mildly.

The voice beside him became even lighter and drier. 'I didn't have to. I've only confirmed it from my own observations since. I was warned off privately, as soon as I came here. By Lesley herself.' There was a brief but weighty pause, and then, as if he had felt oppressed by its suggestive possibilities, he made the mistake of adding, with the same airy intonation: 'Probably she never fancied me, anyhow.'

Gus kept his eyes on the road ahead, and sat stolidly, as though the sharp note of bitterness had passed him by. But from then on he was in no doubt that, whatever this young man felt for Lesley Paviour, it was certainly not indifference.

'In view of all the circumstances,' said George Felse, facing the assembled household in Paviour's study that evening, 'I think it only fair to give you some idea of how this enquiry is progressing. Your professional proceedings are affected, and you have a right to be told why that's inevitable. We want your co-operation. We don't want to upset your routine any longer than we must, or to extend our intrusion a yard beyond what's necessary.'

They were all there, including the young men from the lodge, invited by Lesley to dine at the house. Not an invariable favour, Gus had gathered. Not much doubt that Bill attributed it cynically to his guest's presence.

'Let me substantiate,' said George, 'our claim to move in on your ground. In the first place, the post-mortem on Gerry Boden has shown that he did not drown. There is no penetration of water into his lungs. He died of suffocation, most probably while still stunned by a blow on the head. The time of death, while it's always somewhat more problematical fixing it than is usually supposed, was considerably earlier than the time when, as we have several reasons to believe, he was put into the water. Provisionally, his death occurred somewhere between six and eight in the evening. In other words, about midway between the time when he was last seen, and the time when Mr Hambro was attacked. It's a fair assumption that the attempt on Mr Hambro's life took place because the murderer believed he had seen the boy's body committed to the river. Seen, or heard, or at any rate become aware of something queer going on, something that might make sense to him and be reported later, even if it made no sense then.'

Paviour licked bluish lips, and ventured hesitantly: 'But if there was such an interval, the boy may have been anywhere during that time, not here in Aurae Phiala at all.'

'Oh, yes, he was here. We know that he hid himself in order to stay here and have the free run of the place when everyone else had gone. We know where he hid. And we know where he was hidden, after his death. From under the clump of broom bushes we removed this

101

morning we recovered, as perhaps you noticed, certain small bits of evidence. One was the broken cap of a red ball-pen, fellow to the black one he still had on him when found. It was trodden into the turf, *underneath* those bushes. They were dragged together and heaped over him after he was killed. Another, from among the broom roots, was a sample of hair, which I think will certainly turn out to be Boden's. He was concealed there on the spot, because at the time of his murder it was barely dusk, and the whole of your river-shore is only too plainly visible from the other side. Therefore, that is where he was killed – right there beside the cave-in.'

'But after you came enquiring for him,' protested Paviour feverishly, 'the enclosure of Aurae Phiala was searched. Surely he would have been found?'

'I'd hardly call it searched. We did walk over the site. It was then dark, perhaps dark enough for the murderer to have risked getting him down to the river, if we hadn't been around. But we were not looking for a body then, at least not on dry land. The fact remains, he was there. Further laboratory work should tell us more. His clothes, for instance. They've already told us something of the first import-ance, the reason for his hanging around here until after closing-time.'

He looked round them with an equable, unrevealing glance, a pleasant, greying, unobtrusive man at whom you would never look twice in the street.

'Gerry carried a purse for his loose money. Among the coins in it, which the murderer hadn't disturbed, was a gold aureus of the Emperor Commodus, in mint condition. He can only have found it during the school visit. And he can only have found it there, at that broken flue of the hypocaust.'

'That's an impossibility,' said Paviour hoarsely. 'You'll find this is some toy of his own, a fake, a copy . . . How could you account for such a thing? A freshly-minted coin after years in the ground?'

George picked up the cue, and proceeded to account for it bluntly and clearly, as he had done for Charlotte in the night. He sketched in the figure of the murderer, also waiting for dark, to remove his buried treasure from its perilous position, and his unexpected encounter with the inquisitive boy on the same errand; the instant decision that only the boy's total removal could now protect his profitable racket; and the immediate execution. He described the items of Roman jewellery turning up with inadequate pedigrees during the past year, and the peculiarities of style which linked them, if not necessarily to this site, at least to no more than four or five, of which this was one.

'In short, we believe that someone has been systematically milking Aurae Phiala of small pieces, some very valuable indeed, for a year or more.'

There was a long, tight pause, while he eyed them gently again, his glance passing unrevealingly from face to face round the circle. Then Bill Lawrence said, a little too loudly but with admirable bluntness: 'You mean one of us.'

George smiled. 'Not necessarily. There are a good many people in the village who've been here longer than you have, and known this place just as intimately, some of them before it was organised and shown as it is now. The site could hardly be more open. The riverside path makes access easy for everyone who knows this district, and that includes not only the village, but large numbers of fishermen, too.'

'But only somebody with specialist knowledge,' Bill pointed out forcibly, 'would know how to dispose of articles like that to the best advantage.'

'True enough, but gold is gold, and in certain parts of the world it commands far more than its sterling value, even if it's hard to sell in its original form. There may have been other, larger pieces besides the coins, of course, they'd be a problem to an amateur. The helmet, for instance . . .' he said innocently.

Paviour stiffened in his chair, staring. '*Helmet?*'

'The helmet the ghost is said to wear. You remember Mrs Paviour's interesting account of what she and others saw, or thought they saw? That may be no legend, but a chance find, retained as a property to scare off the superstitious, and divert any curiosity about movements here in the night.'

Paviour gathered himself together with a perceptible effort, sitting erect and taut. 'Such a traffic,' he said firmly, 'would require not just some specialist knowledge, but an expert of the first quality as adviser, if it was to escape detection for long.'

'Such as yourself?' said George.

If it was a shock, he was then so inured to shocks that it made no impression. With bitter dignity he said: 'I am a third-rate sub-expert and a fifth-rate scholar, and the real ones know it as well as I do.'

Lesley whispered: 'Stephen, dear!' and laid a hand appealingly on his arm.

Imperturbably George pursued: 'But other authorities have

visited Aurae Phiala. There have even been brief and limited digs under some of them.' He was gathering up his few notes, and stowing them away in an inside pocket, preparatory to leaving. He looked up once, briefly, at Charlotte, a glance that told her nothing. 'You might give it some thought. Consider who has visited here, and who has dug, during – say – the past year and a half to two years. No, please don't disturb yourself, I can find my way out.'

He was halfway to the door when he added an afterthought: 'One name we do know, of course. It's just about eighteen months, isn't it, since Doctor Alan Morris left from here on his way to Turkey.'

They were still staring after him, motionless and silent, when the door closed gently; and in a few minutes they heard his car start up on the gravel drive.

The inquest opened formally on Saturday morning, took evidence of identification, and at the police request adjourned for one week. George drove the bewildered but stonily dignified pair who were Gerry Boden's parents back to their home, from which he had also conveyed them earlier, because he was by no means sure that Boden was yet in any case to drive. Not that they were making difficulties or distresses for anyone; their composure was chill and smooth and temporary as ice, but though it might thaw at any moment, it would certainly not be in public. Their disciplines included containing their private sorrows. And in a sense Gerry had always been, if not a sorrow, an ambivalent sort of joy, a perilous possession, capable of piling either delights or dismays into their laps at any moment without warning. Life without him was going to be infinitely more peaceful and inexpressibly dimmer. He could have been anything he had put his mind to, good or bad, and now he was a carefully but impersonally reconstructed body put together by strangers to be presentable enough to be released for burial. Boden had already seen him dead. Mrs Boden had not, but would surely insist on doing so when he was given back to them.

Afterwards, of course, they would take up the business of living again, because they were durable, and in any case had not much choice. And in time they would be comfortable enough, being happily very fond of each other, though they had never in their lives been in love.

George went home to do a little thinking, and take a fresh look at the laboratory reports he'd hardly had time to read that morning.

Also to get the taste of despair and disgust out of his mouth and the mildew of misanthropy out of his eyes by looking at Bunty. She was getting a little plumper and a little less sudden now that she was in the middle forties, but her chestnut and hazel colouring was as vivid as ever; and knowing every line of her only made her more of a delightful surprise in everything she said or did. For George had been in love with Bunty ever since he had first heard Bernarda Elliot sing at a concert in Birmingham, while she was still a student, and had never got over her unhesitating choice of marriage with him in preference to a career as a potentially first-class mezzo. Police officers are not considered great catches.

Their only son was busy mending agricultural machinery and driving tractors for an erratic but effective native mission in India, and had just welcomed to the same service his future wife, fresh from an arts degree and a rushed course in nursing. And what Tossa was going to make of the Swami Premanathanand's organisation was anybody's guess, but arguably she would fall completely under the spell of its gentle but jolting founder, as Dominic had done, and lose herself in his hypnotic ambience. George thought of them, and was lifted out of his despond. He withdrew to the study of his morning's professional mail in better heart.

He was halfway through compiling an up-to-date précis when Bunty looked in, unastonished as ever, and announced: 'Miss Rossignol wants to talk to you.' Bunty vanished on the word, and Charlotte, small and trim and magnificently self-possessed, at her most French, came sailing in upon him from the doorway. She looked very determined, and very young.

'Now this,' said George, 'is a pleasure I wasn't expecting. Come and sit down, and tell me what I can do for you.'

'You can tell me,' said Charlotte, looking up intently into his face, 'whether you really meant what you implied last night. Because I've been thinking along the same lines, and not liking it at all. And then, if you don't mind, and it isn't top secret, you can tell me what you know that I don't know about my great-uncle Alan.'

By late morning the diggers had exposed the broken roof of the flue, and half the arch of its slightly damaged neighbour, for a distance of about six feet, and were setting to work in earnest to remove the shattered brickwork and lay bare the channel below. Since this process involved moving sacred relics, and it was a life-and-death matter to Paviour that they should not be damaged or allowed to fall into disorder, both he and Bill Lawrence were now employed, not so much fully as frantically, in trying to label and number everything that emerged, and laying out the materials of the arch in the grass, aside from the affected area. Barnes, out of pure good-nature and some reviving interest in archaeology, lent a hand under Paviour's irritable and anxious direction, but even with three pairs of hands they had all they could do to keep pace. Gus Hambro had taken over one of the small sheds attached to the museum, where there was a sink and a water tap, and removed himself there with all the minor trophies of the first day's work, and with sleeves rolled up, and an array of small nail-brushes for weapons, was carefully washing off the corrosion of soil and dust from dozens of little objects, most of them derisory: fragments of red glaze, one segment of cloudy glass from the lips of a jug, a plethora of animal bones, two plain bone hair-pins and one with the broken remnants of a carved head, and the single interesting item, a bronze penannular brooch with coiled ends to the ring. A boring job, but a vital one. He had good reason to want to be first in discovering and studying whatever there was to be found, but so far the result was disappointing.

It was a little past noon when the door of his shed opened, and Lesley looked in.

'Lunch prompt at one,' she informed him, and came to his elbow to examine the trifles he had laid out on a board beneath the window. 'Dull,' she said, sadly but truthfully. 'Do you need any help?' There was still a heap of grimy objects awaiting his attentions, their nature almost obscured by layers of soil grown to them like rust.

'I shouldn't. You'll get terribly dirty.' And after a moment's hesitation he asked what he had been wondering all morning. 'What happened to Charlotte? I haven't seen her around at all today.'

'I know. She went off after breakfast in my car. She said she wanted to see somebody in town, but she promised to be back for lunch. I offered to drive her wherever she wanted to go,' said Lesley, frowning thoughtfully down at the little bronze brooch, 'but she wouldn't let me, so I saw she didn't want company. Only two days, and you know, I really miss her. I've just got used to having somebody to chatter to, a rare luxury here. Stephen doesn't chatter, or understand being chattered to. Stephen *converses*. When he isn't being totally taciturn, that is.' She laughed suddenly, recognising how fluently she was illustrating her own theme. 'You see? Failing Charlotte, someone else gets sprayed with words. You don't mind being a stand-in, do you? All the others are far too busy, and you can at least go on brushing bones while you listen.'

'You don't know,' he said, 'where she was going?'

'Charlotte? She didn't say, so naturally I didn't ask her. Lend me that bigger brush, I can be whisking the top dirt off these things. I'm no use down there, and there's half an hour or so before I need go back to the kitchen.'

She fell in companionably beside him, and went to work removing the worst of the encrustations from still more inevitable bits of bone and animal teeth. 'Graveyard exercise, isn't it? Like Mr Barnes, I dream of digging up another Mildenhall treasure instead of a cow's incisors, but it's never likely to happen to me.'

She had leaned nearer to him, to drop the despised tooth into the sink, and she felt the slight tension that stiffened the arm she brushed against. She drew back a distinct pace, and kept that distance; but he knew that her eyes were on him, in no sidelong glance, but regarding him widely and directly. The challenge to turn and look as straightly at her was irresistible. Greenish-blue like the off-shore sea under sunshine, her disconcerting eyes were laughing at him, though the rest of her face was mild and grave.

'I suppose Bill's been warning you about Stephen and me,' she said quite placidly.

She had set the key, he might as well follow.

'Shouldn't he have done? I understand you warned him yourself.'

She shrugged. 'Just as well to know where you stand, don't you think? I don't suppose it came as any great surprise to you. Only the very unintelligent could help wondering about us. And you're not very unintelligent. Are you?'

'I'm wondering that myself,' he said.

'The door's open,' she said, smiling. 'Anyone's welcome to walk in. And you could walk out any moment you pleased.'

'Quite. But why, if it's like that, did you walk in? And stay in?'

Perhaps by that time he should have been feeling that the conversation had got out of hand, but he had no such feeling. On the contrary, it was proceeding in perfect control, and not a word had been said on either side without consideration and intent.

'Because I'm a person, too,' she said, sparkling with angry animation. 'He's jealous – all right! But I'm alive and gregarious and talkative, and I'm damned if I'm going to change my nature because he sees more in everything I say or do than I ever put into it. Let him fret that I'm disloyal, if he has to, just as long as I know I'm not. It isn't as if I had any reason to be afraid of him, you know. A gentler, more attentive old idiot never stepped. No, when I went about virtuously warning nice, harmless young men like Bill to keep clear, it was all out of consideration for *his* peace of mind. Now I'm considering mine. I'm what he married. Why should I suppose I'd be doing him a favour by changing into something else? So I've given up the practice. I'm staying the way I am.'

The invitation to equal candour was proffered, palpable on the air. He accepted it. For some reason it would have seemed perverse to refuse it.

'Why he married you,' he said briskly, 'is no mystery to anyone. Given the chance, that is. Why *was* he given the chance? That's the puzzler.'

She had put down the shard of Samian ware she had been brushing, and the brush after it. She leaned with one hip against the edge of the sink, her back half-turned to the window, the better to face him; and even her sea-green eyes had stopped laughing now.

'Because his timing was right. Because he came as such a nice change after the young, handsome, dashing, cold-hearted bastard who'd dropped me into the muck the minute it suited him, and put me off love for life. Or so I thought then. Jilted, I tell you, is no word for what happened to me. And there was Stephen trotting in and out of the office with his little manuscripts, looking rather distinguished and being terribly anxious and patient and kind. So I told him what I hadn't told a soul besides, and he did everything possible to comfort me and make it up to me – as if anyone could! And one of the nice things he thought of was to ask me to marry him. It looked good to me – really, then, it looked like the answer to everything. So I married for what was left, since I'd finished with love. For security, and kindness, for a respectable position, and a crash barrier against all the young, handsome, dashing, frosty-hearted bastards left in the world. The world stopped, and I got off, and that was marriage. And look at me now!'

It was an unnecessary instruction; he was looking at her very intently and steadily, and at a range of scarcely more than a foot. She had turned until she was confronting him squarely, leaning back a little against the stone sink, her hands, grubby from the clinging soil, childishly held up beside her shoulders, with widespread fingers, to avoid dirtying her cashmere sweater. Her short fair hair quivered and seemed to erect itself as if electrically charged, in the small, freakish draught from the window behind her, and through some trick of the fitful sunlight. She had set the pace in all these improbable exchanges, and whether she had now far outdistanced her own intention there was no knowing; but there was no point in trying to turn back, and there might, at least, be something to be gained by following through. For one thing, he doubted very much if she would have revoked on her bargain, even now.

'If it's that bad,' he said deliberately, 'why do you stay with him? The world's still there, if you want to get on again.'

'There's an awful lot of time around, too,' she said. 'I'm waiting. I can afford to wait.'

'For the right moment?'

'Or the right man,' she said.

It was said quite impersonally, almost to herself, but with such abrupt desolation and longing that he was filled with an entirely personal dismay on her account, and instinctively put out his hands to take her by the waist and hold her fast while he found something, however fatuous, however inadequate, to say to her. She was turning slightly away from him when he took her forcibly between his palms. He felt her whole body convulsed by a huge tremor of revulsion and panic, and was distressed into a sharp cry of pity and protest.

'Lesley – don't! My God, I never intended . . .'

She came to life again, her flesh lissom and warm. She twisted to break free, and he held on only to try and reassure her before he let her go, for it was like holding a cat unwilling to be held, the boneless body dissolving between his hands. She reached out to the rim of the sink, to have a purchase for forcing him off, and her fingers missed their grip and slid into the turgid water. She fell against him, drawing breath in deep, transfixing sighs, and suddenly she was silk, clinging with both hands. Her head was against his shoulder, her face upturned close beneath his, with wide-opened eyes and parted lips.

He kissed her, and the passive mouth flowered and burned, in shocked, involuntary acceptance. He felt her hands close on his back, pressing convulsively.

Over her shoulder he saw through the window the whole sweep of grass suddenly inhabited by a single approaching figure, looming large against the driven clouds and gleaming sun, and the distant, skeletal walls. He saw the brisk stride broken and diverted, only a dozen yards away; he saw the long, narrow body lean back, waver and halt. There could be only one reason for such a dislocation. The glass before him had been recently cleaned, and the noon sun shone directly into it. Paviour, coming hopefully up from the dig with a new bouquet of trophies in their plastic sacks, had clearly seen the tableau in the shed.

There was a strange, brief pause, while they hung eye to eye, across all that distance, and perfectly understood that there was now no possibility of disguising their mutual knowledge, that it could only be publicly denied and privately accepted. Then, wheeling to the left with a sudden, jerky movement, Paviour walked away towards the house, still clutching his little plastic sacks. Probably he had forgotten he was holding them.

Gus stood motionless, afraid almost to breathe for fear Lesley should turn away from him in a new access of revulsion, and face the window before that long, stilted, pathetic figure had vanished out of range. It was pure luck that her back had been turned to the light; she had seen nothing. His palms were still clamped with involuntary force on either side of her body, he would have felt any stiffening, any tremor, and she hung fluidly and heavily against him, like draped silk. And Paviour had walked clean out of the frame of the window and out of their sight.

It almost hurt to unclamp his grip on the girl, and separate himself from her, and he did it with infinite care not to offend by the separation as he had offended by first touching her. 'I'm sorry!' he said constrainedly. 'I never meant to scare you.'

She turned aside from him at once, as soon as he released her, reached automatically for her brush and towards the dingy pile of relics awaiting attention. She moved with economy and resignation, and looked curiously calm, as though her recent experience had left her in shock.

'I'm sorry, too. I never thought you did. It simply happens to me. I panic. I can't help it.'

He wondered if he should tell her, if she needed to know. He thought not. She was better off as she was. Her innocence would be impregnable; she had nothing to fear.

'I'd better go,' she said, almost naturally, and put down the brush. 'I've got to see to the lumch.'

She made very little sound, departing, because the door was open, and she moved as lightly as a kitten in her soft walking shoes, so nicely matched to her boyish, slim style in slacks. But he knew the moment when she left, without looking round from his automatic operations on one more fragmentary ivory pin, by the slow, settling tranquillity she left behind her.

Lunch was a minor nightmare only because nothing whatever happened. It cost him an effort to reassemble his stolidly innocent face before he need appear; and then, when he was reasonably assured that his façade was impervious, he had to meet Charlotte head-on at the door.

He had never seen her look quite so un-English or so serenely formidable. There was no wind, and the curled plumes of black hair deployed across her magnolia cheeks might have been lacquered there, they were so steely and perfect. Also he had never realised until that moment how small and slender she was, almost as tiny as Lesley. His mind started involuntarily measuring her waist, and the exercise led on to other highly speculative considerations concerning the resilience of her bones and the scent of her hair, should she ever find herself in his arms, due to an emotional miscalculation on his part and a panic reaction on hers. He failed to imagine it adequately. She didn't look the type. But then, neither did Lesley.

'I missed you,' he said, almost accusingly. 'You've been gone all morning.'

'I had a call to make in town, on personal business,' she said coolly. 'I hope you managed to divert yourself even without me.'

And her thick, genuine, loftily-arched black brows went up, and the eyes beneath them flashed a golden gleam of amusement at his proprietary tone. During the past two days he had given her very little cause to suppose that he attached particular importance to her presence. 'Any interesting discoveries?'

She was referring only to work in progress, and he knew it, and yet every word she said seemed to find a way of probing between the joints of his armour with prophetic force. The defensive reaction she set up in him made him tongue tied when he would most gladly have been fluent; he felt that if he turned his back on her she would see, clean through the tweed of his jacket, the prints of two small, splayed hands, soiled from brushing trivia, clamped against his shoulder-blades.

'If you like,' she said generously, 'I'll be your runner this afternoon, and ferry the bits and pieces up to you.'

'Do,' he said, cheered and astonished. 'I'd like that.' Charlotte darting in and out would be an insurance policy second to none. Against Lesley? When he stood back to consider the incident he couldn't seriously persuade himself that she was likely to come near him again of her own will, however perversely she desired to let off steam. Against himself, then? He flinched from considering it, but it remained a strong possibility.

'We'd better go in,' said Charlotte, only slightly disturbed by his uncharacteristic fervour. 'I'm hungry.'

So they went in. And lunch was the nadir of normality, without an original thought or a perilous suggestion to enliven it. The confrontation through the glass of the window might never have taken place.

By that hour the police had already segregated certain sections of brick and tile marked with recent scars, a few curved shards of pottery from a jar, and covered from injury a small area of flooring within the flue, with its dust still displaying the faint but positive print of the base of just such a ceramic jar. There had been no gold coins in the detritus. No doubt the last of them had been removed in haste after the murder of Gerry Boden. Only the single one from his purse remained to testify.

On Saturday evenings Bill Lawrence, that ambitious and scholarly young man, had an extra-mural class in Moulden. Which meant that the general invitation to dinner issued at lunch by Lesley raked in only Gus Hambro in addition to the curator's household. Bill had generous licence to come along for coffee afterwards, however late, but his class was timed to finish only at nine-thirty, and since it met in the rear clubroom at 'The Crown' it was long odds against the argumentative local savants consenting to go home before closing time, so that his attendance was at best only hypothetical. Moreover, Bill's own attitude was decidedly ambiguous; nobody had to tell him that his commitments were well known, and invitations issued accordingly. He knew when he was, or was not, wanted.

Not that Bill was missing anything, Gus thought, before the evening was half over. The pretence that everything was normal, that they were a party of congenial people enjoying a social get-together, had become downright oppressive, as if everyone was working a little too hard at it. They had an afternoon of unremitting labour behind them, and perhaps were too tired to make a good job of keeping up appearances. Paviour had grown so brittle that he looked as if the least jolt might send all his joints jangling apart; and though Lesley's extrovert lightness of heart was beyond suspicion, it was rapidly becoming unbearable in this context. All very well for her in her innocence, but Gus was in a very different case. Worst of all, there was no chance whatever of making any real contact with Charlotte, and it was exasperating to have her sitting there opposite him, so near and so inaccessible, watching him with the black, acute gaze of a sceptical cat, pupils high-lighted in gold; a look that asserted nothing, merely observed and analysed, stopping short of judgement only, he was afraid, out of indifference.

As soon as he decently could, and on the plea that they were all tired – to which Lesley frankly assented, eliding a yawn into an apology – he excused himself and withdrew to make his way home. He was glad to be alone, and made the most of the ten-minute walk to his bed, taking it at leisure.

It was a restless, luminous night, the kind that late April sometimes casts up between frosts, mild, starry, with a laggard and minor moon. The shape of Aurae Phiala came into being gradually as he walked, looming largely on his right hand, a series of levels marked out by a series of verticals, standing bones of masonry rearing from long planes of turf.

She came silently out of the unregarded spaces on his left, and stood in his path, a small, compact figure quite still and composed; not making any demands upon him, except by being there. He knew which one she was, though the two of them were very much of a build.

'Lesley . . .'

'It's all right,' she said serenely, still neatly enfolded into her own shadowy silhouette. 'Nobody's going to miss me. Believe it or not, I was so tired I went up to bed the moment you left. You surely don't think I share a room with him, do you? Or with anyone!'

'You shouldn't have come out after me,' he said.

'No, I don't suppose I should. What makes you think it was after you?'

'You do,' he said brutally, and stood fronting her, for want of any way by. 'Who else did you think would be making off this way? Don't pretend you *just happened* to choose this way for your evening constitutional.'

'I never pretend anything,' she said, in the soft, mild voice that seemed to belong so aptly to the dark. 'And I never *just happen* to do anything. In any case, it must be quite plain to you that I ran most of the way from the back gate, or I couldn't have got here before you. I simply felt I wanted to talk to you again. But it wasn't much use my finding out how much I liked you, if all I've done is to make you dislike me.'

'Is that what I'm doing?' he said.

'That's the way it looks from where I'm standing.'

'Maybe you can't see very well from there.'

'I could come closer,' she offered.

It was a highly dangerous gift she had, this one of writing both halves of the dialogue. There never seemed to be any possible answer except the one she wanted. Not that he was trying very hard to deviate from the script.

She took two long, slow steps towards him, her arms at her sides, her head tilted back to look up at him. One more step, and the points of her small, high breasts almost touched him. In the darkness her face was serene and pale, and her dilated eyes huge and fixed. He had the impression that she was smiling.

'Do I look any more friendly from there?' he asked, keeping very still.

She said: 'Gus . . .' experimentally, as if she were memorising and tasting his name; and she laughed, very softly, at its ridiculous brevity and inappropriateness. 'Are you waiting for me to explode when touched? Not this time! Something happened to me this morning that never happened before. Try it. Touch me!'

Her face was very close, turned up to him like a white, wide-open flower; and in obedience to the rules of this game he very nearly did take her at her word. But then he changed his mind, and deliberately held still, even when her warmth leaned and touched him. In a voice he had never heard from her before, whispering, almost fawning, and yet still laughing, she said: 'Gus . . .' again, two or three times over, changing the note as though plucking descending strings. 'It's you,' she said, 'you, you, you're the one . . . It was never like that for me – never – not even with *him* . . .'

She put out her hands, and flattened them gently against his chest; and then suddenly her arms were round him, and her body was pressed hard against his, clinging from shoulder to knee. He returned her embrace partly out of pure astonishment, but kept his close hold of her after that out of heady delight. Her intensity was electrifying. Her body moved against him, tensing and turning fluid again, finding every vulnerable nerve. She freed a hand to tug at the buttons of his jacket, and wound her arms about him within it, manipulating the muscles of his back with fierce, hard fingertips. Her mouth reached up to him hungrily, and fastened on his as he leaned to her, in a kiss that left them both gasping for breath. Her lips, progressing by little, biting caresses along his cheek, whispered dizzily: 'Love me, love me, love . . .' until he found her mouth again with his and silenced her.

They were so wildly engrossed in each other at that moment that they heard nothing outside themselves, only the pounding of their hearts and the gusty breaths they drew. Paviour was within six feet of them before they were aware of him. Gus lifted his head and looked over Lesley's shoulder, and there motionless before him, a lean, angular shape in the darkness, the jealous husband stood waiting with bleak courtesy to be let into their world.

Lesley felt the stiffening jolt that passed through Gus's body, and stirred and turned protestingly to look for its reason. There was one strange moment while they both stared at Paviour, and he at them, rather as though they had no shared language between them, and speech could not help them. Very slowly the two tangled bodies drew apart and stood clear; the most important thing just then seemed to be to accomplish this necessary manoeuvre with a little grace and dignity, not in a humiliating scramble. Even when they were separate, their linked hands parted only gradually and gently.

'I'm sorry!' said Paviour with cold civility. 'I regret forcing this intrusion upon you, but you'll agree it's inevitable.' He looked at Lesley, without any perceptible signs of anger; all that Gus could detect in his voice and his stillness was discouragement and grief. 'Go back to the house, my dear,' he said, 'and go to bed. Leave me to talk to Mr Hambro.'

The most remarkable thing was that she did as she was told, not in a manner that suggested any fear of him, or any great desire to justify herself or placate him. Her shoulders lifted in a small, resigned shrug. She cast a glance at Gus, hesitated no more than a second, and then turned and walked away into the darkness, towards the distant shape of the house within its girdle of trees.

'I have no wish to embarrass you,' said Paviour, when the last faint rustle of her steps in the grass had died away. 'That was not my intention.' There was no dislike in his voice, he stood detached and withdrawn into the night, and the lack of precise vision made this encounter easier than Gus would have believed possible. 'But you see, of course, that I had to intervene.'

'You're being absurdly generous, in fact,' Gus said honestly. 'I'm not going to attempt to justify myself. But I can at least assure you, for what it's worth, that things have gone no further than what you've seen.'

'I'm well aware of that,' said Paviour drily; and though it seemed incredible, there was the suggestion of a sour smile in his voice this time. 'And it won't be necessary to defend yourself. I understand the situation perfectly. I should, I've lived with it for some years now. You mustn't think, my dear Hambro, that you're the first. And I can't hope that you'll be the last.'

'I don't understand you,' said Gus, stiffening.

'You will. Do you mind if I walk with you down to the lodge? It's a little cold for standing around, and we can talk as we go.'

Bemused, Gus fell into step beside him on the path. They walked with a yard or so of the dark between them. And after a moment Paviour resumed gently: 'I take it you'll have heard from Lesley about her earlier love affair, and the way it ended. The way, in fact, that we came to get married. I needn't go into that again. And I needn't tell you what's obvious, that Lesley is a beautiful and charming girl, and highly intelligent. But she has an affliction. Not surprising, in the circumstances. That early shock in love damaged her permanently. She was ill – not physically, but you'll understand me – for some time. On that one subject she will never again be entirely well. What has just happened to you is routine,' he said tiredly. 'I'm sorry, but you'll have to get used to the thought. No doubt she'll have told you that I'm pathologically jealous of every man who so much as comes near her – hasn't she? Well, have I behaved like that? Do you really think I didn't see you with her this morning?'

'I know you did,' said Gus. 'I knew it then. That was not quite what it seemed. It happened almost by accident.'

'You think so?' said Paviour, and the bitter smile in his voice was clearer than before. 'My dear boy, Lesley has a temperamental disposition to repeat her ruinous love affair with every unwary male who enters her life. Every presentable one, that is. She behaves with every one of them just as she has been behaving with you today. But heaven help any poor fellow who takes her seriously. The game goes only so far. You may even have detected a rather violent reaction on her part, if you ever got so far as taking the initiative?'

Gus walked dourly beside him, and said nothing.

'Yes – I thought so. The signals turn red very abruptly. You'd get no further, I assure you. She would kill you or herself rather than actually surrender. I have good reason to know. She's emotionally crippled for life, and it's my life-work to protect and conceal her disability, and prevent her from doing harm to herself and others. I married her to take care of her. As I have done already through several affairs, all as fictional as this one with you.'

He felt, and misunderstood, or understood only in part, the obstinate silence walking beside him.

'Yes,' he said challengingly, almost as if defending his manhood against some implied accusation, 'I love her as much as that. It was a little late, in any case, for me to marry for any other kind of passion. This does well enough. It's more than anyone else will ever have of her.'

Gus came out of his own private chaos of speculation and enlightenment just in time to capture the implication, and too late to absorb the shock in silence.

'You mean to say that *even you* . . .' He swallowed the rest of the indiscretion with a gulp, and was thankful for the darkness. His mind had been careering along in quite a different direction, it was too much to ask him to assimilate this all in a moment.

117

'The inference you're drawing,' said Paviour, in a voice thinner and more didactic than Gus had ever yet heard it, 'is a correct one. I knew all about her panic abhorrence before I married her. Sexually, I've never touched her. She is a virgin. She always will be.'

Dignified, pathetic and decent, the man stood there quite obviously telling the simple truth as he saw it, and who was likely to see it more clearly? And it all made sense, or would have done if Gus's blood hadn't still been racing with the remembered persuasion of her body against him, and the ravenous expertise of her mouth, and the ferocity of her nails scoring into his back. That memory confounded the argument considerably. And yet it was true, the initiative had still been hers. All he'd had time to do was go along with her wishes; and if he'd just been reaching the point of having wishes and intentions of his own, he'd been saved by the bell, and she hadn't had to react. Try it! she'd said. Touch me! But deliberately he'd left the next move to her. And now maybe he'd never know which of them was crazy, himself or this elderly masochist – or hero, or whatever he was – who got his satisfaction in cherishing and protecting his wife like a delinquent daughter.

'So you see why it's essential,' said Paviour, gently and firmly, 'that my wife should not see you again. You're not in any illusion that her heart is involved, I hope?'

'No,' said Gus, 'I'm not in any illusion. She won't have any trouble getting over my loss.'

By common consent they had halted well short of the low hedge of the garden at the lodge. The house was in darkness, Bill could not have left the village yet. It would be quite easy, however inconvenient, and there was now no help for it, nothing to be done but what Paviour obviously wanted and expected of him.

'I'll remove myself,' he said, 'totally and immediately. She needn't see me again. I've got my car here, I can pack and get out before Bill comes back, and leave him a note, and my apologies to deliver tomorrow. I shall have had a telephone call. Family business – illness – I'll think of the right thing.'

'I shall be very much obliged,' said Paviour. 'I felt sure I could rely on your good feeling.' And he turned, with no more insistence than that, and no firmer guarantee, and walked away towards his own house, leaving Gus staring after him.

* * *

He did exactly what he had promised he would do, and did it in ruthless haste, for fear Bill should come back too soon. True, the same excuse could be offered to him face to face, but there might be some dispute over whether it was strictly necessary to leave before morning, and moreover, in view of Bill's own remarks on the subject of the Paviour marriage, he was not likely to be deceived. Far simpler to leave a few fresh doodles on the telephone pad, and a note propped on the mantelpiece, and get out clean.

'Dear Bill, Client called home, and they ran me to earth here. He wants me to drive over to Colchester and look at a piece he's been offered and has his doubts about. Rush job, because *if* good it's very good, and there's another dealer in the field, so I'm going across overnight. Didn't want to call the house at this hour, please make my apologies to Mr and Mrs Paviour, and thanks to you and them for generous hospitality. I'll be in touch later.'

Probably Bill wouldn't believe any of it, certainly not the last words, but it would do. And Lesley was no doubt used to abrupt diplomatic departures, and would shrug him off and look round for the next entertainment. Perhaps even give a whirl to Bill, whom she hadn't fancied, but who rather more than fancied her, if everyone told the truth. Better not, that might be a collision she wouldn't shrug off so easily.

He needn't go far, of course, but all the same this was a nuisance just at this stage. They might elect to fetch him off the job altogether, and put someone else in in his place. That couldn't be helped. What mattered now was to get out.

He dumped his case in the car, and drove out from the gate of the lodge, and up the gravelled track that ran within the boundary of Aurae Phiala. Bill would be walking home from the village by the riverside path, and the whole expanse of the enclosure and the bulk of the curator's house and garden would be between him and the way out on to the main road. With luck he wouldn't even hear the car. If he did, he would never think of it in connection with a sudden departure until he read his guest's note. All very tidy.

He had to get out and open the gate when he reached the road. He drove the Aston Martin through, and parked it on the grass verge while he went back to close the gate again and make sure it was fast.

He had the stretch of road to himself, and the late moon, at the beginning of its sluggish climb and rimmed with mist, cast only a faint, sidelong light over the standing walls and pillars of Aurae Phiala. Just enough to prick out before his eyes a single curious spark, that moved steadily along within the broken wall of the frigidarium, appearing and disappearing as the height of the standing fragments varied. It proceeded at a measured walking pace, and at the corner it turned, patrolling downhill towards the tepidarium; and for a moment, where the standing masonry dropped to knee-height, he saw the shadowy figure that walked beneath it, and caught the shape of the glowing crest against the sky. The enlarged head, with its jut of brow, was all one metallic mass, hardly glimpsed before it was lost again in the dark. A helmet, with neck-guard, earpieces, he thought even a visor over the face. Dream or substance, the helmeted sentry of Aurae Phiala was making a methodical circuit of the remaining walls by fitful moonlight.

He left the car standing, and let himself in again through the gate; and even then he took the time to snap the lock closed before he set off at a cautious lope across the grass towards the walls of the baths. Once into the complex, he had to slow to a walk, but he made what speed he dared. The night had grown restless with a rising wind; rapid scuds of cloud alternately masked and uncovered the veiled moon, and drifts of mist moved up from the river in soft, recurrent tides along the ground. A night for haunting. He wondered if there was a policeman standing guard overnight, and felt sure there was not; there are never enough men to cover everything that should be covered. He and the sentry had the place to themselves.

The glimpses he got now of the helmet which was his quarry were few and brief, but enough to enable him to gain ground. It had reached the shell of standing walls at the corner of the caldarium. Clearly he saw it glimmer between two broken blocks of masonry, beyond the low rim of the laconicum. Then it vanished. He approached cautiously, and stood by the edge of the shaft in braced silence, preferring to keep his bearings in relation to this potential hazard, while he waited with straining ears and roving eyes for a new lead.

Cloud blew away from the moon's face for a moment, and a spilled pool of light glazed the tops of the broken walls and blackened the shadows; and there suddenly was the helmeted head burning in the brief gleam. As he fixed his eyes upon it, the figure turned, darkness from the shoulders down, bright above, and stood confronting him, and he caught one glimpse of a frozen, splendid, golden face with empty black eye-sockets, under the bronze peak of the helmet.

It was a rapid displacement of air behind him, rather than a sound, that suddenly raised the short hairs on his neck, and caused him to swing round on his heel, too late to save himself. He caught a chaotic glimpse of a looming shape and a raised arm, a violent shifting of shadows and deeper shadows. Then the contours of earth and the complexities of starlight whirled and dissolved about him, as the stone that should have struck him squarely at the base of the skull crashed obliquely against his temple. An arm took him about the thighs and heaved him from the ground; and in some remaining corner of consciousness he knew what was happening to him, and could not utter a sound or lift a finger to fend it off.

He fell, cold, dank air rushing upwards past his face for what seemed an age, and dropped heavily upon some uneven and loosely shifting stuff that rolled at the impact, and bore him helplessly with it.

The breath was knocked out of him, but he never let go of that last glimmer of consciousness. Something rebounded from the wall of the shaft above him, with a heavy thud and a faint ring of metal, and scraped the opposite wall. The light, the only light, was the faint circle of sky now beginning to glow almost with the radiance of day by contrast with this incredible, dead blackness where he was. In the confused panic of shock he prised himself upwards to run, and struck his head sickeningly against an arched ceiling. All over his body the delayed protests of pain began, outraged and insistent. They helped him, too. They made him aware that he was alive, and acutely aware of other things in the same instant: that he was down the shaft of the laconicum, that the wooden cover had been removed in advance to facilitate his disposal, and that the second object tipped down after him must be his suitcase.

He put his head down in his arms for a moment, feeling horribly sick; and before he had gathered his damaged faculties, the thump and reverberation of falling earth and stones began in the shaft, and disturbed dust silted down over him acridly, choking him. He dragged himself frantically forward as stones began to fall about his legs, and holding by the rough bricks of the floor, found the solid wall ahead of him, and groped left-handed along it into the mouth of an open flue.

The rain of stones went on, heavier fragments now, broken masses from the very masonry of Aurae Phiala, or more likely the rim of the laconicum itself, hurled down to lodge awkwardly in the loose rubble, and pile up until they began to climb the walls.

Then he knew that someone was deliberately filling in the shaft. For a long time there followed a staccato rattle of loose brick and tile, and after that there was already so much matter between him and the outer air that the continuing softer fall of earth over all made only a slight, dull sound, receding until he could hardly distinguish it.

The circle of starlight was quenched. Nothing broke the solid perfection of the dark. He was buried alive in the hypocaust, ten feet beneath the innocent green surface of Aurae Phiala.

Chapter Ten

For a moment he lay flattened over his folded arms, and let himself sag into a self-pitying fury of bruises and concussion. It was more endurable when he closed his eyes; the darkness was no darker, and infinitely more acceptable, as though he had created it, and could again disperse it. And after a few minutes his mind began to work again inside his aching head, with particular, indignant energy. Because somebody had done a thorough job on getting rid of him – somebody? *Paviour! Who else?*– and circumstances and his own carelessness had played into the enemy's hands. His departure was already accounted for, nobody was going to be starting a hue and cry after him. His suitcase, his clothes, his camera, everything that might have afforded a clue to his whereabouts, lay here under the earth with him. All except the car; and since whoever had followed him and struck him down had brought the suitcase to dispose of along with the body, it didn't need much guessing to decide what was now happening to the Aston Martin. A mobile clue that can be removed from the scene of the crime at seventy miles an hour is no problem. He'd known many a car vanish utterly inside a new paint job and forged plates, within a few hours. By the time someone, somewhere, grew uneasy about his non-appearance, he would be dead. He was meant to be dead already. Only that one lucky movement had saved him.

A movement made a shade too slowly and a fraction of a second too late to show him anything more than a looming shadow, a man-shaped cloud toppling upon him, and a descending arm, before the night exploded in his face. The shadow never had a face. But who but Paviour knew how beautifully his tracks were already covered? Who else had just engineered his elimination from the scene, taking advantage of Lesley's sickness, perhaps even sending her after him deliberately, to ease him out of Aurae Phiala without trace? It couldn't be anyone else!

Or could it? There were two of them, he reminded himself, one to bait the trap for me, and one to spring it. Supposing they – whoever *they* were – had been out in the night on their own furtive occasions, and had to freeze into cover within earshot of that scarifying interview? If they had wanted to get rid of him, and hardly dared to take the risk earlier, what an opportunity!

If he kept his senses, if he let his memory do its own work, there ought to be some detail, even in so brief a glimpse, that would resume recognisable identity. In time he would know his murderer. But time was all too limited unless he gave all his mind to his first and most desperate duty, which was to survive. For after all, he thought savagely, maybe I have got one advantage he doesn't know about: *I'm alive!* Let's see if there's any other asset around. Yes, I've still got a watch with a luminous dial, one little bright eye in all this dark, and it's still going. There may not be any day or night, but there'll still be hours. For God's sake, don't forget to wind it! And there's the suitcase. If I can find it. If it isn't buried ten feet deep under all that lumber. But no, it hit the wall and rebounded, and slid down this side. It's not far. What is there in there that might be useful? There's a pocket torch, though it won't run for long unless I'm sparing with it. And leather gloves. I've got no eyes now but my fingers, and they don't see much in gloves, but I can carry the things, and if I have to dig . . .

That brought him to the real point; for there was no sense in studying how to help himself until he had a possibility in mind. And there was not the slightest possibility of digging his way vertically upwards through that settling mass of earth and stones in the shaft. Try it, if you want to know how peppercorns feel in a peppermill! No way out there. And no way out anywhere else . . .

But there was, of course! There was some seven feet of flue laid open to daylight at the far end of this hypocaust, down by the river. Even the inner end of that was blocked by rubble. Not completely, though. There was room at the top for a cat to wriggle through; and the barrier might be thin, would certainly be loose, since the roof still held up, and no great weight had fallen upon it to pack it hard.

His mind was clearing, he could actually think. With his eyes closed he could even draw himself a diagram of the caldarium, and he had seen for himself, in the one flue they had excavated, how the grid ran, with true Roman regularity.

Consider the landward perimeter, one of the shorter sides of the rectangle, as its base. Then the laconicum is located in the bottom left-hand corner, and that's where I am. And the open flue is very close to the top left-hand corner, the length of the hypocaust away, but on my side. He thought of the huge extent of the caldarium on top of him, and felt sick. My God, it might as well be a hundred miles! Better get moving, Hambro, and just hope, because there isn't for ever, and there isn't all that much air down here, and what there is isn't too good.

Careful, though, don't be in too big a hurry to move until you're sure which way you're going, he reminded himself urgently. And he began to think his way back, with crazily methodical deliberation, to his fall. He had come from the road, towards the river, following the bronze spark; and though he had tried to turn at the last moment, his impression was that in falling he had still been facing fairly directly towards the same point, and had been hoisted over in that direction. When stones began to fall after him he had not turned, simply clawed his way forward until he encountered the wall of the flue, and turned left into its tenuous shelter. Therefore he was now facing towards the left-hand boundary of the rectangle, and no great distance from it. His best line was to crawl ahead until this flue terminated in the blank boundary-wall, then turn right along it, and keep straight ahead, and he would be on the right course for the distant corner where the flue was laid open. If the air held out. If he found the brick passages still intact throughout, or at least passable. If the final barrier – supposing he ever survived to reach it! – didn't prove so thick that he would die miserably, digging his way through it with his finger-nails.

All right, that was settled. Better die trying than just lie here and rot. So before he moved off, he had now to edge his way back a few yards, without turning, for fear of losing that tenuous sense of direction, and feel gingerly among the rubble for his suitcase.

Movement hurt, but goaded instead of discouraging him. The sudden small, hurtling body that went skittering over his feet and away along the route he favoured startled but braced him. The rats got in and out somewhere – probably in a dozen places – and if he could find even a rat-sized hole on starlight he would find a way of enlarging it somehow to let his own body out. If there was a hole there would be air, and he was not going to starve for days, at least.

He was beginning to be aware of the minor horrors that up to now had been obliterated in the single immense horror of being buried alive: the chill, the closeness and earthy heaviness of the air, its graveyard odour, the oppression of the low ceiling over his head, and the soft, settled dirt of centuries cold and thick under his hands, so fine that he sank to the wrist in it in every slight depression where it had silted more thickly, and so filthy that every touch was loathsome, though not so disgusting as the foul drapings of old cobwebs that plastered his head and shoulders from the roof.

His left hand groped among stones and soil, disturbing fresh, rustling falls, but he found the corner of the leather case, and patiently worked it clear. The lock had burst open, clothes spilled from it. He found the torch, small and inadequate but better than nothing, and snapped it on for a second to be sure it still worked. Better conserve that. As long as progress was possible along the outermost flue he could do without light. It took him longer to find the gloves, but he did it finally, and thrust them into his pocket. Now forward, and careful at any offered turning. Far better not risk the interior of the maze. Once reach the outside wall, and all he had to do was keep his left hand on it until he reached the far end. *If* . . . My God, he thought, feeling the cold sweat run down his lips and into his mouth, so many ifs!

He had moved forward only a couple of feet, crawling carefully on hands and knees, when he set his left hand upon something smooth and marble-cold, and feeling over its surface with cautious finger-tips, traced in stupefaction the features of a rigid face, and above the forehead rough, moulded bands, and a shallow, battlemented coronal. He sat back on his heels and dug away silting soil that half-covered it, and his nails rang little, metallic sounds against its rim. It seemed to him then that he remembered the ring of metal as the stones began to fall.

He used the torch for the first time. A bronze face sprang startlingly out of the darkness, a hollow bronze head with chiselled, empty, hieratic features and elongated voids for eyes, with a frieze of fighting figures across its forehead, and curls of formal hair for ear-pieces. The visor had broken away at one hinge from the brow, the crown was dented in its fall, but he knew what he was holding, and even here, in this extremity, it filled him with the exultation of delirious discovery. The thing was a Roman ceremonial helmet, of the kind elaborated not for battle but for formal cavalry exercises, complete with face-mask of chilling beauty. He knew of only one as perfect in existence. Moreover, this one had been carefully cleaned and polished, he thought even subjected to minor repairs, to make it wearable at need. He was holding in his hands the moonlit spark that had been used to lure him back to the laconicum and to his death, only half an hour ago, and had here been jettisoned and buried with him.

The Paviour household was at breakfast when Bill brought the news that his guest had departed overnight. Lesley read the note of explanation and apology with a still, displeased face, and looked up once, very briefly, at her husband, before crumpling the paper in her hand with a gesture which alone betrayed something more than consternation, a flash of hurt, highly personal anger. But she said nothing in reproach against the departed, Charlotte noticed; the anger was not with him, nor did she see any point in expressing it further.

'Nothing I could do about it,' said Bill, hoisting his shoulders in deprecation. 'He was gone when I got back. I shouldn't have thought he need have dashed off overnight, but he knows his markets, I suppose. And if you don't work at it, you don't keep your clients.'

'Mr Hambro has a living to make, like all of us,' said Paviour austerely, 'and no doubt he knows his own business best. But it's a pity he couldn't stay longer. He was a very competent archaeologist, from what I saw of him.'

It was that use of the past tense that crystallised for Charlotte everything that she found out of character in this abrupt departure. She looked from face to face round the table, and all three of them were perfectly comprehensible, both on the surface level and beneath it. She could take the situation at its face value, flatly literal like that note lying beside Lesley's plate, or she could delve beneath the upper layer and recall all yesterday's curious emotional signals, and begin to put together quite a different picture. But in both versions she was negligible, without a part to play. And she was well aware that she had been playing a part, one which had now been written out by some alien hand, and that she was not negligible. He would not go away like this without word or hint to her. Word might, of course, be on its way by a devious route, and she could wait a little; but not long. She was uneasy, and convinced she had grounds for uneasiness. She simply did not believe in what she was witnessing.

She went out with Lesley to the site, but George Felse was not in attendance, only Detective-Sergeant Price superintended the enlargement of the cleared section. It was Sunday morning, and the sound of church bells came pealing with almost shocking clarity through moist, heavy air, and below a ceiling of cloud. It had rained all night since about one o'clock, and the water of the Comer, grown tamed and clearer during the last two days, ran turgid and brown once more. Fitful sunlight glanced across its surface like the thrust of a dagger. The edge of the path, glistening pallidly, already subsided into the river.

'We always go to church for morning service,' said Lesley, with perfect indifference, merely stating the routine of the day. 'If you'd like to come with us, of course, do, we'd be glad. But I rather thought it might not be the right brand for you, if you know what I mean.'

Charlotte had been brought up in a household cheerfully immune from any sectarian limitations, and not at all addicted to church-going of any kind, but the opening offered her was too good to miss. She said the right things, and was tactfully left to her own devices about the house when the Paviour car drove away to Moulden church.

As soon as they were gone she rang up George Felse.

It worried her a little that he didn't seem worried. He listened, he was interested, mildly surprised, but not disturbed at all.

'Or were you expecting this?' she challenged suspiciously.

'No,' he said, 'I wasn't expecting it, and I don't know the reason for it. I don't take this sudden errand very seriously, any more than you do. But there could be a good reason for it, all the same. I think it quite probable that he may have gone off after some lead of his own, something he didn't want to make public.'

'He'd still have found a way of communicating with you,' said Charlotte firmly, 'or with me.' She made no comment on the implications of what she was hearing, because time was too precious, and in any case she had had it in mind all along that Gus Hambro was not quite what he purported to be. Indeed, one of the first things she had ever consciously thought about him when he first accosted her was that a face and manner so candid, and eyes so joltingly innocent, marked him out as a man who needed watching. She didn't attempt to explain or justify her last remark, either, George must take it or leave it. Judging by the brief and thoughtful pause, he took it.

'There may well have been no time for that before he left. Say, for instance, that he was following somebody. In which case he'll get in touch as soon as he can.'

'And if he can,' she said flatly.

This pause was still briefer. 'All right,' said George. 'No waiting.

I'll be over there later on, I've got things to do first. But for public consumption his going is accepted as offered. And in the meantime you can do two things for me. How is it you're calling from the house?'

'There's no one here but me. They've gone to church.'

'Good! Then first, go and tell Detective-Sergeant Price what you've told me, and what I've said. And second – what happened to this note? Is it destroyed?'

'No, I'm sure Lesley just crumpled it up and left it on the table. It's probably been thrown out with the crumbs.'

'Find it if you can, and hang on to it. Would you know his handwriting?'

'I've never even seen it,' she said, surprised at the realisation, 'except a weird scribble on a label tied round the neck of a plastic sack.'

'Then get the note and hold it for me. I'll be over before they come out of church.'

Charlotte hung up, and went to turn out the contents of the blue pedal bin in the kitchen, and there was the loosely-crumpled sheet of Bill's graph paper ready to her hand. Quite certainly nobody was attempting to get rid of the evidence; nor had she really any doubt now that it was Gus who had written this mysterious farewell. Which still left the problem of why.

His senses were beginning to wilt in the earthy, smothering air. Twice in the last hour he had found the passage before him partially blocked, and the outer wall of the flue buckled inwards in a jagged heap of brick and soil, but each time there had been space enough for him to crawl through, with some difficulty and a good deal more terror. The tug of shifting earth at his shoulders brought the sweat trickling down over his closed eyelids, but the clogged space opened again, and brought him sprawling down to the brickwork of the floor, with no more damage than the nausea of fear in his mouth.

But the third time he ran his probing hand against a crumbling wall of earth ahead, there was no way through. The brickwork had been pressed down bodily under the weight of soil, and sealed the flue. His straight run home had been too good to be true from the start. There was nothing to be done but work his way painfully backwards, the flue being too narrow to allow him to turn, until he felt the first cross-flue open at his right elbow. If you can't go through, go round, and get back on course as soon as an open passage offers.

He turned right, and then, with a premonition of worse to come, halted to consider what he was doing. What use was a sense of direction, down here in limbo? His only salvation was the Roman sense of order, that laid out everything at right-angles. Suppose he had to keep going on this new line past several closed flues? Keep count, Hambro, he told himself feverishly. Never mind relying on your memory, for every blind alley you have to pass, pocket a bit of tile – right pocket – every shard means one more you've got to make back to the left.

Into his pocket went one fragment of tile fingered out of the dirt. And at the next left turn another one, because here, too, the wall of earth was solid and impassable. And a third, and a fourth. Then it began to dawn on him that he was beneath the open centre of the caldarium, beneath land which had been cleared of its available masonry for local building purposes centuries ago, and for centuries had been under the plough, with a wagon-road obliquely crossing it. Constant use and the passing of laden carts had packed down the soil and settled everything into a safe, solid mass. No choice but to go where he still could, crossing the rectangle towards its right-hand boundary, where he had no wish to go, where there was no way out, and hope to God that somewhere one of these flues would have held up, and let him turn towards the river again.

The first that offered he tried, and it took him a few feet only to close up on him from both sides, and force him back. The second helped him to gain a little more ground before stopping him, and he pushed his luck a shade too hard in his hope and desperation, and brought down a slithering fall of bricks over his left arm. When he had extricated himself, with thundering pulse and shaken courage, and opened his eyes momentarily to blink the dust away, he saw that the luminous second hand in the comforting bright eye of his watch hung still, and the glass was broken. There, at eleven-thirteen in the morning of Sunday, went all sense of time; there was no measure to his ordeal any more.

Sometimes he put his head down in his arms and rested for a little while, where the going was better; but that was dangerous, too, because only too easily he could have fallen asleep, and the urgency of movement hung heavy upon him like the malignant, retarding weight of the darkness. He even kept his eyes open now, to ward off sleep the better. His gloves were in tatters, his fingers abraded and bleeding. And he must have been crazy to bring a damned awkward thing like that helmet with him on this marathon crawl, slung round his neck like the Ancient Mariner's albatross, by his tie threaded through its eye-holes; a clumsy lump hampering his movements at every turn, having to be hoisted carefully aside when he lay flat to rest, slowing him up in the bad patches, where it had to be protected from damage even at the cost of knocking a few pieces off his own wincing flesh. Once an archaeologist, always an archaeologist. It was one of the finest things he'd ever seen of its kind, even if it had all but killed him, and he'd be damned if he'd leave without it.

'He wrote it,' said George Felse, smoothing the crumpled note between his hands, 'and he didn't write it under any sort of compulsion, or even stress, as far as I can see. Does that make you feel any better?'

She looked at him intently, the damp wind from the swollen river fluttering the strands of hair on her cheeks, and said firmly: 'No.'

'It should. To some extent, at any rate. But you can be extraordinarily convincing, can't you?' he said, and smiled at her.

'Does that mean we wait for word of him, and do nothing?'

'No, it means I've already done what needs to be done. For good reasons we don't want any public alarm or any visible hunt. But we've sent out a general call on his car, and an immediate on any news of it or him. Orders to approach with discretion, if sighted, but once found, not to lose. By evening we may hear something. Meantime, not a word to anyone else.'

The air was giving out, or else it was he who was weakening. His head swam lightly and dizzily, like a cork on stormwater, and sometimes he came round with a jolt out of spells of semi-consciousness, to find himself still doggedly crawling, and was terrified that in that state he had passed some possible channel riverwards, or left some crossing unrecorded. He had crawled his way clean through the knees of his slacks, and ripped the sole of one shoe open. There were moments when he felt as if his kneejoints were bared not to the skin, but to the bone, and suffered the alarming delusion that he was dragging himself forward on skeletal hands stripped of all their padding of flesh.

His mind remained, at least by fits and starts, as clear as ever, aggravatingly clear. He had a surprisingly sharp conception of where, by this time, he was. He had started out to proceed in orderly fashion down the left-hand limit of the caldarium to the river, and thence to the open section. And here he was, God alone knew how many hours or weeks later, forced farther and farther off-course to the right, until he must be within a few yards of the right-hand margin, and no nearer the river than when he had set out. Somewhere at this corner there had been a limited dig, he remembered, about nineteen months ago, but they'd filled in the excavation with very little gained. A disappointing affair. My God, he thought, staggered by the astringent precision of his own thoughts while his body was one blistering pain from cramp, exertion and strain, I'm going quietly crazy. I could recite the text of that article word for word, and I'd never even seen this damned place when I got the magazine as part of my briefing.

I will not go crazy, though, quietly or noisily, so help me! I'll crawl out of this Minoan labyrinth on my own hands and knees, or die trying!

It was nearly half past five that Sunday afternoon when a courting couple in a Mini, returning from a spring jaunt and finding themselves with time for an amorous interlude before they need return to the bosoms of their families, drove off the road on the heath side of Silcaster into a certain old quarry they knew of, and parked the car carefully on the level stretch of grass above the abandoned workings. If the boy had not sensibly elected to back into position and drive out again forwards, and his girl friend had not been well-trained in all their mutual manoeuvres, and hopped out without being asked, to make sure how far back the ground was solid after the rain, a very much longer interval might have passed before George Felse got any information in response to his general call.

'Come on, you're all right,' she called, beckoning him gaily back towards the sheer edge of the quarry, still some eight yards or so behind her, and thinly veiled with low bushes here and there. 'Somebody's been back here before us, it's safe enough.' And she glanced behind her, following the course of the tyre-tracks flattened deep and green into the wet grass, and suddenly flung up a hand in warning and let out a muted shriek: 'My God, no! Stop! Eh, Jimmy, come and have a look at this! Some poor soul's gone clean over the edge.'

The tracks ran straight to the rim, and vanished into the void; a little bush of stunted hawthorn, barely a foot high, was scraped clean of all its twigs and leaves on one side, and dangled broken into the grass. In stunned silence they crept forward to the rim of the cliff, and looked over into the deep, dark eye of the pool which had long since filled the abandoned crater. Rock-based, with only a few years' deposit of gravel and fine matter to cloud it, and almost no weed, it retained its relative clarity even after rain, but it was deep enough to cover what it held with successive levels of darkness. Nevertheless, they could distinguish the shape of the car by the still outline of pallor, light bronze forming an oblong shoal with all its sides sloping gradually away into the blue-green of deeper water.

'Oh, God!' whispered the girl. 'It's true! He went and backed her clean over.'

The boy was sharper-sighted, and bright enough to be sure of what he saw. 'He never did! That car went in forwards. Look at it! What's more, look at those tracks!'

By instinct they had walked along the wheel-tracks to the edge of the quarry, the grass being longish and very wet, and the flattened channels the smoothest and driest walking. 'Look there, between the wheel-marks!' She looked, and there beyond doubt ran the curious feather-stitch pattern of two human legs wading through grass, midway between the grooves the tyres had laid down. Not merely walking, but thrusting strongly, for the soft turf, though it retained no details, was ground into a hollow at every step. These marks began only about fifteen feet from the edge, and ended in a patch of more trampled grass about six feet from it. Only a few yards of effort.

'You haven't set foot in there,' said the boy, 'and no more have I. Either I'm crazy, or the bloke that did was *shoving* that car. Put her in gear and let her run, and even then, with this growth, downhill and all she'd need a hand to send her over.'

'What, just getting rid of an old crock?' said the girl, relieved of the vision of two young people like themselves slowly drowning as the car filled. 'Is that all? Well, I know they go to some funny shifts to get shot of 'em, I suppose that'd be one way.'

'I don't know! It doesn't look like a job *I'd* throw away,' he said dubiously, peering down at the pale shape below. 'Suppose it was some car pinched for a job, and then dumped? And it's recent – couldn't be longer ago than last night it was put in there.' He made up his mind. 'Come on, we'd better report it. Just in case!'

133

It was his statement that sent a Silcaster police car out to the quarry less than half an hour later. The colour appeared, the boy had said, to be fawn or light brown. The implications were urgent, with the missing light bronze Aston Martin in mind, and they sent out, after only momentary hesitation, for a skin-diver, to settle the matter as soon as possible, one way or the other. If they were wasting time over an old hulk ditched illegally by its desperate owner, so much the worse. But they couldn't afford to take chances.

The diving unit brought flood-lights and equipment, never being given to do things by halves. The diver went down before the daylight was quite gone, and brought up a report that set the whole circus in motion well into the night.

The first call was put through to George just before seven. 'Got some news of the Aston Martin for you,' said the Silcaster inspector, an old acquaintance. 'Some bad, some good.'

'Let's have the bad first,' said George.

'We've found the car. Dumped in a pool in a deserted quarry up by the heath. Courting couple found the tracks where it had been driven over, and had the sense to report it. We've already had a diver down, and it's the car you want, all right. We're setting up the gear to raise it, but our frogman reckons he could see pretty well into the interior, and—'

'And he isn't in it,' said George, drawing the obvious inference with immense relief. 'That's the good news?'

'That's it. Good as far as it goes, anyhow. No body, no luggage, nothing visible bigger than a rug on the floor. But it leaves you with a problem, all right. Since he isn't there, where is he? Because whoever put his car out of commission down a hole can't have been exactly well-disposed to the owner, can he?'

The air was getting fouler, and he was getting weaker, and he was almost as far away as ever from that unattainable corner where the hypocaust opened one vein to the light of day; though whether it was night or day, and what the hour was, he had now no means of knowing. He had given up hope of finding a way through the centre of the maze. Every hopeful passage he had attempted towards the river had only closed up in front of him and driven him still further to the right, and three times now he had had to turn off to the right even from that line for a short distance, so that he had lost some ground gained earlier. He must now be at the very site, he thought, of that

134

last minor dig, and the one hope he had left was that this right-hand boundary wall might have survived in better case than the opposite one. Since the centre was bedded solid, and the obvious way to his objective had failed him, try the long way round, and pray that it might yet turn out to be the shortest way home. The flues at the rim of the hypocaust had the best chance of surviving, since on one side they backed all the way into solid earth, the brickwork unbroken by cross-passages. And this one towards which he was now crawling, on no remaining fuel but his native obstinacy, would certainly have carried less traffic and less weight during the centuries of cultivation, since the vast bases of the forum pillars alongside it had defied removal even by the ingenious village builders, and baulked all attempts at getting this piece of land under plough. It had always, he remembered from old photographs in the museum, been a scrub hedge between the fields, and a strip of waste ground, good only for blackberrying. This side he might have better luck.

The boundary flue had one other great advantage, considering his present condition of exhaustion and lightheadedness. When he came to it, it would be a blank T-crossing, with no way ahead, and could not be mistaken. He had been telling himself as much, and promising that it would come soon, for what seemed hours, which only indicated how tenuous his grasp of time had become, and how slow his progress. But at every move he still reached out a hopeful hand to flatten against the facing wall that still wasn't there – as now.

But this time it was there. His palm encountered the unmistakable rough texture of brickwork, squarely closing the way ahead. He lay still for a few minutes, his head swimming with the weakness of relief, and also with the thick, smothering odour of the air, which had congealed into a peculiar horror of old, cold physical death. He groped out fearfully towards the left, which was now his way, and the flue beside him was open, and clear of rubble as far as he could reach. He fingered the walls, and they were sound; the ceiling above, and it felt firm as rock. He shifted his weight with labour and pain, carefully moving the dangling mask out of harm's way, and reached out towards the right. If that way, too, the flue seemed whole and sturdy, he would begin to believe that his luck was changing at last, and in time. Because either this air was fouler than any he had encountered yet, or he was losing control of his remaining senses.

The vault to the right held up as strongly as on the other side. He felt his way down from ceiling to floor, and his hand touched something which was not mere dust or the ground fragments of brick, or even thick, foul cobweb, but parted beneath his touch in rotting threads, with the unmistakable texture of cloth.

He couldn't believe it, and yet it revived him as nothing else could have done. The helmet was no find of his, but if this was cloth, then this was all his own. His questing fingers felt shudderingly over the scrap he had detected, passed over a few inches of flooring, and recaptured the same evident textile quality in several more tindery rags. And they had this up, he thought, and never found anything better than a few animal bones and pottery, when they couldn't have been more than a few feet away from here. Curiously, though he had no way of verifying his calculations, at this moment he was absolutely sure of them.

And it was at that very moment that his fingers, moving with wincing delicacy where there might be priceless discoveries to be made, encountered what was unquestionably bone, but exceptional in being not fragmentary, but whole, as far as he could reach, without lesion. Stretching, he touched a joint, where the bone homed into the cup of another mass, as naked and as clean. He searched in his blind but acute memory, and brought up vividly the image of a human hip joint, intricate and marvellous.

He was a hundred per cent alive again, and he had to get out of here alive now if it killed him, because he had to know. There was one minor city, not unlike this one in its history, where they found two human skeletons in the hypocaust, some poor souls who had taken refuge in the empty heating system when the place was attacked, and almost certainly suffocated when most of the town was fired over their heads. The same could have happened here. He forgot how nearly dead he was, and how completely and precisely buried, and quickened to sympathy and pity for this poor soul who had died after his burial, so many centuries ago. Very softly he drew his finger-tips down the mass of the femur, stroked over the rounded marble of a kneejoint, and then reached out tentatively where the foot should be. For a leather sandal might have remained embalmed perfectly all this time, as durable almost as the ivory of the wearer's bones. Quite close to his right knee, under the wall of the flue, his knuckles struck against the erected hardness, and the sound was music to him. A solid, thick sole. He felt from heel to toe, and then round to where the straps should be, and the still-articulated bones of instep and toes within. Gently, not to do damage. Also out of some reverence a great deal older than Christian ethics, the universal tenderness towards the dead.

The leather sole was sewn to a leather upper. Clearly his raw finger-tips relayed to him, with agony, what they found. No straps, no voids between. A very hard, dehydrated shape moulded inwards from the sole, seamed over a smooth vamp, finished at the heel with a hand-stitched band. Above, where the two wings joined over the instep, the small, metallic roundels of eyelets, and the taut cross-threading of laces. The bow he touched parted at the impact, and slid, still formed, after his withdrawing fingers.

Not a fourth-century Roman sandal on this skeleton foot, but a conventional, hand-sewn, custom-made, twentieth-century English shoe.

Chapter Eleven

It was approaching half past seven that evening when George Felse made his appearance at the curator's house, completely shattering Lesley's arrangements for dinner, and throwing the entire household into confusion. He delayed saying what he had to say until Bill Lawrence was summoned from the lodge to join them; and he made no pretence of maintaining a social relationship with any of them while they waited. The atmosphere of strain that built up in the silence might well have been intentional; or he might, Charlotte acknowledged, simply have shut them out of his consciousness while he considered more important things, and the fever might have been their own contribution, a kind of infection infiltrating from person to person, guilty and innocent alike, if there were here any guilty creatures, or any totally innocent. George sat contained and civil and pseudo-simple outside their circle, and waited patiently until it was completed by the arrival of a dishevelled and uncertain Bill.

'I'm sorry, I didn't mean to keep you waiting, but I wasn't even properly dressed . . .'

'That's all right,' said George. 'I regret having to fetch you over here, but this concerns you as being connected with this site, and I can't afford to go over the ground twice. Sit down! You all know, of course, that Mr Hambro left here last night at very short notice. You know that he left a note stating definite intentions, though in very general terms. I am here to tell you that because of certain discoveries Mr Hambro is now listed as a missing person, and we have reason to suspect that the account given of his departure, whether by himself or others, is so far totally deceptive. No, don't say anything yet, let me outline what we *do* know. He is stated to have left here late in the evening, having received a telephone call asking him to give an opinion on an antique offered for sale on the other side of England. He is understood to have packed all his belongings, loaded his car, left a note to explain his departure and apologise for its suddenness, and driven away at some time prior to half past eleven, when you, Mr

Lawrence, arrived home and found his note. Now let me tell you what we also know. His car was driven into a quarry pool on the further side of Silcaster, probably during the night. It is now in process of being recovered, and has already been examined. Mr Hambro was not in it, either dead or alive, nor is there any trace of the suitcase he removed from here last night. We have, so far, no further word of him after he left here. We are treating this as a disappearance with suspicion of foul play.'

The murmurs of protest and horror that went round were muted and died quickly. To exclaim too much is to draw attention upon yourself in such circumstances; not to exclaim at all is as bad, it may look as if you have been aware of the whereabouts of the car all along, and may know, at this moment, where to find the man. Only Charlotte sat quite silent, containing as best she could, like pain suppressed in company, the chill and heaviness of her heart. If she had neither recognised nor even cared to recognise, until now, the extent to which Gus Hambro had wound himself into her thoughts and feelings since he regained his life at her hands, and how simply and with what conviction she had begun to regard him as hers, recognition was forced upon her now. Paviour already looked so sick and old that fresh shocks could hardly make any impression upon his pallor or the sunken, harried desperation of his eyes. Bill sat with his thin, elegantly-shaped, rather grubby hands conscientiously clasped round his knees, carefully posed but not easy. The fingers maintained their careful disposition by a tension as fixed and white-jointed as if they had been clenched in hysteria. Only Lesley, her mouth and eyes wide in consternation, cried out in uninhibited protest: 'Oh, no! But that's monstrous, it makes no sense. Why should anyone want to do him harm? What has *he* ever done . . .'

She broke off there, and very slowly and softly, with infinite care, drew back into a shell of her own, and veiled her eyes. She did not look at her husband; with marked abstention she did not look at anyone directly, even at George Felse.

'I shall be obliged,' said George impersonally, 'if you will all give me statements on the events of yesterday evening, especially where and how you last saw Mr Hambro. I should appreciate it very much, Mr Paviour, if we might make use of the study. And if the rest of you would kindly wait in here?'

Paviour came jerkily to his feet. 'I am quite willing to be the first, Chief Inspector.' Too willing, too eager, in far too big a hurry, in spite of the fastidious shrinking of all his being from the ordeal to which he was so anxious to expose himself. George was interested. Was it as important as all that to him to get his story in before his wife got hers?

'I should like to see Mrs Paviour first, if it isn't inconvenient.'

'But as a matter of fact,' Paviour said desperately, 'I believe I was the last person to see Mr Hambro . . .'

'That will emerge,' George said equably. 'I'll try not to keep any of you very long.'

It was useless to persist. Paviour sank back into his chair with a twitching face, and let her go, since there was now no help for it.

She was quite calm as she sat in the study, her small feet neatly planted side by side, and described in blunt précis, but sufficiently truthfully, how she had slipped out instead of going to bed, and wilfully staged that brief scene with Gus Hambro.

'Not very responsible of me, I know,' she said, gazing sombrely before her. 'But there are times when one feels like being irresponsible, and I did. There was no harm in it, if there was no good. It was a matter of perhaps three or four minutes. Then my husband came.' Her face was composed but very still, in contrast to her usual vivacity. It was the nearest he had ever seen her come to obvious self-censorship. 'My husband,' she said guardedly, 'is rather sensitive about the difference in our ages.'

She had not gone so far as to mention the embrace, but her restraint spoke for itself eloquently enough.

'So he ordered you home,' said George, deliberately obtuse, 'and you obeyed him and left them together.'

Her eyes flared greenly for one instant, and she dimmed their fire almost before it showed. Her shoulders lifted slightly; her face remained motionless. 'I went away and left them together. What was the point of staying? The whole thing was a shambles. *I* wasn't going to pick up the pieces. They could, if they liked.'

'And did they?' George prompted gently. 'You know one of them, at least, very well. The other, perhaps, less well? But you have considerable intuition. What do you suppose passed between them, after you'd gone?'

'Not a stupid physical clash,' she said, flaring, 'if that's what you're thinking.'

'I'm thinking nothing, except what your evidence means, and what follows from it. I'm asking what you think happened between those two men. Of whom one, I would remind you, is now missing in suspicious circumstances.'

She shrank, and took a long moment to consider what she should answer to that. 'Look!' she said almost pleadingly. 'I've been married to an older man a few years, and I know the hazards, but they're illusory. I've known him jealous before, for even less reason, but nothing happened, nothing ever will happen. It's a kind of game – a stimulus. He isn't that kind of man!' she said, in a voice suddenly torn and breaking, and closed her eyes upon frantic tears. They looked astonishingly out of place on her, like emeralds on an innocent, but they were real enough.

'You're very loyal,' said George in the mildest of voices.

Her momentary loss of control was over; she offered him a wry and reluctant smile. 'So is he,' she said, 'when you come to consider it.'

'And your husband joined you – how much later?'

The voice was still as mild and unemphatic, but she froze into alarmed withdrawal again at the question; and after a moment she said with aching care: 'We occupy separate rooms. And we don't trespass.'

'In fact, you didn't see him again until this morning?'

In a voice so low as to be barely audible, she said: 'No.'

'So he left,' said George, 'because you asked him to leave.'

'I didn't have to ask him in so many words,' said Paviour laboriously. 'I made it clear to him that it was highly undesirable that my wife should see him again. He offered to pack up and go at once, and make some excuse to account for his departure. I told you, I make no complaint against Mr Hambro, I bear him no grudge. I'm aware that the initiative came from my wife.'

There was sweat standing in beads on his forehead and lip. He had had no alternative but to tell the truth, since he had no means of knowing how fully Lesley had already told the same story; but his shame and anguish at having to uncover his marital hell, even thus privately, without even the attendance of Reynolds and his notebook, was both moving and convincing. A humiliation is not a humiliation until someone else becomes aware of it.

'And you manage not to hold this propensity against her, either?' George asked mildly.

'I've told you, it's a form of illness. She can't help it. And it can't possibly go beyond a certain point – her own revulsion ensures that.'

'And yet you deliberately kept watch on her last night, and followed her out expressly to break up this scene. You won't try to tell me that it happened quite by chance?'

'It's my duty to protect her,' said Paviour, quivering. 'Even in such quite imaginary affairs, she could get hurt. And she could cause harm to relatively innocent partners, too.'

It was all a little too magnanimous; she had caused plenty of pain, fury and shame to him in her time, by his own account, but apparently he was supposed to be exempt from resenting that.

'Very well, you parted from Mr Hambro close to the lodge, and came back to the house. And that's the last you saw of him?'

'Yes. I had no reason to think he wouldn't keep his word.'

'As apparently he did. We've seen the note he left behind. You can't shed any light on what may have happened to him afterwards?'

'I'm sorry, I've told you I came straight back to the house, and went to bed.'

'As I understand,' said George gently, 'alone.' There was a brief, bitter silence. 'You realise, of course, that no one can confirm your whereabouts, from the time your wife came back to the house without you?'

'I've been here nearly a year now,' said Bill Lawrence. 'I know the set-up well enough to keep out of trouble. Actually I've known the place, and the Paviours, longer than that, I used to come over occasionally during the vacations, when I was at Silcaster university, and help out as assistant. I had to get a holiday job of some kind, and this was right in my line. I'd started planning my book then. So I know the score. No, he's never actually talked to me about Mrs Paviour, but it's easy to see he's worried every time another man comes near her. Especially a young man. It isn't altogether surprising, is it?'

'And Mrs Paviour *has* talked to you about her husband?'

The young man's long, slightly supercilious face had paled and stiffened into watchfulness. 'She warned me, when I came here officially for this year, that it would be better to keep relations on a very formal basis.'

'She gave you to understand, in fact, that her husband was liable to an almost pathological jealousy, and for the sake of everybody's peace of mind you'd better keep away from her?'

'Something like that – yes.'

'And she acted accordingly?'

142

'Always. It was possible to get along quite well – one developed the knack, and then enjoyed what companionship was permissible.'

That had a marvellously stilted sound, and contrasted strongly with the strained intensity of his face.

'And did she act accordingly with – for example – Mr Hambro?'

Dark red spots burned on the sharp cheekbones. Paviour wasn't the only one who could feel jealousy, and there wouldn't be much room here for elderly magnanimity. Bill clamped his jaw tight shut over anger, swallowed hard, and said at last: 'I'm not in a position to comment on Mrs Paviour's actions. You've had the opportunity of talking to her in person.'

'Very true. Mrs Paviour was admirably frank. All right, you can rejoin the others. No, one moment!' Bill turned and looked back enquiringly and apprehensively from the doorway. 'You say you used to visit here before you carne to work here regularly. Did you, by any chance, pay a visit while Doctor Alan Morris was staying here? That was a year ago last October, the beginning of the month.'

'Yes, as a matter of fact, I was invited over to meet him one evening,' said Bill, bewildered but relieved by this turn in the conversation. 'I angled for an invitation when I knew he was coming, and Mr Paviour asked me over for dinner. That's the only time I ever got to talk to a really first-class man on my subject. I was disappointed in his book, though,' he added thoughtfully. 'I got the impression it was rather a dashed-off job. That's the trouble with these commissioned series.'

'Ah, well, you'll be able to offer a more thorough study,' said George with only the mildest irony. 'By the way, you walked to the village and back last night, I believe. So you didn't use the Vespa yesterday? I notice you didn't use it to hop over here tonight.'

'It didn't seem worth getting it out. I'd cleaned and put it away the night before last. It hasn't been out since. Why?'

'How was it for petrol, when you left it?'

'I filled up the day I cleaned it, and it hasn't been anywhere but across here since.' He was frowning now in doubt and uneasiness. 'Why, what about it? What has the Vespa got to do with anything?'

'We borrowed it an hour or so ago, without asking your permission, I'm afraid. You shall have it back as soon as we've been over it. The tank's practically empty, Mr Lawrence. And by the still damp mud samples we're getting from it, it's certainly had a longish run since the rain set in.'

'But I don't understand!' His face had fallen into gaping consternation, for once defenceless and young, without a pose to cover its alarm. 'I haven't had it out, I swear. I haven't touched it. What do you mean?'

'If somebody drove Mr Hambro's car as far as the quarry beyond Silcaster, then – always supposing that somebody belonged here, and had to be seen to be here as usual by morning – he'd need a way of getting back, wouldn't he? Preferably without having to use public transport and rub shoulders with other people. With a little ingenuity a Vespa could be manoeuvred aboard an Aston Martin, don't you think? By the time we've been over your machine properly we may know for certain where it's been overnight. With a lot of luck,' he said, watching the young face blanch and the frightened eyes narrow in calculation, 'we may even know who was riding it.'

He was in the act of crossing to the drawing-room to tell the silent company within that he was leaving them in peace – insofar as there would be any peace for them – for the rest of that night, when there was a loud knock at the side door, along the passage by the garden-room, and without waiting for anyone to open to him, Orrie Benyon leaned in, vast in donkey-jacket and gum-boots.

'Is Mr Paviour there?' He made George his messenger as readily as any other. 'Ask him to come for a minute, eh? I won't traipse this muck inside for the missus.'

His knock had brought them all out: Paviour, Lesley, Charlotte and Bill Lawrence from the drawing-room, instant in alarm because their lives had become a series of alarms, and instant in relief and reassurance when they saw a normal phenomenon of the Aurae Phiala earth leaning in upon them; and Reynolds and Price from the rear premises and the outer twilight respectively, quick to materialise wherever there was action in prospect. Orrie looked round them all with fleeting wonder at their number, and returned to his errand.

'I've just been up as far as the top weir. That path's under water in three places, and the Comer's still rising. She's over to the grass, close by that dig of yours, and fetched down a lot more o' the bank. You're going to have to concrete in all that section and make it safe, after this lot, or we'll be liable for anything that happens to the folks using the path. You'd better come and have a look.'

There was a compulsion about him, whether it arose from his

native proprietary rights in this soil or simply from his size and total preoccupation, that drew them all out after him into the semi-darkness of the evening. After the recent heavy rain the sky had cleared magically, and expanded in clear, lambent light after the sunset, so that it was bright for the hour, and after a minute in the open air it seemed still day to them. The morning would be calm, sunny and mild. Only the river, their close neighbour on the right hand as soon as they let themselves out of the garden, denied that the world was bland and friendly. The brown, thrusting force of the water lipping the land had a hypnotic attraction. Charlotte, slipping and recovering in the wet turf in her smooth court shoes, felt herself drawn to it by the very energy of its onward drive, as though all motion must incline and merge into this most vehement of motions. The pale green, glowing innocence of the sky over it was a contradiction and a mockery.

This path was terribly familiar to her, and walking upstream here was like walking back, against her will, to the moment when Gus Hambro had lain at her feet with his face in the river, quietly drowning. Now she did not even know where he was, or whether he was alive or dead. All she knew was that he had not been in his car when it was driven over the edge of the quarry, nor had he been dropped separately into the same deep pool. And therefore there was still hope that he was extant, somewhere in the world, and no great distance from her. It was no secret now that it mattered to her more than anything else in the world, that the life she had held in her hands safely once should not slip through her fingers now.

Orrie stalked ahead like a prehistoric god on his own territory, huge and intent, never deviating from the path even when he waded ankle-deep in turgid water. The rest went round, not being equipped for wading, Paviour scurrying back to Orrie's shoulder round the incursions of the river, anxious and ineffective in this elemental setting, the others strung out in a line that picked its way with deliberation along the foot of the slope, in the wet but thick and springy grass.

Above the glistening dotted line of wet clay that was the path, the bevelled slope of grass rose on their left, and the untidy fall of loose earth had certainly spilled across into the rising water. They came to the place where the first slip had occurred, and where, above them on level ground, the opened flue lay exposed to the sky. It had yielded nothing of value, either to the police or the archaeologists, except the few evidences of wilful damage. Whatever precious thing had ever rested there in hiding, it had certainly been removed in time. Soon the flue would be carefully built up again, if not covered over. But now the expanse of raw, reddish soil was twice as wide, for both shoulders of the original fall had begun to slide away. They stood in a chilly little group at the edge of the torn area, and looked at the slope in concerned silence. The path was still passable here, but by morning, if Orrie was right and the river still rising, it might well be covered.

'If she comes over and starts eating under this bank,' Orrie said with authority, 'all this loose stuff'll wash away like melting snow, and the bank'll go. Ask me, we ought to put up warning notices, both ends of the path. It'll be us for it, if somebody comes along here, not knowing, and goes in the river, or gets buried under that lot when it gives.'

'I should have been glad to have it closed long ago,' Paviour admitted, 'but you know what happens if one tries to close a right-of-way, however inconvenient and dangerous. However little used, for that matter, though this one does get used. You think the river will rise much more? It's some hours now since the rain stopped.'

'Yes, but it takes a couple of days for the main weight to come down out of Wales. I reckon she may come up another two feet yet afore she starts dropping again. What's more, we'll need to do something permanent about it, besides closing it now. That's not going to be safe again unless we firm up this bank with a concrete lining, and lift the path.'

'That would probably be a shared responsibility,' said George Felse, 'with the local council, but Orrie could be right. Is this the only bad place?'

'No, there's a couple more just close to our boundary. But no falls there, so far. This,' said Orrie, jerking his cropped reddish curls at the slope before them, 'is moving now. Look at it!'

As though some infinitesimal tremor of the earth troubled the stability of the whole enclosure, little trickles of soil were starting down from the raw shoulder, a couple of yards to the left of the exposed flue, and running downhill with a tiny, sibilant sound, resting sometimes as they lodged in a momentarily stable hold, then continuing downhill on a changed course; all so quietly, without haste. The disturbed dead, Charlotte thought, trying to get out. If they could remember what it was like to be alive, she thought with a quite unexpected surge of desolation and dismay, they'd let well alone.

A curious effect, this boiling of the earth. When the pool of Bethesda was troubled, it did miracles. She badly needed a miracle, but she doubted if this narrow well into the depths of history, for all its disquiet, could provide one.

'We'd better have a look at this bit upstream,' said George, 'while we're about it. Orrie's right, you may have to put up those notices, for your own protection, as well as other people's.'

Orrie turned willingly, and led the way again, surging through the shallows, and the others strung out behind him on the dry side of the path, gingerly skirting the shifting pile of loose soil. Charlotte was last in the line, since they had to proceed in single file or wade, like their leader. She never knew exactly why she looked back. Perhaps, being the nearest she heard the slight crescendo of furtive sound that was too small to reach the ears of those in front. The little drifts of earth insisted, and stones began to break free and roll gently and sluggishly downwards. Only small stones, too little to change the world, but they ran, and rolled, and jumped, and the trembling of the well was every moment more urgent with the promise of a miracle; and something prophetic, a small flame of wondering and hoping, kindled in her mind.

So it happened that her chin was still on her shoulder, and she had actually halted and turned in order to watch more attentively, when she saw a sudden small, dark hole burst open in the high mask of earth above her. Not just a hollow, shadowed darker than its surroundings, but a veritable hole upon total blackness. It grew, its rim crumbled away steadily. She saw movement varying its empty blackness, something paler moving within, scraping at the soil. Another biblical image of portent, the cloud, the hole, no bigger than a man's hand, that grew, and grew, like this . . .

It was a man's hand! Feeble, caked with grime, fingers struggled through and clawed at the soil, sending fresh trickles bounding down towards her. A real human hand, alive and demanding, felt its way through into the light with weary exultation.

She was not given to screaming or fainting, and she did neither. She stood stock-still for perhaps ten seconds, her eyes fixed upon that groping, dogged hand, her mind connecting furiously, with a speed and precision she had never yet discovered within herself. The dead

147

were breaking out of their graves with a vengeance. Somebody dumped his car – somebody did this to him – somebody close here, somebody among us. Twenty hours under the earth! He wasn't supposed ever to show up again. Someone is quite confident, quite sure of his work. *I want to know who!* Only one minute, two minutes, she promised silently, and I'll come, I'll get you out of there. But first *I want to know which of them did it! And I want to strike him dead at your feet!*

She turned and called after the dwindling procession winding its way along the riverside: 'Wait! Come back here a moment, please, come and look! I've found something!' The right voice, pleasurably excited, urgent enough to halt them, not agitated enough to give them any warning of more than some minor discovery, some small find carried down by the fall, or the vault of another flue broken open. And that was true, how true, but they wouldn't know the reason. When they turned to look, she waved them imperiously back to the spot, herself planted immovably. 'Come here! Come and see! It's important.'

They came, half indulging her and half curious. She watched their faces as they drew near, and they were all interested, enquiring and untroubled by any forewarning, for their eyes were on her, and the hand, grown to a wrist and forearm now, laboured patiently some feet above her head. She waited until they were all close, and only then did she turn and point, ordering sharply: 'Look! Look up there!'

Two braced arms within the hypocaust thrust at the thinning barrier of soil at that moment, and sent its ruptured fringes scattering. A heaving body, blackened and encrusted with soil, erupted out of its grave, and with a staggering jerk, stood erect for one instant on the shifting slope, before its weight set the whole surface in motion, and hurled it down upon them in a skier's leaning plunge.

She missed nothing. She even took her eyes from him, and let the police jump forward to break his fall, in order to watch all those other faces. There had been a general gasp of fright and horror; no wonder, there was nothing in that to incriminate. Bill Lawrence stood with mouth fallen open in stunned bewilderment, Lesley clapped her hands to her cheeks and uttered a muted scream. Even Orrie, though he stood rooted and silent as a rock, stared with eyes for once dilated and darkened in disbelief. But Paviour gave a high, moaning shriek, and flung his hands between himself and the swooping figure, making an ineffectual gesture of pushing the apparition away. Then, as though he had felt his hands pass clean through its impalpable substance, he plucked them back, and turned blindly to run. Charlotte saw his face stiffen suddenly into blue ice, his eyes roll upwards whitely, and his lips, always bloodless, turn livid. He lifted his hands, spun on his heel in a rigid contortion, and fell face-down on the muddy path like a disjointed puppet.

Gus Hambro reached the grass still upright, in a rushing avalanche of loose soil, and reeled into the arms of George Felse and Detective-Sergeant Price. For a few seconds he stood peering round at them all, and they saw that his eyes were screwed up tightly against the waning twilight as though for protection against a blaze of brightness. He heaved deep breaths into him, dangled his blackened and bloody hands with a huge sigh, and collapsed slowly and quietly between his supporters, to subside into the wet grass beside the enemy Charlotte had terrified herself by striking senseless, if not dead, at his feet.

149

Chapter Twelve

To Charlotte, in her state of minor shock and illogical guilt, the next twenty minutes resembled one of those ancient comedy films in which sleep-walkers stride confidently about the scaffolding of an unfinished building, converging with hair-raising impetus and missing one another by inches: a purposeful chaos with a logic of its own, and all conducted in comparative silence. After the first stupefying moment, exclamation was pointless. Someone, Charlotte supposed it could only have been George Felse, must have given orders, for the whole group, apart from George and Reynolds, dispersed like a dehiscent fruit bursting, Sergeant Price, with Lesley in anxious ward, to telephone Paviour's doctor, Charlotte to rustle up blankets, Bill Lawrence and Orrie Benyon to fetch the sun-bed stretchers from the garden-room, while George and his constable did what they could, meantime, for the casualties. The principle that victims of sudden collapse and probable acute heart failure should not be moved without medical advice hardly held good on a chilly, wet slope of grass beside a steadily rising river, and with night coming on.

At that hour on a Sunday evening it was hardly surprising that Dr Ross, who had been Paviour's doctor for years, should be away from home. His answering service offered the number of his partner on call, but Price preferred to cut the corners and ring up the police doctor, whom he knew well, and to whom he could indicate – Lesley being temporarily out of the room helping Charlotte to collect rugs and pillows from a cupboard in the hall – what the trouble was likely to be.

'Blue as a prime blue trout, and got all his work cut out to breathe at all. Looks pretty bad to me.'

He hung up as Lesley came in, and hoped she hadn't heard. She had hardly spoken a word throughout, and what she was thinking was more than he could guess. For she could connect as quickly as anyone. Not much doubt of that. And who but the man who had put

Gus Hambro underground for good should all but drop dead from shock when the corpse insisted upon rising?

Paviour was laid in blankets on the couch in the sitting-room, livid-faced and pinched, breathing in shallow, rattling snores. She sat beside him, sponging his face and bathing away the sweat that gathered on his forehead and lips. Gus Hambro had been carried straight upstairs to the bathroom to strip him of his wrecked clothes and clean the grime of centuries from his body, and Bill, at his own suggestion, had slipped away to the lodge to bring him some pyjamas and clothes of his own, since the victim's effects were a total loss. Out in the hall by the front door Orrie hovered uneasily, plainly unwilling to leave until he knew what was going on, waiting for the doctor to arrive, and rolling himself one shapeless cigarette after another.

Dr Braby came with an ambulance as escort, having considerable confidence in Price's judgement. The attendant followed him in to await orders, and fetch and carry if required. Lesley relinquished her place by the couch without a word, and stood aside, intently watching, as the doctor turned back the blankets and began a methodical examination. The sight of the sunken, leaden face and the sound of the anguished breathing made him look up at her briefly over his shoulder.

'Will you show Johnson where the telephone is, please? Get the Comerbourne General, and say you're bringing in a congestive heart failure, urgent. I'll give you a note on what he's getting: digoxin, intravenous, fifteen millilitres. We need a quick response, and in his condition I doubt if there'll be any nausea reaction. Hot water, would you mind, Mrs Paviour?'

He spread his bag open beside him, within reach of one freckled, middle-aged hand, and prepared his injection, and very slowly and carefully administered it. For a few minutes afterwards he sat with his fingers on his patient's pulse.

'No history of heart trouble previously?'

'No,' said Lesley, 'he's never complained. He seemed very well, and he didn't bother about regular check-ups, as long as he felt all right.'

'Like most of us. We'll have to send him into hospital, I can't do more for him here. The digoxin will begin to take effect in ten minutes or so, and should reach maximum within a couple of hours. Then he should rally.'

'I'll go along with him,' said Lesley. 'Give me three minutes to put

151

some things together for him.' She looked the doctor squarely in the face. 'You can tell me the truth, you know. Is he going to get over it?'

'No saying yet, I'm afraid. He's bad, but he may pull out of it successfully. Live in hope!'

Was it possible that her hopes inclined the other way? Her voice was so level and her face so still that it was left to the imagination what ambivalent thoughts they covered. If he had really attempted murder, what was there waiting for him if he got over this attack?

'Do you want me to come along with you?' Charlotte asked.

Lesley gave her a faint, brief smile, perhaps detecting the reluctance with which the offer was made. 'No, thanks, you stay here and stand in for me if anyone needs feeding, or coffee, or a drink. I'm going to pack a case for Stephen.' And she went up the stairs at a light and purposeful run, in command of herself and in need of no one to hold her hand, and in a very few minutes was back with her burden. She followed the stretcher-men out through the hall, and there was Orrie still waiting in case he was needed.

He got up when the stretcher came through, his eyes dwelling in fascination upon the swathed body. It looked like a preternaturally long and narrow collection of old bones very imperfectly articulated. There seemed to be virtually nothing under the covering blanket, only two bony feet at one end of it, and a fleshless head with luxuriant grey hair and pointed beard at the other. The face wasn't covered, so he wasn't dead, after all. Just in process of dying. Or pretty near to it, anyhow, touch and go. Orrie looked up at Lesley, and the case in her hand, and understood.

'How you going to get back, then? I tell you what, I'll bring the Morris along to the General after you, and drive you home.'

'Oh, would you, Orrie? It would be a help.' She groped in her handbag and fished out the car keys for him. 'I was going to get a taxi back, but I should be grateful. I'm sorry to spoil your Sunday evening like this.' For ordinarily Orrie would have been in 'The Crown' by this time, or on a fishing day probably in 'The Salmon's Return'. She smiled at him, rather wanly, and went on quickly into the ambulance after her husband; and Orrie went off with the keys in his hand to get the Morris out of the garage.

'Now where's the other one?' Braby demanded briskly, as soon as the ambulance had driven away.

He looked down with astonishment at the slight body in the bath, newly emerged from its indescribable grime. Gus was covered from head to foot with bruises and abrasions, his knees were rubbed raw, and his hands were a mess, but that appeared to be the sum of what ailed him. His state was something between unconsciousness and sleep, but steadily relaxing into simple sleep. He breathed deeply and evenly.

'Now what in the world,' demanded the doctor, 'has been happening to this one?'

'That,' said George, 'is a long and interesting story, and one I intend to tell you, if you can hang around for a while. Because I think you may very well be useful in more ways than one.'

'Tell me now, it might help. And you may as well finish the job you've started, while you're about it. By the look of him, he won't mind waiting for my services.'

George told him, while they lifted Gus out and wrapped him in a bath-sheet, and patted him dry with gingerly care, for there was hardly a square inch of him without minor lesions. They were still busy when Charlotte tapped at the door.

'I've made up a bed for him,' she reported, when George opened the door to her. 'He's going to be fit to stay here, surely? And Bill's brought him pyjamas, and some clothes of his own. They won't fit too well, but they'll be better than Mr Paviour's. Bill's sleeping here overnight, too. I think Lesley'll feel better with a man in the house. It seemed the best thing to do.'

'You're a treasure,' said George warmly, and came out of the room to her, shutting the others in. 'Which bedroom have you chosen for him? Show me!'

She showed him, saying nothing about the fact that it was next to her own, but it seemed that he had divined as much. He looked at her with a small, approving, almost affectionate smile, and she gazed back at him stubbornly and refused to blush. There were more important considerations.

'I understand your choice,' he said respectfully. 'But for my purposes it might not be a good idea. Would you mind changing to another one? Let's have a look at what's on offer.'

He chose a room as remote from the regularly used ones as the large house permitted, its door solitary on a small cross-landing above the back stairs, which were well carpeted. The window looked out on the shrubberies and orchard at the rear, and was out of sight from the sunny front living-rooms where all the activity of the household centred. The room had a large, walk-in wardrobe which had almost certainly been a powder-closet in Queen Anne's day, when the house was built.

'This,' said George, 'will do fine. You make up the bed, and we'll get him into it.'

'It's too remote,' she said accusingly. 'You can't keep an eye constantly on this room. And supposing he came round and called out? No one would hear him.'

'No,' said George, 'they wouldn't, would they?' He met her eyes and smiled. 'Bring the sheets, and I'll help you make the bed.'

She didn't know why she did what he told her, when she distrusted, or felt she ought to distrust, his proceedings. But she went for the sheets, all the same.

Doctor Braby's report on Gus Hambro was made twice over, once informally upstairs, while he examined the patient, and dressed the abrasions on his hands and knees; and once, with more ceremony, downstairs to the assembled company before he left the house. Gus continued oblivious of both the care lavished on him and the indignities to which he was subjected. The only motion he made was when the doctor, with thumb and finger, delicately parted his eyelids, and then his brows contracted protestingly, and his eyes screwed tight against even this invasion of light.

'Perfectly natural reaction,' said Braby, 'after twenty-odd hours of digging his way out like a mole. As soon as he's released from the necessity of struggle he collapses. There's nothing wrong with him but pure exhaustion, a combination of tension – and that's relaxed now – wear and tear – and that can move into the stage of reparation – and sheer want of sleep. I suppose he hasn't eaten anything all that time, either, but that's a comparatively low priority. After about ten hours' sleep he may wake up enough to want something, but don't worry if he stays out even longer. Pulse is like a rock. He'll do all right.'

The second time – it was considerably later – he phrased it rather differently. He came down the stairs with George just after the Morris had drawn up outside. Lesley was coming in at the door, her face set and pale, with Orrie hesitating half-anxiously and half-truculently on the doorstep behind her. But for the master of the household, the cast was complete, for Charlotte and Bill Lawrence were just coming through from the kitchen with coffee and sandwiches, specially prepared against Lesley's return.

'They say,' said Lesley tiredly, in response to enquiries, 'I can telephone early tomorrow, and they'll be able to tell me more then. They said whatever it was you gave him was only just beginning to take effect. I left him looking just the same.' She looked round with slightly dazed tranquillity, seemed faintly surprised to see so many of them, and fixed upon George. 'How is Mr Hambro?'

'I hope you don't mind,' said George. 'We've made free with your house and your bed-linen, and put him into the back bedroom over the shrubbery, where he'll be quiet. He isn't fit to be moved. But we think – we hope – he's going to be all right.'

'Then he's still unconscious?' she said, her eyes widening. 'He hasn't been able to tell you *anything*? About what happened to him? About *who* could have . . . ?' Her voice was carefully hushed and moderate, but she shied away from finishing the sentence. They could almost see the tall, wavering shape of her husband standing behind her, an old man tormented by his inadequacy, and by the youth of every young man who came in sight.

'No,' said George gravely, 'he hasn't come round yet, and he's not likely to before morning. We still don't know whether he ever saw whoever attacked him, or even where and how it happened.'

Bill Lawrence said, with the authority of the half-expert: 'It has to be the laconicum. There isn't any other way he can have got in there. If he'd been exploring from the open flue, he wouldn't have needed to trail around in there for a day and a night. He knew his stuff, he wouldn't lose himself. And there's his car. Whoever made away with that tried to make away with him. Shouldn't we be having a close look at the laconicum right now, whether it's night or not?'

'The laconicum will keep till morning,' said George. 'As for Mr Hambro's actual condition, Doctor Braby can inform you better than I can.'

'Mr Hambro,' said the doctor firmly, 'is suffering from an extreme degree of exhaustion, physical and mental, and however minor his physical injuries may be, they certainly don't help his general condition. At this moment I'd say his nervous collapse has passed into more or less normal sleep, and since his immediate need is for recuperation, I've left him under fairly strong sedation, so that he shall certainly sleep overnight without a break, and probably longer. I realise it's important to get a statement from him – for it seems from his head injury that he certainly was attacked – but from my point of view it's even more important that he should get the long period of total rest which he requires. I'm afraid police enquiries will have to wait until he's fit to deal with them.'

'And will he be fit?' asked Bill. 'I mean eventually? Will he remember, after all this?'

'Remember? Look, we're dealing with a perfectly sound and strong young man, who at this moment happens to be gravely weakened by circumstances strictly temporary. There's no question of serious concussion. Nothing whatever to impair his memory, unless a nervous block occurs, and frankly, I think that very unlikely. Yes, he'll remember. Whether he saw anything of relevance, whether he can identify his assailant, of course, is another matter. But whatever he did record, he'll remember. We may have to wait a day,' he said indifferently, 'to find out what he has to tell, but he'll be perfectly capable of telling it when he does surface.'

He came down the rest of the staircase, passed by Lesley with a sympathetic smile and a general goodnight, and walked out to his car.

'I think,' said George, 'we should all leave you now to get what rest you can. I'm assured that Mr Hambro will be all right until morning, and I'll be in in good time tomorrow to see him.'

'Do you think we should sit up with him?' asked Lesley. 'We would, you know, we'd split the watch. I mean, if he should wake up, and feel lost? After an ordeal like that . . . and in the dark . . .'

George shook his head. 'He won't wake up. The doctor's sunk him for twelve hours or so, I assure you. Sleep is what he needs, and what he's going to get for a while. We shall have to wait. It's only sense, you know.'

He walked out, too, closing the door gently after him. He was not at all surprised to find, before he reached his car, that Charlotte was there in the darkness beside him, though she certainly had not got there by way of the same door.

'You can't do it,' she said in a rapid, indignant whisper in his ear. 'You can't just go away and leave him like this. You've just made it clear that he hasn't said a word yet, but may have plenty to say when he does wake up. Everybody knows it, you've made sure of that. And then you go away and leave him to it!'

'What would you like?' asked George as softly. 'A couple of constables with notebooks sitting by his bed?' He looked at her closely and smiled. 'So you don't accept Paviour's evidence against himself? If the would-be murderer is in hospital at Comerbourne, seriously ill, what is there left to worry about?'

'I don't know! It did look like that. It *does* look like that. All I really know is that Gus is in there asleep, the one person who *may* be able to identify the man who tried to kill him, and everybody knows he hasn't spoken yet, but tomorrow he will. Supposing it wasn't Mr Paviour, after all? People do have heart attacks. I know what I did, I know I meant it, but after all perhaps he was just the most vulnerable. Then there's somebody still around with an interest in seeing that Gus never speaks. That he doesn't live to speak! If it was urgent to kill him last night, it's twice as urgent now.'

The brief and unprotesting silence shook and enlightened her. Dimly as she could see his face, she knew he was looking at her with respect, with affection, certainly with a very gentle and grave measure of amusement.

'That's what you want!' she whispered. 'You've got him all pegged out for bait, like a goat for tigers, waiting for someone to have another attempt.'

'In which case,' said George mildly, 'you may be sure I don't intend the event to go unwitnessed – or uninterrupted.'

'What do you want me to do?' asked Charlotte, charmed into meekness.

'Well, if you insist – it isn't strictly necessary, but it would help. When you're sure everyone else is in bed, you can go quietly down and slip the catch on the back door.'

'I will.' The door at the foot of those well-carpeted back stairs that led to the room where Gus Hambro was asleep; the room, she remembered, with a spacious walk-in wardrobe. 'And what after that?'

'After that,' said George, 'go to bed. And go to sleep.'

'I should have to have a lot of faith in you,' she said, 'to do that.'

'Well?' said George. 'You have a lot of faith in me, haven't you?'

George drove as far as the nearest telephone box that worked, and made two calls, the first being to Barnes, who was standing by for orders, the second to the ward sister in the Comerbourne General Hospital. He was lucky; the night sister on duty was an old friend, and though she was slightly disapproving, she knew him well enough to consent to bend her conscience very delicately to oblige him.

Then he went home to bed.

Barnes let himself in gently by the back door when the house was in complete darkness and silence, eased the catch into place after him without a sound, and made himself reasonably comfortable inside the wardrobe that opened out of Gus's bedroom. Not too comfortable, for fear of drowsiness. He left the door unlatched, but only a hairline open, to admit sound or light should there be either, and adjusted his own line of vision to cover any approach to the bed where the patient still slept, not so much peacefully as rapturously.

He spent a disappointing, even a puzzling night. Nothing whatever was heard or seen to break the serenity. Nothing whatever happened.

Lesley arose very early, to catch the night sister before she handed over duty. She was allowed to ring through to the ward instead of merely making routine enquiries through the office, the case being new and this the first and crucial call.

'Mr Paviour is still unconscious,' said the ward sister, in the carefully bracing voice of one trying to make dismal news sound better than it is, 'but I wouldn't say he's lost ground at all. His breathing is very slightly easier, perhaps, but of course he's very weak. I'm afraid his condition must have been developing for some time without producing warning symptoms. The degeneration is marked. But there's no need to be too discouraged.'

'You mean he isn't really any better?' said Lesley, irritated and demanding. Why must nurses say so much and mean so little?

'Well . . . his condition is much the same. I wouldn't say he's *worse* . . .'

That did convey something, more than it said.

'Do you think . . .' Lesley hesitated. 'Should I visit this afternoon? If he's unconscious, it can't help him . . .'

'Well, I don't think he's going to *know* you, of course . . . I'm afraid he probably won't have regained consciousness. But don't feel discouraged from coming on that account. I think that you'll be glad to feel that you did everything possible . . . In fact, you could arrange to visit briefly at any time that's convenient to you, if you ask at the office. In the circumstances . . .'

'Thank you,' said Lesley, in a small, thoughtful voice, and put down the receiver in its rest.

There was no point now in going back to bed. The morning was bright, clear and still. From the window she could see the river glittering in the first slanting light, like frost-fire. She went down and made coffee, and sat over it for a long time, staring out at the dawn, and going over the telephone conversation word by word, sorting out the grain from the chaff. 'In the circumstances . . .' Visiting hours at the General were generous but fixed; the circumstances that permitted visiting at any time did not need spelling out. But the sister could be wrong, even doctors can be wrong. People confidently expected to die did sometimes turn their backs on probability and decide to come back again, against all the odds. Still . . . ward sisters are very experienced in the prognostication of death. Especially night sisters.

She heard one of her guests stirring overhead in the bathroom, and got up to make fresh coffee and prepare the breakfast. She was busy laying the table, here in the bright, cheerful kitchen instead of the sombre dining-room, when Charlotte came in.

'I'm sorry, I meant to be up before you and start the breakfast, and now you've done everything. I hope you managed to get some sleep?'

'I slept extraordinarily well,' said Lesley, and meant it. 'I don't know how it is. Trust in providence, or what? But I did.'

'You haven't called the hospital yet?'

'I have. I wanted the sister who really knew something, rather than one who'd just come on. She was the one I saw last night, she promised me she'd be standing by for a call from me. His condition is unchanged,' she said, answering Charlotte's unasked question. 'No better. And she insists, no worse. But I'm not sure the lady doesn't protest too much.'

'I'm sorry!' said Charlotte, reading the look more attentively than the words.

'Darling, I married a man nearly forty years older than I am. I've lived all the while with the obvious knowledge that I certainly was going to survive him, probably by many years. All I hope is that I haven't always been awful to him, and he really did get something out of it. While it lasted. It could hardly last all that long, could it? I was grateful, I was contented and happy, and I hope I made all that clear. In love,' she said firmly, 'I never was. Not with him. I don't feel that that was any failure on my part, I never promised it.'

'I don't feel it was, either,' agreed Charlotte, reassured. 'Where do you keep the marmalade?'

They finished the cooking together, just in time for Bill Lawrence's entrance. He was used to breakfasting in pyjamas, unshaven, on the corner of his desk; it did him good to have to face two young women over the breakfast-table. He was scrubbed and immaculate this morning, like the sky, almost arrogantly clean and pure. We must, thought Charlotte, be one of the oddest trios sitting down to coffee in England this morning. How did any of us get here, in Stephen Paviour's house, in this tragic palimpsest of a city without people? And yet everything felt improbably normal and ordinary, like the extraordinary encountered in a dream.

'You didn't look in on Gus?' asked Lesley, looking up at Bill.

'I did, as a matter of fact. I thought maybe I should check. He's still asleep. I'd even say he's snoring now. I hope that's a good sign. I went up to the bed, but he never stirred, so I left him to it. He'll probably sleep until noon.'

It was at that exact moment that the sound exploded above them, somewhere upstairs, remote at the back of the house. A distant, peremptory, wordless bellow of alarm and conflict, curiously like an antique battle-cry. And then a confused thudding and heaving of bodies braced in mute struggle, frightening out of all proportion to its loudness.

They rose as one, strained upright and motionless for the fraction of a second. Then they raced for the doorway, Charlotte first because she had been quivering on the receptive for just such a signal, not only here in the kitchen, but half the night before. They streamed out into the hall and up the stairs in frantic silence.

It was almost over by the time they burst into the rear bedroom where Gus Hambro had been sleeping. Charlotte flung open the door and stood transfixed, a mere witness, with the others brought up short against her braced shoulders.

The sash window stood wide open, the lower half hoisted to its full extent. The top of a ladder projected above the sill; one man was in the act of leaping into the room, a second head loomed just within view behind him. On the bed a large body crouched froglike, leaning with thrusting forearms over an incongruous orange-coloured cushion, which had missed planting itself squarely over Gus Hambro's sleeping face only because, in fact, he had not been sleeping for an hour or more previously, and had hoisted a sharp knee into his aggressor's groin and rolled violently to the right at the moment of impact. He heaved and strained still at this moment, but he was too light a weight to shift that crushing incubus, though nose and mouth were safe from suffocation. It was Detective-Constable Barnes, circling behind him for the right hold, who hooked a steely forearm under the murderer's chin, and hoisted him backwards off his prey with a heave that could well have broken even that bull neck.

The assailant crashed heavily against the wall, and gathered himself as vehemently to battle again; and Barnes and George Felse, one on either side, pinned his arms and wrestled the lunging wrists into handcuffs behind him. He heaved himself to his feet only to find himself bereft of hands. The cushion lay under the chair from which he had lifted it, beside the window; and Constable Collins, climbing in too late to be of more vital assistance, replaced it automatically, and patted it into shape against the wicker back.

'Orlando Benyon,' said George, running rather tiredly through the familiar formula, 'I arrest you on a charge of the attempted murder of Augustus Hambro, and I caution you that you are not obliged to make any statement unless you wish, but that anything you do say will be taken down in writing, and may be used in evidence.'

Chapter Thirteen

Interrogating Orrie Benyon was a more or less impossible undertaking from the first, because silence was his natural state, and his recoil into it entailed no effort. He was far from unintelligent, or illiterate, or even inarticulate, for he could express himself fluently enough when he found it expedient, but it was in speaking that the labour consisted for him, not in being silent. Here, finding himself already charged with an offence that could hardly be denied, with so many eye-witnesses, but might very well be whittled away to a lesser charge which he could embrace without more than a shrug, with everything to gain and nothing to lose by keeping his mouth shut, he did what all his nature and manner of life urged, closed it implacably, and kept it closed.

They brought him down into the small study, and cautiously let him out of his handcuffs, for he had ceased to struggle or threaten, and had too much sense to try against a small army what had failed in more promising circumstances. It was too late now, in any case, to kill Gus Hambro. That charge he would have to ride; other and worse he might still fend off by saying nothing. And while George put mild, persuasive questions, argued the commonsense course of admitting what could not be denied, wound about him tirelessly with soft, reasonable assumptions and invited him to confirm one by denying another, nothing was exactly what Orrie said. From the moment that he had been overpowered in the bedroom, he did not unclamp his lips.

'Why not tell us about it, Orrie? Six of us saw the attack, and it was pretty determined, wasn't it? You meant killing. Because you'd already made one attempt, and were afraid he could identify you, now that he'd reappeared? What made you choose that particular pool to dump the Aston Martin? And are you sure you wiped all your prints off the Vespa, Orrie? Because you won't have the opportunity now, you know. And nobody else but the police has touched it since. Whatever's there to find we shall find. You might as well make a statement. I'm not holding out any inducements, you know you can't lose by co-operating.'

Orrie sat in a high-backed chair, his spine taut, his head raised, looked through them with his blue, inimical eyes, gathered his wits inside that monumental head of his like the garrison inside a fortress, and said nothing.

'And why did you wait so long, Orrie? All those nice, safe hours of darkness, and never a move from you till broad daylight. What were you waiting for? For something that would make it unnecessary for you to take the risk? What did you hope would happen to let you off the hook? Until you realised it wasn't going to happen, and got desperate.'

Orrie looked through him with eyes like chips of bluestone, and made not a sound.

'This is getting boring, isn't it?' said George amiably. 'Perhaps if we enlarge the cast it may get a bit more interesting.' He turned to Collins, who was sitting unobtrusively beside the door. 'Ask all the others to come in and join us, will you?'

'Since Orrie won't talk about recent events,' said George, when they were all assembled, 'I suggest we hear what the other interested party has to say about what happened to him on Saturday night. I'm afraid we rather over-stated Mr Hambro's condition, as you may have gathered. It's true he was in an exhausted state, and slept heavily and long, but he was not under drugs, and his memory is not impaired. He did recover enough to talk to me for a few minutes last night, before I left, and he did tell me what I'm now asking him to tell you.'

And Gus told them, beginning tactfully at the point where he had parted from Stephen Paviour and packed his bag to leave Aurae Phiala. He was still slightly grey and drawn, still mildly astonished at being above the ground instead of under it, and his hands were bandaged into white cotton parcels; but otherwise, apart from presenting a mildly odd appearance in Bill Lawrence's clothes, he was himself again. When he reached the apparition of the helmeted sentry there was an uneasy stir of doubt, wonder and sympathy, as if two at least of his hearers were entertaining the suspicion that he might, after all, be incubating delayed symptoms of concussion. He smiled.

'Oh, no, it wasn't any hallucination. I've handled it, it's real enough. And I know exactly where it is, and we shall be recovering it, all in good time.' All the while he talked he had an eye on Orrie, who sat like a stone demigod, apparently oblivious of them all, but so braced in his stillness that it was plain he missed nothing. 'The wearer I didn't see at close quarters. But it wasn't Orrie. Not big enough. And then, the one who came behind and hit me had to be Orrie.'

He told that, too, the blow and the fall, the rattle of stones and metal as the shaft was filled in over him. 'The rest you know. I made for the river as the only other way out I knew. It took me all night and all day, because there were a lot of places where I had to dig my way through.' The details of that marathon crawl were irrelevant at that stage; he left them to the imagination.

'And could you,' asked George, 'identify the man who hit you and tipped you down the shaft? From that one glimpse you had of him? Describe what you did see.'

'It was dark, but there was fitful light. The man I saw was much taller than me – as tall as Orrie – or Mr Paviour. Though his attitude, leaning and striking, with his arm raised, may have made him look even bigger. He was in silhouette, no chance to see if he had a beard or was clean-shaven. His strength didn't suggest an old man. To be honest, that's all I could say.'

'And could you, then, have identified him positively as anyone you know?'

'No,' said Gus with deliberation, his eyes studying Orrie from beneath their long lashes, 'I couldn't.'

The bluestone eyes kindled for one instant with a fierce spark of intelligence, and were dimmed again.

'So that's why we had to proceed with this obvious invitation to the murderer to try again,' said George. 'We had everything to gain, and he couldn't know that he had nothing. Your mistake, Orrie. There are now no less than seven people who *can* identify you as the man who made a murderous attack upon Mr Hambro this morning. You're not asking us to believe, are you, that there are two men around with the same urge – and the same acute need! – to silence Mr Hambro for good?'

Orrie was not asking them to believe anything. By the Comer, with the man he had murdered breaking out of his grave, he had never quivered or uttered a sound. There was nothing worth calling a nerve in his whole great body.

'But I can't believe in all this!' protested Lesley suddenly, pounding her linked hands helplessly against her knee. 'Look, I know it isn't

164

evidence, but I've known Orrie for years, he's worked for us, and I thought I knew him so well. I still think so. He wouldn't hurt a fly. Why should he do a thing like this? Oh, I know I *saw* him! I can't forget it. But to me that means there's more behind this – or else something's happened to him, a brainstorm – he isn't responsible for his actions any more. Why should he want to harm anyone? What motive could he possibly have?'

'The usual motive,' said George. 'Gain. Not, perhaps, to harm *anyone*. But a very solid motive to get rid of Mr Hambro. Who is, I should mention – though of course you already know it, don't you, Orrie? – Detective-Sergeant Hambro of the Art and Antiques Squad at Scotland Yard, an authority on Roman antiquities. He came here in the process of following the back-tracks of certain valuable pieces which have been turning up in suspicious circumstances in several parts of the world, and which can only have come from a handful of border sites, of which Aurae Phiala is one. Someone, in fact, has been secretly milking this place of treasure over a long period. And whoever he is, he was implicated deeply enough to kill unhesitatingly when an inquisitive boy accidentally stumbled on one gold coin from his remaining hoard, and unwisely hung around to hunt for more. His curiosity could have blown the whole racket wide-open. He had to go. Gerry Boden was suffocated; the same handy method – if you happen to be about twice as strong as your victim – that Orrie was using on Mr Hambro upstairs.'

'But you're not charging him with anything like that,' protested Lesley. 'Only with this attack this morning. How could he know anything about what Mr Hambro was doing here? None of us knew. He never told us anything. It seems you can't even be sure these things came from here. If he'd been helping himself to valuable things like that, and turning them into money, why would he go on working hard for what we pay him here? It doesn't make sense.'

'It makes perfect sense,' George pointed out, 'as long as he still had treasures to dispose of, and kept them hidden here. Things like that can't be unloaded on the market wholesale, like potatoes. It has to be done gradually and cautiously, with long intervals between.'

'I see that,' she admitted unhappily. 'But in that case, what on earth has he done with the money he's already made? He doesn't spend much, that's certain. And personally, I simply don't believe he has much. He doesn't own a thing but his small-holding, not so much as a second-hand car. He hasn't even got a bank account. Stephen and I have sometimes changed cheques for him, if he got paid that way for some of the odd jobs he did in the village.'

It was at this point that Charlotte got up from her place and walked out of the room. In the curious peace of having Gus alive again, and his assailant in custody, she had been sitting back and letting these exchanges pass by her as impartially as she might have watched the Comer flowing by, until a few chance words pricked out of the back of her mind a small memory, a minute thing that fitted like a key into the whole complex of this mystery, and caused it to open like the door of a safe. She closed the door after her, and went purposefully up the stairs to Lesley's room.

When she came back into the study, as calmly as she had left it, and as quietly, Lesley was still warmly arguing the case for Orrie. And Orrie, though he had not turned his head, now and again turned his stony eyes and let them rest upon her.

'But you see how Orrie's behaved throughout, not at all suspiciously, quite the opposite. You agree he told you all about the Boden boy hiding in his shed all that time . . .'

'That was a very intelligent move,' agreed George, 'and he could well afford it. It didn't implicate him in the least – quite the opposite – and it did underline his cooperative zeal. It cost him nothing, and made him look good.'

'And last night,' she pressed on, 'Orrie was urging us to have all that slope concreted up, to make it safe. Would he do that, if he had valuables hidden there?'

'By now,' said George, 'he has nothing hidden there. What was left was almost certainly removed on Wednesday night, immediately after the boy was killed.'

'Then where is it now? If you could find some of these coins and things in his possession, that would go far towards proving it. But I don't believe in it. I'm certain Orrie wouldn't at all mind having his cottage searched, but I'm even more certain you wouldn't find anything guilty there.'

Charlotte leaned forward, and held out in her open palm the smallest of Lesley's keys.

'And I'm sure,' she said, 'that you'd be equally willing to open your safe-deposit box at the bank, where we went to put in a package last Thursday. A small package, but very heavy. For Orrie!'

They had all turned to stare at her, Lesley wide-eyed and mute, her kitten-face pale and bright in wonder. Charlotte had half-expected to have the key indignantly snatched from her, but Lesley hardly glanced at it, only once in a puzzled way, as if she was too stunned at this moment to connect with her usual aplomb. Her smooth brows contracted painfully, frowning back into past occasions, for the first time with doubt and dread. She looked from Charlotte to Orrie, a blank, bewildered question, more than half afraid of encountering an answer. Then at George, as being in authority here, and deserving some part of her attention.

'Yes, that's true, Charlotte and I did go to the bank in Comerbourne. I did have a little box to put in my safe-deposit, Orrie asked me to keep it for him. We've done it before, you know – I don't remember how often, but several times. He lives in rather a lonely place, and these days one hears such . . . We never thought anything about it, why should we? Just keeping things for him a little while, until he needed them and asked for them out. I know he put an old brooch of his mother's in there once, when someone told him it might be valuable, and he was thinking of selling it. They didn't usually stay in long . . .'

She looked at Orrie again, briefly, and the monolith had certainly stirred, and the blue eyes quickened uneasily for an instant. She looked at George, and her own green eyes were wide and gleaming with realisation and disquiet.

'Now I don't know where I am! I don't know anything! *Can it have been that?*'

'If you have no objection to my taking charge temporarily of your key,' said George, 'and if you'll agree to accompany me to your bank and open your safe-deposit, that can be answered, can't it?'

'Yes,' she said in a whisper. And even lower, almost to herself: 'I didn't know! *I didn't know!*'

The key passed into George's hand. The granite monolith had perceptibly moved, heaving its great head round to stare at the small thing changing hands. If stone can shudder, the brief convulsion that shook Orlando Benyon was just such a movement. But his mouth stayed shut; only now tightly, violently shut, as if at any moment it might break open and breathe fire.

'Of course,' said George reasonably, 'there are difficulties in this theory. Orrie has never in his life been out of England, seldom, I imagine, out of Midshire. Two of the objects recovered in this case surfaced in Italy and Turkey respectively. I don't doubt even Orrie could sell or pawn a gold coin in a good many places here in England,

and get away with it, but he'd hardly have the knowledge or the address to work the trade on a big scale. This is a difficult, specialised market – unscrupulous enough if you know where the fences are, and which collectors don't care whether they can ever show their collections, but otherwise rather dangerous. There are plenty of enthusiasts who are quite satisfied with gloating in secret. But you have to know where to find them. Somehow it seems to me that Orrie is hardly in that league.'

Orrie's eyes swivelled again, silently signalling his awareness of every move for and against him, and still reserving his own defence in this defenceless position.

Lesley sat back with a sharp, defeated sigh, seeming for a moment to have relinquished a field that was out of her control. She pondered for a moment in depressed silence, and then suddenly her slight body arched and stiffened, like a cat sighting a quarry or a foe. She seemed to be in two minds whether to speak or hold her peace. Her rounded eyelids, delicately veined like alabaster, rolled back from an emerald stare.

'Chief Inspector, a day or so ago you said there must be an expert involved. I didn't believe in it then, now I begin to see what you mean. You even mentioned a name – Doctor Morris. He was here just before he went abroad for this Turkish year of his. He brought the text of his book about this place. We were just about closing up the small dig we had that autumn, it was October already, but it had been a good season. And you know something? I'd never known Doctor Morris to speak disparagingly of Aurae Phiala until then, never. And yet he went away from here, and spent three weeks on that text in Turkey before he posted it to the publishers. And you know what the finished book is like. Deliberately playing down this site! I can't call it anything but deliberate. Why? *Why?* There has to be a reason! And that dig – it never produced much – not to our knowledge, that is! – it was still open when he was here. Bill will tell you. He visited then, he knows. Wouldn't it account for everything, if Alan Morris stumbled on a really rich discovery while he was here, and kept it dark? If he was tempted, if he moved his finds, put them in a secret place, and left them hidden until he could get them away? He went straight from here to Turkey. And Charlotte tells me nobody's heard from him since.'

She looked at Gus, who was watching her with a guarded face. 'It's your case, you know more about this than I do. If you've been working in contact with all these other countries, and thinking on these lines – I mean about the need for an expert to run the show – then I can't believe that you've never matched up these times, and considered the possibility of a connection between Doctor Morris's exit from England and the beginning of these deals in Roman valuables. I say considered the possibility, that's all.'

'The police of several countries have made the connection,' said Gus drily. 'They could hardly avoid it.' He carefully refrained from looking at Charlotte.

'Then you didn't come here just to look at one of several places that might have been looted – you came here because the connection with Doctor Morris made this the most probable. And you weren't likely to lose interest and go away again,' she added, 'when you ran head-on into Charlotte on the premises, and found out who she was.'

This time Gus did look at Charlotte, fleetingly and rather apprehensively, and even at this crisis he had not lost his engaging ability to produce a blush at will.

'But will someone tell me,' said Charlotte, ignoring the phenomenon, 'why, if my great-uncle found a valuable hoard here and kept his mouth shut about it, he didn't simply pack the lot up and take it abroad with him then?'

'It wouldn't be a practical proposition,' said Gus simply. 'He was booked by air, which means a limit on weight, and too much excess baggage might arouse curiosity. Also some of the things – if there were others like the helmet, for instance – might be quite bulky and very fragile, and need careful transportation. But mostly just plain caution. Someone who knew the ropes would also know the risks. He wouldn't try to smuggle out too much in one go. I don't doubt some of the most precious and most portable things were taken out straight away and disposed of. The rest, we think, were taken from wherever they were found, and hidden in the broken flue of the hypocaust, which seems to have been completely concealed then by the clump of broom bushes. The art of hiding something is to do it decisively, and then go about your business without ever glancing in that direction, as if it wasn't there. The cache was safe enough until the river rose and brought the bank down.'

'There's still another question,' Charlotte pursued. 'Being an expert on antiquities come by honestly isn't the same thing as being expert in disposing of them dishonestly. Would my uncle have had the first idea how to set about it?'

169

'One evening while he was staying here,' said Lesley, 'we were talking about the shady side of the business. About cases he'd known, and how people went about getting rid of rather specialist stolen property. It was the evening you were here, Bill, do you remember?'

'I do,' said Bill unhappily, from the corner where he had sat silent all this time. 'He seemed to know a good deal about it, he went into a lot of detail. Even names. I didn't think anything about it then, after all it was interesting, and we were all asking him questions.'

Charlotte looked enquiringly at Gus, and waited.

'I'm afraid he did know,' said Gus regretfully. 'He acted as consultant for us occasionally, and he probably picked up a good deal about the top fences in the business. The problem collectors he knew already. And then, you see, he had the top-weight to work the racket in a big way, as an amateur couldn't do. His name and reputation would count for as much underground as in the daylight. Collectors would take his word and pay his price.'

'Well, all right!' She had a curious feeling that she ought to be experiencing and showing more indignation, that it was all part of some devious and elaborate charade, of which she understood something, but not enough. She had probably made one mistake in timing already, with that key. Writing her part as she went along was not so easy. But at least her voice had the right edge of irritation and challenge. 'But all you're describing is an absent master-mind in voluntary exile – or sanctuary – somewhere in Turkey. Whoever prowled about the riverside all day on thorns, waiting for everybody to go home and night to fall, so that he could salvage his last instalment of gold, whoever found that poor, silly boy rifling his cache, and killed him and hid his body until night, it certainly wasn't Great-Uncle Alan by remote control from Aphrodisias. *If* he's at the bottom of this affair, then he had an agent here on the spot to keep an eye on the place and feed the remaining stuff out to him gradually – either to him, or wherever he directed. Somebody well-paid and unscrupulous, and once recruited, in for good. They *had* to trust each other, either one of them could destroy the other. So even the assistant was deep enough in to have to kill the boy who blundered into the secret, and try to kill the detective who was getting too close to the truth. Well, at least we all know who made that last murderous attack on Mr Hambro. Do we therefore know who this local agent was? Is that what you're saying?'

There was a brief, expectant silence, in which everyone looked at Orrie; but he maintained his silence as though nothing that had been said bore any reference to him. However delicate your fingering, it's difficult to find a sensitive spot in a being who has no nerves.

'Yes,' said Lesley, slowly and clearly, 'we do know. At least, *I* know.'

She had their attention at once, but more, she had Orrie's. For the first time he turned his whole body – and fixed the sharpening stare of his blue eyes on her, and though the crudely splendid lines of his face never quivered, it was plainly a live human creature who peered through the slits of the mask. She looked back at him for a long moment, steadily and squarely, and it was as if her look was a reflection of his, for her face, too, was motionless and tranquil in its bright purity, but her eyes were alert, uneasy and agitated.

'There's something that happened just over a month ago.' She turned to face George, and addressed herself resolutely to him throughout. 'I never wondered much about it then, I had no reason to, and until now I'd forgotten it. But I can't tell you about it without telling you how I came to be . . . where it happened . . . where I saw it. And if this case is going to come to court, ever,' she said, clasping her hands tightly on her knee, 'this would have to come out in evidence. I can't even ask you to keep it in confidence.'

'I can't promise anything,' said George. 'It may not be necessary to make anything public that would hurt or embarrass you, but I can promise nothing.'

'I know. I'm not asking you to. It's Stephen who would be hurt, and *he* doesn't deserve it.' And after a deeply-drawn breath she said, dearly and steadily: 'I've been Orrie's mistress for eighteen months. I was actually in love with him. There wasn't anything he could have asked of me that I wouldn't have done for him. It was like a disease that turns you blind. I never saw, even for a moment, that he was making a convenience of me, using me as cover while he bled all that gold and treasure out of Aurae Phiala. I didn't believe it even when you charged him. Now I know it's true.'

Even then, it was not the bonds of silence that Orrie Benyon broke. They had all been watching Lesley in such fascination that for an instant no one was watching him. It was like the almost silent explosion of a leopard out of its cover, so sudden and so violent that his great hands were not an inch from her throat when Barnes and

171

Collins pinioned both arms and dragged him off, and even then the blunt nails of his left hand drew a thin red thread down the creamy smoothness of her neck, and a drop of blood gathered and spread in the roll collar of her white sweater. But the most impressive thing was that Lesley never shrank or blinked, only turned a blazing, defiant face and stared him out at close quarters until he was hauled off her and thrust back into his chair. She did not even lift a hand to touch the scratch. There was something superb about her confidence that they would not let him harm her.

Then she sat silent, still fronting him unflinchingly, while he broke his silence at last for want of being able to express himself with his hands, which were always more fluent. Wide-eyed, long-suffering, with all the distaste she felt for him and for her own infatuation in her set face, she listened to the names he found for her, and never tried to stem the flood. Neither did anyone else. It would have been useless. He had been containing it in doubt and patience for so long that no banks could have held it now it was loose.

'Damn you to hell for a lying, swindling whore! Don't listen to her, she's lying, she's nothing but lies right through. Ditch me now, would you, like you ditched him after he'd served your turn? Drop the whole load on me to carry, and you stroll out of it as pure as a lily, you dirty, cheating devil! But it isn't going to work! Not with me! Deeper than the sea, I tell you, this bitch – look at her, with her saint's face! And *she* began it, *she* called the tune – not only about the bloody gold, but the sex kick, too. You think she ever wanted that old man of hers, except for cover and an easy meal-ticket? Winding herself round him with that tale about being let down, and her life ruined – poor bloody misused innocent, needing his pity! But she didn't want any of *his* bed, bargain or no. Kidded him she was a sex-nut-case, a virgin nympho who couldn't stand being mauled but couldn't help asking for it! But it didn't take her long to pick up the clues with a real man, I tell you! With me she was all nympho! You wouldn't credit all the games that one knows. You think she intended to stick it out here with that old fool for life? Not a chance! We were going to clear up the lot, and then take the money and get out together – the cheating sow, *I thought we were!* – No hurry, we'd got our ways of passing the time while we waited. Every time her old man's back was turned – in her bed and mine, in the shed, in the orchard, down in the hollow where the bloody Roman jakes was, and that was hell on them stones, but she liked it to be hell sometimes, she'd think up ways to make it hell, ways you'd never dream of. Nails, teeth and all, she knows the lot! Six more weeks, and we'd have been ready for off, somewhere safe and soft for life. And then that bloody river had to come up and start the damned bank slipping . . . !'

His voice, even in murderous rage, was a deep, melodious thunder, the singing western cadences like a furious wind in strings. Although no one was holding him now, he heaved and strained against his own grip on the arms of the chair, as though he were chained. 'I'll fix her, though! I'm going to make a statement that'll see her off, the dirty, cheating bitch, the way she's trying to see me. There's nothing in her but lies, and lies, and lies. You can't twist fast enough to have her. You can only kill her! I *will* kill her! I'll . . .'

The pealing thunder snapped off into abrupt silence. He shut his mouth with a snap, biting off words too dangerous to utter. For he was charged only with the attempt as yet, not the achievement.

'You shall have your chance to make a statement, all in good time,' said George, to all appearances unstartled and unmoved. 'Go on, Mrs Paviour. Say what you were going to say.' She would not be interrupted again; Orrie had made his point and could bide his time.

'I realise,' said Lesley quietly, 'that it's my word against his. I realise that my recoil from him now makes him want to drag me down as low as he can. I can only tell the truth. I never knew anything about any thefts from the site, but I do admit the affair with him. I wish I needn't. It wasn't even a happiness while it lasted – not for long. My own fault! Yes, I was going to tell you . . . We did meet in his cottage sometimes. That was what I had to explain, how I came to be there in his bedroom.' She took a moment to breathe; she was quite calm, even relaxed, perhaps in resignation now that the worst was over. 'The last time was about a month ago. I don't remember the exact date, but it was in the last few days of March. He had a letter with a foreign stamp on the table by the bed, and I was surprised and picked it up to look at the stamp, out of curiosity. I didn't know he knew anyone abroad. It was a Turkish stamp, and the postmark was the twentieth of March. When he saw me looking at it he took it out of my hand and dropped it into a drawer. But afterwards I kept thinking I knew the handwriting, and couldn't place it. It was addressed in English style, the lay-out and the hand. I had the feeling that it was familiar in some special way, that some time or other I'd copy-typed from a hand like that. I had. I know now. I happened to turn out some notes I typed up for him while he was staying here. It was Doctor Morris's handwriting.'

'She lies!' said Orrie, shortly and splendidly, without weakening emphasis. 'There never was any such letter.'

'A month ago?' said George sharply. 'Dated the twentieth of March? You're sure it wasn't old? From a previous year?'

'Quite sure. The date was plain. It was March of this year.'

'Then about six weeks ago Doctor Morris was unquestionably alive and well, and still in Turkey?'

'He must have been. He addressed that envelope, I'm certain of that.'

'Where in Turkey? Could you read the postmark? Was there anything to give you a clue to where he could be found now?'

She shook her head. 'I can't remember anything more. It was the date I noticed—' She turned and looked full at Orrie. 'But *he* can tell you. He must know where Doctor Morris is. He's always known.'

The briefest of glances passed between George Felse and Gus Hambro; and Gus, who had been silent during all these last exchanges, said suddenly, briskly and forcibly:

'I doubt if he does. *But we do*. We know exactly where Doctor Morris is. He's down in the flues of the hypocaust, luggage, briefcase, typewriter and all, and he's been there ever since he left your house to catch his plane, nineteen months ago.'

She had had no warning, none at all; for once her sixth sense had failed her. She came out of her chair with a thin, angry sound, quivering like a plucked bow-string, torn between panic acceptance and the lightning reassertion of her terrible intelligence; and in the instant while the two clashed, she shrieked at him: 'You're lying! You can't have been near where we put hi . . .'

The aspirate hissed and died on her lip, and that was all, but it was fierce and clear, and just two words too many. She stood rigid, chilled into ice.

'He wasn't on the direct route, no,' agreed Gus softly, 'but my route was a good deal less than direct. There's hardly a yard of flue passable in that hypocaust where I haven't been. Including the near corner where – "we" – put him. I left your bronze helmet with him for safekeeping. As soon as you're in custody we're going to set about resurrecting them both.'

The deafening silence was shattered suddenly by a great, gusty, vengeful sound, and that was Orrie Benyon laughing. And in a moment, melting, surrendering, genuinely and terrifyingly amused by her own lapse, Lesley Paviour dropped back into her chair and laughed with him, exactly like a sporting loser in a trivial quiz-game.

Chapter Fourteen

She laughed again, when she was alone with George in his office at CID headquarters in Comerbourne, with no shorthand writer at hand and no witnesses, and he asked her, with genuine and unindignant curiosity – since indignation was quite irrelevant in any dealings with Lesley: 'Do you always contrive to have not merely one fall guy on hand in case of need, but at least two? And doesn't it sometimes make things risky when you decide to change horses in midstream?'

'I never plan,' she said with disarming candour, 'not consciously. I just do what seems the clever thing at the moment.'

All too often, he reflected, it not only seemed clever, but was. She had matched every twist until the last, the one she hadn't foreseen even as a possibility. For some built-in instinct certainly acted to provide her with escape hatches and can-carriers well in advance of need. Why, otherwise, had she gone out of her way to let Charlotte not only see but handle the package still waiting to be reclaimed from the bank? And to tell her guilelessly that it was Orrie's, and not the first time he had put similar small items into safe-keeping? Thus underlining for future reference his involvement and her own naive innocence. She had even scattered a few seeds, according to Charlotte, concerning Bill Lawrence's solitary and furtive prowlings about the site, in case she should ever need yet another string to her bow. Lesley collected potentially useful people, and used and disposed of them like tissues, without a qualm.

'I'm not sure,' he said, 'it was so clever to write off Orrie. I wonder at what stage you made up your mind to throw him to the lions? You did allow him the chance to drive you back from the hospital last night. Hadn't you decided then? He'd been waiting on hot coals for a chance to talk to you alone. He wanted you to do your share, didn't he? You were in the house, it was your turn to do the necessary killing. Even a delicate little woman could press a cushion over the

176

face of a man fast asleep under drugs after an exhausting ordeal. But you never intended sticking your neck out for him. Why didn't you tell him so? Obviously you didn't, or he wouldn't have left his own attempt so late. He waited all night, hoping you'd do the job for him. And I don't doubt you slept soundly.'

'Never better,' she said.

'Was it more fun letting him sweat? Was it just to make sure he *would* mistime it and be caught? Or were you afraid you wouldn't get back alive from the hospital with him if you pushed him too far?'

'I'm never afraid,' she said, and smiled. 'I don't drive through red lights, but I'm not afraid.' He believed that, too.

'And of course,' he said, 'it was only going to be your word against his, since your husband was going to die. And if you were winding up the operation and getting out with the proceeds, Orrie was going to be a liability as well as an expense, wasn't he? But what would you have done if he'd refused to put his neck in the noose, and decided to take a chance on Gus, and sit it out?'

'I'd have thought of something,' said Lesley confidently.

'In the end even you had to make one slip.'

'I shan't make another. I knew your thumbs were pricking about me,' she said without animosity, 'when you encouraged me to do poor old Stephen out of his alibi for the night. I could hardly do that without pointing out that I hadn't got one myself, could I? But even now, what are you going to charge me with?'

'Concealing a death will do to begin with.'

Lesley laughed aloud. 'You'll never make even that one stick. Not without Stephen's evidence, and you're going to have to go rather a long way to get that, aren't you?'

'Just as far,' said George, 'as the General. It's a mistake to be too clever at reading between the lines. Neither Doctor Braby nor Sister Bruce told you any lies, they just didn't tell you the whole truth. Sister told you repeatedly he wasn't any worse. She didn't say he wasn't any better. He is, very much. Digitalisation is taking effect excellently. He's out of danger.'

'But she told me,' said Lesley, genuinely indignant at such duplicity, 'that he was dying!'

'She did nothing of the sort. She told you simply that you could visit any time, even out of visiting hours. What you read into that is your worry. So you can visit, if you'd like to – under escort, of course.'

177

She made a small, bitter kitten-face, wrinkling her nose. The jolt was shrugged off in a moment; she adapted to this as nimbly as she did to everything. 'Thanks, but in the circumstances perhaps it wouldn't be tactful. It certainly wouldn't be amusing. But even if you do get to talk to him,' she said, strongly recovering, 'he won't say a word against me, you know.'

'You may,' said George, rising, 'find you've over-estimated even his tolerance. How will you get round it then?'

'I'll think of something,' said Lesley.

It was two days before Stephen Paviour was sufficiently recovered to be visited briely in hospital, and even then George put off what he really had to tell and ask him for two days more, and consulted his doctors before taking the risk of administering a new shock. By Thursday evening his condition was so far satisfactory as to allow the interview.

In all his life of half-fulfilment, of disappointments and deprivations, of loving without being loved, he had perhaps become accustomed to the fact that no one ever came to break good news. It was better to hear the whole story at once than to put it off, since his forebodings were almost always worse than the reality. And with long experience he had acquired a degree of durability against which even this might break itself and leave him unbroken. All the same, George approached the telling very gently and very simply. Flourishes would only have made sympathy intolerable.

Paviour lay and listened without exclamation or protest. There was offence and pain in it for him, but beneath the surface there was no surprise. When it was over he lay and digested it for a minute or two, and strangely he seemed to lie more easily and breathe more deeply, as though a tension and a load had been lifted from him.

'They both admit this? It's been going on – how long?'

'Since before Doctor Morris's visit. Perhaps two years. Perhaps even more.'

'I was rejected,' he said slowly. 'I had to respect her morbid sensitivity, and cherish her all the same, and I did it. That I could bear. And all the time she was wallowing with that beautiful draught-horse, that piece of border earth. While she fended me off with those elaborate lies, because I was too dull, too civilised, too old to serve her turn.' He thought for a moment, and there was colour in his grey face, and a spark in his normally haggard and anxious eyes. 'I'll tell you,' he said, 'exactly what happened, though I see now that it was not what happened at all, since there's no truth in her. This propensity of hers – to provoke men and then recoil from them – this feigned propensity . . . She used it on Alan Morris, too. You know he was a ladies' man? But a gentleman, and experienced enough to be able to deal with her. I was not worried at all.'

It was a bad moment to interrupt, but George had thought of one thing he needed to ask. 'Do you remember one evening during his visit, when young Lawrence came to dinner? Was there a conversation then about the criminal side of the archaeological interest? About how to market stolen antiques?'

Paviour looked faintly surprised, but the intervention did him good by diverting his own too fixed bitterness.

'I do remember it. I couldn't understand then why she should be so interested in such things. I understand now. She was picking his brains. I took it simply as her way of engaging his attention. I'm sure it was she who began the discussion.'

She had, George thought, such a housewifely sense of economy. She never threw away a solitary detail that might some day, suitably perverted, turn out to be useful.

'I'm sorry, I put you off. Please go on.'

'The last night of Morris's stay I had a lecture in the village, one of a series the county education office was putting on. When I came back I found Lesley sitting on the steps of the garden-room, in a hysterical condition. She was wet and cold and crying.'

No doubt, thought George, she can cry at will. God help the jury that has to deal with her!

'She said,' went on Paviour in a level, low voice, drawing up the words out of a well of anguish, 'that she had gone out for a walk with Alan by the river, and he had attacked and tried to rape her. And she had fought him off and pushed him into the Comer. It was credible, you understand, I had experience of the violence of her revulsion. She was very convincing in my case! And I loved her, and let her be. With someone who didn't understand – yes, there could be a tragedy. I didn't question it. She said she had got him out, but he was dead. She swims very well, you know, she was born by the river. I coaxed her to take me where he was. He was dead. There was no mistake. I knew – *then*, of course! – that exposure of such an affair, however accidental it might be, however innocent she might be, would destroy her totally. Her balance was already so precarious, you see.

So I hid his body in the hypocaust. We were in process of closing the small dig we'd managed to finance that year, at the corner of the caldarium. It was pitifully small, and we got almost nothing from it. But it did afford a grave. I did it all myself, by night. I'd kept back his typewriter, and all his documents, and a suit of his that fitted me best. There was nothing to be done but take his place, his flight was booked, and it would account for his leaving. We were much the same build, and of course the same age. That goes a long way towards making a passport photograph acceptable, unless the officers have reason to suspect something, and they had none. I had to shave off my beard, but he wore a moustache, that was a help. He was not really very like me in the face, but the same general type, I suppose. And I was wearing his clothes, his hat, his glasses. It worked quite smoothly. We'd talked about his plans, I knew what was needed. And if I'd forgotten anything, I realise now, she would have prompted me. She did prompt me, many times. I took up his air reservation, his hotel reservation in Istanbul. And I worked over his text there, on his typewriter, and made sure that the manuscript he sent to his publishers on Aurae Phiala should put off all enquirers thereafter. It had to. There must never be a full-scale dig here, never.'

'The purpose was not, in fact, to conceal any valuable find,' said George. 'Just a body.'

'I never knew of any valuable find until now. No . . . I was hiding poor Morris. It wasn't a grave he would have rejected, you know.'

'We've found him,' said George. 'The pathologists may still be able to tell us how he died. I very much doubt if it was by drowning. I should guess he walked slap into one of their meetings, and found out what they were doing. In the circumstances, I doubt if he'd hold anything against you.'

'I hope you're right. I always envied him, but we were good friends. After I'd posted his book – yes, that he *would* hold against me, wouldn't he? That must be put right! – I telephoned his friend at Aphrodisias, and apologised for a change of plans, and paid my bill and went to the railway station. I changed to my own clothes in the baths there, and then flew home on my own passport. We'd left the last segment of the hypocaust open on purpose. I put all his other effects underground with him, and covered him in again with my own hands. It was not easy. None of it was easy.'

Very gently and reasonably George asked: 'Will you, if the issues we have in hand come to trial, testify against your wife? I promise you shall be fully informed of the weight of evidence against her with regard to any charges we prefer.'

'I'll testify to the truth, as far as I know it,' said Paviour, 'whether it destroys her or no. I realise that I myself am open to certain charges, graver charges than I understood at the time. Don't hesitate to make them. I have a debt, too. I made her possible.'

'No wonder the poor soul nearly dropped dead with shock when you came heaving out of the earth,' said George, two days later, in a corner of the bar at 'The Salmon's Return', with a pint in front of him, and Charlotte and Gus tucked comfortably into the settle opposite him. 'He took you for his own dead man rising. You'd hardly credit the difference in him now it's all over, now he doesn't have to live with his solitary nightmare, and there's no hope and no horror from her any more. The tension's snapped. Either he'll collapse altogether for want of the frictions that have kept him on edge, or else he'll look round and rediscover an ordinary world, and start living again. Just now I'd say all the odds are in favour of the second, thank God!'

'Do you think he'll really testify against her?' Charlotte wondered. 'He may feel bitter against her now, but what about when it comes to the point?'

'He'll testify,' said George with certainty. 'You can't love anyone that much, and be betrayed as callously as that, and not find out how to hate every bit as fiercely. Not that we know yet who did kill Doctor Morris. If those two decide to talk, of course, *she*'ll say *he* did it, and forced her to trick her husband into covering up for him. What he'll say I wouldn't bet on, except that it's more likely to be true than anything we get out of Lesley.'

'Who do you think actually did it?' asked Gus.

'Ordinarily she was the teller and he was the doer. But supposing Doctor Morris really did drown, in this case she may very well have done it herself. If he started taking a suspicious interest because of all her leading questions, *she*'s the one he'd be watching and following. There's a skull fracture, not enough to have killed him, probably, but it does bring Orrie into the picture. We may get a conviction for murder against both, but at least we can fix her as an accessory. Paviour will see to that.'

'Did you know when you set your trap,' asked Charlotte, 'that it was Orrie you were setting it for?'

181

'It wasn't for him,' said George simply. 'It was for *her*. I had a queer hunch about her, even before Gus came round and told me what he could. Two people were involved. And the cast wasn't all that big, even if I did make soothing noises about the village and the fishermen not being ruled out. And all of them male but Mrs Paviour, and all, somehow, so accurately deployed all round her, like pawns round a queen. If Gus was being stage-managed out of the world, who was more likely to be the stage-manager, the one who initiated that scene in the night, or the one who interrupted it? And if she had an accomplice, who was it likely to be but a lover? I did toy with the idea of young Lawrence. He was obviously jealous, though that could be regarded as evidence either for or against. And the Vespa was his, but his consternation when he heard about it being used rang true. And then, which of them was Lesley more likely to choose? The nice, dull, civilised scholar, her husband in embryo? Not on your life! So I was betting on Orrie, yes, but I didn't *know*! I was beginning to feel we might make a respectable case against him for Gerry Boden, though it would be mostly circumstantial. The boy had inhaled fibres from a thick, felted woollen fabric. I hope we'll be able to identify them as coming from Orrie's old donkey-jacket. His brand of wood-dust, fertiliser and vegetable debris should be pretty unique. And so's he, in his way. He must have slipped back from the vicarage garden as soon as it began to get dusk, caught the boy grubbing in the hypocaust, killed him and hid his body until it should be dark enough to get it down to the water, collected his aurei, and gone calmly back to his work. He almost certainly had the gold pieces in his pocket when Price called on him at home around nine o'clock to ask about Gerry's disappearance. And even after that he was cool enough to call in at 'The Crown' before he went back to Aurae Phiala to send the body down the river. Not a nerve anywhere in him.'

'So you were following up his movements all the time,' said Charlotte, 'while you hardly ever seemed to look in his direction.'

'Never let wild creatures know you're watching them. They tend to go to earth. If you carry on as if you haven't even noticed them they may emerge and go about their business. Not that it paid off with Orrie. There'd have been gaps in his time-table, if we'd had to proceed on the evidence, but we couldn't have proved how they were spent. Still, I'd have taken the risk of charging Orrie. On her I had nothing. I hoped – so did Orrie! – that she'd attempt the job herself.

Then we'd have had her red-handed. *I* hoped she'd be frightened enough. *He* hoped – he *believed* – she cared enough. But we were both wrong. So I had to bluff it out the hard way, and hope to get through her guard somehow.'

'And I thought I'd wrecked it,' Charlotte said ruefully, 'going off at half-cock like that over her key. I'd only just realised what was going on. I wasn't very clever.'

'Not a bit of it! Once I had that key she had her back to the wall. Oh, she could have stuck to her story that she knew nothing about the coins. But she'd have had hard work accounting for the rest of the deposit.'

Stephen Paviour had authorised the opening of the box two days previously, and it had yielded, in addition to the coins, a highly interesting collection of documents concerning Lesley's buoyant financial situation, though without a word to explain it. She must have made good use of her holidays abroad with her husband, and the few occasions when she had accompanied him to digs in other countries. Nor is it always necessary to go abroad to find the kind of collector who asks no questions, and doesn't mind keeping his acquisitions to himself, well out of sight.

Charlotte thought of those tormented and tormenting lovers, so unevenly matched except in beauty, who now stood charged jointly with the murder of her kinsman. 'Would she ever really have gone away with him, as he thought? If their plans had gone on working out, right to the end?'

'Not a chance!' said George. 'Not with a crude, handsome, lumpish piece of earth like Orrie. She had all the money at her disposal, she could vanish and be rich. He'd helped her to put away plenty, mostly in banks in Switzerland. And what a trusting soul he was, everything was in her name! No, he'd given her a lot of pleasure, and been a lot of fun, but she'd have sloughed him off without a qualm. The world is full of men!'

'Not,' said Charlotte, torn between satisfaction and unwilling pity, 'the world where she's going.'

'Don't be too sure!' warned Gus feelingly, thinking with almost superstitious dread of the kitten's emerald eyes and sharp, insidious claws. 'Even if we do fix her, come eight years or so, and she'll be out on the world again – sooner if the charge is reduced. She isn't going to deteriorate, she isn't going to forget anything, only learn new tricks, and never in this world is she going to change. She'll come out ripe and ready for mischief. Give her half a chance, and she'll be popping up in another mask to lure another poor sucker to his death. No, my girl, you save your sympathy for me and the world that has to cope with her.'

George finished his beer, collected their glasses, and brought them another round. They had been installed here with Mrs Lane all the week, and they seemed, he thought, to be getting on very satisfactorily together. Gus was involved in the documentation of the case from two angles, and could also claim to be a convalescent, entitled to take his duties at a rather leisurely pace, but it was questionable whether he would have strung out his work locally quite so long if Charlotte had not been still at 'The Salmon's Return'. Tomorrow Gus was leaving for London and duty at last; and it could hardly be coincidence that Charlotte was going to town by the same train, to confer with her solicitor and make preparations for the reburial of her great-uncle. He had known even stranger circumstances bring people together. In a sense, Gus Hambro had been a dead duck from the moment he drew Charlotte after him on his nocturnal rush to have one more look for a missing boy. When you have given someone his life back, it may be magnanimous to give it wholly and go right away and forget the benefit, but it's very human to keep a thin, strong string attached, and retain a proprietary interest.

'I'll leave you to it,' said George. And he looked at Charlotte with the private look that had somehow developed between them. 'It's a big step, you know. I'd sleep on it, if I were you.'

'Your wife didn't,' said Charlotte.

They halted at the crest of the bowl to look back over the shallow, undulating expanse of Aurae Phiala. The flood water had passed, the weather was settling into the pure spring-like hush that sometimes comes before a turbulent May. The river ran deeply green and tranquil under its shelving banks. Away to their right, round one corner of the caldarium, tarpaulin screens fenced off the enclosure where the police had dug Doctor Alan Morris out of his grave. The inquest had not yet opened. But there would be no problem of identification there, with all his belongings securely buried round him, like a pharaoh.

'I wish he could have come out of it alive,' said Charlotte. 'But I'm glad he comes out of it with credit. In a sense he was defending the ethics of the profession, if he died because he suspected their thefts and tried to prevent them. For a time you thought I might be here as his agent, didn't you?'

'And for a time,' he said, 'you thought I might be behind the racket myself, didn't you?'

'You knew so much about it, too much. How was I to know which side you were on? I always knew you weren't what you seemed. And I knew you'd latched on to me after you found out my name, not for my charm.'

'Only half true,' he said. 'I don't believe you were ever in doubt for a moment how I felt about you.'

Their voices were as tranquil as the evening sky, and they were standing hand in hand.

'There was a time,' she owned serenely, 'a very brief time, though, when I did wonder just what you were feeling for Lesley.'

'I'd never given her a thought of any kind,' he said firmly, 'until she began to make a dead set at me, after she'd whisked my jacket away to dry and brush it, when I got buried that time. She'd begun to have suspicions already, because she seized that opportunity like a pro. And I was fool enough to carry stuff on me that I shouldn't have done – my passport with the bill from that Istanbul hotel still in it, and some notes, and even a drawing of that gold triskele brooch from Italy, the one that started me on the case. She couldn't very well mistake it. She sold the thing in Livorno. After that it was all "do stay to lunch", and "move in with us, we've got plenty of room". You she wanted under her eye to find out what you were up to, me to dispose of permanently. Not that I realised it then. I just played her shots back to her, to find out what the game was. She'd made up her mind I had to go for good. Underground. I was getting a lot too near to what I was after.'

He remembered with a convulsion of painful rapture and guilt the clinging frenzy of that small body, which this one beside him must some day wipe out of mind. Aloud he said: 'Those scenes with me were staged for him. She could manipulate him like modelling clay. His job was to interrupt us and very politely, very considerately, ask me to leave. So that she and Orrie could entice me back to the caldarium and dispose of me, with everything accounted for, a farewell note waiting, and no questions asked.'

The moon, a filigree wafer of silver foil, was rising, and the Welsh shore had dimmed into a deep, twilit blue of folded hills. Aurae Phiala was as beautiful as ever, and as pure. No part of this greed, violence and deceit had done more than glance from its present-day surface, which was only illusory. It had outlived all its own tragedies long ago.

'I went to see Mr Felse at his home on Saturday morning,' said Charlotte, 'after he flew that kite about Great-Uncle Alan, and started Lesley thinking what a convenient scapegoat he'd make. And he told me about the Yard enquiries, though not about you, and said they'd led inevitably to considering my uncle as one possibility. And then I asked him again if *he* believed in it. And he said, personally, no. He said scholars are seldom rich, but no matter how great the temptation to personal gain, if a find of that magnitude did turn up, the strongest temptation of all would be the innocent one, to the excitement and glory and public admiration. I loved him for that. Because, you see, until then I hadn't been quite so sure myself. But he was right. And because I wanted him to be right, I began to take his word for everything.'

'So that was when you met his wife,' said Gus, remembering George's enigmatic valediction. 'What was that all about, anyhow? What was it his wife didn't do?'

They had begun to walk back, turning away from the crude tarpaulin shape and the scarred ground. And they forgot all the dead of Aurae Phiala in the blessed conviction of being themselves rather more than usually alive.

'She didn't back away and demand time to sleep on it,' said Charlotte, 'when she was asked if she'd consider marrying a policeman.'

THE END

Flight of a Witch

Chapter One

Driving along the lane from Fairford, at four o'clock on that half-term Thursday in October, Tom Kenyon saw Annet Beck climb the Hallowmount and vanish over the crest.

A shaft of lurid light sheared suddenly through the rainclouds to westward, and lit upon the rolling, dun-coloured side of the hill, rekindling the last brightness in the October grass. The rift widened, spilling angry radiance down the slope, and a moving sapphire blazed into life and climbed slowly upward through the bleached and faded green. The blue of her coat had seemed dark and unobtrusive when she had stood at the gate, holding him off with eyes impenetrable as stone; it burned now with the deep fire of the brighest of gentians.

And what was she doing there, in the cleft of brightness between rain and rain, like and apparition, like a portent?

He pulled in to the curve of rutted grass in front of the Wastfield gate, and stopped the car there. He watched her mount, and nursed the small spark of grievance against her jealously, because for some reason it seemed to him suddenly threatened by some vast and obliterating dark that rendered it precious and comforting by contrast.

Westward, the folded hills of Wales receded into leaden cloud, but on the near side of the border the Hallowmount flaunted its single ring of ancient, decrepit trees in an orange-red like the reflected glow of fire. The speck of gentian-blue climbed to the crest, stood erect against the sky for an instant, shrank, vanished. And at the same moment the rent in the clouds closed and sealed again, and the light went out.

The hill was dark, the circle of soft October rain unbroken. He turned the ignition key, and let the Mini roll back over the glistening, pale grass on to the road. Maybe three hours of daylight left, if this could be called daylight, and with luck he could be home in

Hampstead soon after dark. His mother would have a special supper waiting for him, his father would probably go so far as to skip his usual Thursday evening bridge in his son's honour, and more than likely Sybil would drop round with careful casualness about nine o'clock, armed with some borrowed magazines to return, or some knitting patterns for his mother; having, of course, a matter of weeks ago, taken care to inform herself as to when Comerbourne Grammar School kept its half-term, and whether he was coming down by car or by train. She would want to hear all about his new school, about his sixth form and their academic records, and his digs, and all the people he had met, and all the friends he had made, to the point of exhaustion. But if he told her any of the essentials she would be completely lost.

How do you interpret a semi-feudal county on the Welsh borders to a daughter of suburbia? Especially when you are yourself a son of suburbia, a townie born and bred, quick but inaccurate of perception, brash, uncertain among these immovable families and seats of primeval habitation, distracted between the sophistication of these elegant border women, active and emancipated, and those dark racial memories of theirs, that mould so much of what they do and say? Sybil had no terms of reference. She would be as irrelevant and lost here as he had been, that first week of term.

Mathematics, thank God, is much the same everywhere, and he was a perfectly competent teacher, he had only to cling firmly to his work for a few weeks and the rest fell readily into place. He knew he could teach, headmasters didn't have to tell him that. And all things considered, the first half of his first term hadn't gone badly at all.

The school buildings were old but good, encrusted with new blocks behind, and a shade cramped for parking space, though with a Mini he didn't have to worry overmuch about that. He hadn't been prepared to find so many sons of wealthy commuting business-men from the Black Country at school here in the marches, and their lavish standard of living had somewhat daunted him, until he ran his nose unexpectedly into the headmaster's characteristic notice on the hall board:

'Will the Sixth Form please refrain from encroaching on the Staff parking ground, as their Jaguars and Bentleys are giving the resident 1955 Fords an inferiority complex.'

That had set him up again in his own esteem. And the long-legged seventeen- and eighteen-year-olds who emerged from the parental cars, in spite of their resplendent transport, were not otherwise hopelessly spoiled, and had a shrewd grasp of the amount of work that would keep them out of trouble, and an equable disposition to produce the requisite effort, with a little over for luck. They seemed to Tom Kenyon at once more mature and developed and more spontaneous and young than the southern product with which he was more familiar, and on occasions, when they were shaken out of their equilibrium by something totally unexpected, alarmingly candid and abrupt. But they were resilient, they recovered their balance with admirable aplomb. Usually they were pulling his leg before he'd realised they no longer needed nursing. They weren't a bad lot.

Even the staff were easy enough. Even the three women for whom he hadn't been prepared. Jane Darrill, the junior geographer, could be a bit offhand and you-be-damned when she liked, but of course she was very young, not above twenty-five. Tom was twenty-six himself.

It was Jane who had suggested he should move out to the village of Comerford for living quarters, and put him in touch with the Becks, who had a house too big for them, and an income, on the whole, rather too small.

'If you're going to be a countryman,' said Jane, with her suspiciously private smile, that always made his hackles rise a little in the conviction that she was somehow making fun of him, 'you might as well go the whole hog and be a proper one. Come and be a borderer, like me. Comerford is the real thing. This dump is rapidly becoming a suburb of Birmingham.'

That was an exaggeration, or perhaps a prophecy. Jane was blessed, or cursed, with an appearance of extreme competence and cheerfulness, round-faced, fair-complexioned, vigorous, pretty enough if she hadn't filed her brusque manner to an aggressive edge in order to keep the Lower Sixth in healthy awe of her. Sometimes she liked to offset the impression by leaning perversely towards cynicism and gloom.

Tom looked out of the common-room window upon a Comerbourne which appeared to his urban eye small, limited, antique and charming. He could see the tops of the limes in the riverside gardens, a thin ribbon of silver, the balustrade of the nearer bridge over the

Comer. A provincial capital of the minor persuasion, still clinging to its weekly country market, still drawing in, to buy and sell, half the housewives and farmwives of a quarter of Wales as well as Midshire itself. Back-streets straight out of the Middle Ages, a few superb Tudor pubs, a dwindling county society more blood-ridden and exclusive than he'd thought possible in the mid-twentieth century, still conscientiously freezing out intruders, and pathetically unaware that its island of privilege had long since become an island of stagnation in a backwater of impotence, and was crumbling away piecemeal from under its large, sensibly-shod feet; and round it and over it, oblivious of it, swarmed the busy, brisk, self-confident rush of the new people, the new powers, business and banking and industry and administration, advancing upon an expanding future, brushing with faint impatience and no ceremony past the petrified remnants of a feudal past.

That was what he saw in Comerbourne; and to tell the truth. the encroachments of the industrial Midlands into the fossilised life of this remote capital rather attracted than repelled him. But he'd never lived in a village, and the idea still had a (probably quite misleading) charm about it. He thought vaguely of country pursuits and country functions, and saw himself adopted into a village society which would surely not be averse to finding a place for a young and presentable male, whatever his origins. He could have the best of both worlds, with Comerbourne only a couple of miles away, near enough to be reached easily when he needed it, far enough away to be easily evaded when he had no need of it. And it's always a good idea to put at least a couple of miles between yourself and your work in the evenings.

'What are these Becks like?' he asked, half in love with the idea but cautious still.

'Oh, ordinary. Middle-aged, retired, a bit stodgy, maybe. Terribly conscientious, they'll probably worry about whether they're doing enough for you. Not amusing, but then you needn't rely on them for your amusement, need you? Mr Beck used to teach at the Modern until a couple of years ago. He never made it to a headship. Not headmaster material,' she said rather dryly. Tom Kenyon, confident, clever and ambitious, was obvious headmaster material, and, moreover, knew it very well.

'He hasn't got a son here, has he?' asked Tom sharply, suddenly shaken by the thought of having his landlady's darling under his feet, with a fond mamma pushing persuasively behind. He wished it back the moment it was out. A silly question. Jane wouldn't be such a fool as to land him in any such situation, it would be against all her teacher's instincts, and they were shrewd and effective enough. And blurting out the horrid thought had only exposed himself. But she merely gave him the edge of a deflationary smile, and rattled away half a dozen rock specimens into the back of her table drawer.

'No sons at all, don't worry. "He has but one daughter, an uncommon handsome gel".'

'Go on!' He wasn't particularly interested, but he produced the spark in the eye and the sharpening glow of attention that was demanded of him, and straightened his tie with exaggeratedly fatuous care. 'How old?'

'Eighteen, I think! She was seventeen last spring, anyhow, when the row—' She frowned and swallowed the word, shoving away papers; but he hadn't been listening closely enough to demand or even miss the rest of the sentence.

'Eighteen, and uncommon handsome! That does it! They won't look at me, they'll be after some old gorgon of a maiden aunt for a lodger.'

Jane turned her fashionable shock-head of mangled brown hair and grinned at him derisively. 'Come off it!' she said. 'You're not that dangerous.' It had been a joke, and all that, but she needn't have sounded so crushingly sure of herself. Girls had never given him much trouble, except by clinging too long and tightly, and at the wrong times.

'What's her name?' he asked.

'Annet.'

'Not Annette?'

'Not Annette. Just Annet. Plain Annet.'

'What's plain about it? Annet Beck. That's a witch's name.'

'Annet is a witch, I shouldn't wonder,' Jane looked thoughtfully back into the past again, and refrained from calling attention to what she saw. Witch or not, neither of them was greatly concerned with Annet; not then. 'Go and take a look at the place, anyhow,' said Jane, offhand as usual. 'If you don't like the look of the border solitude, you needn't take it any further.'

And he had gone, and he had taken the recommended look at Comerford. Along the riverside road, through coppices scarlet and gold with autumn, and thinning to filigree; out of sight and memory of the town, between farms rising gently from water-meadows to stubble to heath pasture, over undulations of open ground purple with heather, and down to the river again.

The village closed in its ford from either bank, a compact huddle of old houses, considerably larger than he had expected, and comparatively sophisticated, with beautifully converted cottages and elegant gardens on its fringes that told plainly of pioneering commuters or wealthy retired business people in possession. The town had, in fact, reached Comerford, it was almost a small town itself. He looked at it, and was disappointed. But when he lifted his eyes to look over it, and saw the surging animal backs of the enfolding hills, time ran backwards over his head like silk unwinding from a dropped spool.

Ridge beyond ridge, receding into pallor and mist, filmed over with the oblique beams of light splayed from behind broken copper cloud, Wales withdrew into fine rain, while England lay in quivering, cool sunlight. Meadows and dark, low hedges climbed the slopes. Away on the dwindling flank of the hog-back to north-westward the horizontal scoring of ancient mine levels showed plainly. Lead, probably, worked out long since, or at any rate long since abandoned. Round the crest of the same hill the unquestionable green earthworks of an Iron Age fort, crisp and new-looking as though it had been moulded only yesterday. The long green heavings of turf, the deep ditches, the few broken, black mine-chimneys and the gunmetal-coloured heaps of old spoil nestled together without conflict, and the village with its smart new façades and its congealing shopping streets settled comfortably in the lee of the scratched Roman workings, and thought no wrong. All time was relative here; or perhaps all time was contemporaneous. Nothing that was native was alien or uncanny here, though it came from the pre-dawn twilight before man stood upright and walked.

He drove through Comerford, village or town, whatever it was, and the hills melted and reassembled constantly as he drove, drawn back like filmy green curtains to uncover further recessions of crest beyond crest. Arthur Beck's house was beyond, shaken loose from the last hand-hold of the village itself, a quarter of a mile along a narrow but metalled road that served a succession of border farms. On his right the river narrowed to a trickle of trout-stream in its flat meadows along the valley floor, winding bewilderingly, the hills grown brown and fawn with bleached grass and sedge and coarse heather behind. On his left a long, bare ridge of hill crowded the road implacably nearer and nearer to Wales. A ring of gnarled, half-naked trees, by their common age and their regular arrangement clearly planted by man, showed like a top-knot on the crest. One outcrop of rock broke the blonde turf halfway up, another had shown for a few moments over the comb of the ridge, a little apart from the trees on the summit. Sheep-paths, trampled out daintily over centuries by ancestors of these handsome, fearless hill-sheep he was just learning to know for Cluns and Kerrys, traced necklets round the slopes, level above level like the courses of a step-pyramid.

For the first time he was driving by the Hallowmount. The mid-afternoon sun was on the entire barren, rustling, pale brown slope of it, and yet he felt something of shadow and age and silence like a coolness cutting him off from the sun, not unpleasantly, not threateningly, rather as if he was naturally excluded from what embraced all other creatures here. He was the alien, not resented, not menaced, simply not belonging. And suddenly he was aware of the quietness and the permanence of this utter solitude, which seemed unpopulated, and yet had surely been inhabited ever since men began to tame beasts, before the first experimental grass-seeds were ever deliberately sown, before the first stone scratched the earth, and the developing tools were smoothed to a rich polish in the manipulating hands of the first artisans.

A turn to the right, just before the track plunged into half-grown plantations of conifers, brought him down towards the river again, past the gate of Wastfield farm, through a small coppice to Arthur Beck's gate at the end of the farm wall.

There it was: Fairford. An old house, or rather a new house made from two old stone cottages, mellow, amber-coloured stone from higher up the valley. A walled garden in the inevitable autumn chaos, a glimpse of rather ragged lawn, a tangle of trees too big for a garden, but beautiful. Why should he care that the leaves would be a nuisance, tread into a decaying mush all over the paths, and silt down into a rotten cement in the guttering? He wouldn't have to maintain the place; all he would have to do would be live in it and enjoy it. He imagined the summer here, and he was enchanted. Even the name wasn't an affectation, there was a fair ford only fifty yards on, where the river poured in a smooth silvery sheet above clear beds of amber and agate pebbles, bright as jewels in the sun. The masonry of the original cottages looked – how old? – three centuries at le The place had probably been Fairford ever since the advan of the Danes clawed a toehold on the Welsh bank of the river here, only to be rolled back fifty miles into England, and never thrust so far again.

He was almost sure then that he would come and lodge here; but some instinct of caution and perversity turned him back from opening the gate then and advancing to the massy door. He parked the car by the open grass along the riverside instead, and went for a long walk up the flank of the hill until it was time to drive back into Comerbourne.

'Not bad,' he said to Jane, in the common-room during the next free period they shared, 'but I don't know. All right in the summer, but a bit back-of-beyond for a bad winter, I should say. You could get snowed-up there for weeks.'

'They ought to charge you extra for that as an amenity,' said Jane, bitterly contemplating some gem in the homework of Four B, who were not her brightest form. 'Imagine having a cast-iron alibi for contracting out of this madhouse for weeks at a time! But don't kid yourself, my boy. They kept that road open even in 1947. The Wastfield tractors see to that. Snow or no snow, nobody gets away with anything around here.'

She didn't ask him what he thought of doing, or he might, even then, have gone off in the opposite direction, sure that everybody has an angle, and she couldn't be totally disinterested. She lived in Comerford herself, he knew that, and hadn't failed to allow for one obvious possibility. But she showed no personal interest in him; and even if she was biding her time she wouldn't find him easy to keep tabs on, with her family's cottage a quarter of a mile this side the village, and Fairford well out on the opposite side. He'd had plenty of practice in evading girls he didn't want to see, as well as in cornering those he did. No, he needn't worry about Jane.

So he went back to Fairford on the Saturday afternoon. The westering sun smiled on him all the way along that journey back into pre-history, confirming his will to stay. By the time he drove back the dusk had closed on the Hallowmount, and black clouds covered the hills of Wales; a chill wind drove up the valley, crying in the new plantation. And he might have changed his mind, even then, if he hadn't been already lost from the moment when he rattled the knocker at Fairford, and listened to the rapid, light footsteps within as someone came to open the door to him.

He was lost, then and for ever; because it was Annet who opened the door.

There is a kind of beauty that produces wolf-whistles, and another kind of beauty that creates silence all about it, taking the voices out of men's mouths and the breath out of their throats. Nobody but Annet had ever struck Tom Kenyon dumb. He lived in the same house with her, he'd been rubbing shoulders with her now almost daily for half a term, and still he went softly for awe of her, and the words that would have come to him so glibly with a girl who meant nothing to him ebbed away clean out of mind when he was face to face with this girl. And yet why? She was flesh and blood like anyone else. Wasn't she?

(But why, why should she be climing the Hallowmount in the rain and the murk in a dank October twilight? Distant and strange and elusive as she was, what could draw her up there at such an hour of such a day?)

She was not much above middle height for her eighteen years, but so slender that she looked tall, and taller still because of the lofty way she carried her small head, tilted a little back to let the great, soft masses of her hair fall back from her face. When she wanted to hide she sat with head bent, and the twin black curtains, blue-black, burnished, smooth and heavy, drew protective shadows over her face. She wore it cut in a long bob, not quite to her shoulders, uncurled, uncoloured, unfashionable, parted over her left temple, the ends curving under to touch her neck. He never saw her play with it; the most she ever did was lift a hand to thrust it back out of her way; and yet every gleaming hair clung to the sheaf as threads of silk cling, alive and vital, and even after streaming in the wind the heavy coils flowed back massively like water into their constant order and repose.

Between the wings of this resplendent helmet her face was oval, delicate and still, with fine bones that impressed their pure, taut shapes through the creamy flesh. Passionate, eloquent bones, if the envelope that enclosed them had not imposed its own ivory silence upon them. There was little red in her face, and yet she was not pale; when he saw her first she had the gloss of the summer still upon her, and was tinted like honey. Her mouth was grave and full, often sullen, often sad, quick to smile, but never at any joke he could share, or any pleasure he could afford her. And her eyes were the deep brilliant, burning blue the sun had just found in her coat on the crest of the Hallowmount, the blue of the darkest gentians, between blue-black lashes as dark as her hair.

She had showed him the room, and he had taken the room, hardly aware of its pleasant furnishings, seeing only the movement of her hand as she opened the door, and the long, courteous, unsmiling blue stare that had never wavered as she waited for him to speak. Her own voice was deep and quiet, and only now did he realise how few words he had ever heard it speak, to him or to anyone. She moved like a true eighteen-year-old, with a rapid, coltish grace. What she did about the house was done well and ungrudgingly, but with a certain impatience and a certain resignation, as though she were making ritual gestures which she knew to be indispensable, but in the efficacy of which she did not believe. And her attendance on him was of the same kind; it hurt and bewildered him to know it, but he could not choose but know.

For him life in Fairford had only gradually taken shape as a frame for Annet, and all the kaleidoscope of other faces that peopled his new world was only a galaxy in attendance upon her. Arthur Beck, handsome in a feeble, pedantic way, wisps of thin hair carefully arranged over his high crown, glasses askew on his precipitous nose, bore about with him always an air of vague and puzzled disappointment, and a precarious and occasionally pompous dignity. Ageing people shouldn't have children, when they were doomed to be always so hopelessly far from them. Even the mother must have been nearly forty at the time. Who can jump clean over forty years?

Mrs Beck, solider and more decisive than her husband, was one of the plainest women Tom had ever seen, and yet revealed a startling echo of Annet's beauty sometimes in a look or a movement. Dark hair without lustre, waved crisply and immovably, dark blue eyes faded into a dull greyish colour, like blue denim after a lifetime of washing, an anxious face, kind but troubled, a flat, practical voice.

Dull, impenetrable people, at least to a newcomer with more self-assurance than patience. And that incredible bud of their age flowered with face turned away from them, as though her sun had always risen elsewhere.

The children of ageing marriages, so he had heard, are often difficult and strange, like deprived children; in a sense they are deprived, a lost generation cuts them off from their roots, they have grandparents for parents. These were not even young grandparents at heart, but dim, discouraged and old. Sometimes gleams of wistful scholarship showed in Beck, and brought a momentary eagerness back to his face. Mrs Beck kept up with village society, and dressed like a county gentlewoman, but for God's sake, what good was that when county gentlewomen were themselves a generation out of date, living anachronisms, museum pieces even here, where the past, the genuine past, was as real and valid as tomorrow?

At first he had thought, with his usual healthy confidence in his own charms, that he would bring a breath of fresh air into Annet's enclosed life, and provide her with the young company she needed. But in a week or two he had found that she was, in fact, almost never in, and appeared to have gallingly little need of him. She had a job that took her away during the day; she acted as secretary to Mrs Blacklock at Cwm Hall, a privilege which gave great satisfaction to her mother, if she herself accepted it without noticeable emotion. The lady needed a secretary, for she ran, it seemed to Tom, everything in sight, every local society, every committee, every charity, every social event. Nothing could take place in and around Comerford without Regina's blessing. Her patronage of Annet, therefore, was balm to Mrs Beck's heart. Annet, as Tom heard from various sources – but never from Annet! – would have liked to uproot herself from this backwater and go and get a job in London, but the Becks were terrified to let her, and stubbornly refused to consent. Maybe because they knew they were hopelessly out of touch with her, and were afraid to let her out of their sight; maybe because she was their ewe lamb, and they couldn't bear to part with her. She was safe with Mrs Blacklock. Regina was inordinately careful and kind. Regina never let her come home alone if she was at all late, but sent her in the car. Regina wouldn't let her strike up any undesirable acquaintances, Regina saw to it that she knew everyone who was presentable and of good repute.

For God's sake, thought Tom impotently, she was eighteen, wasn't she? And intelligent and capable, or the Blacklocks wouldn't have kept her. And did she behave as if she needed a chaperone?

She lived a busy enough life. Choir practice on Friday nights, dances in Comerbourne on Saturdays, or cinemas, and Myra Gibbons from Wastfield usually went with her. Their escorts to dances were vetted carefully; Mrs Beck had old-fashioned notions. But the sorry fact remained that Annet had no need of Tom

Kenyon. There wasn't a young man in Comerford who hadn't at some time paid tentative court to her. There wasn't a young man in Comerford who had got further with her than he found himself getting.

Remote, alien and beautiful, Annet floated upon the tide of events, submitted to parental control without comment or protest, and kept her own secrets. He didn't know her at all; he never would.

The rest revolved about her. They had made him welcome, adopted him readily into their activities, found him a part to play; more than she ever had. Yet he saw them only by her light, at least those nearest to her: the Blacklocks, the vicar with his hearty voice and his uncertain, deprecating eyes, the Gibbons family, all the population of Fairford. Lucky for him that some of the denizens of his Sixth lived in Comerford, and their parents opened their doors to him readily: Miles Mallindine's young, modern parents, Dominic Felse's policeman father and pretty, shrewd, amusing mother. Policeman was the wrong term, strictly speaking; George Felse was a Detective-Inspector in the Midshire CID, recently promoted from Detective-Sergeant. The progeny of these pleasant couples tolerated him and kept their lordly distance, behaving with princely punctilio if they were left to entertain him; the parents welcomed him and never worried him. Privately they laughed a little, affectionately, at their own sons. Tom found them a pleasure and a relief. And they delivered him, at least, from feeling himself dependent upon Annet's charity, when he had dreamed of extending to her the largesse of his own.

He drove through the dim rain, and he saw all the procession of new faces, one by one, passing before him. But always Annet, always Annet. And always with gentian eyes fixed ahead, and face turned away from him.

Eve Mallindine had given him a lift once, when the Mini was in the garage for servicing, and run him into town from the Comerford bus-stop. It was pure chance that he had mentioned Annet to her; if anything connected with Annet could be called chance. More probably he was so full of her that he couldn't keep her name out of his mouth. Had he even betrayed that he was jealous of the young men who danced with her at the Saturday hops in town, and resented her mother's prim care of her? He was horribly afraid he might have done. Well for him it was Mrs Mallindine. Everything a sixth-former's mother should be, young and sophisticated and pretty, with a twinkle in her artfully-blue-shadowed eyes, and legs like flappers used to have before the fad for impossible shoes spoiled their gait and made them the same thickness from ankle to knee. Incidentally, she wore stiletto heels herself. How did she manage to walk like a proud filly in them? And how on earth did she drive so well?

She looked along her shoulder at him briefly, and returned her golden-brown eyes to the road ahead. She pondered for a moment, and then she said: 'I'd better tell you, Tom. Do you mind if I call you Tom? After all, you're almost *in loco parentis* to my brat.'

He hadn't minded. He couldn't remember when he'd minded anything less. Just sitting beside her was enough to make him feel a few inches taller, and he needed every lift he could get, when he remembered Annet.

'Barbara Beck isn't so mad as she looks to you,' said Eve Mallindine, with a wry little smile. 'Annet nearly made a run for it, early last spring. With my blessed hopeful. And don't you dare let him know I told you, or I'll wring your neck. But you wouldn't, you're not the kind. Excuse a mother's partiality. I wouldn't like him hurt. And if I'd been seventeen and male, I'd have jumped at the chance, too. They didn't get any farther than Comerbourne station. Bill got wind of it, somehow – I never asked him how, I was far too busy pretending everything was normal and I hadn't noticed the row going on. Bill took Annet home, and then brought the pup back and shut himself in the bedroom with him. I'm sure they both behaved with the greatest dignity – not even a raised voice between 'em! Miles was past seventeen, and nearly six feet high, and so damned grown-up – well, you know him! Poor Bill must have felt at a hopeless disadvantage – if he hadn't been in a flaming temper. I don't know which of them I was sorriest for. I kept out of it, and made a cheese soufflé. It seemed the most sensible thing to do, they are both crazy about my cheese soufflés, and even a broken-hearted lover has to eat.' She cast a glance at him again, even more briefly, and grinned. 'They argued for an hour, and neither would give an inch. Poor darlings, they're so alike. Don't you think so?'

He didn't. He saw Miles Mallindine every time he looked at her. Miles wasn't the most unattractive member of the Upper Sixth, not by a long way. But all he said was, somewhat constrainedly: 'Where were they heading?'

'They had one-way tickets for London. Poor lambs, they were twenty minutes early for the train. A mistake! The trouble I had, getting Miles thawed out after that catastrophe. It's awfully difficult, you know, Tom, for a seventeen-year-old to believe one doesn't blame him. But I didn't. Would you? You've seen Annet.'

'No,' he said; with difficulty, but it sounded all right. 'No, I wouldn't blame him.'

'Good for you, Tom, I knew you were human. But poor Bill has a social conscience, you see. I only have a human one. They made each other pretty sore. Bill felt Miles ought to come right out and confide in him. And Miles wouldn't. They ate the soufflé, though,' she added comfortably, rightly recollecting this as reassurance that her menfolk were not seriously disabled, physically or emotionally. 'And to tell the truth, I laced the coffee. It seemed a good thing to do.'

Was he allowed to ask questions? And if so, how far could he go? There must be a limit, and the most interesting questions probably stepped well over it. Such as: why? Why should Miles find it necessary to plan a runaway affair with Annet? Many escorts a good deal less presentable were allowed to take the girl about, provided they called for her respectably at the house, and were vetted and found reliable. The Becks wouldn't have frozen out a good-looking boy with wealthy parents, excellent prospects, and charm enough, when he pleased, to call the bird from the tree. If he'd wanted Annet, he had only to convince the girl, her parents would certainly have smiled upon him from the beginning. So why? Why run? Apparently there was no question of previous misbehaviour, no girl-in-trouble complications that made a getaway and a quick marriage desirable.

'It's all blown over now, of course,' said Eve, slowing at the first traffic lights on the edge of Comerbourne. 'Nobody else ever treated it as more than a romantic escapade. But Mrs Beck still thinks Miles planned her poor girl's ruin. I thought I'd better tell you how the land lay, you might feel a bit baffled if it came up out of the blue.'

Somehow it was too late by then for the 'why' question. All he could say was: 'And is he still – I mean, has he got over her by now?'

'I don't know. I don't ask him. What he wants to tell he'll tell, what he doesn't nobody can make him. Me, I don't try. But getting over Annet might be quite an arduous convalescence, don't you think so?'

'It well might,' said Tom, with brittle care. She was a dangerous woman, she might see all too readily that Miles wasn't the only chronic case.

'Ah, well,' she said cheerfully, putting her foot down as the orange changed to green, 'he'll be going up to Queens' next year, and he'll have more than enough to keep him busy. I hear he's coming camping with you next weekend. Thirty juniors to ride herd on, he says. Heaven help you all!'

'We'll survive,' said Tom. If you were the youngest male member of staff, and owned an anorak and a pair of clinkered boots, you were a sitter for all the outdoor assignments, and it was your bounden duty to look martyred and moan about it. No matter how much you actually enjoyed skippering a party of boys up a mountain or under canvas, you could never admit it. 'Drop me along here by Cooks', would you? I've got to see about some maps I ordered.'

And as he got out of the car and leaned to offer thanks for his ride, glad to be seen with her, complemented by the greetings he shared with her, the amazing woman smiled up at him confidently and calmly, and said: 'You won't take them on the Hallowmount, will you?'

She wasn't even going to wait for an answer, so completely did she trust him to accept and understand what she had said. She gave him a little wave of her hand, and expected him to withdraw head and hand and close the door; and when he didn't, she sat looking up at him with a quizzical, slightly surprised smile, no doubt thinking him as endearingly male and stupid as her own pig-headed pair.

'Not take them on the Hallowmount?' said Tom cautiously, to be sure he had not mistaken her.

'No – but naturally you wouldn't. Silly of me!'

'Why not, though? Or is that a stupid question? And why naturally not?' He had been feeling so close to her, so comfortable with her, and suddenly he felt alien and out of his depth. There she sat, in her amber-and-bracken autumn suit that wouldn't have looked abashed in Bond Street, with her smooth brown beehive of hair and her long, elegant legs and incredibly fragile and impractical shoes, as modern as tomorrow, as secure and confident as money and education and travel and native temperament could make her; and without mystery or constraint, as though she were reminding her husband to lock the garage door, she warned him off from taking his week-end camp on the Hallowmount.

'Oh, we just wouldn't,' she said, vaguely smiling, eyes wondering at him a little, but making allowances for him, too, as the incomer, the novice in these parts. 'We just don't. I wouldn't worry too much myself, but some of their mothers might. You weren't thinking of going there, were you?'

'Well, no, I wasn't. Too exposed, anyhow, for October. I was thinking of taking them up between the Westlyns.'

'Good! Fine!' said Eve Mallindine, satisfied, and slammed the door shut. She looked up and smiled at him through the open window. 'No need to go yelling for trouble, is there?' she said serenely, and shot away up Castle Wylde before the lights at the Cross could change colour again.

And he had not taken them on the Hallowmount. Once, he suspected – and the glance back at himself when younger was revealing – he would have gone there on principle, having been warned to keep away. Not now. Besides, she hadn't pressed him, hadn't exactly warned him off. She'd merely indicated to him that the plate was hot, so that he shouldn't burn his fingers. She'd taken it for granted that no more was necessary where a sane and sensible adult was concerned. And whether it could be considered a sign of good sense and maturity or not, he hadn't taken them on the Hallowmount.

But in the gathering dark over the remnants of the fire, up there in the shelter between the ridges of the Westlyns, with one ear cocked for sounds of forbidden horseplay from the Three B tents, he had turned his head to stare thoughtfully at the distant ridge of the Hallowmount, with its top-knot of trees and rocks black against the milky spaces between the stars. And he had asked the son what he had never had time to ask the mother.

'How did it get its name – the Hallowmount? And why is it taken for granted one doesn't take boys camping there?'

'Is it?' said Miles vaguely, flat on his back on a spread ground-sheet, with the faint glow of the fire falling aslant across his smooth, high-boned cheek and broad forehead. Mild wonder stirred in his tone and recalled Eve's look and voice, but he wasn't paying very much attention. 'I suppose it would be, come to think of it. They wouldn't mind by daylight, but at night they'd probably think it wasn't the thing to do. On the principle that you never know, you know.'

'I don't know,' said Tom. 'You tell me. What about the name, for instance?'

'I don't think anybody knows much about the name, to be honest, but a lot of them will tell you they do. It goes back into pre-history—'

'Or thereabouts,' said Dominic Felse dubiously, demurring at such imprecision in his friend.

'Let's not argue about a few hundred years. Anyhow, whenever it was, we don't know how it arose. Something not quite canny. But all this region and its inhabitants are a bit uncanny, I suppose.' He opened his eyes wide at the sky and sat up, feeling it, perhaps, hardly dignified to conduct a discussion from the supine position. 'Take the old lead mines,' he said thoughtfully. 'There couldn't be anything more practical, but there couldn't be anything more haunted, either. We have knockers – like in the Cornish tin mines. And Wild Edric's down there, too, with his fairy wife Godda. And half a dozen others, for all we know. It's the same with the Hallowmount. Some say it's "hallow" because it was holy, a place of sacrificial mysteries in the pre-Christian cults. And some say it's really "hollow", and not for nothing. They say people have stumbled on the way inside sometimes, and vanished.'

'Or come back years later,' said Dominic helpfully, 'like Kilmeny, with no memory of the time between, and as young as when they disappeared.'

'Oh, that's common to every country in Europe,' said Tom, disappointed. 'Nearly every hill that has a striking shape or has been the site of occupation from very early times gets that tale attached to it. Are you sure King Arthur isn't down there, waiting for somebody to blow a horn and wake him up?'

'No, sir, we use Wild Edric instead round these parts, we don't need any other saviours.' That was Milvers, the third of his only-slightly-dragooned sixth-form volunteers for this week-end chore. A clever one, Milvers, stuffed with the history and legends of the borders, all the more because he was not himself a borderer. He might be able to tell more than Miles Mallindine about the documentation of the Hallowmount; but nothing he could say would be as revealing, as perfectly direct and simple as Miles's mild: 'All this region and its inhabitants are a bit uncanny, I suppose.' Without pretensions and without reluctance he had included himself in that verdict, in just the same way as his mother dealt herself in. They found nothing incongruous in having one foot in the twentieth century and one in the roots of time.

'And some say a witch-coven used to meet there,' said Milvers, warming to the assignment. 'Did you know that outcrop of rock is known locally as the Altar?'

He hadn't known, but it didn't surprise him. Just a place of acquired ill-omen, after all, an accumulation of ordinary super-stitions.

'So that's it,' he said. 'Just bad medicine.'

'Oh, no, not really. Not *bad*. Any more than lightning's good or bad. Or fire. Or the dead.' Miles straightened and quivered to the sudden energy of his own thoughts, the thick brown lashes rolling back widely from bright, intent eyes. 'Did somebody tell you it was bad luck, or something?'

Tom told him, in a strictly edited version, about that lift into town. 'Your mother evidently thought it was a place to fight shy of. I suppose that's the legacy of the witches.'

'I don't believe there ever were any witches. Just that chain of lives going back so unbelievably far, and a kind of impress left from them all—' He couldn't find the words he wanted, and wouldn't descend to substitutes; he shut his arms helplessly round his knees, and rocked and scowled, still mining within his mind for the means of fluency. When not stirred, he could be a little lazy; it was an effort getting into gear.

'Then why should everyone be afraid of it?'

Dominic looked at Miles, and Miles looked at Dominic. Tom had seen just such exchanges pass before, and the two mute faces relax in absolute agreement, as now. After that it was always a toss-up which of them would do the talking, but it was a certainty he would be talking for both.

'We're not *afraid*,' said Miles, carefully and kindly keeping his smile in check. 'Why should we be? We were born here. We're in the chain, we don't have to be afraid of it. We belong to it.'

'In awe of it, then.'

They considered that with one more bright and rapid glance, and as one man accepted it.

'Oh, in awe, yes, but that's quite another thing, isn't it?'

'Is it so far from being afraid?' said Tom, unconvinced.

Miles scrambled to his knees, leaning over the faint glow of the fire;

206

in a little while now they would have to smother it for the night. 'When my mother drove you into town, did she get caught at the lights by the technical college?'

'Yes, I remember they were at red.' He saw no connection yet, but here again was the twentieth century taking hands simply and naturally with the primeval darkness, and he felt the continuity tightening, and his palms pricked with the foreknowledge of a revelation that would leave him mute.

'And was my mother afraid?'

Patiently, willing to learn – and wasn't that something new for him, too? – Tom said: 'Of course not.'

'No, sir, of course not. You're not afraid of traffic lights at red, it would be silly, wouldn't it? But you don't drive through them, either – do you?'

And he hadn't been able to pin any of them down more precisely than that, until Jane Darrill handed him over to the mercies of the Archaeological Society. Basely and deliberately, as it turned out, for she must have known very well that once they had received him as an enquirer they wouldn't let him escape until he had imbibed every word that existed in manuscript or print about the Hallowmount. They wrangled among themselves, but they spared him nothing.

Well, he'd asked for it! The vicar primed him with the parish records, and dragged him along to Miss Winslow, who kept the local archives, and Miss Winslow in turn hustled them both into the damp, dark but lovely splendours of Cwm Hall, which was middle Elizabethan black-and-white, and excellent of its period.

Regina Blacklock was president of the Archaeological Society as of

most such bodies, and Peter Blacklock functioned as usual, good-humouredly and resignedly, as secretary and her dutiful echo. The weight of birth and position and money was all on her side, it was rather overdoing things that she should also have so strong and decisive a character. Who could stand against her? She was an authority on everything to do with Comerford and district; where the folklore of the borders was concerned, what she said went. She poured details over Tom's head in a merciless stream, buried him under evidence of the Druidic goings-on which had once enlivened the Hallowmount on midsummer night and at the solstices. The vicar, pink with enthusiasm, acted as chorus whenever she drew breath. Devotees both, and no need to suspect that their passion was anything but genuine. But somehow Miles had been more convincing in his vagueness, and acceptance, and serenity.

'You must go to the Borough Library, Mr Kenyon,' said Regina, radiant with helpfulness and ardour, 'you really must. I'll telephone Mr Carling in the morning and tell him to expect you, and he'll have the Welsh chronicles ready for you whenever you like to call him and arrange a visit. And he has the aerial photographs of the Iron Age Fort – Maeldun's Ring, you know, the one on Cleave. You should look at those, they're a revelation. Peter has a few here, but not all. Peter, darling, where are those enlargements now?'

And Peter darling brought them. Blessedly he brought a large whisky and soda in the other hand, and a small, mild, rueful smile that warmed his long, rather tired face into a very acceptable sympathy. A tall, slender, quiet man, of spare, gentle movements and thoughtful face. Goodlooking, too, in a somewhat disconsolate way, and even his mournfulness enlivened now and then by fleeting gleams of humour, affectionate when his eye dwelt upon his formidable wife, but satirical, too. They appeared to understand each other very well, but it was inevitable that she should be the one on top, since she was the last of the Wayne-Morgans, and proprietress of half this valley and one flank of the Hallowmount. Peter Blacklock had been a local solicitor by profession, though he didn't practise now, being fully employed in running his wife's estates, and making, as everyone agreed, a conscientious job of it.

How old would they be? Forty-five maybe. Not more than a year or two between them, and it could be either way. She was a very striking woman, if only she wouldn't work so hard at it; but that tremendous energy had to go somewhere, and if there were only small channels at hand to receive it they were bound to get overcharged. She expounded the history of the border as if it was the future of man. Eve Mallindine wouldn't have thought her forebears anything particular to shout about.

How well he remembered that evening. Regina talked with passion, leaning towards him across the deep, blonde sheepskin rug; a big woman, red-haired but greying a little, interesting bands of silver in the short, russet hair; a broad, rather highly-coloured, energetic face, smooth and blonde, ripe blue eyes, arched brows plucked rather too thinly; a plump, full, firm body in good country tweeds. And Peter Blacklock in his elderly, leathery-elbowed sports jacket and Bedford cords, comfortable and distinguished, as though he had been born to the game. And the vicar, a contemporary, hard and athletic in body, eager and juvenile in mind, genuine echo to Mrs Blacklock's full song. There were no pretences here, these were the real people. Tom had never known such, and bludgeoned as he was, he could not fail to be fascinated by them.

And in the background, of course, distant, indifferent and aware, but as though her soul remained absent, Annet. Working a little late that night, as she sometimes did, bored, probably, with them all, waiting to go home. Large-eyed, motionless of face, thinking of God knew what, she watched them all and was herself so withdrawn that she might have been in another world. The heavy, soft curve of her hair shadowing her face was like the undulation of one of the cords that held the world in balance. The whisky had been so sympathetically large that it affected his vision, and endowed her with, or perhaps only uncovered in her, cosmic significances.

'In the seventeenth century,' said the vicar, glowing with ardour, 'we're told there was a witch-coven in these parts that used to meet on the hill-top.' His voice sounded somehow light-weight and breathless, emerging from that big, lean, shapely body. I'll bet he was a Rugby blue, thought Tom inconsequently, and felt a small shock again at the uncertainty and shallowness of the face. For all his regular features, he looked more like a sixth-form schoolboy than sixth-form schoolboys themselves do nowadays. And why should he be so anxious to get in his Black Mass and his coven and his devil? But of course, he had, in a way, a vested interest in these basphemies. Where would his profession be without them?

'Coven, nonsense!' said Regina roundly. 'There isn't a particle of evidence for that tale, and I don't believe a word of it.'

'But how can you dismiss Hayley's diary so lightly? One of my predecessors in office, Mr Kenyon, the incumbent in the mid-seventeenth century, left a very circumstantial journal—'

'Your predecessor was a demented witch-hunter,' objected Regina firmly. 'He left a reputation, as well as a journal, and personally I think I'd rather be called a witch than the things some of his contemporaries called him. By all accounts he'd have had half the village searched and hanged if he'd had his way, but luckily the local justices knew him too well, and were pretty easy-going country fellows themselves, so he didn't do much damage. But *don't* quote him as evidence! No, Mr Kenyon,' she said, fixing Tom with a smiling but authoritative blue eye, 'the occasional people who strayed into fairyland, or limbo, or whatever is inside magic mountains, I'll stand for. I don't mean they necessarily happened, these Rip-Van-Winkle vanishings, but I do accept that people here *believed* they happened. But witches, no! There never have been and there never will be any witches on the Hallowmount!'

And that was the sum of what he had got out of the evening, that and the fifteen minutes of unbelievable anguish and bliss on the way home, with Annet silent beside him in the passenger seat. That was the night he began to realise fully that this was different, that he couldn't make use of it and wasn't capable of disentangling himself from it; that he would never get over her, and never again be as he had been before he had known her. What he had thought to be a mild infatuation, only a little more serious than half a dozen others he had lived through and exploited, had grown and deepened out of knowledge, until it filled all his world with its new sensitivity, inordinately painful and disturbing. Annet was like that. He should have known at sight of her. But at sight of her it had already been too late to back away.

And then this afternoon, half-term Thursday. He had had a free last period, and got away early to pick up his case and set out on the drive home; and as he slid out of the car at the gate Annet had come out in her dark-blue coat, a nylon rain-scarf over her hair, three letters in her hand. At sight of him she had checked and recoiled very slightly, and the kind, careful, palpable veil of withdrawal had closed over her face. She knew his wants and was sorry; she did not want him, and was a little sorry for that, too, or so it seemed to him. If she had not liked him she would not have troubled to evade him, she would not have shrunk from so small an encounter, but she liked him, and preferred not to have to remind him at every touch that she had nothing to give him that could ever satisfy him.

'You'll get wet,' he said fatuously, 'it's coming on to rain. Let me take them for you.'

'I don't mind,' she said. 'I want a breath of air, I don't mind the rain.'

'I'll run you down, then, at least let me do that.'

'Thank you, but no, please don't. I just want to walk.' She saw the next plea already quivering on his lips, and staved it off rapidly and gently. 'Alone,' she said, the deep voice making it an apology and an entreaty, while her eyes stood him off with the blue brilliance of lapis lazuli in an inlaid Egyptian head.

'I'm sorry!' she said. 'Don't be hurt. I should only be horribly unsociable if you did come, and I'd rather not.'

She had even gone to the trouble to find several small, kind things to say to him, she who had no small-talk, softening her enforced rejection of him – and why had he forced it? – with reminders of his family waiting at home, of the long journey before him, and the advisability of making an early start and taking advantage of the remaining daylight to get as far as the M1. And he had followed her lead gratefully, glad to return to firmer ground.

'Your people must be looking forward so much to having you home again.'

He said he supposed they probably were. What could he say?

'Have a pleasant journey! And a nice week-end!'

'Thank you! And you, too. See you on Tuesday evening, then. Good-bye, Annet!'

'Good-bye!'

She went up the lane towards the postbox outside the Wastfield gate. He went into the house, drank a hasty cup of tea, finished the packing of his single case, and set off again in the Mini towards Comerford.

And chancing to lift his eyes to the long, rain-dimmed hog-back of the Hallowmount as he drove, just as the clouds parted and the quivering spear of light transfixed it, he saw the moving sapphire that was Annet climb the hillside and vanish over the crest.

Chapter Two

It was after eight o'clock on Tuesday evening when he lifted and dropped the knocker on the front door of Fairford, and listened with pricked ears to the footsteps that advanced briskly from the living-room to open the door to him. He hadn't taken his key south with him. There were only two, and the whole family would be in on a Tuesday evening, so there was no question of his being locked out.

He said afterwards that he knew as soon as the knocker dropped that something was wrong; but the truth was that the hole in his peace of mind really showed itself when he recognised the footsteps as belonging to Mrs Beck. There was no reason in the world why that should be a portent of any kind; but we make our own superstitions and our own touchstones, and it had been Annet who opened the door to him first, and she should have opened it to him now. If she had, he would have believed that he was being offered another chance, a new beginning with her, if he had the wit to make better use of it this time. But the steps were heavier and shorter than hers, the hand that turned back the latch was sharper and clumsier with it; and he knew it was Mrs Beck even before she let him in.

'Ah, there you are, Mr Kenyon!' She held the door wide. The hall was in half-darkness; the brittle brightness of her voice might have been trying to make up for the want of light on her face. 'Have you had a nice week-end?'

Had he? Back from a brief re-insertion into a vacancy which no longer seemed large enough for him, back to a desired but elusive right of domicile which had not yet fully admitted him, he couldn't find much comfort anywhere. But he said yes, he had, all the more positively for the nagging of his doubts. What else can you say? Everybody'd been almost overglad to see him, and made all the fuss of him even he could ever have wished; that ought to add up to a nice week-end, according to his old standards.

'We've missed you,' said Mrs Beck, making a production of taking his coat from him and hanging it up. He unwound his college scarf, and was stricken motionless for a second in mid-swing, arm ridiculously extended, at a statement so disastrously off-key. She didn't say things like that. She was too correct and practical, and they hadn't, so far, been on that kind of terms. It was then he began to feel the ground quake under him with certainty that something was wrong.

There was no Annet in the living-room, no glossy black head lifting reluctantly from her book to speak faint, warm, rueful civilities over his return. Only Beck, with his glasses askew and his lofty brow seamed and pallid, almost mauve beneath the light. Too ready with a rush of welcoming conversation, missing his footing occasionally in his haste, like his wife. But unlike his wife, lurching at every mis-step; and his eyes, distorted by the lenses of his glasses, liquefying at every recovery into anxiety and fear.

'Annet working late?' asked Tom, himself shaken off-course by this inexplicable disquiet.

If the pause was half a second long, that was all; if they did exchange a look across his shoulder, it touched and slid away in an instant.

'No,' said Mrs Beck, 'she's gone into Comerbourne with Myra, there was some film they wanted to see. One of these three-hour epics. They'd have to miss the end if they caught the last bus, they'll stay overnight with Myra's aunt in Mill Fields.'

She must have seen his face fall, if she hadn't been so busy desperately holding up her own. But he accepted it; he swallowed it whole, and gave up expecting to see Annet that night. Flat and cold the evening extended before him; and if he hadn't succumbed to his hideous disappointment and taken cravenly to flight from the prospect of keeping up appearances face-to-face with her parents through all those dragging hours, the course of events might have been radically changed. But he did succumb, and he did resort to flight. Better drive over to the local club in Comerford than sit here trying to keep his mouth from sagging. He made his excuses winningly, and had the discomfiting sensation of having hurled himself at an unlatched door when they received them almost eagerly, without even formal regret at being deprived of his company.

He withdrew himself thankfully as soon as supper was over; he'd have skipped that, too, if he'd been less hungry, or if there'd been much prospect of getting a meal in Comerford at this hour. In the

213

hall he wound himself up again in his scarf, and then, remembering that he was wearing his scuffed driving shoes, opened the large clothes-cupboard to fish out some more presentable ones.

And suddenly something fell into place, a doubt, a premonition, a memory, whatever it was that put his own intended moves out of mind, and set him searching through the many coats on their hangers, looking for the dark gentian blue one with the large collar. Her best amber-gold one was there, the new one she had bought only a few weeks ago. Her second-best tweed raincoat was there. But not the blue. When did Annet ever go into town to the cinema in her everyday coat? He looked for the blue nylon head-scarf, that she used to drape casually over the rail, since it could hardly be creased even if one tried. He couldn't find it. And her shoes, the shoes she had been wearing that rainy Thursday afternoon, strong half-brogue walking shoes suitable for such weather – where were they? Her more prized pairs she nursed carefully in her own room, but her walking shoes stayed down here. Where were they now?

Slowly he went back into the living-room. They both looked up at him with a quick, oblique uneasiness, and fastening on his face, calmed and stilled into a kind of resigned despair.

'It's a fine night,' he said, with what sounded even in his own ears like horrible inconsequence. 'Stars shining, not a sign of rain. Did she go off wearing her rain-hood, and her heavy shoes, a night like this?'

No one, apparently, noticed his effrontery in making deductions unasked about Annet's movements, no one bridled at his asking these questions as though he had a right to an answer. The Becks looked at each other with a long, drear look, and crumbled before his eyes.

'She isn't out with Myra – is she?'

'No,' said Mrs Beck, and straightened her back and met his eyes wretchedly; not resenting him, almost grateful for him. As a pair they only depressed and degutted each other, those two, they grasped at a third, now that it was inevitable, like drowning men at a good solid log. 'No, she isn't.' She dropped her hands in her lap, and let them lie, let the breath go out of her body in a great, helpless sigh.

Tom moistened his lips. 'She went out on Thursday,' he said, 'just as I came in. She was wearing that blue coat she wears around, and those shoes, and the rain-hood. That makes sense, it was raining then. But where I've been it hasn't rained again all the week-end. I don't know about here. But the roads were bone dry all the way.'

'It hasn't rained here, either,' said Mrs Beck in the same flat, drearily angry tone. Beck made an inarticulate sound of protest, and she rode over him, raising her voice. 'What's the use? He may as well know. At this rate everybody'll know before long. Where's the sense in thinking we can keep it quiet? She did go out on Thursday afternoon. She said she was going to post the letters and then have a quick walk before tea. She said she wouldn't be long.'

'Mother!' said Beck in reproachful appeal. She turned her head for a moment and gave him a startled, wondering, almost derisive look in return for the incongruous word; but her eyes came back almost at once to Tom's face. If she was pinning her hopes to anyone at this minute, he realised, it was to him.

'And she never came home,' said Mrs Beck.

Once it was out they could all breathe and articulate again, and by an appreciable degree the tension eased. Things admitted can be faced. They have to be, there's no choice in the matter. But they were all trembling; and the relationship between them, that had been so decorous and neutral until that moment, would never be the same again.

Very carefully, so as not to unbalance himself and them, Tom asked: 'Have you notified the police that she's missing?'

They had not. They shook their heads mutely, eyeing each other, each willing the other – he should have foreseen it – to tell him the reasons that were so obvious to them and should have been incomprehensible to him. They imagined him seeing Annet, with her perilous beauty, dead in a ditch; they couldn't know that he was seeing her rather as they saw her, alive, resolute and passionate, in the company of some other man. Or boy. Or whatever sixth-formers are these days, with their prodigiously advanced bodies and their struggling half-adult minds, so mutually hurtful, so impossible fully to reconcile. He almost went along with their instinct for conceal-ment, and concealed his own knowledge; but then he shook off the temptation and slashed his way through to the truth. For what mattered was not their sensitivities but Annet's safety.

'I know about that last time,' he said. 'I know why you kept it quiet. But what does that matter, when she may be in trouble worse than that? Someone has to find her. And they've got the best chance, the best facilities. You'll have to go to them.'

'Yes,' said Beck, grey as cobwebs, 'I suppose we shall. But you see, once before she went off of her own will – or tried to. And now again. People will say – they'll call her— We didn't want that. No more scandal round her name, not if we could avoid it. What will her life be like, if—? It's for her own sake!'

'And ours, too,' said his wife flatly and coldly. 'Because we know we're to blame, too. We're out of touch with her, we don't know how, we don't know why. We've no influence over her. But that makes it our fault as much as hers. Where did we fail? Where did we lose contact with her?' She turned her rigidly-waved head and looked at Tom with fierce, helpless eyes. 'Who told you? Are people still talking?'

'No. Not the way you mean. Someone told me rather with the opposite intention, to soften the effect if anyone else should gossip, that's all. But I can see that you hoped she'd just come home in her own good time, or write to you, and nobody else any the wiser. Did you *look* for her?'

A fool's question; or maybe a lover's, someone who can't trust anyone else to value his divinity or exert himself for her fittingly. Of course they'd looked for her. Beck had tramped the lanes and combed Comerford all the evening and half the night, and then gone off by bus to his sister's house in Ledbury, and his cousin's Teme valley small-holding, in case she had turned up there; Mrs Beck had sat at home over the telephone, calling up with careful, ambiguous messages anyone who might, just might know anything, anyone who had a window overlooking the railway station, or a teenage son who could, in some way, be brought into the conversation and eliminated from the enquiry. But there were plenty of mothers of young sons with whom she wasn't on telephoning terms, plenty of dancing partners who didn't move in her orbit at all. And she had got nowhere.

'And Mrs Blacklock? Hasn't she been on the line wanting to now where her secretary's got to?'

'Regina's away. She's been away all the week-end at some conference in Gloucestershire – something about child psychology. She gave Annet the whole week off. If Annet came back now, no one would know – no one but us three. Mrs Blacklock won't be back until tomorrow night.'

She offered that as a life-line, and as such he clutched at it. Because if that was the case, Annet also might come back tonight, or tomorrow, in time to be stonily in her place when next Regina looked for her. That was if this was not final; if she meant it only as a fling, a gesture, a statement of her own will and her determination to go her own way. That was what her mother was hoping for, he saw that. Damage there would still be, irreparable after its fashion; but the worse damage is the known damage, and this, barring the last cruelty of fate, wouldn't be known. If he hadn't been so acutely tuned to everything that touched Annet, not even he need have known it.

'She's clever,' said Mrs Beck strenuously, 'and strong-willed, and capable about practical things. She can take care of herself, and she's no fool. We thought she'd come home in time. We did what we could to find her ourselves, but we didn't want to start a hue and cry. If we did, she'd be ruined.'

'You must see that,' said Beck, pleadingly. He might have been an old man in his dotage, looking to his son to save something for him out of his life's wreckage.

'I do see it, I can understand it. But it's five days! And no message, no letter, nothing!'

'Nothing!'

'And what if it isn't what you think? Haven't you been afraid of that? What if she's come to some harm through no fault of her own, while we're writing her off as her own casualty? We've got to go to the police. What matters now is to find her.'

Deliquescing, disintegrating before his eyes, they owned it. They dwindled, leaning on him. If he could bring her back safely and keep them their faces and their respectability through this they would give her to him gladly. Only he didn't want her given, he wanted her to come of her own will, as of her own will she had turned her back on him. All manner of perversity he read into her actions, but he would have cut off his own hand to have her back intact, whether she ever came his way or no.

'I saw her,' he said deliberately. 'Last Thursday, when I left. I was driving along the lane past the farm, and the sun came out on the Hallowmount. I saw Annet then. She was climbing up the side of the hill, towards the top. I saw her go over the crest and disappear. Do you know what she could have been doing there?'

Staring at him without comprehension, almost unbelievingly, they shook their heads. But even at that straw they clutched eagerly.

'Are you sure? Then she couldn't have been heading for the station, or the bus. And she had no luggage,' said Mrs Beck, her face flushing into life and hope again.

217

'Not with her then. But she could have left a small case somewhere to be collected.' How could they, how could he, talk of her like that? Not some common little delinquent, but Annet, whose erect, flaming purity he saw now for the first time. And yet she was gone, and surely not alone. Why should she go at all, if she was alone? She knew very well how to seal up her solitude against all comers, she needed no distance between herself and men. But what could he do but go on fighting for her in these small, corrupt, prosaic, impertinent ways? She was in the world, they must reckon with the world if she would not.

'It was Miles Mallindine last time,' he said. 'At least I can go and see that he's safely at home this time. Bill won't mind my dropping in, I can make some excuse.' They were on 'Bill' terms then, he was welcome in their house whenever he dropped around, and they wouldn't know he was riding herd on their son, he'd see to that. Eve, who hadn't blamed the boy, wouldn't blame the girl too much, either. Eve had a fair, sweet mind. He wished Annet had had her for a mother, and Miles for a brother. There might have been no problem then.

'We ought to go to the Hallowmount,' said Beck, astonishingly. And as they stared at him blankly: 'She went there. It's the last we know of her. There might be something to speak to us. How can we be sure there isn't? We ought to go. At least to look where she went.'

'We can look,' said Tom without enthusiasm, for if there was one thing certain it was that they wouldn't find her there. Whatever she had wanted on that solitary hill, it was over long ago. Her case? But why there?

'Please! On our way to the Mallindines', it wouldn't take us long. There's a moon.'

And they went, the two men together, in the light of the newly-risen moon, whiter than daylight and almost as bright.

'You'll stay in the car at Mallindine's,' said Tom firmly, rolling the Mini out on to the bone-white ribbon of the lane.

'Oh, yes, I will. They won't know.' He would have promised anything. He was shaking like an old, old man. He loved his daughter, after all, or else he was sensible of some secret dismay of guilt, and heartily afraid.

'She was here,' said Tom, calf-deep in the bleached autumn grass, panting from his climb. 'When I first saw her, that is. About here.

And she went on climbing on this line. Fast.'

He climbed. The hog-back of the hill heaved above him, white in the moonlight; here and there an encrustation of heather, but most of it pale, withered grass, dehydrated, dying. Like fair, tangled, lustreless hair. The night was still, starry above, bone-naked in its pallor below. And yet a little curl of wind spiralled upward in front of his feet, coiling through the grass on the path Annet had taken up the steep. Coiling, twining, bending the strawy stems, just in front of his feet all the way. Some trick of displacement of air, alien humans intruding on the filled and completed spaces of the night. What else could it be? Or a small groundwind that never reached his knee. Or something light going before him, inviting, showing the way, itself unseen. Showing the right way, or the wrong?

Beck laboured behind him, panting heavily, but he couldn't wait for him, the quivering of the grass drew him on, hypnotically alluring. They had left the lower outcrop of rocks behind on their right hand, jagged in black and white like broken teeth. Against the skyline, faded periwinkle blue and faintly luminous beyond that enormous moon, the tips of the rocks at the Altar just showed clear of the grass. At close quarters they stood thirty feet high, a horseshoe shape with a worn space of grass enclosed in their uneven arms, a picnickers' delight. The ring of squat trees, stooping, misshapen pines half-peeled of their bark, still lay out of sight on the summit.

He turned his head, and saw the bowl between the border hills drowned, drained of all colour, a landscape solitary and strange as the craters of the moon. He withdrew his eyes from it with a wrench, and leaned into the slope as though his life, or a life incredibly becoming almost dearer than his own, depended on his reaching the top of the hill. Though there could be nothing here for them, nothing at all, no sign. If she had left her prints charmed into the grass, this acid whiteness of the moonlight would have bleached them all away.

There was a real wind up here, no longer a mysterious tremor that trod out the path for him, but a steady, light breeze that blew from behind him, from the hills of the west. So it was that he heard nothing as he breasted the last yards of the slope towards the Altar, panting, and saw suddenly before him the small, slender ankles moving in a rhythm of confidence and peace, the light feet furrowing the grasses. No colour in the shoes, the stockings, only gradations of grey, no colour in the narrow skirt gripping her thighs as she came. No colour in the coat now, no gentian blue, only a deeper, dimmer grey, soft-textured, melting into the night. And within the hoisted collar the abrupt darkness of blue-black hair, the more abrupt whiteness and clarity of an oval face.

His eyes reached the face, and he had to halt and stiffen his legs under him to sustain the weight of relief and gratitude. Everything else could wait, the incipient rage, the anxiety that would surely close in again within minutes to impede all contact between them. What did they matter? He was looking at Annet. Annet, alive, intact and alone.

She came dropping down the slope towards them with her soft, lithe stride, not hurrying, not delaying, one hand in her pocket, one holding up her collar to her chin. He saw her face pale and still, with great eyes enormously dilated. She was aware of him; she saw them both, converging upon her, and knew them very well, and yet it seemed to him that she was looking through them rather than at them, that her mind and her heart were somewhere infinitely distant and inaccessible. He could not put a name to the disquiet she roused in him, or the quality of the pale, charged brightness that vibrated about her moonlit movements. But he knew he was frightened, that he dreaded the unavoidable questions to which he didn't want to know the answers. And all the time she was drawing nearer, her steps quickening a little; and there was no escaping the moment and the spark.

But when the spark flashed Beck was breathless, and Tom was dumb. It was Annet who looked wonderingly from face to face, and asked in a voice shaken between offence and uneasiness: 'What are *you* doing here? Is anything the matter?'

Was anything the matter! As though they had offended her by coming out to meet the last bus, as though they could not trust her to come home alone. The same erected head and faintly, gravely hostile face, unaware of having given more cause for anxiety than she did every day by being aloof and independent of them. Or was it quite the same? Her eyes were so wide and opaque and strange, as though she had only just awakened from sleep, and deep within the blankness a small, remote flame of disquiet kindled as he watched. But not fear; only disquiet, as though they were the unaccountable ones.

He said: 'We came to look for you.' What else could he say?

Still out of breath, her father said with feeble anger:

'Where've you been? When you went out you said you'd be in to tea.' Fantastic, the commonplaces that came most readily to the tongue; maybe wisely, for what could words do about it now?

'I know,' said Annet, her voice almost conciliatory, something like a smile playing over her face for the absurdity of all this. 'I meant to. I know I'm horribly late, I went a long way, farther than I realised. I couldn't believe it was so late, it seemed to drop dark all at once. But you didn't have to send out a search party, surely? I thought you'd be home by now, Mr Kenyon. You didn't stay because of me, did you?'

And then she did smile, vaguely and sweetly and penitently, softened and eased by the night and the silence and that something in herself that kept her lulled and still like a dreaming woman; and the smile died on her lips and left them parted on held breath as she saw their fixed and wondering faces. Their own wariness, incomprehension and quickening fear stared back at them from her dilated eyes.

'What's the matter? I'm sorry I'm late, but why should you be alarmed about a couple of hours? I really don't see— I'm not even wet, it's stopped raining. What is the matter?'

Carefully, in a breathy voice that hurt his throat, Beck asked: 'And what about the five days in between?'

She looked from one face to the other, and the smile was as dead as the skeleton rocks bleaching in the moonlight below them. She moistened her lips and tightened her grip on the raised folds of her collar. In the great dark eyes the little flames of fear burned high and bright.

'I don't know what you mean,' said Annet in a thin whisper. '*What five days?*'

Chapter Three

He got up as soon as it was light, and dressed and went out. What was the point of staying in bed? He hadn't slept more than ten minutes at a stretch all night. He couldn't stop hearing her voice, patiently, desperately, wearily going over the recital time after time, unshakable in obstinacy.

'I went out to post the letters, and met Mr Kenyon at the gate. He offered to take them for me, but I wanted some fresh air, so I walked. What else can I tell you? That's what I did. I went for a long walk, right over the Hallowmount and along the brook. I meant to come back round by the bog, but it got dark so quickly I changed my mind and climbed back over the top. And then I met them, and that's all. It's Thursday. Whatever you say, it must be Thursday, it was Thursday I went out with the letters. What's happened to you all?'

And the two of them at her, one on either side, frightened and angry but afraid to be too angry, afraid to drive her further from them; anxious, bitter, piteous, throwing the same questions at her over and over.

Where did you go? Where did you spend the nights? Who went with you? What's come over you? Do you expect us to believe a fairy-tale like that?'

He had driven them home, and then torn himself away as inconspicuously as he could, but he hadn't been able to help hearing the beginning of it. What right had he in that scene? Annet didn't want or need him, and he didn't want to hear them call her a liar. He got out of the house, and took the car and drove into Comerford. All the way along the quarter of a mile of solitary, moonlit road, under the flank of that naked slope, he was repeating to himself that at least she was alive and well, and that was everything. Wherever she had been, whatever was the truth about her lost five days, she was alive and well, and home. But by the ragged, chaotic pain that frayed him he knew that that was not quite everything. And he knew that she would win, that in the end, true or not, they would all be committed

222

to the same uneasy silence and acceptance.

One thing he could do, and he did it. He parked the Mini in the drive of Bill Mallindine's modern house by the riverside, and made returning a borrowed book the excuse for his unexpected call. Eve was out at some improbable feminine meeting, but Bill gave him a drink and a chair by the fire, and welcomed him gladly. And he hadn't even had to ask any questions. At a table in one remote corner of the multiple living-room – heaven knew how they heated it so successfully, the crazy shape it was – Miles Mallindine and Dominic Felse were devotedly disentangling finished cassettes from cameras, and securing them in their little yellow bags ready for the post. Their heads together over the work, they gave him the polite minimum of attention. It was Bill who teased Miles to display some of his best pictures, and volunteered the information that the two had spent the half-term camping and climbing near Tryfan. The two pairs of boots, bristling with tripe hobs and clinkers, carelessly off-loaded in the hall, should have spoken for themselves.

So that, as far as it went, was that. Miles was home, with enough paraphernalia to provide him with an alibi, and with a reliable ally to bear witness for him into the bargain. And if they'd really planned anything together, Annet and he, wouldn't they have taken care to cover her tracks as well as his?

And besides, there was the incredible conviction with which she had carried off her return, the dozen details that couldn't be shrugged away. The mention of her surprise at seeing him, when he should have been well on his way home, the reassurance that she wasn't even in danger of getting wet, because it had stopped raining, when it hadn't rained for five days. And her charmed, distant face, and the suddenly engendered fear and wonder as the ground shook under her feet. Could she, could anyone, act like that? It was hard to believe.

Almost as hard as that the earth had opened and admitted her into secret, terrible places, and given her back at the end of five days with no memory of the time between, not a minute older than she went away. Late, late in a gloaming Kilmeny had come home, all right, but whether from some fairy underworld or a cheap hotel God-knew-where, that was more than he dared guess. Bonny Kilmeny! She was that, whatever else she might be. And Kilmeny, you'll remember, he said to himself bitterly, driving home, was pure as pure could be. Who are you, to say Annet isn't?

It wasn't over when he got home. He had prayed that she'd be in bed, and her parents too exhausted to harrow the barren ground over again for him. But she was still there, and all that was changed was that the passion was clean gone out of her repeated affirmations, nothing left but the simple repetition of facts, or what she claimed were facts. She was indifferent now, she spoke without vehemence; if they believed her, well, if they did not, she couldn't help that. She was tired, but eased; and there was something still left in her face and body of a strange, rapt, content. The strongest argument for her, if she had but known it. They might plead, and argue, and lament; she had only to withdraw into her own heart, and she was secure from all troubling. He could feel the truth of that, at least. The source of warmth and joy and security was within her, some perfection remembered. Not remembered, perhaps, only experienced still. My God, but it couldn't be *true*! *Could it?*

And when they all said good-night, like relatively civilised people, suddenly it was clear that they would speak no more of this. She could not be shaken. She could only be convinced by the production of a letter received in answer to one she had posted on Thursday, by the torn-off leaves of the calendar, and their collective certainty. Confronted with these, she shrank in bewilderment and fright, and from accusing they had to reassure her. Did any of them believe? Was it even possible to believe? Elsewhere he would not have credited it, but here on the borders the frontiers of experience grew generously wide and imaginative. They winced from pressing her too hard, probably they were grateful that they had not been able to catch her out in any particular. Wasn't it better to let well alone, and pray a little? Dreading, nevertheless, what revelation might yet erupt to confound them all.

Nobody knew! That was sanctuary, that nobody knew but the four of them, and please God, nobody ever would. He was so tangled into their household now that he would never get clear. Maybe he had drawn too close to Annet, in everything but blood, ever again to be considered as more distant than a brother.

Perhaps that was why he couldn't sleep, why he arose before dawn, and went like a sensible modern man to look over the ground by daylight. Painfully new daylight, but clear enough to show details the moon had silvered over. Because she must be lying. (*Mustn't she?*) And if she was lying, where had she been? Farther away than the other side of the Hallowmount. And what had she been doing?

(*And with whom?* But that was the question he would not entertain, he pushed it out of sight as soon as it reared its head.) Even granted the simple possibility of amnesia, she must have been somewhere. And from that somewhere she had returned precisely to the Hallowmount, as if only through the medium of that incalculable place could she reach her home again. That made this as surely a translation back from fairyland as if the earth had truly opened and let her go.

Again he climbed the hill, this time in the grey first light of a dull morning. Once over the crest he looked down upon the shallower undulations of another moorland valley, open heath grazing on both sides of the narrow brook that threaded it. An unpopulated, bare, beautiful desolation in changing tints of heather and bracken and furze. Not a single house in sight. No one here but sheep to stare at him and wonder as he dropped in long strides down the hill. On a wet Thursday afternoon there'd be no picnickers, no hill-walkers, no one to watch Annet Beck disappear into the underworld. Not like venturing on to Comerbourne station with a suitcase in broad daylight, among hundreds of people who knew her. But if this was to be considered as an escape route to somewhere else instead of fairyland, then there had to be a means of leaving this bowl of waste land, and faster than on foot. Footpaths were here by the dozen, trailing haphazard across the country from nowhere to nowhere, apparently, skirting the patches of bog where the cotton grass fluttered ragged and frayed. With a pony you could cover the ground here at a good speed, but Annet wasn't one of the local jodhpurs and 'ard 'at sorority, and with a pony she would in any case have been courting notice when she did encounter human beings. Could a car be got up here? He had been long enough in these parts now to realise that there were comparatively few places round these border uplands where the local people couldn't get cars to go. They had to; they lived in every corner of the back of beyond.

The long, oval, tilted bowl of pasture rose to northward, towards Comerford, and dipped to southward, in the direction of Abbot's Bale. Both were out of sight. In a tract of land without cover you could still be private here; all you needed was neutral colours and stillness, and you were invisible.

The easiest run out of the bowl would surely be towards Abbot's Bale. And beyond the brook, in the broad bottom of the valley, there sprang to life irresolutely a tiny, trodden path, that broadened and paled as it followed the ambling brook downwards, until it showed bared stones through here and there, and had grown to the dimensions of a farm cart, with two deep wheel-ruts, and the well-trodden dip where the horse walked in the middle. Where it tunnelled through the long grass it dwindled again, but always to reappear. Where it passed close to the marshy hollows the bright emerald green of fine, lush turf invaded it. In the distance there was a gate across it, and beyond probably others. But gates can be opened. Most gates, anyhow. A motor-bike could be brought up here with ease, even a small car, if you didn't mind a rough ride. And whoever had met Annet here and taken her away wouldn't be noticing a few bumps, or even a few scratches threatening his paint.

To Abbot's Bale, and from there wherever you liked, and no one in Comerford or Comerbourne any the wiser, for neither need be touched. Her everyday coat, a sensible rainscarf, no luggage: Annet had taken no chances this time. No one should suspect; no one should have any warning. Afterwards? Oh, afterwards the flood, the price, anything. What would it matter, afterwards?

He jumped the brook and made his way along the cart-track. Deep ruts on both sides of him, in places filled with the moist black mud of puddles that never dry up completely. Brown peat water deep between the tufted grasses, distant, solitary birds somewhere calling eerily. The hoof-track on which he walked had been laid with stones at some time, and stood up like a little causeway, only here and there encroached upon by the richer grass. There seemed to be no traces of a car having negotiated this road recently. Nor had he heard any sound of an engine break the silence last night, when she returned, but that great hog-back of rock had heaved solidly between, and might very well cut off all sound.

Five dry days, and a brisk wind blowing for three of them; the ground was hard and well-padded with thick, spongy turf. Only in the green places where the marsh came close would there be any traces to be found.

He came to the first of them, and the stony foundation of the track was broken there, and the ground had settled a little, subsiding into a softer green tongue of fine grass. Moisture welled up round the toe of his shoe, and he checked in mid-stride and drew his weight back carefully. The wheel-ruts still showed cushioned and smooth on both sides; no weight had crushed them last night, or for many days previously. But in the middle of the path a single indentation showed, the flattened stems silvery against the brilliant green. Too resilient to retain a pattern of the tread, the turf had not yet quite recovered from the pressure of somebody's motor-bike tyres.

There was no doubt of it, once he had found it. He followed it along almost to the first gate, and found its tenuous line three times on the way, to reassure him that he was not imagining things. Nowhere was there a clear impression of the tread; for most of the way the path was firm and dry, and where the damp patches invaded it the thick grass swallowed all but that ribbon of paler green. But he knew now that he was not mistaken; someone had brought a motorcycle up here from the direction of Abbot's Bale no longer ago than yesterday. A motorcycle or a scooter; he couldn't be sure which.

The sun was well up, and he was going to be late for breakfast; they'd be wondering, next, what had happened to him! He turned back then, and scrambled up the slope towards the ring of trees.

Miles Mallindine had a Vespa. And however many young men had danced with and coveted Annet, there was no blinking the fact that Miles had already got himself firmly connected with her comings and goings once, and could hardly expect to evade notice when something similar happened for the second time. Others might be possibles, but he was an odds-on favourite.

But he'd been camping somewhere near Llyn Ogwen and climbing on Tryfan with Dominic Felse. Or had he? All the long week-end? With a Vespa he could cover that journey quite easily in a couple of hours. And would young Felse lie for him? Neither of them struck him as a probable liar, and yet he was fairly sure that for each other, where necessary, they would take the plunge without turning a hair.

If you want to know, he told himself with irritation, lunging down the westward side of the Hallowmount, there's only one straightforward thing to do, and that's ask. Not other nosy people who *may* have seen something, not his friend who'll feel obliged to put up a front for him, but Miles himself. At least give him the chance to convince you, if there's nothing in it, and to get it off his chest if there is.

As if that was going to be easy!

It took him all morning to make up his mind to it; but in his free period at the end of the morning school he sent for Miles Mallindine.

* * *

'You wanted to see me, sir?'

The boy had come in, in response to his invitation, jauntily and easily, brows raised a little; unable to guess why he was wanted, you'd have said, but long past the days of instinctively supposing any summons to the staffroom to be a portent of trouble.

'Yes, come in and close the door. I won't keep you many minutes.' They had the room to themselves for as long as they needed it, but the thing was to keep it brief and simple; and tell him nothing that wasn't absolutely essential. 'You own a Vespa, don't you?'

'Yes, sir,' said Miles, agile brows jumping again.

'Did you go up to Capel Curig on it this week-end?'

'Yes. It's a bit of a load, with two up and the tent and kit, but we've got it to numbers now.' He was filling in the gaps, kindly and graciously, to avoid leaving the bald, enquiring: 'Yes' lonely upon the air between them. But he was wondering what all this was about, and testing out all possible connections in his all too lively mind.

'Spend the whole time up there? When did you leave? And when did you get back yesterday?'

'Oh, left about half past five on Thursday, I think, sir. I called round to pick up Dom first, and we did the packing at our place. We'd been in about half an hour when you looked in at home last night – just long enough for a wash and supper.'

He didn't ask point blank: 'Why?' but the slight tilt of his head, the attentive regard of his remarkably direct and disconcerting eyes, put the same question more diplomatically; and a small spark deep within the eyes supplemented without heat: 'And what the hell's it got to do with you, anyhow?' '*Sir!*' added the very brief, engaging and impudent smile he had inherited from his mother.

Tom was tempted to soften this apparently pointless and unjustifiable interrogation with a crumb of explanation, or at least apology; but the boy was too bright by far. To try to disarm him with something like: 'I'm sorry if this makes no sense to you, but *if* it makes no sense you've got nothing to worry about!' – no, it wouldn't do, he'd begin tying up the ends before the words were well out. No use saying pompously: 'I have my reasons for asking.' He knew that already, he was only in the dark at present as to what they could be, and at the first clue he'd be off on the trail. The fewer words the better. The more abrupt the better. They took some surprising, these days, but at least he could try.

'Did you take your Vespa out earlier on Thursday afternoon? A trial run, maybe, if you'd been working on her? Say – round through Abbot's Bale to the track at the back of the Hallowmount?'

If Miles didn't know what it was all about now, at least he knew the appropriate role for himself. He had drawn down over his countenance the polite, wooden, patient face of the senior schoolboy. It fitted rather tightly these days, but he could still wear it. Ours not to reason why; they're all mad, anyhow. Ours but to come up with: 'Yes, sir!' or: 'No, sir!' as required. The mask had an additional merit, or from Tom's point of view an additional menace; from within its bland and innocent eye-holes you could watch very narrowly indeed without youself giving anything away.

'No, sir, I didn't. I had her all ready the night before, there was no need to try her out.'

'And you weren't round there yesterday, either? Before you got home?'

'No, sir.'

He waited, quite still but not now quite easy; he was too intelligent for that. And something subtle had happened to the mask; the young man – not even the young man-of-the-world – was looking through it very intently indeed. Tom got up from his chair and turned a shoulder on him, to be rid of the probing glance, but it followed him thoughtfully to the window.

'I take it, sir, I'm not allowed to ask why? Why I might have been there?' The voice had changed, too, frankly abandoning the schoolboy monotone, and far too intent now to be bothered with the experimental graces of sophistication that were its natural sequel.

'Let's say, not encouraged. But if you've told me the truth, then in any case it doesn't matter, does it? All right, thanks, Mallindine, that's all.'

He kept his head turned away from the boy, watching the dubious sunlight of noon scintillating from the thread of river below the bridge. He waited for the door to open and close again. Miles had turned to move away, but nothing further happened.

After a moment the new voice asked, with deliberation and dignity: 'May I ask one thing that does matter?' No 'sir' this time, Tom noted; this was suddenly on a different level altogether.

'If you must.'

'Has anything happened to Annet?'

It hit him so hard that the shock showed, even from this oblique view. He felt the blood scald his cheeks, and knew it must be seen, and felt all too surely that it was not misunderstood. This boy was dangerous, he used words like explosives, only half-realising the force of the charge he put into them. Has anything happened to Annet! My God, if only we knew! But the simpler implication was what he wanted answered, and surely he was owed that, at least. Even if he was the partner of her defection, lying like a trooper by pre-arrangement, and sworn to persist in his lies, that appeal for reassurance might well be genuine enough, and deserved an answer.

'I hope not,' said Tom with careful mildness. 'I certainly left her fit and well when I came out this morning.'

He had his face more or less under control by then, the blush had subsided, and he would not be surprised into renewing it. He turned and gave Miles a quizzical and knowing look, calculated to suggest benevolently that his preoccupation with Annet, in the light of history, was wholly understandable, but in this case inappropriate, not to say naive. But the minute he met the levelled golden-brown eyes that were so like Eve's, he knew that if anyone was involuntarily giving anything away in this encounter, it wasn't Miles. He knew what he was saying, and he'd thought before he said it. Fobbing him off with an amused look and an indulgent smile wouldn't do. Shutting the door he'd just gone to the trouble to open wasn't going to do anyone any good.

Tom came back to his table, and sat down glumly on a corner of it. 'You may as well go on,' he said. 'What made you ask that?' Even that fell short of the degree of candour the occasion demanded. He amended it quite simply to: 'How did you know?' If he was the lover, he had good reason to know, but no very compelling reason to show that he knew; and if he wasn't – well, they were all a bit uncanny round here, so he'd said, cheerfully including himself. Maybe Eve was a witch, and had handed on her powers to him for want of a daughter.

'My mother had a telephone call on Thursday evening,' said Miles with admirable directness. 'From Mrs Beck.'

There couldn't have been much communication between those two ladies during the last few months, no wonder Eve's thumbs had pricked.

'She made some excuse about asking when the Gramophone Club was starting its winter programme. But then she worked the conversation round to me, and fished to know what I was doing over the week-end. My mother told me, when I came back last night. I didn't think there was anything in it, actually, until you began asking

– related questions. Oh, you didn't give anything away,' he said quickly, forestalling all observations on that point. His head came up rather arrogantly, the wide-open eyes dared Tom to stand on privilege now. 'My mother can connect, you know. But so can others. And I don't suppose our house was the only one she phoned – if it's like that.'

We ought to have known, thought Tom. In a small place where everyone knows everyone else's business, where half the women compare notes as a matter of course, we ought to have known it would leak out. How could she hope to go telephoning around the whole village and half Comerbourne, without starting someone on a hot trail?

'No,' he said flatly, 'I'm afraid it wasn't.'

'She wouldn't realise,' said Miles generously. He might not have occult powers, but he had a pair of eyes that could see through Tom Kenyon, apparently, as through a plate-glass window. 'My mother had good reason to look under the mat – if you see what I mean. But some of 'em don't need a reason, they do it for love. And my mother doesn't talk. But plenty of them do.'

How had they arrived at this reversal? The kid was warning him, kindly, regretfully, like an elder, of the possible unpleasantness to come; warning him as though he knew very well how deeply it could and did concern him, and how much he stood to get hurt. Without a word said on that aspect of the matter, they had become rivals, meeting upon equal terms, and equally sorry for each other.

It was high time to close this interview, before somebody put a foot wrong and brought the house down over them both. They had to go on confronting each other in class for the best part of a year yet, they couldn't afford any irretrievable gaffes.

'Too many,' he agreed wryly. 'But gossip without any foundation won't get them far. And I take it that you and I can include each other among the non-talkers, Mallindine.'

'Yes, sir, naturally.'

'Sir' had come back, prompt on his cue. This boy really wanted watching, he was a little too quick in the uptake, if anything.

'If there's anything you want to ask me, do it now. But I don't guarantee to answer.'

'There's nothing, sir. If—' He did waver there, the elegantly-held head turned aside for a moment, the eyes came back to Tom's face doubtfully and hopefully. '—if Annet's all right?'

'Yes, perfectly all right.' He had nearly said: 'Of course!', which would have been a pretence at once unworthy and unwise in dealing with this very sharp and dangerous intelligence. He dropped the attitude in time, but a faint, rueful smile tugged at Miles's lips for an instant, as if he had seen it hovering and watched it snatched hastily away. The young man was back in charge, and formidably competent.

'Thank you, sir. Then that's all.' For me it is, said the straight eyes, challenging and pitying; how about you?

'Right, then, off you go. And I shouldn't worry.'

Wouldn't you? said the flicker of a smile again, less haughtily. Either Tom was beginning to see all sorts of shades of meaning that weren't there, or that last, long, thoughtful, level stare before the door closed had said, as plainly as in words: 'Come off it! You know as well as I do there was another fellow in the case – nothing for you, nothing for me. Now tell me that doesn't hurt!'

He knew, as well as he knew his own name, that if he questioned Dominic Felse on the subject of the weekend in Wales, Dominic would go straight to Miles and report the entire conversation word for word; and yet it seemed to him that he had very little choice in the matter. Since he'd begun this probably useless enquiry, he couldn't very well leave an important witness out of it. He might be primed already, he might lie for his friend; but that was a hazard that applied to all witnesses, surely. And for some reason Tom felt sure that Miles would not yet have unburdened himself about that morning interview; he took time, when it was available, to think things out, and he had himself been considerably disturbed. He might not keep it quiet, but he wouldn't run to confide it until he knew what he wanted to say.

So Tom sent for Dominic Felse, half against his conscience and a little against his will, but already launched and incapable of stopping. Dominic confirmed that he and Miles had spent all the week-end together. Yes, they'd packed up together and left about half past five, maybe a little earlier. No, they hadn't been separated at all during the whole trip, except for half-hour periods while Miles took the scooter and went shopping, and Dominic cooked. Miles was no good as a cook. Yes, they'd come straight back to the Mallindines' for supper.

Why?

Dominic was nearly a year younger than Miles, and less impeded by his dignity and sophistication from asking the obvious questions. Moreover, he was the son of a detective-inspector, and had a consequent grasp of the rights of the interrogated which made him an awkward customer to interrogate. With sunny politeness he answered questions, and with reciprocal interest asked them. Tom got rid of him in short order, for fear of giving away more than he got.

He met the two of them in the corridor as he left when afternoon school ended. They gave him twin civilised smiles, very slight and correct, and said: 'Good-night, sir!' in restrained and decorous unison.

The sight of the two of them thus, shoulder to shoulder, with similarly closed faces and impenetrable eyes, settled one thing. They had pooled everything they knew, and were preparing to stand off the world from each other's back whenever the assault threatened.

He had seen it coming, and he didn't make the mistake of thinking that either of them would as lightly confide in a third party. All the same, he began to regret what he had set in motion. Would it really do any good to find out what had happened, and who had made it happen? Wasn't it better to creep through the next few days and weeks with fingers crossed and breath held, walking on tiptoe and praying to know nothing – not to have to know anything – like Beck and Mrs Beck? Thankful for every night that closed in with no trap sprung and no revelation exploding into knowledge; frightened of every contact in the street and every alarm note of the telephone, but every day a little less frightened.

Annet came and went with fewer words than ever, but with a tranquil face. Something of wonder still lingered, and something of sadness and deprivation, too, and sometimes her eyes, looking through the walls of the house and the slope of the Hallowmount into whatever underworld she had left behind there, burned into a secret, motionless excitement that never seemed quite to be able to achieve joy. She went to Cwm Hall in the morning, and Regina Blacklock's chauffeur drove her home in the evening, and nobody there seemed to notice anything wrong with her or her work. Thank God that was all right, anyhow! There were bushels of Regina's notes from the conference to decipher and type out, and a long report to her committee, which Annet brought home to copy on Thursday evening. On the incidence and basic causes of delinquency in deprived children!

She was working on it when Tom came through the hall after supper to go out and stable the Mini for the night. He heard the typewriter clicking away in the dingy little book-lined room Beck still called his study, though all he ever did in it was accumulate endless random text-notes of doubtful value on various obscure authors, with a view to publishing his own commentaries some day. No one believed it would ever be done, not even Beck himself; no one believed the world stood to gain or lose anything, either way.

Tom opened the door gingerly and looked in, and she was alone at the desk. It was the first time he had been alone with her, even for a moment, since her return. He went in quickly, and closed the door softly at his back.

'Annet—'

She had heard him come. She finished her sentence composedly before she looked up. He could see no hardening in her face, no wariness, no change at all. She looked at him thoughtfully, and said nothing.

'Annet, I want you to know that if there's anything I can do to help you, I will, gladly. I'd like to think you'd ask me.'

She sat and looked at him for a long moment, looked down at her own hands still poised over the keys, and back slowly to his face. He thought he caught the bleak, small shadow of a smile, at least a shade of warmth in her eyes.

'You'd much better just go on thinking me a liar,' she said without reproach or bitterness. 'It's nice of you, but I really don't need any help.'

'I hope you won't, Annet. Only I'm afraid you may. I know, I feel, it isn't over. And I don't want you to be hurt.'

'Oh, *that* doesn't matter!' said Annet, startled into a rush of generous words. 'Not at all! You mustn't worry about me.'

She smiled at him, the first real, unguarded smile he had ever had from her. If she had asked him to believe in fairyland then, he would have done it; any prodigy he would have managed for her. But the moment was over before it was well begun; for it was at that instant that the knocker thudded at the front door.

He shivered and froze at the sound. Annet's smile had grown suddenly, mockingly bright. 'It'll be Myra, coming for me,' she said, quite gently. 'What are you afraid of?'

But it wasn't Myra. They heard Mrs Beck cross the hall, quick, nervous steps, running to ward off disaster. They heard the low exchange of words; a man's voice, quiet and deep-pitched, and Mrs Beck's fluttering tones between. He was in the hall now; only a few steps, then he was still, waiting.

The door opened upon Mrs Beck's white, paralysed face and scared eyes.

'Annet – there's someone here who wishes to speak to you.'

He came into the doorway at her shoulder, a tall, lean man with a long, contemplative face and deceptively placid eyes that didn't miss either Tom's instinctively stiffening back or Annet's blank surprise.

'I'm sorry to interrupt your work, Miss Beck,' said Detective-Inspector George Felse gently, 'but there's a matter on which I'm obliged to ask you some questions. And I think, in the circumstances, it should be in your parents' presence.'

235

Chapter Four

From the very first she seemed startled and bewildered, but not afraid; a little uneasy, naturally, for after all, George Felse was the police, and clearly on business, but not at all in trouble with her own conscience.

'Of course!' she said, and slid the bar of her typewriter into its locked position, and stood up. 'Shouldn't we go into the living-room? It's more comfortable there.'

'But Mr Kenyon—' began Mrs Beck helplessly, and let the words trail vaguely away. An old, cold house, where was the paying guest to sit in peace if they appropriated the living-room?

'That's all right,' said Tom, torn between haste and unwillingness, 'I'll get out of the way.'

But he didn't want to! He had to know what he had let loose upon her, for he was sure this was his work. He should have let well alone. Why had he had to question Mallindine, and then go on to confirm what he well knew might still be lies by dragging in Dominic Felse? They'd compared notes almost before his back was turned; and young Felse had promptly gone home and let slip the whole affair, with all its implications, to his father. How else could you account for this?

But no, that wouldn't do; as soon as he paused to consider he could see that clearly. If Dominic had informed on Annet, it was because something else had happened during that lost week-end, something that could be linked to a strayed girl and an improbable fairy-story. Something of interest to the police, whose sole interest in a pair of eighteen-year-old runaways would be to restore them to their agitated parents, and let the two families settle it between them as best they could; and even that only if their aid had been sought in the affair. No, there must be something else, something that had frightened Dominic with its implications, and caused him either to blurt out what he knew unintentionally, or driven him to deliver it up as a burden too heavy and a responsibility too great to be borne.

'It's just possible,' said George Felse, eyeing him amiably but distantly from beyond the rampart of his official status, all the overtones of friendship carefully excised from a voice which remained gentle, courteous and low-pitched, 'that I may need to see you for a few moments, too, Mr Kenyon, if you wouldn't mind being somewhere available, in case?'

He said he wouldn't, numbly and reluctantly, and turned to go up to his own room. He didn't hurry, because he wanted to be called back, not to be excluded. In a way he would have given anything to escape, but since there wasn't going to be any escape, anyhow, and he had already been dragged into the full intimacy of the family secret, what point was there in putting off the event? And before he had reached the stairs Beck was there, framed in the doorway of the living-room, wispy and grey and frightened, and looking desperately for an ally.

What is it? Did I hear you say you want to talk to Annet, Mr Felse?' His eyes wandered sidelong to Tom, who had looked back. 'No, no, don't go, Kenyon, this can't be anything so grave that you can't hear it. Please, I should be glad if you'd stay. One of the household, you know. That's if you have no objection to being present?'

Panic gleamed behind the thick lenses of his glasses; not for anything would he be left alone with Annet and his wife and the threat George Felse represented. His wife would expect him to spread a male protective barrier between his womenfolk and harm; or she would not expect it, but watch his helplessness with a bitter, contemptuous smile, and that would be worse. And Annet would act as though he was not there, knowing she had to fend for herself. No, he couldn't do without Tom. He laid a trembling hand on his arm, and held him convulsively.

'It's rather if Felse has no objection,' said Tom, watching the CID man's face doubtfully.

'No, this is not official – yet. Later I may have to ask you to make a formal statement. That will depend on what you have to tell me.'

He was looking Annet in the eyes, without a smile, but with the deliberate, emphatic gentleness of one breaking heavy matters to a child. He had known her since she was a small girl with pigtails; not intimately, but as an observant man knows the young creatures who grow up round him in his own village, the contemporaries of his own sons and daughters. He'd had to pay similar visits to not a few of their homes in his time, he knew all the pitfalls crumbling under their uncertain feet.

'I'll tell you what I can,' said Annet, brows drawn close in a frown of bewilderment. 'But I don't know what you can want to ask me.'

'So much the better, then,' he said equably, and followed her into the living-room, and turned a chair to the light for her. She understood that quite open manœuvre, and smiled faintly, but acquiesced without apparent reluctance. The parents hovered, quivering and silent. Tom closed the door, and sat down unobtrusively apart from them.

'Now Annet, I want you to tell me, if you will, how you spent last week-end.'

George Felse sat down facing her, quite close, watching her attentively but very gently. If he felt the despairing contraction of the tension within the room he gave no sign, and neither did she. She tilted back her head, shaking away the winged shadow of her hair, as if to show him the muted tranquillity of her face more clearly.

'I can't tell you that,' she said.

'I think you can, if you will.' And when she had nothing to say, and her mother only turned her head aside with a helpless, savage sigh, he pursued levelly: 'Were you here at home, for instance?'

'They say not,' said Annet in a small, still voice.

'Let them tell me that. I'm asking you what *you* say.'

'I can only tell you what I told them,' said Annet, 'but you won't believe me.'

'Try me,' he said patiently.

She looked him unwaveringly in the eyes, and took him at his word. Again, in the same clipped, bare terms she retold that fantastic story of hers.

'Mrs Blacklock gave me practically a whole week off, from Thursday morning, beacuse she was going to the child care conference at Gloucester. She asked me to come in again on Wednesday – yesterday – and clear up any routine correspondence, and then she came home in the evening. So I had five free days. I hadn't made any plans to do anything special. I meant to go to choir practice on Friday night, as usual. Maybe to the dance on Saturday, but I hadn't decided, because Myra was going with a party to the theatre in Wolverhampton, so I hadn't anyone to go with. They must have missed me at choir practice, and at church on Sunday. If I'd intended not to be there, shouldn't I have let them know?'

'He rang up on Friday night,' said Mrs Beck, a little huskily. 'Mr Blacklock, I mean – after choir practice. He was worried because she didn't turn up, wondered if she wasn't well. I told him she had a bit of a cold. He was quite alarmed, and I had to put him off, or he'd have been round to see her. I said it was nothing much, but she was in bed early, and asleep, so he couldn't disturb her, of course. He rang again on Sunday morning, after church, to ask how she was.'

'He only has four altos,' put in Beck with pathetic eagerness. 'And she never lets them down. Mr Blacklock knows he can always rely on Annet for his alto solos.'

Annet's clenched lips quivered in a brief and wry smile. It was all a part of the well-meaning communal effort to keep Annet busy and amused, everyone knew that. The Blacklocks had been taken into Mrs Beck's embittered and indignant confidence, after that abortive affair with Miles Mallindine, and with her usual competence Regina had stemmed every gap in the fence of watchful care that surrounded the girl, and poured new commitments into every empty corner of her days. Probably the choir was one of the things she'd enjoyed most. Regina couldn't sing a note; it was Peter, with his patient, fastidious kindness, who manipulated the casual material at his disposal into a very fair music for a village church. No wonder he rejoiced in Annet's deep, lustrous, boy's voice. And as charged by his wife, he always brought or sent her home in the car; that was a part of his responsibility. If Annet ever defected again, it mustn't be while she was in their charge.

'So from Thursday morning you were free,' said George mildly, undistracted by these digressions. 'What did you do with your freedom?'

'I was home all Thursday afternoon. I washed some things, and played a few records, and wrote one letter. And my mother had two more to post, so about half past three I said I'd go and post them, and then go for a walk. I said I'd be back to tea. I met Mr Kenyon just at the gate, and he offered to post the letters for me, but I told him I wanted some air and was going for a walk. It was just beginning to rain, but I didn't mind that, I like walking in the rain. I posted the letters in the box by the farm, and then I went on up the lane and over the stile on to the Hallowmount. I climbed right over the hill and went down into the valley by the brook, on the other side. I remember coming to the path there, this side of the brook. I can't remember how much farther I walked. I can't remember noticing which way I went, or when it stopped raining. But suddenly I realised it was dark, and I turned back. It wasn't raining then. I thought I'd better get home the shortest way, so I climbed over the hill again, and there the grass was quite dry, and so were my shoes, and the moon was out. And just below the rocks there I met Mr Kenyon and my father, coming to look for me. They *said* they were looking for me. It seemed silly to me. I thought I was only a couple of hours late. But they said it was Tuesday,' she said, eyes wide and distant and grave confronting George Felse's straight regard. 'They said I'd been gone five days. I didn't believe it until we got home, and there was a letter for me, an answer to the one I'd posted. But I couldn't tell them any more than I've told you now, and I know they don't believe me. All the week-end, they say, they've been trying to find me, and covering up the fact that I wasn't here.'

George sat silent, studying her thoughtfully for a moment. Nothing of belief or disbelief, wonder or suspicion, showed in his face; he might have been listening to a morning's trivialities from Mrs Dale. Annet knew how to be silent, too. She looked back at him and added nothing; she waited, her hands quite still in her lap.

'You met no one on the hill? Or along by the brook?' It was hardly likely on a rainy Thursday afternoon, but there was always the possibility.

'No.'

'Mr Kenyon saw her,' said Mr Beck quickly.

'I was driving back along the lane about four,' confirmed Tom, 'on my way home for the week-end, and I happened to look up at the Hallowmount just as the sun came out on it. I saw her climbing towards the crest, just as she says.'

'Could you be sure it was Annet, at that distance?'

'I'd seen her go out, I knew just what she was wearing.' Carefully he suppressed the aching truth that he would have known her in whatever clothes, by the gait, by the carriage of her head, by all the shape and movement that made her Annet, and no other person. 'I was sure. Then, when I got back here on Tuesday evening, and found she's been missing all that time, I told Mr and Mrs Beck about it, and we went there on the off-chance of picking up any traces. We didn't expect anything. But we found her.'

'She was surprised to see us,' said Beck eagerly. 'She asked what we were doing there, and if anything was the matter. She said she knew she was very late, but surely we didn't have to send out a search party.'

'She was particularly surprised to see me,' added Tom. 'She said she thought I should have been home by then, and surely I didn't stay behind because we were worried about her.'

They were all joining in now, anxiously proffering details of the search for her, of her return, of the terrible consistency of her attitude since, which had never wavered. George listened with unshakable patience, but it was Annet he watched. And when he had everything, all but those tyre-tracks of which her parents knew nothing, and which Tom must mention only privately if he mentioned them at all, it was still to Annet that he spoke.

'So you went up the Hallowmount,' he said, 'and vanished out of time and place, like Tabitha Blount in the seventeenth century. And came back, also like Tabby, sure you'd been there no more than an hour or two, and never strayed out of this world. She never could give any account of her fairyland. Can you do any better?'

'I know I was happy,' said Annet, disregarding all but what she wished to hear; and suddenly the blue eyes deepened and warmed into such a passion of triumph and anguished joy that George was startled and moved. 'Happy' was a large word, but not too large for the blaze that lit her for a moment.

'There's nothing more you wish to tell me? And nothing you want to amend? It's up to you, Annet.'

'There's nothing else I can tell you,' she said. 'I told you that before I began. Ask them if I've changed anything. I told you they didn't believe me. I can't help it if you don't believe me, either.'

'I don't,' said George simply. 'Nor do I believe that your parents or Kenyon here have accepted it, never for a moment. Your missing five days were spent somewhere. As you very well know. I think, though I may be wrong, that you also know very well where, in every detail. I strongly advise you to think again, and tell me the truth, as in the end you'll have to.'

Her father was at her side by this time, feebly fumbling her cold hand. Her mother was close on her left, gripping the arm of the chair.

'Mr Felse, you must allow for the possibility of – of— More things in heaven and earth, you know— How can we presume to know everything?' Beck was tearing sentences to shreds in his nervousness, and dropping the tatters wherever they fell.

'She's been utterly consistent,' Tom pointed out, trampling the pieces ruthlessly. Someone had to sound sane, and put the more possible theories. 'I don't argue that you should believe in fairies – but you'll notice that Annet hasn't asked you to. She's made no claim at all that anything supernatural ever happened to her. She says she doesn't remember anything between going over the crest of the Hallowmount and coming to herself to realise it had grown dark, and then hurrying towards home. There's nothing fantastic about that. It doesn't happen often, but it happens, you know of cases as well as I do. Of course those five days were spent somewhere, we know that. But it may very well be true that Annet doesn't know where.'

'Amnesia,' said Mrs Beck, too strenuously, and recoiled from the theatrical impact of the word, and said no more.

Why were they arguing like this, what was it they were trying to ward off? What did the police care about a truant week-end, provided no laws had been broken?

'It was a fine, dry week-end,' said George reasonably, 'About ten per cent of the Black Country must have been roaming the border hills on Saturday and Sunday, and the odds are pretty good that a fair proportion of them were on the Hallowmount. They couldn't all miss a wandering, distressed girl. If any locals had seen her they'd have spoken to her. Everyone knows her. And did she reappear tired, hungry, anxious or grimy? Apparently not. She came down to you completely self-possessed, neat, tidy and fresh, asking pertinent questions. From fairyland, yes, perhaps. From amnesia one's return would, I fancy, be less coherent and co-ordinated.'

He hitched his chair a little nearer to Annet, he reached and took her hands, compelling her attention.

'I don't doubt the happiness, Annet,' he said gently. 'In a way I think you've told me a kind of truth, a partial truth. Now tell me the rest while you can. You were no nearer the underworld than, say – Birmingham. Were you?'

Hard on the heels of the brief, blank silence Beck said, in a high, hysterical voice: 'But what does it mean? What if she actually was in Birmingham? That's not a crime, however wrong it may be to lie to one's family. What are all these questions *about*? I think you should tell us.'

'Perhaps I should. Unless Annet wants to alter her story first?'

'I can't,' said Annet. Braced and intent, she watched him, and whether it was incomprehension he saw in her face or the impenetrable resolution to cover and contain what she understood all too well, he still could not determine.

'Very well. You want to know what the questions are about. Last Saturday night, around shop-closing time,' said George, 'a young girl was seen, by two witnesses independently, standing on the corner of a minor – and at that hour an almost deserted – street in Birmingham. She was idling about as though waiting for someone, about forty yards from a small jeweller's shop. The first witness, an old woman who lives in the street, gave a fair description of a girl who answers very well to Annet's general appearance. The second one, a young man, gave a much more detailed account. He spoke to her, you see, wasted five minutes or so trying to pick her up. He described her minutely. Girls like Annet can't, I suppose, hope to escape the notice of young men.'

'But however good a description you had,' protested Tom, 'why a girl from Comerford, of all places, when this was in Birmingham?'

'A good question, I'm coming to that.'

'I suppose your son told you Annet was missing during the weekend,' said Tom, bitterly and unwisely.

George gave him a long, thoughtful glance from under raised brows.

'No, Dominic's told me nothing – but thanks for the tip. No, the Birmingham police came to us because this girl, according to her unwelcome cavalier, was filling in the time while she waited, as one does, by fishing the forgotten bits out of her pockets. Everyone has an end of pencil, or a loose lucky farthing, or a hair-grip, or something, lost in the fluff at the seam. This girl had a bus ticket. She was playing with it when he accosted her, and she was nervous. That amused him. He paid particular attention to the way she was folding it up into a tiny fan – you know? – narrow folds across in alternate directions, then fold the whole thing in the middle. When he was too pressing – though of course he doesn't admit that – she drew back from him hastily, twisted the fan in her fingers and threw it down. He says he left her alone then. If she didn't want him, he could do without her. But when they took him back to the corner next day he knew where the ticket had lodged, close under the wall, in a cranny of the paving stones. And sure enough, they found it there, and he identified it positively.

'It turned out,' said George flatly, 'to be a one-and-fourpenny by

Egertons' service between Comerbourne and Comerford. With that and the description it wasn't so hard to settle upon Annet, once they came to us. Unfortunately no one saw the person for whom she was waiting. She told the youngster who accosted her she was waiting for her boyfriend, and he was an amateur boxer. So he didn't hang around to put it to the test.'

'But what of it?' persisted Beck feverishly. 'Why are they hunting for this girl – whoever she may be?'

'Because, around midnight that night, when a policeman on the beat came along, he saw that the steel mesh gate over the jeweller's doorway wasn't quite closed. All the lights in the shop were off, the gate was drawn into position, but when he tried it he found it wasn't secured. And naturally he investigated. He found the till cleared of cash, and several glass cases emptied, too, apparently of small jewellery. The loss is estimated at about two thousand pounds, mostly in good rings.

'And the proprietor – he was an old, solitary man, who lived over his shop – he was in his own workroom at the back. His head had been battered in with a heavy silver candlestick,' said George, his voice suddenly hard, deliberate and cold. 'He was dead.'

The gasp of realisation and horror that stiffened them all jerked Annet for the first time out of her changeling calm, and out of her chair. She was torn erect, rigid, her face convulsed, her hands clutching at the empty air before her. The great eyes dilated, fixed and blank with shock. The contorted mouth screamed: 'No – no – *no!*' and her voice shattered on a suffocating breath.

Tom sprang wildly towards her; but it was George Felse who caught and lifted her in his arms as she fell.

'Call her doctor,' said George, over the limp, light body. 'I'd rather he was here.'

He put off Mrs Beck, who was clawing frantically at her darling and spilling unwonted and painful tears, with a lunge of one shoulder, and carried his burden to the couch. 'Tom, you get him. Use my name, he'll come all the quicker.'

Tom got as far as the telephone before he realised that he did not even know which doctor they favoured, and there being no emergency notes on the scratch-pad to enlighten him, he was forced to come and drag Beck away from the couch to supply the information he needed. Annet was lying motionless and pale by then, a pillow under her cheek, her body stretched carefully at ease, the narrow skirt drawn down over her knees, surely by George Felse. Tom dialled with an erratic finger, hating George more for his deftness and humanity even than for his official menace. What right had he? What right? To strike her down, and then to be the one who held her in his arms, and laid her down so gently among the cushions, and stroked back the tumbled hair from her eyes with such assured fingers.

'Doctor Thorpe? I'm speaking for Mr Beck at Fairford. Can you come out here at once, please? Yes, it's urgent. Miss Beck – Annet – she's in a faint. Detective-Inspector Felse is here, he told me to ask you to hurry. I don't know – a degree of shock, I suppose – he urges you to come as soon as possible. Good, thank you!'

He hung up, and his hand was shaking so that the receiver rattled in the rest. He went back to the living-room with Beck clinging close on his arm.

Mrs Beck had control of herself again; the traces of her few and angry tears mottled her cheeks, her ruled dark hair, dull from many tintings, was shaken out of its customary severity, but she was herself again, and would not be overwhelmed a second time. George had withdrawn and left Annet to her; not, it seemed, from any embarrassment or incompetence on his own part, rather to provide her with something urgent and practical to do, for he did not withdraw far, and he watched her ministrations with a close and sombre regard.

'Is she subject to fainting fits?'

'I've never known her faint before.' She gave him a furious look over her daughter's body. 'You frightened her. You shocked her.'

'She could have read most of the same details in tonight's paper,' said George, 'but I doubt if they'd have had the same effect. She wouldn't have realised then what she knows now – that it happened forty yards away from her, while she was waiting for her – friend. There are things she knows that I didn't have to tell her. Such as where he was while she stood waiting for him. If he'd been round the other corner in the tobacconist's, buying cigarettes, I think Annet would have stood the shock of an unknown old man's death without collapsing.'

'But, good God!' protested Tom, twisting away from the thought, 'you're making out that she kept watch for him on the corner while he did it.'

'That's one possibility. There are others.'

He didn't go into them. He stood looking down at the pale, motionless face on the cushions, pinched and blue at the corners of the closed lips, a strange, faint frown, austere and distant, clenched upon her black brows. The silken wings of her hair spread blue-black on either side, buoyed up on the resilient down of the pillow like a drowned girl's hair afloat on water.

So slight, and so remote; and so incalculable. Was it possible to know her so well that she would some day be able to take down all the barriers and be relaxed and at peace with you? He'd never had much close contact with her. It might be only that unbelievably touching beauty of hers that made him feel her exile from her fellow-men to be something imposed from without, and not chosen. That, and her age. She could have been Dominic's year-older sister. He would have liked a girl. So would Bunty, but there'd just never been one. Did she remain closed like an ivory box with a secret spring even when she was with X? Or open like a flower to the sun? The inescapable X. X who must be found, because he had almost certainly killed a solitary, eccentric, miserly old man for the contents of his till and the sweepings of three show-cases.

'You haven't proved she was even there,' said Beck, stirred to the feeble man's desperate bravery. 'There must be many girls who fit the same description equally well. You see Annet's ill. She never faints. She was wandering somewhere all the week-end, and she's ill and frightened, and you have to use her so brutally.'

'I'm sorry if you think I was brutal. I don't think I was guilty single-handed of cutting the ground from under Annet's feet. Someone else did that. When he hit the old man. No,' he said, looking down bitterly at the slow, languid heave and fall of Annet's breast, 'I haven't proved she was there. I haven't proved she was the girl on the corner. I didn't have to. Annet told us that, pretty plainly. The only thing she has told us yet.'

But it wasn't; not quite. She had told him, however unwillingly, the depth and height and hopelessness and helplessness of the love that was eating her alive. If they hadn't seen it, if they had no means of measuring or grasping it, that was their failure; and it looked as if that inadequacy in them might yet be the death of Annet. A little honest brutality might have cheered and warmed her, and brought her close enough to confide.

He looked up and caught Tom Kenyon's eye upon him. There was one who wasn't going to dispute his contention that Annet had betrayed herself. He'd wanted a reaction from her, and he'd got it at last, and it identified her only too surely.

'But you realise, don't you,' said Tom with careful quietness, 'that she's absolved herself, too? Oh, I know! If it wasn't Annet your witness saw, why should this be such a shock to her? But since it is such a shock, she can't have known. Can she? She *can't have known* anything about the murder, maybe not even about the robbery. She was there, yes, but quite innocently, waiting for him. She thought he was buying something, maybe a present for her. It was only because of their joint escapade that she wouldn't admit where she'd been. To keep him out of trouble, yes, but not *that* trouble – because she knew nothing about that until you just told her. Why else should it drop her like a shot?'

George said: 'You make a pretty good case. If this is genuine, of course.'

'*If* it's genuine! My God, man, look at the poor kid!'

No need to tell him that, he'd hardly taken his eyes off her. But he didn't commit himself to any opinion about the nature of this collapse. He'd been in the world and his profession long enough to know that deception has many layers, and women know the deepest of them. No question of Annet's unconsciousness now, no doubt of her anguish; but he had known self-induced illnesses and self-induced collapses before, as opportune as this, as disarming as this, sometimes even deceiving their victims and manipulators. When you can't bear any more, when you want the questioning to stop, when you need time to think, you cut off the sources of reason and force and light, and drop like a dead bird off its roost in a frosty night. And as long as you stay darkened and silenced, no one can torment you.

Annet remained dark and silent a disquietingly long time. Cold water bathing her forehead brought no flicker to her pinched face.

'We'd better get her to bed,' her mother said. 'Arthur, help me with her.'

'I'll carry her upstairs for you.'

George stooped and slid an arm under the girl's shoulders, very gently easing her weight into balance against his breast. Her head rolled limply upon his shoulder, the black wing of glossy hair swung, and hid her face. Inside the loose collar of her yellow sweater a narrow thread of black velvet ribbon lay uncovered against the honeyed pallor of her neck. It moved with her weight, dipping between her little breasts.

He held her cradled against him, and ran his fingers round her neck beneath the fragrant drift of hair. There was a neat little bow tied there in the ribbon; he eased it round until he could untie it, and she never stirred, not even when he laid the loosened ends together, and drew out the treasure she had concealed between her breasts.

He held it out for them all to see, dangling on its ribbon: a narrow circlet of gold, a brand-new wedding ring.

They were upstairs with her a long time, the mother and the doctor, but they came down at last. George, who had sat all the time looking down with a shadowed face and dangling the ring by its ribbon, rose to meet them. He could think of nothing in his life that had filled him with so deep a sense of shame as the act of filching that tiny thing from her while she lay senseless; the most private and precious thing she possessed, the symbol of everything she wanted, and he could not let her keep it. He weighed it in his hand, and it was heavier than it should have been with all the inescapable implications that clung to it.

The old man's assistant, who had left him just preparing to lock up on Saturday night, had made an inventory of the stolen pieces, as far as his memory served him. There was no question as to whether he would be able to identify the ring; a tiny private mark was scratched beside the assay marks inside it, whoever had had it in his stock would know it.

'Has she come round?'

'How is she?'

Two of them asked together; Arthur Beck, suddenly piteously old and withered, only trembled and waited.

'Yes, she's come round.' Doctor Thorpe closed his bag and looked from one to another of them with quick, speculative grey eyes. 'But you won't be able to question her any more tonight.'

The slight antagonism in his voice was human enough, in the circumstances, but George's ear was becoming acutely tuned to every inflection that concerned Annet. Thirty-five, not bad-looking, in professional attendance on her for five years or so – on those rare occasions, at least, when she needed attention: yes, this might very well be another of her many mute, unnoticed victims.

'I wasn't thinking of trying. Is she going to be all right?'

'Physically there's not much the matter with her. It was a long faint, but she came out of it fairly well in the end. She seems to be in a state of deep and genuine shock, but physically she's as strong as a horse, there'll be no ill effects. Just leave her alone for tonight, that's all.'

'Will you come in and see her tomorrow morning? I'd like to have your all-clear before I talk to her again, and, I'll go very gently. But it's urgent that it should be as soon as possible.'

'Very well,' said the doctor with tightening lips, 'I'll look in and see her before surgery. Call me about nine, and I'll give you my report.'

'When she's slept on it she may be willing to talk to me freely. I think you must see it's the best, the only thing she can do to help herself now. If you have any influence with her, try to get her to realise it.' He included all of them in that request, and saw the doctor's tight, reserved face ease a little. 'I've got a job to do, but it isn't to hurt Annet. A part of it is to save whatever can be saved for her.'

'I'll bear it in mind,' said the doctor.

'Do one thing more for me, will you? With your permission, Mr Beck, I want to put a constable on guard here in your grounds. I'd be obliged, doctor, if you'd stay here with Annet until he arrives.'

They stared eye to eye for a second, then the doctor said quietly: 'Very well, I'll go back to her.

Beck turned and shuffled his way to the stairs after him, a wretched, wilted figure, babbling feeble daily platitudes, trying to pretend there was a grain of normality left in his life, where there was nothing but a waste of wreckage like a battlefield.

'I'll be off now,' said George, glad, if anything, to be left confronting Mrs Beck, with whom, it was clear, he would have to deal if he wanted to get sense out of anyone. 'I shall have to take this ring with me, you understand that?'

'Yes, I understand.' She looked down pallidly at the thin, bright circlet. 'Do you think – is it possible that they—?'

'I think it very unlikely. This is a symbol, that's all. And a promise. It isn't so easy to get married in a hurry without a fair amount of money, and you see they can't have had much between them.'

She flinched at that, his sound reasons for thinking so were only too clear.

'And in the circumstances,' he said gently, 'I think you should hope and pray that they didn't manage it.'

She whispered: 'Yes!' hardly audibly.

'Don't let her go to work tomorrow, even if she wants to. I want you to keep a close guard on her, and hold her available only to us. Don't take anyone into your confidence, not yet, at any rate. Better telephone Mrs Blacklock in the morning, and say Annet has a return of her cold.'

'Yes,' she said again, dully, 'I expect that would be best.'

'And I need, if you have one, a good recent picture of her.'

Photographs of Annet were so few in the house, now Tom came to think of it, that their rarity shed light on her absence of vanity. When had he even seen her peering at her make-up in a mirror with the devoted attention of most girls? Mrs Beck brought a postcard portrait, the latest she had, and George pocketed it after one thoughtful glance again at the lovely, troubling face.

'Thank you. You shall have it back, I promise you.' Would she get the original back as surely? He wished he knew the answer to that. 'I'll leave you in peace now. And believe me, I'm sorry!'

'I'll see you out,' said Tom, and followed him from the room and out through the dim hall, into the moist, mild night. The front door closed almost stealthily upon the tragedy within.

'It can't be true!' said Tom, suddenly in total revolt. The rupture was too brutal and extreme between this immemorial border stability, the continuity that made nothing of wars and centuries and dissensions, and that abrupt and strident descent into the cheapest and shallowest of ephemeral crimes. A mean little incident, a quick raid and a random blow, merely for money, for the means to buy things for Annet, to take Annet about in style – everything Annet didn't want. The offence against her, the debasing of her immoderate love, almost as capital a crime as the killing of the old man. She couldn't have known. It was the death of everything she had wanted from love. No, she couldn't possibly have known.

'It can,' said George grimly. 'It happens all the time.'

Did he mean merely this sordid, characteristic latter-day killing for profit, or the unbelievable misunderstanding and profanation of love implied in it? There was no knowing; he was so much deeper than he seemed, you only saw the abyss when you were already falling.

'We think we have sound relationships,' said George, answering the doubt beyond doubt, 'and suddenly there's a word said or a thing done, so shatteringly out of key that you find yourself alone, and know you've never actually touched your partner at any point, or said a word in the same language. And it doesn't always even absolve you from loving, when it happens. That's the hell of it.'

'There's nothing I can do,' said Tom, 'except tell you everything I know. There's only one thing you haven't heard already. They don't know about it, I never told them, but I went over the Hallowmount yesterday morning, early, to see if there were any signs of a vehicle having been up there recently. I found tracks of a motorbike or a scooter, there's no telling which.' He described them, and traced them again to the first gate. 'It seemed to me that someone must have brought her back that way, the night before. After the showers this afternoon the grass and moss will have sprung back and smoothed them out, most likely, but there may be a trace left here and there. And I can show you exactly where they were.'

'Then you shall, early tomorrow. If you wouldn't mind turning out about seven? The track up from the south – Abbot's Bale and beyond. Yes, I see that,' said George, musing darkly under the hollies by the gate. 'But why the same route back? She left in broad daylight, without luggage, in her everyday clothes, and that improbable way. All very understandable. But in the dark he could surely have come round and dropped her quietly at the corner of the lane.'

'But not without using up quite a bit more time over his return, because he'd have had to come right round the hill, one end or the

other. And maybe it was urgent that he should get home. He may
have watchful parents, too,' said Tom with a hollow smile.

'Probably has! They often turn out to belong to the most
respectable citizens around,' reflected George wryly, 'and they're
always at a loss to understand what they've done to deserve it.'

'But Annet—' He looked up briefly and bitterly at the lighted
window; no shadows moved across the pale curtains. 'Do you have to
put a police guard on her? Where could she run to, even if she tried to
get out?'

'I wasn't thinking so much of Annet running,' said George in a
deceptively mild and deprecating voice. He caught the wondering
glance that questioned his purpose and said more abruptly, with no
expression at all: 'Hasn't it dawned on you that this lover of hers has
killed once already? And that only Annet knows who he is?'

He walked away into the dark. Shaken to the heart, Tom protested
softly and wildly after him: 'He wouldn't hurt *her*? Damn it, he *loves*
her!'

'He did,' came wafting back to him hollowly as the car door
slammed. 'Before he was frightened for himself.'

Mrs Beck was nowhere to be seen when Tom went back into the
house; and Beck was sitting slumped in a chair, clutching a glass that
shook in his hands and slopped shivering waves of whisky and soda
on to his trousers. When he lifted it to his mouth it chattered against
his false teeth, when he propped it steadyingly against his body it
chattered against his waistcoat buttons. His glasses sagged sidelong
down his nose, exposing one moist, hopeless eye, while the other was
still seen monstrously magnified behind the lens. He must have
downed one drink already, and spilled half of it. And he hadn't
forgotten to get out a second glass. Tom's heart sank at sight of it,
though he needed at least one shot, perhaps, to steady him. If this
was going to be the way of escape, he wanted no part of it, he needed
all his wits, he had thinking to do. And yet how could he go away and
leave this wretched wreck to sweat and shiver alone? He wasn't fit to
be left.

'He's gone, is he? Come and have a drink, Kenyon. I don't usually
indulge, but I felt I needed something to steady my nerves.' He cast a
hunted look towards the ceiling. 'My wife's with Annet. I don't
know! You don't think it could be all a mistake?' he pleaded
pathetically, and shrank from the direct encounter of their eyes. 'No,

I suppose not. If the man's dead— But it's some mistake about Annet. She couldn't have picked up that sort of young man. But as it is with her, I'm sure that can't be true. She wouldn't encourage the wrong type of boy. She's hard to please, our Annet. She never liked the flashy type. These teddy boys, they used to ask her to dance, and she'd dance with them, and be polite, but they never got anywhere with her. Myra always tells us what kind of evening they have.'

Myra always tells us! Not Annet. And Annet knew, none better, that Myra always told them, that her very function was always to tell them. The closer you watch, thought Tom, the more you do not see. You didn't trust her – I wonder why, in the first place? There must have been a time when she was to be trusted absolutely – you didn't trust her, and you wouldn't let her have her soul to herself, but she got it in spite of you, and shut you out from it. And it's too late now to complain of what she did with it, unaided and unadvised.

'But you haven't got a drink, my dear boy, do help yourself to a drink. I'm sure you need – we all need a little reinforcement. Please! Let me!'

He struggled to rise and reach the bottle, and there was nothing to be done but forestall him. Tom made his glass pale with soda, and hid its insipid colour with a careful hand.

'And then, in Birmingham, is that feasible! I ask you! No, no, there's some mistake, it was another girl. How could Annet know a young man in Birmingham? She's hardly ever been there even overnight, only once or twice with Mrs Blacklock to educational conferences or extra-mural classes, you know. And now and then shopping, of course, with her mother, or with Myra, but only for the day. It's absurd! With so little opportunity, how could she possibly have formed an intimate association with a young fellow in the city? It's a mistake, isn't it? It must be a mistake.'

'If it is,' said Tom encouragingly, though encouraging was the last thing he felt just then, 'the police will find out. You can be sure of that. The best possible thing Annet can do is tell George Felse everything she did during the week-end. There'll be people who've seen her, and can confirm her story, if only she'll speak.'

'Yes – yes, that's true, isn't it? There are always ways of verifying such statements. If only she'll tell us! And even here at home, you know, Tom, where does she ever go alone for more than an hour or two? Myra's always with her when she goes to dances, and we see to it that they have reliable escorts. And even if she works late the

253

Blacklocks always send her home by car. From choir practice Mr Collins walks her home, or Mr Blacklock brings her himself. It isn't as if we've been neglectful. All our friends think the world of her, and care for her like their own. When *can* she have formed an undesirable acquaintance? We should have known. Someone would have warned us.'

Only too surely they would. That was why she had to learn to cover every trace, to erase the very prints of her feet where she had passed, to open her own escape hatches into the underworld below the Hallowmount.

'There was the affair of young Miles, of course. But that was understandable folly. And since then we've watched her even more carefully.'

What was the sense in telling him now that that was where they'd made their mistake? And in fact it was only one in a wilderness of mistakes, and not, Tom felt, the fatal one. Something else had gone wrong with Annet's daughterhood, something basic and incurable.

'Don't upset yourself, that won't help. You've always done your best for her, everybody knows that.' He leaned and extracted the quivering glass from Beck's fingers, for it was slipping slowly through them as he watched. Beck did not seem to notice its going, only in a distant way to be relieved to find his hands free. He took his quaking head between them, staring blindly through a mist half drunkenness and half tears.

'We did do our best. They'll find out they've made a mistake. It wasn't Annet. It couldn't have been.'

But he was crying his denials because he knew it had been. Her charged stillness, braced to bear whatever pressures were loosed on her, and still cover up her known sins for the sake of her partner; this spoke loudly enough. And her cry of passionate denial and fearful realisation when she was forced to contemplate the sin of which she had not known; and the violence of her retreat into a semblance of death; and the ring on its ribbon round her neck.

The old man was weeping feebly, without even knowing it, letting the tears find a desultory way down the furrows of his grey, despairing face.

'It wasn't good enough, that's all, our best wasn't good enough. Where did we go wrong? Was it my fault? I never carried much weight, you know, not with anyone. Managing the children at school was too much for me sometimes, They always know,' he said drearily, 'who can hold his own with them, and who can't. I never could find out how it was done. But to fail with Annet! To fall short even with her!'

'Nonsense, of course you haven't always fallen short. You mustn't think like that, what good does it do? The best girl in the world can very well throw away her affection on a bad lot, we all know it happens. Is that your fault?'

Tom's voice was gentle and reasonable; he marvelled at himself, while his mind dallied with the thought of filling the old man to the brim with whisky, and sinking him completely. Then at least he cold be manhandled to bed, and he'd be blessedly silent, affording a respite for himself and everyone else. But he'd probably be sick, and not even put himself happily to sleep. No, better not risk it. Let him talk. If it helped him, at least somebody was getting something out of it.

Drearily, drearily the fumbling voice, thickening a little now, proceeded lead-footed along its inevitable downhill toad of confession, laying out his inadequacies like pilgrim stones along the way.

'But then, why should I be expected to succeed with her? You don't know, Tom, do you – about Annet? I've never told you. We never told anyone. It isn't the sort of thing you write to your friends—'

He was laughing now, and still crying. Maybe the whisky was taking hold, and he'd pass out. Tom put a hand on his arm and shook him gently.

'That's all right, there's nothing you need to tell me. Wait till tomorrow. There'll be new developments then, maybe they'll have found the real girl they're looking for.'

'They have found her,' said Beck with dreadful clarity, and gripped Tom's arm in his heavy, trembling hands. 'I want to tell you. It's been on my mind so long, I've got to tell someone. She isn't mine, you see. Things might have been different if she had been. I never understood her, I never had any influence over her. I was always ashamed and afraid, because she isn't even mine.'

He sagged into Tom's shoulder and lay there, as it seemed, thankfully, almost comfortably. And, my God, what do you say now? What can you say?

'You're a little tight, you know, better come to bed and rest. You don't mean this. All parents have these doubts sooner or later, it's one of the hazards of fatherhood.'

His own voice sounded to him like the phoney effort of one

privately in acute pain. He got to his feet brusquely, wild to break up this inconceivable party, and lugged Beck up after him, propping him against the arm of the chair until he could get a firm hold on him. And Beck yielded. When had anyone pulled or pushed or propelled him, that he had not yielded? But he went on talking, too, with remorseless misery, all across the room and all along the empty hall.

'You don't believe me. But it's true. *My wife told me*,' he said with self-mutilating satisfaction. 'She'd waited long enough for me to give her a child. In the end she got one where she could. She never told me who. She said what was that to me? I couldn't help her. She held it against me. She still does.'

Somehow, he was never very clear how, Tom got him up the stairs and into his bedroom, and there frankly abandoned him. Sick with disgust and pity, he shut himself into the bathroom and washed the sweat and the prickling of shame from his face in cold water. He felt like vomiting, but he hadn't had enough whisky. Maybe he ought to go down again and put himself out for the count. It would be one way of shutting the door on all this for a little while.

Was it true? Had she ever really told him such a thing? She might have, she was a woman who could if driven to it, and he was a man to whom it could be done, so crushable that in the end there might be nothing to be done with him but crush him once for all, and finish it. But even if she had told him that, need it necessarily be true? Or a gesture of hatred and cruelty engendered by the bitter frustration of their marriage?

Tom went over and over the bleak sentences he had tried hard not to hear and could not now forget, and for the life of him he couldn't judge what was truth and what wasn't.

But Annet herself was the heart of the evidence. Was there anything of Beck there, in her clear-cut, self-contained, fastidious dignity? And if she was alien, and the root of their alienation, she might well be wandering, lost, trying to find her own way in a desert without asking for help from anyone. And if she knew—? How could she know? No one could be so inhuman, so insanely self-centred as to tell her? But *if* she knew—

And there was nothing he could do for her. Nothing to help or comfort her. Nothing, nothing to make her aware of him.

They came down from the Hallowmount in the fresh morning light, and separated on the road below, Tom heading for school, George for the southern end of the ridge and the straggling village of Abbot's Bale in the long, bare cleft of Middlehope.

There was an hour yet before he could call the doctor and receive his verdict on Annet; and when he went to Fairford this time he must have a sergeant and a constable with him. Meantime, he could view the escape route and its strategic possibilities, the filling-stations, the natives, the chances of picking up evidence. Annet was striking in any circumstances; even flying past on the pillion of a motor-bike (probably stripped of its silencer and ridden with vile technique and viler manners), she might be noticed. If they'd halted at a filling-station with healthily normal young men in the forecourt instead of girls, she certainly would be. Someone might remember.

'So Miss Myra Gibbons always reports back, does she?' said George sceptically. He had received a half-account of last night's unsought confidences, but it stopped well short of the revelation about Annet's parentage. If anyone re-told that tale, short of the most desperate emergency, it would have to be Beck himself.

'Not as fully as Father supposes, I fancy. I bet I know one or two things that never got back to the parents. As, for instance, that a couple of uniformed men had to show up at the hall late one Saturday night, to stop what promised to be a first-class fight. Over Annet. Not her fault, unless she's to blame for looking like she does. A handful of the local ton-up club have taken to looking in at the ballroom about ten to ten, just in time to beat the no-entry or re-entry after ten rule. They know a good-looker when they see one, and they think a good-looker ought to go for their kind. Annet didn't do anything except dance with the leader of the bunch when he asked her. It was her escort who objected when he promptly asked her again. There've been other clashes, too, occasionally, less serious.

Oh, yes, even among the respectable and ultra-respectable Annet can set the sparks flying.'

'Then this youngster who tried to corner her had a motor-bike,' said Tom hopefully. 'All the round-the-houses brigade seem to have big, powerful jobs, five hundreds mostly. What beats me is they never seem to do anything or go anywhere with them – only round and round the block.'

'Oh, they do now. They go all the three-quarters of a mile between their favourite roosting-ground on the corner of the square and the Rainbow Café on the edge of town. And back. One or two,' admitted George on reflection, 'might have the enterprise to get as far as Birmingham. One or two, literally, might get a good deal farther and venture a good deal more, but I wouldn't put it higher than two. And one of 'em's the youngster who fancied her at the dance. And he works,' said George reflectively, sliding into the driving-seat of his almost-new MG, 'at a haulage concern in Abbot's Bale.'

'He does?' A spark of hope kindled professionally in Tom's eye at the thought that the hunt might veer so blessedly away from the school. Not one of ours! One of the black-leather lads, born scapegoats! But could so close an association be formed over a few dances, without a single strictly private meeting? Maybe it could, but the odds seemed against it. He'd never, for instance, taken her home afterwards. She always went home with Myra. Or did her parents merely suppose that she did?

'Of course,' he said dubiously, 'it seems more likely, on the whole, that it was someone from Birmingham, someone who came here to fetch her, and isn't necessarily known here.'

'With Annet planning the operation and telling him exactly where to wait for her and how to get there? It could well be.' It could; she had the stuff of command in her, and passion enough for two if the partner proved deficient. 'We're checking at both ends, anyhow,' said George. 'Properly speaking it's Birmingham's case, not ours.'

He was turning the key in the ignition when Tom came loping across to ask: 'You didn't ask your boy, did you? About my questioning them both?'

He was glad to have the full story of that incident off his chest, but very reluctant indeed that it should get back to Dominic. Nothing had been published yet about Annet. Nothing would, if they could get the information they urgently needed some other way; and surely, surely she'd talk this morning, and save herself? It would be superhuman to keep silence still. Supposing she told everything, did her best to co-operate, and she herself turned out to have known nothing about the crime, then her part in the affair, even if it could not be suppressed, would be for ever toned down to its most innocent, and maybe need never erupt into the headlines at all.

'I asked him about their week-end. He told me what he told you.' George's eyes did not commit him at all as to how completely he had believed; but the ghost of a rather rueful smile showed for a moment. 'I didn't say I had any deep motives for asking, and I didn't say you'd tipped me off – even inadvertently. But I suspect he already smells a sizeable rat.'

'Did he say anything to make you think so?'

George's smile lost its sourness for an instant. What Dominic had actually said, and very belligerently, was: 'What business is it of Brash 'Arry's, anyhow?' But there was no need to broadcast that. 'My thumbs pricked, that's all.' This time he did turn the key. 'So long, Tom, and thanks!'

He drove southward along the flank of the Hallowmount, past the turning to Wastfield, past the new plantations, on towards the slow, descending tail of the ridge, that took such an unconscionable time to decline far enough to permit the passage of a road. Yes, if the boy had needed to keep a strict time-table on his return home he might very well be forced to cut that long drive round, and drop Annet where he had picked her up, to climb back over the hill. But why not simply drop her on the bus-route to the village, and let her ride the last stage home as though she'd been to a cinema? Who would have thought anything about her appearance on an evening bus? It might even have disarmed some who had been gleefully scenting a trail of fresh trouble. But half the 'why's' involved in any crime must be answered without too nice a reference to logic. At our best we are not creatures of absolute reason and consistency. Having killed, we are not at our best.

Not much time to do more than run into Abbot's Bale, and take a quick look at the upland road which soon dwindled into a cart-track, plunging at last through a farm-gate to climb the first rough pasture; and then fill up at Hopton's as an excuse for a word with old man Hopton, who was sure to be the only one pottering about the forecourt at this hour. A powerful, bowed, cross-grained little elderly man with an obstinate, surly face that never took anyone in for long. It was one of the very few places where George and the probation officer had ever been able to place their most perilous problem-boys with goodwill and confidence. If they failed there, you were on your way to despairing of them. Some did fail; there was more than enough to despair about in human nature, twentieth-century style. Some, against all the odds, stuck it out and got a stout foothold on life again; there was plenty of ground for hope, too.

George asked after the latest of them, as Hopton flicked his leather squeaking across the windscreen. Hopton opined that the latest was an idle, cheeky layabout with a chip on his shoulder as big as a Yule log; he reckoned he'd shape up about average. Rightly interpreting this as a considerably more encouraging report than it sounded, George turned to the matter that was nearer his heart.

'Ever see young Geoff Westcott these days? He's still driving for Lowthers, isn't he?'

'Hear him more than I see him. Comes clattering in to fill up sometimes, week-ends. Oh, ay, he's still there. Good driver, too, on a lorry. Pity he leaves his manners in the cab when he knocks off. He's hell on that three-fifty of his.'

'Fill up last week-end?' asked George.

'Didn't see him. Why? You got something on him?' The shrewd old eyes narrowed on George's face expectantly. 'Didn't see him since Thursday, come to think of it.'

'He's clean, as far as I know,' said George amiably. 'When on Thursday? Just a little job involving a motor-bike, nothing special on him, just eliminating the barely-possibles.'

'He was in in the middle of the afternoon. I remember young Sid asked him what he was doing romping around in working hours, and he said he had three extra days saved up from the summer holidays, and was taking 'em before the weather broke altogether.'

George digested this with a prickle of satisfaction stirring his scalp. He fished out from his wallet one of the barely-dry copies the police photographer had made him from Annet's photograph.

'What poor girl's he standing up for what other poor girl, these days?'

'Mate,' said Hopton, very dryly indeed, 'you got it wrong. These days the girls ain't surplus round here like they used to be. It's the men who get stood up, even the ones with three-fifties. And if they don't like it, they know what they can do. They're relieved if they can get a girl to go steady, they lay off the tricks unless they want to be left high and dry.'

'You're not telling me young Geoff's got a steady?'

'Hasn't he, though! Wouldn't dare call Martha Blount anything but steady, would you?'

'No,' owned George freely, 'I wouldn't!' If Martha Blount meant marriage, the odds were that she wasn't wasting her time. There were still Blounts round the Hallowmount, nearly three centuries after Tabby blundered in and out of fairyland. 'How long's this been going on?'

'Few weeks now, but it's got a permanent look about it.'

'Ever seen him with this one? Before or since.' George showed the grave and daunting face, the straight, wide eyes that made it seem a desecration to mention her in such light and current terms.

'Oh, I know *her*. That's the old schoolmaster's girl, from up the other valley. Used to teach my nephew, he did, they nearly drove him up the wall before he got out of it and moved to Fairford. She's a beauty, that one,' he said fondly, tilting his head appreciatively over Annet's picture. 'No, I've never seen *her* with Geoff Westcott. Wouldn't expect to, neither.'

No, and of course they'd know that, whether they ever acknowledged it or not, and take care not to affront the village's notions of what was to be accepted as normal and what was not. Still, one asked.

'Now if you'd said *him*,' said Hopton unexpectedly, and nodded across the street.

Outside the single hardware shop a young man in a leather jacket of working rather than display cut had just propped a heavy motorcycle at the pavement's edge, and was striding towards the shop doorway. A tall, dark young man, perhaps twenty-five, scarcely older, possibly younger; uncovered brown hair very neatly trimmed, a vigorous, confident walk, none of the signs of convulsed adolescence about him. And a striking face, dark and reticent as a gipsy, with a proud, curled, sensitive mouth. He was in the shop only a minute, evidently collecting something which had been ordered and was ready for him, tools of some kind; a gleam of colour and of steel as he stowed the half-swathed bundle in his saddle-bag, straddled the machine with a long, leisurely movement of his whole body from head to toes, kicked it into life, and roared away from the pavement and along the single street. In a few moments he was out of sight.

'Seen her with *him* times enough,' said Hopton, as if that was perfectly to be expected.

'Have you, indeed! And who is he? I don't even know him.'

'Name of Stockwood. He's another of 'em. See him behind the wheel of the Bentley, and butter wouldn't melt in his mouth. Put him astride one of them there BSAs they keep for running up and down to the plantations and the farms, and he sprouts horns. He does look after them, though, I will say that. They come in now and again to be serviced – some rough rides they get, the estate being what it is – and you can tell a machine that's cared for.'

'Are you telling me,' asked George intently, light dawning, 'that that's Mrs Blacklock's chauffeur? Since when? There used to be a thin, grey-haired fellow named Braidie.'

'Retired about three months ago, and this chap came. I've seen *him* driving the Beck lass home often enough.'

George stood looking thoughtfully after the faint plume of dust that lingered where the rider had vanished. So that was the reliable human machine that guarded Annet from undesirable encounters by regularly driving her home. Pure luck that he should be seen for the first time not with the car, but with one of the estate utilities, and consequently out of strict uniform. Chauffeurs are anonymous, automatic, invisible; but there went a live, feeling and very personable young man. Was it quite impossible that Annet, startled and disarmed by the change from Braidie's elderly, familiar person, should steal glances along her shoulder in the Bentley, on all those journeys home, and see the man instead of the chauffeur?

'All right,' said George, 'break off. No use going on like this, leave me
alone with her.'

He got up from his chair and went to the window of the living-room, and stood staring out vaguely through a mist, as though he had been wearing glasses and steamed them opaque with the heat of his own exhaustion. Sweat ran, slowly and heavily, between his shoulder-blades. Who would have thought she had the strength in her to resist and resist and resist, fending off solicitude as implacably as reproaches? She looked so fragile that you'd have thought she could be broken in the hands; and it seemed she was indestructible and immovable.

He heard them get up obediently and leave the room, Price first with his note-book, that had nothing in it but a record of unanswered questions, then Sergeant Grocott, light-footed, closing the door gently behind him. Mrs Beck had not moved from the chair by the couch.

'Alone,' said George.

'I have a right to be present. Annet is my daughter. If she wants me—'

'Ask her,' he said without turning his head, 'if she wants you.'

'It's all right, Mother,' said Annet, breaking her silence for the third time in two hours. Once she had said: 'Good morning!' and once: 'I'm sorry!' but after that nothing more. 'Please!' she said now. 'Mr Felse has a right. And I don't mind.'

The chair shrieked offence on the polished floor. Mrs Beck withdrew; the door closed again with a frigid click, and George and Annet were alone in the room.

He went back to her, and drew a chair close to the studio couch on which she was ensconced in the protective ceremony of convalescence. Mrs Beck, surely, had arranged the tableau, to disarm, to afflict him with a sense of guilt and inhibit him from hectoring her daughter. He doubted if Annet had even noticed. Silent, pale and withdrawn, the small, painful frown fixed on her brow as though she agonised without respite at a problem no one else could help her to solve, she looked full at him while she denied him, as though she saw him from an infinite distance but with particular clarity. Bereft even of her fantasy wedding ring, she clung at least to her silence, an absolute silence now.

'Annet, listen to me. We know you were there. We've got a firm identification of you from two witnesses now. And your ring came from the dead man's stock. All this is fact. Established. Nobody's going to shake it now. We know there was a man with you. We know you waited for him on the corner. We know the exact time, and it fits in with the medical estimate of the time the old man died. This is murder. An inoffensive old man, who'd never done anything to you, who didn't even know you. Who'd never seen his murderer before. Just a chance victim, because the time was right and the street was empty, and there was money just being checked up in the till. A quick profit, and what's a life or so in the cause? That's not you, Annet. I know society is dull and censorious and often wrong, I know its values aren't always the highest. But if you diverge from its standards, it surely isn't going to be for lower ones. There's only one thing you can do now, and only one side on which you can range yourself. Tell me what happened. Tell me the whole story.'

She shook her head, very slightly, her eyes wide and steady upon his face. She let him take her hands and hold them, tightly and warmly; her fingers even seemed to accept his clasp with more than a passive consent. But she said nothing.

'Have I to tell it to you? I believe I can, and not be far out. You were coming past the shop together, maybe the old man was just putting the mesh gate across, ready to close. Your companion stopped suddenly, and told you to wait for him. Probably you were surprised, probably you wanted to go with him, but he wouldn't let you. He stood you on the corner, well out of earshot of what he intended to do, and told you he was going to buy you something, and it was to be a surprise. And you did what he wanted, because you wanted nothing else in the world but to do everything he wanted, because all your will was never to deny him anything. And maybe what he intended, then, was only robbery, if he hadn't hit too hard. Frightened boys turning violent for the first time frequently do.'

The hands imprisoned in his suddenly plunged and struggled in their confinement for an instant. Her face shook, and was still again.

'I know,' said George, sick with pity. 'I told you, none of this goes with you, nothing except your loving him. That happens, who can blame you for that? Personally, I don't think you knew a thing about either robbery or murder until I sprang it on you last night. He came back to you and gave you the ring, and so much of you was concentrated on that – as a gift and a promise, as a kind of private sacrament – that if he was agitated or uneasy you didn't notice it. He hurried you away, and all you knew was that he'd bought you a wedding ring, on impulse, on a sentimental impulse at that, with money he couldn't really afford. A sweet, silly thing to do. But he left Jacob Worrall dead or dying in the back room, switched off the shop lights and drew the gate to across the doorway. And nobody saw him. Nobody knows who he is. Nobody but you, Annet.'

He had got so far when he saw that she was crying, with the extraordinary tranquillity of despair, her face motionless, the tears gathering heavily in her dilated eyes, and overflowing slowly down her cheeks. No convulsive struggle with her grief, she sat still and let it possess her, aware of the uselessness of all movement and all sound.

'Surely you see that the best thing you can do, ultimately, even for him, is tell me the whole story. Who is he, this young man of yours?

Oh, he loved you very much – I know! He wanted to be with you, to give you things, because he loved you. He wanted more than a stolen week-end, he wanted to take you away with him for good. But he had to have money to make that possible. A lot of money. And he took what he thought was a chance, when it offered. But think what his state must be now, Annet! Do you think it's enviable to be a murderer? Even the kind that gets away with it? Think about it, Annet!'

And maybe she did think about it; she sat gazing at him great-eyed, perhaps unaware of the tears that coursed slowly down her face, but she never spoke. She listened, she understood, there was a communication, of that he had no doubt; but it was still one-sided. He could not make her speak.

'If you love him,' said George, very gently and simply, 'and I think you do, you'll want to do the best for him, and save him from the worst. And being convicted, even dying, isn't necessarily the worst you know.'

The word passed into her with a sharp little jerk and quiver, like a poisoned dart, but it did not startle her.

'You see, I'm not lying to you. This is capital murder, and we both know it. It may not come to that extremity; but it could. But even so, Annet, if it were me, I'd rather pay than run. You can't save him now from killing, but you can spare him the remembering and hiding and running, the lying down with his dead man every night, and getting up with him every morning—'

Still she kept her silence, all she had left; but she bowed forward suddenly out of her tranced grief, felt towards George's shoulder with nuzzling cheek and brow, and let herself lie against him limp and weary, her closed eyelids hidden on his breast. He gathered both her hands into one of his, slipped the other arm round her gently, and held her as long as she cared to rest so. He made no use of the contact to persuade or move her; the compassion and respect he felt for her put it clean out of his power.

She drew away from him at last with a sigh that was dragged up from the roots of her body. She looked up, while his face was still out of focus to her, and in a soft, urgent voice she said: 'Let me go! Don't watch me! Take your man away from the house, and let me go.'

'Annet, I can't.'

'Please! Please! Take him away and leave me free. Tell them not to watch me. You could if you would.'

265

'No,' said George heavily, 'it's impossible.'

She took her hands from him slowly, and turned her face away, and the silence was back upon her like an invisible armour through which he could not penetrate. He got up slowly, and stood looking down at her with a shadowed face.

'You realise, Annet, that if you won't give us the information we need, we must get it elsewhere. So far we've kept you from the Press, but if you won't help us we shall have to make use of your name and photograph. There'll be people who'll remember having seen you during the week-end. There must be someone who knows where you spent those nights in Birmingham. Time is very important, and you can't be spared beyond today. You understand that?'

She nodded. The averted face shivered once, but she made no protest.

'I ask you again to make that unnecessary. Tell me, and we shan't have to put you in the pillory.'

'No,' said Annet absolutely; and a moment later, in indifferent reassurance: 'It doesn't matter.' He understood that she was disclaiming any consideration for herself, and acknowledging his right and duty to expend her if he must. More, after her fashion she was comforting him.

He turned his back on her wearily, and went out without a word more. He could get tears from her, he could get warmth from her, but he could not get words. What was the use of persisting in this impossible siege? But he knew he'd be back before the day was out. How could he leave her to destroy herself?

'I'm leaving a man on guard,' he said to Beck in the hall. 'And I want you to let me place a policewoman in the house with Annet, as an additional precaution. It's for her protection, you surely realise that. Make sure that somebody's always with her, don't let her out of your sight. And don't let anyone in to her but the police.'

He wasn't going to lose Annet if he could help it, however wantonly she was offering herself as a sacrificial victim. Let me go, indeed! George shrugged his way morosely into his coat, and went to report total failure to the Chief of the County CID.

'Do you want her arrested, or don't you?' demanded Detective-Superintendent Duckett, before the tale was finished. 'Seems to me you don't know your own mind. If she was my girl, I'd hustle her behind bars and heave a sigh of relief. And I'd make sure of putting her out of reach before the evening paper rolls out on the streets at one o'clock. We've done it now.'

'Had to,' said George grimly. 'There's nothing to be got out of her, and we can't afford to lose today. I warned her. She knows the odds. Not that that lets us out.'

'Well, if you've put the brightest girl we've got in the house with her, and left Lockyer on guard outside, I don't see what harm she can come to.'

All the same, they had crossed a Rubicon there was no re-crossing, and they knew it. Once the regional *Evening News* hit the streets all the world would know that Annet Beck was 'expected to be able to help the police' in their enquiries into the Bloome Street murder; that she had been identified by witnesses as having been in the district at the time; and that further witnesses to her movements in Birmingham were being sought, with a photograph of Annet to remind them in case they were in doubt of the face that went with the name.

'No,' said George, 'I don't want to arrest her. I admit I was tempted to do it the easy way, and put her clean out of his reach. He may not have much faith in her silence; and however surely he committed the crime for her – in a sense – in the first place, his terror now is liable to be all for himself, and all-consuming. He must have been wildly uneasy already; he'll be frightened to death when he sees the paper. But there it is – I don't want to bring her in, because I'm convinced she's absolutely innocent – apart from this damned mistaken loyalty of hers after the event.'

'Well, let's hope the photograph will bring in somebody who saw and remembers them in Birmingham. Somebody who can give us a good description of the boy. Up to now, what do we really know about him? No one's admitted to seeing him, he left no distinguishable prints on the glass cases or the latch of the door or the candlestick – soft leather gloves, apparently. Trouble is, they all know the ropes by now. He's still totally invisible and anonymous, to everybody but the Beck girl. He may be from anywhere, he may be anyone. All we can say with reasonable certainty is that he must be someone young enough and attractive enough to engage a girl's attention. And what does that mean? Most of the young ones you see about, these days, you wouldn't expect a smart girl to want to be seen dead with, but they break their hearts over 'em just the same. And what else do we know about him? That he's got no money. He has to get it the quick, modern way in order to be able to take his girl about in style. But which of 'em have got money? They make what most of us used to keep a family on, but they're always broke before the end of the week. And that's it. A blank.'

'Except that he *may* have a motor-bike,' said George, and stuffed his notes sombrely back into his pocket. '*If* we accept that the tracks down in Middlehope are relevant. Nothing positive from London yet on our friend's week-end?'

'Nothing conclusive. He was home, that's true enough, but in and out a good deal, apparently. I asked them to fill in Saturday evening, and let the rest go. From London to Birmingham is an evening out these days. Coaches do it in no time, up the M1. I called them again half an hour ago, but they won't be rushed. I hoped we'd get that, at least, before we had to issue the hand-out, but it makes no difference. We'd have had to publish, the grapevine was getting in first. So how does it stand from the other end now? How's your list of possibles?'

'Wide open. Her parents think they had a boy-proof fence erected round her, but you and I know there's no such thing. There were three or four rather dull and respectable lads they allowed to squire her to dances, but always with the Gibbons girl in tow. But who knows whether they stay dull and respectable once they're out of sight of the older generation? Here are the names of the approved, and we're checking up on them, but I'm not expecting much from them. Still, you never know. Then there's young Geoff Westcott, who would certainly *not* have been approved by mother. He's danced with Annet several times, and started a fight over her at least once. And he chose to take the few days' holiday Lowthers owed him from the summer this last week-end, and filled up at old man Hopton's on Thursday afternoon. Scott is nosing around to find out what he did with his time. And then there's an interesting outsider. I saw him this morning in Abbot's Bale. Mrs Beck always reassured herself that the Blacklocks took care to send Annet home in the car when she worked late, or whenever the nights dropped dark early, or there was bad weather. If Regina or hubby didn't drive her home, they sent her with the chauffeur. All very nice and safe, and when could she possibly have struck up an undesirable acquaintance? But was it so nice and safe? Braidie was sixty-five and past caring, but Braidie, it seems, retired about three months ago. The fellow they've got now – I wonder if the Becks have even noticed? – is one Stockwood, twenty-fourish, good-looking and altogether presentable. And because Mrs Blacklock was away at her conference, and Blacklock prefers to drive himself, Stockwood was given the week-end off after he'd driven Mrs Blacklock down to Gloucester, and he reported back only to fetch her home on Wednesday. Annet had the opportunity to get to *know* him, all right. Probably three, four times a week he's had her in the car alone with him.'

'And that's all?'

George said, with his eyes fixed on the roofs of Hill Street outside the window, and the small crease of personal anxiety between his brows, 'It wouldn't do any harm to get on to Capel Curig, and ask them to check up on the boys and their camp-site, I suppose. Shouldn't take them long, we can tell them exactly where they were supposed to be.'

'I did,' said Duckett smugly, and grinned at him broadly through the smoke of his pipe and the stubbornly un-military thicket of his moustache; and anything that could raise a genuine grin that day was more than welcome. 'I should have told you sooner – you can cross off young Mallindine. They were there, all right, both of 'em, we found people who saw them regularly two of three times a day, one couple who climbed with them all day Sunday. Saturday night, around the time we're interested in, know where they were? In the local, with a couple of half-pints. The barman remembers, because he asked 'em, by way of a leg-pull, if they were eighteen. He says one of 'em looked down his nose at him and said yes, and the other blushed till his ears lit up.'

'Good God!' said George blankly, manfully suppressing the thankful lift of his heart. 'I didn't know he could.'

'Plenty of things you don't know about your Dom, you can safely bet on that. But his friend's in the clear over this, and your boy hasn't had to tell any lies for him. As for his crime against the Licensing Act, you take my tip, George, don't waste it. Save it up till the next time he gets uppish with his old man, and then flatten him with it. You'll have him walking on tip-toe for weeks, thinking you're Sherlock Holmes in person.'

'I wish to God I was!' owned George, sighing, and rose somewhat wearily to put on his coat. Something was gained, at least, if Miles was safely out of the reckoning. Only let there be someone observant and reliable somewhere in Birmingham at this moment, reading the noon edition over his lunch, and suddenly arrested by Annet's recognised and remembered face. Let him be able to set another face beside it, clearly, quickly, before that other turned the same page, to

269

swallow his heart and pocket his shaking hands, and ponder at last, inescapably, that it was Annet or himself for it.

'I'm going to snatch a meal,' he said, picking up his hat from Duckett's desk. 'I'll be back.'

He had the door open when the telephone rang. Very quietly he closed the door again, and watched Duckett palm the hand-set, his shaggy head on one side, his thick brows twitching.

'Ah, like that!' said Duckett, after a few minutes of silences and monosyllables, and emitted a brief and unamused snort of laughter. 'Yes, thanks, it does. Clears the decks for us, anyhow, and leaves us with at least a glimmer of a lead. Yes, let us have the reports. Thanks again!' He clapped the receiver back and thrust the set away from him with a grunt that might have meant satisfaction or disgust, or a mixture of both.

'Well?' said George, his shoulder against the door.

'One more you can cross off. His parents didn't see him for most of Saturday, he came in after midnight. But there's a girl. A clinger, it seems. All Saturday afternoon and evening she never let go. You can take the story he told to you as being on the level, tyre-tracks and all, for what they're worth. Whoever knocked old Worrall on the head, your Number One didn't.'

Chapter Seven

The evening paper wasn't dropped into the Felse family's letter-box until the last edition came in at about five o'clock. Bunty Felse was alone when it came, with the tea ready, and neither husband nor son present to eat it. Dominic was always late on rugger practice afternoons, but even so he should have been home before this time. And as for George, when he was on this kind of case who could tell when she would see him?

She sat down with the paper to wait for them patiently, and Annet Beck's face looked out at her from the front page with great, mute, disconcerting eyes, beneath the query: 'Have you seen this girl?'

'Anyone who remembers noticing the girl pictured above,' said the beginning of the text more precisely, 'with a male companion in the central or southern districts of Birmingham during last week-end, should communicate with the police.'

Bunty read it through, and in fact it was as reticent as it could well be and still be exact in conveying its purpose and its urgency. She sank her head between her hands, threading her fingers into the bush of chestnut hair that was just one shade darker than Dominic's, and contemplated Annet long and thoughtfully. 'A male companion,' 'it is believed,' 'helping the police in their enquiries' – such discreet, such clinical formula, guaranteed non-actionable. But a real girl in the middle of it, and somewhere, still hidden, a real boy, maybe no older than Dominic.

They were pretty sure of their facts, that was clear. They knew when they laid hands on the partner of Annet's truancy they would have Jacob Worrall's murderer. What they didn't know, what nobody knew but Annet, was who he was. And Annet wouldn't tell. Bunty didn't have to wonder or ask how things were going for George now, she knew.

No one could identify him but Annet. And she wouldn't. Why, otherwise, should they be reduced to appealing to the public for information, and displaying Annet as bait? He might be anyone. He might be anywhere. You might go down to the grocer's on the corner and ask him for a pound of cheese, and his hands might be trembling so he could hardly control the knife. You might bump into him at a corner and put your hand on his arm to steady yourself and him as you apologised, and feel him flinch, recoiling for an instant from the dread of a more official hand on his shoulder. He might get up and give you his seat in a bus, or blare past you on a noisy motor-bike at the crossing, and snarl at you to get out of his way. He might be the young clerk from the Education Department, just unfolding the paper in the bus on his way home. He'd killed a man, and he was on the run, but only one girl could give him a face or a name.

How well did he know his Annet? Do you ever know anyone well enough to stake your life on her? When all the claims of family and society and upbringing pull the other way? If he was absolutely sure of her loyalty, there was a hope that he wouldn't try to approach her at all, that he'd just take his plunder and make a quiet getaway while he was anonymous, leaving Annet to carry the load alone. Could she love that kind of youth? Plenty of fine girls have, owned Bunty ruefully, why not Annet? It might be the best thing, because if he started running he would almost inevitably lose his nerve and run too fast, and just one slip would bring the hunt after him. Somewhere away from here, where he couldn't double back to remove, in his last despair, the one really dangerous witness.

But if he couldn't be sure of her, if he feared, as he well might, that under pressure she might break down at last and betray him, then from this moment on Annet's life was in great danger. If you're frightened to death, you stop loving, you stop thinking or feeling but in one desperate plane of reference, you fight for your life, and kill whatever threatens it. These, at least, thought Bunty, must be the reactions of an unstable young creature, not yet mature, the kind of boy who could have committed that brutal, opportunist crime in the shop in Bloome Street. The commonplace of today, the current misdemeanour, cosh the shopkeeper, clear the till, run; quick money to pay for this and future sprees, in three easy movements. It happens all the time. Preferably old men or old women in back-street shops, because they're so often solitary. No, the boy who did that wouldn't keep his love intact for long when it was his life or Annet's.

Bunty got up suddenly and went to the telephone in the hall. It wasn't so much that she was really anxious about her offspring; just a sudden unwillingness to be alone with this line of thought any longer, and a feeling that company would be helpful. It might even help her to think. How could she leave alone a problem that was tormenting George?

'Eve? You haven't got Dominic there, have you?'

'I did have, sweetie, for about ten minutes, but that was half an hour ago. They blew in and went into a huddle in the corner, and then they up and made a phone call, and went off again. They brought the paper in with them. I did wonder,' said Eve Mallindine, resigning the idea reluctantly, 'if they'd come to you. They never said a word. And when I looked at the *News* – well, you'll have seen it.'

'Yes,' said Bunty, and pondered, jutting a dubious lip. 'Eve – they *were* where they said they were, surely? Over the week-end? They couldn't, either of them—'

'No,' said Eve, firmly and serenely, 'they couldn't. Neither of them. Not in any circumstances.'

'No, of course not! My God, I must be going round the bend. It's such hell growing up, that's all. And I'm afraid to think we've got angels instead of boys – such arrogance! And there *was* the first time, for Miles – don't shoot me down in flames, but it did happen.'

'Listen, honey,' said Eve's bright, confident voice, for once subdued into a wholly private and unmocking tenderness, 'it *didn't* happen. Not even that once. Don't tell anyone else. I promised Miles I wouldn't ask him anything, or tell anything, and I wouldn't now if we weren't all in a pretty sticky situation. Miles never tried to run away anywhere, with or without Annet Beck. So you can put that out of your mind.'

'But they were picked up at the station,' said Bunty blankly, 'with two cases. And two tickets to London.'

'So they were. Two cases. But both of them were Annet's.'

'*Both* of them? But Bill would have *known*! For goodness' sake! He took Annet home with one case, and brought Miles back with the other. Do you mean to tell me he doesn't know the family luggage?'

Eve said, with curiosity, wonder, and not a little envy: 'You know, George must be a tidy-minded man, to inspire such confidence in husbands. Bill?' A brief, affectionate hoot of laughter patted his name on the head and reduced him to size. 'Bill doesn't know his own shirts. Every time we dig the cases out of the attic to pack, he swears he's never seen half of them before. "When did we buy this thing, darling?" "I don't remember this – did we pinch it somewhere?" I could filch a tie out of his drawer and give it him for his birthday, and he wouldn't know.'

'But how, then? I mean—'

'I don't know, I never asked. When Bill dropped on them and jumped to conclusions, Miles arranged it that way, that's all. And she let him. I got the case back to Annet afterwards. *I* took advantage of Regina Blacklock's car to do it, but she never knew, and you knew Braidie, he was so correct he was stone-deaf to everything but what he was supposed to hear. It was very easy, I just telephoned to Annet at the hall, and asked her to get Braidie to call here when he took her home, some day when her parents would be out. So I know what I'm talking about, my love. I'd thought the poor lamb had bought it specially for the jaunt, you see, and I started to unpack it, out of pure kindness of heart and helpfulness. Thank God Bill wasn't there! All Annet's best frocks! You should have seen Miles's face! After he'd covered up for her so nobly, and then to see me meddling. I tell you, I had the honour of all mothers in my hands.'

'I'll be cheering in a minute,' said Bunty, swallowing a sound that indicated other possibilities. 'All right, I'm grateful, you preserved our reputation most nobly. But if you expect me to live up to your record, and not ask questions—'

'Wouldn't be any good, darling, I don't know any more answers.'

'Not even who the second ticket was for?'

'That least of all. Because Miles doesn't know it, either.'

'Then I give up! *Why* should he?'

But she stopped there, because there could be only one reason, and it made her stand back and look again at young Miles, with sympathy and respect, and a sudden flurry of consternation and dismay. If he was reaching after maturity at this rate, without any childish desire for acknowledgement or payment or praise, how far behind could Dominic be? She didn't want them men too soon, she needed a little time yet to get used to it, even though the symptoms had begun already so long ago. She caught her breath in a rueful giggle, and said: 'Eve, do you suppose there's an evening class we could join – on growing old gracefully?'

She expected something profane and cheering from Eve in return, but there was blank silence, as though her friend had withdrawn altogether and cut off the connection. On Bunty, too, the abrupt chill of realisation descended, freeing her where she stood.

'Bunty—' said Eve's voice, slowly and delicately.

'Yes, I'm still here. Are you thinking what I'm thinking?'

'I shouldn't wonder,' said Eve. 'Great minds!'

'*Could* it be the same person? Since it wasn't Miles, that time – *could* it be? Then anything Miles knows – anything! – may be vital. Anything she ever said to him then, a name or something short of a name. Anything he noticed about her. Anyone he saw her with. She relied on him, she let him help her, she may have trusted him with at least a clue.'

'No,' said Eve, her voice anxious and still. 'Miles doesn't know. *He* – whoever he may be – was always a secret, from Miles, from everybody, just like this time. Terribly like this time, now you come to mention it.'

'But there might be something that he does know, without even realising it. Eve, he must talk to George.'

'You took the words out of my mouth. Call me if he shows up there. And if he comes back here,' said Eve with grim resolution, '*I*'ll see to it that he comes round to your place and gets the whole story off his chest like a sensible man – if I have to bring him along by the ear!'

No one, however, had to bring Miles along by the ear. About seven o'clock Bunty looked out as she drew the living-room curtains, and saw them striding briskly and purposefully up the garden path towards the front door, Dominic in the lead. Not merely two young, slender shapes, but three. Somewhere along the way, Bunty thought at first, they'd picked up a third sixth-former who had an uneasy conscience about something he knew and hadn't confided; but when she ran to let them in, and they came into the light of the hall, she saw that the third was Tom Kenyon.

Of all people in the world she would least have expected them to run to him for advice. He was too perilously near to them, and yet set apart by the invisible barrier that segregates teacher from pupils; too old to be accepted as a contemporary, and too young to have any of the menace or reassurance of a father-figure. They liked him well enough, with reservations, these hard-to-please, deflationary young gentlemen, even if they had christened him Brash 'Arry, jumping to conclusions about the middle initial H on his brief-case; but to go to him in their anxieties was quite another matter.

'Hallo!' said Bunty, from long habit reducing even the abnormal to normality. 'Come in! You're in time for coffee, if you'd like some.'

275

'I'm sorry if we look like an invasion,' said Tom, with a brief and shadowed smile, 'but this may be urgent. Is George home yet? We've got to see him.'

'Yes, come along in.' She threw the door wide and passed them through. Her son went by with a single preoccupied glance of apology for his lateness. Miles, always meticulous, said a dutiful: 'Good evening, Mrs Felse!' Tom marshalled them before him with an air of dominant responsibility that made Bunty smile, until she remembered the occasion that had almost certainly brought them here. 'Visitors for you, darling!' she said, and closed the door on them and went to reassure Eve.

George had his slippered feet on the low mantelpiece, and his coffee-cup in the hearth by his chair. He looked up at their entrance with tired eyes, not yet past surprise at this procession.

'Hallo, Kenyon, what is this? Are you having trouble with these two?'

Two reproving frowns deplored this tone. Tom Kenyon didn't even notice.

'They came to me after they'd seen the paper tonight. It seems they'd been comparing notes and putting two and two together, and they came to the conclusion they had some information and a theory that they ought to confide to somebody in authority. Your boy naturally wanted to come straight to you, but Miles preferred to try it out on me first, before bothering you.'

That was one way of putting it. He knew very well why, of course. At first startled and disarmed by their telephone call, he had been tempted to believe that he had done even better than he had supposed during this first term, and established himself as the natural confessor to whom his seniors would turn in trouble. But he had too much good sense to let his vanity run away with him for long. A careful glance at the circumstances, and he knew a better reason. Neither of them would have dreamed of coming to him, if he had not betrayed himself so completely to Miles in that one brief interview. If there was one thing of which Miles was quite certain, after that, it was that Brash 'Arry would be guided in this crisis not by pious thoughts of the good of society or his moral duty, but by one simple consideration: what he felt to be in Annet Beck's best interests. If he listened to their arguments, and then gave it as his opinion that they must go to the police, to the police they would go, satisfied that they were doing the best thing for Annet.

And he needn't think he had the advantage of them as a result of this consultation, either; what it meant, he told himself ruefully but honestly, was that they had discovered in him weaknesses which could be exploited. And boys can be ruthless; he knew, it wasn't so long since he'd been one. They might, on the other hand, be capable of astonishing magnanimity, too. There was stuff in Miles that kept surprising him; his address in this crisis, the direct way he approached his confession, without hesitation or emphasis, the way the 'sir' vanished from his tongue, and the greater, not less, respect and assurance that replaced it. Maybe there were things this boy wouldn't use even against a schoolmaster, distresses he wouldn't exploit, even to ease his own.

'I didn't wait to hear all they have to say, but I've heard enough. I said we ought to come straight to you, and tell at once. So here we are.'

Had his own motives, after all, been quite as single and disinterested as they had calculated? Anything that might uncover the identity of Annet's lover he would naturally bring to George at a run, because it might remove the danger that threatened Annet's life. And remove with it, prodded the demon at the back of his mind, the unseen rival, the tenant of that tenacious heart of hers, leaving the way free for another incumbent. He was afraid to look too closely at this dark reverse of his motive, for fear it should prove to be the main impulse that moved him. My God, but it was complicated!

'Sit down!' said George, getting up to pour coffee. 'All right, Miles, we're listening. What's on your mind?'

'I've been taking it for granted, of course,' said Miles directly, 'that I'm on the list of suspects, until you check up on our week-end. Because of the last time. I haven't asked Mr Kenyon if he knows about that—'

'I do,' said Tom.

'—but I know *you* do, of course. And this is going to sound as if I'm just trying to slide out from under, I realise that, but I can't help it.'

'Don't let that worry you,' said George. 'We've already checked, you *are* out from under. We know where you were on Saturday evening, and what you were doing. Just go ahead.'

'Oh, good, that makes it easier. You see,' said Miles, raising sombre brown eyes to George's face in a straight, unwavering stare, 'I never did plan to go away anywhere, that last time, it wasn't what it looked like at all. I've never said anything before, and I wouldn't now, except that somebody did plan to go away with her then, and it

277

might – I don't know, but it *might* – be the same person who took her away this time. There's been one murder,' said Miles with shattering simplicity, 'and there may well be another. Of Annet herself. If we don't find him.'

The 'we' was significant. He watched George's face, unblinking. 'That's right, isn't it?' he said.

'That's right. Go on.'

'So we have to find him. And the devil of it is that I didn't try to find out anything about him when I had the chance. I never asked any questions. She asked me to help her to get away. She wanted to go to London. I knew she wasn't happy. I knew they didn't want her to go, and it was wrong, in a way, to help her to leave them high and dry. But she asked me, and I did it. She said her parents would be out when she was supposed to go for her piano lesson in the village that Friday afternoon, and she'd have her cases packed, and would I fetch her and take her to the station at Comerbourne. And I said yes. I'd only just passed my test about three weeks before, I wasn't supposed to touch the car yet unless Dad was with me. But I said yes, anyhow. And I asked her, did she want me to get her ticket for her, so that she could slip in without being noticed at the booking office. And she said it was two tickets she wanted, not one. Singles.'

He had paled perceptibly, and for once he lowered his eyes, frowning down at his own hands clenched tightly in his lap. But only for a moment, while he re-mustered his forces. 'And I booked them for her,' he said, 'the day before she planned to leave.'

'It sounds,' said George, carefully avoiding all emphasis, 'as though she made fairly shameless use of you.'

'No! No, you don't know! It wasn't like that at all. She was perfectly honest with me. I could have said no. I did what I wanted to do. I helped her, and I didn't ask her anything. If she needed to go, as badly as that, I was for her. She didn't owe me anything. And it was for me to choose what I'd do, and I did choose. I booked the tickets for her, and the next day I skipped my last period, and went down to where Dad leaves the car, just round the corner from his office, in the yard at the back. You can't see it from his window, I knew that, and I had the spare key. I fetched Annet and her two cases from Fairford. Her parents were due home in half an hour, but they wouldn't expect her back from her class until six, so she had a couple of hours' grace. I took her to the station. We were a good twenty minutes early, but the train backs in well ahead of time. She said *he* would get on the train independently, with only a platform ticket, and then join her on board. So we went in together when there was a slack moment, and I took a platform ticket from the machine to get out again. We wanted both London tickets punched normally, you see, no queries, nothing to wonder about at all.'

'And you never asked her outright who he was? Or even looked around to see if anyone was casing the pair of you? Anyone who might be the boy she was going to meet?'

'No,' said Miles, and flamed and paled again in an instant, remembering stresses within himself that had cost him more than his dignity was prepared to admit.

'All right! This isn't a matter of betrayal now,' said George practically, 'it's Annet's safety. I believe you didn't ask, I believe you didn't look for him. Leave it at that for now. Go on.'

'Well, you know how it ended. Or rather you don't, quite. I meant to have the car back in the yard before Dad ever missed it, and ninety-nine days out of a hundred I could have done it, but that was the hundredth. He had a call from a client who was breaking a train journey for one night at the Station Hotel, and had some bit of business he wanted to clear up quickly. And of course there was no car. He thought it had been stolen – there were several taken around that time, if you remember, locked and everything – some gang going round with a pocketful of keys. Anyhow, he reported it to the police, so after that there wasn't going to be any hushing up the affair, naturally. And then he took a taxi across to the station, and the first thing he saw was his own car parked down the station approach. Well, of course he tipped off the constable from the corner to keep an eye on it, and he came down to the booking-office and the ticket gate to ask if anyone had seen it driven up and parked there. They know him – everybody does. And of course—'

Miles hunched his shoulders under the remembered load.

'That was it! There we were on the platform, with two suitcases, and I had the two tickets in my hand. And he was furious already about the car. I didn't blame him. Actually he was damn' decent, considering. But after a bit of publicity like that it was all up with Annet's plans, anyhow. We just let it ride, let him think what he was thinking. We didn't have to consult about it, there wasn't anything else to do. There'd be fuss enough about me, why drag the other fellow into it? All Annet could save out of it was her own secret. Dad said, back to the car, please, and back to the car we went like lambs. He drove out to Fairford, and handed Annet out of the car, and then he looked at the two cases, and neither of them meant a thing to him, but then he never remembers the colour of his own from one year to another. Mummy buys them for him, for presents, when the old ones are getting too battered. *He* wouldn't notice. So I handed him one of them, it didn't matter which, and gave Annet the item with one eye, and she caught on at once. Mummy got the other back to her, afterwards.'

'You mean your mother *knew*?' said Tom, startled, his respect for Eve's unwomanly discretion soaring.

'Oh, yes! I don't think it would have taken her long to get the hang of it, anyhow, because Mummy *does* notice things. But she opened the case that same night, meaning to put my things away, so the cat was well and truly out of the bag.'

'And she never said a word! Not even to your father?' asked George.

'No, she never did. She could have got me out of some of the muck, of course, but then we'd have had to leave Annet deeper in it, you see, and that was the last thing I wanted. *I* was all right, in any case, my parents never really panic. And at least nobody was pestering Annet about who, or how, or why, the way things were, because they thought they knew. If somebody'd crossed me out they'd have begun on her in earnest. Mummy let me play it my way, and that way there weren't any questions. But you see,' said Miles, contemplating his involuntary guilt with set jaw and dour eyes, 'that that makes what's happened since partly my doing. I stood in for him, and he stayed a secret. She still had him, they could try again. This time she didn't ask anyone for help, they didn't risk trains or places where there were people who might know them. And this time they pulled it off, if only for a week-end. A trial run for the real flight, maybe. Only this time,' he said with the flat finality of certainty, 'he ran out of funds and killed a man.'

'It doesn't necessarily follow,' said George cautiously, 'though I admit it's a strong probability.'

'I think it does follow. I think if there'd been any doubt, Annet would have spoken. As soon as she knew about the murder, she seems to have known whose life was at stake. Why else should she close up like this?'

'Even Annet could be wrong,' said George. 'She never gave you any clue? You never noticed anything? Saw her with anyone special?'

Miles shook his head decidedly. 'Maybe I was trying not to, I don't know. I've tried all this evening to dredge up something that might be useful. But what I have is only deduction. He was from somewhere round here. That's certain, because of the tickets. She wasn't lying to me about that, I'm sure, he was going to board the train in Comerbourne. That time they were bound for London, this time it was Birmingham. That all ties in. She's never been away from Comerford for long, it's far more likely she'd get involved with someone here, someone she saw often, someone close at home. And someone hopelessly unsuitable,' he said, watching George's face steadily. 'Even more unsuitable than I am now. I wasn't warned off until after that fiasco. This one, whoever he is, would never have been allowed near her at all. That's plain. There was a young fellow who drives long-distance lorries. Good-looking chap who danced—'

'We know about him,' said George.

'Not that I know anything against him, mind you, only that they wouldn't even have considered him for her. Or there's a clerk from Langfords' drawing-office, who used to make trips to London for the firm sometimes. He took her out once or twice, but there are tales about him, and her mother didn't like him, and soon put a stop to it. Someone like that fits the picture. Someone who travels a fair amount and knows his way around. Because she doesn't really. With all her assurance, and everything, she's a milk-white innocent.'

The urgent, practical, purposeful level of his voice never changed, but suddenly it was sharp with an unbearable concentration of beauty and longing, as though he had charmed Annet into the middle of their close circle. There passed from one to another of them the electric tension of awareness, and every face was taut and still, charged with private anguish. Tom stared sightlessly before him with eyes that had reversed their vision, and were struggling with the uncontrollable apparitions within him. Dominic watched Miles protectively and jealously, and kept his lips closed very firmly upon his personal preoccupations. George saw them momentarily isolated hopelessly one from another. Loneliness is the human condition; we grasp at alleviations where we can find them, but most of the time we have to get by with tenuous illusions of communion. Only families, the lucky ones, and friends, the rare and gifted ones, sometimes grow together and inhabit shared worlds too securely for dispossession.

'And then,' pursued Miles, too intent upon his hunt to be aware of any checks and dismays, even his own, 'there's the matter of her reappearance. Nobody seems to have realised how odd that is, and how suggestive.'

'And what do you know about her reappearance? There was nothing in the paper about that.'

'I know, but Mr Kenyon began asking us some pretty significant questions the day after half-term, about where we'd been – about where *I*'d been,' amended Miles more precisely, 'over the week-end, and about the cart-road at the back of the Hallowmount. And Mrs Beck had been on the telephone to my mother, fishing about my whereabouts, too. So we knew there was something wrong at Fairford that *I* should naturally be blamed for unless I had an alibi, and that the track behind the Hallowmount had something to do with it. It *had* to be Annet, or why get after me? But Mr Kenyon said, when I asked him, that Annet was safe at home. So why all this about the road at the back of the hill, unless they knew she'd gone or come back that way? But that's not all. The grape-vine's got it now, with trimmings. Putting all the bits together, and adding what they fancy, as usual. They're saying Annet was found wandering on the Hallowmount at night, and swore she hadn't been anywhere, that she'd only been for a walk and was on her way home. They say she'd been lost to the world for five days under the Hallowmount, like those village girls in the eighteenth century, and remembered nothing about it. They say it in an ambiguous sort of way, if you know what I mean, half believing it really happened, half sniggering over it as a tall tale invented to cover what she was really up to all that time. Round here they're expert in having it both ways.' He looked from George to Tom, and back to George again. 'Is it true?'

'Substantially, yes. Mr Kenyon saw her climb over the Hallowmount on Thursday, and he and her father went up there on Tuesday night, and met her just coming over the crest.'

'And she did tell that tale? Pretending she knew nothing about the five days in between?'

'Yes,' said Tom.

'Then she did it for a pretty urgent and immediate reason. Dom and I have been thinking about this. Nobody knows better than I do,' said Miles with authority, 'how Annet behaves in a jam like that. I've been through it with her once. She never told a single lie. She walked in at home again with a ruthless sort of dignity, told what she pleased of the truth, and wouldn't say another word. She didn't let me out of it, because I'd shown her I didn't want that. But she never admitted to anything against me, either. She'd have done the same again. That was what she meant to do, I'm certain. If you're thinking she cooked up that tall story as an alibi for the week-end, and turned up on the Hallowmount to give colour to it, you're way off target. No, the boot's on the other foot. She told it *because she was caught there*.'

'What you're saying, then,' said George intently, 'is that Annet was there on the hill for some private and sound reason of her own, and was taken completely by surprise when she came over the crest, intending to go straight home, and ran full tilt into her father and Kenyon.'

'Exactly. And she did the best she could with it on the spur of the moment. She'd have done better if she'd had time to think, but she didn't, she had to act instantly. So she fell back on the old tales, not to cover her lost week-end, but to distract attention from what she was doing *there, at that moment*.'

'Go on,' said George, after an instant of startling silence that set them all quivering like awakening sleepers. 'What do you think, in that case, she *was* doing there?'

'She could,' said Dominic, out of the long stillness and quietness he had preserved in his corner, 'have been hiding something, for instance. Something neither of them wanted to risk taking home with them.'

'Such as?'

'Such as two thousand pounds worth of small jewellcry, and what was left of the money after they'd paid their bills.'

'No!' protested Tom Kenyon loudly, rigid in his chair. 'That's as good as saying she was a party to the crime. I don't believe it. It's impossible.'

'No, sir, I didn't mean that. She needn't have known at all. Suppose he gave her a box, or a small case, or something, and said, here, you keep this safe, it's all I've managed to save, it's our capital. Suppose he told her: Put it somewhere where we can get at it easily when we've made our plans, and are ready to get out of here together. *He*'d know what was really in it, and how completely it could give him away if it was found, but *she* wouldn't, she'd only think he was afraid of his family prying, and getting nosey about his savings, maybe even pinching from them if it happens to be that sort of family. And it easily could. He may be in lodgings, he may have a father who keeps a close watch on him, or scrounging brothers, there could be a dozen reasons why it would be safer to trust to a hiding-place in the footways of the old lead mines, or in one of the hollow trees up there, than to risk prying eyes at home. *She* wouldn't know how urgent it really was, but it would make sense even to her. And you see the one solid advantage of putting it somewhere outside rather than having it at either home – if by bad luck it *was* found, there'd be nothing to connect it directly with him. She wouldn't question. She'd do as he asked, and think no wrong until you sprang the murder on her, two days later. *Then* she'd understand.'

'In that case, why didn't he persuade her to run at once – permanently – instead of coming home at all? He had the girl, he had the money. Why not make off with them both while he had the chance?'

'Because he was comfortably sure there was nothing in the world to connect him with the murder, and to run without reason just at that time would have been the quickest way of inviting suspicion. Wouldn't it?' challenged Dominic earnestly, brilliant eyes clinging to his father's face.

'You're forgetting,' said Tom, 'the roaming Romeo who tried to pick her up.' He caught himself up too late, and met George's eye in embarrassed dismay. 'I'm sorry, probably I shouldn't have mentioned that. It hasn't been published, has it?'

'It hadn't, but since we seem to have embarked on a full-scale review, it may as well be.' He recounted the episode briefly. 'There's certainly a point there. When he heard of that incident he'd know there was a possible witness who'd be able to tie in Annet, at least, to the scene and time of the murder. It isn't difficult to give a recognisable description of Annet. It would be impossible not to recognise any decent photograph of her, once you'd seen her at close quarters.'

'But she wouldn't know there was any urgent reason to warn him that a witness existed, because she knew of no crime. And without an urgent reason,' said Miles with absolute and haughty certainty, 'she wouldn't say a word to him about a thing like that.'

'Not tell him, when she'd been accosted by a street-corner lout?'

The very assumption of intimate knowledge of her, even at this extremity of her distress and need, could prick both these unguarded lovers into irritation and jealousy. Kenyon had allowed himself to slip into the indulgent schoolmaster voice that brought Miles's hackles up, Miles was staring back at him with the aloof and supercilious face that covers the modern sixth-former's wilder agonies. The minute action and reaction of pain quivered between them, and made them contemporaries, whether they liked it or not. Dominic's very acute and intelligent eyes studied them both from beneath lowered lashes, and what he felt he kept to himself. But the air was charged with sympathy and antagonism in inseparable conflict, and for a moment they all flinched from the too strident discord of the clash.

'No,' said Miles, more gently but no less positively. 'It was a thing she wouldn't confide. Especially not to him.'

'Well, if you're right about that, he'd have no idea that there was going to be anyone to give a description of either of them. He knew he'd left no traces, he thought he was quite clear. Every reason why he should hope to lie low for a reasonable time, and let the robbery in Birmingham blow over. Yes, that makes sense,' agreed George. 'It seems possible that he may not even have known, at first, that the old man was dead. Most probably he hit and grabbed and ran, and left him, as he thought, merely knocked out.'

'And even when he knew it was murder, there was nothing, as far as he knew, to connect him with it. The obvious thing to do was come inconspicuously home again, and go back to work, and act normally. Hide the money and the jewellery,' pursued Dominic, returning to his trail tenaciously, 'or get Annet to hide them, somewhere where naturally he hoped they'd stay safely hidden, but where at any rate they couldn't incriminate him any more than anyone else if they were discovered. But now it's gone past that. There *was* a witness he didn't know about, and Annet has been identified. The case is tied firmly to Annet and the man who spent the week-end with her. And only Annet's resistance stands between him and a murder charge. That's the situation he finds himself in now.'

'There's another point.' Miles frowned down at the hands that had tightened almost imperceptibly on each other at every repetition of her name, and carefully, painfully disengaged them. 'Supposing this is a good guess of ours, and she was entrusted with the business of hiding the money, then of course they may have agreed on the place beforehand. It may even be a place they've used for other things before now. But it may not. Supposing nobody but Annet knows where the stolen jewellery and money is now? He knows his life depends on her keeping silent. If he gets to the point of being terrified into running for it, he can't even get his loot and run without contacting Annet. And if he does—'

'He can't,' George said reassuringly. 'We've got a constant guard on her, inside the house and out. The degree of her danger hasn't escaped us. And we don't intend to take our eyes off her. You can rely on that.'

'Yes—' And he was grateful, a pale smile pierced the preoccupied stillness of his face for a moment. 'But he's got nothing to lose now unless he can get the means to make his break. And if he can find a way to her somehow, he's liable to remember that she— that nobody else can identify him—'

Miles carefully moistened lips suddenly too dry to finish the sentence.

'Yes, I realise all that. But I've got a man outside the house, Miles, and a policewoman inside with her. And however desperate he may be, we're dealing with only one man. The essence of his situation is that he's alone.'

'Not quite alone,' said Miles almost inaudibly. 'He's got one person who might help him to get to her, if ever you so much as turn your back for a minute.'

George stood off and looked down at him heavily, and said never a word in reply to that. It was Tom Kenyon, still fretting against the arrogance of the boy's certainty, who demanded: 'Who's that?'

'Annet,' said Miles.

They had talked themselves into dead silence. The two boys sat with the width of the room between them, braced and still, their eyes following with unwavering attention every quiver of George's brooding face, while he told over again within his mind the points they had made, and owned their substance. They had good need to be afraid for Annet, and very good reason to look again and again at the looming, significant shape of that long hog-back of rock and rough pasture that linked her with and divided her from her lover. Was it necessarily true that Annet had had a particular purpose in being on the Hallowmount that night of her return? Wasn't it simply her road back? Wasn't it natural enough that they should use the same route returning as departing? She wouldn't be afraid of the Hallowmount in the dark. But in that case, according to Miles, she wouldn't have troubled to cover herself and her movements with that fantastic story, even when she was taken by surprise on top of the hill. She drew her veil of deception because she had something positive and precise to hide. Who should know better than Miles?

But even if she had indeed been entrusted with the hiding of the plunder on her way home, was it likely that she had put it somewhere unknown to her partner? Possible, at a stretch, but certainly not likely. What appeared to George every moment more probable was that they had some hiding-place already established between them, and frequently used, their-letter-box, their private means of communication, accessible from both sides of the mountain without difficulty and without making oneself conspicuous. Given such a cache, tested and found reliable from long use, it would not even occur to them to hide their treasure anywhere else. And it would be the most natural thing in the world for Annet to undertake the job of depositing it, if the spot was directly on her way home. The boy had his motor-bike to manage, and his own family to manipulate at home; and by consent, so it seemed, they made use of the Hallowmount as the watershed of their lives, and the act of crossing it alone had become a rite. It was the barrier between their real and their ideal worlds, between the secret life they shared and the everyday life in which their paths never touched, or never as lovers. It was the hollow way into the timeless dream-place, as surely as if the earth had opened and drawn them within.

What was certain was that they had between them a treasure to hide. What was likely was that they had a place proved safe by long usage, in which to hide it. What was left to question was whether it was still there. Up to the appearance of the evening paper, probably he had no reason to see any urgency in its recovery, and every reason to avoid going near it. But now?

For some hours now he had known how closely he was hunted. Frightened, inexperienced, unable to confide in or rely on anyone but himself, how long would it take him to make up his mind? Or how long to panic? He might well have retrieved the money already. But he might not. And whether they were justified in all these deductions or not, there was nothing to be lost by keeping a watch on the Hallowmount, in case he did betray himself by making for his hoard. Heaven knew they had no other leads to him, except the mute girl in Fairford.

Price wouldn't thank him for a chilly, solitary night patrolling the border hills, but anything was worth trying. George excused himself, and went to the telephone. When he came back into the room none of them had moved. They all looked up at him expectantly.

'I'm putting a man on watch overnight,' said George, 'in case he goes to recover it during the dark hours. You may very well be right about it being hidden there, somewhere on the hill. Night's the most likely time for him to go and fetch it, if by any chance he does know where to look, but covering the ground by daylight won't be so easy. The last thing I want to do is put him off, and the sight of a plainclothes man parading the top of the Hallowmount would hardly be very reassuring. And man-power,' he owned, dubiously gnawing a knuckle, 'isn't our long suit.'

'We could provide you with boy-power,' said Tom Kenyon unexpectedly. 'Plenty of it, and it might be a pretty good substitute. Miss Darrill's taking out the school Geographical Association on one of their occasional free-for-alls tomorrow. They were having a field-day on Cleave, but there's no reason why they couldn't just as well be switched to the Hallowmount. It's geologically interesting, it would carry conviction, all right. And if we deploy about forty boys all over the hill it will make dead certain nobody can hunt for anything there without being spotted. As well as giving us three a chance to do some hunting on our own. If you gentlemen,' said Tom, looking his two sixth-formers in the eye with respectful gravity, 'wouldn't mind joining in for the occasion?'

They had stiffened and brightened, and looked back at him as at a contemporary, measuring and eager, only a little wary.

'If it would be any help?' said Miles, casting a questioning glance at George. 'And if you think we should involve Miss Darrill? We should have to tell her why.'

'It would give me a day,' said George. 'the most important day, the day he's likely to break. He knows now how he stands. Of course Miss Darrill must know what's in the wind, but nobody else, mind. And if she does consent, she's to do nothing whatever except what she was going out to do, take her members on a field expedition and keep them occupied in a perfectly normal way. All I need is that you should be there, and prevent him from getting near any possible hiding-place on the hill. If he's collected his loot already, it can't be helped. But if he hasn't, that's our only working lead to him.'

'Jane will do it,' said Tom positively. 'And what if we should find the stuff ourselves? What do we do?'

'You leave it where it is, but don't let the spot out of your sight. I'm going to have to be in Birmingham part of the day, but before the daylight goes I'll be ready to relieve you. Can you hold the fort until then?'

'Yes, until you come, whenever that is.' It was the only way he had of helping Annet. She might not be grateful, she might hate him for it, but there was no other way.

'Good! I'll try to be back in the station by four-thirty. Will you call me there then? If anything breaks earlier, I'll get word to you as soon as I usefully can.'

'I'll do that. And may I call Jane Darrill now? Better give her what warning we can, if we're upsetting her bus arrangements.'

He called her, and the light, assured, faintly amused voice that answered him manifested no surprise. Curious that he should be able to hear in it, over the telephone, wry overtones of reserve and doubt he had never noticed in it in their daily encounters.

'That means switching tea to somewhere in Comerford,' she said, sighing. 'There won't be time to take them out to the Border. And what do you suppose the Elliots will do with the provisions laid in for forty hungry boys?'

'I didn't think about that,' he said, dismayed. 'Well, if you can't do it, of course—'

'Who said I couldn't do it? Twenty-four hours notice is required only for the impossible. Don't worry, I live here, I can fix tea, all right. By the way, who's asking me to do this, you or the police?'

'Me,' he said simply, without even the affectation of correctness.

'Just as long as we know,' said Jane, a shade dryly. 'All right, it's on.'

She hung up the receiver, and left him troubled by tensions newly discovered in himself, when he had thought that Annet had exhausted all his resources of feeling and experience. He wondered, too, as he went back to report to George in the living-room, why he should feel ashamed, but he had no leisure to indulge his desire to examine the more obscure recesses of his own mind. There had been, throughout, only one person who really mattered, and for the first time in his life it was not himself.

'That's that,' he said. 'It's arranged. I think we'd better call it a day now, if we're going to be on patrol between us all day tomorrow. Come on, Miles, I'll run you home.'

In the hall he hung back and let the boys go out into the chill of the night ahead of him. There was still something he had to ask George. He could not remember ever feeling so responsible for any boy in his charge as he did now for Miles; the act of confiding had drawn them closer than he found quite comfortable, and probably the boy was chafing, too.

'It's definite, isn't it?' he asked in a low voice, as they emerged on the doorstep. 'What you said about young Mallindine? They were up there in Snowdonia the whole time?'

'Quite definite. We've already checked on their week-end.' George remembered the mental clip over the ear that was in store for Dominic when the time was ripe, and smiled faintly in the dark. The two boys were talking in low tones, out there beside the Mini, small, taut, tired voices studiously avoiding any show of concern with the things that really filled their minds. 'Don't worry about them, they're in the clear.'

'I shouldn't think you've ever been so glad to cross off your prime suspect,' said Tom, feeling his own heart lift perceptibly, even in its passionate preoccupation with that other hapless young creature for whom there was no such relief.

'Well, he wasn't that, exactly, he was rather down the list, as a matter of fact. Though as it turns out,' said George with soft deliberation, 'we've lost Number One as well.'

'You have? Who—?' But perhaps he wasn't allowed to ask; it was all too easy to assume that goodwill entitled you to the confidence of the authorities. 'Sorry, I take that back. Naturally you can't very well talk about it.'

'Oh, in this case I think I could.' George cast one brief glance at him along his shoulder, and saw the young, good-looking, self-confident face paler and more thoughtful than usual, but unshakable in innocence and secure as a rock. 'Number One was an obvious case for investigation. In close contact with her daily, then clean away from here for the week-end just as she vanished. Involved closely in her reappearance, too, as if he knew where to look for her, and was interested in creating the atmosphere for her return. Anxious to be around when I began to ask questions, very anxious to know the odds. And falling over himself to point out to me indications that someone else had been on the scene.'

Tom was staring back at him blankly, searching his mind in all the wrong directions, and still quite unable to see this eligible lover anywhere in the case.

'But there wasn't anyone. The trouble from the beginning was that there was no one in close contact with her like that—'

'No one?' said George with a hollow smile. 'Yes, there was this one fellow. Right age, right type, and rubbing shoulders with her every day. You mean to say you never noticed him? But we've checked up on his movements all the week-end, too, and he's well and truly out of it. He went home like a lamb, just as he said he was going to, and he was in a theatre with another girl when Jacob Worrall was killed. For God's sake!' said George between irritation and respect, 'do you want me to tell you what they saw?'

Then it came, the full realisation, like a weight falling upon Tom and flattening the breath out of him. He froze in incredulous shock, heels braced into the gravel, staring great-eyed through the dark and struggling for words, confounded by this plain possibility which had never once occurred to him. What sort of complacent fool had he been? He stood off now and looked at himself from arm's-length, with another man's eyes; and that, too, was a new experience to him.

'You mean to say you never realised? Why do you suppose I asked Doctor Thorpe to stay with Annet, that night, until my man came to keep watch on her? Who else knew at that time that we were on to her? Who else could have known that she was a threat to him? Did you think I was protecting her from her father? You weren't a very likely murderer in yourself,' said George gently, propelling the stricken young man along the path towards the waiting boys, 'and you could hardly have been her partner in that first attempt at flight, six months ago, that's true. But even now it isn't by any means certain that the man we're looking for is the same person, it's merely a fair probability. And on circumstantial evidence alone, until Miss MacLeod put you clean out of the reckoning today, you were undoubtedly Number One.'

Chapter Eight

George came to Fairford very early in the morning, intent on being unexpected, appearing when Annet was still in a housecoat, pale and silent and unprepared for the renewed assault. But it seemed there was no time of the day or night when she was not armed against him and everyone. Her great eyes had swallowed half her face, the fine, clear flesh was wasting away alarmingly from her slender bones. She looked as if she had not slept at all, as if she had stared into the dark unceasingly all through the night, gazing through her window at the ridge of the Hallowmount, stretched like a slumbering beast against the eastern sky.

He asked her the old questions, and she was silent with the old silence, patient and absolute. He sat down beside her and told her, in clipped, quiet tones, everything he knew about Jacob Worrall's narrow, harmless, shabby life, about his poor little backroom hobby of collecting local Midland porcelain, about the two blows that had splintered his fragile skull and spilled his meagre, old-man's blood over the boards of his workroom. He chose words that made her tremble, and pushed them home like knives, but she never gave him word or sound in return. The room was full of pain, but the only words were his words. He wanted to stop, but she had to speak, she had to be made to speak.

It occurred to him at length, and why he did not know, to send Policewoman Crowther out of the room, to wait below until he should call her back. As soon as the door had closed behind her Annet leaned and took his hand and smoothed it between hers, entreating him with clinging, frantic fingers and desperate eyes.

'Let me go!' Her voice was only a breath between her lips, a small, broken sound. She held his hand to her cheek, and the drift of her dark hair flowed over it. 'Take her away from me, take them all away, and let me go! Oh, please, please, take them all away and leave me alone!'

'No, Annet, I can't do that. You know I can't.'

How well Miles knew her, and how deeply he understood the real threat to her now. Whether she understood what she was trying to do was another matter. All George was sure of was that he had only to remove all restrictions from her, and sit back and watch, and she would lead him to her lover; and that he could not let her do it, that he would not risk her even to catch a murderer. He could not make her speak, and she could not make him grant her the freedom of action she wanted, to throw her own life away after the old man's life.

'You must! Please! I've done nothing. Let me go! You must let me go!'

'No.'

'Then there's nothing I can do, nothing, nothing—Oh, please help me! Help me! Take everyone away and let me go free!'

The dark hair slipped away on both sides to uncover the tender nape of her neck, and its childishness and fragility was more than he could bear. He took his hand from her almost roughly, and walked out of the room, and her long, shuddering sigh of despair followed him down the stairs.

'No,' he said wearily, meeting her mother's questioning eyes in the doorway of the living-room. 'Hasn't she said anything to you that could offer us a lead?'

'She says nothing to me. She might be struck dumb. She's like this with everyone.'

'And no one's asked to see her? Or to speak to her on the telephone?'

'Not to speak to her, no. The vicar rang up to ask after her. And Regina, of course.' Even in this extremity she could not suppress the little, proud lift of her voice, at being on Christian name terms with Mrs Blacklock of Cwm Hall. 'Last night, that was, after the papers came. She and Peter were both very distressed about her. They asked if there was anything they could do, and if they could come and see her. I told them you didn't wish anyone to see her yet. Though she isn't charged with anything,' said Mrs Beck, staring him hard in the eye, 'and we have a right if we choose—'

'Of course you have. But you also have the good sense to understand the sound reasons why you should listen to me and do what I say. When you stop agreeing with me, let them all in,' said George patiently.

'We know you have a job to do, of course. And I suppose it gives an impression of activity to mount guard on my girl, when there's nothing else you can think of doing. Naturally you want to keep up your reputation—'

'What I chiefly want,' said George, walking past her to the door, 'is to keep Annet alive.'

He went out into the bright air of morning, and the sun was high above the Hallowmount, climbing in a sky washed clean of clouds. Thank God for a fine Saturday for Jane Darrill's field-day with the Geographical Association. No one would wonder too much at seeing forty small boys let loose over the hills on a sunny October afternoon, no one, not even themselves, would suppose they were there to fend off a thief and murderer from recovering his gains (if, of course, he had not already recovered them), and no one would think that even their supervisors and elders were looking for anything more sensational than samples of the local flora, and of the conglomerates, grits and slates of the ridge, or the occasional fragment of galena, or bright bits of quartzite from the outcrop rocks.

Thanks to them, George thought as he slammed the door of the car and drove along the lane to Wastfield, he had this one day's grace; and it hung heavy upon his mind that that was all he had, and that he must make it bear fruit. Time trod so close and crushingly on his heels that he had difficulty now in remembering that the murder of Jacob Worrall was, in the first place, Birmingham's case and not his.

He had extracted a list of Annet's closest schoolfriends from her mother; he checked it with Myra Gibbons, who had been closest even among these, and she supplied, with some encouragement, details of their subsequent whereabouts and fortunes. It might be time wasted, but it might not. No one had yet provided any clue as to where Annet and her partner had spent their nights in Birmingham, though by this time the hotels were all eliminated, and even the bed-and-breakfast places dwindling. One of Annet's GCE class, it seemed, was now reading English literature at Birmingham University, and another was studying at the School of Art. Probably both in respectable supervised lodgings, but sometimes they found flatlets which afforded them privacy enough to abuse the privilege. And even if they had not given her a bed, they might have been in touch with Annet while she was there. No need for them to have seen the boy, he could easily be kept in the background. But even there, there was at least a chance.

He telephoned Duckett from the box at the edge of the village, and reported his meagre gains: three addresses where there might be something to be gleaned, the two girl students, and an old, retired teacher who had once been on unusually good terms with the fourteen-year-old Annet at the Girls' High School in Comerbourne.

'They'd have come forward,' said Duckett positively, 'if they'd known anything about her moves. The teacher, anyhow.'

'You would think so. But we can't afford to miss anything. Have you talked to them again at that end? I take it they've got nothing?'

'Nothing? Boy, they've got everything, except what they want. The usual lunatic fringe ringing up from everywhere else but the right places, reporting having seen everybody but the right girl. They creep out from under every stone,' said Duckett bitterly, 'and run to the nearest telephone. But no sense so far. And yet they must have slept somewhere. And even with dark glasses and a different hair-do and whatever, you couldn't hide that girl every minute of the day. Somewhere in the ladies' room of a café she'd be sure to re-do her hair, somewhere she'd take off her hat, if she was wearing one.'

'I don't believe she ever tried to disguise herself,' said George. 'She was committing only a private sin, and she wasn't ashamed or afraid, once she was away from Comerford, once she'd got what she wanted. I don't believe she ever even tried very hard to hide from anyone. If she had, she might have been noticed more. And yet, as you say, they slept somewhere, they ate somewhere. Public transport they didn't need, if they had the motor-bike. And if they walked the streets together, they did it in the dark. The two witnesses who came forward and identified her as the girl on the corner wouldn't have been much use to us, either, if she hadn't stood under a street-light.'

'As you say. For one who wasn't trying, she made a pretty good job of being invisible.'

'Agreed, but largely accidentally. You see she didn't mind being seen that night. She did stand under a light, she didn't try to withdraw even when the Brummie lad came along, she only froze him out when he got too oncoming. She didn't know of any more pressing reason for hiding herself or her lover than the mere preservation of their week-end together. But somehow the circumstances of their stay in the town were such that they did remain unnoticed. That's how I read it.'

'You could be right,' said Duckett. 'Try it out.'

'Nothing new? Has Scott reported anything further on Geoff Westcott?'

A spurt of laughter exploded in George's ear. Duckett laughing meant trouble for someone, but decidedly not hanging trouble.

'Has he! And very interesting it all is, too, but I doubt if it'll do much for you, George. No, the thing is, Geoff told Scott yesterday he'd been down in South Wales with that side-kick of his, Smoky Brown, staying with Smoky's cousins in Gower. Said the whole clan would bear him out. Scott didn't doubt that, knowing our Browns, so he didn't ask 'em, he went straight to Martha Blount, before Geoff could get away from Lowthers' last night. Told her Geoff had told him he'd travelled south for the week-end with *the Browns*, to stay with their cousins, and asked her if she could confirm it. Innocent style, she'd be sure to know, and all that. And Smoky Brown's sister being the only other Brown in the reckoning, and a very hot little number into the bargain, Martha jumped to the inevitable conclusion, and all but went through the roof. The rat, she says, so *that's* what he meant by doing a long-distance driving job as a favour to a friend! And me believing every word, like a damned fool! All Scott had to do was put in the right questions whenever she stopped for breath: What friend? Where to? What was he carrying? She came out with everything he'd told her, and what he'd told her was the truth as far as it went, and it went one hell of a long way. He didn't tell her where they'd lifted all the lead from, but would you believe it, he told her in confidence where he was delivering it. Two trips, two lorry-loads, to a back-street yard in Bolton. Love's a terrible thing.'

'Doesn't mix with business, anyhow,' agreed George wryly. 'Think they'll be in time to pick up the goods?'

'With luck, yes. How are the receivers to know he'd be such a fool as to tell his girl the real reason why he couldn't take her out Saturday? Didn't tell her his cargo was pinched, of course, but he only pulled himself up just short of that.'

So that was another one off the list of possibilities, thought George as he hung up the receiver. Poor Martha! But at least if she made up her mind she was well rid of Geoff, no one was going to die of it. And if she cut her losses and made the best of him, with her force of character she might keep him out of gaol in future. Once having told her the truth, it wouldn't be any use telling her lies thereafter, she would always be on the look-out and ready to shorten the rein. And if young Geoff really wanted her, as seemed, oddly enough, a strong possibility, he must have thrown such a scare into himself this time that he'd do almost anything in future rather than take the risk of losing her again. She might, even, find it easy to forgive him and wait for him, in the relief of finding that he was not unfaithful, but merely a minor criminal.

Their small story, at least, need not occupy him. A few more such intrusive comedies, and his list of possibles would be dwindling out of sight.

He drove through Comerford and over the bridge, and round the eastern flank of the long, triple-folded range to Cwm Hall. The long drive unrolled before him, the vista of the park and the hollow square of the stable-yard over to the left, aside from the house and by two centuries younger. To the rear of the beautiful, E-shaped house lay the farm buildings, barns and dovecote so tall that they showed above the mellow red roofs.

Regina was at her desk in one of the large windows, ploughing her way remorselessly through her morning's correspondence without Annet's aid. She saw the car sweep round the wide curve of the drive to halt on the apron of gravel, and waved a hand and rose at once to come out to George on the doorstep.

'Mr Felse, I'm so glad to see you. I've been longing to telephone Mrs Beck again, but it seems cruel to pester the poor woman.' The alert, commanding blue eyes looked a little startled behind the distorting lenses of her reading glasses. The briskness and decision of her movements and words, undaunted by death, suspicion or suffering, sprang to meet him almost roughly; no wonder those on whom she conferred her quite genuine visitations of sympathy often reacted with bristling hackles and tongue-tied offence. And yet she was a kind, sincere woman, and the one thing she would not do for those in distress or need was leave them gently, self-sacrificingly alone.

'Do tell me about Annet. This is such a terrible business, I don't understand how she *could* have become involved. We were always so careful of her. And she isn't a deceitful child by nature, I'm sure she isn't, there were never any signs. How *could* we have failed to see that there was someone on her mind? How is the poor girl now?'

'Physically,' said George, bracing himself and digging in his heels against the force of her energy, 'she's well enough.'

'You don't want us to see her yet? I don't want to make things more difficult for you in any way, but do let us know as soon as we can go to her. We're very concerned. If there's anything we can do in the meantime, please do ask, we should be very glad if we could help her.'

So would a great many people, thought George, remembering Tom Kenyon and Miles Mallindine eyeing each other across his rug in an anguish bitterly antagonistic and helplessly shared. Some with better rights even than yours.

'Do you want to talk to Peter? He's down in the stable-yard with Stockwood, I think, working on one of the cars.'

'It's with Stockwood I wanted to have a word, as a matter of fact.'

'Oh!' she said, drawing back a step to measure him with blue eyes wide and wary. 'I thought he'd already satisfied you about his moves. One of your men was here yesterday afternoon to talk to him.'

'I know. Just a detail I'd like to check with him myself. If you've no objection?'

'I have no objection, of course. But I think I should tell you that I feel every confidence in this young man. I haven't had him long, that's true, but I can usually make up my mind fairly soon about people. I see,' she said with authority, 'why you must consider him as a possibility. But I'm sure you'll be wasting your time.'

'He's simply one man who at least has been in occasional contact with Annet. You must take my word for it that that's enough to make this necessary.'

'And personable,' said Regina, suddenly running her fingers deep into the orderly waves of her short red hair, and clenching them there for a moment. 'And young!'

The faint, astonished tang of bitterness the word had for her made her mouth twist. Had she looked too often and too closely at the chauffeur herself? It wouldn't be the first time that had happened to a busy, self-confident, indulgent woman suddenly shocked into awareness that youth had left her. If so, she had surely never done more than look; she was too certain of herself to sacrifice a part of her personality to an employee, whatever the momentary temptations.

'How much more do you know about him? He came to you with references, of course?'

'One,' she said, 'from his last employer, a business man down in Richmond. But of course you can see the letter if you want to. Before that he says he was in Canada for a year, driving or doing any job he could get. So far we've found him completely satisfactory.' It was a royal 'we,' and George recognised it as such; Peter had no use for a chauffeur, and no interest in this one provided Regina was happy.

'Oh, I don't doubt that. And he lives in Braidie's old quarters?'

'In the south lodge.' It was behind the house, and hidden from it by the older plantations Peter had brought to such excellent growth and condition.

'Alone? Or is he a married man?'

'He has been married. His wife got a divorce from him – at least, it won't be absolute for a month or so yet. Over an incident with another woman. You see, he was very frank with me about his circumstances when he applied for the job.'

'So he does live alone?' In that minor lodge on a very quiet road, out of sight of the house, where coming and going would be easy. 'And does for himself?'

'Yes, very economically and neatly, so I'm told.' She smiled for an instant, but wryly. 'Our head gardener has a rather forward daughter who has made it her business to offer her services, but she hasn't got anywhere so far. He doesn't seem to have any use for women, by all the signs.'

No, maybe not. But then he wouldn't, for other women, if he had Annet in his sights.

'I'll go round and join them, if I may.'

'Do, of course. You know your way.'

George walked round the wing of the house and down the slope of grass. The eighteenth-century stable block sat four-square about a large courtyard, two-storeyed, many-windowed, like a mansion in itself. There were still three riding-horses on the place, but the cars had nearly elbowed them out of their own yard. Peter Blacklock, in slacks and an old polo-necked sweater, was bending into the bonnet of the E-type Jaguar that was credibly reputed to be Regina's last birthday present to him. Stockwood, in overalls, was washing down the Bentley. He turned his head at the hollow sound of footsteps under the stable archway, and showed that proud, dark face of his, withdrawn and defensive as a Romany. For a moment he was motionless. Water streamed from his rubber brush down the flanks of the car, and flowed away into the drain.

Peter Blacklock took his head out of the car's innards, and shook back the lank fair hair from his forehead with a nervous toss of his head.

'Oh, hallo, Felse!' Something of consternation, something of resignation, showed in his long, hypersensitive features for an instant, and then was gone suddenly, leaving only his unusual faintly weary but beautifully modulated politeness. 'I'm sorry, I didn't hear you come. Were you looking for me?'

He leaned into the car and switched off the purring engine, and stood wiping his hands on a tangle of cotton-waste. 'Am I allowed to ask about Annet? We've beeen – we *are* terribly anxious about her. There's nothing new?'

'No, nothing new.' He didn't want to talk to anyone about Annet, he didn't want to show to anyone else even a part of what she had made him experience. 'We're still filling in details wherever and however we can – about all the people we can. Do you mind if I ask Stockwood a few questions?'

'If you must,' said Peter, frowning. 'But I thought you'd already done with him. He accounted for himself to one of your fellows yesterday. Something the matter with the liaison, or what?'

'Nothing the matter with the liaison. Just a double check for safety's sake. And you might fill in the timing of the week–end for me yourself first, if you will. Mrs Blacklock went off to Gloucester on the Thursday afternoon. Stockwood drove her down and brought back the car, because she was meeting a friend ther who could run her about locally. You then gave him the whole long week-end off, I understand. Exactly when did he leave here, and when did he return?'

In the very brief moment of quietness Stockwood leaned and turned off the tap. He laid down the brush and took a step towards them, waiting in readiness, dark colour mounting in his face and blanching again to pallor.

'He garaged the car about a quarter to five,' said Peter in a thin, brittle voice, his long face sagging with reluctance and distress. 'I told him he could consider himself free until the following Wednesday noon, and then come in for the Bentley and fetch my wife home. I told him if he liked he could make use of one of the BSAs for his week-end, and he said yes, he would like to. I don't know what time he left the lodge, but it was all in darkness before six o'clock. He came back prompt at noon on Wednesday, and drove to Gloucester to bring Regina back.'

'You didn't ask him where he was going?'

'I didn't. I don't. Nor where he'd been when he came back. He's my wife's employee, not mine, but even if he were mine I shouldn't think that gave me any right to ask him where he spends his free time.

Only his working hours are bought and paid for.' He added gently and wearily: 'Your business, of course, it may very well be. *You* ask him.'

The young man dried his hands carefully, automatically, confronting them both with a wary face and narrowed eyes. He had left it too late to protest at being interrogated again, and far too late to pretend surprise or indignation. He waited, moistening his lips, a glitter in his eyes that might have been anger, but looked closer kin to desperation.

'I think,' said George after a moment of thought, 'I'd better talk to Stockwood alone. If you don't mind?'

Blacklock did mind, that was abundantly clear; he felt a degree of responsibility for all the members of his wife's staff, and was reluctant to abandon any of them to the mercies of the police, however implicit his faith might be, in theory, in British justice. He hesitated for a moment, swung on his heel to pick up his jacket from the stone bench in the middle of the yard.

'All right! I'll see you when you've finished, Felse. Look in at the house for a moment if I'm not around, will you?'

He went out through the deep archway between the coach-houses with his long, nervous stride, and vanished up the slope of the field towards the hall.

'Well?' said George. 'Where *did* you spend the week-end?'

The young man drew breath carefully between lips curled in detestation and fright. 'I've told you already. I told your bloke who was here yesterday—'

'You told him you went to a fishing inn up the Teme valley – I know. Not having a home of your own to go to.'

Stockwood's head jerked back, the gipsy face took fire in a brief blaze of defiance quickly suppressed.

'You thought the landlord was a friend of yours, and quick on the uptake, and would see you through. Maybe he promised you he would, when you phoned him. Maybe he really would, up to a hold-up or a smash-and-grab. But as soon as he smelled murder he packed it in. He'd not be getting lumbered with any part of it, boy. And you weren't at the Angler's Arms last Saturday night. So where were you?'

The colour had ebbed from Stockwood's face so alarmingly that it seemed there could not be enough blood in him to keep his heart working. George took him by the arm and sat him down, unresisting, on the stone bench. The lean young face, self-conscious and proud, stood him off steadily; and in a moment the blanched lines of jaw and mouth eased.

'That's better. Take it quietly. It's very simple. You gave us a phoney tale about where you spent your free week-end. Now all I want is the truth, and for your own sake you'd better produce it. You'd have done better,' he said dryly, 'to stick to it in the first place, when you came here after the job. Why didn't you tell Mrs Blacklock you had a prison record? Oh, no, I haven't told her, either, so far this is just between you and me. But you must have cased the job and the people before you tried it, you should have been able to judge that she'd take you even with a stretch behind you – maybe all the more.'

'I didn't know,' said the young man through tight lips. 'How could I? I wanted the job, and I was on the level. I didn't dare to risk what she'd do if she knew.'

'I'm telling you, she'd have taken you on just the same. She'd pride herself on giving you your chance.'

'That's what you fellows always say. And that's what women like her always say. But when it came to the point how could I be sure? I've done the job properly,' he said, stiffening his neck arrogantly, and stared up into George's face without blinking. 'Didn't take your lot long to get after my record, did it?'

'It doesn't, once we've got the idea, once we know you're lying about your movements last week-end. We can connect. It doesn't follow,' said George, 'that we think you necessarily did the Bloome Street job. It's a long way from helping to hi-jack a load of cigarettes to killing a man. But nobody lies about his movements without having something to hide. So where were you?'

Stockwood's jaw clamped tight to shut in whatever words he might have been about to blurt out furiously in George's face. He sat for a moment with his hands clenched and braced on the edge of the stone seat. There was no hope of success with a second lie, and all too clearly he had no new line of defence prepared. After a brief struggle his lips opened stiffly, and said abruptly: 'With a woman.'

'Miss Beck?' said George conversationally.

'*No, not* Miss Beck!'

'Rosalind Piper again?'

Or was it 'still' rather than 'again'? But there was as little reason for him to hide a connection with her as there was to continue or resume it. According to the records, she had cost him a year in gaol by involving him in the gang in the first place; and she had cost him his marriage, too, it seemed, since there was a divorce hanging over him. Briefly George wondered what she had looked like. A blonde decoy with a brazen face, or a little innocent creature with big blue eyes? The boy could have been only about twenty-one or twenty-two at the time, and not long married, probably a decent enough young man with good prospects, but the usual, ever-present money difficulties; and a quick share-out from one big haul must have seemed to him an enticing proposition, especially the way the experienced Miss Piper had pictured it for him, with herself as a bonus.

'No!' Stockwood spat the negative after her memory, and turned his head obstinately away.

'I have no interest,' said George patiently, 'in your private affairs, as long as you're breaking no laws. You'd better give her a name. If she bears you out, I can forget it.' If she bore him out, it would be the truth.

'*You* might,' said Stockwood. '*She* wouldn't.'

'If she didn't grudge you the week-end, she won't grudge you an alibi. What harm can there be in asking her to confirm your story? If, of course, it's true this time.'

'It's true!'

'And if you did nothing the law would be interested in.'

'No. I didn't do anything wrong. You won't be able to prove I did, because I didn't.'

'Then don't be a fool. Tell me who she is, and help yourself and me.'

'No – I can't tell you!'

'You'll have to in the end. Come on, now, she won't be inconvenienced, we have no interest in her. But unless you name her you're putting yourself in a nasty spot, and casting doubt on every word you have told me.'

'I can't help it,' said Stockwood stubbornly, and licked a trickle of sweat from his lips. 'I can't tell you.'

'You can't because she's as big a lie as the fishing week-end. She doesn't exist.'

'She does exist! Oh, my God!' He said it in a sudden, soft, hopeless voice to himself, as though, indeed, she was the only creature who did exist for him, and of her reality he was agonisingly unsure. 'But I can't tell you who she is.'

'You won't.'

'*All right, I won't!*'

George walked away from him as far as the hollow shadow under the archway, walked his heat and exasperation out of him for a few minutes in the chill of it, and came back to begin all over again. It went on and on and on through the sparse, barren exchange, two, three, four times over; but at the end of it, it was still no. Quivering with tension, exhausted and afraid, Stockwood looked up at him with apprehensive eyes, waiting for the inevitable, and still denied him.

'All right,' said George at last, with a sigh, 'if that's how you want it, there are more ways than one of finding her.'

But were there? Had he discovered even one way yet of finding the man who had picked up Annet and taken her to Birmingham? The city might be, must be, more productive.

'We'll leave it at that,' he said, 'for the moment. And on your own head be it.'

'Are you taking me in?' asked the young man from a dry throat.

'No. Not yet. I don't want you yet, and you'll keep. But you won't do anything rash, will you? Such as deciding to get out of here, fast. I shouldn't. You wouldn't get far.'

'I'm not going anywhere,' said Stockwood steadily, and sat with his clenched hands braced on his knees, tense and still, as George turned and walked out of the stable block.

Peter Blacklock was waiting in the leaf-strewn border of the drive, just out of sight of the windows of the house.

'Well, did you satisfy yourself?' His kind face was clouded, his eyes anxiously questioning. 'You know, Felse, you're barking up the wrong tree. I'm sure Stockwood had nothing whatever to do with it.'

'I've finished with him for the time being,' said George noncommittally, his voice mild.

'I'm glad. I was sure—'

He fell into step beside George, shaking his head helplessly over his thoughts, and feeling for words.

'You know, Regina and I are very worried about Annet. One can't help realising, from what was published in the papers, that she's very deeply implicated. What I wanted to say— to ask— You do realise, don't you, that she must have been dragged into this terrible position quite innocently? We know her, you see, very well. It's quite impossible that she should willingly hurt or wrong anyone. She can have known nothing, nothing whatever, about the crime – before or after the act.'

He waited, and George walked beside him and said nothing.

'Forgive me, but I had to tell you what we feel about her, we who know her, perhaps, as well as anyone. We're very fond of her, Mr Felse. I'm sure you can understand that.'

'I can understand it,' said George. 'I'm beginning to think I know her pretty well myself.' And could be very fond of her, too, his mind added, but he kept that to himself.

'Then you must have realised that she can't have known anything about murder or theft.' He looked up into George's face with the shadowy, emasculated reflection of his wife's confidence, authority and energy. 'I know this isn't professional conduct, but I should be very grateful to you for some reassurance – a hint as to how you're thinking of her—'

'I think of her,' said George, goaded, 'as a human creature, not a doll, a whole lot more complicated and dangerous than any of you seem to realise. She isn't anyone's hapless victim, and she isn't a pawn in anyone's game, and when I pity her I know I'm wasting my time. But if it's any consolation to you, I *don't* think she's a murderess.'

He climbed into the MG, swung it round, hissing, on the apron of rosy gravel, and drove away down the avenue of old lime trees, leaving Blacklock standing with a faint, assuaged smile on his lips and the deep grief still in his eyes; slender and tall and elegant in his ancient and excellent clothes, like a monument to a stratum of society into which he had been drafted just in time to decay with it.

George telephoned Superintendent Duckett from home, over the hasty lunch Bunty had spent so much time and care preparing, and he had now no leisure to enjoy.

'The bike again,' said Duckett hopefully. 'If you can find where they stayed there may be a real chance of finding out if anyone saw the bike around. And if so, then it's looking unhealthy for our friend. But why, for God's sake, say he spent the week-end with a woman, if he really is the one who was off with the Beck girl? You'd have thought he'd turn out absolutely any tale rather than go so near the truth.'

'He did, originally. It fell down under him. This time he was pushed. And of course,' said George cautiously, 'there's always the chance that it may be true – even provably true, if it's that or his neck. He's a good-looking chap, and there could be other women, besides Annet, who'd think so. Even some others he might risk a good deal before he'd name.'

'You've got one in mind?' said Duckett alertly, hearing the note of wary thoughtfulness he knew how to interpret.

'I have, but it's far-fetched. I'd rather plough other ground first, it's more likely to yield.'

He could picture in Technicolor Duckett's face if the receiver should blurt out baldly in his ear: 'Well, he *could* have gone off back to Gloucester, and spent the week-end amusing Mrs Blacklock between lectures and discussions. She's noticed him, all right. She speaks up for him, as well she might if she knows where he was but doesn't want to have to say so – and a little more freely than you would normally for a good chauffeur you'd had only three months, and who otherwise meant nothing to you. And what would be more likely to shut his mouth, and make him stick out even the threat of a murder charge rather than come out with the real facts? A blazing scandal, her reputation gone and his job, and where would he get another in a hurry? If it was Regina, it all makes sense!'

No, that was all true enough, but not for publication, and for the moment non-essential in any case. It couldn't catch their murderer for them, even if they proved it, it could only cancel out one more possibility. The elimination of Stockwood could wait its turn.

'I'm making for Birmingham now,' he said, aloud. 'It looks the more profitable end at the moment.'

'Give 'em my love,' said Duckett. 'And keep off their corns.'

George drove to Birmingham, and conferred with his opposite numbers there briefly and amicably. They had worked together on other occasions, and understood each other very well. Hag-ridden and undermanned, the city CID were hardly likely to chill their welcome for someone who came with a handful of suggestions, however dubious; all the more if he was willing to investigate them himself.

The sum of their own discoveries, up to then, was two shop assistants who had sold clothing to Annet in one of the big stores, and one elderly newsboy from whom she had bought a paper on Friday evening.

'Never reads the damned things himself,' complained the Superintendent bitterly, 'except the racing page. Says he's seen too many of 'em to care. Waving the girl's face in front of the rush-hour crowds, and never noticed it himself!'

'She was alone when they saw her?'

'Every time.'

'Well, let's see if we can get anything out of her old class-mates.'

The student of literature was out of town for the week-end; he should, of course, have thought of that. But her lodgings were easy enough to find, shared with three other students, and presided over by a competent matron of fifty, who had reared a family of her own, and knew all the pitfalls. It was clear within ten minutes that it would be quite impossible for any irregularities to creep into her well-ordered household, or any of her girls to misbehave herself or entertain a misbehaving visitor within these walls. Contact with Beryl there might have been, but on the whole even that was improbable. The one girl who was spending the week-end in town, over a crucial essay, had never heard Annet mentioned, and never seen her, and from her George gathered that Beryl's time and attention was very largely taken up by men friends rather than women. He wrote that one off, and made for the retired teacher who had enjoyed Annet's liking and confidence.

Miss Roscoe was rosy and grey and garrulous, of uncertain memory, but certain that she had not heard from or seen Annet Beck for over a year.

It took him some time to run the art student to earth, for Myra Gibbons had known no exact address for her, and before he could find her he had to find the secretary of the school. But he had luck, and when at last he located the small old house in a quiet road, and the side-door in the yard which led directly to the converted first-floor flatlet, it was Mary Clarkson in person who opened the door to him.

No, she had not seen Annet Beck during the weekend, because she had herself been home in Comerbourne for a whole week, and left the flat closed up. She knew, of course, about Annet's picture being in the paper, and the appeal for information about her, but she had had no information to give. She was terribly concerned about her, of course, but mostly just plain astonished, because it seemed so incredible.

They wrote to each other very occasionally. When had she last written? Oh, maybe a month ago. And had she mentioned that she would be going home for such a long visit at half-term? Yes, she

believed she had, now that he came to suggest it. It was terrible about
Annet, wasn't it? But no, she'd never told Mary anything about
boys, or not about any special boy. Annet didn't confide that kind of
thing. No, nothing at all, never a word to indicate that she was either
in love or in trouble. She was quite sure. She'd have been curious
enough to read between the lines and try to work it out in detail, if
ever there'd been the slightest hint.

It appeared that he had drawn a blank again, and the hours of his
single and irreplaceable day were slipping away from him with
nothing gained. But when she was letting him out, and he looked
round the yard and saw how securely enclosed it was, with no
window overlooking it, and no other door sharing it, his thumbs
pricked.

'Where's the actual door of the house?'

'Oh, that's round the corner in the other street. This was the back
door originally, but when she had the flat made to let, she made use
of this door to serve it, and walled it off from the kitchen and the
passage. That's what makes it so beautifully private.'

And so it did, so beautifully private that now he could not be
mistaken, and he could not and would not go back with nothing to
show for it.

'Has Annet ever been here?'

'Oh, yes, two or three times. She stayed with me once, just
overnight, but that's a long time ago.'

'She never asked about coming again? Or suggested that she might
borrow the flat when you were away?'

'No, not exactly. I mean, *she* didn't. But I remember *I did* tell her,
when she was here, that she could make use of it if ever she wanted to
be in Birmingham, even if I wasn't here. I told her to ask Mrs
Brookes for the spare key, if she needed it. And I told Mrs Brookes
about it, just in case she came. But she never did—'

She let that ending trail away into silence. She stared at George.

'I think,' said George, 'we'd better have a word with Mrs Brookes.'
He made for the yard door, and the girl came eagerly after, hard on
his heels. 'When did you get back into town?'

'Only this morning. We haven't got any classes until Monday, but
I'm meeting someone tonight, or I should have stayed over until
tomorrow evening. I haven't seen her to talk to yet. Do you really
think—?'

'Yes,' said George, and headed round the corner at speed to ring the bell at the coy blue front door. 'Were there no signs of occupation?'

'Not that I noticed. Everything was tidy, and just as I left it. But it would be – she was always tidier than I am. And I haven't really looked for anything, why should I? I never even thought of it.'

The door was opened, softly and gradually. A thin, small, elderly woman in black, of infinite gentility, glanced enquiringly over George, and smiled in swift, incurious understanding, reassured, at sight of the girl beside him.

'Ah, there you are, my dear,' said Mrs Brookes. 'I caught just a glimpse of you this morning when you came in with the shopping, but I thought you'd look in during the day sometime. Your friend was here last week-end – I expect she left a message for you, didn't she? I gave her the key, and she promised she'd leave everything nice for you. Such a pretty child, I was so glad to see her again. And no trouble at all,' she said serenely, smiling with vague benevolence at the remembered image of Annet, shy, silent and aloof, clenched about her secret. 'Quiet as a mouse about the place. And she thanked me so sweetly when she brought the key back on Tuesday evening. If only all the young girls nowadays had such pretty manners, I'm sure there wouldn't be any occasion for all this talk about what are the younger generation coming to.'

'She's seventy-one,' said George, reporting over an acrid cup of tea and a Birmingham sausage roll that represented all the meal he was going to have time for. 'A widow, no relations very close, a few friends, but they don't pop in at all hours. She's not very active or strong, her groceries and laundry are delivered, no dog to walk— Astonishing how completely isolated and insulated you can be in a city, if you let it happen. And she's the kind that doesn't mind, not even particularly inquisitive. She doesn't take a newspaper, except on Sundays, because she gets all the news the modern way. Where we made our mistake was bothering about the Press at all, it seems what we should have done was put the girl's photograph on television. She follows that, all right, religiously. As it was, she simply didn't know – after all this labour she really didn't know – what our girl looked like. Not that she's been able to tell us very much even now, but at least we know now where Annet and her boyfriend spent their nights. And knowing that, it's surely only a matter of time finding out more. Mrs Brookes may not be the nosy type, but there must be somebody in that street who spends her time peering through the net curtains to watch everybody's comings and goings. Somebody will have seen them – some other old girl who doesn't see the papers, or didn't want to get mixed up in the business. They still come like that our way, I don't know about Birmingham.'

'They still come like that here, too,' the Superintendent assured him grimly, and went on with his notes.

'Even some old soul too blind to identify a photograph may have a pretty good eye for general appearances, height, walk, the basic cut of a man. The knocking on doors begins now, all along the street. Thank God that's your job, not mine.'

'Not mine, either,' said the Superintendent with a tight smile, 'if I know it. A hate of leg-work got me where I am. Check on this for me. The girl came for the key on Thursday evening about seven by which time it was dark – reminded Mrs Brookes that her friend had given permission for her to use the flat any week-end. And Mrs Brooks remembered and obliged. Girl said she didn't need anything, she had everything, and old lady left her alone to run her own show. The entrance is private, a motor-bike could lie in the yard there and not be seen. Old lady saw her three or four times during the week-end, coming home with shopping. Not only food, but fancy bags from a dress-shop, very natural in any girl. But always alone. Two or three times they chatted for a few minutes, but that was all. Never saw a man there. Voices don't carry through the walls – that I can believe, those are old houses, and solid. No mention of a man, no glimpse of a man, but with her windows facing the opposite way, and her eye on television most of the time, anyhow, that doesn't mean much. Anyhow, she can tell us nothing about a man, and she won't hear of one. Not in connection with this angelic girl. And on Sunday morning Beck was in the local church for morning service, alone, which only reinforces Mrs Brookes's opinion that we're misjudging her cruelly. On Tuesday evening she brought back the key, said thank-you prettily, and left, by what means of transport Mrs Brookes doesn't know. We could,' he said sourly, 'have done with a more inquisitive landlady, that's a fact.'

'There'll be a neighbour with a flattened nose somewhere around. The girls who sold Annet the dress and the nightdress didn't add much, either.'

'She shopped alone. Every time. And in city shops and a supermarket, never in the small local places. If he was with her, he waited outside. Most men do. So that's it. That's the lot. But at least we've moved, and now we can keep moving.'

'That's the lot. And I've got to be on my way,' said George, pushing away his empty cup. 'Mrs Brookes promised me to try and dredge up every word they said to each other, or anything she can remember about the girl. If she does come through with anything, call me, will you? I'll give you a ring as soon as I get in at the office, and give you anything new we've got at that end. Not that I expect anything,' he said honestly, turning up the collar of his coat in the doorway against the thin wind that had sprung up with dusk. 'Yet,' he said further, and went round to the parking ground to pick up the car.

He was later than he'd said he'd be, getting back to the office in Comerbourne. Tom Kenyon had telephoned once already, with nothing to report but a blameless day of chaotic activity among the geographers, and a continuing watch on the Hallowmount, which would be faithfully maintained until he and his helpers were either called off or relieved. He had promised to ring again in half an hour, which meant he might be on the line again at any moment.

But when the telephone rang again, and George leaned across to pick it up, the voice that boomed in his ear belonged to the Superintendent in Birmingham.

'Thought you'd be making it about now,' he said with satisfaction. 'Two bits of news for you, for what they're worth. First, we've found a small boy who lives three doors away from Mrs Brookes's back premises, and plays football in the street there. They will do it. He kicked the ball over the wall into Miss Clarkson's yard on Friday morning, and knowing she was away, opened the door and let himself in to fetch it. He says there was a motor-bike propped on its stand inside there. A BSA three-fifty. That fits?'

'It fits,' said George, aware of a sudden lurch forward, as though he had been astride just such a mount, and accelerating along a closed alley between blank walls. 'He didn't, by any chance, collect registrations?'

'No luck, he didn't. Bright as a button about what interests him, he's completely dim about the number. But if it was there, somebody else must have seen it, if we look hard enough. Somebody will have seen the rider, too. It's only a matter of slogging, now we know where to look. And the second thing. Mrs Brookes has had an afterthought. Don't ask me what it means, or even if it means anything. Myself, I'd be inclined to suppose she made it up to bolster her own picture of the visiting angel, if she didn't in other ways strike me as being scrupulously honest in her observations, if not exactly acute. She says there *was* mention of a man. It didn't occur to her when she was talking to you, because it was so obvious that you were enquiring about someone very different. But she remembered it afterwards, and thought she ought to correct her statement, however irrelevant this information may be.'

'I recognise,' said George, 'the style.'

'Good, now make sense of the matter. So far, I can't. She says when Annet Beck fetched the key on Thursday, she told her that she would probably be having a visitor during the week-end. Said he had to be in Birmingham, so he'd be looking in to see her—'

'He?' said George, ears pricked, suddenly aware that this was going to be the place where the cul-de-sac ended, and he must brake now, and hard, if he wanted to keep his head unbroken.

'He. The man for whose presence she was apparently preparing Mrs Brookes, just in case he should be seen. The only man in the case. And know who she said he'd be? This'll shake you! *Her father!*'

Chapter Nine

Promptly at five-thirty Tom Kenyon telephoned again.

'Nothing new here. It was a good day out, but nothing whatever happened. I suppose that was exactly what we could expect, with forty-two of us clambering about all over the rocks. If there is anything here to be found, you can stake your life nobody came for it today. But we didn't find it, either.'

'Were you able to do any looking?' It wouldn't be easy, with a handful of sharp-eyed juniors on the watch for every eccentricity in their elders.

'Some. Not to attract attention, though, and that means we could only look very superficially at the outcrop areas where the kids were swarming. We had a go at the ring of trees, and the old footways down below, until the boys came down to hunt over the tips for crystals among the calcite. But all we collected was pockets full of Jane's rock specimens. She always loads them on to the nearest human pack-mules to carry home for her. Women know what they're doing, having no pockets.'

'They've all come down by this time, I suppose?' said George.

'Ostentatiously. I thought it might be a good idea to leave with as much noise as possible, in case someone somewhere was waiting his turn. But Mallindine and your boy are still up there,' he said reassuringly, 'keeping an eye on things from cover until I go back. I'm on my way now, I'm going to send them down to get tea here at the pub.'

'The others have gone?'

'Yes, into Comerford with their coach, for tea. Jane arranged it. And then home to Comerbourne and disperse. Dead quiet up there now.'

He could feel the quietness of the Hallowmount moving, growing, pouring through the dusk towards the village, flowing round and over Fairford and Wastfield, drowning this isolated telephone box on the edge of the wilds. Down the darkening flanks the streams of silence ran softly and slowly, curling round the scattered buildings of the farm, sweeping greenly over the roof of the Sparrowhawk's Nest. All day waiting like a great beast asleep, the long ridge stretched and stirred now in the first chill of twilight, and the little, quivering, treacherous ground-wind awoke and began curling its tremulous pathways up through the long grass.

'Can you hold on there until I come out to meet you?'

'Yes, I'll be somewhere on top. I've had tea. I'll send the boys down and wait for you.'

'Good! I'll be along as soon as I've talked to the Superintendent. And had a look in at Fairford, perhaps, if you don't mind hanging on another half-hour or so?'

'I don't mind. Whenever you can make it, I'll be here. Don't pass up anything you should do first.' He hesitated, unsure how much right he had to ask questions but aching with the effort to contain them. 'Did you turn up anything useful at your end?'

'Maybe. Difficult to tell as yet. We've found where they stayed. Not a hotel – they borrowed a flat rented by a friend of Annet's. The motor-bike appears again. No one saw the man. But according to the old lady round the corner, the owner of the house, Annet told her she was expecting a visitor. Annet described him to her as her father.'

The indrawn breath at the other end of the line hissed agonisingly, as though the listener had flinched from a stab-wound. 'Her *father*?'

'Does that suggest anything?'

It suggested far too much, things Tom had never wanted to hear, and did not want to remember, possibilities he could not bear to contemplate. He choked on exclamations that would unload a share of the burden on to George's shoulders, bit them back and swallowed them unuttered. They lay in his middle like lead.

'It sounds as if we have to revise our ideas, doesn't it?'

'It does,' said Tom, his throat constrained.

'Why say that, unless it was to prepare the way in case she was seen with this man? A man obviously, in that case, respectable enough to pass for her father. *And old enough*.'

'Not a teenager run wild,' said Tom.

'Not even a youngster in his twenties. A father-figure. If only just. One could pass for Annet's father at around forty, maybe, but hardly earlier. Any ideas?'

The distant voice said hoarsely, aware how little conviction it must be carrying: 'No ideas.'

'You be thinking about it,' said George, and rang off without more words.

And what did that mean, on top of all the confusions that had bludgeoned him since noon? What was it young Tom Kenyon knew that George didn't know, concerning some man who might be, but was not, Annet's father? And why, feeling as he felt about Annet, and longing as he must long for an end to this uncertainty that held a potential death for her, why had he gulped back his knowledge from the tip of his tongue in panic, and resisted his solid citizen instinct to plump it into the arms of the police and get rid of the responsibility?

George turned out the lights in the cold office, locked the door after him, and went to make his report in person to Superintendent Duckett. But Annet's father, and Annet's fictional father, and Annet's father's lodger, and the accidental intimacies and involuntary reactions of proximity mingled and danced in his mind all the way.

It was nearly half past six when he reached Fairford. He didn't know why he felt so strongly that he must go there, he had no reason to suppose that anything new had happened there, least of all that Annet would have unsealed her lips and repented of her silence. Nor was he going to try to prise words out of her by revealing any part of what he had found out. That he knew from ample trial to be useless. It was rather that he felt the need to reassure himself that there was still an Annet, a living intelligence, an identity surely not dependent on any other creature for its single and unique life, a girl who could still be saved. Because if she was past saving, the main object of this pursuit was already lost. The old dead man had his rights to justice, but the young living girl was the more urgent charge now upon George's heart.

He turned in at the overgrown gate, into the darkness of the untrimmed, autumnal trees, the soft rot of leaves like wet sponge under his wheels. He came out of the tunnel of shadow, and sudden lances of light struck at his eyes. The front door stood wide open, all the lights in the house were blazing, the curtains undrawn. In the shrubberies down towards the brook someone was threshing about violently. In the garden, somewhere behind the house, someone was bleating frantically like a bereaved ewe, and until George had stopped the engine and scrambled out of the car he could not distinguish either the voice or the words. Then it sprang at him clearly, and he turned and ran for the house.

'Annet! Annet!' bellowed Beck despairingly, crashing through the bushes.

George bounded up the steps and into the hall, and Policewoman Lilian Crowther leaned out of the living-room doorway with the telephone receiver at her ear, and dropped it at sight of him, and gasped: 'Thank God! I was trying to get through to you. She's gone!'

'When?' He caught at the swinging telephone and slammed it back on its rest, seized the girl by the arm and drew her with him into the room. 'Quick! When? How long ago?'

'Not more than five minutes. We found out a few minutes ago. Lockyer's out there looking for her – and her father. She can't be far.'

'You shouldn't have left her.'

'She collapsed! Like that other time. She was lying with her head nearly in the hearth, and I couldn't lift her alone. I ran for her mother to help me—'

The window was wide open, the curtains swinging in the rising wind of the evening. Mrs Beck blundered past through the shaft of light, running with aimless urgency, turning again to run the other way, her face contorted into a grimace of weeping, but without tears or sound. As though death was all round the house, just outside the area of light, and everyone had known and recognised it except Annet; as though she was lost utterly as soon as she broke free from the circle and ran after her desire, and none of them would ever see her again. As though, plunging out of the window, she had plunged out of the world.

George vaulted the sill and landed on the edge of the unkempt grass. Mrs Beck turned and stared at him with dazed eyes, and caught at his arm.

'She's gone! I couldn't help it, no one could stop her if she was so set to go. It isn't anyone's fault. What could we do?'

'I'm not blaming you,' he said, and put her off, and ran through the trees to the boundary fence, leaving her stumbling after him. No moon, but even in the starlight of half a sky the emptiness about Fairford showed sterile and motionless. He had met no girl on the road. She would keep to the trees as long as she could. He circled the grounds hurriedly, halting now and again to freeze and listen. He heard Beck baying at the remotest edge of the garden, and met Lockyer methodically threading the shrubberies.

'No sign of her?'

'No sign, sir. I heard your car. Crowther'll have told you—'

'Keep looking,' said George, and turned back at a run towards the house. He overtook Mrs Beck on the way, and drew her in with him.

'Here, sit down by the fire and be quiet. Lilian, close the window and get her a drink.' He shut the door with a slam, and leaned his back against it. 'Now, what happened?'

'I told you, she collapsed, she almost fell into the fire. How could I know it was a fake? I ran for Mrs Beck – she was upstairs, she didn't hear me call. When we came back Annet was gone.'

'She climbed out of the window,' said Mrs Beck, hugging her writhing hands together in her lap to keep them still. 'Without even a coat – in her thin house-shoes!'

'Yes, yes, I know all that.' And Lockyer, patrolling dutifully outside, couldn't be on every side of the house at once. Annet could move like a cat, she hadn't found it difficult to elude him on her own ground. 'But before! Something happened, something gave her the word. Why tonight? Why now? She chose her time, she had a reason. Has she had any letters? Telephone messages?'

'No,' said Lilian Crowther positively. 'I've been with her all the time until she dropped like that. And Mrs Beck reads her letters – but anyhow there haven't been any today.'

'And no visitors,' said George, fretting at his own helplessness, and caught the rapid flicker of a glance that passed uneasily between them. 'No visitors? Someone *has* been here?'

'I asked him to come,' said Mrs Beck loudly. 'I asked him to talk to her and do what he could. What else is he for, if not to help people in trouble? I thought he might get something out of her. It was last night being choir practice that made me think of it. I telephoned him, and asked him to come in today. There couldn't be any harm in that. If she couldn't see her own vicar – even criminals are allowed that.'

'All right,' said George, frantically groping forward along this unforeseen path, 'so the vicar came. No one else?'

'No one else. You must admit I had the right—'

'All right, you had the right! Was he left alone with her?'

'No,' said Lilian, defensively and eagerly, 'I was with her all the time. Mrs Beck left them together, but I stayed in the room.'

'Thank God for that! Annet didn't object?'

'She didn't seem to care one way or the other.'

And yet she had bided her time, and torn herself resolutely out of their hold. Something had passed, something significant. Why otherwise should she have chosen this particular hour, after waiting so long and so stoically? 'Well, what did they have to say to each other? Everything you can remember.'

She dredged up a number of embarrassed, agonising platitudes through which the adolescent rawness of pity showed like flesh through torn clothing. The vicar was back in the room with them, convulsed with sympathy and hideously unable to contain it, or spill it, or wring his inadequate if kindly heart open and give it to her frankly; an ageing boy with only a boy's heaven to offer anyone, and stunted angels with undeveloped wings like his own.

'He said he was to tell her the choir had missed her at practice, and sent her their prayers. He said they took comfort in the thought that they would meet her at six-thirty at the altar. If only in the spirit, he said. And that was about all,' she concluded lamely, scouring her memory in vain for more vital matter. 'It doesn't seem anything to set her off like this.'

And yet she had received, somehow, the summons that sent her out into the dusk. He could not be mistaken. If it was not here, in this trite comfort, then there must be something else, something they had missed.

'Nothing else happened? He didn't give her a note from someone else?'

'No, honestly. He never went near enough to hand her anything. You'd have thought he was afraid of her – I suppose he was, in a way,' said Policewoman Crowther, with more perception than George would have given her credit for.

'She didn't see the paper?' He hadn't seen it himself, he didn't know if there was anything in it to speak to her, but somewhere the lost thread dangled, and must be found again.

'No, she never tried to. She never showed any interest.'

Perhaps, thought George, because she knew they wouldn't let her have the papers even if she wanted them. Perhaps because she had waited with such fatal confidence for the only message she needed, and knew it would not come that way.

But then there was nothing left but those few, bald sentences, brought from the outside world by the vicar; and if the clue was nowhere else, it must be there. The choir had missed her – Mrs Beck must have telephoned him just before he went over to the church for practice, and he had unburdened his heart to her colleagues to spread the load. And nobly they had responded. Or had they? The tone of the message was surely his, or a careful parody. It sounded as though he had dictated, and they had said: Amen. They sent her their prayers. They would meet her at six-thirty at the altar. If only in the spirit. Six-thirty was the hour of evensong, that was plain enough. Yes, but it belonged to tomorrow, not today. Why did it send her out tonight? George sweated through it word by word, and darkness, rather than light, fell on him in the moment of discovery, stunning him.

Six-thirty at the altar. Six-thirty at the Altar! All the difference in the world.

Six-thirty!

Twenty to seven by his watch, and she was somewhere out there in the dark, with a quarter of an hour's start on him at least, bursting her heart on the steep climb to her lover.

He tore the door open and was out of it and down the steps in a couple of raking strides, before they realised that he had found what he was looking for. Racing towards his car, he shouted peremptorily for Lockyer, and by the time he had the MG turned recklessly in the confined space and pointing down the drive, the bushes threshed before the constable's galloping body, and Lockyer was running beside him. George slowed, and shoved open the door.

'Get in, quick! Never mind searching, you're not needed here. I know now where to look.'

Lockyer fell lurching into the seat beside him, and slammed the door. They rocked out through the gate and swung left into the narrow road.

'Where are we going?' Lockyer clung to the dashboard, and hefted his big body to speed the turn, panting after his run.

'Top of the Hallowmount.'

'For God's sake, what's she doing rushing up there?'

'Meeting her lover. He sent for her.'

Her lover, if he still was that, after being hunted for days, and nursing for days the knowledge that the case against him depended entirely upon her. More likely by now it was her murderer she was going to meet. One can run faster and live more cheaply than two, hide more easily, remain anonymous more surely. And besides, the bulk of the evidence would die with Annet. Even when he made up his mind to run, he couldn't, he daren't, run until he had silenced her. God alone knew what she thought they were going to do. Run away

319

together, maybe, to the ends of the earth, ditch the BSA somewhere, hitch lifts, reach the sea and the chance of a passage over to France.

Maybe! Or maybe she had something else in mind, something passionate and individual and her own, not to be guessed at too confidently by anyone in the world; because no one in the world knew Annet well enough to be sure what she would do, but George Felse by this time knew her at least well enough to wait with humility, and wonder, and acknowledge that she was a mystery.

Past the Wastfield gate, bounding and wallowing over the cart-ruts, and on between the rough pastures, fenceposts blurring into a continuous flickering wall of pallor alongside. Half the sky dark over them, but glimmerings of starlight still. Pale objects shone lambent out of the darkness, a tall gate-post where the plantation began, the wall of a barn in the field opposite. Before them the Hallowmount loomed, cutting off the dapplings of the sky, its great bulk languid but aware.

'But *how* did he get word to her? Or was it all arranged between them before?'

All arranged, maybe, though they'd expected to make their bid for freedom in other circumstances than these. All arranged but the time and the place, perhaps even the place accepted, established by old usage. And the time he had appointed, and she was keeping her appointment. Without even a coat. In her thin house-shoes.

'Her visitor brought the message this afternoon.'

'Her visitor? But there wasn't anybody, except—'

Members of the clergy, like doctors and postmen, tend to be invisible, but that big, comely, well-meaning figure sprang into sharp focus now, became male, personable and possible in Lockyer's eyes. He swallowed, appalled. 'What, the *vicar*?' He swallowed again, swallowed voice and all, and sat stunned.

Her father! Well, he was old enough to fill the bill, if only just old enough, he made sense of the description; and nobody had enquired into his movements. Why should they? Certainly he was at choir practice, that night when Annet missed it, certainly he was at church and fulfilling his usual duties on the Sunday. But a man can be in Comerford church at half past seven, and in Birmingham by nine o'clock, or shortly after. One man had.

'But – the *vicar*!' persisted Lockyer, gulping dismay and disbelief.

George said nothing to that, he was busy holding the car steady over the worst patch of road without slackening speed. He knew now. This time he couldn't be wrong, and he wasn't in any cul-de-sac, with a blank wall at the end of it waiting for him to crash at speed.

He saw the rough grasses of the slope put on form behind the wire fence, the crouching bulk of the hill withdraw into its true dimension. He brought the car round into the arc of short grass by the second plantation gate, and scrambled out of the driver's door and through the wires of the fence with Lockyer pounding at his back. Head-down, lungs pumping, he breasted the first slope, got his rhythm, and began to climb the Hallowmount faster than he had ever climbed a hill in his life.

Tom Kenyon sat in a niche of the rocks on the highest point of the Altar, and stared along the ridge. It was the first time he had ever been up here alone, and the strangest thing to him was that it did not feel like the first time. The silence that had flowed down into the valleys with the dropping twilight was absolute now, it lay like a cloak over the whole great, wakeful shape of rock and pasture, smoothed and moulded to the stretched body. Sometimes he felt a rhythm stirring under him, like deep and easy breathing, and found himself tuning his own breath to the same measure. Sometimes he fell, without realising it, into such a stillness that the faintly-seen shapes of his own circling arms and clasped knees seemed to have acquired the texture and solidity of rock, as though he had grown into the quartzite of the Altar. He had no sense of undergoing a new experience; this was rather a recollection, drawn from so deep within him that he felt no desire to explore its origins, for that would have been dissecting his own identity, or to question its validity, for that would have been to doubt his own. He felt the tension of long ages of human habitation drawing him into the ground, absorbing him, making him part of the same continuity.

Miles had been right, fear was inappropriate and irrelevant. Awe remained with him, and grew, but not fear. And if Miles had been right about that, too, then belonging was all. It could happen to you without any motion on your part. Suddenly it was, and you were in it. You belonged, you respected, you partook, you contributed, this earth and all its layers of ancestral bones accepted you; a better and safer, a more impregnable security than belonging to a tribe or conforming to a society could give you.

How strange that you should have to clamber alone into some

remote, wild place like this, into this articulate silence and this teeming solitude, to discover where you came from and where you were going, and in what company. I belong, therefore I am.

The ground-wind had dropped, the grasses were motionless. The cold, clear air hung still. He heard, with some detached sense that did not suffer his deeper silence to be broken, light, distant sounds from the edges of Comerford, the faint, far hum of cars on country roads, a motor-cycle climbing steadily, small synthetic echoes from other worlds.

And all this time, side by side with this unbelievable serenity of mind, the horror possessed him that had fallen upon him when George Felse had said: 'Annet described him as her father.'

There was nothing new to be thought or felt about it now, but he could not let it rest, his mind trod round and round the same path endlessly, agonised and finding no reassurance.

George had taken it to mean merely that she was preparing the way for some man respectable enough and old enough to pass for her father, in case they should be seen together. But supposing she had been using the term more precisely than that? Supposing she really meant the man everyone thought of as her father?

He had tried to get the idea out of his mind, but it would not leave him. All the details that might have presented discrepancies, and delivered him from the nightmare, came treacherously and fell into place. Beck had been home all the week-end? Oh, no, by his own account and his wife's, he hadn't. He'd tramped the lanes and the streets of Comerford most of Thursday night, but after that he'd gone off by bus to his sister's place at Ledbury and his cousin's small-holding in the Teme valley, in case Annet had turned up there. He'd come home only on Monday night. Nobody had checked his statements, why should they? Not even his wife. Nobody knew that he wasn't really Annet's father, nobody except Mrs Beck and Tom Kenyon.

Unless Annet knew. That was the whole point. *Did* Annet know? And if so, how long had she known? He pondered that painfully, and he could not avoid the fear that she did know it, and had known it for a long time. It accounted all too reasonably for her inaccessibility, her estrangement from them both. From Beck as father, that is. But Beck as a man?

Was it too far-fetched? It would be an appalling tragedy, but it could happen. There was an even worse thought peering at him relentlessly from the back of his mind: that Beck had told her the truth himself, because he could not feel towards her as his daughter, knowing she was not, and his sick conscience would not let him rest until he had made confession. He was a stickler for truth and duty in his ineffective way, he might even have meant it for the best.

And she – how could you ever be sure about Annet? She might have reacted with warmth and indignation and tenderness, from which the slippery path to love is not so far. And granted that as a possibility, into what a desperate and piteous situation they had trapped each other. Flight, robbery, murder might well come to look like legitimate ways out of it, if no other offered.

He wished now that he had told George, he even made strenuous resolutions to tell him as soon as he came; but in his heart he knew that he never would. He could not repeat what he had heard from an over-wrought and drunken man; he had no right to break that lamentable confidence.

As often as he reached the end of this reappraisal, and turned to look at the whole idea with a more critical eye, he was convinced that he was mad, that it was impossible, that he had a warped mind; but as soon as he began a feverish examination of the details, in the hope of throwing it out altogether, he knew that it could happen, that such things had happened, that there was no immunity from the abnormal even in a world of careful normality, and no place to hide from love if it came for you. Look at his own case! Had he ever wanted to love her? Does anybody ever want to walk into the fire?

Half past six by his watch. The small, luminous pinpoints of the figures were the only brightness in this calm, immemorial, secret dark. He stirred, finding his limbs cramped by the gathering chill, and slid down from his perch into the grass. George would surely be here soon. And almost inevitably the two boys, though told to go home after their tea, would use their own obstinate judgement, and come back to share what was left of his vigil. More than likely even Jane, having packed her coach-load off to Comerbourne in charge of a couple of prefects, would return to see how he had fared. It couldn't be long now.

He would be sorry, almost, to have his solitude shared by the living. For all the innumerable generations of the dead, dwindling far into time past, before the Romans came mining for lead, before the Iron Age fort on Cleave was dug, before the chipped flints of Middlehope were made, he had no need of speech in order to communicate, no need to exert himself in explanations or response. He was at one with them without effort of any kind, without rites, without ritual.

Regina was surely right. There were not, there never had been, any witches on the Hallowmount. They would have been inappropriate, derisory, redundant, alien, false. Incantations were for outsiders.

He thought, I'm going queer from being alone, getting fanciful; there's a twentieth century somewhere around, and we're in trouble in the middle of it, and no way out that I can see.

And it was then that the small sound that had been hammering for some minutes at his senses, unnoticed, achieved actual presence, and made itself known to him. Time came back with it, and stress, and the inescapable memory of Annet, mute in the heart of her pathetic dream of happiness, with wreckage all round her. He moved out of the enclosing ring of the rocks, to hear more clearly.

Busy, regular, persistent, the hum of an engine climbing steadily, not on the Fairford side of the hill, but down there in the highest reaches of Middlehope. From the western flanks of the Hallowmount the sound would be cut off completely; here on the crest he heard it plainly. And when he moved out to the edge of the slope, looking down over the shallow bowl of the valley head, he saw the small glow-worm of a headlight weaving its way up by the sheep-path from Abbot's Bale. Light and sound drew steadily nearer, crossing the boggy patches with assurance, mounting into the dry pasture where the path vanished like a smoke-trail on a pale sky. Close beneath the Altar, in the throat of Middlehope, the motor-cycle halted, and in a moment the engine stopped.

Like a cloud of birds disturbed, the silence wheeled, circled, and settled again. The tiny light went out. A small, dark figure detached itself from its mount, and began to climb the slope.

He drew back hurriedly into the circle of rocks about the Altar, the beat of his heart suddenly violent against his ribs, the tatters of time past shuddering away from him. The grating of stones under his own feet sounded like an avalanche to him. He felt with stretched toes for the silent patches of short turf, groped his way round bony elbows of rock into a deep niche of darkness, braced his feet firmly in grass, and took hold on the harsh faces of spar with cautious fingers. With his head drawn back into cover, his cheek against the stone, he could watch the faint, lambent spaces of sky between the outcrops, overhanging the descent into Middlehope. If he failed to see where the intruder emerged, he would surely hear him come.

A motor-bike, and a solitary rider climbing purposefully towards this unlikely place in the night! They had not been so far out in their guesses, they had not wasted their day. And here was he alone, not empowered or equipped to do more than observe and identify. Above all identify. That he must do, at whatever cost. Because this could not be coincidence, it could not be innocent. The man climbing the hill was Jacob Worrall's murderer.

How many minutes to mount from the last faint smear of the path above the brook? The head of the valley was shallow and bare, it could not take long. He waited with breath held, but the thudding of blood in his own ears deafened him to more distant sounds, or else there was no rising current of air to lift to this place sounds from too close below. Minutes dripped by like the slow drops of sweat trickling between his shoulder-blades, and still nothing. He began to think the newcomer must have swung away from the Altar to traverse towards the trees.

Then he caught the sudden rattle of a stone rolling under a foot, and the grunt of a sharply-drawn breath, both startlingly close. He shrank and froze in his cranny, cheek turned painfully against the rock, eyes on the paler levels where sky and earth met.

A head and shoulders, stooped into the effort of climbing, and all but shapeless in consequence, heaved from the dead black of the earth and hunched into the dim blue-black of sky. In lunging strides the shadow lengthened, came over the rim panting with exertion, and straightened and stretched with a sigh of relief as it stepped on to level ground. Against the sky he was a long silhouette, against the rocks, as he came forward, he was shapeless movement, almost invisible, and rapid movement at that. He knew exactly where he was going, and felt no doubt of his solitude.

Tom heard the slur of his steps along the short grass, the deep, whistling breaths he drew, still panting with the exertion of his climb. He was moving diagonally across the space within the rocks, somewhat away from where Tom lay in hiding. Sounds rather than vision traced his passage, and it was straight as an arrow to the furrowed faces of spar at the base of the Altar.

Craning out of his hiding-place, straining vision and hearing after identity, Tom gathered every detail only to doubt it the next moment, where so much was guessed at blindly. Now the shadow shrank, dropped together. He heard the effortful subdued movements that did not belong, surely, to the very young. And that fitted, now that the woman in Birmingham had given them the clue. The man was on his knees, close against the piled boulders of the outcrop, the buttresses of the Altar. Huddled, headless, the dull shadow hunched forward, reaching with both arms into a crevice of the rock face. The laboured breathing steadied cautiously, the faint sob at the end of every inhalation swung like a pendulum.

The sound of cautious groping, and a whispered curse, and then a strong and certain sound, the grating of stone against stone, as though a heavy stopper was being withdrawn carefully from the unglazed neck of a stoneware bottle. The stooping shoulders heaved back, the bent head reappeared. Something was laid aside on the grass with a soft thud, and he leaned and groped forward again, and again drew back with full hands. A deep sigh of thankfulness. He turned on his knees to face away from the rock, and held his prize before him on the grass.

Tom's heart repeated vehemently and certainly: Not Beck! Not because of the motor-bike. Beck had never openly owned such a thing, true, but motor-bikes can be hired, or if necessary bought and kept secretly. And however grotesque it might seem to associate Beck's narrow, unworldly nature and mild scholarship with such things, the fact remained that many even odder and more unlikely characters rode them. Not Beck, when it came down to it, only because he so desperately desired that it should not be Beck. But he clung to his certainty, and would not be dislodged from it.

A glow-worm of light sprang up abruptly between the arched body and the circling rocks, trained upon the grass. By the tiny pool of pallor it made, it could be only one of those thin pencil-torches that clip in a breast pocket, and even so the kneeling man held it shrouded in his hand, for his fingers were dimly outlined with the rose-coloured radiance of his blood. He could not risk showing a light openly on top of the Hallowmount, but neither could he handle his prize, it seemed, without using the torch for a moment or two.

Sharp in the gleam sprang the black outline of a small leather briefcase. He held it flat and steady with a knee, the torch cupped over it closely, while with his free hand he turned a key in the lock, tipped the case upright, peered and fumbled within. He had to satisfy himself that his treasure was intact, it represented his funds, his hope of escape, the only future he had. He wanted two hands to manipulate it, and leaned aside for an instant to wedge his torch in a crevice low in the rocks, turned carefully on the briefcase and shaded by his draped handkerchief. Now if only he would turn his head, if only the wind would rise and whisk the handkerchief away, so that the shrouded thread of light could expand and reach his face. But the air hung still, charged with indifference and silence.

Turning back feverishly to the examination of the contents of the case, he set his knee astray on the sharp edge of the flat plug of stone he had drawn from the crevice, and winced and gasped, but neither the hissing indrawn breath nor the painful exhalation had any voice to identify him. That cavity within the rocks must have been known to them for a long time, served them as letter-box and safe-deposit on more than one occasion, but it had surely never had to guard two thousand pounds' worth of small jewellery before. Could so small a case hold all that value in jewellery? Tom supposed it could. Most of it had been in good rings, and diamonds and sapphires and a few gold watches will lie in a very little space.

And it seemed there had been room left in the case for something else, besides the stolen jewellery. The motion of the hurrying hands brought it halfway out into the light, the right hand gripped it momentarily with a convulsive clasp, the shape of the hold defining it clearly, even before Tom's straining eyes caught the short black thrust of the barrel.

A tiny thing, a compact handful. Some small-calibre pistol. He knew nothing about guns, he had never handled one. Some time, somewhere, this man had; the hand knew the motions, though it performed them as in a momentary and terrifying absence of mind. Men of an age to pass for Annet's father had almost all of them been in uniform during the last war, and the trained hands don't forget. And plenty of them had brought home guns at the end of it, and never bothered to hand them in, even after police appeals.

He was satisfied now, he sat back on his heels with a sigh, and thrust the gun down again into the case. His hand was swallowed to the wrist when the sudden sound came, lifted over the crest between them on a random current of air from the west, from the Fairford side of the ridge. Somewhere below there it might have been fretting at the edges of their consciousness for a minute or more, and they had been too intent to notice it; for now it was startlingly near and clear and resolute, for all its quietness, the soft slurring of light feet in the grass, running, stumbling, slipping, recovering, hurrying uphill to the Altar.

The kneeling man heard it, and wrenched round frantically to face it, plucking the gun from the discarded briefcase and bracing it before his body. His lunging shoulder swept the handkerchief aside and dislodged the torch after it; it fell and rolled sparkling along the ground, and he leaned after it with a hoarse gasp and snapped it off into darkness. But for an instant it had illuminated his tense and frightened face as it fell.

Tom clung shaking in his niche, the blurred oval of light and fear still dancing on the darkness before his eyes. Not Beck! No! Not any of the young bloods who gathered on the corner of the square in Comerbourne to compare the noisy and ill-ridden mounts that were their pathetic status symbols. Not young Stockwood. Not some mercifully expendable stranger. But Peter Blacklock, estate manager and husband to the wealthiest woman in West Midshire, secretary of half a dozen worthy bodies that operated under her shadow, choirmaster, organist, general factotum of the village, the prince-consort of Cwm Hall.

With the face everything fell into proportion, coherence and certainty, instantly, before the whorls of light had ceased to float in front of him in the darkness, and long before he relaxed the half-hysterical grip of his abraded finger-tips on the rocks.

Her father! Yes, he would do for that, she could have produced him before Mrs Brookes without a qualm. Forty-four or so, pleasant and charmingly-spoken, mild, easy-humoured, with a twist of rueful fun in him, and an uncle to her in her parents' eyes – who could have filled the bill better? And he made sense of so much more than that, by the qualities he had not, by the voids he offered for her to fill. He was as inevitable as he was impossible.

Who else had been in such close contact with her? Thrown together by the hour, casually and practically, in Regina's house, forced together by Regina's pitiless committee work, those two, being what they were, might easily fall together into the abyss of love, and drown, and die. It wasn't as if you were offered a choice. The time might well come when they could not bear it any longer, when they had to escape, had to be together somewhere out of her shadow. And once tasted, how could they let that desperate ecstasy go? Even the opportunist robbery, which at first seemed so improbable in one who had everything, fell implacably into place. *Because he was penniless!*

It was staggering, but it was true. What did he have of his own? From the time he'd married Regina her estates had taken up all his time. And what did he want with a profession when she would gladly buy him or give him anything he wanted? Except, of course, the one thing he had wanted to death, and couldn't ask her for. For that he'd had to provide himself.

Poor devil!

All this passed through Tom's mind by fitful glimpses, like light from a guttering candle, in the few seconds while he listened to the fervent footsteps his heart recognised now only too well. He wanted to call out to her to go back, while there was time, but he'd hesitated too long, and it was too late. Annet was there against the sky, her hair streaming.

Blacklock had lowered the gun; he knew her now, and sprang with open arms to meet her. But the true impetus that flung them together, strained breast to breast in a ravenous embrace, was hers, and had always been hers. She wasn't his victim; he was hers. She had destroyed him by loving him. If she'd never even noticed him, except as a middle-aged man, a father figure, he'd have mastered his feelings for her. But she'd opened to him, she'd loved him, he'd been forced to turn longing and dream into action. No, Annet was nobody's victim, she had done what she had chosen to do, taken him because he was the weakest, the most helpless, the least effective, the unhappiest of all the men it might have been. All good reasons, and there was no going back on them now.

Blacklock said: 'Annet!' as a man dying of thirst might have said: 'Water!' He had his arms locked round her, the gun, still in his hand, pressed against her back. And then there was a silence that tore at Tom's senses, while they kissed and he burned.

'I thought you weren't coming. I was afraid!'

'I came as soon as I could. You knew I'd come.' And again the silence, aching and hurried and brief. 'Darling! Darling!' Her deep voice throaty and charged with agonising tenderness, the implications in its tones of stroking hands, and the deliberate, assuaging pressure of her body, reassuring, caressing, protecting.

'Yes, I knew! If you could, I knew you'd come. But I was afraid. We've got to hurry,' he said urgently. 'The bike's down below. If we can get an hour's start we can shake them. They won't look for us westwards. And from Ireland—'

He broke off there to take her in more exactly. 'You haven't even got a coat! We must buy you one somewhere tomorrow. You can wear my windjacket for tonight.' He stooped to snatch up the briefcase from the ground, and caught Annet by the wrist. 'Come on, hurry, they'll be after us soon.'

They would go, he would tow her down the hill in his wake and drag her into his crime, she who had done nothing criminal yet. It was more than Tom could bear. She must not do it. She must not make herself an accessory after the fact, an outlaw and a felon, not even for love's sake. To hold her back from that was something worth dying for.

He didn't know what he was going to do until he had done it. Scrambling, shouting, he broke out of the shadow of the rocks and flung himself between them and the edge of the slope.

'Annet, don't! Don't listen to him! Don't go with him! Don't make yourself a murderess! Don't—'

Blacklock uttered a soft, terrified cry of panic and despair, and loosed Annet's arm. Hugging the briefcase to him, he fired blindly at the half-seen figure that distorted the darkness, fired rather at the shouting and the threat than at any corporeal opponent. The impact of the bullet sent Tom staggering backwards, and swung him partially round before he dropped.

He groped along the ground, astonished, lucid and without pain for an instant, dazed by the whirling of stars over him, and the chill and shock of the ground under him. Then the pain came, knifing at his shoulder a full second after the impact, and he cried out in bitter indignation, one brief, angry shout of agony. The earth and the sky stilled, he knew himself lying at Annet's feet, and felt the stillness of horror holding her paralysed over him. Fumbling at his left shoulder, he felt the hot stickiness of blood; and when he tried to lift himself on one elbow, he fell back ignominiously into the grass.

Darkness lurched at him, withdrew, stooped again. He fought it off, straining upwards obstinately towards Annet's unseen face and frozen stillness.

'Don't go! Don't let him make you.' His own voice sounded grotesquely faint and far, and faded like a weak radio signal. He thought he had uttered more words than he heard, and some had been lost, but he went on trying. It was all he could do for her now. 'You didn't kill anyone – you didn't steal— Don't let him make you what he is.'

There was no way to silence him but one. Shaking, sweating and half-blinded, Blacklock passed his forearm across his eyes to clear them, and reached the hand that clutched the briefcase to push Annet out of the way.

'Annet, go on ahead!'

He pointed the gun carefully at the patch of muted darkness heaving on the ground. His finger tightened convulsively on the trigger. The voice *had* to stop. It was like a barrier between them and freedom, there was no escape until it was silenced.

She woke to realisation and awareness, starting out of her daze of horror.

'No, don't!' She flung herself between them with arms spread.

'Annet, please!' He dropped the briefcase then to grasp her by the arm and pluck her out of the way, his voice a wail of despair.

Annet tore herself out of his grip and dropped like a bird, stretching her body upon Tom's on the ground, winding her arms about him fiercely. Her cheek was pressed against his, her hair spread silken and cool over his forehead and eyes. Breast to breast, her chin upon his shoulder, she clung to him tenaciously with all her slight, warm, dear weight, covering him from harm.

'*Annet!*'

'No, you shan't, I won't let you!'

And she felt nothing for him, nothing at all! That was worse than the drain of blood out of his burning shoulder, worse than the terror of death. She felt nothing for him, all her agony and resolution was to save her darling from damning himself beneath a still greater load of guilt, a second and more deliberate murder.

Faint and sick, Tom lay quaking with his new knowledge of her. She had never needed him to show her her duty. He should have known it. She had run up here to her meeting without even a coat, without so much as a handkerchief by way of luggage. *She never meant to go!* It was for something quite different she came. And all he had done, with his interference and his disastrous want of understanding, was at best to subject himself to her humiliating pity, and at worst to destroy himself. Live or die, this was the only way he would ever have her arms round him.

He braced his one good hand feebly against her shoulder and tried to push her away from him, outraged by this admission to her mercy while he was excluded from her heart. Light as she was, she clung and would not be dislodged. He was too weak to lift her weight from him. He could not even break her hold. He felt the tears burst from his closed eyelids and dew her cheek, but she did not seem to be aware of them, and he could not even turn his head aside and spare her his humiliation and distress. There was no help for it; he had to submit, he had to hear them fight out their last conflict over his body.

'Get up, Annet! There's no time—' Blacklock was all but weeping.

'No! You shan't touch him, I won't let you. Not again!'

'Let him live, then, I don't care! Anything, whatever you want, only come, quickly! Get up – I won't hurt him, I won't touch him. Only come on, we've only got a few hours at the most.'

She unwound her arms from Tom very gently and carefully, and rose from the ground. She kept her body between the wounded man and the gun still, her hands spread on the air, ready to turn and cover him again at the first false word or gesture. Slowly she drew herself upright, and faced her lover.

Low and clearly: 'No,' she said, 'I'm not coming.'

He could not believe it. He stared, the gun drooping and trembling in his hand. '*Annet!*'

'Peter, don't go! Come back with me, it's the only way. Come back and face them. Oh, *why* did you? *Why did you?* There wasn't anything I wanted, except you. Surely you knew that? And now there's nothing we can do except go back together. Can't you see that?'

He repeated: '*Annet!*' whimpering, unable to understand but already transfixed with terror.

'I'll stay with you, don't be afraid.' She went towards him, her hands out to touch him, and he gave back before her as though she had been an advancing fire. 'As long as they let me, I'll stay with you. I won't forsake you. Only don't run, and hide, and kill again. You'd have to, once you began running. Stop now! *That poor old man!*' she said, and her voice was a soft, dreadful cry of pain. 'Come back with me and give yourself up. Darling, darling, trust me and come! I can't bear the other way for you, it's too horrible.'

He couldn't believe it. He drew breath, sobbing, fumbling towards her and starting away again. 'You must come! You said you'd come! Oh, God! Oh, God! Annet, you can't abandon me!' No louder than the stirring of the breeze that came so late, his voice wept and raged, and Tom could not stop hearing it.

'I'm not abandoning you, I'm here with you. As long as they let me I shall be with you. Always, everywhere. But I won't go away with you. What we've done we've done, we have to stand to it now. Come back with me!'

Helpless under their feet, the blood draining steadily out of him into the ground, Tom shut eyes and ears and willed his senses to withdraw from them and leave him darkened and out of reach. But there was no escape. He tried to turn on his face, clawing at the ground with his one good hand, struggling to drag himself away by the fistfuls of long grass that brushed cold along his cheek; but he could move only by inches, and there was no place to hide.

Where was his conception of love now, beside this tormented passion? They had forgotten him. For each of them no one existed but the other; he pleading with her to escape with him, refusing to go without her, refusing as desperately to turn and go back with her; she absolute and inflexible to save him from further evil, begging him, willing him to turn and walk of his own volition towards his expiation and salvation.

'You want me taken! You want them to hang me!'

'You know I don't. I want you intact, I want you free. There isn't any virtue unless you choose it freely.'

How could he choose it? He was too feeble and too afraid.

'You don't love me,' he moaned, helpless to go or stay.

'It's *because* I love you!'

'Then you've got to come with me. You *shall* come with me,' he said in a broken howl of despair, 'or I'll kill you. I'd rather that than leave you behind.'

'Yes!' Incredibly she seized on that as the answer to her deepest anxiety. Her voice lifted into joy, her broken movements towards her lover took fire in a sudden blaze of confidence and eagerness. 'Yes, kill me! That would be best. Kill me! I want you to.'

She had taken two soft, rapid paces towards him, she had him by the hand that held the gun, and was raising it softly, softly, towards her breast, with infinite care not to startle or frighten him. Her long fingers gentled his wrist, encircling and caressing him.

'Yes, kill me, Peter. I mean it. Then I'll be there waiting for you, and you won't be alone or afraid. Don't be afraid of anything. I won't forsake you. I love you! Kill me!'

Passionate, persuasive and sincere, the voice insisted. Dominant and assured, the hand lifted and guided his hand. Oh, God, oh, God, she really did mean it! There was nothing she would not do for him, dying was not even the ultimate gift she was offering him, she had the hereafter in the other hand, patient companionship through purgatory, half his guilt on her shoulders, and no deliverance for her until he was delivered.

Tom rolled over on his face, and braced his good arm under him to prise himself up from the ground. He had to get to them, there was nobody else. He shouted, or thought he shouted, but they seemed to hear nothing. Red-hot tongs gripped his left shoulder, and his dangling arm fouled the balance of his body and swung grotesquely in the way of the knee he was laboriously hoisting under him. When he got foot to ground, the ground rolled away and brought him down again on his face, sobbing with pain and desperation; but he touched rock with his outflung hand, and groping his way up it inch by inch, got a firm hold, and dragged himself up again to his knees, to his feet. Swaying, lurching, holding frantically by the rock, he struggled round to face the two who did not even know he was there.

He gripped his bleeding shoulder in his right hand, and thrust himself off from the rocks, blundering towards them in a top-heavy run; and then the crushing darkness swirled round him again in strangling folds and brought him down, and for a moment vision and hearing deserted him, and nothing was left but the agonised sensitivity of his finger-tips, flayed and quivering from the very touch of the withered grass.

So he never saw Annet draw the muzzle of the gun to her breast and settle it, smiling – though the darkness would have hidden the lovely and terrible quality of the smile – against her heart.

* * *

Hearing came back to him with a crash, swollen sounds battering his flinching ears like bomb-bursts. Then as suddenly they dwindled and separated, congealing into recognisable order, though for some seconds they made no sense, because he had no strength to turn his head. He thought there was a voice urging something, and that must have been Annet, and another voice that recoiled and refused, in helpless horror, and yet with so little strength or conviction that it was plain it could not long go on refusing. And then a clipped impact, a sharp, faint cry, and something falling.

Two things falling. One of them flew and rolled, ricocheting from the rocks, and at the end of its course along the grass stung his outstretched hand. He closed his fingers on it, and it was hard and heavy, and fitted snugly into his palm. A flung stone. Not just any stone, he knew it by its weight and texture. One of Jane's specimens of galena. One of the boys must have had it in his pocket. It didn't belong on top here, it came from below, by the old lead workings.

One of the boys! That shook him into full consciousness again, and drove him to his knees, heavy head thrust erect by main force, clouded eyes straining. The mated shadows under the Altar had been torn apart, something small and metallic had whined against stone in falling. The gun, struck clean out of Blacklock's hand, lay three yards away in the grass, a pencil-beam of light from his little torch searched for it frantically and found it. On either side shadows came running, a ring of footsteps circled him like a chain, as he flung himself after the gun and snatched it from the ground.

He was straightening up with it in his hand when another light found him, pinned him, held him transfixed and dazzled. Someone had come scrambling round the slabs of the Altar, running with the rest, and there halted suddenly to launch and steady the beam of a strong torch upon him. For a long moment he crouched blinded in the glare, his head thrown back, his eyes dilated and blank as glass in a contorted face of desperation and anguish, quite motionless.

He could have fired into the light, he could have taken one at least of these encroaching shadows with him out of the world, but he did not. They were all round him, they knew him, there was no escape. He knew it was all over. It stared plain in the tragic mask of his face that he knew, and had accepted his end. He looked full into the light, and suddenly lifted the gun to his own temple and squeezed the trigger.

The shot and Annet's brief, heart-rending shriek of grief and loss exclaimed and recoiled together from rock to rock, eddying away into infinite distance. The beam of light quivered in a shaking hand, and dropped after the collapsing body into the grass.

When George Felse reached the spot half a minute later, with Lockyer hard on his heels, when Jane Darrill came forward on unsteady legs, the torch dangling in her hand and the two boys silent and shaken beside her, Dominic still clutching a fragment of barytes in his hand, Annet was crouched in the trampled grass with her lover's body cradled in her arms, her cheek pressed against his head, the small, powder-rimmed hole in his temple hidden by the fall of her black hair. Body, arms, head, she was folded about him with all her force, as though she would never again unclasp and separate herself from him. She did not move when they came to her, or speak, or show in any way that she was aware of them.

Faintness like a smothering velvet curtain swung between Tom's eyes and the figures that closed in from either side. Snatches of voices reached him. He heard George telling somebody to 'see what you can do for Tom,' and then there were hands carefully taking hold of him, turning him on his back, detaching his rigid fingers from the tuft of long grass by which he had been trying to drag himself along. Someone raised him a little against a knee. Through his own personal darkness he was spasmodically aware of light turned upon him. The hands that were busy at his blood-soaked shoulder were a man's, but the light touch that supported his head was surely a woman's. He opened his eyes and looked up into Jane's face, softly lit from below, drawn, subdued, gaunt-eyed with shock.

The pendulum of consciousness reached its steadiest, and the light its brightest. He lifted his head with an effort, craning round Jane's supporting arm. Someone stood between him and Annet, a young, tall silhouette, frozen still for awe of death.

'Dom, go down and phone from the box,' said George's voice. 'Call the station and tell them it's an ambulance job, urgent. Then call Superintendent Duckett, and tell him what's happened. And then go home. You hear?'

Low-voiced, Dominic said: 'Yes,' and offered no argument. He uncrooked his aching finger from about the piece of barytes he wouldn't, after all, have to throw, and let it fall dully into the ground; then, remembering that Jane had wanted it, groped for it again and returned it to his pocket. He felt beneath the dangling plummet of specimens for coppers, and his hand, numbed from long tension, fumbled clumsily with pennies it could not feel except as coldness. He dragged his gaze from Annet and went as he was bidden, walking to the edge of the westward slope with the abnormal firmness and matter-of-factness of one still in shock; but once over the edge he came to himself, and set off running and leaping down the traverse of grass like a hare.

His going uncovered the two fingers clasped insissolubly together in the grass. Annet had not moved. Withdrawn into herself in the sealed silence of bereavement, she crouched in the classic shape of mourning. Tom strained to kep his eyes upon her, and his own pain was only an irritation that fretted at his bitter concentration without bringing him ease, a threat that filmed his vision over with faintness when most he desired to continue seeing. He moaned when they eased the coat away from his wound, but he shook the encroaching dark from him, and fastened on Annet still like a famishing man.

George had dropped to his knees beside those motionless, fused lovers, and was putting back gently the curtain of black hair that shrouded their faces, to look closely at the wound that had brought them down together. But even when he had satisfied himself, what was there he could have to say to Annet? She knew Peter Blacklock was dead; there was no need for anyone to break that news to her. There was no need for words at all; there was no aspect of this death and the survival she had not already understood. And George had nothing to say. But without fuss, as one doing what was there to be done, he took her chin in his hand and lifted her head erect, gently loosened her fingers from their rigid clasp, and unwound her arms from about her head. He lifted the limp body out of her embrace and laid it down in the grass, and taking Annet by the hands, drew her to her feet.

And she turned to him, not away from him! She turned to him voluntarily, leaning forward into his shoulder with a broken sigh. He held her for a while, gently and impersonally; and when she raised her head and stood back from him he took away his arms gently and gradually and let her stand alone.

'Miles!'

He had not said one word or made one movement until then, only stood motionless and apart in the darkness by the rocks, biding his time. Tom had forgotten him until he heard the measured and muted voice say: 'I'm here.'

'Take Annet down to my car, and drive her home. She'll go with you now.'

Chapter Eleven

He came up out of a well-shaft of weakness and slight fever, tossed into half-consciousness, aware of faces bending over him, and of a bright, bare whiteness which was a small room at the Cottage Hospital, though he did not know that until later. He said aloud the most urgent thing he had drawn up with him out of his uneasy dreams, not realising how often he had said it before.

'Annet didn't know. She had no part in it. She knew nothing about murder – or robbery.'

The faces showed no surprise. They soothed him quickly: 'It's all right. We know. Nobody blames Annet.'

'She only wanted to go to him to persuade him to come back with her and give himself up.'

'Yes, don't worry. Don't worry about anything. We know.'

'She said – it had no virtue unless he chose it himself. She refused to go away with him. She wanted—'

'Yes, you told us. It's all right, we know everything.'

She wanted him to kill her, he had tried to say, but it stuck in his throat and filled him with such a leaden burden of pain that he sank again into the drowning depths of his isolation. None of them had heard what he had heard, or suffered what he had suffered. They could look her in the face again, live within touch and sound and sight of her and find it bearable. But he never could. He didn't even ask after her. It was no use, there was nothing there for him. His only right in her was to proclaim her immaculate; and that he did as often as he drifted back into consciousness, purging his over-burdened soul and bleeding his frustrated love out of him in anxious witness to her innocence.

'Don't let them blame Annet. She didn't do anything—'

'No, no, don't worry. Annet will be all right.'

Later, when he was convalescent, propped up in pillows with his shoulder swathed, they all came to see him, bringing with them

338

fragments which were not now so much pieces of a puzzle as handfuls of stones to pile on a cairn, marking the place memorable for a disaster or a death. Or maybe an achievement. Or a discovery. Such as his own limitations, or the child's discovery, uncomfortable but salutary, that fire burns, or if you get out of your depth you may drown.

It was George Felse who brought him the few pieces that actually were gaps in the puzzle: the inquisitive small boy who had reported the motor-cycle in Mrs Brooke's backyard, the message the vicar had brought, and the precise reason behind Annet's flight from Fairford.

'The bike seemed to point to Stockwood, who had the loan of one of the estate BSAs for the week-end. He couldn't have been the first fellow, six months ago, but that didn't let him out altogether, there was no certainty they were the same. And he'd let himself in for suspicion, anyhow, first by lying about his whereabouts, and then by saying he'd spent the time with a woman, but refusing to name the woman.'

He said nothing about his own barely tenable theory that the woman might, just might, have been Regina Blacklock; a theory they'd never had to investigate, after all, thank God!

'Moreover, he had a prison record. He did a year for his part in a hold-up job, through getting mixed up with some girl, and his wife got a decree nisi against him into the bargain. He was an obvious possibility. But when Mrs Brookes came up with the item of evidence about Annet's *father*, that let Stockwood out. He wasn't old enough by years. When I spoke to you on the phone I had a kind of idea that *you* knew something you weren't exactly rushing to tell, something that seemed to fit.'

'I did,' said Tom, remembering that, too, as something infinitely distant and unreal. 'I thought I did. But it doesn't matter now. It was wrong, anyhow. So you didn't have to find out who Stockwood's woman was.'

'No, we didn't have to, but as it turned out, we did. The Superintendent let his name drift into the hand-out to the evening paper on Saturday, and she came forward in a hurry, all flags flying, to say he'd been with her. She was his wife, you see. She *is* his wife,' he corrected himself with a broad smile. 'Talk about good out of evil, the Bloome Street case put paid to that divorce, once and for all. I doubt if he could lose her again even if he tried.'

Side-tracked out of the too-deeply-worn cutting of his own

obsessive grief, Tom followed this strange by-product of murder with awakening wonder. 'But if it was his wife, why wouldn't he say so?'

'Because it had taken him months to get her even to talk to him again, and he wanted her back, and had just brought her to the point of surrender. It was a triumph that she'd let him work his way in and stay those few days. But he knew he was still on probation, and he was terrified that if he gave it away that he'd lived with her again she'd think he was trying to fix her, force her hand by preventing the divorce from going through. He knew her well enough to know she has a temper, and she was badly hurt the first time. She might very well have turned on him and told him to go to hell if she'd thought he was framing her. But when she heard the police were interested in his movements, she came like a fury to protect him. That's one happy ending, at least, even if we only reached it by accident.'

'I'm glad somebody got some good out of it,' said Tom.

'So we were left with a motor-bike that could be one of the three they keep at Cwm, but didn't have to be, and this idea of the man who could pass for Annet's father. When it turned out that the vicar had brought the message that sent Annet out that night, that seemed to make him a possibility, at first sight. But obviously he spent the whole of Sunday at Comerford – he had Communion and two services, and he always puts in an appearance at Sunday School, too – and in any case there were immediately other inferences to be drawn. The message he brought was from the choir, so he said, but in practice that meant from the choir-master. Peter Blacklock – well, who had such privileged access to Annet as he did? He could and did ride one of the estate three-fifties up and down to the plantations when it suited him – nobody in his senses would use an E-type Jag for a job like that, where he wanted to be inconspicuous – and he could very well pass for Annet's father. And it was only a startling thought at first sight,' said George, looking back at it sombrely from the light of knowledge, 'and then not for long.'

'But he was at church, too. And at choir practice on the Friday night. He rang up afterwards and asked why Annet hadn't come – whether she was ill.'

'That was part of the campaign. He had to know whether they'd done anything decisive, like going to the police. Annet was sure they wouldn't, but he wasn't happy, he wanted to know. He divided his time very delicately. On Thursday he took Annet to Birmingham. On Friday at dusk he left her there and came back to choir practice, and went through that little performance of enquiring after Annet, offering to go round and see her if she was fit to have visitors. And then he went back to her, and stayed with her until Sunday morning. What happened on Saturday night you know. It wasn't planned, of that I'm certain. It happened out of desperation and chance opportunity. He never intended murder, but he needed money. He needed it badly, and it was there winking at him, and only this old man in the way. He gave Annet the wedding ring, and neither she nor we will ever know exactly why. It may have been just cover for what he'd done. Or it may be the real reason why he went into the shop, to buy the thing for her, the symbol of the permanence of their love and the secret dream-marriage that was all they would ever have, and the other thing may have happened on a disastrous impulse, because the time and the circumstances offered, and he was fuller of longing for her than he could bear. I don't know. In some ways I underestimated him, maybe I'd better not even try to guess.

'Well, that was Saturday. And on Sunday he came to morning service in Comerford, to be seen, to be fortified by other people's assumption of his normality until he almost believed himself that everything was normal. He didn't know until he went back that the old man was dead. He'd asked his deputy to play on Sunday evening. That happened sometimes, no one thought anything about it. And he didn't come back until he brought Annet home on Tuesday evening, and parted from her behind the Hallowmount.'

'And it was Annet who hid the briefcase?'

'Yes, that was Annet. She hid it in their old place, and walked over the crest and came face to face with you.'

With difficulty, his face turned away, Tom asked: 'She told you about it?'

'She told us. No reason why she shouldn't now.'

'But she didn't know what it was. He can't have told her.'

'All she knew was that it was their savings, the only funds they had, and they wanted it ready to hand, because soon – very soon, they were determined on that now – they were going away together for good.'

Tom turned from that because it cut too near, and he could not bear to look at it yet. 'I should have thought it might have been

341

awkward with the servants. I know there was no reason to go closely into his movements, but if you had, they'd have told you he was absent most of the relevant time.'

'What servants?' said George simply, and smiled. 'The days of resident staffs are over, even in houses like Cwm. Hadn't you realised? Well, why should you, come to think of it, it wouldn't be a revolution that hit you, any more than it did me. Nobody has servants, these days. You have dailies who come in to clean, mornings, and maybe one who cooks if you're lucky, but only during the day, at that, and not week-ends. Week-ends Madam does her own cooking now, and if she's away, her husband eats out. Stockwood had been sent off to his wife, and delighted with the opportunity, Mrs Bell had said she had her daughter and the baby coming over at the week-end, so she couldn't oblige, and Blacklock had said that was all right, he could manage it. Their regular early girl, who came first thing in the morning to clean, had a key, and most often she never saw him, anyhow. No, there was no difficulty there. One appearance at choir practice and one at church, and everyone had a normal picture of his week-end, and was convinced he'd spent it here.'

'I suppose,' said Tom, staring fixedly at the stiff hem of the sheet, 'It must have been going on for some time – between him and Annet?'

'That depends what you mean. I think he must have loved her almost from the moment she began to work for his wife. Certainly very soon afterwards.'

Very soon afterwards! How could he help it, married to that busy public figure whose capacities for private warmth he must have exhausted long ago, and brought into daily contact with that glowing, ardent, conserved potential of beauty and passion, whose very extravagence would be like drink to him in a desert?

'I don't know when he made the fatal mistake of betraying it. Probably not long before they planned that first abortive flight together. I think it must have been a new discovery then. She couldn't, I think, fail to respond as soon as she knew. And once she loved him,' said George, weighing the words and dropping them on to the cairn one by one, 'he was done for. Between the two of them he didn't have much chance.'

'*She* didn't make him a murderer,' said Tom, taking fire. 'I don't see how anyone could blame Annet.'

'*I*'ll go with you on that. So would most people. Everyone

probably,' said George ruefully, 'except Annet. *She* knew. When it was too late, she knew what she'd done. If she'd failed to respond he would have made himself content with what he had, glimpses of her, proximity, company, the pleasure of working together, until time and his glands eased up on him, and turned the whole thing into a nice, gentle, father-and-daughter affection. She made the mistake of taking him at his word. It was only a very little step from that to loving him. And once she began, *she* was the dominant. She'd dragged him unwittingly into a situation that wasn't beyond her scope, but was more than he could bear. To her love was for loving, not a passive thing, and once she'd accepted him he couldn't go on fondly dreaming it, he was forced to turn it into action. The first try was a failure, but the second – more cautious this time, just a rehearsal – came off. When they wandered past Worrall's shop that Saturday evening they'd had just two nights together, and the world was on fire. Once he'd tasted that, how could he let it go? They had to get away together, for good this time. Nothing else would do. But for that he had to have money, a fair sum of money, not the twenty pounds or so for petrol and day-to-day spending he kept in his pockets by Regina's grace, but enough to break free and start again somewhere else. And money in that quantity was what he hadn't got – almost the only thing he hadn't got.'

'I know,' said Tom, low-voiced. 'It takes a bit of realising. The cars, and the clothes – and everything.'

'He was a pretty good solicitor once in his own right, but when he married her the administration of her estates took up all his time. It never occurred to her that she ought to pay him for it, everything she had was his. He only had to admire something, only to like it, much less want and ask for it, and she'd buy it and give it to him. There wasn't anything she wouldn't give him – except the solid salary his work was worth to her. She wasn't possessive about her money, she just didn't think about it, and it never occurred to her that he could feel cramped and humiliated by having to ask her for what she never grudged. Maybe he didn't miss it himself until he wanted something he couldn't ask her to buy for him. So like any adolescent kid pushed to desperation, he took the twentieth-century short cut – a quick attack and a clean sweep of the most expensive-looking cases in the shop. But like any adolescent kid frightened out of his wits by his own first act of violence, he hit too hard, and there was more than a headache and the insurance money to pay for it. No, between those two he didn't have much chance. But Annet had the honesty and the courage to look squarely at her own part in it, and take rather more than her share of blame on her shoulders. She was quite prepared to give her own life away to save him from making bad worse, to try to make some sort of restitution to him and to the world. Regina is and will always be injured and blameless.'

'And yet she thought the world of him,' said Tom, honestly baffled. 'And she *is* a good woman.'

'A good woman, but not a good wife. She was kind but not considerate,' said George reflectively, 'lavish but not generous, intelligent but without imagination.'

Chilled by the rounded knell of the falling phrases, Tom said: 'It sounds like an epitaph.'

'It turned out to be an epitaph,' said George, 'only not hers.'

Miles and Dominic came, brought him fruit and cigarettes and dutiful greetings from their parents, and sat by his bed making somewhat constrained conversation for half an hour. They told him the ordinary things, scraps of news from school and the harmless social calendar of the village. They were punctilious in addressing him as 'sir,' and retaining, with an effort they hid, on the whole, very well, traces of the schoolboy in their own phraseology. He understood, as once he would not have understood, that this was a delicate device on their part to restore the distance between them that would make life easier for him.

And he played their services back to them neatly, and was grateful, as once he would not have been grateful.

The Becks came, side by side in tacit truce, united by the catastrophe that had overtaken them. Whether Mrs Beck had lied or told the truth, for all practical purposes Annet belonged to both of them, and for her sake they were compelled to draw together. They explained to him that they planned to give her and themselves a fresh start by moving south to a new home. They had found a small house in a village near Cambridge, which was Mrs Beck's native district. There'd be a job for Annet there, within easy reach, and new friends, new scenes, a new life would soon set her up again. But of course he must come back to them when he came out of hospital, next week; they would still be at Fairford for several weeks yet, and he would need time to look round and find fresh lodgings.

He breathed the more easily for knowing that they were leaving. But for that he would have had to hand in his resignation and get away to fresh fields himself. It would be impossible to live in daily contact with her now, having witnessed what he had witnessed. There are things that should not be seen.

He asked after her; it was like devouring his own heart. He didn't, after all, need their answers, he could see her plainly enough moving through her sunless days, the shell of Annet, silent, secluded, drained deep in unhappiness, surviving her loss because she must. Life can't just stop. Their version softened the picture, made it more encouraging. They offered him a sad little greeting from her; he did not believe in it, but he could not imagine why they should make it up.

Only after they had left did it occur to him that they regarded him as blessedly safe, as one who would be good for her, as the means of turning their perilous liability into a tamed, respected, domesticated schoolmaster's wife. They wanted him to take her off their hands, and provide her with the halo of a real wedding ring.

Oh, no, he thought, not me. I've drawn back into my depth. I've given up. I know when I'm licked. On Annet's plane of love there are precious few of us can operate with dignity, and, God help me, I'm not one.

And Jane came. Jane came oftenest. She was as off-hand as ever, didn't make any great fuss of him, didn't try to tell him he'd done anything heroic when he knew he'd done something stupid and short-sighted, of which he was ashamed. She told him that Regina, shocked beyond words in her respectability, but surely in her heart, too – for there was a heart somewhere under all the crust of offices – had taken up her roots for a while and gone abroad.

'And the Becks have got a cottage somewhere down south – Cambridgeshire, I think. They hope to be in before Christmas.'

'I know,' he said, 'they told me. It's the best thing they could do, for Annet and themselves.' He hesitated over what he wanted most to ask, but it came out of itself before he was aware: 'Have you seen Annet?'

'Yes,' said Jane, giving him one of those slightly disconcerting looks that had once made him speculate on whether she had designs on him, but now only warned him that she was probably making allowances for him.

'She'll live,' she said shortly, before he could feel himself forced to ask. And as quickly she looked up again, herself startled by the brusque sound of it. 'Not being flippant about it,' she said crossly. 'I meant it literally. She *will* live – a hundred per cent, some day. Well, ninety, say. Which is more than most people manage. She's far too positive and alive ever to have wanted to die, no matter what debts she conceived she owed and was willing to honour. If you think the stuff she has in her can be battered out of shape by this or any other experience, my boy, you can think again. Don't worry about Annet. And don't feel sorry for her. But don't kid yourself, either,' she added honestly, 'that you'll ever get her, because I don't think you will. Sorry, but there it is.'

He didn't say that he agreed with her, or that he had already withdrawn from the field and acknowledged defeat. He didn't say that he was just becoming reconciled to the idea of setting his sights, some day, on a less impossible target. There was only one Annet, now and forever out of reach; but in his new humility he was prepared to listen respectfully to the small, dry voice deep within him, assuring him that he could think himself damned lucky if some day he was able to settle for someone like Jane.

When he came out of hospital and returned to Fairford it was already November. The Hallowmount withdrew itself at morning and evening into mist, shrouding the Altar and its ring of decrepit trees. He wondered if the small, unaccountable ground-wind had abandoned, until next spring, its nightly ascent by the old paths to the old places where Annet had vanished for a while into her secret world, and whether the reverberations of her tragedy had already seeped away like spilt blood into that already saturated soil.

He had found new lodgings in Comerford, and he began to assemble his belongings in preparation for the move. He was in the hall one evening, digging out his windjacket and climbing boots from the cupboard, when the knocker rapped gently to announce a visitor.

Tom dropped his boots and went to open the door. Miles Mallindine looked at him across the threshold, composed, dogged, dignified, with a handful of late roses. In the sheltered garden close to the river they bloomed until Christmas unless discouraged.

Not everyone knows when he's beaten. Not everyone can recognise when he's out of his class. There was – wasn't there? – an obligation. In pure kindness someone ought to warn him.

'May I come in? Mrs Beck said I could drop round tonight.'

He was in already. He had a very unobtrusive way of moving, that took him where he wanted to go, even against opposition, without actually looking aggressive or even noticeably determined. And he held the roses as one neither embarrassed nor ashamed at displaying his intentions. He wasn't smiling; sieges like the one he was contemplating are no joke.

'Oh, of course! Annet's in the study, doing some typing for her father, I think.' Never had she been so gentle with his pretensions, or so willingly segregated herself behind the clacking of the keys, over his interminable notes.

He let Miles go halfway across the hall, and then he couldn't let him go the rest; not without a word of caution, at least, because he was heading gallantly in full armour for a sickening fall.

'Miles—'

Miles halted and turned, surprised and wary, brown eyes wide. The curled lashes arched towards his brows. Faint colour came and went in his thin, shapely cheeks. He looked like his mother; Eve disarmingly young and apparently vulnerable, but already, beyond mistake, a dangerous person.

'Miles, I shouldn't. There's nothing there now for you. The best's gone.'

'I know,' said Miles, not retreating a step.

He was doing this badly, but he couldn't stop now. The detachment they had so considerately restored to him he was endangering again, but at least this was between himself and Miles, man to man again with no witnesses.

'She won't want to look at any man, not for a long time yet. And even if she ever does, what she's got left to give—'

'I know,' said Miles, honestly, ruefully, even gratefully, but without the slightest intimation that it made any difference.

It was something in the voice that made Tom pause. He caught the maturing intonations of patience and forbearance, and turned with the sudden shock of recognition to confront himself. Here we go again, he thought. You were going to save Annet, weren't you? You, without a clue to what went on inside her, or what she was capable of! Now you're setting out to save Miles, and just about as likely to find him in need of it, and just about as well-equipped to make a hash of it. How do you know what he has it in him to do? Just because you've bitten off more than you can chew, and been forced to own it, does *he* have to give up, too? Wake up and stand by for a shock: you *can* be outdone!

He drew back into silence, carefully, respectfully, and looked at the whole set-up again. But what future was there in it? Next week Annet was going with her parents to Cambridgeshire, and if there was one thing certain it was that they'd never come back to Comerford.

Well, next year Miles was going to Queens', wasn't he? Not that the issue depended on such small, convenient accidents as that, he thought, studying the boy's courteous, wary company-face. There was nothing here now for Tom Kenyon, no. But might there not be something for Miles Mallindine? Some day, if his patience held out?

For Miles there'd have to be. Because he had no intention of ever giving up. He knew what he wanted, he meant to have it. The whole, or half, or whatever there was to be won at last. He was never going to settle for any substitute.

And Annet, whole or broken, sick or convalescent, had her values right. Sooner or later she'd recognise what it was she was being offered.

'All right, forget it,' said Tom. 'You go ahead your own way. And good luck!'

Miles said: 'Thank you!' and for a moment it was touch-and-go whether he would add: '—*sir!*' It was on the tip of his tongue, but he snatched it back generously, flashing for one brief instant the engaging and impudent smile he had inherited from Eve. Then he turned, patient, stubborn and profoundly sure of himself, and went in to Annet with his roses.

THE END

Funeral of Figaro

Chapter One

It was curiously appropriate that he should arrive just in the middle of '*Deh vieni non tardar*,' at the precise spot in the fourth act when he was later to make his exit. The purposeful chaos of a piano rehearsal disguised the significance of the moment, and dulled the impact of his coming into a mere natural quiver of interest and awareness; but afterwards they remembered it as if with a quickened vision, and even believed they had had premonitions of disaster.

Slumped on his back in the front row of the stalls, with his crossed feet on the balustrade of the orchestra pit, Johnny listened with delight to Tonda, and kept his eyes closed to avoid seeing her. It wasn't that she was ugly; far from it, she was thought by some sound critics to be rather like her celebrated countrywoman Gina Lollobrigida. In Susanna's bell skirts and tightly-laced bodices she looked enchanting, but she was rising forty, and she really ought not to come to rehearsals in black ballet tights and thick mohair sweaters. She hadn't acquired the nickname of Tonda for nothing, and the impression of a ball of angora knitting wool transfixed by black plastic needles was overwhelming. But she sounded wonderful, worth every lavish pound he was paying for her three roles in the season's repertoire.

Some Susannas made '*Deh vieni*' too arch, some too ethereal, the utterance of a disembodied spirit. Tonda knew better. Her Susanna was a flesh and blood woman and her voice took up the deliberate, maliciously seductive invitation to love with all the vengeful subtlety of which the female is capable, tormenting her listening lover with the certainty that she was not addressing him, and then gradually in the middle of her teasing she forgot her grudge, forgot the very face of the Count, and was indeed singing to Figaro, pouring out to him all the rapture and excitement of her wedding night in soft, thrilling, aching cries of passion. And still the fool didn't realise!

That was what Tonda could do with her voice, make you believe in the profundities of human love even at rehearsal, and turn back the convoluted leaves of comedy one by one to delve into the deepest places of the heart after Mozart. Provided you didn't look at her there was no limit to the marvellous potentialities she could suggest. Johnny kept his eyes closed, even when by the faint stirring of the air and the fragrance of *muguet* he knew that Gisela had slipped round to take the seat beside him. He turned his face towards her and smiled blindly, and she touched his hand with ome finger, and they listened together.

Count Almaviva, in grey slacks and a sports shirt, stood with folded arms in the wings, listening attentively. Cherubino, in toreador pants and one of Johnny's old sweaters – seemingly sweaters were just the right size these days if you could get into 'em twice over – copied his attitude and his gravity, her fair head tilted, her grey eyes fixed respectfully upon the singer.

Across the stage from them the Countess, tall and stately and immaculate in a closely-tailored suit that made her Scandinavian legs look even longer and more delectable than usual, divided her critical attention between Tonda and the Count.

He was young for the rôle, a rising star out of Austria, not yet used to being famous. What he had in voice and natural ability he still lacked in experience, and it was no small honour for him to be asked to sing so important a rôle opposite Inga Iversen. She had been at pains to be gracious to him. It was necessary that someone should take him in hand, or the predatory Italian woman would ruin him. And that would be a pity, for he had a fine voice and some acting ability. And such eyes! Blue as gentians, and of a heart-rending innocence. Also he was that marvel, a partner tall enough for her. Inga had suffered untold embarrassments at the hands of short, tubby Counts.

In the most remote corner of the orchestra pit Doctor Bartolo and Don Basilio sat cheek by jowl, shirt-sleeved and comfortable, their backs propped solidly against the wooden barrier, their cynical elderly eyes swivelling knowingly from Tonda's rapt face and heaving bosom to Inga's aristocratic calm, behind which the feline claws flexed themselves thoughtfully in secret.

Doctor Bartolo was lean and cadaverous and dignified, and as English as a wet summer, and his name was Max Forrester. Don Basilio was short and rosy, pepper-and-salt haired, and with the Welshman's bold, strongly-marked bones and tough, weathered flesh. He had sung Don Basilio so often in his thirty years on the stage that he sometimes had difficulty in remembering that his name was Ralph Howell. Tenor character parts of any quality are comparatively few and far between, he had taken some pains to corner the best of them as soon as he became resigned to being forty years old. They were conducting a laconic conversation in an almost soundless, almost motionless style that would have done credit to two old lags under the warder's eye.

'What did I tell you?' said Don Basilio, digging an elbow into his friend's lean ribs. 'You're on a loser, boy. Tonda's got him dazzled.'

'They're only warming up yet,' returned Doctor Bartolo confidently. 'Wait until Inga gets to him with the great forgiveness phrase at the end.'

'Ah, a couple of bars, man, what's that after a brainwashing like this? Look at him! Ravished to the soul, poor lad! You might as well pay up now, you've said good-bye to that fiver.'

'I'll still put my shirt on Inga. Want to raise the stake?'

'Double it,' offered Don Basilio promptly, surveying the ample charms of the lady who carried his money, and dwelling with professional pleasure on the melting ease with which she turned the lovely high phrase and sank in a series of soft falls, like a dove descending. Backstage half a dozen of Johnny's ship's company were listening to it no less appreciatively, straightening and stilling among the surrealist detail of their half-assembled sets. Perhaps the greatest love song ever written for a woman sank to its close in triumphant stillness, like a folding of wings.

'Mate,' said Stoker Bates, scratching thoughtfully at the back of his grizzled neck, 'that's a bit of all right, that is. You can have all your *Traviatas* and your "Oh, my beloved daddies" for one drop o' Mozart.'

The dove settled and nestled, soft as down.

'*"Ti vo la fronte incoronar – incoronar di rose."*'

Old Franz Hassilt at the piano echoed the rounded cadence and drew breath to croak the indignant comment of the missing Figaro, for whom he delighted to do duty; but the interjection was taken clean from his lips by a great voice that spat the '*Perfiaa!*' over their startled heads from the doorway on the right of the stalls.

'"Traitress! So all the time she meant to betray me!"'

Cherubino flashed round open-mouthed, forgetting the trill she had been about to launch after Figaro's line. Johnny opened his eyes abruptly and came leaping to his feet, Franz whirled on the piano stool, and every head turned expectantly to examine the Leander Theatre's new bass-baritone.

His fame had come before him, and they were curious and wary, for they had to measure their powers side by side with his from now on. It was only by luck Johnny's agent had been able to sign him up at all; after the loss of Raimondo Gatti in the plane crash at Vienna they might well have had to make do with a minor artist and be thankful, but fate in the shape of an army cabal in Latin America had effectively cancelled a prior engagement, and presented them with the chance of a lifetime to get Marc Chatrier, and Jimmy Clash had jumped at it. Johnny could stand the racket; grand opera was the one undertaking on which Johnny had ever managed to lose money, and he needed it to ease his tax position, so he said. One of the biggest sums even he had ever paid out was very well spent on the greatest living Figaro.

And there he was, just within the doorway, looking them over with calm, quizzical eyes and visibly selecting Johnny from among them as the man to be reckoned with. Johnny came bounding like a Saint Bernard dog, shoving out a brown fist and beaming.

'Mr Chatrier, this is wonderful! We didn't expect you to show up this morning, after your journey. I'm sorry I couldn't meet you myself at the airport last night, but I hope Mr Clash looked after you properly.'

Jimmy always looked faintly bewildered when he was referred to as Mr Clash. He was so used to being Number One or Jimmy the One that the rare occasions when he got his proper name, for the benefit of newcomers who couldn't yet be expected to understand the peculiarities of the Leander Theatre, jolted him like being suddenly confronted with a distorting mirror. He beamed back happily at his employer and friend, proud of his errand and of the acquisition he had brought them.

'Are you comfortable at the Grand Eden? It's a longish drive out here, but there'll be a car at your disposal for the season.'

'All your arrangements worked admirably,' said Marc Chatrier in his black velvet voice, 'and the hotel seems excellent.'

They were much of an age, and matched each other in vigour and glow so evenly that the meeting of their hands should have started a flurry of sparks. Johnny was brown and bright, with thick russet hair greying at the temples, and an uneven, mobile, responsive face.

Chatrier was black-haired and black-eyed and self-contained, with the quirk of a slightly quizzical smile never far from his lip. The experienced face was a little lined, the dark eyes a little world-weary, but he knew how to wear even these ominous signs as added graces.

'What's the betting,' murmured Ralph Howell, eyeing this formidable new competition, 'the girls don't switch their attentions?'

Doctor Bartolo considered the possibility thoughtfully for a moment, and shook his head resolutely. 'No. Youth has it. They'll stick to the coming lad. This one's been. He's on his way back.'

'Come and meet everyone.' Johnny had an arm lightly about his new Figaro's shoulders, and a hand outstretched for Franz Hassilt. 'You must know our musical director – everyone knows Franz. Without him we could never have made our reputation in such a short time. Without me, of course, he'd have managed it in half the time. We fight a lot, but he always wins.'

The old man, wonderful hair erected like a blazing silver aureole, gaudy shirt a dazzle of greens and reds, peered narrowly from the intelligent eyes that could be so gentle and so fierce, and said sharply: 'Johnny is a humbug. He treats opera like a toy, but Johnny loves his toys. Nobody crosses Johnny in his play.' He blinked up at the tall man whose hand he held, and said with satisfaction: 'Mr Chatrier, at last I get a Figaro who menaces instead of blustering. Now we show them a production as it should be.'

'We can at least try,' agreed Marc Chatrier gravely.

'And here's our Countess, Miss Iversen. Miss Gennoni, your Susanna. And Cherubino – my daughter Hero.'

'Enchanted!' said Marc Chatrier, dividing the small gallantries of glance and smile and caressing voice between the three of them. Not quite evenly.

A brittle Norwegian icicle whom he already knew, a plump Italian kitten, and a boy-girl in trousers and sweater. Honey-fair, grey-eyed. The girl held his eyes longest. So millionaire Johnny Truscott had a daughter, had he? Could she really sing, or was the impresario only a fond and foolish father who thought she could? Well, he could afford to pay for both their fancies.

Hero said: 'Hallo!' airily, like a blunt but assured boy, the approximate blend of gaucherie and self-confidence turned out by the English public school.

'You can see she's well into the skin of the part,' said Johnny, grinning. 'Dress her up in a party frock now and take her out, and you're liable to get run in. She swaggers about as if she had riding-boots on under her skirt – like Octavian in the third act of *Rosenkavalier*.'

'It's your own fault,' said Hero, grinning back. 'You shouldn't have given me such a silly name if you didn't want me to get complexes. I'm going to sing all the transvestist parts, Mr Chatrier. Ending up with Octavian.'

'I imagine the process will take a few years,' he said, and smiled fully for the first time.

'I imagine it will. But Cherubino's a good beginning.'

'And here's Max Forrester,' said Johnny, 'our Bartolo. And Ralph Howell, who sings Basilio.'

The alert black eyes assessed, pondered, discarded. Forrester was a good second-rate artist of the kind England bred in considerable numbers, Howell one of the perennial Welsh tenors who end up entertaining at smoking concerts.

'And the Count – you haven't met Hans Selverer?' Johnny was proud of him. 'Believe me, he's going to make the critics sit up when we open with this production.'

The young man wasn't yet used to being famous, he blushed when he was praised. At first glance a big, good-looking simpleton; at second glance a stubborn, detached intelligence standing off the newcomer and measuring him as exactly as he was himself being measured.

'Selverer!' Chatrier was smiling; the quality of the smile was still ambivalent, perhaps it always would be. 'I recall that name.' Several eyebrows rose at that; the past year had seen a great deal of newsprint lavished on the boy's achievements. 'No, no,' said Chatrier easily, 'I mean from some years ago, when you can have been no more than a child. Was your father also a musician?'

'A conductor,' said Hans, a little grave and constrained as always when too much attention began to concentrate at close quarters on his person or his affairs.

'Yes – that's it! I believe I met him once in Vienna, just before the war.'

'It could be so,' said the young man, but without volunteering more.

'I lost sight of him after that. Is he still conducting?'

'He is dead. He died during the war.'

'Ah, I'm sorry! A great pity!'

'And Marcellina – you must meet our Marcellina,' said Johnny, delicately snapping off this tightening thread of conversation before it could stretch too cruelly thin. 'Where *is* Gisela? She was with me only a few minutes ago.'

'I'm here,' said Gisela's serene voice, and she came out of the shadows under the circle stalls. So that was what she'd been up to, restoring her make-up for the occasion. A new, firm bow to her mouth, and every hair in place. A faint, astonished sting of jealousy pricked Johnny's heart. Since when had she gone to the trouble to put on a new face for any man? She never bothered for him.

'Marc Chatrier – Gisela Salberg. Gisela is our Marcellina, and much more than that. I don't know what we should do without her.'

She stepped into the light, and he saw her fully. A slender woman of middle height, with a great sheaf of black hair coiled on her neck, and the pale oval face that went with such hair, magnolia-skinned and still, only the large dark eyes and the mobile lips quick with suggestions of humour and feeling. Forty-five, perhaps. Very elegant. She looked up at him steadily, the social smile just curving her lips. A nerve quivered in her cheek. Marc Chatrier smiled at her from under half-lowered lids, hooding the smile from the light and the onlookers, but not from her.

'We're very fortunate to have so notable a Figaro,' said Gisela in her dear, cool voice. 'I hope we shall be able to work well together, Mr Chatrier.'

God, thought Johnny, he must have made an impression. When did she ever go so far upstage for me?

'I'm sure we shall, Miss Salberg, I'm sure we shall. After such a charming welcome,' said Chatrier, smiling at her, his voice heavy and smooth as cream, 'I feel that you and I are old friends already.'

'But the crew don't like him,' said Johnny, raking with worried fingers through his erected hair, and slamming a drawer of his desk shut on the rest of the cares of the day.

'Who says they don't?' objected Gisela mildly from her perch on the end of the desk.

'No one says, they don't have to say. I know that gang too well to need any telling. You'd think they had an instinct about him. And yet he took them in his stride, you saw that, never batted an eyelid. And you must admit they can be disconcerting on first acquaintance. And he's all right at rehearsals, isn't he?' Chatrier had been working with the cast for ten days now, if there was anything to be discovered against him it should have begun to show at the rubbed edges. 'Franz seems to be thoroughly happy about him.'

'With reason. He's a splendid artist. He isn't too easy to work with, perhaps, but it's because he's a perfectionist. I know he's lavish with advice and suggestions, I know he can be exacting. But he's nearly always right. He wouldn't have Franz's goodwill if he wasn't. What are you worrying about? Rehearsals have gone well, and you're going to have a very fine production.'

'Yes,' he admitted more cheerfully, 'yes, I think so. But I wish he wouldn't treat young Hans as a raw recruit – and slow on the uptake at that! The boy's as fine in his way as Chatrier—'

'That could be the trouble,' said Gisela, with a wry smile.

'Yes, I suppose it could.' He brightened; jealousy was a very human reaction from a man at the peak of his career towards a youngster who had soared to the front rank in no more than three seasons, and had at least twenty-five years of fame before him with any luck. 'And I hand it to the kid, he's as obstinately good-tempered as a saint. And yet there's this odd way the boys draw in their horns whenever Chatrier comes by. They've been with me a long time, they've developed a kind of feeling for when things are going right and when they're off the rails. And they don't like him. Sam used to smell bad weather before it came, and now I see him sniffing the air just the same way. They go about quietly, not saying anything, just watching. Damn it, sometimes I think they're uncanny myself.'

He didn't mean it, he was only being faintly peevish after a long, tiring day. To him there was nothing at all to set his ship's company apart from ordinary people, except the mutilations and disabilities they had suffered under his leadership during the war, and by those he was bound to every one of them for life. The theatre was full of his staunch pensioners, though he would have objected strongly to that word. He paid them a good wage, and they did what they could in return for it, and sometimes Johnny was afraid that left him a long way in their debt.

It was because of them rather than as an expression of his own nostalgia that he had given his theatre its name; so many of the survivors of *Hellespont*'s crew shifted its scenery and minded its stagedoor and stoked its furnaces that it could have no other name but one closely recalling their old ship. And they had adopted it with all the enthusiasm they had given to the ship, and ran it like one of their old secretive, ramshackle, effective naval operations.

Probably no one now even remembered what discerning genius at Admiralty had recognised in Johnny Truscott, aged twenty-three and in his first command, a born buccaneer, and seconded him and his cockleshell to secret duties; but whoever he was, he had done well by England and by countless refugees and prisoners of war in Europe, and very well, in the long run, by Johnny himself. They'd taught him how to smuggle, how to infiltrate through even the strict and wary controls of wartime, how to ferry saboteurs and information into occupied territory, and wanted persons and more information out again; and Johnny had found his métier and bettered the instruction, until not even his instructors knew the half of what he was up to.

If his raids were also highly profitable to himself, at least England had no cause to complain of any losses on him. And was it his fault if he couldn't settle down to a quiet, law-abiding life after the war, and went on with his old business? Not always to England's satisfaction then, it must be admitted; as, for instance, the Israel period. By then he'd had three ships, all busy running illegal immigrants. Now he had ten, and they seldom smuggled anything more reprehensible than wine and brandy.

The spice had departed to some extent with the need; he was so rich that there was no point in exerting himself to grow even richer. Johnny himself fondly imagined that he was settling down and becoming middle-aged and respectable, whereas the truth was that he was as restless and venturesome at forty-five as he'd been at twenty-five. And as attractive, thought Gisela, looking down at the tangled brown shock-head he nursed in his hands, and the blunt, bold, sunburned face of an experienced and formidable but still ardent boy. Hopeful of all things, curious about all things. All he'd done was to pour his surplus energy into a new channel. He had approached grand opera dubiously, for Hero's sake, but he had fallen for it with one of the biggest bangs in history, and no one had been more surprised than he.

'And you're unsettled, too,' said Johnny unexpectedly, turning his head abruptly and catching her eyes thus brooding upon him. 'I can feel it. It's all since he came.'

'No,' she denied half-heartedly.

'Yes, I always know by the look on your face when you start looking back and remembering.'

'Don't be silly, what earthly difference could he make to me? I do look back sometimes, but haven't I good reason?'

'Not any more. You should have forgotten all that by now.' Johnny rose and stretched himself. 'Come on, I must drive you home.'

She had a service flat in a new block no great distance from his house at Richmond, and they made their journeys to and from the theatre companionably together.

'*Cosi* went well to-night,' said Johnny, reaching his hat down from the peg behind the door; and the warmth of delight came back lightly into his voice as he returned to his passion.

'Yes, very well.'

'Franz is at the top of his powers. Seventy-five years young.' He took her arm, hugging it to his side in a convulsion of pleasure at the perfection of his toy, and her shared delight in it. 'Three days to the première of *Figaro*. It is going to be good, isn't it?'

'Of course, you know it is.'

He didn't really need her reassurance, he was only exulting and inviting her to exult with him. As she'd been doing now for twenty years, ever since he'd dropped a tree across the road, and snatched her out of the car that was taking her to the clearance camp for Jewish women, en route for Ravensbruck. She had been one of very many who owed their lives and liberty to Johnny and his contacts, but to her he had come as a restoration of man to grace, a kind of miracle when she had felt herself discarded, forsaken and utterly without faith. What use was it for him to tell her she should forget? To forget the betrayal would have been to lose the revelation of faith regained. Gisela preferred to keep both.

Or perhaps it was all so much simpler than that. Perhaps she had merely clung to him ever afterwards for the most female of all reasons, because she loved him. And his wife, and his child, and his shipmates, and all the waifs and strays he accumulated around him, and every little dog that had the sound judgment to stop and speak to him in the street.

She caught one last glimpse of Eileen's photograph in its silver frame on the desk, before Johnny switched off the light and closed the door. Grey-eyed and black-lashed and honey-fair, like her daughter; and fifteen years dead. Poor Johnny! The bad partners never die young.

They went down the carpeted stairs together, Johnny's hand at her elbow. The lavish, rambling spaces of the theatre were growing quiet, the lights going out in the corridors. Glasses clinked softly to a murmur of tired, contented voices in the circle bar, and Dolly Glazier called a good night to them as they passed. Below in the foyer old Sam Priddy rolled across the dim, splendid purple and gold carpeting on his two odd legs, both shortened after the explosion in the engine-room, but shortened unevenly so that he went always with a heavy list to port. He opened the door for them, and roared: 'Hey, Codger!' over his shoulder; and in a moment Codger Bayliss came running eagerly with his knitting rolled up under his arm, the steel needles clacking to his ungainly gallop.

Johnny was never allowed to get into a car without Codger being present to open the door for him and shut it with a conscientious slam. If Johnny ever fell out of a car in motion, it wasn't going to be because Codger hadn't closed the door properly.

'You want to watch out to-night,' said Sam, eyeing with a frown the overcoat he did not consider warm enough for November. 'There's a thin wind come up. Shouldn't wonder it'll drop in the small hours and there'll be frost.'

'I'll be careful, grandma. Went well to-night, Sam. How did you like Inga's Fiordiligi?'

There had been a time when Gisela had wondered if Sam really liked opera, or whether it was only a reflected glow from Johnny's pleasure that made him burn bright when it was mentioned. Now she accepted his passion, and did not question its nature.

'Smashing, skipper!' Sam whistled a line of the lady's melting and agitated self-reproaches; he knew whole operas by heart.

And there was the Bentley, just drawing up smartly at the foot of the steps, the wheel almost invisible within Tom Connard's enormous, gentle hands. Codger reached for the handle of the door and held it open for them.

Since his disaster Codger never aged, never worried; a kind of dim understanding of essential things like daylight and warmth and love moved behind the mute and arrested face, and sometimes there was a faint tremor of wonder and disquiet, as though recollection stirred for a second; but never for longer. The large, calm, chiselled features, lit by those big, devoted eyes, had a beauty he had certainly never possessed while the mind behind them had troubled and racked him.

Johnny smiled at him and twitched at the dangling end of green wool, but only to tease him, not hard enough to drag a stitch from the needle.

'Thanks, Codger! Sorry I kept you waiting. Now you get Dolly to pack up quickly, and I'll send the car back for you.'

Codger lived with Sam, and Dolly had a flat in the same house, and looked after them both. The house belonged to Johnny, and the rent they paid for it was a sop to their independence.

Johnny looked back as they drew away, to see the lighted façade of his darling recede and dwindle until he lost it at the first corner. The Leander Theatre. Fifth winter season. Within easy reach of London by bus or underground. The only enterprise on which Johnny Truscott lost money regularly and heavily. But it was worth ten times his losses to him.

'Just imagine,' said Johnny, sliding down on to the small of his back with a deep sigh of content, 'if there'd been no Mozart! What on earth would it have been like, trying to live without him?'

Franz Hassilt rapped irritably for the tenth time, gathered the phlegmatic attention of his orchestra with snapping fingers, and ordered: 'Gentlemen, gentlemen, once more! We are tired, I know, but once more. From: "*Cognoscite, Signor Figaro, questo foglio . . .*"'

The four people on the stage drew breath wearily, for he had worked them hard. Susanna and the Countess hovered uneasily on either side of the Count, Figaro confronted him assured and smiling. It was the smile, perhaps, that unnerved Hans, and caused him to miss the beat on which he should have made his stern attack, flourishing the letter.

First dress rehearsals always go badly, but that was the worst moment of a bad morning. His mind fell blank and his mouth dry; and smiling, helpful, condescending, Marc Chatrier came in for him, prompting him like a Sunday school teacher rescuing a backward boy who has forgotten his catechism:

'"*Cognoscite . . . Signor . . . Figaro . . .*"'

Syllable clearly intoned after syllable, with meaning nods of encouragement, to complete his humiliation. Killing with kindness. The fiery red surged up out of his lace cravat and dyed him crimson to the roots of his hair, but with healthy rage as much as embarrassment. He refused to pick up the proffered thread, looking over his tormentor's shoulder straight into Franz Hassilt's eloquent eyes.

'I am very sorry, that was my fault. Again, please, be so kind!'

This time his blood was up, and he made a good job of it. No Figaro had ever been bawled out with more authority.

There was no doubt about which side the women were on; they hovered caressingly, complimenting the scowling Count with speaking eyes all the while they were conspiring with his manservant against him. Tonda leaned close to one elbow, Inga hung upon the other arm. And the red in the Count's cheeks did not subside, it merely changed in some subtle way to a milder and more pleasurable shade.

If he only knew, thought Hero critically, hugging her knees in Johnny's stage box, what an ass he looked, shiny with complacency at being courted by two goddesses at once, publicly and blatantly – like a ridiculous latter-day Paris! Uncomfortable he might be, but he couldn't help being flattered even in his discomfort. And she had carefully dissociated herself from the contest, ostentatiously flourished her boyishness under his nose off-stage as well as on, and where had it got her? Had he relaxed with her? He had, and only too thoroughly!

He proceeded to demonstrate it by taking refuge with her in the box as soon as they drew the act to a close and were released for a quarter of an hour's break after their labours. He climbed in to her over the front of the box from the stage, none too deftly because of his elaborate breeches and stiff embroidered coat-skirts. He didn't mind being clumsy in front of her; he would have minded very much if she'd been Tonda or Inga.

He was still flushed, but he'd got over his anger; the twin pussies had purred him into a good humour and an excellent conceit of himself.

'*Himmel!*' he said in a great sigh of relief, and dropped into the seat beside her.

'You made a fine idiot of yourself that time,' said Hero, with the unflattering candour that was expected of her.

'I know it! What will Franz say to me when he gets me alone? But now I am all right. It will not happen again.'

'Well, they certainly did their best to kiss it better,' agreed Hero, straddling the crimson plush rail with the studied maleness she had cultivated for Cherubino's sake until it was almost second nature. 'You know, you'll really have to put 'em out of their agony soon. You can't have both, my boy. Take one and let the other go. This is *Figaro*, not *Seraglio*.'

And he was fool enough to do it, she thought bitterly, if only he could make up his mind which. Luckily he couldn't. And they were both at least twelve years older than he was!

He turned and gave her a speculative look and a tempted grin. 'You want I should drop you overboard, Master Cherubino? With your commission also?'

'You and how many more? 'said Hero derisively.

He could move fast enough when he chose, but she could have ducked and rolled out of reach if she had really wished. He held her between large, well-shaped and very capable hands, dangling her backwards over the rim of the box. Oh, yes, she'd succeeded in putting him at his ease with her, all right! She tried to reach his chest with her small fists, but he had her fast by the upper arms, and all she could reach was the satin of his sleeves.

'Let me up, you big ape! I'm falling!'

'Only as far as I shall let you. You are quite safe. Beg my pardon nicely for being impudent!'

But she didn't; and as soon as she allowed the hint of a whimper to complicate her breathless laughter he hoisted her gently back into the box, shifting one hand to a fistful of her hair. He shook her by it softly, and let it go without so much as noticing that it was a fascinating colour between corn and honey, and very thick and fine. No, she'd miscalculated badly, these tactics were getting her nowhere. He never really saw her at all.

However, she probed forward experimentally to be sure of her ground.

'A good thing for you,' she said, shaking her ruffles back into order, 'that I'm not the predatory type, too.'

'Dear God, yes!' he said, with such heartfelt gratitude that she turned open-mouthed to stare at him, suspicious for a moment of such improbable simplicity; but his face was as open as a sunflower at noon, and fervently friendly.

She could hardly believe it. Could anyone really be as modest as that in his disarming vanity?

'At least you feel safe with me, don't you?' she said with wincing care. The note that should have warned him crept in, all the same, withering the edges of the words like frost browning the rim of a leaf. But he never noticed it.

'But of course!' he said blithely.

So that was that. He meant it; he had no qualms at all.

That was one plan cancelled; and now something drastic would have to be done to shake him out of his complacency and make him take another look at what he was slighting. No use turning feminine now, that would only make her one of three in pursuit of him, and lose her even this maddening intimacy which was all she'd gained. No, let him stay feeling safe until he began to feel himself injured and deprived by his security. She could be as feminine as she pleased with someone else; not exactly under his nose, but somewhere just in the corner of his vision.

She cast one comprehensive glance over the available field, and there was only one man in it at all suitable for her purpose. Her grey eyes lingered speculatively on Marc Chatrier's straight shoulders and long, erect back, so elegantly filling the coat of the Count's gentleman's gentleman. Maybe Hans would wake up if she began to demonstrate that a man with twice his experience found her irresistible.

And she wouldn't even have to make the running. As soon as she turned her serious consideration upon Marc Chatrier she became aware what extremely serious consideration he was devoting to her.

'The poor man's Glyndebourne, Johnny calls it,' said Hero over coffee. 'It was Gisela who started him on opera. She told him I had a good ear and a good voice, and he ought to have me properly taught. And he did, and it turned out opera was what I was best suited for, as well as what I wanted most. So he took up opera and fell wildly in love with it. He built the Leander, and got Franz to take over the musical direction, and we were off. *Hellespont* was the name of his ship, you know, the one he lost the last year of the war. That's why it had to be the Leander Theatre.'

'And that's why you are Hero?'

'Oh, yes, that was inevitable. The *Hellespont* changed Johnny's life, it comes out like a rash all over. She was torpedoed, you know, blown to shreds. They lost half the crew, and a lot of the others were disabled. Well, you've seen them. You must have noticed Sam Priddy, the lame one. Chief deck-hand, so to speak. He was Johnny's bos'n, with him all through the war. They think the world of each other.'

'So that explains your rather startling staff,' said Chatrier, smiling. 'I won't pretend I hadn't wondered.'

'Yes, well . . . We're nice,' said Hero firmly, speaking up loyally for her family, 'but let's face it, we *are* a bit odd. There's Sam, and there's Dolly Glazier – her husband was drowned when the *Hellespont* went down. And there's Stoker Bates, who has only one hand, and Chips, and Mateo. And there's Codger Bayliss, the big one who sits in Sam's box and knits. Codger was torpedoed once before he came to Johnny's crew, and then again with the *Hellespont*, and he was about forty hours in the water that time before they found him. They didn't think he'd live, but he did, only now he can't speak, and the shock did something to his mind. We taught him to knit to keep him busy and happy. It's the one new skill he's managed to pick up since it happened to him, and he's so proud of it he almost never stops. Haven't you noticed how many sweaters we all have?'

He laughed. 'Your father seems to have had an adventurous war.'

'Oh, he did. They were on secret duties, a sort of roving commission. Suited them, they were all born anarchists. They brought out no end of people from occupied Europe, you know. Gisela was one of them,' said Hero proudly.

'She was?' A flicker in the dark eyes. 'I didn't know that.'

'She had some heel of a husband who divorced her as soon as she became a bit of a drag on his career – she's half-Jewish, you see. She'd have gone to Ravensbruck if it hadn't been for Johnny.'

'No wonder,' said Chatrier softly, 'no wonder she's become such a devoted friend to him.'

'Gisela's a darling,' said Hero warmly. 'And she did something just as wonderful for him when she introduced him to opera. She never expected him to go head over heels for it like he did, or to launch out and build an opera house of his own. But Johnny had so much money he didn't know what to do with it. And nothing was too good for me, being the only child, you see.'

The kind, attentive, flattering eyes which had been appraising her silently all through lunch did not change their expression, yet her thumbs pricked suddenly. Nothing, just a shiver of awareness. A slight, infinitely slight tremor of response to those words of power, 'only child' and 'money'. It illuminated everything, the expert compliments, the indulgent attentions he had been paying her.

She thought, no, I'm imagining it! He's world-famous, he has plenty of money already, why should he care? He just likes me, and enjoys playing with the children, that's all. But the obstinate seed of doubt would not be quieted. Had he necessarily got plenty of money, just because he ranked amongst the greatest singers of the world? He must have made plenty, but that was another matter; probably he spent it as fast as he made it. And when you're – what would he be? Forty-eight or forty-nine? – when you're nearly fifty you can't reckon on the funds being inexhaustible for ever. And then, an opera house thrown in!

Well, she would soon see. If he stopped to speak kindly to Codger Bayliss, now that she'd clearly demonstrated her own partiality, she would know exactly why.

And he did. Somehow she had been sure he would.

Codger was alone in Sam's room by the stage-door, knitting away for dear life, and he lifted his fine, blank eyes at them as they came by, and focused upon Hero the sudden, struggling glimmer of recognition and love that belonged to all Johnny's chattels. The hands that shook and dangled aimlessly when they were disengaged, with an almost spastic compulsion, were steady enough on the steel needles. He was clean and closely shaved, and always neat in his person; Sam saw to that, and the legacy of the navy years helped. The big, well-shaped head with its motionless features might have been carved in wood, except when convulsed with the effort at speech, eternally painful and vain.

'That's a splendid pattern,' said Chatrier gently, halting to smile at him and finger the green pullover. 'Some day, if I earn the favour, I'm going to ask you to knit one like it for me.'

Very nicely done, the touch and the voice. Like those odious people who take children on their knees to ingratiate themselves with their mothers, though they don't want them, and the children don't want to be nursed. Such people ought always to be confronted, and indeed usually are, with just such a cold, distant stare.

So now she knew. It came as a shock to her vanity to realise that the man she had been making use of was also making use of her. But at least it eased her conscience of the slight compunction she had felt towards him.

They went on along the corridor to the stairs. Twice he allowed his hand to touch hers, and each time closed his fingers momentarily and very delicately, as though the touch had been accidental, and his elaboration of it a motion of deference and apology.

'Hero—'

He drew her to a halt in the dimmest corner, and she turned to face him, speculating behind a placid face on what might be coming next. It was too soon yet for extremes, unless he thought her very impressionable.

'Hero, if you're free this evening will you come and have dinner with me in town? I should like just once to be quiet with you, before the excitement begins. Drive in with me after rehearsal. I'll bring you back in good time.'

'Oh, no, I should have to go home and change,' she objected, fending off the necessity for answering with a definite yes or no. 'I couldn't possibly show up at the Grand Eden without my best frock. And I did half-promise to look in on my grandmother to-night.'

'Come later, then, come for dinner at any rate. Grandmothers should be in bed early. She'll spare you by eight o'clock?'

She clutched at that. By eight o'clock she would surely have made up her mind, and if she wanted to back out she could think of some excuse, telephone him. All she wanted now was not to have to promise to go with him, to have time to think. 'Yes, I could probably make it by eight. Yes, I'm sure I could.'

'Good, then I shall expect you at eight. You won't forget?'

Probably she would have let it rest at that, if her quick ear had not caught and understood the faint creak of the stagedoor swinging as someone with a light, long step bounded in from the street.

She knew that gait very well. Suddenly she lifted her face with the defenceless confiding of a child, in a half-invitation there was no mistaking. She saw Chatrier's eyes kindle warmly in self-congratulation, and momentarily closed her own, as he drew her gently to him by the shoulders, and kissed her on the mouth.

Only when the hasty footsteps rounded the corner and baulked wildly, did Chatrier disengage himself and turn, too late to see more than a hastily receding back in a light raincoat.

Hero, emerging from the kiss chilled and stiff with doubt and self-reproach, caught one fleeting glimpse of Hans Selverer's face as he skidded to a halt, hung for one instant dumbfounded and motionless, and then spread a hand against the wall, swung round, and retreated precipitately round the corner. If it was any satisfaction to her, at least he'd seen her this time. She carried the vision of his outraged and startled face with her as she drew herself quickly away and turned to scurry up the stairs.

'You won't forget?' said Chatrier, letting her go by stages, his fingers slipping smoothly down her arm.

'I won't forget,' she said, and ran for her dressing-room.

It was what she'd wanted, what she'd intended to happen; yet now she wished it undone. It wasn't the thought of Hans that had shaken her with this sudden storm of doubt and dismay, it was the memory of the embrace she had just provoked, so accomplished, so restrained, so gentle, so calculated. It was the first time in her life she had ever been kissed without the least trace of affection, and it had made her aware that she was playing with something considerably more dangerous than fire.

All the same, she wasn't giving up now, whatever the hazards. Not when Hans Selverer was just beginning to notice her existence!

'Pay Johnny to keep an eye on that little madam,' said Sam Priddy, watching them pass singly across the end of the corridor and climb the stairs; first the girl, flushed and in a hurry, then the man, at leisure and smiling faintly, the light of amusement and satisfaction in his eyes.

'She's all right,' said Stoker Bates comfortably. 'Our kid's got all her buttons on, don't you worry.'

'I know she has. But that's one bloke I don't like, that Chatrier. Johnny should have left him where he was, as good a Figaro as he may be. Asks too many questions round here, and answers too few.'

'He can sing like nobody's business,' said Stoker positively.

'He can that, I don't deny it. But he treats young Hans like a half-witted beginner, and he's pretty offhand with Miss Salberg, too. And now he's making a dead set at Butch. I don't like it. And the hell of it is,' said Sam, tugging irritably at his thick grey hair, 'I keep thinking I've seen that superior pan of his somewhere afore. What's more, I believe Johnny has the same idea. I've seen him looking sideways at the bloke sometimes, as though he was bashing his brains to remember where he'd run up against him, and couldn't fix it. Maybe it's only an illusion, maybe we're just recalling photographs we've seen of him, or something. I just wish I could feel sure about it, that's all. I just wish I knew.'

Chapter Two

'I shall be out to-night, darling,' said Hero, half-obscured by the cloud of fair hair she was industriously brushing. The powdered wig was hot to wear, and crushed her feather cut. She kicked off Cherubino's buckled shoes, and sank on to the stool before her mirror. 'I've got a dinner date, but I promise I won't be late back.'

Johnny, half-submerged in the big tub chair by the window, looked up sharply.

'Who're you meeting?'

It didn't occur to him, until she turned to stare, how far he was stepping out of character. He never asked her where she had been, or with whom, he'd never had to. Usually she told him, and if she didn't it was because she forgot, and then he trusted her. And now suddenly he sat upright and bristled at the mention of an unnamed date, and wondered that she gaped at him almost anxiously, as though he'd shown signs of growing old, or sickening for something.

'I like to know these things, Butch,' he said placatingly, subsiding again, but warily. Fathers get that way. You wouldn't be flattered if I just said: OK, push off, who cares!'

'Johnny, dear,' said Hero, levelling her hairbrush at him admonishingly, 'I'm getting a big girl now.'

'I know,' said Johnny moodily, 'that's the trouble. Other people are beginning to notice it. And since we're on this subject, let's say it right out loud – you're a well-heeled girl, too.'

She finished arranging her hair, and said nothing. He waited, growing a little anxious but sure he wouldn't have to insist; but when she still said nothing he pursued doggedly: 'So who're you meeting?'

She didn't know why she hadn't told him at once; there must be something very slightly wrong with her conscience. Surely there was no reason in the world why he should be displeased, and yet she knew he would be. And she'd begun this all wrong in any case, because she hadn't even made up her mind whether to go or not.

She eyed her father in the mirror, steadily and warningly, and said: 'It's Mr Chatrier, if you want to know.'

Johnny came out the chair as if he'd been stung, and hung over his daughter stiff with dismay, but not, she noted, with surprise. This was what he'd had in mind when he popped up like a jack-in-the-box and scowled at her.

'Oh, it is, is it?' said Johnny ominously. 'Well, let me tell you something, Hero Truscott. I've been hearing things already about your goings-on with the great Figaro, and that's one association I'd rather see kept strictly professional. You hear?'

All she had really heard was the offensive description of her strategy, and she took fire at it. If there had been no goings-on at all – as indeed there so nearly had – she would have laughed at him and probably reassured him; but the one kiss, so clearly invited, stuck fast in her mind and wouldn't be swallowed down. She turned on him with all the rage of her sore conscience.

'Goings-on! Johnny Truscott, them's fighting words! So you've been hearing things, have you? You never had the decency to come to me and say so straight out, and ask me what I had to say, did you? What am I supposed to have done? Go on, tell me! And who runs with the tales? Somebody with a pretty vivid imagination – and you swallow every word, I suppose.'

It had only just dawned on her that one person at least might have something factual to report, and her eyes and mouth rounded with indignation. 'Well, the stodgy great prig!' she gasped. 'Just wait till I see him!'

'You leave Sam alone, he never said a word against you. *I*'m the one who called them *your* goings-on. Sam was only worried about you getting hurt. And why shouldn't he be? And why shouldn't he talk to me about it?'

'Oh,' said Hero in a subsiding breath, and smiled again for a fleeting minute, 'oh, *Sam*!'

'What do you mean—"*Oh, Sam*?" Dolly as well, if you must know. Damn it, we all take an interest in what you do, how can we help it? Anyhow, I've been noticing things myself the last couple of days. And I don't want you to spend your time with Chatrier. He's old enough to be your father, and let him sing as well as he will, he's a man I find I don't like. You be friendly with him while you're at work, but don't get involved with him.' He linked his hands under her chin and turned up her face to him, smiling down at her anxiously, willing to be conciliatory if only she'd help him. 'You won't go, will you,

Butch? Ring him up later, and say you've got a headache.'

'Johnny! What a dirty trick!'

She had to sound scandalised, because it was exactly what she'd been thinking of doing; and no sooner had she given utterance to this judgment than she had to accept it. She would go. Why shouldn't she? If she didn't she would be wasting all the trouble she'd already taken, and Hans would soon forget the salutary shock of seeing her devoting to someone else attentions she never bothered to lavish on him.

'I promised to go,' she said, all the more firmly because it was not strictly true.

'Well, you can easily get out of it—'

'And I *want* to go.'

'Then this time,' said Johnny flatly, 'want will be your master, that's all.'

'Are you telling me I can't go?' She couldn't believe it, such a thing had never arisen between them before, and she didn't know how to deal with it without being furiously angry or melting into tears from pure shock.

'Just that! I'm forbidding you to go.' He didn't trust her! After all the years he'd known her, he couldn't rely on her to have a sense of values, to know what Marc Chatrier was and rate him accordingly. That was what hurt her most, that and the sting of knowing that she was to blame, and he was at any rate partially justified. Worse, he was justified without knowing it. And now she was fairly in it, and she had to go, or lose her self-respect for ever. Johnny's daughter couldn't back out, and mustn't admit defeat.

'I'm going!' she said.

'Is that so?' said Johnny, his own temper flaring. 'Now, look, I'm giving you one minute to see sense and promise me you'll ring him and call it off.'

'Why should I? I'm nineteen, and I've never given you reason . . . You've no *right* to be like this. All I'm going to do is have dinner with him, what is there in that? If you think you're going to begin choosing my friends for me at *this* stage, Johnny Truscott, you can damn' well think again.'

'You're going nowhere but home to-night,' said Johnny, sticking out his jaw. 'Make up your mind to that.'

'Oh, yes, I am, I'm going to the Grand Eden. Try and stop me!'

'I mean to,' he said promptly, and turned and plunged upon her clothes, that lay in a frothy little pile upon a chair. He scooped them up in one arm, wrenched open the wardrobe and gathered her dress and coat from their hangers. She flew to intercept him, but he evaded her with a swerve that would have done credit to a rugby forward, and was out of the room with her stockings floating behind him.

The door slammed; incredulously she heard the key turn.

She banged furiously on the panels for one moment, and then gave up. This time he'd gone too far. He expected her to laugh, and rage, and argue, and finally allow herself to be appeased and cajoled into giving way gracefully. He'd find out his mistake. She wasn't his daughter for nothing.

She stood silent, glaring at the door, beyond which the expectant silence gradually lengthened out into an uneasy hush. She could practically see him standing there, the pig-headed old autocrat, waiting for her to speak first.

At last he drummed his fingertips suggestively against the door, and said in a carefully level voice that couldn't quite disguise his baffled disquiet: 'I'll be back in an hour. If you're ready to talk sense then you can come out.'

Poor Johnny, he'd wanted the whole thing to break down in laughter; maybe even in a rough-and-tumble, so that they could go off home cronies as thick as ever. She steeled her heart and said equally constrainedly: 'And if I'm not?'

'Then you can stay there till you are.'

'You'd better start phoning round for a substitute Cherubino, then,' said Hero coldly. 'Good night! Don't bother to come back in an hour, you'll only be wasting your time.'

Johnny exploded with the kind of oath he thought he'd forgotten, and stamped away along the corridor and left her to her obstinacy. The toe of a nylon drooped derisively from the crack of the door. She damned it and sat down to scowl at her own face in the mirror. Now how on earth had all that come about, when neither of them had wanted it?

She curled up in the tub chair and waited for Johnny to come back, sure of his surrender if only she stood her ground.

He made her wait the full hour, and then she heard his fingers rap softly at the door again. Cajolingly, close to the panel, he said: 'Butch!'

No answer.

'You ready to come home yet?' coaxed Johnny.

'On what terms?' said Hero.

'Now don't be an ass. What's so important about this business, anyhow?'

'The principle,' said Hero grimly.

'All right, then! On *my* terms. You stop this nonsense and come home with me, or I'll leave you here until after the performance tonight, and see how you like that,' said Johnny, beginning to shout again, 'you obstinate little hellion!'

'Good night,' said Hero; and Johnny went.

Now she'd really done it. He wouldn't come back until the house lights went out for the night, and then, in a way, he'd have won, and that was unthinkable. She couldn't get out, no use even shouting for someone else, because Johnny'd taken the key. She'd be late for her date now in any case. And she had no clothes, and if she sneaked back to the house to change she might get caught. Even supposing she could get out in the first place, which she couldn't.

It took her half an hour more to remember the hatches Johnny had had run through the walls in the three end dressing-rooms on this side, because the windows were not suitable for an outside fire escape. They had never been used, and no one thought of them; even Johnny had forgotten. But there in the corner was the low square trap, and all she had to do was slip through it into the dressing-room next door and walk out blithely into the corridor.

It was as simple as that! And as for clothes – well, these were good enough for the eighteenth century, why not for the twentieth?

Her eyes had begun to dance as soon as she saw her way to a victory. She scrambled back into Cherubino's embroidered coat, smoothed on the powdered wig with its neat black ribbon queue, and shot her ruffles with a swagger in the mirror. Gleaming pale-blue satin breeches, white silk stockings, black buckled shoes, full shirt-sleeves knotted with black ribbon billowing in the wide cuffs of the sky-blue coat, and pearl-grey waistcoat stiff with silver thread. Nothing could possibly be more respectable.

No, wait a minute, why not go the whole hog? Off came the coat again, and she settled the ribbon of rainbow silk that was the baldric of Cherubino's smallsword across the breast of the silver waistcoat, and eased the scabbard comfortably at her hip. The finishing touch.

This she was really looking forward to. This would be the biggest free publicity stunt any première of *Figaro* had ever had, and Johnny could like it or lump it, whichever he liked.

She twisted the full skirts of her coat before the mirror a last time, clapped the silver-braided tricorne on top of her wig, and slid open the panel in the wall.

'West End, here I come!' said Hero, and ducked through the hatch and ran for the back staircase.

The commissionaire who opened the door of the Aston Martin in front of the discreetly lit portal of the hotel gaped and stared for an instant at the vision that slid nimbly out of the car. Two leather-coated young men halted and whistled, and even respectable elderly gentlemen turned their heads and loitered to watch, faint grins of pleasure and speculation dawning gently on their disillusioned faces. London, accustomed to every fantastic manner of dress the world provides, sometimes still shows mild surprise and sophisticated wonder at the tricks chance can play.

Most of those who lingered to admire Hero's vainglorious progress up the steps and in at the glass doors put her down to the vagaries of the film world or the advertising business, but that did not lessen the pleasure she gave them.

The diminutive page-boy who was just crossing the foyer as she entered had more imagination. At first sight of her his jaw dropped so far that he almost dislodged his pill-box cap, but the next moment he had laid a white-gloved paw on his heart and swept her a prodigious bow.

'Good evening, m'lord!'

Hero twirled her ruffles and flourished her hat, and made him an even more elaborate return, and they parted with solemn faces, magnificent in make-believe. After that the grown-ups with their goggling astonishment, smoothly hooded at once behind profes-sional serenity, were a sad come-down. The middle-aged gentlemen sitting over drinks in the open hall showed candid appreciation, but she ignored them; in or out of fancy dress, they were easy game.

The women were more interesting. Eyebrows signalled indulgent amusement, mild curiosity, and cool, well-bred, expertly disguised jealousy. Hero slowed her progress towards the reception desk to give them their money's worth, and accentuated the delicate swagger she had cultivated for Cherubino until she had every eye in the room upon her. It was good practice for achieving the same effect on the stage. It was also slightly alarming, and very pleasant.

Two round, dark waiters, plainly Italian, achieved the feat of pouring out drinks flawlessly while their eyes followed her with eloquent and perfectly frank delight the length of the room. A male clerk had mysteriously materialised from some hidden regions, and unobtrusively elbowed the woman aside from the precise area of the desk at which the vision might be expected to arrive. An invisible spotlight accompanied her. All the other women might as well not have been there at all, nobody was looking at them.

She was very late, presumably Chatrier had given her up. She leaned a satin elbow on the desk, tilted her smallsword cockily, and said nonchalantly: 'Will you be so kind as to acquaint Mr Chatrier with my arrival? He expected me earlier, but unfortunately I was unavoidably delayed.'

'Certainly, *sir*!' said the goggle-eyed clerk, a shade heavy-handed with his co-operation. 'What name shall I say?'

'Cherubino,' she said grandly, and turned to let her gaze rove tranquilly over the audience in the foyer.

She had practically put a stop to conversation there, even business held its breath a little. One of the Italian waiters moved slowly out of sight through a service door, his chin on his shoulder, and his eyes devouring her to the last moment when the door swung to between them.

A tall young man had just come in from the dining-room, and was looking round in some wonder for the focus of the prevalent hush. He found it, and halted as abruptly as if he had run his good-looking nose into a brick wall. The blue eyes opened very wide, directing at her a long, roused, dubious stare. Better and better! She had forgotten in her single-minded obstinacy that most of the company's principals, including Hans Selverer, were at the same hotel.

She continued to gaze past him, contemplating the florid decoration of the far wall, but acutely aware of what was going on behind his cloudy face, none the less. He was making up his mind; he was beginning to thread his way between the chairs and tables towards her. Not yet, she thought firmly, and not here, and turned again to the beaming clerk, who was just cradling the telephone.

'Mr Chatrier will come down at once.'

He was coming down at that very moment, and precipitately.

The first glimpse of his face was interesting. Through the blaze of conscientious delight she sensed the careful motions of a mind busy balancing solid satisfaction at her coming, with all its implications, against irritation at the difficulty in which she'd landed him. This was far too public and unorthodox for his plans. She'd alert her father too soon – if, indeed, she hadn't done so already.

'Hero, my dear!' He took her hands, looking her over with magnificently dissembled dismay. 'I'd given you up. What has happened?'

'I know,' she said quickly. 'I'm sorry, I couldn't get away earlier.' Out of the tail of her eye she observed that Chatrier's arrival had stopped Hans Selverer in his tracks. He frowned, hesitating whether to meddle; if she wasn't quick he'd make up his deliberate but formidable mind and move in on the spot, and Johnny might take a dim view of his daughter playing the leading part in a public scene.

'Can we go somewhere quiet?' she said appealingly. 'I didn't really *want* to sail in here looking like a refugee from pantomime.'

'Of course! Come up to my suite, I'll have them bring dinner there for you.'

He shepherded her hastily up the staircase in his arm, bending over her with elderly gallantry for the benefit of the spectators. The gallantry he would display upstairs would probably be of another kind, though equally discreet and expert, but with Hans Selverer's black scowl scorching her back she felt pretty secure. The only question was whether, between the two of them, she would get any dinner that night, and that represented a risk she felt to be justified in the circumstances.

'I'm afraid,' said Chatrier softly in her ear, 'you've been running into rough water for my sake. Come and tell me. If there's something wrong I must know. I don't want to complicate your life.'

Somewhere in the velvet solicitude of his voice there was hidden a thin, clear stream of silent thought that she could almost translate aloud. This girl is going to be a push-over. She wouldn't have come here like this, nuisance though she is, if she hadn't got it badly. Take it easy to-night, but better get her tied up quickly and irrevocably, so that marriage on civilised terms will seem the best thing even to her father.

The sudden chill of warning trickled down her spine. If she had been less sure of Hans Selverer, gnawing his lip down there in the foyer, she would have turned back then.

She needn't have worried. The tap at the door of the sitting-room came before they had even finished the first drink. She had had, as it happened, no intention of finishing hers; she knew her limitations, and she knew a calculated inhibition-loosener when she tasted one.

Chatrier had seemed, if anything, rather relieved to see her lack of interest in it. Probably the drinks had been ordered beforehand, and he had regretted his too-comprehensive planning when he guessed that Johnny was already in arms. Possibly he was as relieved as she was when the door, opening in response to his invitation, admitted Hans Selverer instead of the expected waiter.

'Please forgive this intrusion,' said Hans, closing the door firmly behind him, 'but I have a message for Miss Truscott from her father.' He fixed his eyes upon Hero, curled in the deep chair with the half-emptied glass at her elbow, and set his young jaw at her like a bulldog. 'I have told him that you are here, and quite safe. I think you must know that he has been looking for you everywhere, and was very alarmed about you. I have reassured him that you are about to leave for home. Under my escort.'

'You have,' said Marc Chatrier, coming hotly to his feet, 'the impudence of the devil, Mr Selverer.'

But he hesitated then, visibly checking his natural anger in face of a sudden doubt. He turned upon Hero, too; he came across to her and stood looking down at her with a slight, troubled frown.

'Hero, you didn't tell me that your father had no idea you were here. Is it true?'

The part was developing real possibilities. She hugged her satin knees and lowered her eyes uneasily, admiring Chatrier's resourcefulness and her own versatility. She hedged, protesting that she had been about to tell him the whole story, that Johnny must have *known* where she would be, though actually – well, there'd been no time, she'd just hopped into the car and come. Why not? What difference did it make?

The cue was admirably taken.

'What *difference*!' sighed Chatrier. 'Oh, my dear girl! You should have told me. How can I possibly . . .'

He turned away with a small gesture of gentle exasperation, and came eye to eye with Hans, who had not moved from his place by the door.

'You say you've spoken to Mr Truscott? Why did you not have the courtesy to speak first to me? You must have known that I would not dream of doing anything behind his back. What have you told him?'

'Simply that Miss Truscott is here. I dissuaded him,' said Hans grimly, 'from leaping into his car and coming to fetch her, but he made it plain that he did not know she was here, and did not wish her

378

to remain. He has authorised me to drive her home, and I shall do so.'

'I'm not coming!' said Hero loudly and indignantly.

She didn't really want a fight, she wasn't sure that she could cope with it, though the potentialities had a certain allure; but it would look altogether too complacent in her if she fell into line without putting up a struggle.

'Yes,' said Hans, very pale and very precise, 'you will come.'

'I won't! And please go away. Your interference in my affairs is insufferable.'

'I am sorry. All the same, you are going home.' He grew grimmer by the moment. 'After that you need not be troubled with me any more.'

She was comfortably certain that he didn't mean it; his voice held too much vehemence and too little conviction. She began to look forward ardently to that drive home, and didn't know for the life of her how to get to it gracefully; but she need not have worried, Chatrier was equal to this as to all situations.

'Hero,' he said very gently and reasonably, leaning down to take her by the shoulders, 'you don't realise. This is something I can't countenance. I had no intention of deceiving your father, and we must put it right at once. This young man may be insufferable, as you say, but he is undoubtedly right. You must go home. I would take you myself, but your father wishes and expects that you should go with Selverer, and I have no right whatever to quarrel with what your father wants.'

He drew her to her feet, kindly but firmly, smiled at her, and turned to cast one light, disparaging glance over the stiff young sentry by the door. 'You will undoubtedly be quite safe with Selverer,' he said.

Who would have thought that could be turned into such a deadly insult? And one that couldn't be resented, either. Hans reddened slowly to his hair, but said not a word.

'So, please, dear child,' said Chatrier, turning his back scornfully on his enemy, 'do as I ask you, and as you know you ought to. Go home and make your peace with your father. You will be glad afterwards.'

She let herself be persuaded. 'Well – if *you* say so.' Disconsolate, devoted, all he could wish. A push-over.

He escorted her to the door, and there, as though there had been no uncompromising figure grimly guarding it, he kissed her lightly on the forehead. Oh, the fatherliness of it, the forbearance, the breathtaking hypocrisy! 'Good night, Hero!'

'Good night!' she said, gruff and small, and went out meekly with Hans watchful at her elbow.

On the stairs he took her by the arm, and she felt what did not show in his face, the full tension of his rage. He was furiously angry with her, she had only to prod him a little and the fire would blaze. This was better than that young-brother stuff at least, this was something she could enjoy; and now that she was out of Chatrier's sight she needn't even contain her enjoyment.

She hardly felt the reviving glances that provided a guard of honour for her exit, and Hans was not aware of them at all. The first check came when he had marched her out at the door and down the steps to the Aston Martin. He transferred to her the glower he had fixed on the car.

'Your key, please!'

She gave it to him, trying not to look too complacent about it. 'Like me to drive?' she said innocently.

For answer he opened the passenger door for her, and bundled her into the seat, slamming the door upon her with the first tremor of temper he had betrayed. He settled himself beside her dourly, and switched on the engine.

'Are you sure you can drive it?'

He approached it with caution, but he soon showed her if he could drive it. Once he had got the feel of it, she had never been whisked out of London at a smarter pace. True, he set off at first in the wrong direction, his experience of the streets of London being sketchy as yet; and when she thought fit to point it out, he extricated himself from a one-way street by means of a U-turn which would have landed him in court if there had been a policeman handy; but of his technical ability there could be no doubt.

'You're still going the wrong way,' said Hero helpfully.

'You will please direct me,' he said through his teeth.

'Why should I?' she objected reasonably. 'I'm in no hurry to get home. You're the one who said we were going there. I don't mind if we end up in Bath – and we shall, if you keep tearing along the A4 at this rate.'

Hans braked suddenly and brought the car to the side of the road. He turned on her furiously; even in the dark she felt the blue, outraged glare he fixed on her.

'Everything is play to you. You are *irresponsible*. To come here to London *so* when you knew your father did not wish it, and to allow yourself to go to that man's room like – like—'

'Be careful!' said Hero, flaring dangerously.

'—like a half-witted *child*. And all out of vanity, because you must have your own way. You don't care that your father is worried and waits for you. You don't care what trouble you cause, only *you* must be amused and indulged. And so *stupid*, to put yourself in the hands of such a man.'

'What's the matter with him? What have you got against him? So far he's behaved towards me a great deal more considerately than you ever have, you – you virtuous busybody! That's what you are, a meddlesome, priggish busybody!'

'And you,' he said furiously, 'are a spoiled, self-willed, ill-natured child! Your father should *beat* you.'

'Why don't you advise him to? You fancy yourself at correcting other people's behaviour, why stop at mine? You could put him wise to his parental mistakes – maybe he'd be more grateful than I am.'

For a moment she thought he was going to take her by the shoulders and shake her, at the very least; instead, he jerked away from her with a set face, and seized the wheel.

'I must go more to the left. You will tell me where to turn, or else I will lock you in the car while I go to telephone your father and tell him where we are.'

That wouldn't have suited her, but not for the reason he supposed. She had still several miles of wrangling to look forward to, as things were, and she hadn't half-finished the fight yet. So she told him, only prolonging the ride by a few modest prevarications here and there. The battle raged every yard of the way, and was the most gratifying event of her day. Whatever he felt towards her now, it wasn't indifference; and it wasn't the blind, benevolent affection of an elder brother, either.

The battle with Johnny was less satisfactory. For one thing, he had been really frightened, when he weakened and went back to release her, only to find her gone; and that made her feel horribly guilty. For another, he was still blinder than any bat, and that infuriated her so much that she had no difficulty in transferring the load of her guilt to him.

He ought to have known her better, after all they'd been to each other all her life. He ought to have been looking for her real motives – no, he ought to have felt them by instinct, without even having to look for them. He ought to have recognised that admittedly hair-brained trip to London as what it was, a commando raid into enemy territory, undertaken for strategic reasons – well, partly strategic and partly prestige. After all, he had practically dared her to do it. And here he was, fussing and lecturing in a heavy-handed way, actually convinced that she was genuinely infatuated with Marc Chatrier.

It hadn't occurred to her until then that anyone but Marc Chatrier himself, and with luck Hans Selverer, could seriously believe that she was attracted to the man. And that Johnny should swallow it so easily, Johnny of all people! She felt as if a gulf had suddenly yawned between them, the revelation set him so far from her.

She had walked straight into his arms on arrival, and kissed him, and apologised for scaring him, all in the best filial style, more than willing to make amends, but desiring also that he should admit his own folly. And how where were they?

She'd never thought the day would come when she'd hear Johnny carrying on like a father. And no end to it! She finished the sandwiches she'd brought in with her providently from the kitchen, and poured the last cup of coffee.

'You ought to take lessons from Hans,' she said bitterly. 'You ask him, some time, how to deal with daughters. He knows it all.'

'Now, Butch,' said Johnny reproachfully, 'do I deserve that tone? I can't help being anxious, when I see you going overboard for a man I don't like and don't trust. You take my word for it, he isn't worth any hard words between you and me—'

'God!' said Hero incredulously. 'We sound like a cut-price soap opera.'

'You're only just nineteen,' said Johnny doggedly, 'and I'm responsible for you, and whether you find it corny or not, my girl, I'm going to *be* responsible for you. You think about it overnight, and don't kid yourself I'm fooling. If you're not to be trusted with a car, right, I'll get rid of the Aston, and if you're not to be trusted with money to spend I'll tie up your allowance so you can't get at it.'

That did it. Outraged, Hero marched across the hearth to stare him closely and fiercely in the eye. It wasn't the threat that infuriated her, it was his sheer, monumental stupidity.

'You can do all that,' she said, 'but *still* you won't be able to dictate to me whom I shall love – or even like.'

'Maybe not,' said Johnny, equally grim, 'but I can put a whole lot of obstacles in the way of your making a go of it.'

'You might alter my ideas about some of the people I used to *like* though,' said Hero as a vicious afterthought, and stalked out of the room shaken to the heart by the cruelty of the barb she hadn't even suspected she was going to throw.

Franz Hassilt had called an extra rehearsal for the next morning, bent on worrying out a few rough edges he had detected in the immensely complex and delicate structure of the last act. It went well and ended early; and Marc Chatrier was just opening his late mail in his dressing-room when Johnny Truscott tapped at the door and walked in upon him.

'Can you spare me five minutes? This won't take longer.'

He had closed the door behind him with the finality of a man going into action, and his lively, inquisitive face had about it the settled look it must always have worn when he entered dangerous waters. Johnny was as capable of subtlety as anyone, but what he hated was inaction when action was ultimately inevitable. Moving in, he always looked the happier for it.

'At the risk of appearing both obvious and crude,' he said, declining the chair Chatrier swung round for him from the table, 'I've got something to say to you. Keep away from my daughter.'

'At the risk of appearing equally obvious,' said Chatrier, suddenly erect and attentive, 'I would point out that you seem to have committed your daughter to pretty close contact with me, since you allow her to sing major rôles in your theatre.'

'Figaro,' said Johnny crisply, 'I don't mind. Figaro I can stomach. Chatrier, to be blunt, I can't. And I'm telling you again, leave my girl alone. I pay you what your agent asked, you give me, amply, what I'm paying for. Leave it at that, and we can respect each other and work together. But lay off Hero, or I pitch you out of here, and you can make it cost me what you like, it'll still be very well worth it. And, if you'll overlook a further crudity, the publicity will do you more harm than it will me – the stage you've reached.'

'Ah!' said Chatrier in a soft voice, and faintly smiling his ambiguous smile. 'It's like that, is it?'

He folded the letter he had been reading, and slipped it back into its envelope with deliberately graceful movements of long, elegantly-shaped fingers.

'My dear Truscott, I am comfortable here, I have no intention

383

of moving out, and none of suing. And I like your daughter.'

'That I can believe. But it doesn't alter the way I feel.'

'Ah, but isn't the way *she* feels of more importance?'

'Not,' said Johnny, 'if you want the gold mind as well as the girl. And don't pretend you'd be very interested without it, however much you might like her.'

'Oh, come, how little faith you show in the charms of a very delightful young lady.'

'I've warned you,' said Johnny, unmoved. 'I don't say things twice.'

He turned and walked to the door, and his hand was already outstretched to open it when the soft voice behind him said conversationally: 'How's the export-import business doing, Truscott? How much per body these days, and in and out of where? Or have you become a hundred per cent legitimate? I dare say you're rich enough to be able to afford to.'

The door remained closed.. Johnny stood a moment with ears pricked, considering the implications, and they spread widening circles into recesses of his life of which he had not thought for a long time.

He turned slowly, and came back into the room, gazing down at Chatrier with a thoughtful face. The agreeable mask, turned up to him smiling, could have been covering a mind of knowledge or a monumental bluff.

'Really well-informed bastards,' said Johnny in a sweet, small voice, 'talk less.'

'They talk just enough to convey what they mean. I can be an interesting conversationalist when I lay myself out to please. Your authorities, for instance, would be interested in some of the stories I could tell about your old passenger lists. There would be names on them they never knew – wouldn't there? Not all those pathetic refugees of yours came in like Gisela, all open and above-board – did they? There were others . . .'

Johnny relaxed his cramped fingers in his trouser-pockets, and wrote off the hope that this was simple bluff. The fellow knew about Gisela. She was all right, she had nothing to hide; nothing about her had ever been hidden, except the worst of her experiences, which she kept for ever to herself. But there had been others. There had indeed!

He remembered a Spaniard, tainted with a mild trade-union background, who had been just one jump ahead of a long prison term, without means, and without a hope of getting legal admittance to Britain. He'd be old now, but he could still be extradited if they caught up with him. And the Algerian girl who was still wanted by the French, if only they had known where to look for her.

Even some of the wartime waifs, whose political past, honest enough and innocent enough in Johnny's eyes, had contained elements which made their admittance by ordinary channels dubious, at a period when there was no time to brief counsel and argue the matter out. And since then, certain scholars and artists of intractably independent mind who would not, simply would not, endorse theories and acts they held to be immoral. A long procession of his crimes passed before his eyes and warmed his heart.

Maybe there were one or two questionable cases among them, but on the whole he was proud of them. Those who could pay had paid, and those who couldn't, hadn't. The costs had been met, somehow. And then, the Palestine days. The active nights along that inhospitable coast, the crowded, passionate, desperate, resolute and tragic cargoes, shaken loose from their past, and bent with all the hoarded fire of their natures upon reaching their future. Of them, too, he thought with pleasure and warmth, and gratitude, too, because they at least were safe, nobody was going to extradite them any more. All they could do, if the record came to light, was sink him in the hottest water of his life. But the others could be hounded out of their new and fragile security back to countries that had ill-used them and codes that were waiting to kill them.

Not, thought Johnny behind his placid face, if I know it.

'You tell me,' he said. 'It's your story.'

Chatrier leaned back in his chair at ease, and lit a cigarette. He was smiling, and the sparkle in his black eyes looked entirely confident, but he was an actor off the stage as well as on, and who could be sure what sort of a hand he really held?

'It would take too long,' he said, 'and you'd find it tedious. Perhaps just one little instance will settle your mind. You took off a certain party once from Italy, when Mussolini was cracking and the Germans were taking over. I could name the police official in Rome who was your contact and acted as go-between, but names are indiscreet. A fat fellow with a short beard – you remember?'

Johnny continued to regard him with the bright, impartial interest of a helpful pupil taking pity on a dim teacher.

'Yes, I think you remember. They shot him afterwards, did you know that? There were five people, all of them artists of one kind or another, all wanted by the Germans. But they weren't official business, and they weren't the kind that are easy to dispose of. A travelled lot, not wanted in several countries. Some of them got through eventually with legal papers, and some had to do without. But they all found asylum. Two of them in this country – and I could name both of them. I know what else you took aboard, too. Three very valuable canvases stolen from a German who had himself undoubtedly stolen them in the first place, and quite an assortment of smaller works of art – most of them in America now, I should imagine. They'd be very interested in that privateering sideline, too, but to do you justice I don't suppose that worries you very much. But the people, Truscott, the people would worry you a great deal.'

He shouldn't have lingered with such particular emphasis on his single instance; Johnny had him now. Eighteen years is a long time, and men change, but it was not for nothing Johnny had been scouring his remoter memories for that precise turn of the black head, and the rich music of the voice.

He hadn't been known as Marc Chatrier then, and he hadn't yet consolidated even the ground of his present reputation. Five people, all artists of one kind or another, and all in imminent danger of arrest; and one of them a young singer, born in Alsace, admittedly no hero, admittedly somewhat compromised in his complaisant dealings with Nazi authority, but due to be picked up within a day or two, and certain to be done to death rapidly or slowly thereafter. Johnny groped after the name, but it still eluded him. The face, hardened, polished and aged, smiled up at him through the smoke of Chatrier's cigarette fom narrowed black eyes.

That made things clearer, if not easier. It meant that he really had knowledge he could use to harm at least two people besides Johnny. But in all probability it also meant that that was the sum of his knowledge.

Did that make him less dangerous? Hardly. What mattered was not what he himself could uncover, but what was there to be uncovered once he set the process in motion. If they followed up one case and found it proved, they would set about stripping all the rest. And even if they stopped at one or two, what use was that? They were none of them expendable.

Johnny relaxed; he knew now where he stood. No need to dispute what they both remembered very well; there were no witnesses.

'Well, well!' he said. 'So that's what became of the starved tom-cat baritone from the Rome opera. You *have* got on in the world, haven't you? No wonder I couldn't quite place you. All this time I've been fretting over little things about you, trying to decide who it was you reminded me of. And I shouldn't wonder if you weren't on the run at all, if only I'd had time to go into it a bit more thoroughly.'

'Oh, yes, I was on the run, and only just ahead of the axe, too. It was a little private matter that had made Rome too hot to hold me – a little affair of a woman who belonged to a German general.'

'It would be!' said Johnny, sighing. 'Women are your line. If only I'd known you then as well as I'm getting to know you now, you needn't have given any of them any more trouble.'

'Ah, but this is different.' The malicious smile caressed him shamelessly. 'This is the love of a lifetime, my dear Truscott, and my intentions are honourable.'

'Like all hell!' said Johnny.

They studied each other long and steadily.

'Think about it,' said Chatrier, 'think about it in the calm of solitude, my dear fellow, and I'm sure all your lame dogs can rely on you not to let them down by doing anything foolish.'

Johnny looked at him for a long moment in considering silence, with nothing in his face to indicate either anger or uneasiness, and then without haste turned and walked out of the room, closing the door quietly behind him. There was no point in wasting energy in words or gestures now; thought was indeed indicated, and pretty urgently, too.

Even if Hero made a healthy recovery from her infatuation, this man would continue a potential danger to all those helpless people he had threatened. As long as he lived there was always the possibility that he might some day find it to his advantage to set the hunt in motion, for gain or for spite, or simply for sport if the fit took him.

Johnny happened to be down in Sam's box by the stage-door when Marc Chatrier came down from his dressing-room and strolled along the corridor to the door, where the car Johnny had put at his disposal was waiting for him. They watched him pass, hat at a debonair angle, whimsical mouth smiling faintly, eyes dreamily pleased with life and the sunlit noon. They did not take their eyes from him until the car slid forward from the kerb and vanished round the corner. In the corner by the window Codger knitted away with silent devotion, his steel needles clicking merrily, his large eyes fixed fondly on Johnny. In his presence they never strayed.

'Marriage of Figaro!' said Johnny bitterly, staring after the acquisition he had hailed with such innocent pride not so long ago. 'That fellow's ripe for a funeral, if everybody had what I wish him!'

Chapter Three

Johnny closed the door, and the faint, quivering, distant tremor of the strings leading into '*Porgi amor*,' one of the most melting sounds in the world, was cut off sharply, as if by a blow. The second act beginning, the house full and responsive, and the mysterious fine thread of splendid tension already lifting players and audience out of their everyday selves, into a world of superhuman achievement and supernormal sensitivity of apprehension; the two halves of a magic, making between them one of those miracles of a night that send human beings out renewed, never to be quite the same again. And Johnny shut the door on it with a clouded face.

'What's the matter?' said Gisela, turning from the glass. Marcellina's mantilla lay discarded on the ottoman by the wall, but she still wore the black lace dress with its tight, boned bodice of stiff silk. She had not the operatic figure; he could almost have shut her waist in his two hands. He tried it, smiling faintly as he stretched his long fingers; and all with that shadow still heavy on his eyes.

'Something's happened,' said Gisela with certainty. 'What is it?'

'Yes, something's happened, all right. Yesterday, after the rehearsal. I tried to get you on the phone afterwards, but you were out. And I didn't have time to speak to you alone before the curtain went up tonight.'

'I knew there was something, or you'd have been in your box.' Gisela swept Marcellina's lace gloves from the long stool before her mirror, and drew him down there beside her. 'Tell me.'

He told her, as simply and bluntly as if he had been confiding in a man. She listened in silence, her eyes intent upon his face. The shadow that lay upon him communicated itself to her. At the end she said, slowly feeling her way back through the years to a time she had often been adjured not to remember: 'You say you took him aboard there in Italy? Are you sure of him?'

'Yes, now I am. Ever since he came I've had an uneasy feeling at the back of my mind that I'd seen him somewhere before, that I ought to know him. But from photographs I did know him – who doesn't? – and I put it down to that. But as soon as he mentioned that trip I had him. I'm quite sure.'

'Then he really does know about two people, at least. *Could* he make trouble for them? After all this time, would anyone want to follow it up, even if they did get in with faked papers?'

'I think they still might. I think so. *She'd* probably be all right, she's getting old, and she lives in retirement, they've never had any trouble with her. But the professor has one of those consciences you can't shut up. He's up to the eyes in nuclear disarmament, and you know how popular that would make him. It's taken his friends all their time as it is to keep him out of the active group and jail. And even if he was behaving like an orthodox lamb,' said Johnny, ploughing deep furrows through his thick brown hair, 'government departments don't like being by-passed. They're only too well aware that three parts of 'em are useless as it is, it doesn't pay to rub it in.'

'So he must not set the machinery in motion,' she said, 'whatever happens.'

'No, he mustn't. I could put up a good running fight over my own record, if it came to it, but I couldn't protect them. And now we know what cards he holds, it seems to me he'll always be a danger. Even if I did stand out of his way and give him a free hand with Butch – and I'll see him in hell first – I should never feel safe from him. The first time he chose to feel himself cramped, and start angling for some new concession, out would come the same threat. I could start an inquiry into his own record, and there might well be stuff there that would shut his mouth tight enough if we could get at it, but that's going to take time. It isn't even a question of Hero so much now,' he said, scrubbing anxiously at his forehead. 'I saw that as soon as the cards were down. He's served me with notice that he reckons he can do as he likes round here, or else. And a set-up like we've got here is a powerful attraction to a man whose voice isn't going to be getting any better from now on. I see a sort of dreamy look in his eye, as though he's seeing himself as director of productions here in a year or two. Can you think of a better old age pension for a man like him?'

'Open the door, Johnny,' said Gisela. 'You'll miss "*Voi che sapete*".'

He looked hastily at his watch and jumped to obey. To this room the sound from the stage came up faint but clear. Hero was already in full song; the notes soared light and true, pouring out all the agitation and ardour and haste of the boy in love with love.

Johnny stood with his head inclined, vulnerably fond and proud, smiling like an idiot, and Gisela, taking her eyes from him for a moment to stub out her cigarette, caught the same look on her own face, and smiled through her preoccupation.

'She's good, isn't she?' said Johnny, whispering, as shy as if he praised himself.

'She's *very* good, Johnny. And she'll be better yet, much better.'

She waited until he had closed the door again on the busy voices of the Countess and Susanna, a faint, mingling murmur in which he was no longer vitally interested. Then she said: 'It worries me, Johnny, about Hero. She has usually such a good instinct about men, how could she be taken in by him? Are you sure you're not mistaken?'

'I'm not sure of anything with her now,' he admitted disconsolately. 'I thought I knew her so well, and now she's got me baffled. But love does do funny things with very young girls – doesn't it? They go overboard for the most revolting specimens, you've seen it.'

That was true enough; but still she frowned dubiously over this particular infatuation. 'You know – it seems I must have been wrong, but I did think she was a little interested in Hans.'

'*Hans?*' Johnny uttered a short howl of laughter? 'I only wish she was. She hates the sight of him since his performance of two nights ago, even if she didn't before. Every time they come near each other now they're scrapping. Didn't you see them in the first act?'

His worried eyes gleamed momentarily at the memory.

'It's working out very well for the performance, as a matter of fact. I've never seen a *Figaro* where the Count and Cherubino really struck sparks from each other before. Gives it more body, you get the absurd rivalry between the jealous rooster and the chick, and at the same time a touch of reality in the heart of it, just the foretaste of a genuine rivalry to come, and no holds barred. It's taken his mind off Tonda and Inga, too, and that's all to the good. They were round his neck before, and much good that is, when they're supposed to be fighting him tooth and nail. Now their blood's up, and they're really tearing into him.'

'I've noticed it,' agreed Gisela dryly, and smiled with him for one pleased moment, warmed by his delight in his perfect plaything.

The first act had gone wonderfully; the spring was wound, and the play and counterplay of characters moved with a taut precision that fused them all into one reality and one conviction; and the music clothed the drama in a translucent splendour of sound that made it timeless and universal, transmuting the Count's autocratic tantrums, Cherubino's quivering romantic temerity, Figaro's sly, subversive fire, Susanna's shrewd, resourceful charm, all into the stuff of immortality. Franz, directing from the harpsichord, was incandescent with inspiration. Everything that happened on the stage seemed to emerge out of an inner certainty that possessed them all, like a dream in which you cannot put a foot wrong. Even when the Count, hauling Cherubino angrily out of the great chair, had dealt him a resounding slap on his neat satin behind to go with the thundered: '*Serpente!*' it had merely seemed to be an inspired improvisation arising inevitably out of his lordship's jealous frustration.

But hadn't it rather, thought Gisela, suddenly enlightened, been simply one opportunist blow in the off-stage battle those two were conducting, and nothing at all to do with da Ponte's libretto? A coincidental felicity! Maybe, after all, Johnny was worrying about nothing where Hero was concerned. Maybe!

There remained, however, the others. The problem was not resolved, and at the end of every flight they came back to Mare Chatrier.

'Yes,' said Johnny, arriving by his own more circuitous route at the same insurmountable obstacle. She had taken up the black mantilla, and was arranging it carefully over her piled-up hair. He stood behind her, his eyes holding hers in the mirror, while he draped the folds over her shoulders. 'Of course, I could kill him,' he said thoughtfully.

'Don't talk such nonsense!' said Gisela fiercely. 'Give me my gloves, it's nearly time I went down. And you'd much better come down with me and watch the performance.'

Johnny smoothed out the long strands of lace, looking down at them with a closed and unrelenting face.

'But when you think,' he said, 'how many men we wiped out between us, just in the way of our daily work, not so long ago. Experts we were – had to be. And now we can't rub out a snake to prevent him from biting. Does it make sense?'

She took the gloves from him, stroking them on and rolling them up to her elbows. When it was done she took him by both hands, and he looked up into her face speculatively, keeping his own counsel.

'You won't have to do any killing,' she said. 'Whatever happens, neither you nor anyone you care for shall suffer at Marc Chatrier's hands. Don't worry about Hero, don't worry about the boys. You go and enjoy your triumph, and don't let anything spoil tonight for you. To-morrow's time enough for him.'

Johnny stood mute for a moment, regarding her with a slightly rueful smile. Then he stooped his head impulsively and kissed her on the cheek.

'You're a great old girl, Marcellina. But you stay out of this, and leave the vermin-clearance to me. Come on, grab your contract and let's be after that lawyer of yours, or your husband will get away.'

He checked suddenly in the act of towing her towards the door, turning on her a horrified face.

'Only suppose he really was your husband, girl! What a ghastly fate that would be!'

Before he left the bar, during the main interval, he stopped to have a word with Codger, who hovered greedy for his attention, struggling with the inevitable convulsion of all his disorganised features for speech.

Everybody made the extra effort for Codger. People who were in flaming tempers because of somebody else's idiocy or their own mistakes contained themselves and spoke gently and equably to their mascot. Even Franz, when everything went wrong at rehearsals and his language to his company outdid that of a drill sergeant handling an awkward squad, muted the explosions when Codger appeared within earshot.

'A new sweater, Codger! I never noticed.' It was a pleasant blue-grey this time. The welt was nearly finished, two inches of neat ribbing stood stiff on the bright blue plastic needles. Dolly always bought the wool for him; he couldn't manage the smallest such commission himself, though she sometimes took him with her to choose a colour, and no one ever objected if he selected a pastel pink or a luridly fashionable purple. 'Did you finish the green one? Who's going to get this one when it's finished?'

Codger mouthed and gestured, agonising after the expression that always eluded him.

'It's for his lordship,' translated Sam indulgently. 'Took a liking to that lad, Codger has.'

392

'Well, I'm sure it'll suit him,' said Johnny loyally, 'and look even handsomer than that satin waistcoat.'

The effort to find something nice to say to Codger was always pathetically over-rewarded. He want away with Sam, beaming, satisfied with so little, understanding so little, so terrifyingly tenacious of what he did understand; and Johnny went to have a word with Hero before going round to his box for the third act.

He wasn't sure if she was still punishing him for turning into a heavy father at this late stage, so he tapped at the door with a not entirely light-hearted parody of trepidation; but the reluctant officer, very trim in her laced coat and white breeches, looked round and grinned at him, too preoccupied with the business in hand to remember any incidental grudges.

'Hi, Butch!' said Johnny.

'Hi, skipper! How'm I doing?'

She was busy laying out the dress she had to wear over her male clothes half-way through the act, so that she could dive into it and be laced up in the shortest possible time.

'You're doing *fine*,' he said fervently, and loped over impulsively to kiss her. She lent him her cheek amiably, and returned him a hasty hug, but apparently she hadn't so much as noticed that he'd been missing from his box all through the second act. He was so proud of her he could hardly speak without spilling over.

'I'm going to be a case for Freud by the end of this business,' said Hero, pushing him off as the warning bell sounded. 'You've no idea how complicated it is trying to be a girl pretending to be a boy pretending to be a girl. Isn't it *odd* how the type persists? Thank *goodness* the composer in *Ariadne* doesn't dress up as a woman! Wouldn't you think they'd let a "breeches part" *be* a breeches part?'

'You *would* be a transvestist,' said Johnny, and patted the seat of her smart regimentals and fled, somewhat cheered on one issue at least. She might be annoyed with him, but it didn't go very deep. They could get back on to their old terms, if only the stumbling-stone could be removed. Removed. It had an easy, as well as a final, sound; but the word had no magic, and Marc Chatrier would not vanish for the sake of a wish.

Johnny watched the third act from his box. The complicated plot unfolded with a galloping impetus, so full of clichés, on the face of it, that it should have creaked at every turn, but so magically manipulated on the dazzling stream of the music that its very banalities illuminated the deepest places of the human heart, and the puppets blazed into a life more intense than realism could ever have given them. Marvellously still, the crowded house was uplifted and held taut on the tension of the ravishing sound.

Susanna pretended surrender, the Count swung in a few moments from triumph to frustrated malevolence, and his hoped-for vengeance melted and slipped through his fingers in the absurdities of the sextet, a whole novelette in itself. Long-lost son and long-bereaved mother (unmarried) embraced each other.

That cost Johnny his single lurching fall out of the alchemy of Mozart into the reality of his own predicament, the sight of Gisela and Marc Chatrier locked in each other's arms. The sudden furious ache of his anger astonished him. She ought not to have to touch the fellow. And yet it was doubtful if at that moment she was even aware of him except as Figaro, for they had achieved the rare and timeless miracle, and they were no longer players, but the very creatures of Almaviva's castle of Aguas Frescas, near Seville, acting out their immortal day unaware of being watched or overheard.

And there went Cherubino, the infant officer, slipping across the stage hand-in-hand with the gardener's daughter to hide himself among the village girls. And here came the Countess, tall and pale and noble and distressed, to dictate to her maid the letter that should bring her jealous husband headlong into a trap.

Then the village girls bringing their flowers to the Countess, and the shy country cousin, gawky under his unaccustomed skirts – modern play-clothes made for good Cherubinos – was first favoured and then unmasked and scolded. And how little effect it ever had on him! Young Nan Morgan, who played Barbarina, took a deep breath and poured out her plea for him in a piping flood, innocently blackmailing the Count into letting him off yet again.

And then the procession of the two wedding couples, with that splendid, stylish march. How had one man managed to draw up out of the well of sound so many superlative tunes? And how was it there were any left for later genius to find? You'd have thought Mozart had taken them all. Tunes that seemed to glide so lightly over the dimpling face of human experience, and yet pierced so deeply into the unfathomable places of the personality, far beyond anywhere the loud, portentous boys could reach, as lofty and as deep and as far-ranging as the spirit has room at its largest.

Her uncle the gardener led Susanna to kneel before the Count and receive her wedding veil from him. Figaro brought in his mother Marcellina to receive the same favour at the hands of the Countess. The march paraded all its bravery and gaiety as they crossed the stage hand-in-hand, Gisela's lace skirts swaying majestically about her.

They entered from the side opposite to Johnny's box, and he had their faces in full view and an excellent light. They smiled, the lightly linked hands were easy. But he saw their lips moving, very slightly and carefully and coldly.

He reached for the glasses in the pocket under the rim of the box; ordinarily he seldom used them. The smiling mask of Gisela's face leaped at him. It was a long time since he'd done any lip-reading, and the performance of professionals is a very different matter from the open speech of unsuspecting people; but he still had the accomplishment, one of many he had acquired for deadly purposes during the war. He watched, and rcad as best he could, missing words where there was not enough movement to give him a hold. He saw, framed almost imperceptibly on Gisela's lips, his own name.

'—touch Johnny,' she said.

Chatrier was harder. His head was turned towards her, so that Johnny got only a partial view, but he saw the shape of 'prevent me?' and then, strangely, with every implication of astonishing intimacy: '—my dear!'

'I've warned you,' said Gisela clearly, and hand in hand with him she swung to face the Countess's chair. The last glimpse Johnny caught said distinctly: 'You won't live to hurt him.'

Marcellina sank to her knees, with a deliberation nicely distinguished from Susanna's lissome youthfulness, before the Countess. Figaro stepped back from her to his place bcside his own bride, and the girls burst into their song of praise to their lord and master the Count. The mad day of Aguas Frescas drew to its climax and the end of the third act.

Johnny closed the glasses and put them away. The hand that snapped the catch of the pocket was not quite steady.

Figaro held the stage alone, the darkened stage shadowy with trees, the dim shapcs of the two arbours discreetly withdrawn to left and right. He had set the scene for his revenge on the whole race of women, his witnesses were planted, his reproaches already prepared. He sang his raging aria with a contained but formidable passion that ripped the livery from his manhood. How could so small a spirit control so great a gift? On the bitter last line he withdrew into the stage pine grove, gradually melting into the darkness until he vanished utterly from sight.

They were using a slightly cut version which omitted Basilio's aria, and transposed to this spot Barbarina's giddy little recitative about the supper she had begged for her hidden Cherubino.

'I had to pay for this with a kiss – but never mind, someone else will pay it back!'

The girl was going to be good, the secret fire of the evening had kindled a small flame in her, too. She heard the approach of Susanna and the Countess, and scuttled into the left-hand arbour with a tiny squeak of alarm. Oh, those arbours, stock properties of comedy like modern bedroom doors, tumbling out unexpected bodies at the end to confound everyone! Who would ever expect, if you wrote down the ingredients in cold blood, that something so transcendent could be made of them?

Barbarina had vanished, and the small conspiracy of women appeared, the Countess, Susanna and Marcellina all bound together by women's enforced loyalty to one another in face of the stupidity and unreason of men. They knew all about the invisible listener, and two of them sweetly withdrew to leave the third to pay out her lover for his suspicions by twisting the screw another turn or two. Marcellina followed Barbarina into the left-hand arbour, the Countess slipped away into the trees.

'"Now we shall see the great moment,"' sang Figaro savagely out of the darkness; and again, echoing Susanna's demure teasing with aching ferocity: '"To take the air – to take the air!"'

Time had brought them full circle from the moment when Chatrier first came in. Johnny's mind, suddenly harking back to that hopeful entrance, recoiled in unreasonable revulsion from '*Deh vieni non tardar.*' Tonda's voice was as limpid as spring water; she stood with the whole stage to herself, her pretty head thrown back, her round throat shaping and spilling the heavenly notes like floating pearls. Johnny drew back from her, and slipped away out of his box without a sound.

Perhaps the greatest love song ever written for a woman sank to its close in triumphant stillness, like a folding of wings. The dove settled and nestled, soft as down:

'"*Ti vo la fronte incoronar – incoronar – di rose.*"'

The whispering postlude followed on her heels as she drew back into the trees, dwindling like a candle-flame withdrawing into the night. Then, just as Figaro should have hissed his: '*Perfida!*', just as Cherubino tripped out of the wings with the trill poised on his lips, and the Countess moved softly forward from the bushes, Tonda hit a high note that was not in the score, the high note to end all high notes, soaring like a dart vertically to the roof of the theatre and sheering through it to split the night.

Cherubino, in the middle of a flushed and flustered entrance, jumped as though the steely point of that sound had pierced his flesh. The Countess dropped her handkerchief and swung about with an audible gasp. Faces loomed in the wings. The audience rustled uneasily and clutched at one another. And Tonda, drawing breath in a long, heaving cry, screamed and screamed until Franz signalled frantically from the orchestra pit, and the curtain came down between two uproars.

The stage lights went up, glaring white as the whole cast came running. Tonda was in a whimpering heap on the boards, her hands clutching her cheeks, her eyes staring in horrified shock at the body of Figaro, flat on his face among the stage trees with a pretty little dress rapier upright and quivering in his back.

Chapter Four

'Yes,' said Hero,' I do recognise it, of course. It's mine. I don't mean just that I had to wear it in the opera. I had, but also it belongs to me. My father bought it for me once in Salzburg. It was made for a minor princeling, I forget his name, but he was thirteen years old, I remember that. I knew it was a real sword, not a toy.'

She stood before Inspector Musgrave sturdily, her pale face fixed and resolute, her grey eyes flickering from his deceptively mild regard to the note-book on his knee. A grey, precise man of about fifty, in a dinner-jacket. Light-lashed eyes slightly magnified behind thick lenses, sharp, irritable features that suggested an experienced and intolerant law clerk rather than a policeman. But the thick, self-assured body in its good clothes indicated something rather more prosperous, perhaps an autocratic but on the whole benevolent company director out for an evening at the opera.

It was for a doctor Johnny had appealed, he hadn't bargained for a detective-inspector as well. Who would expect to find a Scotland Yard officer in the third row of the stalls?

Musgrave's right hand was busily drawing and writing all the time he questioned; she could see the layout of the last act briefly sketched upon the page, and a lot of dots distributed about it. A dot which must be Tonda in mid-stage. A dot which could only be Inga in the dimness of the trees close to the right-hand arbour. An X which was the dead man, here where he had fallen. Hero looked down at the empty place on the boards from which they had removed the body after the photographers and the surgeon had done with it. There was a small, irregularly-shaped stain of blood there now to mark the spot. But so little! Who would think a man could die and leave so little trace?

'And you were supposed to be wearing it as part of your costume,' said Musgrave. 'I saw it of course. You had it on when you ran through the hall with Barbarina in the third act. Then you made your next appearance with a dress over your uniform. Did you wear the sword then?'

'No,' said Hero. 'It's a nuisance under the petticoats, you know.'

He placed a tiny circle carefully in the wings on his plan, and wrote two names against it: Max Forrester and Ralph Howell. Together, so they said, at the moment when the alarm was given. And in the wings on the other side, ready for his impending entrance, the Count, this young Austrian Selverer. And here, close to Forrester and Howell, the girl, just tripping forward on to the stage, a shade flushed, a shade flustered – and without her pretty little smallsword.

'I see. And when did you last see it, then? You didn't have it during the fourth act, did you?'

'Well – I did. But then I . . .' She drew breath and swallowed the unsatisfactory opening to start again. 'I meant to wear it again in the fourth act, and I actually put it on. But then I – the baldric broke. While I was still off-stage, that is. I . . . it was broken in an altercation.' The word had a triumphantly legal sound about it, she didn't know from what recess of her mind she'd dredged it in this emergency.

'Oh?' said Musgrave mildly. 'An altercation with whom?'

'With Mr Chatrier,' she said in a hurried gasp.

Young Hans Selverer had been slowly and stealthily inching his way round the circle of tense and watchful people towards her, but at this he stood frozen, watching her across the few yards of intervening air with a heavy, anxious frown.

Musgrave had looked up from his labours sharply. Points of light gleamed behind his disguising glasses, and made him look less mild.

'You mean you were actually involved in some sort of struggle with him?' He had the scabbard across his knees, he handled it delicately through a handkerchief, lifting the frayed end of the rainbow ribbon. It had broken, apparently, in front, where it would cross her breast, and what was particularly notable about it was that the shorter end thus left, perhaps eight inches of it, had been torn away from its moorings. Only a few floating threads coiled and fluttered round the silver trappings of the scabbard at the front fastening. The length of ribbon was clean gone. The other end, long enough to span her slender back and reach down to her breast, was still firmly anchored to its silver buckle.

'This wouldn't take much force to break it, I realise that. But it can't have been ready to part of itself, all the same. What happened to break it? *Were* you struggling with him?'

'Yes,' said Hero faintly.

'Please,' said Hans, reaching her half a second ahead of Johnny, and supporting her with a large young arm, 'do not make her—'

'Butch,' said Johnny anxiously, hemming her in on the other side, 'do you know what you're saying? If he accosted you, why didn't you come to me? I . . .'

She shook them both off gently but firmly, and stepped a pace nearer to Musgrave, who had waited and watched with interest during this brief interlude. 'I'm all right, really I am. Why shouldn't I be? And I *want* to tell him.'

'A very sensible attitude,' said Musgrave, inserting the dot which represented Marcellina, cosily in the left-hand arbour with the young one, that Nan child who played Barbarina. Two together again, lucky for them. He cast one glance at Gisela, who sat with folded hands on the property marble bench at the edge of the circle, patient and self-contained, her dark eyes ranging with quick intelligence from face to face.

'What was this altercation of yours about?' he asked, flashing back to Hero. 'A commonplace amorous assault?' In a brief interval in her father's theatre it seemed hardly likely. He said so. Hero hesitated, her pallor suddenly flushed.

'Well, it's partly my fault. To some extent I – I suppose I'd been leading him on.'

'Butch,' said Johnny hastily, 'that's making too much of it. You know there was nothing to it. You haven't, I suppose,' he said hopefully, turning upon Musgrave, 'got any just-grown-up daughters, have you? Pity! You'd know what it's like if you had. All she did to encourage him was have lunch with him a couple of times, and accept one dinner invitation. If I hadn't been a shade over-anxious she wouldn't even have thought of it as leading him on. Ridiculous phrase to use!'

'I see. You just had dinner with him once.'

'Well, I didn't, actually. I meant to, but . . .'

She didn't know how to get round that incident, and before she knew where she was it was out. Better from her, perhaps, than from the staff of the Grand Eden. She thought of that, and took heart to tell almost the whole of it; and probably what she didn't tell Musgrave guessed for himself.

'Mr Selverer happened to have to telephone my father over something, and he mentioned that I was there in the hotel, and my father asked him to drive me home at once. And he did,' said Hero, simplifying somewhat drastically.

He didn't question it. He looked down critically at his drawing, and said mildly: 'So Chatrier had some grounds for feeling encouraged. And to-day he presumed a little too far on your goodwill. When did this scuffle take place, and where?'

'It was in the corridor outside my dressing-room, not long before – before he was killed. It was while Gisela was singing that aria of Marcellina's. You know, when Figaro has rushed off threatening vengeance, and his mother says she'll warn Susanna, because women must stick together – and then she has that quite long aria—'

'I'm very well acquainted with the opera, thank you. I know the place you mean. So he had only just come off-stage, and you were coming from your dressing-room, all ready for your entrance in the middle of the act.'

'Yes, but I had loads of time. I met him in the corridor, and he – he wanted me to stop and talk to him, and I didn't want to. And – I pushed him off and broke away, and he grabbed the baldric and it broke. So I just ran back into my dressing-room and left him holding it. I locked the door, because I knew he had to go on again in a few minutes, before I did, so I only had to wait. He tried to coax me out, and then I heard him drop the rapier outside my door and go away.'

'Did you open the door and take in the sword?'

'No, I waited several minutes to make sure he'd gone. I wasn't in any hurry. And when I did open the door there wasn't any rapier or baldric there, it was clean gone.'

'Had you heard anyone pass during the interval? Anyone who might have taken it?'

'I didn't notice. There are often people about, naturally, but I wasn't paying any special attention. I wasn't listening, if that's what you mean, because I knew he had to go on, it was only a matter of waiting a few minutes. I . . .' This time she flushed darkly. 'I had another go at my make-up, it was slightly mussed.'

'So the sword was gone. And you didn't see it again? Not until it turned up in these – peculiar circumstances?'

'No, I didn't.'

'And you haven't any idea who could have taken it from outside your door?'

'No, not the least idea.'

Musgrave carefully spiced his plan with a few question marks which indicated the probable positions of supenumeraries like Sam Priddy. He looked up at Johnny with a strictly controlled smile.

'It seems you were wise to feel some misgivings about your

daughter's association with the dead man, Mr Truscott. May I take it that you didn't like Chatrier? Or was it merely a matter of his age? I quite understand that Miss Truscott may attract admirers who are not invariably – disinterested, shall we say?'

'I didn't like him,' said Johnny firmly. It would appear in any case, better from him than from others. 'I had reason to think that he saw my girl as a fortune, and my attitude towards him was what you surely might expect it to be. Professionally I had no quarrel with him. He was a splendid artist.'

Undoubtedly, thought Musgrave, eyeing him steadily, this was not a man who would need any help in managing his own affairs in the ordinary way, without resorting to such extrcmes as murder. The young fellow was more likely to be pushed hard by his jealousy of an older man who had apparently been shown some favours. All the same, daughters can be the devil, and it was always possible . . .

Musgrave added a small, neat mark of interrogation to the wandering dot representing Johnny, an infinitesimal drawing of a man in orbit between his stage box and the wings. Hans Selverer already had his own question mark. The waiters at the Grand Eden would be able to fill in some necessary details.

'Well, I think I now have an idea of everybody's movements during the material time. What's remarkable is that we have such a short period to fill in. The last time anyone can be certain they saw or heard Chatrier alive was when he sang the final: "*Il fresco – il fresco!*" during Susanna's short dialogue with the Countess before "*Deh vieni*". By the time Susanna withdrew into the trees at the end of that aria he was dead – or at least the attack that killed him had already been made. A matter of no more than ten minutes. With a brisker tempo it wouldn't have been so long.'

'You found my tempo too slow?' said Franz, bristling. 'You want Susanna should gallop through "*Deh vieni*", and there should be no sudden catch in the breath in the middle of all the horse-play? You will teach me to conduct *Figaro* like I could teach you to catch murderers.'

'I don't wish to be unduly critical. I could quote excellent authorities.' For the first time the mild eyes really took fire; it seemed the man had a passion, and his ticket hadn't been a gift from a missionary friend, or a concession to an aspiring wife. 'I may say I was very surprised,' he said belligerently, 'to see that a *cut* version of *Figaro* was being used in *this* theatre.'

'Cut,' said Johnny, catching the spark, 'at my wish, and not to save time, either. Cut, and all the better for it.' His voice said plainly: 'Want to make something of it?'

'To take out the "ass's skin" aria – a very fine aria—'

'Hear, hear!' murmured Ralph Howell tenderly from the background. 'And the only one Basilio has to himself, mind you, bach!'

'A very fine aria,' snapped Johnny, 'and nothing whatever to do with the business of the act. We axe it because I prefer it that way dramatically, and transpose Barbarina's recitative to that spot because it makes the timing smoother. We never cut anything for any reason except to get a heightened tension.'

'We've got that, all right,' said Forrester dryly, shooting a modern wrist-watch from under Doctor Bartolo's great laced cuff. 'Two in the morning, and we have to go from murder to musical criticism. What I want to know is, when can we at least send these girls off home to bed?'

'Very shortly now.' Musgrave recovered the thread of business hastily. What would the local inspector think of him? And after accepting his prior presence so mildly and amenably, too. 'If no one has anything to add to these provisional statements, I think we might let the ladies go.'

He looked round the circle of feminine faces, brightening with the hope of release, losing the betraying lines of tiredness. The local man, who had said little during the interrogation, had fixed a thoughtful stare on the Countess, in whose pale blue Scandinavian eyes showed a gleam of purpose which held a certain promise.

'Miss Iversen, you wanted to add something?'

The sergeant poised his pencil hopefully. Inga looked out of the corner of her eye at Hero. Cherubino's sky-blue sleeve nestled gratefully into Hans Selverer's glittering brocade side, and his fingers clasped the boy-girl's elbow firmly and protectively. There had been a little too much of the boy-girl, but Inga was no longer deceived.

'I wait,' she announced clearly, 'for Miss Truscott to correct her statement, but she does not do so. I am a truthful person. I ask myself, what must I do?'

Herself, apparently, was ready and waiting with the answer.

'This I do not mention earlier, because I do not at first realise it is important. But I was a witness of this – altercation between Miss Truscott and another person. I regret, I much regret, she makes it

403

necessary for me to tell it, but it was not Marc Chatrier who broke the ribbon of her sword.'

She savoured her moment, the dismay in the grey eyes that were alone eloquent in Hero's wooden face, the flare of anxiety and apprehension in Johnny's.

'It was Mr Selverer,' said Inga with intense satisfaction.

The hum and vibration of suppressed excitement, shaking them all, sent the blood coursing up into the Count's ingenuous face, and tightened his fingers upon Hero's trembling arm.

'You saw them?' said Johnny, bristling. 'Where were you, then?'

'I happened to cross the corridor, coming from my dressing-room . . .'

Tonda emitted an explosive snort of laughter. 'Do not believe her. She is jealous because the little one here puts her nose out of joint with him. She will say anything, that one.'

'You are calling me a liar, *madam*?' Inga's icy claws came out; the northern lights spat and flickered in her eyes.

Tonda bounced up from her chair joyfully. 'Yes, I say it! Worse than that you would do to pay her for being so young, after all the fury you have put into chasing him all in vain—'

'And you?' shrieked Inga. 'You Italian washer-woman with skirts kilted up to run after him faster – you dare talk of chasing him? *You*?'

'Me, I do not pretend. I amuse myself, but if I lose I lose, there are plenty of men. For you perhaps he was the last hope.'

Johnny took Tonda about the waist just in time, Ralph Howell and Max Forrester closed in from either side upon Inga, and bloodshed was averted by the length of a finger-nail. The Countess, freezing into dignity again, brushed off the restraining hands, composed her maid's muslin skirts about her, and said with deadly simplicity:

'Ask her.'

All eyes came back to Hero, who had grown paler by fierce degrees as Hans Selverer had grown redder.

'All right,' said Hero with resignation, 'it was Hans. But all the rest of it was true. I only altered the identity of the man.'

'Only!' said Johnny in a frantic whisper meant for the ears of a higher providence. 'My God, women!'

'Well, what's so surprising about that?' said Hero, goaded. 'What harm could it do Marc Chatrier now, my saying it was him? After all, we're a company, we don't go round throwing suspicion on one another—'

'*Some* of us do not,' snorted Tonda.

'—and it couldn't hurt him, so I made it him.'

'So you thought,' said Musgrave, 'that Mr Selverer might have made use of your sword, once he had it, to kill Chatrier, and you set out to divert suspicion from him.'

'Of course not! I *knew* he didn't. In the first place he wouldn't, and in the second place I keep telling you he didn't take the thing away with him, he left it outside my door. But I thought *you*'d start thinking he'd done it.'

'Couldn't you trust the police not to jump to conclusions quite so easily?'

'No,' said Hero simply.

She caught her father's speaking eye, and protested indignantly: 'Well, *do* people? Ever? You don't suppose he's got as far as being an inspector without knowing that, do you?'

Musgrave crossed out the two question marks with which he had flanked the dot which was Cherubino. They were no longer appropriate; she was too devastatingly reasonable to be associated with such equivocal symbols.

'Then I'm to take it, am I, that you would always lie for your friends if you thought it necessary? Even on oath?'

That made her face solemn for a moment. She thought about it, pulling at the curls of her wig, and then she said: 'That would make it a bit dicey. But yes, I suppose so. If I was sure they hadn't done anything wrong. Wouldn't you?'

Don't answer that, Musgrave! Plead the fifth amendment if necessary, but don't answer it.

'Then how am I supposed ever to trust anything you say? How am I to tell the difference when you tell me something true?'

'I don't know,' she owned. 'That's a sort of occupational hazard, isn't it? Maybe I might look less sure of myself when I wasn't telling the truth – or maybe more, to compensate? It's hard to say.'

He resisted the temptation to pursue this unexpected philosophical by-way, and got back to the matter in hand. 'Well, suppose you tell me the truth now, and see if I recognise it.'

'It happened just like I've told you, and just at the time I told you, only it was Hans. We'd been quarrelling, rather – most of the evening. About my being spoiled and selfish, and his being bossy and priggish. We were still at it then, and I'd had enough, and he wanted to make me listen to him, that's all. He grabbed the baldric, and it broke, and I ran off and locked myself in. He tried to get me to talk to him, and when I wouldn't he said, oh, very well, he'd leave the rapier propped up in the doorway for me. And he did.'

She was emphatic on that point; she wanted him to have no doubts of her truthfulness this time. But there remained the doubt which she herself had raised: when lying, would she be more or less convincing?

'How do you know he didn't take it away with him, after all?'

'Because if fell down after he'd gone. I heard the point of the scabbard slither on the polished floor, and then the hilt clattered on the boards. It must have rolled half across the corridor.'

A nice detail, but one she had not mentioned before; that might be mere chance, for the point was a small one, but there was not doubt she was quick at picking her way through thorns.

He turned his attention to Hans, whose angry colour had not yet subsided.

'Mr Selverer, do you wish to support this version?'

'It is true,' said Hans, and restrained himself from adding: 'this time.'

'Why did you not correct the previous one?'

'Oh, don't be silly!' cried Hero reproachfully. 'How could he, when I'd just told it in front of everybody? He never had a chance.'

To everyone's surprise, Hans shook her sharply by the arm, and said in a tone Johnny found himself envying: 'Be quiet! You have made quite enough trouble for everybody.' More surprisingly still, she said: 'I know! Sorry!' in a meek tone, and was quiet.

'Did you leave the sword there, as she says?'

'I did.'

'And you didn't see it again until after Chatrier was dead?'

'No, I did not.'

And yet they could still be in collusion. One story had fallen down because of the accident of Inga's intervention, they palmed another one with all the dexterity of old hands.

'Did you get on well with Chatrier, Mr Selverer?'

'I respected his gifts and his knowledge,' said Hans stiffly. 'Working with him was not easy, but it was rewarding. As a man I did not care for him so much.'

'But Miss Truscott did?'

'As Miss Truscott's father,' said Johnny peremptorily, 'I strongly object to that question. And if you've finished with her now I'd like to send her home.'

Musgrave smiled, cocking an eyebrow at his colleague; 'Very well, I think we can let all the ladies go now.'

Marcellina, the quiet one, rose with a quick, reassuring look at Johnny Truscott, and he nodded at her gratefully, committing his troublesome daughter to her care without a word.

Hero kissed her father. '"*Pace, pace, mio dolce tesoro!*"' she whispered placatingly in his ear, and went off stumbling and yawning to take off Cherubino's finery.

Once he was in the theatre, there was no way of getting him out. Wherever they turned, in the store among the sets, in the wardrobe, in the dressing-rooms, round the switchboard, down in the orchestra pit, there Musgrave would turn up, silent, still, and unbelievably obtrusive. The local man, though he took over the official business of statements and interviews, seemed to be able to go and come without creating those pregnant silences round about him, or drawing the deck crew prowling on his heels. The sergeant and his underlings who did the routine work of searching dressing-rooms and watching the comings and goings of the company were ordinary human beings, with whom casual communication was possible. But Musgrave did not so much visit the theatre as haunt it.

'That man's just about had this place to pieces already,' said Dolly Glazier, polishing glasses in the circle bar before the evening performance of *Alceste*, three nights after the catastrophe of *Figaro*. There had been no pause in the activities of the Leander Theatre; one morning rehearsal had been cancelled to allow the exhausted Franz to sleep late, but that had been the only concession. 'We're a commercial undertaking,' Johnny had said, magnificently if not strictly truthfully, 'and we keep faith with the public'. *Arabella* had gone on according to plan on the night after the tragedy, and *Don Giovanni* the next night, with every man on his mettle. 'What's he after now,' said Dolly, 'that's what I want to know.'

'Keeping an eye on the lot of us,' said Sam. 'Thinks if he hangs around long enough, somebody's going to lose his nerve and give himself away.'

'But what's he looking for, anyhow?'

'A bit o' ribbon,' said the old man, soft-voiced, 'off our kid's sword-belt. That's my guess, anyhow. That's the only thing that went missing. Drop it in the furnace if you find it, girl, that's what I say.'

'Destroying evidence!' said Dolly reprovingly. 'Not that I'd go a step out of my way to help round up the one who knocked off that Chatrier fellow, that's a fact. I don't believe it was any of Johnny's folks, mind you. But it's a bit too close for comfort, all the same.'

'I wouldn't mind,' said Stoker Bates heatedly, 'if he'd stick to detecting, but he don't. Takes on to learn me to scene-shift – *me!* Tells the old geyser how to conduct, very nearly. The other day, when Jimmy the One was in, blow me if this chap wasn't telling him what was wrong with the casting, and who he should have signed up instead of half the company. And you know what? . . . He thinks Wagner's better than Mozart!'

'*No!*' gasped Dolly, scandalised.

'True as I'm standing here. I heard 'em at it yesterday. Mozart, he says – *Figaro*, he says – *pleasant enough pastiche*, he says. Now *Tristan* . . . Teutonic bluster, says Johnny. Not that he means it, not really, but what can you do with a bloke like that? *Pastiche!*'

They looked at one another in mute decision, writing off Musgrave from that moment. A policeman has his job to do, they could have forgiven him that; even his unnerving ways of erupting under their feet were perhaps only the symptoms of an occupational disease. But a man who could prefer Wagner to Mozart was beyond the pale.

'He's here again,' said Sam, putting his head in at Johnny's office door on the sixth morning after the final exit of *Figaro*. 'Siegfried without his helmet! Wants to see the maestro, he says. Right now he's busy lousing up the piano rehearsal. I reckon if we don't get him up here out of Mr Southall's hair pretty soon there's going to be more murder done.'

'Damn!' said Johnny, and rose to switch off the tape recorder. They were playing through their two-year-old production of *Rosenkavalier*, in preparation for planning the new one to take pride of place in their next winter repertoire, and to call a halt in the middle of the rising excitement of Octavian's arrival, with the argument about Hero still far from settled, was frustrating, if not a kind of blasphemy. 'Oh, well, must co-operate with the law, I suppose. Send him up.'

Franz took his slippered feet off the desk, and fretted irritably at his silver mane. 'I tell you the child can do it. If we can find her a Sophie who is young enough also, she can do it, and the work will gain.'

'She isn't ready,' repeated Johnny. 'She says she isn't, and who am I to shove her into such a responsibility until she feels able to carry it?'

Gisela rose and shook together the preliminary drawings for the costumes. 'I'd better leave you to it. Personally, I'd love to see an

Octavian who really was still in his teens. What do you say, Sam?'

'Our kid?' said Sam, divining the cause of this mild dispute. He flicked a gesture of confidence at them with thumb and forefinger as he walked out. 'Do it on her head,' he said scornfully, and rolled away down the stairs with his ungainly but nimble gait.

Presently they heard Musgrave's deliberate feet ascending.

'No, don't go, Gisela,' said Johnny, drawing her back as she would have made for the door with the portfolio of sketches. 'Maybe he won't stay long.'

'He seems to be practically a permanent resident,' she said with a resigned smile; but she sat down again.

Musgrave came in brisk and large as ever, the slight expression of superiority provoked by Franz's belligerent deputy still on his precise features. He couldn't resist commenting. If he came with a warrant for me in his pocket, Johnny thought sourly, he'd still have to stop and tell us we were taking the second act finale too fast.

'You've put *Figaro* back into rehearsal, I see.'

'It won't be out of the programmes more than a fortnight,' said Johnny, pushing the cigarettes and the desk lighter towards him.

'Your substitute seemed to me to be doing very well.'

'A lightweight,' said Franz. 'A small voice and no presence. He does his best, but it will be a travesty.'

'Hm, I see Chatrier has at least one mourner.'

He had not many, it seemed; his connections were professional only. A married sister in Colmar had written but not put in an appearance, and it had been left to his American agent to claim his body and set in motion the preparations for his funeral. But the musical critics of the world's Press, at least, were weeping ink for him by the column.

Musgrave settled his briefcase comfortably beside him, and leaned back in his chair.

'I won't keep you from your work long, Dr Hassilt, but I think you may be able to help me. The international musical world isn't so big that artists of your calibre can revolve in it as long as you have without encountering most of the others of the same rank. And opera has always been your speciality. Tell me, did you ever hear of a baritone named Antoine Gallet? It would be some time ago, about the end of the war, or even during it.'

Franz was regarding him narrowly from under knitted brows. 'Yes, I have heard of him.'

'Ever meet him?'

'Once, in Vienna, in 1942. He sang at one of the last concerts I conducted before I left Austria.'

He had left it, like so many others, just ahead of the axe. It was a long time ago, and he never talked about it. Probably he seldom even thought about it. Music is a present world, perpetually renewed.

'I did not know him personally, apart from that.'

'But you knew his reputation? It seems he was known as a collaborator. Born in Alsace, apparently, and he began to make extensive tours and to claw out a fairish living for himself after the Germans occupied France. Ditched his wife in the process, incidentally. They can't have been married more than a couple of years. Divorced her and let her be herded off to a concentration camp. And later he seems to have been responsible for several similar incidents. The records tend to be blank, so much having been destroyed. But rumour says he got several musicians into trouble whle he was in Austria, including a certain conductor who ended up in Auschwitz. Died there, about a year later. Did you know all that about him?'

'Not the details, no. Certainly not about his wife. I knew he was looked upon as – pliable, and that he was quick to extricate himself from any association that might compromise his own safety. People were expendable. Every man for himself. He was young and he was frightened. Frightened people are not at their best.'

'And did you know that he went to America after the war, changed his name – though he seems to have changed it once or twice already, for that matter – and made quite a new life and reputation? I think you did. You seem to have welcomed him,' said Musgrave, pouncing happily, 'when he came here in his new identity to sing Figaro for you.'

Franz leaned forward, his irascible old face constrained to lines of laboured patience.

'*Meester* Musgrave,' he said gently, 'I am seventy-five years old. I no longer think I have the right to judge men and write them off for life, because in certain bad circumstances they have failed to behave like heroes. Gallet – that was twenty years ago, and what profit is it to harrow over it any more, if he is now another man? When Mr Clash cables that he has signed up Marc Chatrier I am simply glad, because now I have the best Figaro now alive, and my job is to get as near perfection as a man can. If he deserves only good of me now, good he shall have—'

'And if not?' said Musgrave quickly. 'How if he turned out to be the same even when he wasn't young and frightened? How if he began making hell all around him, for the people you like?'

'If he made trouble I could deal with him. I could protect my friends and colleagues.'

'I see. He got the benefit of the doubt, though you knew he was Gallet . . . You agree you did know that?'

'I knew it.'

'—and if he made trouble, you would feel responsible for the security and peace of mind of your friends, and take steps accordingly.'

'Such as with a sword, Franz, my boy,' said Johnny bitterly. 'Don't put words into my musical director's mouth, Mr Musgrave, you've got two independent witnesses here if you do. Motives don't come much thinner than that.'

Musgrave was smiling. 'Thank you, Dr Hassilt, that's really all I wanted. And now if I could just have a word with Mr Selverer before I leave you—'

'I am going down,' said Franz, ruffled and breathing hard, 'I will ask Hans to come up to you.'

'If you don't mind, I'd rather you stayed here.'

An instant of sheer, uncomprehending surprise, and then Franz understood. He sat down again with a look of faint contempt, and Johnny, resigned, picked up the telephone.

'Stoker, my apologies to Mr Southall, and would he mind asking Mr Selverer to come up here for a few minutes.'

Hans came up flushed and preoccupied from rehearsal, and checked sharply in the doorway at sight of Musgrave. In his presence all faces were guarded, he was used to that, and accomplished at reading even between the lines they smoothed away. The young man came in with eyes full of reserve, in a face held very still. He looked aside once at Gisela, and she smiled at him. Was it imagination that the tension of his jaw and mouth eased a little?

'I'm sorry to take you away from rehearsal,' said Musgrave with all his deceptive mildness flowing like honey. 'This won't take a moment.'

It sounded ominously like a dentist's reassurance before the pouncing extraction of a tooth, and that was much the way it turned out. The question came briskly and brightly this time, before the boy had even settled himself in a chair.

'Do you know the name Antoine Gallet, Mr Selverer?'

Hans jerked up his head with a wild start that made an answer

411

unnecessary. His hands gripped convulsively in the upholstery of his chair for a moment, and then with painful care relaxed their tension.

'Yes,' he said.

'Ah, I thought you might. Did you ever see him? Or photographs of him, perhaps?'

'I never saw him in person. Photographs I may have seen, but I do not now recall it. It would be a very long time ago. Why do you ask me about him? Surely he is dead?'

Musgrave's particular smile, come and gone in an instant and leaving no ray behind, touched his grey countenance and fled. 'Oh, yes – he's dead! Tell me what you remember hearing about him.'

Hans moistened his lips, and pondered the wisdom of complying, though the look in his ingenuous eyes suggested pure bewilderment and mistrust rather than any personal disquiet.

'I know he was a singer who used to have a certain modest reputation during the war. I have heard my mother speak of him. But I have not heard the name now for many years.'

'Yet you hadn't forgotten it. Well, it seems I'm better informed than you. He had another kind of reputation, too, for taking care of his own career by all manner of questionable tricks. There was a case, for instance, involving a conductor who was already suspected of anti-Nazi sympathies, and Gallet chose to bolster up is own position by refusing to work with this man, and getting him thrown out of his job, and finally he died in a concentration camp. His name, it turns out,' said Musgrave deliberately, 'was Selverer. Richard Selverer.'

He looked up into fixed blue eyes that were staring at him in detestation. 'A coincidence, would you say?'

'You know you are speaking of my father. If I did not choose to speak of this myself, it is because I did not and do not see what it has to do with you. I do not like this intrusion.'

'You'll see the application very soon. When Antoine Gallet came here a little while ago to sing Figaro in this new production . . .'

Hans was on his feet, quivering. 'What are you saying? I don't understand. Are you seriously trying to tell me that *Marc Chatrier* was Antoine Gallet?'

'My dear Selverer, are *you* seriously trying to tell me that you didn't know?'

'How could I know? I never saw him. I thought he was dead long ago, the name had vanished. It is only something I remember from a child. I never associated Chatrier with him. Why should I?'

412

'Ah, but you see, there was someone here who could very well have told you. Doctor Hassilt knew.'

' I have told him nothing,' said Franz flatly and coldly, 'and you will certainly never prove that I did. Sit down, boy, sit down and calm yourself. The man is trying to get you to incriminate yourself, and so far, I must say, he is failing. But ludicrously!'

'And, for God's sake!' protested Johnny.' The boy must have been about seven years old. How tenacious do you think a child can be?'

'Oh, I'm not suggesting it's been on his mind all this time as a filial duty, not at all. But when the man unexpectedly turns up here in the person of this great man Chatrier, right here on the spot, rubbing shoulders with the son daily as he once did with the father – well, you see there could be a powerful compulsion there.'

Hans sat down slowly, and let out his breath in a fierce sigh. 'I think there could,' he acknowledged grimly. 'But I tell you again, until you just told me yourself, I had not the least idea that Chatrier was Antoine Gallet.'

'That may or may not be true, we have only your word for it. But the background is suggestive. Then there is also this added element of your rivalry with Chatrier over Miss Truscott.'

'We are *not* rivals,' protested Hans, flaming. 'You have no right to speak so of Miss Truscott—'

'—and there is the plain fact that you are the last person known to have handled the sword with which Chatrier was killed. Your prints are on both hilt and scabbard. The only other prints found on it are those of Miss Truscott and her father.'

Hans frowned with distaste at the sturdy, well-shaped fingers which had supplied the sample prints to implicate him now more deeply. 'I handled it, of course,' he said. 'But I left it there propped in Hero's doorway, just as she told you, and I did not see it again until after the murder.'

Gisela rose, crushing out her cigarette in the silver ash-tray beside her chair, and came forward to the desk. She had sat all this time in silence, only her eyes ranging from face to face as they talked, and once at least widening and flashing at Hans Selverer in what might have been either a reassurance or a warning. Musgrave had almost forgotten she was there; Marcellina was always the quiet one. He looked up in surprise to find her close at his elbow.

'I think,' she said mildly, 'it is time *I* said something, before you fall too deeply in love with the idea of Mr Selverer's guilt. No doubt

413

you'll come to the conclusion that all women are as unscrupulous as Hero warned you. But I think that won't surprise you.'

Hans was struggling to catch her eye, signalling alarm and entreaty. She let her hand rest upon his shoulder to hold him still and silent.

'He was not the last person known to have handled the rapier, Mr Musgrave. *I* picked it up in the corridor that night. I'd forgotten my fan, and I went back to my dressing-room to get it after I'd sung my aria and made my exit. I have to pass Hero's door. She told you the truth on one point, at least. The rapier had slipped down and rolled into the corridor, and I kicked it accidentally – those enormous skirts, you know, one's feet tend to be unguided missiles. So I picked it up and brought it down with me into the wings.'

'Your prints don't appear on it,' said Musgrave, almost indignantly.

'Chance is so inconsiderate, I am sorry. It's with no evil intent that Marcellina always wears long black lace gloves. I never even thought how useful they were being.'

'And *why* did you pick it up in the first place?'

'It occurred to me suddenly,' she said, looking him calmly in the eye and uttering the words without emphasis, 'to kill Chatrier with it.'

Johnny was on his feet, his hand gripping her arm.

'Gisela, *shut up*!' He turned on Musgrave, who was staring intently, the deep inward gleam of the hunter in his eyes tempered by a certain wild distrust. 'She's trying to confuse the issue to cover everyone else, that's all this is. What she says *can't* be true, you know that already. She was in the arbour with Nan before Chatrier was killed, and she didn't leave it until Tonda screamed and we all came running. You *know* that – you were there, too.'

'I didn't say,' protested Gisela reasonably, 'that I killed him. I said I took the sword because I *thought* of killing him. Oh, no, I didn't *do* it.' She put off Johnny's hand very gently from her arm.

'Then what did you do with the rapier?' demanded Musgrave.

'I propped it outside the left-hand arbour. When I went on-stage I had to hide in that arbour – but you know all the details of the libretto.' She smiled; he had told them so often enough.

'If Barbarina hadn't got bored and wandered off until the finale, as she very well could have done, I was going to send her to fetch something from my dressing-room. If she'd gone already, then the coast would have been clear for me without any trouble. Then I was simply going to walk out at the back of the arbour, pick up the rapier, and kill Figaro with it. In the darkness of our stage forest it wouldn't have been difficult to come up behind him – theoretically, at any rate.

414

And the rapier is a very fine piece of eighteenth-century swordcraft, and extremely sharp, as you must know – it's your Exhibit A. In practice, of course,' she said, a tremor convulsing her calm face for a moment, 'I expect I shouldn't even have found it possible when it came to the point. It didn't arise, anyhow. Barbarina was still there, and before I got rid of her I felt out at the back of the arbour, where I'd propped the sword, and it wasn't there. It hadn't fallen, or anything. It was gone. So I just stayed there with Nan, and didn't do anything deadly, after all. And I think I was glad.'

'But if this is true,' said Musgrave, thin and sharp, 'anyone could have taken the thing. Any one of you.'

The case was wide open again. Selverer was still a possibility, but not more so than any of the others who darted about backstage in the fevered comings and goings of that last act. And even Truscott himself – he had been in his box just before Susanna embarked on '*Deh vieni*,' but he had certainly not been there by the time she withdrew into the trees at the end of it. He'd been prowling back and forth all through the performance like a lost soul.

'Well, not quite anyone,' said Gisela. 'I couldn't, Nan couldn't, and Tonda couldn't. But it certainly leaves it rather open.'

Musgrave looked up at her in silence for a long moment, and then asked the final, the inevitable question. She was quite ready for it. The large eyes stared back at him unwaveringly.

'Why? Because I could not tolerate that he should disrupt the lives of others as he once disrupted mine, and go on all his life ruining and hurting people. I don't suppose you followed up the record of his marriage far enough to find out his wife's maiden name? A mistake, Mr Musgrave. As you said, the international musical world is not such a large one. She was also a singer from Alsace. Her name was Gisela Salberg.'

For one instant of utter silence they stared at her and held their breath.

'She'd been very much in love with him,' said Gisela, low-voiced. 'You can imagine what it did to her, when he threw her to the wolves to save his own skin, and snatched back even his name from her. Yes,' she said bitterly smiling, reading the mind that calculated frantically behind Musgrave's startled eyes, 'isn't that a wonderful motive for murder? Better than the one you dug up against Hans, and far better than the one you were trying to foist on to Doctor Hassilt. What a pity, what a pity Nan was with me in the arbour every moment of the time!'

Chapter Five

Musgrave came and went by the stage-door these days, like a member of the company who had rights there; yet most unlike, for wherever he passed a slight chill followed, a stillness and a hush. Hands froze on what they were doing, voices dried up for a moment in contracted throats, heads turned stealthily, stiffly, trying not to be caught at it. He was like walking bad luck, the evil eye on two legs. Mateo, who was Maltese and not quite canny himself, actually marked a thumb-sign surreptitiously on his thigh as the alien went by.

Playing solo in Sam's box during their lunch hour, they felt him enter, and the cards hung suspended over the table until he had passed. Hero, sitting in with a hand while Stoker Bates shopped for his missus, looked up with the ace poised in her hand, and could not put it down until he had gone past the glass hatch and vanished. It was wrong, it was cruel; he wasn't even a bad fellow, and yet they all felt leagued against him, drawn into a solid phalanx of enmity as soon as he appeared. Why? Did they really believe one of their own people had killed Chatrier?

Yes, they did. They really believed it. She felt that intensely as she played her card and made her solo. Did they also have clearly conceived ideas about who the murderer could be? When she came to consider it, she was sure that they had; but they were hiding them even from themselves, and no two of them had quite the same theory.

Stoker Bates, by his more than usually protective attitude, favoured herself. She had never thought of it in that light before, and it caused a shudder of mingled horror and gratitude to run down her spine. They would love her even if she'd killed a man! They would close in round her more formidably than ever. Then was that why Sam was following Johnny about so faithfully, more than ever like a devoted guard-dog?

The shadow had withdrawn from them, and the silence went with him. Only Codger, who experienced their fears and forebodings dimly as a tremor of dread shaking his flesh, sat uncomprehending and mute knitting away industriously at Hans Selverer's blue-grey sweater, his large, confiding and yet unfathomable eyes fixed upon her. She was Johnny's; in the absence of Johnny himself she represented him, and Codger watched her jealously and lovingly, the sum and symbol of faithfulness.

'I thought we might be shut of *him*,' said Mateo, dark eyes following the sound of Musgrave's feet along the corridor while his head never turned, 'once the inquest was over.'

'He hasn't found his bit o' ribbon yet,' said Sam, shuffling the cards. 'Likely he never will, and we shall have him running round grey-headed, give him time, like Lord Lovell looking for his bride. That isn't the way I like the ghost to walk. Your call, Chippy.'

'*Is* the inquest over?' asked Hero, sorting her cards between her fingers with expert speed. 'I thought they adjourned it.'

'They did, love, for a week, but the week was up yesterday. They brought it in murder against persons unknown, like you'd expect.'

'And it *was* my sword that killed him?' Somehow at the back of her mind she'd always preserved a dream-like hope that it wouldn't be.

'There was a lot of technical bits about the wound, this wide and that deep, and such and such an angle, and how it penetrated the heart, and all that stuff. But yes, that's what it added up to. Why, what else were you thinking might have done it?'

'Oh, I don't know, I just thought you never *know*. I'd rather it hadn't been my sword. I don't think I want it back.'

'You stop thinking too much about that and too little about the hand you're holding, or these thugs'll have the dress allowance out of your pocket. You got a winning streak if you keep your mind on it. Come on, now, call!'

'Abundance!' she said, rallying valiantly.

'Make it!'

She made it. It looked as if the wool fund, where her winnings invariably ended up, was going to be in pocket as a result of Stoker's shopping expedition. She had to take their money if she won, it was a matter of honour.

'Who d'you reckon *he* thinks done it?' asked Mateo, low-voiced, jerking his head after the enemy.

'I wish I knew. Mate, I only wish I knew.'

'He'd like to think it was Miss Salberg, only he can't because the young 'un was with her the whole time. And he'd like to think it was

417

Johnny, if he could prove Johnny knew about this bloke being the bastard who did the dirty on her years ago, but he can't. And he'd like to think it was the maestro, only he was tinkling the blooming continuo until the balloon went up. And he'd like to think it was his lordship the Count, only he didn't get the right sort of rise out of him when he sprang it on him Chatrier was this other fellow. Or any two of 'em or any three of 'em in conspiracy,' said Chips morosely, collecting tricks with a large brown hand that was minus the upper joints of three fingers, 'he's not fussy. And I'm not saying Johnny might not have felt like doing it, for that matter, *if* he'd known.'

'Shut up about it,' said Sam, drawing hard at his foul old briar, that gurgled and plopped like the crater of a small boiling geyser, 'and deal the last hand. It'll have to be the last. You lot o' layabouts have got to get old Astro-what's-her-name's flying machine assembled before to-morrow morning's rehearsal, as well as three major shifts to-night. And it'd better work, too! Our Queen of the Night's in a bad enough temper already since she ain't been speaking to Miss Gennoni. If that thing drops her we've all had it!'

They played out the hand, and went off wrangling about the drop of the cards. Hero lingered still, sitting by Codger's side and stroking out the curling grey-blue sleeve that dangled from his needles. She talked to him softly and sadly, her heart not quite in it; and he made the low, loving, animal noises that were as near as he could get to speech.

She was watching the glass hatch and listening for the click of the stage-door opening.

Hans had hardly spoken to her for six days, and never once asked her to go out to lunch with him. He was kind and correct, and a little distant, and impossible to pin down; and she felt in her heart that she'd made a hash of it again, and made him dislike her for life. It seemed she could have had a gentle, sexless intimacy with him, and she hadn't been satisfied with that; and now all she'd got in its place was complete rejection. He just didn't like spoiled, self-willed girls. He'd take care of them if they'd got themselves into a spot, but not out of love or even liking, only because he was the conscientious sort. And be glad to drop them as soon as he could. Small blame to him, either.

Sam patted her shoulder, and said: 'Stop fretting, kid, it can't go on for ever. Mr Nosey Musgrave'll get tired and go away, just give him time.'

'Sam,' she said, letting her head rest gratefully against his hip, 'Johnny couldn't really have done it, could he?'

'Who am I to say who could and who couldn't do things? We all could, very likely, if the chips happened to fall a certain way. But what's better than couldn't – Johnny didn't. You keep hold o' that, and never mind anything else.'

'Oh, Sam! And it's all my fault, isn't it? I'm no good to Johnny, and I'd be no good . . .'

She didn't finish it, because she had caught back Hans Selverer's name in time; and she never heard Sam's indignant abuse and reassurance, because the click of the stage-door slamming open had brought her to her feet instantly, eyes brightening wistfully, ears pricked.

The step was the right step. She was out of the door and walking nonchalantly along the passage before Sam could blink away the dazzle of enlightenment.

'Oh, hallo!' said Hero brightly, slowing her step and continuing to occupy almost the centre of the corridor, so that he should not be able to pass her politely, and speak briefly, and hurry on.

'Hallo!' said Hans perforce, curbing his pace to hers because there was no way of escape. The small, constrained frown did not leave his brow, but it shook for a moment, as though he would have liked to smile, and dared not. He was stiff and, she felt, wary. He kept his chin up and his eyes forward as though it might be dangerous to look at her. Taking no chances, she thought dolefully. But she tried her best.

'Have a nice lunch?'

She disliked that as soon as it was out; it sounded too much like a reproof for not asking her to join him. But what else was there neutral and safe to talk about while they went through the difficult approach steps? My God, what we've come to, she thought dismally; we even talk about the weather.

'Yes, thank you. And you?'

'Johnny had it brought in to-day, nobody can get him away from the sets for next year's *Rosenkavalier*. He's up there with Mr Fawcett now, they've got all the little pieces out, moving and assembling them like kids with a toy train. They're nice!' said Hero, warming into a flush of hope and pleasure. 'Would you like to go up and see them?'

'I would, of course – but – not now, perhaps. Franz wants me for just half an hour, and then I must go back into town. Perhaps to-morrow.' His voice was careful and gentle, feeling its way painfully, trying not to hurt. He still did not look at her.

'But Franz is up there, too, he's as bad as Johnny. He wants everything different. They always fight about sets.'

They had reached the shadowy corner at the end of the corridor. She turned her face up to him gallantly, but the smile had never given her more trouble. His arm touched her breast inadvertently for an instant, and she felt him shrink from the contact.

'I – no, not now, Hero. Excuse me!'

She turned squarely to face him then, a faint flush of returning indignation colouring her cheeks.

'All right, I know. I'm sorry, I shouldn't have pushed you into having to say it. You don't want anything to do with me off-stage. I can understand it, but . . . I just hoped . . . I know it's all my fault,' she said, 'and I know what you think of me, but I thought at least we might try making the best of it. I *am* trying—'

'Hero,' he said agitatedly, 'you *don't* know! I *don't* blame you. How could you think—?'

He wrenched his head aside to break the compulsion his eyes felt to devour her too openly.

'To-morrow,' he said desperately and not very coherently, and slipped past her and went up the stairs as fast as dignity would let him, and perhaps a little faster.

The sets for *Figaro* came out of store after a fortnight's banishment, and were assembled ready for the smooth transitions on which the deck crew of the *Hellespont* prided themselves.

Johnny prowled the wings from piece to piece, his eye all the time on Musgrave, who lurked in the orchestra pit, desultorily pulling the first act design to bits and reassembling it nearer to his heart's desire. He made no attempt to pass unnoticed, there was nothing stealthy about him; sometimes Johnny wondered if he really came in the hope of discovering anything new about the death of Marc Chatrier, or whether his monomania had fettered him for ever to the only opera house to which he had ever had completely free access. It was a nightmare thought, that they might have him for ever, the voice of something too extreme to be called criticism, something close to disintegration.

'—all that ring-o'-roses round the arm-chair, that's a pure comedy convention. You ruin it by all this realism – having an elaborate love-seat really big enough to hide in. It's too heavy-handed. And the realistically darkened pine-grove in the last act – all those *commedia del arte* characters in disguise don't really have to carry *conviction*.'

'They do in this theatre,' said Johnny, his pulses tingling again at the thought of the darkness in that pine-grove. But for that insistence on conviction Marc Chatrier would have been still alive. A little more light, and no one would have dared.

'You're taking Mozart out of his world.'

'All worlds belonged to Mozart,' said Johnny. 'All inhabited worlds, anyhow. The word is universal. And you know what? . . . That's why he vanished. His body couldn't be in one place. "The dewdrop slips into the shining sea." The lad's everywhere.'

'I always understood that as meaning the loss of the dewdrop,' said Musgrave with his faintly superior near-smile, threading his way between the angular, silent music-stands.

'You would!' said Johnny. 'It's one of the fundamental divisions of humanity – like warm people and cold people, and people who eat the top of their iced-cake first and those who save it till last.'

He was out of sight of his antagonist at that moment, the defence in depth of the standing sets between them. He stood under the arched entrance of the left-hand arbour, where Nan and Gisela had retired that night of the tragedy, and inadvertently given each other the firmest alibi possible. A series of flat washes on canvas under full light, a magic of branches and deep shadows by stage lighting, and within, light or dark, this framework of stiffened canvas and hessian on two-by-four.

He moved deep into its recesses from the lecturing voice that pursued him, his fingertips running affectionately up and down the woodwork and dimpling the fabric. Here at the back Gisela had reached out her hand and felt for the sword. He still could not believe in the strange events of that night, or rather his mind believed in them but his senses could not adjust themselves to the idea of Gisela steeling herself, putting out her gloved hand for the weapon she had laid ready.

He repeated the gesture. Nothing. And then she was free. She, but not the other person, the one who had lifted the burden from her.

He drew back his hand. Close to his eyes as he turned, wavering gently in a faint current of air, a floating thread of red, fine as a hair, signalled from the crevice between the wood and the canvas. A thread of frayed silk, one strand from a thread, rather. He pulled it, and it parted at a touch, clinging to his fingers with the living vigour of silk. But short and bright, a thicker end of blue followed it into the light, a down of white, the infinitesimally tiny corner of a scrap of material.

He inserted his fingertips very carefully, and felt along the folded edge of a small, flat thing wedged tightly between canvas and stay, close to where they were fastened together. The feel of the silk, vibrant, organic, tingled through the nerves of his hand, and set the hairs on his wrist erect. Folded in three, fine as gossamer, it took up very little room. He smoothed even the last delicate filament out of sight. He dared not do anything else; the didactic voice was drawing nearer, coming to look for him; Musgrave was out of the orchestra pit, and up on the stage.

Johnny went out to meet him, calm of face and empty of eye, went past him and stood in mid-stage looking round upon his assembled toys.

'The trouble with you, Musgrave,' he said, 'is that you've lost the capacity for honest, generous delight, and because you can't enjoy it you're damned if anyone else shall. The critical faculty to you means a weapon by which you can spoil things for other people, people who would have been quite happy with them, and rightly, if you'd kept your mouth shut.'

'Oh, I know,' said Musgrave, following him closely, grinning the superior grin that meant his blood was up, 'you'd have us all become as little children.'

Johnny had got him to the other side of the stage now, step by step away firom the tiny folded thing hidden in the arbour. Keep the argument going, and he was like a hooked fish. But how difficult it is to argue when your own mind is caught inextricably in another matter, a matter of life and death, which must at all costs be kept secret.

'Oh, no, I wouldn't say that,' he objected, eyeing his opponent critically. 'You must have been a horrid child, come to think of it, for ever sticking pins in other kids' balloons, and all for their own good. No, my dear chap, you stay as adult as you please, and wallow in your chilly intellectual experiences. But don't espect to enter the kingdom of heaven, either.'

Off the stage now. Get him well away from it, ask him up to the office, if necessary, to look at the *Rosenkavalier* toys. '*Pastiche*,' he'd call that marvellous, inspired heir to *Figaro*, without doubt, but let him. Anything, as long as his attention was never for a moment drawn to the arbour.

'I shall be staying through your performance of *Figaro* to-night,' said Musgrave, pacing elbow to elbow with him along the corridor.

'By all means. Use my box, if you'd like to.'

'Thanks all the same, but if it's all one to you, I'd like to hang around backstage.'

He would! Johnny saw him for ever looming up, angrily smiling, between him and the small, damning thing that must be extracted and destroyed. There'd be no touching it again until to-night's performance was over; but some time, praise be, the man must go home and sleep.

Alone behind closed doors, Johnny sat down to think it out. Twice he reached out for the telephone to call Gisela, and once he even began to dial her number, only to drop the instrument in its cradle again without completing the call.

What, after all, could he tell her? And what could he ask her?

He knew now where the length of embroidered ribbon torn from Hero's baldric had vanished to, he knew where to lay his hand on it this minute, if only the watch-dog below could be called off for a quarter of an hour. Poppies, cornflowers and wheat embroidered on white silk and edged with gold thread, part of a ribbon from a Bohemian bridal headdress, converted to serve as trappings for a child prince's dress sword, nearly two centuries ago. His fingers still burned with the touch of it, soft and fierce and clinging.

And no one but Gisela could have put it there.

That was a certainty. She had stood there concealed during Tonda's aria, and it seemed she had known already that she must get rid of this delicate, dangerous thing at once. She had to hide it there, where she was, before she went out to face the disaster that had fallen upon them all. It could easily be done without Nan's noticing, there in the dark.

Once done, the thing could not be undone; Musgrave's men were always about the place, there was nothing to be done but leave the thing where it was and show no interest in it, and hope that the enemy would go away. But the enemy had not gone away.

She had hidden it. She had known that she must hide it. She had known the reason for its importance, because she had known, she must have known, that Chatrier was already dead. Whatever might be the truth about that night, Gisela had lied.

* * *

The final curtain came down on a *Figaro* as disappointing as it seemed to have been successful. Eight or nine curtain calls, a conservatory of flowers; but Johnny knew better, and so did all his team, even the brave and unlucky substitute Figaro who realised only too well that he was out of his class and struggling against the odds. The audience had the wrong feel about it; half of the seats, at least, were occupied by people who would not normally have gone near a Mozart opera, and had done so now only out of morbid curiosity, dropping in on the scene and setting of a sensational tragedy for kicks.

The same attitude would be reflected in the more popular notices, and the better ones would hold fastidiously aloof and be more critical than usual to avoid joining a fashionable stream. Unsatisfactory to everyone. Johnny was sorry for his Figaro. The boy had worked hard and done as well as it was in him to do, and it's bitter having to swallow the knowledge that your best isn't good enough.

He went out of his way to say a few words of appreciation and comfort to him at the end of it; not too effusively, because the boy was by no means a fool. I could make a fine artist of him, thought Johnny, if I could have him for a couple of seasons and find him the parts that are within his range. Why should he have to put up with being a bad Figaro when he has the makings of a pretty good Masetto?

The house was emptying rapidly, the receding hum of satisfied excitement, familiar but tonight curiously off-key, vibrated in Johnny's ears as he stood in the wings. The members of the orchestra were clattering out of their pit through the low doors, hoisting their instruments and drifting away to put on their coats and make for home. Their talk was of the iniquity of the licensing hours in these parts of London's outer fringe, and where you could get a drink notwithstanding, and the horse that fell down in the three-thirty, and Spurs' chances in the European Cup.

That was all right with Johnny; he knew all about the small realities as well as the great ones, and saw no quarrel between them. Some of Mozart's jokes were distinctly off-colour, and he had all, repeat all, the attributes of humanity. But the music – oh, the music!

The lady harpist, of course, was more genteel; she knitted in the intervals while the others played pontoon.

Johnny stood saying: 'Good night! . . . Good night! . . . Good night!' to this one and that, and letting the evening disintegrate round him. He had seen no sign of Musgrave since the curtain fell. There had been three other plain-clothes men about the place, but none of them was in sight now.

Johnny set a course across the stage, in such a way that it would bring him close to the back of the left-hand arbour; and there under cover of the canvas he halted to light a cigarette. No one paid any particular attention to him, no one was close.

He knew already what he would find, but he slid his fingers between the wood and the canvas, and felt upwards to the spot where the folded ribbon had rested.

There was nothing there now. Only an infinitesimally tiny fibre of white silk, three-quarters of an inch of thistledown, clung to the edge of the two-by-four where it had been.

She had had to wait a long time for her opportunity, but *Figaro* had provided it at last. The same hand that had hidden Hero's torn baldric had retrieved it again during the last act.

He made his way slowly and miserably to Gisela's dressing-room, knowing that he could not let it rest at that. He had never before hesitated to knock at her door; this time it cost him an effort. And even when she called him in, smiling over her shoulder from tired, dark eyes, he knew that he couldn't begin to ask her about it. After all the time they'd known each other, suddenly he found himself at a loss with her.

'Well?' said Gisela. 'How did it go?'

She was still in Marcellina's black gown, with the stiffly boned bodice and the tiny waist. He came to her back, and stood looking down into the steady eyes that watched him from the mirror. She smiled, and he returned the smile; which of them had to make the greater effort was a question.

'As well as we could expect, I suppose. Pretty well, really. After what's happened we couldn't hope for an honest audience.'

'It will pass,' said Gisela, as though she could find no better comfort for him or for herself.

'I'm sorry, I thought you'd be dressed. I'll go away, shall I?'

He let his hand rest in the lace that made her milky shoulders whiter. She turned her head a little, her lips parted and her lashes low on her cheeks, as though for a word or one more touch she would have laid her cheek against his hand and rested so. He had never seen her look so tired. There were tiny, fine lines at the corners of her mouth, others like them round her eyes. His heart melted in him with so sudden and sad a fondness that he could hardly speak.

'Oh, girl, if only you'd told me!'

How often had he said that to her in the last few days? And how often looked it, even when he was silent?

'Oh, my dear, don't! How could I? By the time I knew he was coming it was too late, we couldn't have gone back on the contract. What would have been the use of making you miserable, and starting all that again? I thought we could make it work. I thought I could carry it.'

'But if I'd known! I'd never have let you.' He drew back hopelessly, sighing. 'I'll go away,' he said. 'You get dressed, and I'll take you home.'

'No, don't go, you sit down here. I'll manage.'

Her wardrobe had large double doors; she retired behind their shelter, and he heard the long zipper of her gown shirr softly downwards as she unfastened it.

'Hero was a little subdued to-night,' said her muffled voice from under the hooped petticoat as she lifted it over her head.

'Aren't we all?' he said bitterly.

'She did very well. But a little muted, all the same.'

Her handbag lay on the dressing-table, close to his hand. He had already known for some minutes what he was going to do, but doing it was one of the hardest thing he'd ever undertaken. His body was between her and his hands, so quiet there on the dressing-table close to the black calf bag. His broad shoulders would hide both the act and the image of the act in the mirror; from her, not from him. He would have to live with it, and with himself after it, as well as he could. And it might be all for nothing. A silly, obvious, frightening place to put something so dangerous, but women are queer about handbags, they regard them as sacrosanct by some special magic, even apart from any granted privacy.

'You're very quiet,' said Gisela, installing Marcellina's dress on its padded hanger, and reaching for her own black jersey suit. 'What's the matter? More than usual, I mean,' she added wryly, for the weight of the shadow that burdened them all had become daily harder to bear.

'Nothing. Same complaint as Butch's, I suppose – just subdued.'

His fingers eased open the clasp of the bag, very gingerly for fear of a sound she would be sure to recognise; but the rustle of the voluminous lace and taffeta skirts in the wardrobe covered his offence.

She was a tidy person, even her handbag was a model of order. Make-up, comb, purse, keys, handkerchief, cigarette case, lighter, two or three opened letters. Nothing more. Yes! In one of the letters, something soft and smooth that wasn't paper. He parted the folds, and there it was, the sudden bright, burning gaiety of gold and red and blue and white, putting out fine, wavering filaments to fasten on his skin like tentacles.

Between forefinger and middle finger he drew it out and unfolded it. Seven or eight inches of it, with a torn hem at one end, and strands of coloured threads trailing at the other; and obliquely crossing it, approximately midway, a straight, narrow line of dark, brownish-red, hardly thicker than a pen-stroke, and like a pen-stroke more strongly marked at its edges, where it frayed out a little, like an ink-stain.

A thin line of blood, incomprehensible but unmistakable, the blood of Marc Chatrier.

Chapter Six

He heard her light step behind him, and felt the cold sweat break in the palms of his hands with shame and agitation. The ribbon was folded back into its envelope, the clasp of the bag closed, everything as she had left it, except for the stinging colour in Johnny's cheeks. The faint waft of *muguet* that shook out of her movements reached him and set him quivering. He had never been so acutely aware of her as now, when she couldn't confide in him, and he didn't know what to do to help her.

Her eyes met his in the mirror. He got up slowly, and turned to face her. For a long moment they were out of words. She hugged the collar of her fur coat to her pale cheeks, and picked up her bag.

'Johnny . . .' she said in a muted gasp.

He thought for one moment that she was going to pour it all out to him, but he should have known better; all she wanted was an hour off, time to regroup before the next engagement.

'Johnny, take me out somewhere. Anywhere, I don't care. Let's go and have supper at the Mezzodi Club, or something.'

'If you like,' he said, startled. 'If you're not too tired.'

'I'm not *tired*. I'm just wild to go somewhere else and do something else, and not see Inspector Musgrave's face while I'm doing it.'

'I'll send Hero home with Tom,' said Johnny eagerly, 'and we'll borrow her Aston and run into London.'

'You don't mind?'

'Mind? I'll be glad. I need to get out of here, too.'

And that was true enough, perhaps, but the answer to his problem wasn't going to be found in London any more than here, and how could he ever speak to her of what he knew? For years he'd relied on Gisela, worked side by side with her, thought aloud to her without a qualm, shown her the worst of him as well as the best, and trusted her to accept both and make do with him as he was. And she'd never attempted to restrain or change him, but neither had she ever withdrawn her loyalty and friendship from him.

He took her arm as they went along the corridor to Hero's room. The handbag nestled between their bodies, the symbol of her silence and solitude. She hadn't given him the trust he'd always given to her. And how could he wrest from her what she hadn't offered? There was no way round it. Nonplussed and miserable, he held her gingerly, afraid even the touch of his hand might betray how much he knew.

Where did he stand now? What was he to do? How was he to help her if she wouldn't ask for his help? And he felt her there against his side, so slender and so quiet, dearer than ever he'd imagined she could be, a revelation. She must be preserved, at all costs. Nothing was any good to him without her.

'We're going out to supper,' said Johnny, putting his head in at Hero's door. 'You don't mind going home with Tom, do you, Butch, and lending us the Aston Martin for to-night? Nella will have a drink waiting for you, and a sandwich. And sleep well, love. You haven't got a rehearsal to-morrow, you stay in bed.'

'Anybody'd think I was an invalid,' said Hero affectionately, and bundled her coat into his hands for the pleasure, as she said, of being helped into it by her favourite male. How easy it had been to recover the old terms with Hero.

'It's just that you've looked a bit down, gal, the last few days.' He wrapped his arms round her with the coat and hugged her warmly, her rumpled fair hair against his cheek. 'Anything the matter?'

'Everybody in this theatre,' said Hero resignedly, 'seems to be going round asking everybody else if anything's the matter. Not really, darling. We had a murder on the premises, that's all. Funny, the way it upsets people. You'd never expect it.' But she turned and hugged him in return. 'Sorry! I'm all right, duck, don't you worry. You run off and spend all night dancing, or something. Do you both good.'

They took her down with them. Her presence there between them on the way afforded them a kind of ease, because she put immediate confidences out of their reach, and enabled them to make believe fondly that but for her innocence they could have spoken freely.

In the foyer Sam was waiting for them, and as soon as they appeared he bellowed for Codger, who came running jealously to guard his privileges.

'He's outside,' said Sam, in the tone which could only refer to Musgrave. 'Been standing there ten minutes or more, swopping news with a couple of his buddies. Watch out he ain't got a cordon round the house when you get home.'

'We're not going home, Sam. Butch here is, she has to get her beauty sleep. But us young ones are going out on the tiles.'

'Prodigal parent I've got,' said Hero, gallantly playing up to him. She didn't even look round for Hans Selverer; he'd be gone long ago, and in any case, he'd shown pretty clearly, for all his half-hearted denials, what he thought of her, and on what terms he wanted to continue his association with her. Nobody, thought Hero sadly, is getting much out of this deal. 'You come home tight and dent my car,' she said warningly, 'and see what you get.'

Sam and Codger followed them out to the Bentley. It was early November, and moist and mournful, with a thin slime on the streets and a thin mist in the air, so that all the lights had faint grey aureoles round them. The decorative trees that fringed the semi-circular forecourt of the theatre had long since turned crimson, and there had been no frost as yet to bring down the leaves; but the sodium lighting and the moist air took from them all their colour and texture, and they hung shivering like faintly luminous grey rags on the branches, silent and sad.

In the apron of light the Bentley stood drawn up at the foot of the steps, with Tom Connard idling beside it, his great hands in his pockets, his enormous jut of bony brow ape-like over the kindest and most knowing eyes in the world. The cigarette that clung to his lower lip was whipped smartly out and trodden into the thin mud as soon as he saw his skipper approaching. The details of their relationship were laid down by Tom, not Johnny; Johnny had never been a stickler for the hierarchies even in the Navy, and not much of a respecter of ranks and persons himself, for that matter.

There were still a few other cars about the forecourt, just warming up and switching on their sidelights to drive out to the road. And there was Musgrave's black Austin, pulled right round into a strategic position close to the exit end of the sweep of tarmac, where he could make a quick, smooth and unobtrusive departure at whatever moment he pleased. Even the lights tailed out there into dimness, and the glisten from every moist surface of road and coachwork and kerb and masonry tended to blend the car deep into its background.

Midway between the Bentley and his own car, Musgrave himself stood on the bottom step talking to two of his men. As though on an expected signal, he broke off his colloquy as Johnny reached the pavement, and walked away towards his Austin at a brisk but casual pace.

Johnny's thumbs pricked. The way the car was positioned might be the fruit of experience and instinct, the lingering until he came and the departure when he came might mean nothing but that Musgrave wanted to assure himself that events were pursuing their normal course this night as on other nights. But added together they suggested a more exact and deliberate concern with his movements than he liked to contemplate. For himself he didn't care, it could hardly matter less how much sleep Musgrave lost over him; but the little, folded thing in Gisela's bag turned his heart sick when he thought of it.

'You've only got me to-night, Tom,' said Hero. 'We're swopping cars for once, Johnny's going on the town.'

'Very good, miss,' said Connard, generously giving way so that Codger could open the door for her.

'No, the front, Codger, love, I'm going to ride with Tom. That's fine!' She turned back for a moment to offer Johnny a chilly cheek. 'Good night, darling! Good night, Gisela!'

'Hey, how about your keys?' said Johnny.

'In the car. I garaged it, so I didn't bother to bring them out.'

Codger slammed the door firmly upon her, pulled to make doubly sure his work was good, and stood back, beaming. The Bentley pulled away. Round to the left the black Austin had its lights on and its engine running and was heeling round very, very gently towards the road. It let the Bentley go by, halt at the exit, and turn majestically into the open road. It had seemed that the Austin was about to follow, but it did not. Its exhaust continued to breathe faint blue fumes for a moment, its engine to purr experimentally, then it was drawn more closely into the side again, and the hum of the motor ceased. In a moment the driver's door opened.

So that was it. And now they knew where they stood; but at least Hero was off home out of it. He didn't want her, he wasn't interested in her. As soon as he saw that she was alone in the car apart from the driver, he abandoned the Bentley. He was waiting for other game.

'The bastard!' said Sam softly between his teeth, watching him start back towards them. The two plain-clothes men had turned and mounted the steps into the theatre to keep the watchman company. It wouldn't be difficult to find something that ought to be said, in ordinary courtesy to the owner of the place.

Johnny thought of Gisela and himself shut into the car shoulder to shoulder, as close as lovers and as far apart as the poles, unable to communicate, unable even to face this danger as one creature, as they had always faced everything from their first flight together in the dark. Always they had had that unity. Even the broken, shocked creature he had snatched out of the ambushed transport had instinctively fastened in him the last remaining root of her faith in man, from which the whole marvellous plant had sprung again. Now they had nothing. He, who had always taken it for granted that he would be the first person she'd come to for help, was powerless now to help her.

Suddenly such a desolation of rage seized him that he shook from head to foot, and the approaching figure of Musgrave quivered before his eyes like a broken reflection in a pool.

'Blast him!' he said through his teeth, in a muted howl of frustration and despair. 'I wish somebody'd do me the favour of knocking *him* off!'

For that one instant he meant it; it was like a convulsion of pain jerking through him, turning his blood to gall. Then it was ebbing, and he shook with the feebleness and shame it left behind. He licked his lips, and the bitter taste of sweat was there, and his forehead was dewed with cold.

'You don't have to worry, son,' said Sam at his shoulder, only just above his breath. 'There's nothing he can do. You hear, Johnny?' A hard old fist rapped at his ribs behind, knocking home the text. 'You'll be all right,' said Sam.

'Famous last words,' said Johnny, with a grin that hurt him, but looked all right.

The weakness and nausea ebbed away after the mutilating rage; he took hold of the affair as it was, and stopped thinking of what it should have been, because Musgrave was very close now, and there was no time left. He didn't think anything was due to happen here; he thought Musgrave was more interested in letting them go their own way for the moment, and waiting for things to happen of themselves, provided always that he was there to see. But because of the ribbon in Gisela's handbag the danger was acute. She couldn't be left alone with Musgrave now, not even for the time it took to fetch the car round from the garage.

'Sam,' he said, in a voice now quite calm, 'would you mind giving Norrie a ring and asking him to bring Butch's car round? And don't you bother to come out again, it's chilly out here.'

Luckily Musgrave probably hadn't learned enough about the Leander Theatre yet to realise how out of character it was for Johnny to ask to have his transport brought round for him at all when Tom Connard wasn't there; ordinarily he'd have been round the corner himself after it, like a terrier after a rat. But those were the aspects of things that Musgrave didn't pick up so quickly.

'We'll be all right,' agreed Johnny softly, and returned Sam his nudge in the ribs to start him up the steps.

He looked round then for Codger, but Codger had already disappeared. He'd be back; no good telling *him* not to bother, shutting Johnny safely in the car was one of the main moments of his day, and he wouldn't care which car it was, either.

'I think I ought to tell you,' said Musgrave, blandly arriving, 'that I'm leaving a man here overnight. You've no objections?'

'No, I've no objections,' said Johnny. 'Would it be indiscreet of me to ask whether you're expecting something to happen?'

'Not expecting. But no harm in hoping. And he can put in his time studying stage furnishings, without the complications of rehearsals and performance going on all round him.'

'He has my permission to poke wherever he fancies. I hope he likes his tea strong? That's the way he'll get it if he hasn't brought his own. Or there might be stout, if he's lucky, Martin isn't a beer man. What is this, a last fling?'

'We never give up,' said Musgrave, with a not unpleasant smile. 'I know you gave me a blanket permission to go ahead at the beginning, but I thought I'd just mention it.' He drew back a step, his eyes slipping smoothly from face to face. 'Good night then, Mr Truscott! Good night, Miss Salberg!' And yet another step. He was turning on his heel as he said: 'A very creditable performance to-night.'

'The patronising bastard!' said Johnny under his breath, a faint but controlled gust of the old fury shaking him. He had it in better focus now, he knew that by rights it did not belong to Musgrave. But the ache within him would not be eased. She stood silent in his arm, so pale and mute and calm that he could not bear it. If only she'd let him in!

The Aston Martin came sliding sweetly round into the arc of tarmac, and Norrie, who looked after all the cars and lived over the

433

garage, hopped out of it grinning with pleasure, and held open the door for them. Poor old Codger was missing his treat; in his own way he'd complain of it for days, and everyone would have to devise new excitements for him in compensation. Johnny expected him to come darting down the steps anxiously at the last moment, but he must have been somewhere out of sight and earshot, safe with Sam, for he did not appear.

Musgrave was just climbing leisurely into his Austin as the sports car slithered by and halted at the exit. Very nice timing, hardly a pretence at all, only a cloak of decency for the benefit of both hunted and hunter. Not a disguise, merely clothing. It argued at least a kind of respect for his opponent.

Johnny swung the car left, towards London. Traffic was light, and the moist night curiously silent. They might have been a thousand miles from the city, and yet all the unpeopled trappings of town life were strung along the way, eerie and pale, livid in the ghostly lights on either side of them. A few walkers on the footpaths, but so few that they, too, were muted and distant, like ghosts.

'Speak, girl!' said Johnny, his eyes on the mirror. 'How will I know I've got a woman with me, if she won't talk?'

The Austin had rounded the curve into the road after him, and was following sedately on his tail, not bothering to lie close.

'He's following us,' said Gisela, small and still against his shoulder.

'I know. Don't worry, I can leave him standing once we're in the decontrolled stretches.'

He was driving very demurely, because he had to think as well as drive, and because he wanted her, with all his heart, to take this opportunity of confiding in him. There was nothing he wouldn't do for her, if only she'd let him, but she was still mute, she asked for nothing.

What was he to do if she still shut him out? What *was* he to do about this woman of whom he found he was so damned fond?

If she wouldn't talk, that made his thinking all the more urgent. She had lied, and she was hiding evidence. Not evidence that would in itself convict anyone of murder, but extremely suggestive evidence, none the less; and more damning than the thing itself was the act of hiding it, and the persistence and length of her silence about it. The ribbon had been torn from the baldric of the sword used to kill Chatrier, and it had Chatrier's blood on it.

And it had been found where only she could have hidden it.

So the provenance of the thing alone made it legitimate to begin to reason from the premise: *If* she killed her husband . . .

He went on from there; the Austin all the while following him at a civil distance.

If she killed her husband, then it cannot have been after she entered the arbour, for from that point on she was with Nan Morgan until after Tonda fell over the body and screamed. That is absolute, whatever objections there may be to it.

Therefore Figaro was dead *before she entered she arbour*.

But he sang his two asides afterwards. No, *he* didn't, because he couldn't have done, he was dead, that's given. Correct the former statement: *Somebody* sang his two asides after she entered the arbour. There was no doubt at all that Figaro had sung his aria himself, for he had had the stage to himself and been in full view of hundreds of people until the end of it, when he retired into the trees. Only those two lines from hiding could have been sung by someone else. Could they? By another baritone, even a good mimic, as so many singers are? Yes, in this case they could. Angry, sardonic asides, hissed in a half-tone, with hardly more personality than a whisper. Yes, another baritone could have done it.

Hans Selverer.

Too clearly, too positively, Johnny saw the whole course of that evening. A joint revenge. Gisela had picked up the rapier as she had said, but she had not disposed of it as she had said, she had quite simply brought it down into the wings in her voluminous skirts, walked into the darkened pine-grove and used the sword on Chatrier, and then calmly gone on-stage; and Hans, with two short lines, had given her an alibi afterwards. Hardly more than five minutes in all had been gained by that act, but it had been enough to place her well clear of suspicion. Perhaps an instantaneous conspiracy, all achieved in those few minutes, perhaps an impulsive act on the spur of the moment, undertaken by Hans of his own volition.

There remained a number of unanswered questions. Why did she take the baldric away with her afterwards? There was blood on it, yes, but all the same, why didn't she just drop it with the scabbard, beside the body There was nothing in the thing itself to connect it with her more than anyone else. If she'd left it there, what would it have told the police more than they knew already? Bloodstain and all?

435

'He's closing up on us,' said Gisela, her chin on her shoulder, her eyes narrowed against the following headlights. The street lighting was thinner here, they had left the shops and cinemas behind, and were threading row upon row of suburban dwellings, with elaborate pubs on every crossroads; but still in such a ghostly quietness. The country has no such solitudes as the less frequented urban spaces at night.

'I know,' said Johnny bitterly. 'And I'm doing forty. He's a cop, he can afford to shove it up above the legal figure, but he needn't think he's going to get me picked up for speeding.'

He couldn't read anything in Gisela's voice; she merely made the remark as though she had gathered from his manner that he might be interested, as though the whole thing had nothing to do with her.

And what resolution and self-control she had shown throughout, simply hiding the ribbon in the best place available to her, and then for a whole fortnight never casting even so much as a glance in its direction, never making the fatal mistake of trying to recover it until the next performance of *Figaro* ensured that she could do so in privacy. And now to have it actually on her person the very night when Musgrave chose to keep her under observation!

If I weren't here, thought Johnny, she could quite simply wind the window down and throw the thing out, once we pull away from Musgrave over the heath. By the time it's lain in the gutter overnight and had a few wheels or feet over it, nobody's even going to stop to look at the colours, much less pick it up. The roadmen would sweep it up with the rubbish, and nobody any the wiser. But she can't do it, because Musgrave isn't the only one who mustn't know. *I* mustn't know. And I can't tell her that I know already, not only because I'm ashamed of spying on her, but even more because having trespassed once doesn't give me any right to trespass again. And he thought again, my God, what am I going to do if he decides to take a chance and pick her up to-night, before she has an opportunity to get rid of it?

The derestriction sign waved its bar dexter at him. The lights, strung thinly here like gold beads on a chain, made scattered islands of radiance in a thicker haze between the trees of the open heath. The houses fell away, and left them in a startling urban solitude.

The Austin was close now, but lying decorously back from the Aston's tail. Johnny's foot went down smoothly, and the little car leapt forward like a hound let off the leash.

He was drawing steadily away when he saw in his wing mirror an abrupt and unaccountable convulsion seize the Austin's lights. They lurched sideways towards the verge, recovered for an instant, and then suddenly plunged wildly across the road at speed, out of control.

Gisela turned in the passenger seat, her fingers cold on his arm, her eyes flaring.

'Johnny, what's happening? He *can't* . . .'

Tyres screamed ineffectively, sliding on the moist road. The crash shivered the night's quiet into fragments. A broken beam of light bowed into the bottom of the hedge; the second eye was blinded. Another crash, dull and echoless, like metal crushing under an enormous foot, followed the first. By then Johnny had braked fiercely, and had his door open and was out of it and running back along the road almost before he had cut the engine. Shuddering, the quietness came back, settling like a startled bird reassured. Only Johnny's running footsteps troubled its placidity. The Austin was still enough now.

Gisela clawed her way out of the car and ran after Johnny, her handbag clutched under her arm; even in emergencies women cling to their handbags.

She saw Johnny come close to the crumple of metal that was the Austin, and baulk at what he saw. He heard her coming behind him, and turned to catch her in his arm.

'Go back! Please! This isn't for you.'

'Yes,' she said, panting, 'I'm all right, I can help. What *happened* to him?'

'God knows!'

He put her behind him, he had no time to argue with her. He turned to the shattered car. It had hit the lamp standard head-on, and wrapped its broken face about the metal base until the bent shaft was nearly hidden in the crumpled sheets of black paintwork and chrome. The left headlight dangled loose from the wreckage, spilling wiring, like a gouged-out eye. The upper part of the standard had snapped clean off and dropped across the roof of the car, crushing it. The front passenger seat was collapsed like a tin can in a press; but when Johnny darted round to the right-hand side he saw that the driver's door lolled open and undamaged, scraping the ground, and a huddled figure prostrate on the road was just dragging his feet after him from the interior of the car.

He hoisted himself up groggily from the slimy tarmac, and got his feet under him, stunned eyes wide open but blind, just in time to mouth a throatful of incoherent sounds and collapse into Johnny's arms. But he had stood, he was alive, death had discarded him.

Johnny took the weight neatly, dropping to put a shoulder under Musgrave's hips. He hoisted him carefully to the grass under the trees at the roadside, propping his head with the scarf he stripped from round his own neck. Musgrave was breathing, hoarsely but regularly, and Johnny could find no obvious signs of injury.

'My God, but some folks are lucky! If that door hadn't burst open . . .'

Musgrave's glasses had flown off when he was flung out of the open door; they lay broken in the gutter, their splintered lenses refracting gleams of faint, sourceless light.

Behind Johnny's back Gisela said,' Johnny . . .'

Her voice was low and muted; it took him a moment to realise why it made his hair rise in the nape of his neck. That hushed sickness of horror brought his face round to her wary and still.

'Johnny, there's somebody else in the car.'

There couldn't be. It was absurd. Musgrave had clambered into his car alone, and certainly stopped nowhere on the way. Yet Johnny laid the unconscious man's head hurriedly back on the folded scarf, and came to his feet in frantic haste.

'In the back seat. Somebody—'

She was half in at the hanging door, kneeling in the frost of broken glass that whitened the driving seat, squeezing her shoulders against the unbelievably crumpled junk of metal that sagged into the rear of the car. A hand and an arm lolled over the back of the driving seat. She was feeling her way with shivering, tentative fingers up the sleeve towards a shoulder trapped and flattened cruelly under the weight of the standard and the roof as it was driven in. Shallow and hard, moaning breaths gushed out of the tangle of wreckage from a face close to hers. There was blood on her hand.

Johnny took her round the waist and drew her back, and she turned suddenly with a cry of understanding and love and pity, and wound her arms about him.

'Johnny, it's *Codger*!'

He didn't say anything, he just froze in her arms, for one instant absolutely stiff and still; then he had put her aside and was in the car, thrusting, heaving, tearing hands and wrists on jagged edges as he fought to lift away the weight that held the crushed body prisoned. His hand touched a feebly moving jaw, stroked its way up a cheek sticky with blood.

'Codger, old lad, I'm here, Johnny's here. Hold on, boy, I'll get you out. It's me, Codger . . . it's Johnny . . .'

A faint sound, between moan and speech, answered him out of the tangle, and something in the very tone of it told him he was known. Whether his voice had penetrated the darkened and lonely mind, or whether his very presence spoke its own languag to some inner sense, Codger was aware of him. Johnny worked his left hand painfully under Codger's armpit, gripping hard in the stuff of his coat.

'Gisela—'

'Yes,' she said, quivering at his shoulder.

'See if the rear door will open.' He rested while she tried, keeping his hold, spreading his back against the sagging roof. 'It's buckled.' She had a foot braced against the running-board, her weight thrown back, pulling with both hands.

'I know – but I think the catch has burst, it might give. Careful, don't hurt yourself.'

The top of the door gaped, started out of place. With a hideous grating of metal the lower part gave to her pull, and the door was open. She leaned into the car, stretching an arm to support Codger about the body. Her sleeve tore against jagged edges of metal, but she gripped and held.

'Good girl! If I can shift this an inch or two, try to ease him clear.' Crouching, he got a foot on the seat, and thrust upward with braced shoulders, panting, setting his teeth. He had felt the slight lurch above him of a weight settling afresh; it was not so much a matter of lifting it as of disturbing it. The lamp standard had crashed on the left side of the car and crushed it. Johnny's contortions shook the lopsided shell, and the weight slid farther to the left. The buckled metal, relieved of the oppression from above, lifted slightly with the force of its own tensions, and Johnny felt it give, and heaved with all his force.

Codger slid backwards out of the vice, and Johnny, scrambling after, helped to lower him with aching care and anxiety into Gisela's arms.

'Let me take him.'

He came round to lean into the car behind her, and she let his arm replace her own, and edged past him to stand clear, waiting until she could lift Codger's trailing legs and help to carry him to the grass.

Johnny held the distorted, crushed body in his arms, stooping over it, his forehead running with sweat as he wiped blood away from the battered face.

The large, blank eyes opened wide, staring unfocused into the night. A convulsion of doubt and loneliness and fear quaked through him. A core of solitary terror, deep within and tenacious to the end, beat frantically about its prison for company and comfort.

'I'm here,' said Johnny, close to his ear. 'I've got you, it's all right.' Nobody had ever heard Johnny's voice sound like that, except Hero, perhaps, when she was three years old, and he had suddenly to be two parents instead of one.

Codger's mouth moved, fought for a moment with the old constrictions, and then forgot them utterly. A thread of a voice, heart-rendingly apologetic for failure, said faintly but coherently: 'Sorry, Johnny! I done it all wrong – botched it . . . Sorry!'

'You did fine,' protested Johnny staunchly, not even understanding then what he meant, not even realising that his poor mute had expressed himself plainly at last; and he kept on saying it, steadily and soothingly, until it penetrated his senses that Codger had stopped listening.

Chapter Seven

Johnny laid his burden back in the grass, and got stiffly to his feet.

'I'm going to take the car and go back to the first house there, and call the police. See what you can do for Musgrave.' He took a couple of steps, and looked back for an instant. 'You don't mind being left?'

'I don't mind,' she said.

Almost inevitably some car or other would be along and stop at the scene any moment; the marvel was that they had had the night to themselves so long, though it had been no more than ten minutes in all, he found, when he thought to look at his watch. Better wipe his face and hands, and not burst in on some suburban housewife looking like a murderer fresh from his crime. He used a handkerchief as best he could on his scratched cheek and stained palms, and whirled the car round in the width of the road. There was a house only a hundred yards or so back, the last of its kind for half a mile, and certain to be on the telephone. Better call the ambulance, too, while he was about it. It wouldn't be any use to Codger, but Musgrave might need it.

He drove like an automaton, and said and did what was needful. He felt nothing yet, only a stunned coldness that was probably shock. He didn't think, he didn't reason, the functions of his own personal mind had stopped; social man, civic man, did what was required of him.

When he got back to them Musgrave was sitting up in Gisela's arm under the hedge, and there was a dark Morris drawn in close to the wreck. The newcomer had provided brandy, apparently, for Gisela had a flask in her hand. Better still, the kind donor was by no means anxious to linger if he could be of no further help; no doubt he had a wife at home waiting for him, and by the look of him probably a family, too. If the police and the ambulance were already summoned, and there was nothing more he could do, he thought he'd better be on his way.

Johnny thought so, too. He wasn't anxious to have any unofficial observers present during what was to come.

'Then I'll leave you my card, in case I should be needed.'

He was still addressing himself to Johnny, but with a respectful eye on Musgrave, too, an accurate measure of the inspector's rapid and dogged recovery.

'Thanks,' said Johnny, 'but I don't suppose they'll have to bother you. We'll stick it out. We have to, anyhow, but that's enough.'

'Terrible thing,' said the relieved Samaritan, gratefully withdrawing. 'So sorry about your wife – dreadful for her. Wonderfully brave!'

He drove away uncorrected. Maybe there really was something about them that made them look married, or maybe it was the done thing to assume that two respectable-looking middle-aged people driving about together late at night should have the benefit of the doubt.

The words stayed in Johnny's bludgeoned mind when the speaker was gone, like a spark in bracken, smouldering unseen in the roots of his thoughts. My wife. A long time since he'd even run the phrase over his tongue. It had a bitter-sweet taste, stimulating and evocative.

He took a rug out of the car, retrieved Gisela's coat, and gently covered Codger's body. It seemed already to have contracted, to be strangely low and at home in the grass, as though it were already returning to earth. Johnny closed the large, puzzled, patient eyelids over the fixed eyes, and turned abruptly to those who were still alive.

'Here, girl, better put this on. I'm sorry we've managed to ruin it for you.' He turned her about like a child, and fastened the single great button under her chin. 'Sit in the car, love, and try not to feel too much of anything. As soon as I can I'll take you home.'

He wasn't too surprised when she didn't do it. Women had always liked Johnny, but they'd never obeyed him; and that was odd, considering how little trouble men had ever given him in that way. She was close beside him as he lunged forward quickly to lend Musgrave an arm to lean on, for the inspector was climbing unsteadily to his feet.

'Now, take it easy, man, your fellows will be here soon. I've called them, and the ambulance, too, and you'd better stay a patient for tonight, I should think.'

'I'm all right,' said Musgrave obstinately. 'This is my case, as long as I'm on my feet. I'm quite capable of carrying on now. You got him out, didn't you? Miss Salberg told me. Where is he?'

He kept hold of Johnny's arm to hold himself upright, for the world swung when he turned his head; but the dry authority had come back into his voice as soon as he was master of his senses.

Johnny nodded silently towards the place where the car rug was spread over Codger's body. He still found it hard to grasp that that was all, that one of his friends, dependants, children, was gone; troublesome, no doubt, in his way, but does that make you feel any differently towards your children?

Musgrave went down on his knees gingerly, and turned back the rug. The dead face ignored him, already sunken into its own inscrutable fantasy, where he had no rôle at all, either as friend or enemy.

'He tried to kill me,' said Musgrave quietly, his voice suddenly fully alert and aware. 'Or did you know that already?'

'*He did what?*' said Johnny faintly, hearing his own words echo to him out of an infinite distance, and unconscious even of Gisela's hand closing warmly on his arm.

'Tried to kill me.' Musgrave repeated it no less quietly, looking up at him over the silent body. 'You didn't know, then? What *did* you imagine he was doing here?'

'*Codger?*' He clutched his head, holding his disintegrating mind together. 'He was the gentlest soul who ever breathed, he wouldn't hurt a fly.'

'Oh, yes, I think he would – if he thought you were being threatened, Mr Truscott. You, or anyone belonging to you. Was he the gentlest soul who ever breathed when he graduated through that special training course of yours during the war? And what do you think *this* was for?'

He had pushed back the rug from the right arm, and lifted the large hand that curled indifferently at Codger's side. He drew up the cuff and showed a thin cord dangling from the clenched brown fingers. Not long, no more than eighteen inches, tethered to a waisted toggle at either end. Black cord, close-textured, probably waxed.

'And how do you think I got *this*?'

Musgrave pulled down the collar of his shirt and strained his chin upward, to show a thin groove scored across the right side of his neck, strung here and there with beads of blood.

'And this?'

He held out his left hand before Johnny's eyes, and a similar groove marked its back, and broke the skin below the base of the little finger

'He was in the back of the car. Quiet as a cat. All I saw was a change in the degree of light in the mirror, suddenly, as though something had cast a shadow. I didn't hear a thing. I don't know why I put up my hand, but that's the only reason I'm alive now. Just a reaction against a feeling of movement behind me. The cord went round hand and all, and he couldn't tighten it. I half blacked out, and lost control. But I'm alive.'

Death had kicked open the driver's door and ejected him. The dog it was that died.

'Ever seen a thing like that before?'

Musgrave laid down the hand in the grass, and clambered weakly to his feet again. Johnny was standing staring down at the trailing cord with dilated eyes, his face motionless and numb.

Yes, he had seen similar cords many times. Just one of the many ways of killing silently. Men who were to survive and continue useful in Johnny's wartime trade had had to know as many of them as possible; no man can master them all. Codger's unco-ordinated mind had never excised those skills, his hands had never forgotten them. There'd been no spastic tremor when he flicked the cord round Musgrave's throat and drew it tight; only the blind instinct of fear and the upflung hand had saved him.

Johnny stiffened knees that threatened to buckle under him, and suddenly the fingers closed tightly upon his arm seemed to be all that held him upright, or kept him from covering his face and howling his anguish to the night.

He knew now what it was Codger had botched. 'I done it all wrong . . . Sorry, Johnny! Sorry!' Only now did he understand what he had heard.

'Oh, my God!' he said helplessly. 'My God, my God!'

The hum of cars coming rapidly, not yet shut between the trees; the distant alarm of an ambulance bell at the last crossroads.

'That won't be needed,' said Musgrave, and went down on his knees again to feel his way through the dead man's pockets, without any great hope of revelations; what could such as Codger Bayliss be carrying about with him? The garrotte was an atavism, a mechanical memory, violence re-enacted in innocence; there wouldn't be two such prodigies.

444

'I don't know or care,' said Johnny, in a voice that creaked with effort, 'whether you'll take my word for this, but for my own peace I want to say it. I didn't send him. I had no idea what he meant to do.'

'He knows,' said Gisela in a whisper.

Musgrave looked up, his bruised eyes flashing from her face to Johnny's. 'Strange as it may seem,' he said, 'I don't doubt you. I can imagine you doing murder, Truscott, but not getting somebody else to do it for you. Not even a man in his right wits. If it came to it, I'm pretty sure you'd do your own killing.'

'Thank you. I suppose I should be grateful for that. And yet you understand, don't you, that he wasn't to blame, that he couldn't be held responsible for what he did. I took on the responsibility for him, and this is how I've carried it.'

I done it all wrong – botched it . . .. Sorry, Codger! Sorry!

'Your conscience doesn't come within my province,' said Musgrave dryly. 'You must sort that out yourself.'

'Blast you, I wasn't offering it to you, or asking your advice about it, either. I'm telling you we've somehow managed to kill off an innocent between us, no matter what you choose to call him.'

'I'm concerned only with facts. Facts like a length of cord round my neck, Mr Truscott. Or . . .'

His hand came out of Codger's left-hand jacket pocket holding something that looked at first like a rolled-up handkerchief. It uncoiled on his hand like a living thing, bursting into a glow of colours under the headlights as a sleepy fire bursts suddenly into flames.

'Or this,' said Musgrave, his voice sharp and quivering with eagerness, vented in a great sigh of achievement; and he stretched out in his two hands before Johnny's eyes eight inches of embroidered silk ribbon bright with poppies and cornflowers and ripe golden wheat, the torn end of Hero's baldric, slashed with Mare Chatrier's blood.

'I'll go, then,' said Johnny, halting just inside the door. 'If you're sure you'll be all right?'

'You won't come in? I think you need a drink, Johnny.'

'Not now. We'd better get some sleep.'

It was nearly three o'clock. The world seemed to have completed an entire revolution in those three hours of the night.

She watched his face with hollow dark eyes, hazed with weariness, and felt him withdrawing from her moment by moment into a private place where he kept his deepest griefs, and where, it seemed, even after all these years she was not allowed to enter.

'Johnny, are you all right?' Ridiculous phrase, but one used it for every degree of well-being from the merest subsistence to bliss; and he would understand.

'I'm all right,' he said.

'Do you know you never said one word all the way home?'

'What was there to say?' he said drearily. 'He's dead. He tried to kill Musgrave, and Musgrave is about to prove that he killed Chatrier. And I made a fine mess of taking care of him, if I couldn't keep him from getting involved in this job. But it's too late to say anything. It's done.'

'I wish you could have been spared this,' she said in an aching whisper, meaning the bereavement and self-reproach and the pure pain of Codger's death.

'I wish I could,' said Johnny, meaning the knowledge he would have given his right hand not to possess, but of which he could never now be rid. He hadn't said a word, he'd let the thing happen as she'd willed it, because he wasn't supposed to know, and what good could it do Codger now to turn and betray Gisela? Hadn't he been thrashing his mind for a way in which she could get rid of the baldric safely, without even admitting him to the secret, since it seemed she'd die before she'd do that? Well, she'd found a way.

Still half-dazed, Musgrave had never questioned his discovery. Why should he? He'd opened his eyes to find two people bending over him, and one of them an innocent stranger, whose very presence was a guarantee of the correctness of Gisela's behaviour. Why should he inquire exactly when the convenient witness had arrived on the scene, and whether Gisela had been there alone for some minutes before his coming? He had one murderer, why be in too big a hurry to look for another?

Maybe in her place, thought Johnny, I should have done the same. There was Codger dead and safely out of it, and Musgrave unconscious, and no one else by, and it was now or never. Codger couldn't be hurt any more. Maybe I should have planted the thing on him, too. How can I tell? Who am I to blame her? Was it so terrible to leave him to carry both loads, when he'd already incurred one? Who am I to judge her? Who am I, for God's sake, to judge anybody, the mess I've made of my responsibilities?

Let it go, then. He felt that Musgrave was satisfied, that he would never be able to resist this neat, well-rounded ending. Somehow every detail would be fitted into the pattern of Codger's jealous and protective passion. It would be interesting to see the pieces of the puzzle ingeniously tailored into place. Why look for a second criminal, where one so obligingly offered himself?

Then – if you won't come in—'

'No, I'd better get home. In the morning I shall have to tell Hero.'

He saw Gisela flinch, and suddenly, as though a curtain had been drawn from between them, he saw every least imprint and mark of her history in her face, the set of her lips, indrawn and pale, the tight white lines that marked her slender bones in jaw and cheek and brow, as though they were fretting their way through the skin, and above all the silent, uncomplaining endurance of her eyes.

In all the time he had known her he had never seen tears in them, but he knew the look they had when there should have been tears, and her reticence and courtesy insisted on containing them.

'Good night, then, Johnny.'

'Oh, girl, girl!' he said in a great sigh of pity and resignation and bewilderment, and reached and drew her to him, folding his arms round her and holding her to his heart. Her cheek was cold against his. He kissed her very gently, and turned and went away without saying another word, suddenly so tired that when the door was safely closed between them he could hardly fumble his way down the stairs.

'So the case,' said Musgrave, 'can be regarded as closed. You must have been expecting that, I suppose. With one would-be murderer already known, it hardly seemed very probable that there should be another one hanging around in the same comparatively restricted group of people. It could happen, once in a while, but the odds are all against it. But this – this turning up in his pocket more or less clinched it.'

He spread out the strip of silk on Johnny's desk, leaning over it with a thoughtful frown, and with something of human satisfaction, too, in the set of his features. New glasses with a more fashionable winged shape had given him an oddly quizzical expression, and made him look younger. The thin line on his neck, like a faint brown pencil-mark, was fading rapidly. His brush with death had left, as far as could be detected, no other mark on his nature or his mind, not even a touch of awe and humility.

Johnny sat looking down at the beautiful, radiant bit of brightness, the gold-thread ears of wheat, the scarlet and blue of the flowers.

'A normal man would have burned it long ago,' said Musgrave, kindly explaining to him the workings of the minds of all men but himself. 'He had plenty of opportunity. I suppose he kept it because it was so pretty, and gave him pleasure to handle and look at.'

'I suppose that could have been it,' said Johnny woodenly.

'So he carried it around with him, a fortnight and more after the murder. Curious that after all the hunting we'd done for the thing, it should be put into our hands so simply at the end of it.'

'Extraordinary,' said Johnny, without joy or wonder.

He put out a hand, and moved one fingertip gently back and forth above the torn end of the baldric, and the fine, waving filaments of silk rose and clung to his finger. Magical stuff, silk. You could smooth it on to the wall, and it would cling there, too. Or perhaps the weight of the embroidery would be too much for it and bring it down. He touched the ruled line of dull brown that was all that remained of Marc Chatrier's blood.

'You're wondering about that,' said Musgrave with a slight smile.

'In a way, yes. Such a curious sort of mark. No doubt it tells a detailed story to you, but I haven't been able to make much of it.'

'Well, I suppose these are small professional mysteries. You have others as complex in your own field.'

'But I leave you yours,' said Johnny, with the first faint gleam of humour and malice. 'You're sure you're not making too much of this? Does it really make a complete case in itself? It looks a bit flimsy, lying there alone.'

'Possession of it was almost more revealing than even what the ribbon itself can tell us. The thing has been missing ever since the night of the murder, it was clearly torn away in the course of the murder; and after that it turns up again for the first time in Bayliss's pocket. Who but the murderer was likely to have torn it loose and removed it? I admit I didn't pay enough attention to Codger Bayliss in the first place. He seemed to me too simple and harmless to conceive such an act, let alone carry it out. These cases can be very complex. Who knows what goes on inside their minds?'

'Who, indeed?'

The thought of Codger, imprisoned within his speechless world and struggling to communicate with the world outside, made Johnny's heart turn in him with a convulsion of sickness. And yet had Codger been more isolated than the rest of human kind? If he could not reach a hand to Gisela, nor she to him?

'And that stain . . . that *is* blood, I suppose?'

'It is, and the same group as Chatrier's. There can be very little doubt that it *is* Chatrier's. Which takes us a step further. And then, the form of this is peculiarly interesting. And so were some of the details of the wound, though I didn't tell you that earlier. It seems that the point of deepest penetration showed signs of a double thrust, as though an attempt had been made to withdraw the blade, and then, finding it too difficult and having no time to make a job of it, the murderer had thrust it back in and abandoned it. At the farthest point of the wound, for no more than a minute fraction of an inch, this dual penetration showed.

'Now, what we think happened is something like this. Bayliss was upstairs with Mrs Glazier in the bar all through the third act and for part of the fourth, then he slipped away unnoticed, and he was down in the wings when the alarm was given. No one was clear about exactly when he arrived there, but with so many people moving about that isn't surprising, and they were all quite used to him. It seems probable that in his own way he had been disturbed for some days by the unrest he felt around him, and by a feeling that Chatrier was making himself a nuisance and perhaps even a danger to you. He's in the wings when Chatrier sings Figaro's last-act aria and withdraws into the pine-grove to hide. Chatrier's back would be to Bayliss, his eyes naturally on what was going on on the stage. Bayliss has found Miss Truscott's sword where Miss Salberg put it ready to hand. It's a pretty thing in itself, and the broken baldric is even more attractive. He's playing with it when Chatrier backs towards him. I've seen he was used to ways of silent killing, and you've confirmed that he had training in those techniques. Was he also, in his time, expert with knives and bayonets?'

'He'd handled every kind of steel. But it's a long time ago.'

'He hadn't forgotten what to do with a cord, had he? So he has a very fine, keen sword in his hand, and your enemy backing on to it . . . and he follows his instinct, and kills.'

'So efficiently? Not a murmur out of Figaro?'

'I didn't tell you this, either, but Figaro's lips were, as you might expect, marked by slight but unmistakable bruises. A hand was clamped over his mouth. And the sword, I think, was gripped through the baldric, which is why there were no fingerprints on it but yours, Selverer's and Miss Truscott's. Figaro falls, and dies probably within a minute. Bayliss knows enough to lower him gently to the boards. He then tries to pull out the sword, but it's lodged fast, and he hardly succeeds in moving it. But in that attempt, which he very soon abandoned, I think this mark was made.

'He can't shift it by pulling from the hilt, he tears off this end of the baldric, which is already dangling loose, and through it grips the blade with his right hand, close to the body, and so tries to ease it out. He moves it a little, and in doing so encourages the very slight bleeding. I don't know if you've noticed, or if you remember off-hand, but the sword has some very fine chasing up the edges of the blade near the point, and the blood had been drawn *up* these grooves for a few inches. Here he held the blade through this ribbon, and the edge over which the silk was folded left this stain on it. You can see what a thin, straight line it is.'

'I had noticed. It was puzzling me. You make everything very plain. And the other edge didn't mark it, or cut it?'

'Try holding a very sharp blade through a fold of silk. You don't shut your hand on it, you fold the silk round the edge that's towards your palm, and hold the centre of the blade firmly between fingertips and thumb. The rest of the ribbon hung free. The threads weren't cut because there was no actual pressure against the edge, and no friction. But these very fine roving strands took up the blood and retained this stain. And then he gave up, because it was inevitable the alarm must be given any moment. He left the sword and scabbard, but he took his piece of ribbon away with him – perhaps at first hardly realising he was still holding it, but afterwards he kept it because he liked it, and it seemed no harm.'

'I see. Everything explained,' said Johnny, with a hollow smile.

'It leaves nothing unaccounted for, I think.'

'Nothing. I congratulate you.'

Musgrave folded the strip of silk again carefully, and slipped it back into the plastic folder in which he had brought it.

'I know you were fond of the fellow, Mr Truscott. I know it's a tragic case. But be thankful it's over. You can go ahead with your work, now, with an easy mind.'

'May I tell my people the case is closed? To some extent the cloud's been over us all.'

'Yes, of course, tell them. They have a right to know.' He rose, buckling the straps of his briefcase. 'Miss Truscott's sword can be returned to you very soon. And the inquest – yes, an ordeal, I know, in the circumstances, but it'll soon be over.'

'I don't think Hero wants the sword back,' said Johnny, going to the door with his visitor. 'She's upset enough about Codger, I don't want her to see it again. But there's one thing I did want to ask you . . .'

Musgrave halted in the doorway, looking back with an encouraging smile. 'Yes?'

'After the inquest – I don't know the drill when a case ends like this, without a trial. Shall I be able to claim his body? I'd like to take care of the funeral.'

'Yes,' said Musgrave, after a long moment of studying him in silence, 'I think I can promise you that you shall have his body.'

The word had gone round within the hour.

A shadow lifted from the Leander Theatre and its company as the news passed from lip to lip. Johnny told Franz, and Franz told the morning rehearsal of *The Magic Flute*. Inga, a truly electrifying Astrofiammante, spoke to Tonda, her Pamina, for the first time in ten days voluntarily and even civilly. Max Forrester, an imposing Sarastro even in slacks and a sweater, remarked to Monostatos that celebrations would be in order, and Monostatos agreed that the Blackcock's Feather, just round the corner, would be open any minute.

In the regions backstage the shadow that had fallen some days ago kept the sky still cloudy and Codger's place in the corner of Sam Priddy's box ached with emptiness. But even there some urgency of heart began to lift from them, and left them looking forward instead of back.

But the news fell with the most profound effect of all upon Hans Selverer.

Papageno turned with a face suddenly full of shining purpose, put down his magic chime of bells with a ringing peal, and walked unnoticed out of the rehearsal. When next they should have heard his voice there was blank silence, and the birdcatcher was nowhere to be found. Such a thing had never been known to happen before; he was normally a very conscientious young man.

Hans was looking for Hero. He knew she had come to the theatre with her father that morning, though he had not seen her since. She was not anywhere about the stage, she was not in Johnny's office, she was not in her own dressing-room. Hans knew at least where to ask after her next.

He put his head in at Sam's box, and there she was. She was sitting lonely in the most retired corner, where Codger Bayliss had so often sat with his knitting, and it seemed she had inherited the function with the seat, for she had Codger's unfinished sweater on its plastic needles before her, and was counting stitches with a deep frown of concentration. She went on counting even when Hans came in. The narrowings at the top of a sleeve can be tricky when you have no pattern, and are following in the steps of somebody who has left you no clues.

'Hero!' said Hans, and halted, unsure of his English though not of himself.

She looked up quickly, grey eyes flaring wide. For two days they'd lost their clarity and brightness, crying in private over Codger; but she was nineteen, and her world was full enough of people to repair the hole torn in it by the passing of one among so many. The sadness that lingered in her face was the impending shadow of maturity. She looked at him in doubt and astonishment, and with something of offence, too. He had been avoiding her for days, and now he walked in on her with a bright, possessive face, as if he owned her.

'Hero, have you heard that this case of Figaro is now closed? But officially. Franz has just told us, and he had it from your father.'

He sat down beside her, and looked grave for her sake, but still he could not help shining.

'I know you are sad, and I am sorry about Codger, you know I am. But now I am able to come to you and ask you something, a thing I could not ask before.' He took the knitting firmly out of her hands, careful not to spill the stitches, and laid it down at a safe distance; and because the spark of indignation was alight suddenly in her eyes and her colour was rising, he made haste to take possession of the hands he had thus emptied, in case she should slip out of his reach and run away from him.

'I wish to ask you if you will marry me,' said Hans firmly, looking her in the eyes with those gentian-blue eyes of his that had been so steadily staring in the opposite direction for the past week and more.

The kindling flush left her cheeks abruptly, her lips fell apart in a gasp of astonishment, wariness and, of all things, consternation. She had imagined such a moment fondly in her own private fantasies times out of number, and while there had seemed no possibility of its ever being translated into reality it had seemed to her the last prodigy of human bliss. She had even imagined her own response to it; but never like this. Now that it was suddenly pitched into her lap in good earnest she reacted to it with a strong impulse of panic and recoil.

It was too soon, too sudden, she wasn't ready. She was only nineteen, and it wasn't something you could undo in a year or so if you didn't like it – not the way the Truscotts understood it, anyhow. And she hadn't been anywhere yet, or seen anything, or sung half the roles she wanted to sing. And then, just *one* man, and you couldn't whistle up another one when you got bored, or sort your dates by the half-dozen and shut your eyes and draw for it. Even if you did want him very much, even if you were sure you loved him very much, it took a bit of thinking about to jettison everything else for him. And the end of it was unreasoning rage, for he shouldn't have sprung it on her like this, without any warning or any time to think.

'No!' she said, not manoeuvring any longer, but in plain and resolute retreat. She tried to withdraw her hands, but it wasn't so easy. He was taken aback, but he held on; perhaps he couldn't believe his ears, or perhaps he simply didn't intend to give up so easily.

'Hero, you must know that I am in love with you. These things women always know.'

Someone must have told him that, perhaps one of the older women who found him so irresistible. Inga, maybe.

'You have a nerve, Hans Selverer!' she said hotly. 'All this time you've been avoiding me as if I had the plague, you could hardly say "Good morning" to me. And now you come making up to me, and expect – expect—'

'Not *you* had the plague, Hero, but *I*. Don't you see how hopeless was my position until this case was solved? That Inspector Musgrave, he believed that I had done it. He knew about my father, and he thought – he was sure I had killed this man. How could I ask you to have anything to do with me? How could I try to make you like me better, when I was suspect like that?'

'I don't believe you care anything about me,' she persisted, holding her reeling defences together against the assault of his near presence, with treason already budding in her soul. 'It isn't much of a way of showing you love a person, to refuse her a share in your worries. *Anybody* can be generous with the good things.'

'If I was wrong I am sorry. I could only do what I thought was right. But now I am free to tell you how much I love you, and to ask you—'

'But you don't, you can't! You called me a spoiled, self-willed child.'

She turned her head away from him, straining out of reach, aware of the crumbling walls of her resistance, and fascinated by the spectacle they made as they toppled. The very crash might be rather glorious.

He loosed her hands and took her by the shoulders, drawing her to him. He was smiling, not too confidently, but with some childlike trust in her ultimate will to acceptance, as though he knew her better than she knew herself, but didn't want to flaunt his knowledge too openly.

And after all, she was beginning to think, resigning herself to the next world like a drowning woman, there might be compensations. Just one man might not be a bad thing at all, provided he was the nicest, the most gifted, the most attractive man around, and the one every other girl coveted. And there was also the consideration that when a man like that did ask you, you couldn't afford to take any chances on whether he'd feel like asking you a second time.

'*You* called *me* a priggish busybody. And it was not true, I was only very alarmed for you, and very jealous.'

'You mean it *was* true what you said about me. You said Johnny ought to beat me'—

His arm slid round her shoulders. She flattened her palms against his chest, but they seemed to have no force, and in a moment her right hand stole up the lapel of his coat and round his neck, and settled there with fingers spread in his hair and the taut lines of his nape fitting snugly into the palm. He was at once warm and cool to the touch, and sent tremors of delight to her heart.

'I didn't mean it,' he said against her cheek, 'I was only angry. And you know, in opera it is always the wife who beats the husband – like Susanna and Figaro. So marry me . . .'

'No!'

He kissed her so nimbly that it was possible to pretend she had never uttered that negative, and he had never heard it. And then he was moved by a stroke of inspiration to invite himself into the family by a formula she could not resist.

'"*Pace, pace, mio dolce tesoro!*"' pleaded Hans very softly in her ear.

She heaved a deep, helpless, happy sigh, and: 'Yes yes!' she said, and tightened both arms round his neck.

The walls fell, and the crash was glorious.

Hans went up the stairs with a firm tread, a bold face, a smudge of lipstick just in front of his left ear, and no doubts at all of his reception until he reached the door of Johnny's office. After all, he was a person who had something to offer, a rising reputation, ambition, a sufficient income, tastes triumphantly in common with Hero's, and a character which was now threatened by no shadow. All the same, the inevitable constriction gripped his middle as he rapped at the door and answered Johnny's somewhat restrained: 'Come in!'

'Mr Truscott,' said Hans, looking at his prospective father-in-law across the desk with a face of such earnestness that Johnny's mouth fell open almost before the shot was fired, 'I have the honour to ask you if I may pay my addresses to your daughter.'

Now I wonder, thought Johnny, charmed in spite of his astonishment, what wonderful phrase-book he got that out of!

'Well, well!' he said, swallowing down the shock with difficulty. 'This comes a bit suddenly, a man needs time to think about it. And ultimately, let's face it, fathers don't have much say in the matter these days. You sit down and keep quiet while I get my breath back.'

Hans declined the chair he was too restless to stay in, and demonstrated his nervousness by going on talking.

'I love your daughter very much, but you will understand I could not address her while I felt myself to be under suspicion.' Luckily he had no way of knowing how that ran into the quick of Johnny's senses. 'And it matters to me very much that we should have your approval.'

Johnny got up from his chair, to be free of the blue, disconcerting eyes, and walked to the window to stare down into the forecourt littered with dull, dead leaves.

'And Hero,' he said without turning his head, 'how does she feel about it?'

That was pure stalling, because he had to have time to think. He'd seen the little pink bow that decorated the boy's ear, and the ravages that hadn't quite been combed out of his thick brown hair. Give him that, he'd hardly been able to get up the stairs fast enough for Father's blessing. And it made sense of things he hadn't understood, things that had complicated all their lives. Not that he ever would understand his daughter. Or women in general, for that matter.

'She has done me the honour to accept me. If we have your permission, of course.'

'Hero never said *that*,' said Johnny positively, and a brief, lop-sided grin shook his face out of its anxiety for a moment. 'Oh, I know, I know! She's a good kid, she wants me to be happy about it, too. But look, I need time to think. I've got to get used to the idea. I've hardly realised yet that I've got a grown-up girl, and here I am threatened with losing her. She's only just nineteen, and if she's going to get herself set up for life I need to be sure she's getting it right.'

'Naturally,' said Hans, 'that I perfectly understand. If you wish us to wait, to make sure – *I* am sure, but I will wait for her as long as you think right.'

'Yes, well . . . Suppose you leave me to think it over now. Don't worry, I won't keep you waiting long, but I'd like to be left alone to-day to come to terms with the thought. Take her out somewhere until this evening, take her home after the performance. Take care of her, and come and talk to me to-morrow.'

He felt acutely the confusion of mind in which he was sending Hans away. He'd expected, perhaps, a pretty thorough grilling, but an inevitable welcome into the family in the end. Why shouldn't he? He knew his worth. There was something wrong here, some reservation he didn't understand. And yet to be told to take the girl out for the day argued that her father had a certain amount of confidence in him.

'As you please,' said Hans stiffly, discouragement damping his voice; and he went away with somewhat subdued dignity. What he would tell Hero Johnny couldn't guess. Maybe it would bring her hot-foot up the stairs to confront her awkward parent and demand to know why he hadn't flung his arms round her suitor's neck at once, as apparently she had. But no, she wouldn't do that. In deference to her new lord she'd be all duty and loyalty, and leave him to conduct his own business. She might even feel for the old man, thought Johnny wryly, and want to make the upheaval as little of a shock to him as possible. She was a nice kid, even if she was a handful. Maybe he ought to have asked Hans if he knew what he was tackling.

And now he was alone the problem lay there before him in all its crudity and ugliness, and not all the contortions he might essay in the effort to put himself in other people's places could make it look any better to him. He couldn't very well feel happy about entrusting his girl to a young man who had been an accomplice in a murder, and who apparently didn't in the least mind letting a poor old imbecile take the blame.

A fine singer, a potentially great artist, a pleasant and good-natured young man, he was all that. It wasn't that Johnny had any holier-than-thou thoughts about him, it wasn't that he didn't like him; he did like him, very much. But giving him Hero was another matter.

So now there was no help for it. He would have to talk to Gisela.

Chapter Eight

The Countess stepped out of the right-hand arbour, alone, erect, regal even in Susanna's pert soubrette clothes, her voice clear and still as it severed the clamour of recriminations and pleadings and rejections seething round her disguised maid. Frozen, they stared at her, even their exclamations hushed to awed undertones; and Susanna slowly uncovered her face, the deception happily over and the battle won.

The Count, who had sung like a man possessed all the evening, cajoling and menacing and lording it as never before, excelled himself now in his moment of utter defeat; and suddenly it was clear how right Mozart had been to give him only those last four words to say for himself, without bluster or anger or defence of any kind, simply:

> '"*Contessa, perdono,*
> *perdono, perdono!*"'

Clear, too, why the answer came so simply, the lovely, rounded, melting phrase of forgiveness. When she told him: 'I can't say you nay,' she was telling the final, absolute truth not only about the end of this adventure but about their turbulent married life. No one could have resisted this Count. He could have led any woman a dog's life with his caprices and his jealousy, and still wound her round his finger at the end of it when he gave in and admitted his enormities thus engagingly. Even though she would know, as doubtless his Countess knew, that the whole thing would happen all over again within a month.

Inga extorted her tribute of dimmed eyes and absolute silence, melting and wringing all hearts. The whole group echoed the same caressing phrases. And then the end of the finale, fresh and gay and harking back strongly for the wind of happiness, ready to dance all night.

457

The curtain came down on forgiveness, reconciliation, hope.

Johnny left his box and went round into the wings as they came off-stage after their flurry of curtain calls. The fine, satisfying sound of an audience going away happy soothed his ears; he knew that full, fed note of content very well, now, he was sensitive to every variation in it.

Cherubino, seeing him there, made a brief, impetuous detour into his arms, hugged him breathlessly, and was hugged again almost too exuberantly.

'Hey, my *ribs*! Were we good to-night?'

She knew the answer, she was glowing with achievement.

'It was *him*! He got us all on the run. Even Inga's forgotten she was standing on her dignity. She *congratulated* us! Imagine that!'

'Oh, so he's taking it for granted he's got you, is he?' said Johnny, nettled.' Bragging about his luck already!'

'No, *he* isn't. I told them. It's all right, isn't it? I didn't exactly tell them, actually, it just sort of started busting out all over me, and I had to explain.'

She had no doubts at all, no qualms about his reactions. How could anyone resist her Hans? She locked her arms about Johnny's neck, and hugged him again warmly.

'Darling, I'm so happy! It's all right if I go and have a little supper with him, isn't it? I'll be right home afterwards.'

'Since when,' said Johnny,' do you ask my permission before you have supper with a bloke?'

She blushed at the reminder, but without any dimming of her state of bliss. 'Since right now. Not that I'm afraid of you, just make a note of that. I love you, that's all.'

'Well, come to that, I'm pretty soft on you.'

He turned her about in his hands. 'Go on, then, get off with you, you baggage, and be good.' He started her off with a pat in the fluted skirts of her blue coat, and she took to her heels and ran like Cherubino himself for her dressing-room and her own clothes. The rapier that danced at her hip now was a mere property sword; nobody would ever commit murder with that.

So it seemed the whole company must know by now that Hero considered herself engaged to Hans Selverer. Time and events were hemming Johnny in, even her innocence and confidence conspired to force his hand. There was no help for it, he must go to Gisela and have it out with her to-night.

'Good night!' he said to the members of the orchestra on his way along the corridor, and: 'Good night!' to Nan, slipping out blushingly in the arm of the youngest 'cellist. 'Good night!' to Don Basilio and Doctor Bartolo, hurtling out as one man, headdown for the stage-door, en route for the Blackcock's Feather round the corner; they had practically five minutes left before closing-time. 'Good night!' to Tonda, tripping down the stairs in her mink, her arms full of flowers and her eyes full of self-satisfaction, energy and mischief. Business as usual in the Leander Theatre, it seemed, and everything back to normal, even tempers. The hole Codger had left behind him would soon heal, except for the few who had had large tracts of their own lives and whole aspects of their own personalities torn out with him.

Johnny climbed the stairs with a tired step, and knocked at Gisela's door.

She was sitting before the mirror in her old candlewick robe, taking off Marcellina's make-up. Mezzo-sopranos are perpetually condemned to sing mothers and duennas and housekeepers. He had once had a great scheme for presenting her as Carmen, but she had firmly put her foot on that. She hadn't the voice for it, she said, and she hadn't the temperament. And she'd been right, as usual, he'd had to admit it in the end. Annina, the intriguer, with the foreign accent and the itching palm, would be a pleasant change from middle-aged frumps when they staged their new *Rosenkavalier* next season.

He closed the door behind him, and stood for a moment leaning against it, watching as she loosed her long hair out of the elaborate dressing and began to brush it. He knew she had seen him come in, their eyes had met for a moment in the mirror. Words did not come so easily now, the effort that preceded speech made the very air in the room seem tight and rarefied, too thin to keep alive. They still drove home together as before, always hopeful that the old ease would return, always straining with small, hesitant acts of consideration and tenderness to conjure it back again. They could not draw together again, and they could not separate; separation was unthinkable. Apart, they would die.

'Good audience to-night,' he said, coming to her shoulder.

Her eyes lifted to his face quickly, sensing something more than usually askew about the mirror image.

'What's the matter?'

When she questioned him directly, like that, her voice intent with partisan affection and anxiety, the impalpable barrier between them shuddered and almost cracked, but never quite.

'Nothing,' he said. 'Merely a little problem in responsibility. Young Hans came to see me this morning, after Musgrave had gone, after I'd told Franz to let the company know it was all over.'

'Ah!' said Gisela with a pale, bright smile.

'Yes . . . you've heard, of course. Everyone seems to know already. It seems he's been nursing a notion that he was still suspect number one, and now that he finds he isn't he's come right out and told me he wants to marry Hero.'

Her face had kindled into affection and pleasure, and even a brief, flashing glimmer that might have been laughter, until she saw the shadow that hung on his lowered eyelids.

'You see, that was how the wind was blowing, after all. When they took to being so polite to each other I thought I'd been mistaken. To-day she's been shining so, no one could miss it.'

The silence when she stopped speaking was marked. She laid down her hairbrush, watching him with eyes suddenly wide in wonder and anxiety.' You're not glad. She's in love with him, Johnny. This isn't just play. They're in earnest.'

'Apparently,' said Johnny. He had picked up the silver ribbon that had bound her hair, and was twining it round his fingers.' She'd left her brand on him plain enough.' His voice was as cloudy as his face. She watched him, alert and still, the dark curtain of her hair half-veiling her eyes.

'I know, Johnny. It is very early. She is very young. But it was bound to happen. Just look at her! And he's surely a very suitable match for her, and a very good young man. You won't be losing her,' she said, touching very delicately where she supposed his pain was.

'No, I know. Not losing a daughter, but gaining a son. I know! Though I admit it does come as a jolt to know it's on me so soon. They grow up too fast, you can't keep pace with them.'

'What have you said to him?'

'I haven't given him an answer, not yet. I told him to come and talk to me to-morrow.'

'But Hero seemed to be sure—'

'But I'm not,' he said, with a sudden flare of trouble and anger. He put down the ribbon, and came round to the side of the mirror to have her face to face. She saw how compulsively he closed his hand upon the edge of her dressing-table; the large, long bones stood white in the brown of his fingers.

'Marriage is no joke, Gisela, marriage is for life, and don't forget this is my responsibility. She isn't of age. I can at least hold things up for nearly two years if I think it necessary – long enough to give her time to think better of it. Not that I don't like him. I do. But—'

He had arrived at it by ill-judged and unhappy ways, but he had arrived. It came out not angrily or cruelly, but with a helpless and inflexible simplicity.

'What am I to do? *You* tell me! He was your cover, wasn't he? He sang the two lines that put you out of the running, safe in the arbour with Nan. And Codger being written off as the killer doesn't seem to worry him, he's as happy as a sandboy now he's in the clear. Not that I can blame either of you for hating the fellow,' admitted Johnny, 'and not that I've any right to judge. Still . . . A man prefers his son-in-law not to be an accessory in a murder. But what am I to say to Hero if I turn the boy down?'

Gisela had heard him out in stillness and silence, the sudden blaze of understanding in her eyes burning down into a steady glow. Her hands lay in her lap stiff and motionless. It seemed to him that for a moment she held her breath.

'I know where the lost piece of Hero's baldric was hidden,' said Johnny, 'because I found it there. And I know nobody but you could have put it there, and nobody but you could have taken it away again. You or Nan, and why should Nan do any such thing? But I made sure,' he continued doggedly. 'I looked in your bag, while you were changing that night. So I knew it was you who put it in Codger's pocket afterwards. And if *you* had killed Chatrier, then it happened earlier than we thought, before you went into the arbour. So there had to be somebody who sang Figaro's asides for him after he was dead. And that was Hans – wasn't it?'

Her lips moved, saying soundlessly: 'Yes.'

'So what am I to do? Liking him is one thing, but giving him my girl is something very different. It isn't that I'm so spotless a lamb, God knows! But this is Hero's future, not mine. If you know the answer, you tell me.'

She sat staring at him for a long moment still, her eyes wide and deep and stunned, and then the calm of acceptance came upon her, and the whiteness of strain began to fade out of her face. She got up quietly and went to the wardrobe, and lifted out of it Marcellina's rustling black dress. She brought it to him in her arms. 'Look,' she said, and unzipped the slender, boned bodice.

Marcellina was a compound of anachronisms. Not only did a zipper close her laced gown, but the busks that stiffened the bodice were slightly flattened spirals of wire covered with smooth plastic, instead of whalebone. A whole cage of springy supports ran from neck to hip, and the two front ones, one on either side of the zipper, were slightly larger than the others, and slightly stiffer. The seams were not sealed at the neck, but only closed by the fold of the lace-trimmed hem, so that the busks could be withdrawn at will. Gisela turned back the fold from the left-hand one, and drew out the top of the plastic-coated spiral a few inches. It was more rigid than would have been expected, and in a moment Johnny saw why. She turned the open end downwards and shook it, and with finger and thumb coaxed out of it something long and bright, with a small round knob at the end. As soon as she had the knob clear of its sheath the rest came out easily, and she held it up in her hand for him to see.

A strong steel knitting-needle, the old-fashioned kind nobody uses in these days of improving plastics. About nine inches long, but in its knitting days it had been longer; and filed down to a long, needle-sharp point that turned it into an efficient and deadly dagger.

He took it from her and looked at it closely. A faint film of a stain dulled the point end for several inches, though there was nothing material there under his fingers, only the discoloration. He looked up at her over the incomprehensible thing, and she saw that his hands were trembling.

'Sorry!' said Johnny. 'I'm dumb, you'll still have to tell me.'

'Did you not see that he had some new blue needles for his eternal knitting? Hero has been trying to finish his work for him – go and look at it, if you wish. And then remember how many years he had these.'

The trembling had reached his body. He moistened his lips with a tongue almost as dry, and said in a creaking whisper: 'Are you really trying to tell me that *this* – ? *Not* the sword? But the sword was in him.'

'Yes, the sword was in him. But the sword didn't kill him.'

'Girl, do you know what you're saying? Are you sure?'

He took her by the arms and held her before him, shivering suddenly, shaking her with his bewilderment and exhaustion and grief, and the tiny flame of hope and ease at the heart of all. 'How can you be so sure?'

'I'm sure,' she said, 'because I saw him killed. In front of my eyes, almost within touch of me. And I'm sure about the needle being the thing that killed him, not the sword, because, God help me, I know he was dead when I pulled out the needle, and drove the sword into him in its place.'

Deep within the turmoil of his mind a small core of quiet came into being, as there had been, so it seemed, a core of justice, however lame and inadequate, at the heart of the tangle of Marc Chatrier's death. He took the foaming bundle of Marcellina's skirts out of her arms, drew her with him to the ottoman by the wall, and made her sit down there. He went on his knees beside her, and held her fast by the hands. He did not yet realise for the chaos she had made of his ideas that the barrier and the distance between them had been wiped out. He could touch her, he could hold her hands, he could question her and answer her questions.

Codger's mutilated knitting-needle lay beside her on the green brocade. A dual penetration in the last fraction of an inch of the wound, Musgrave had said – signs that the sword had been slightly disturbed in an attempt to withdraw it, and then thrust back again. Musgrave could fit everything into his theory. It seemed it was perfectly possible to pick the right man and get everything else wrong.

'You didn't really think,' she said, her hands clinging suddenly to his with a desperation that belied the composure of her face,' that I could make a good job of sticking a rapier into a man's back? Silently – while he was *alive*?'

'Girl, how could I know what you had it in you to do? You or any other woman? Or any man? I don't know much of anything, and what I do know I get all wrong. You tell me. You should have told me then, right from the start.'

'How could I? Above all, I wanted you not to know. I couldn't feel that he – that the guilt . . . And you loved him!'

'And don't I love you?'

He shut both her hands gently in one of his, and with the other stroked back the long hair from her forehead and cheek. He didn't even know what he had said, it had slipped from his tongue so naturally.

'So that was why you took the needle away and hid it, because

463

knitting-needles would have led straight to Codger. I know! I can imagine!'

For years they'd all been sharing the responsibility for Codger. How could she let him go bewildered and frightened into custody, and then to trial, however kind the law might prove, however surely he would be found unfit to plead? How could she, being the person she was, let him be taken away and shut up in an asylum? She must have acted so quickly, so instinctively, that thought had hardly been involved at all.

'I told you the truth about picking up the sword and bringing it down with me,' she said, 'but not about the reason. I never thought of killing anyone. I did try talking to him, I did threaten him, even, to make him leave you alone. I said I could make trouble for him if he made trouble for you, and so I would have done. What would it have looked like for him if I'd told some Sunday newspaper the whole story of our marriage, and what he did to me? But that was all, because I was sure it would be enough. He had as much to lose as you, maybe more, and he wasn't a fool. And then I tripped over Hero's rapier in the passage outside her door, and I saw the baldric was broken. So I brought it down with me. I didn't stop to ask any questions about how it got there, because I thought at first that if we were very quick we could put a few stitches in it to hold it for the rest of the evening, and give it back to Hero, but then I saw there wouldn't be time. And that's why I had it in my hands when I came into the wings.'

It was all entirely in character. She was the tidier-up, the mender and tranquilliser and smoother of ends about the place. It was always Gisela who took care of the little things.

'I was early for my entrance. And you know how dark we had the stage, and how complex the set is. Tonda and Inga were somewhere to my right, but nowhere near me, Max and Ralph were over on the other side. And *he* was on the stage singing his aria, and then he backed into the pine-grove, almost towards me. There was someone standing there under cover, waiting for him. I didn't see or hear him until he moved a little to keep directly behind Figaro. And I didn't understand, I never realised . . . we were all so used to seeing him about the stage, he went where he pleased. There was no reason why I should even wonder. And then – he simply slipped his left hand over Figaro's mouth, and the needle into his back, there in front of my eyes, before I could move or speak. It didn't seem possible it could be done so smoothly. He just lowered him in his arm and let him lie, and he never made a movement again.'

Her voice had grown thin and fine with wonder and terror, not of death so much as of its silence and suddenness. Even killing a chicken, even hooking a fish, had more struggle and conflict about it than this. He held fast to her hands, and thought of the act almost as an achievement; for that was the spirit in which Codger had learned the art of silent killing. He made no mistakes about the things he did know. He had forgotten the names of his brothers and half the events of his own life, but he never forgot his acquired skills, and his hands could still reproduce them.

'He was dead,' she said, 'before I even touched him. He'd left him there just – lowered him to the boards and slipped away and left him. And I . . . the knitting-needle was so childish, so obvious. I thought of him on trial, and of you . . . Or perhaps not thought, I doubt if I did think. It simply happened to me. I pulled out the needle. There was almost no blood. It wasn't even difficult. I tore the loose end off the baldric, in case, and held it with that, but there was nothing, not so much as when you cut your finger. I wiped the needle on the piece of silk so that had to vanish, too . . .'

As simple as that, the curious diagonal line over which Musgrave had exercised so much ingenuity. Nothing to do with the chasing on the blade, just the thin mark left where she wiped the needle.

'And then I unsheathed the rapier, and put the point to the wound at the same angle, and . . .'

A sudden convulsive shudder ran through her, but her face remained fixed in a stunned and wondering calm, and her hands, starting and quivering for an instant like frightened wild things in his, sank again into a warmer ease.

'The wound would have given away almost as much as the weapon, I *had* to mangle and disguise it somehow. You can do anything if you have to. I don't remember much about it now,' she said, staring back wide-eyed into the memories she had disturbed, 'except that I did it.'

Just as well, thought Johnny, seeing before his eyes the thin, tell-tale stroke of blood on the bright silk, and the slender blade swaying upright, its point in Chatrier's back.

'And how did Hans get into it?' he prompted gently. Keep her talking, make her pour out the whole of it, empty the darkness and share the last of it with him, so that there should never again be so much as a shadow between them. He knew now that he couldn't bear another such banishment.

'He didn't do anything, he didn't know anything, there wasn't any conspiracy. He simply came into the wings ready for his entrance, and he must have seen me get up from the body and run on-stage. I was nearly late on my cue. I didn't know he was there until I turned to go into the arbour, and then I looked quickly to see if the body showed at all, and there he was. Standing right beside it, staring at me. I knew by his face he'd seen me, I knew what he was thinking. Such horror, and such pity! I couldn't guess what he would do. I couldn't do anything about it, whatever he did. So I just went on into the arbour. Then I was all right, then I had time to think, time to hide the ribbon where you found it, and slip the needle into the busk of my dress.'

'And Hans gave you what he thought you needed, an alibi.'

The boy must have made up his mind in about twenty seconds, for Figaro's first indignant comment came only three lines after Marcellina's retreat into the arbour. Johnny heard again vividly with his inward ear the final bitter: ' "*Il fresco – il fresco!*" ' Maybe Hans had had qualms about his act afterwards, maybe he'd deeply regretted it, but he'd stood to it stoutly even when he feared he was himself beginning to figure as chief suspect. No, there was nothing there that need make a man hesitate to confide his daughter's future to Hans Selverer. On the contrary, such stubborn loyalty was not easily to be found, and Johnny knew how to value it.

'He never had time to think, either,' she said, 'only to feel sorry for me.'

'Does he know now? That it – wasn't you? That you only intervened to protect Codger?'

'Yes, he knows now.'

'And when the alarm was given and the police took over, of course, you had to leave the ribbon where it was, and let it take its chance. And the needle, too? Do you mean to tell me that thing's been in your dress ever since? Even when the dressing-rooms were searched?'

'They were searched for the first time while I was still wearing it. And then, they were looking for the baldric, not for a knitting-needle. I knew there was a certain risk in leaving it where it was, but it seemed to me much more risky to try and move it while the police were always here among us. I knew I could get the ribbon back as soon as we gave *Figaro* again, and the best way not to draw attention to it until then was not even to look towards it or think about it. It wasn't so surprising that they didn't find it, you see, because it was perhaps the one place where they took it for granted it couldn't be . . . Nan and I being in there together, by their reckoning, from before the murder was committed until after it was discovered. When I did recover it I meant to get it away out of the theatre and burn it. But you know what happened.'

Yes, he knew. After all her patience and courage and resolution, after the days and nights of going about her business with a composed face and keeping her own counsel, all to save Codger, Codger had undone all her work with his own hands.

'When you left me alone with them, that night, I didn't know what to do. Codger was dead then. He couldn't be saved, and you couldn't be spared. It was too late to do anything but pick up what few pieces I could, and it seemed to me the best thing I could do was hand Musgrave his evidence, let him make his case as it stood. There was no way of getting Codger out of the blame this time, and he couldn't be hurt now. So I put the baldric in his pocket for Musgrave to find. Maybe it was the wrong thing, I don't know. I was frightened of the complications I'd made, now that they were no more use I only wanted to be rid of them.'

'Girl, girl!' said Johnny, drawing her into his arm with a groan of self-reproach. 'What you've gone through alone!'

'It wasn't quite so bad then. Not even quite so lonely. After that night I told Hans . . . to put his mind at rest. And it did something for my mind, too. He's a good boy, Johnny, he'll never let her down, you can be sure of that.'

'But why didn't you tell *me* the truth then? You could have, then. It was over for Codger, there was no need to hide it any longer.'

'If I'd known you knew the half of it, like him, of course I'd have told you the rest. But I didn't know, you never said anything. Why didn't you tell me you knew I had the baldric? Then I should have told you everything.'

Why didn't you tell me? They were both asking it; they could lose so soon the sense of helplessness and isolation, shake off so soon the state of separation where speech was a burden and confiding an impossibility, however much goodwill, however much love they brought to the struggle.

'And then, I didn't want to involve you in anything I'd done. I thought you were better out of it. One of us was enough to be tangled in all that. Poor Codger!' she said, and turned and rested her smooth forehead for a moment against Johnny's cheek.

'Poor Codger! But better that way than the other. If they'd taken him away from us he'd have died of fright and loneliness. But that you should have to go through all that for him!'

'It was mostly for you,' said Gisela with the shadow of a smile warming the drained pallor of her face.

'Well, don't you ever do anything like that for me again, that's all. It scares the living daylights out of me when I think I've lost touch with you. We'll dispose of this thing now. You and I, together. We can, now. Musgrave's gone, and the case is closed.'

And not, it seemed, so unjustly as he had thought.

There was a kind of providence in it, after all. After she was back with him, he saw her clearly, his voice could reach her, they were saved. Never risk that again, never in life. He knew now that he couldn't manage without Gisela.

She drew herself gently out of his arm and rose, drawing breath deeply as though she had cast off a burden as great as the one she had lifted from him. 'I must dress. No, you sit there, don't move. And you won't have to turn Hans down, after all, you see. All he did was take pity on me.'

'I'm glad,' said Johnny. 'He's a fine boy, and they'll make a grand team. If he can manage her.'

'He'll manage her. She'll see to that.'

It sounded like a recipe for a pretty good marriage. Johnny, thinking of his darling, began almost to look forward to the excitement and promise of her dazzling career beside Hans Selverer; each of them would be a stimulus and a challenge to the other. Gisela watched him from the mirror, and the warm, heavy, lingering smile of her love played upon him without concealment. She thought he was safely clear of all his doubts and reservations concerning the death of Marc Chatrier; but suddenly the shadow was back in his eyes, and he harked back to it again, as it seemed she must be prepared for him to do many times yet before the place in his mind healed.

'One thing bothers me,' said Johnny. 'Codger never thought of that by himself, you know – either time. He never hurt anybody in his life off his own bat, only when he was told. Someone told him to do it. And I'm horribly afraid it was me. I know I said something about knocking off Musgrave – you remember?'

'But he'd often heard things like that said, and never taken them seriously.'

'But that time I meant it. I did mean it! Only for a minute, but . . . From other people he had to have orders spelled out, but from me a hint was enough. He might have sensed that I was in dead earnest – I wish to God I knew!'

'You were *not*,' she said quickly and fiercely.

'Then he must have thought I was. Damn it, I don't know myself. And something comes back to me now about the other time, about Chatrier. I said something about him, too, a day or so before it happened. Something about him being due for a funeral, not a wedding, if everybody had his deserts. I didn't say it to Codger – but Codger was there. Gisela, Codger only did what he thought I wanted! In the end I'm to blame.'

'Oh, Johnny!' she said, and turned suddenly and took his face between her hands. 'Oh, Johnny; oh, my darling, don't! I love you, and I can't bear any more. Let it alone, let it alone, and don't kill me!'

She got him to the bottom of the stairs safely, silent and dazed between the revelations of his wretchedness and his happiness. They were very late. The theatre was hushed and still, but its emptiness felt warm and at ease, without a qualm for dead Figaro. In Sam's box by the stage-door there was an ache where Codger had been, but even there, it seemed, there could be no permanent void. Sam's voice, gruff and querulous, addressed some unseen presence within:

'Take your tail out o' that fire, you daft mutt, and get from underfoot.'

The dog Buster, a stray with one wall eye, had walked in and insinuated himself into Sam's room yesterday morning, draggled with rain. Not an attractive beast, nor a bright one, but bright enough to recognise encouragement beneath what had sounded like the opposite. Probably Sam wouldn't have welcomed a more presentable specimen. The vacancy wouldn't have fitted anything but a helpless, well-meaning creature doomed eternally to be a liability and a nuisance.

In the corridor Johnny halted abruptly.

'Wait a minute!' he said, labouring with a new thought. 'New blue plastic knitting-needles! He had those the night before the murder, I remember seeing them when he showed me the sweater he was knitting for Hans. Who gave him those? Codger couldn't shop for the simplest thing, that was one thing Dolly never left to him.

Someone provided him with those needles – *before he killed Chatrier.*'

'Johnny, let it rest.'

'I can't. Somebody planned it, somebody made use of him. It wasn't just that I said something that set him off – because somebody acted, somebody gave him the new needles and took the old ones . . .'

Sam had heard their voices, low as they were, and emerged from his box, the dog at his heels. He seemed to have shrunk since he had lost Codger, the big frame hung lank inside his clothes, the lines of his face were fallen into a mournful mask.

'I thought you'd decided to stay the night,' he said. 'Tom's been kicking his heels outside twenty minutes, waiting for you.'

Johnny seemed not to have heard a word of this. He stood staring at the old man with the flare of a wild suspicion in his eyes, and fought to bring the point-blank question out of his throat, where it was stuck fast and choking him.

'Sam, tell me something. And tell me the truth. Did *you* put Codger up to killing Chatrier?'

They looked at each other for a moment in silence, the shock almost palpable on the air between them. Sam's ancient eyes, that had seen Johnny grow from an insubordinate cadet to the man he was now, and never underestimated him and never gone in awe of him, fixed him with a steely gleam of indignation that could not quite burn into anger.

'No,' he said, 'I did not. What do you think I am? Me, that's looked after the poor beggar like a nursemaid all these years? No, I didn't. And if you ever ask me a thing like that again, so help me, Johnny Truscott, I'll clout you.'

Johnny knew the truth when he heard and saw it, at least in Sam. He heaved the horrible doubt off his chest in a gasping sigh of relief.

'So help me, you should have done it this time,' he said. 'I beg your pardon, Sam. I ought to have known better.'

And indeed he ought. Who had been more constant in his care for the poor wreck the sea had left of Codger? The night he'd mislaid his charge he'd had Martin out helping him to scour the neighbourhood, frantic with anxiety, until Johnny had telephoned from the police station to break the news to him. Without his burden he'd lost the obstinate energy that had been the mainspring of his life. Johnny saw suddenly and piteously how old he was, how the hard flesh had begun to dry up on his bones. What sort of friend was it who couldn't do him the bare justice he himself had received from Musgrave?

'That's all right, lad. We're all a bit out of ourselves. Get on home to bed, and forget it.'

He saw them out to the top of the steps, and the car was waiting below in a dim, desultory haze of rain. The long-legged dog pressed close at Sam's heels, leaning against his twisted knee; it had chosen its place, and did not intend to be dislodged.

'Don't come down, Sam,' said Gisela. 'You go back inside, out of the rain.'

'All right, if you say so. Good night, miss!' He dug a hard fist into Johnny's ribs, administering painful comfort. ''Night, Johnny!'

'Good night, Sam,' said Johnny, shivering with unreasonable shame, and went down the steps to the car confused and sad and resigned and hopeful all at once, with Gisela in his arm.

'All the same, *someone*—' he said.

'No, not necessarily. What do we know about the country of his mind, Johnny? We're all without maps, there. Maybe he understood more than we knew, maybe he could do much more than we thought – when it was for you. Let him rest, Johnny,' she said in his ear. 'Stop now. There's a time to stop, for everybody's sake.' Her cheek stooped briefly to his shoulder in a muted caress that made his heart lurch in him. 'Stop before you break things,' she said.

She felt then that his will to resist her was being lulled to sleep, that she was the certainty and the comfort in the chaos of his mind, and that she had only to remain close beside him and his hopeless inward inquiries would cease. Already the urgency was ebbing out of him, the tension slackening out of his tired body and troubled spirit. Let it alone now. Let him rest.

They had reached the bottom of the steps when she said suddenly: 'Oh, wait a moment for me, please, I shall have to go back. I left a letter behind . . .. Sam told me there was one by the late delivery, and I never collected it. He must have forgotten it, too. I won't be a moment.'

'I'll go,' said Johnny.

'No, you wait for me. I'll only be a moment.' And she ran back up the steps before he could insist, and vanished through the swinging door.

Sam had been scraping out the bowl of his foul old pipe with a penknife worn down to a sliver of steel, and was testing the result without much optimism. He blew, and the stem bubbled like a boiling kettle; he sucked, and drew distressing noises from it, like a cow proceeding with ponderous deliberation through a swamp. A bit of dottle, disturbed by the knife, had lodged deep in the bottom of the bowl. He couldn't displace it with the blade; he stretched one hand to his table drawer, rummaged in it blindly, and prodded discontentedly in the bottom of the offending briar with the first implement that came to hand. It wasn't much good for the job, too long and too thick, but he persevered obstinately. The point grated sadly in the charged wood, the rounded knob wagged by Sam's right ear.

A voice from the doorway said quietly: 'Sam!'

He dropped his unwieldy tool into the drawer, and shut it to with a quick but calm movement, and turned to face Gisela. She had come in so silently that even the dog had done no more than elevate one shaggy ear and open one disconcerting white eye. She closed the door gently behind her, and stood leaning against it, her dark eyes wide and still.

Sam got to his feet with the rocking motion peculiar to his maimed legs, and the dog, stretched out at his feet, kept its chin possessively across his toes and cocked a wild eye at Gisela. Sam's eyes had never been more tranquil. He looked at her without a smile, thoughtfully, almost expectantly, and said mildly: 'Forget something, miss?'

'Yes, Sam. A letter, for Johnny's benefit. And for yours, just something I had to say.'

She left the door and came forward a few steps into the room, her gaze steady and kind and sad upon his face.

'Simply that you needn't worry. Johnny'll be all right, I'll take care of Johnny. He'll never know anything more from me than he knows now.'

He looked back at her uncomprehendingly, with eyes blank as pebbles, as though she had spoken to him in a foreign language; but she caught some communication that came from deeper within and needed no visible expression, for she smiled wanly, and answered what he would not ask.

'No, *I* didn't lie to him, either. Like you, I didn't have to. There was no need for me to tell him *who* it was I saw in the wings that night. *He* told *me*. He made it easy for both of us. And that's the way it must stay, Sam, for Johnny's sake. He's lost one man he was fond of, he shan't lose two. Not for a Marc Chatrier.'

The old man's eyes, opaque and still, watched her and made no acknowledgement.

'It was wickedly foolish,' she said, a tremor shaking her voice for an instant, 'to use a weapon that pointed so obviously to Codger – when he was close at hand there, and sure to be suspected. But who am I to talk? I did worse than that to him when he was dead. And I did it knowingly, with intent. I thought he wouldn't grudge it, for Johnny. Or for you.'

He shook his head slightly, and continued mute. What was there to say that wouldn't be better left unsaid? She was the one who knew how to put things. Some day she'd even get around to working out how carefully he'd installed Codger upstairs with Dolly, and how sick he'd felt when he'd seen him there in the wings, and realised that the poor old fool had slipped off after him, and left his nice, safe alibi behind him. No need to tell her; when she thought a bit, she'd know.

'But you can't foresee everything,' said Gisela sadly, as though she had followed the mournful trajectory of his thoughts. 'We're all so tangled up together, guilty and innocent, there's no point now in trying to sort it out. Codger's dead, and the act that killed him was at least his own act. Maybe that half absolves the rest of us. God knows!'

'I dare say you're right, miss,' said Sam, like an old man humouring a child whose chatter he has not even heard properly, much less troubled to understand.

'So good night, Sam, and don't worry.'

In the doorway she checked again for an instant, and looked back. 'Oh, and Sam—'

'Yes, miss?'

Her dark eyes lingered for a moment upon the table drawer. She looked up into the old man's face, and the veil of isolation was drawn back from between them for one blinding instant before she turned her eyes away.

'Get rid of it, Sam,' she said, rapid and low. 'Now, before Martin comes on duty. I'll buy you some proper pipe-cleaners to-morrow.'

She was gone. He heard the outer door swing after her, and her light steps running down in haste to Johnny; and in a moment the car purred away round the forecourt and out on to the road.

Sam pulled the drawer open, and took up with blunt brown fingers the solitary steel knitting-needle that lay among the litter of small things within. She was right, of course, it would have to go. He wondered what they would do with the other one, or what they had already done with it. Something safe and final.

He took his foot, not too brusquely, from under the dog's reluctant and protesting chin; and Buster, heaving himself out of his half-sleep with a gusty sigh, followed his lame god down to the furnace.

THE END